Critical acclaim f

'A genuinely engaging story. Ju[...]
position as a prolific writer of bestsellers'
The Age

'A glorious summer read'
Woman's Day

'What stands out in *Heritage*, Judy Nunn's new and absorbing
tome, is the quality of the background research . . .
Nunn's narrative pace never falters'
Sydney Morning Herald

'A great story and a thought-provoking meditation on the
history of the Australian migrant experience . . . Explosive
with surprise twists'
Sunday Telegraph

'One of Australia's most popular writers returns with a
tale of rebirth and redemption . . . A moving story of
struggle and survival'
New Idea

'Nunn specialises in sweeping, larger-than-life sagas . . .
a deft storyteller'
West Australian

'Judy Nunn at the height of her powers in this passionate
and fast-paced tale'
Geraldton Guardian

'A passionate saga about true survivors, a lesson in tolerance,
and a tribute to those who helped forge the Aussie spirit'
Adelaide Advertiser

'A moving story set against one of the greatest events
that forged our country'
Illawarra Mercury

From stage actor and international television star to blockbuster bestselling author, Judy Nunn's career has been meteoric.

Her first forays into adult fiction resulted in what she describes as her 'entertainment set'. *The Glitter Game, Centre Stage* and *Araluen*, three novels set in the worlds of television, theatre and film respectively, each became instant bestsellers.

Next came her 'city set': *Kal*, a fiercely passionate novel about men and mining set in Kalgoorlie; *Beneath the Southern Cross*, a mammoth achievement chronicling the story of Sydney since first European settlement; and *Territory*, a tale of love, family and retribution set in Darwin.

Territory, together with Judy's next novel, *Pacific*, a dual story set principally in Vanuatu, placed her firmly in Australia's top-ten bestseller list. Her following works, *Heritage*, set in the Snowies during the 1950s; *Floodtide*, based in her home state of Western Australia; and *Maralinga*, have consolidated her position as one of the country's leading fiction writers. Her eagerly awaited new novel, *Tiger Men*, will publish in November 2011.

Judy Nunn's fame as a novelist is spreading rapidly. Her books are now published throughout Europe in English, German, French, Dutch and Czech.

Judy lives with her husband, actor-author Bruce Venables, on the Central Coast of New South Wales.

By the same author

The Glitter Game
Centre Stage
Araluen
Kal
Beneath the Southern Cross
Territory
Pacific
Floodtide
Maralinga
Tiger Men

Children's fiction
Eye in the Storm
Eye in the City

Heritage

JUDY NUNN

This book is a work of fiction. A number of well-known historical figures are incorporated, but with the exception of several locals whose real names I have used, all other characters are fictitious. The work camp of Spring Hill is also fictitious and is loosely based on my research of the existing work camps of the time.

An Arrow book
Published by Random House Australia Pty Ltd
Level 3, 100 Pacific Highway, North Sydney NSW 2060
www.randomhouse.com.au

First published by Random House Australia 2005
This Arrow edition published in 2006, 2007, 2011

Addresses for companies within the Random House Group can be found at
www.randomhouse.com.au/offices

National Library of Australia
Cataloguing-in-Publication Entry

Nunn, Judy.
Heritage / Judy Nunn.

ISBN 978 1 86471 249 0 (pbk)

Snowy Mountains Hydro-electric Authority – Fiction.
Refugees – Fiction.

A823.3

Typeset by Midland Typesetters, Australia
Printed in Australia by Griffin Press, an accredited ISO AS/NZS 14001:2004
Environmental Management System printer

In fond memory of Bob and Rita Duncan

'Give me a man who's a man among men
Who'll stow his white collar and put down his pen
Who'll blow down a mountain and build you a dam
Bigger and better than old Uncle Sam.

Sometimes it's raining and sometimes it's hail
Sometimes it blows up a blizzardy gale
Sometimes it's fire and sometimes it's flood
And sometimes you're up to your eyeballs in mud.

Give me bulldozers and tractors and hoses
And diesels to ease all my troubles away
With the help of the Lord and of good Henry Ford
The Snowy will roll on her way.'

Extract from the song 'Snowy River Roll'

PROLOGUE

'**W**e can say goodbye to old Berlin, Mannie.'

Mannie Brandauer had never forgotten the look on his father's face the day he said those words, or the sorrow in his father's voice. And, from then on, Mannie noticed, whenever his father talked of the golden days of the Twenties, he always referred to 'old Berlin'.

'Before President Hindenburg was forced to appoint that awful little thug as Chancellor,' Stefan Brandauer would say to his wife, Margit, recklessly careless of his young teenage son's presence. Then Margit would gently warn Mannie that he was not to repeat his father's views in public.

Far from heeding his wife's concern, Stefan voiced his opinions with equal vigour to his close circle of like-minded friends, those who still gathered regularly at the Brandauers' grand house on diplomats' row in Tiergarten-strasse, overlooking the magnificent parkland which had once been a royal game reserve.

Stefan had been Director of Protocol in the Weimar Republic for ten years and, having been retained by Hitler for his brilliance in foreign diplomacy, such inflammatory conversation was certainly not in keeping with Stefan's position. But then, as he pointed out to Margit, he had never before socialised with thugs and vulgarians, and if he was now forced to do so in the workplace, then he would at least recognise them for what they were. He was not impressed, he said, by their uniforms and their pistols, nor was he intimidated by their loutish behaviour and bullying tactics.

But it was not Stefan's political views that finally brought about his demotion; it was the company he kept. Despite his impeccable Aryan lineage and his staunch belief in the Roman Catholic faith, it was noted that the Director of Protocol was a Jewish sympathiser and the decision was made that he should be posted abroad. But not until after the Olympic Games.

Stefan Brandauer – multilingual, urbane, well known and well liked by the majority of visiting ambassadors – was an invaluable asset during the 1936 Olympics, when Hitler sought to disguise the anti-Semitic policies already strongly in place, and to impress upon the world Berlin's sophistication and fairness. But when the Olympics were over and the dignitaries and tourists had departed, the placards of condemnation inspiring hatred and urging boycotts reappeared, the anti-Jewish publications returned to the newsstands, and Hitler refocussed on his major objective: purifying the city. It was then that Stefan was posted to London and obscurity, his duties at the German Embassy being those of any other minor civil servant.

By that time, Mannie was in his first year of Law at Berlin University and so he didn't accompany his parents. He bade them a fond farewell, knowing that he would miss them sorely. As his father would miss 'old Berlin'. He moved into a modest flat near the university with his child-hood friend and fellow first-year student, young Samuel Lachmann.

On a clear summer evening in mid July, 1943, Mannie hefted his knapsack of groceries over one shoulder and walked down Kurfürstendamm through the gathering dusk. He thought, as he so often did, of his father and 'old Berlin'.

Along either side of the broad boulevard, cafes, bars, theatres and nightclubs still bravely opened for business, despite the increasing bombing raids that were systematically destroying the city. Life went on for the Berliners. But Kurfürstendamm catered to a different society these days. It had been a swaggering clientele at first, one of strutting uniforms and self-importance, loud, coarse and vulgar. Then, so quickly that it seemed to happen overnight, the same thugs had been empowered with the right to commit acts of shocking brutality. They were no longer mere louts showing off in their finery. They had become the feared Gestapo ordered to hunt out Jews, or they were the murderous Schutzstaffel – the SS – Hitler's elite corps of race guardians bent on the annihilation of all 'undesirables' who tainted the purity of the Fatherland.

Mannie vividly recalled the 'old Berlin' of his childhood, and the circle of his father's friends. He'd been ten years old when Stefan had taken him to the opening night of the outrageous new musical *The Threepenny Opera*. It had been staged at the Theater am Schiffbauerdamm, and he'd met its creators on a number of occasions. Both Bertolt Brecht and Kurt Weill were regular visitors to the house in Tiergartenstrasse, as were many members of Berlin's thriving artistic society. Painters and writers, composers and musicians, actors and film-makers all gravitated to the salon created by Stefan Brandauer, where they could freely vent their anger at the 'counter-renaissance' movement which was already noticeable in 1928, the twilight of the golden age. Where were those artists now? Mannie wondered. All gone. Some had fled, but most had been murdered.

He turned into Joachimstalerstrasse, passing a playground which still bore the sign *Arischen und nichtarischen Kindern wird das Spielen miteinander untersagt.* These days there was no point in banning Aryan and non-Aryan children from playing together, he thought. There were no non-Aryan children left to play. The children, like the artists, were gone. They'd been forcibly removed. Unconsciously, Mannie quickened his pace. *And nobody's doing anything about it!*

Just along from the house in Tiergartenstrasse had been the Papal Nuncio's residence, and Mannie remembered how, as a child playing in the park, he'd watched the men in their sombre black occasionally venture out to stroll beside the meandering streams and bridle tracks of the Tiergarten, or to sit in quiet contemplation by the lake. Having been brought up a devout believer in the Church of Rome, Mannie had found the men impressive. They were men of the cloth; they had been called by God.

One of the men he'd seen walking in the park had been Cardinal Pacelli, the Vatican Secretary of State who'd spent nine years in Berlin. Mannie thought about him a great deal lately. Cardinal Pacelli was now Pope Pius XII – *why wasn't he doing something about it?*

Manfred Brandauer was tortured by the Vatican's silence. As a Roman Catholic he had felt a personal sense of guilt when the Pope first refused to speak out against the sickening persecution of the Jews. And now, years later, the Pontiff continued to maintain his silence. Mannie's shame overwhelmed him. His own priest, the man who heard his weekly confession, had no answers about why the Vatican wasn't protesting. Indeed, the priest had not wished to discuss the matter: 'It is not for us to question the Holy Father, my son.' Mannie had even visited the Cathedral in search of answers. 'Why is Rome, the Vatican, the Holy Father himself, not taking a stance?' he'd demanded. Still no answers came. So Mannie continued, day after day, month after month, to feel his ever-deepening shame.

Walking briskly, he rounded the corner into Viktoria-Luise-Platz, a picturesque square with a central park and fountain surrounded by townhouses. The flat Mannie rented was on the third floor of a six-storey apartment block built in the 1890s, in the 'new Baroque' style that had been so fashionable at the time. With ornate balconied facades, it was a gracious building.

Mannie's best friend, Samuel Lachmann, lived in the apartment below him. The two no longer shared accommodation as they had in their student days. Both twenty-five years of age, Samuel was now a married man with a baby daughter, and Mannie was a qualified lawyer. But they remained as close as they had been throughout their lives. Closer than brothers, they both agreed. 'You can choose your friends,' Samuel always said, with that cheeky gleam in his brown-black eyes.

Samuel hadn't changed, Mannie thought. Even as the times had grown darker, Samuel Lachmann had remained as cheeky and buoyant as he had been throughout their shared childhood, and Mannie admired his friend's strength. But he worried incessantly for Samuel's safety, and for that of his wife, Ruth, and their little girl. They should have left Berlin long ago – he'd been nagging them to do so for years – but it had been Ruth who'd been adamant about staying. Just as she had been in 1938 following the murder of her father.

It had been on the evening of November 9, Kristall-nacht, the 'night of broken glass', when hordes of rioters, bent on a bloodbath, had smashed the windows of Jewish shops and businesses. Hyram Stein, along with many others, had been dragged into the street and bashed to death by the mob.

'This is my father's home,' Ruth had said of the apartment in Viktoria-Luise-Platz, when Mannie had urged her to leave. 'I have lived here with my father for over fifteen years, ever since my mother died. Papa was my world and I will live in his home.' The patrician, honey-haired looks that Ruth Stein had inherited from her Gentile mother not only belied her father's Jewish blood, but the indomitable strength that lay beneath her beauty.

Ruth's uncle, Walter Stein, had fled with his young family following the death of his brother, but Ruth had refused to accompany them. She had shouldered her grief, completed the second and final year of her degree in languages and, eighteen months after her father's death, she had married Samuel. The two of them had set up home in the old apartment, and when the flat upstairs had become vacant, they had suggested Mannie rent it.

'We are family, after all,' Ruth had insisted, and Mannie had readily agreed to the arrangement. It meant that he could be of assistance to them in these increasingly threatening times.

When Jews were denied regular employment, Samuel had accepted odd jobs labouring for those he could trust, while Ruth had worked from their apartment as an English tutor, many of her pupils being the children of wealthy Jews preparing to flee Germany. These days, however, she had only one pupil, young Naomi Meisell, the daughter of her friends who had a ground-floor apartment on the opposite side of the square. Eighteen-year-old Naomi, always a rebellious girl, fearlessly refused to forgo her English lessons.

In the Thirties, the vibrant suburb of Schöneberg had been home to a vast Jewish community; now it appeared that Ruth and Samuel and the Meisells were the only ones left. They didn't know for certain: they didn't dare enquire.

Hyram Stein and Efraim Meisell, both forward-thinking businessmen, had many years previously purchased their apartments under fictitious non-Jewish names. It had been their intention to protect their investments, but their prescience was now protecting their families. Jews were not allowed to own properties, and the families lived in secrecy in the prisons of their homes. Occasionally they would venture out to purchase meagre supplies or to scavenge for food. But every such excursion was fraught with danger, for it was imperative they wear the yellow Star of David, emblazoned with the word '*Jude*', on the left side of their outer garment. To be discovered without their badge could mean death. But always, upon leaving their apartments, and upon their return, they clasped a bag or some other object to their chest to cover the Star. Jews no longer lived in Viktoria-Luise-Platz.

Mannie bounded up the two flights of stairs to the Lachmann apartment and gave the secret knock on the door, which then opened immediately.

'Mannie!' Her arms were about him, her soft cheek against his, warm and welcoming, just like the sister she'd always been.

'You haven't lost a brother, Mannie,' she'd told him when she'd married Samuel, 'you've gained a sister.'

There had been a time during their days at university when Mannie had wished with all his heart that Ruth could be more to him than a sister. But Ruth had had eyes for no-one but Samuel. It had been love at first sight for them. Although Ruth was a freshman studying languages and Samuel was in the second year of his engineering degree, they would study together side by side in the reading room, and they would hold hands as they strolled across the campus to the library. They'd been inseparable from the outset. And Mannie could do nothing but embrace the sisterly friendship Ruth offered, and be happy for the man he considered his brother. It had been a painful time for him, but he'd accepted his lot. Now he merely worshipped from afar, or rather from the apartment upstairs.

'Mannie! Mannie! Mannie!'

Little Rachel was toddling comically towards him as fast as her two-year-old legs could carry her. Mannie closed the door, picked up the infant and dumped the knapsack of groceries on the living room table.

'How's my favourite girl?' he said to the child as he followed Ruth through the open archway into the kitchen. 'Something smells good.'

'Chicken soup.' Ruth stirred the pot on the stove. 'Fresh stock. Samuel had a job this afternoon and he came back with five chicken carcasses – isn't that wonderful? We'll have real soup for a whole week.' She didn't look at him as she spoke; she knew Mannie would be cross. And he was.

'Read story, Mannie, read story.' Rachel was tugging his hair demanding her customary bedtime story, but Mannie put the child down.

'Not just now, *liebchen*. Why did he go out looking for work, Ruth? You know how dangerous that is. Where did he work? For whom? Is he here now?'

'He's washing, he came back filthy.' She continued stirring the soup. 'It was Hoffmann's Garage in Wilmersdorf, we can trust Hoffmann. And they paid him well. But then you know how good Samuel is with cars – he says he shouldn't have bothered studying engineering, he should have been a mechanic . . .'

'Yes, yes, I know how good he is with cars. But to actually look for work! Someone could have reported him. They could have followed him back here! It's too . . .'

'Too dangerous, I know.' She turned to face him at last. 'I tried to warn him, but he just said he was off to make some money and we were going to have chicken soup.'

'But I've brought the groceries, Ruth. He didn't need to . . .'

'Darling Mannie.' She kissed his cheek fondly. 'What would we do without you?' She turned down the flame under the pot. 'Let it brew, come and sit down.' She picked up Rachel and they walked into the living room to sit at the table that looked out over the balcony to the square below, although these days the gauze curtains were always drawn.

'I saw Sharon Meisell this morning,' Ruth said. 'She told me that they're getting out. Efraim has arranged false papers.'

She looked weary, Mannie thought. Not the ever-present signs of fatigue that resulted from inadequate diet and lack of exercise, but a weariness that came from deep within. It was hardly surprising under the circumstances, but Mannie was unaccustomed to seeing what he perceived as sadness in Ruth's eyes. Clear blue, they were always alive and positive. Like her husband, Ruth was a creature of humour and spirit, of resilience and determination; the two were made for each other. Concerned, Mannie waited for her to continue.

'I never thought the Meisells would leave. Well, not of their own accord,' she added, her tone heavily laced with irony. 'They've been here longer than my father. It came as a bit of a shock, I was so sure that we'd all stick it out together. We were the strong ones, we agreed at the beginning, the Meisells and the Lachmanns. Now Sharon says that we were the foolish ones, and I've no doubt she's right.

'Anyway,' Ruth bounced the child on her lap, Rachel raking her tiny fingers through the fair honey-brown of her mother's hair, 'I suggested to Samuel that we should try to get out too. Sharon's given me the contact for the false papers.'

'Excellent,' Mannie agreed enthusiastically. 'I'll pick them up for you. I'll do whatever I can . . .'

She interrupted him. 'Samuel won't go.'

'Why?' he asked, but she wasn't listening.

'He would have, years ago when you said that we should. Samuel would have listened to you, Mannie. But he stayed because of my stubbornness. No,' she corrected herself with a rueful raise of her eyebrows, 'my selfishness. My determination to live on in my father's home, regardless of the danger to my husband and child. And now Samuel's the one who refuses to leave.' She disentangled the child's fingers from her hair and put Rachel down on the floor. The child toddled over to Mannie to tug at his trouser legs.

'Samuel says that "the tide has turned",' she continued. 'He says that it's only a matter of time before Germany is defeated, and we must "weather the storm".' Ruth smiled as she imitated her husband. 'You know Samuel, Mannie – the constant optimist, and how he does love a cliché when he's being dramatic.' A humorous twinkle returned to her eyes as she fought to lighten the moment. Besides, she realised, she did feel better now that she had admitted her guilt, and to the person to whom her admission was most important. 'He always thinks if he says something passionately, and often, it will come true.'

Mannie remained silent, but he nodded.

'So we shall "weather the storm" together. Who am I, having demanded we remain in the first place, to now decide otherwise? Then he said he was off to earn some money and we were to have fresh chicken soup. I told him if anyone should risk going out to work it should be me. He looks so damn Jewish!' She shrugged, refusing to admit to the fear she had felt all afternoon, and her laugh was one of loving exasperation.

Ruth's laughter was normally contagious, but this time Mannie didn't join in. 'I'll speak to him, Ruth. I'll convince him.'

'Speak to me about what? Convince me about what? No, no, don't tell me. You're going to read me the riot act.'

Mannie rose, and Samuel, a towel around his neck, his black hair wet and tousled, gathered his friend in a boisterous hug. 'No lectures until after the soup, though,

Mannie, we're dining early – I haven't eaten since breakfast and I'm starving.'

'Someone has to talk sense to you, for God's sake . . .'
Mannie began as soon as he could extricate himself from
the embrace.

'After the soup!' Samuel had picked up Rachel and was
whirling her about, the child squealing excitedly. 'No
lectures until after the soup, promise me.'

'All right, all right,' Mannie agreed. 'When Rachel's
gone to bed.'

'Read story, Mannie, read story,' the little girl called at
the mention of bedtime.

'After the soup.' It was Ruth giving the orders, as she
rose and crossed into the kitchen.

Mannie followed with the bag of groceries, unpacking
the bread, the powdered eggs, several tins, and producing,
with a flourish, a precious small brown paper bag.

'Coffee!' Ruth exclaimed delightedly upon opening it.
'How on earth did you manage that?'

'We lawyers have excellent black-market connections.'
He grinned, proud of himself and pleased by her reaction.

Upon Ruth's instruction, Mannie rejoined Samuel and
Rachel in the living room and, through the open archway,
Ruth watched the men play with the child as she stacked
the supplies into the cupboard and cut up the bread. Chalk
and cheese, the two of them, she thought, but such a bond
they shared. They'd both spoken to her a great deal about
their childhood. Samuel was always the one who got them
into trouble, they said, and Mannie was always the one
who got them out of it.

'Son of a diplomat,' Samuel would say. 'It obviously
rubbed off.'

Ruth had never met Stefan Brandauer but she'd seen his
picture many times in the newspapers. Stefan Brandauer
had been a prominent member of Berlin society, and
Mannie looked just like his father. Tall, fine-boned,

elegantly handsome, his hair always groomed. A tidy man. The antithesis of Samuel. She smiled as she watched Samuel piggy-backing Rachel around the living room. Nuggetty, athletic, his dark curly hair refusing to be tamed – not that he'd care to try anyway – Samuel was an unruly man in every way.

But the differences between them had always meant nothing. Just as being Gentile and Jew had had no influence upon their friendship. It never had. They'd been children of Berlin, they both maintained. 'True Berliners, and proud of it,' Samuel always said. That's why it had been such a shock when he'd been dismissed from university before he'd completed his degree.

'They say I'm not a German,' he'd told her, hurt and bewildered. 'They say that I'm a Jew. What's wrong with being both? I'm a German who happens to be a Jew.'

Samuel had never thought of his Jewish heritage in terms of race. His upbringing had been unorthodox, and Ruth remembered, when she'd first met him, being faintly shocked to discover he ate ham with gusto, jokingly calling it smoked salmon. His father had been a professor of physics at the University of Berlin, an intellectual and, like Stefan Brandauer, a staunch patron of the arts. Leonard Lachmann and Stefan Brandauer had become firm friends, and it was in the Brandauer house at Tiergartenstrasse that the lifelong friendship of their sons had been forged. Leonard had lost his position at the university around the same time as Stefan had been posted to London. 'A sign of the times,' Stefan had wryly remarked, then more seriously he'd added, 'We'd best pray for our sons.' Shortly after Stefan's departure, Leonard Lachmann, too, had left Berlin, having accepted a post at Zurich University.

'So there we were,' Samuel had told Ruth when he and Mannie had given her their potted history, 'thrown out into the storm, left to fend for ourselves, two lonely orphans.'

'Two lonely orphans whose fathers paid for their education, set them up in a flat, and forwarded regular allowances,' Mannie had corrected him.

'It sounded better my way. Don't listen to him, Ruth. He never lets me get away with anything.' Samuel had cast a caustic look at his friend. 'What on earth would I do without you, Mannie?'

What indeed? Ruth thought as she spooned the soup into the bowls.

They ate at the kitchen table, Ruth helping Rachel messily devour her soup and Mannie staring thoughtfully through the gauze curtains at the Meisells' ground-floor apartment opposite. Their curtains were also drawn, but the light within was clearly visible. He prayed that the Meisells would get out safely. Just as he prayed that Samuel would heed his advice, and in his mind he rehearsed his 'lecture'.

When they'd finished dining, Ruth stacked the bowls and cutlery, preparing to leave the men alone for their talk.

'Read story, Mannie, read story.'

Ruth shared a smile with Mannie. He had always been Rachel's favourite bedtime storyteller.

'I'll take her to the bathroom and get her into her pyjamas and you can put her to bed, Mannie.' She dumped the soup bowls in her husband's hands. 'Samuel will do the washing up, after which we'll have coffee, and he'll give you his full attention. Won't you!' Her look defied Samuel to disagree.

'Yes, yes, I said I would. Not that it'll make any difference anyway.'

Samuel and Ruth were making the coffee together, measuring out the precious grinds and taking care that it didn't boil over, while Mannie read out loud to Rachel, tucked in her cot, the latest chapter of her favourite story. She never tired of Hans Christian Andersen's 'The Snow Queen'.

Then the quiet of the night was shattered by the clatter of boots in the street and, for a brief moment, all four of them, even the child, froze in a breathless silence.

Barely a second later, Mannie rose and turned out the bedroom light, noting the Meisells' apartment opposite also plunge into darkness. Dear God, he thought frantically, was there time to get the family upstairs to his flat? Then he heard the stamp of the boots on the wooden stairs. There wasn't. He gathered Rachel in his arms, whispering for her to be quiet.

In the kitchen, Ruth had turned out the light and Samuel had dived into the living room to extinguish the lights there. The boots were in the hallway now. Samuel returned to the kitchen and held Ruth close as they waited silently in the dark.

The boots stopped at the front door and there was a banging of fist on wood.

In the bedroom, Mannie clasped Rachel to him.

In the kitchen, Samuel and Ruth remained frozen.

'No,' she said, as he finally made a move. 'Let me go. I might be able to bluff them.'

She went into the living room, stared at the front door, then took a deep breath and turned on the light. There was another pounding, and she opened the door to a man in plain clothes. A Gestapo officer, she knew it immediately. Beside him was a uniformed Oberleutnant and behind them three troopers, also in the immaculate grey of the SS.

The Gestapo officer marched straight in, the SS men following, the Oberleutnant's pistol drawn, the troopers' rifles at the ready, all eyes surveying the room.

'You are Frau Lachmann, the owner of this apartment?' the officer demanded.

'I believe you are mistaken,' Ruth replied, disguising the tremor in her voice, her tone firm but respectful. 'This apartment is the property of Herbert Klauptmann.' She gave the fictitious name in which her father had purchased the apartment. 'The records will clearly show that he purchased it over twenty years ago.'

The Gestapo officer was momentarily confused. This woman was Aryan, and patrician at that. She was no Jew. He glanced at the Oberleutnant. Perhaps they had the wrong apartment. Perhaps they should check the records.

But the Oberleutnant did not acknowledge the officer's querying look. 'It has been reported that the Jews Lachmann live here,' he barked. 'Man, wife and child. Your papers.' He held out his hand peremptorily, and Ruth knew that all was lost.

'I am Lachmann.' Samuel appeared from the kitchen and the troopers immediately trained their rifles upon him. He walked slowly to Ruth, careful to give the men no cause for alarm, and put his arm protectively around her.

'Where is the child?' It was the Gestapo officer, annoyed at the Oberleutnant for issuing the orders, but more annoyed at himself for his moment of indecision.

'The child is not here,' Samuel answered. 'The child is staying with friends.'

'It is not wise to lie to the Gestapo, Herr Lachmann. Search the apartment.' The officer indicated the bedroom door, which was ajar, and two of the troopers started towards it.

'No!' Ruth ran to the door trying to bar their way, an act of sheer desperation. 'No, please!'

One of the men grabbed her by the hair and threw her to the floor, the other pointing his rifle at her. Samuel roared and leapt at the man. Two shots rang out from the Oberleutnant's pistol and suddenly Samuel was sprawled on the wooden floor, blood seeping from his head.

Ruth crawled to him, screaming hysterically, but one of the SS men dragged her to her feet. Then the door to the bedroom slowly opened, and Mannie stood there, Rachel in his arms. He was wearing Samuel's coat which always hung on the peg behind the door, the coat with the Star of David stitched on the left side of the chest.

'We will go with you quietly,' he said. 'We will cause no trouble. Come, come my dear, Rachel needs you.' The child was crying, and he held her out to her mother. The SS man released Ruth and she took the little girl in her arms, burying Rachel's face against her shoulder so the child wouldn't see the body of her father.

'The report stated there was a family of three in this apartment,' the Gestapo officer said. 'The family of Lachmann. Man, wife and child.'

'That is so,' Mannie said, his arm about Ruth. She was controlling her hysteria for the sake of her daughter, but her horrified gaze was focussed on the ever-increasing pool of blood around her husband's head. Mannie pulled her close to him. 'I am Samuel Lachmann, this is my wife Ruth, and this is our child.'

'And what of this man?' the officer demanded, pointing at the body on the floor.

'My brother – he was visiting us.'

'His bad luck,' the Oberleutnant sneered, and the other SS men exchanged smirks. The only good Jew was a dead one, they all agreed.

The Gestapo officer did not approve of the remark, just as he did not approve of the shooting. His job was to conduct good, swift roundups, neat and efficient. Get the Jews out of his jurisdiction and down to the Grunewald Goods Train Station. The gun-happy thugs of the SS made things messy. There were three more raids to be conducted that night, and God knew how many more bodies there would be for his men to collect in the morning.

'You are permitted to pack one suitcase. You have three minutes,' he ordered.

'We are packed already,' Mannie said. He knew where Samuel and Ruth kept the suitcase. They had been prepared for such a moment for the past two years.

One of the SS men accompanied him into the bedroom and watched while Mannie slid the suitcase out from under the bed and took Ruth's coat with its Star of David from the peg behind the door.

Mannie didn't know why he was doing what he was doing. Perhaps it was to assuage his shame as a Roman Catholic, although he was sure his death would serve little purpose. Perhaps it was his love for Ruth and his instinctive desire to protect her. Who could say? He only knew that what he was doing was right, and that he was prepared to pay the price.

He draped the coat over her shoulders and Ruth, in a state of shock, allowed him to guide her to the door. Mannie glanced back briefly at the body of his friend, the stream of Samuel's blood now gathering about one of the legs of the dining room table. Then, both oblivious to the officious barking of the Oberleutnant, he and Ruth stepped out into the hall.

'*Juden raus! Raus! Schnell! Schnell!*'

The Gestapo officer switched off the light and pulled the door closed behind them. How he wished the man would shut up.

BOOK ONE

BOOK ONE

CHAPTER ONE

They came from everywhere. Within a matter of months, the mountain work camps and townships of the Monaro rang with a cacophony of unfamiliar accents and languages which confused both the locals and the hundreds of their fellow countrymen who had flocked to the area looking for work. Even city-bred Australians, who'd bumped into the odd 'Wog' and considered themselves relatively sophisticated, were confounded. They were outnumbered by the Europeans, and bewildered by the sudden onslaught of foreign accents and the sights and smells of strange foods. Garlic wafted from the kitchens of the Italians; the Poles and the Czechs ate evil-looking, thick sausages; the Germans downed sauerkraut by the bucket-load; and the Norwegians, incomprehensibly, relished soused herring and pickled rollmops with their beer. The previously sheltered Australians didn't know what to make of this avalanche of new sensations.

It had been on August 1, 1949 that fifty-three-year-old William Hudson was appointed Commissioner of the Snowy Mountains Hydro-Electric Authority. 'Ahead of us lie many years of toil, numerous obstacles to be surmounted and, I have no doubt, many disappointments,' he announced in his radio broadcast to the nation. 'But these are what make the achievement worthwhile. The nation has accepted the Scheme and if I judge Australians rightly, we will see that it goes through.'

The people of Australia listened in awe as Hudson unfolded the plans for the massive construction scheme, the most ambitious ever to be undertaken in their country.

The waters of the Snowy River were to be diverted from their path to the sea by a series of tunnels under the Great Dividing Range. The waters would be channelled westwards into the Murrumbidgee and Murray Rivers, whose flow would be regulated by the provision of two main water storage areas, Jindabyne and Adaminaby Dams. The Snowy Scheme had two principal purposes: the irrigation of dry inland areas, and the creation of a massive source of electrical power. As the accumulated waters were diverted through the system of tunnels and reservoirs, the energy generated by their movement would be stored at various stages in power stations where it would be converted into electricity. It was estimated that the Scheme would require the construction of approximately fifty miles of aqueducts, ninety miles of tunnels, sixteen large dams and seven power stations.

Commissioner Hudson set about the task with all the energy and commitment for which he was renowned. Overseas contractors were employed, not only for their engineering expertise and the supply of heavy equipment and vehicles, but for the construction of temporary 'townships' at the many work sites.

The Snowy Scheme was to be a long haul – twenty-five years in all – and men couldn't live in tents forever, especially during the bitterly cold winter months.

Most important to the success of the Scheme was the supply of workers, both skilled and non-skilled. An undertaking of such magnitude demanded legions of workers along with the hundreds of specialists required and, with a population of only eight million and a critical post-war shortage of men, Australia had to look overseas for labour. The call went out.

The Australian Government's offer resonated throughout war-torn Europe and was answered in droves. Those whose lives had been destroyed by the ravages of war felt a new world was opening for them.

The Snowy Mountains Hydro-Electric Authority considered the combination of so many nationalities a potential danger and initially established separate camps for the local and migrant workers. An 'Aussie' camp and a 'New Australian' camp were erected on opposite sides of the Snowy River, just downstream from Jindabyne. The latter quickly became known as 'Wog Camp', the Aussies choosing to ignore the official term 'New Australians', referring instead to their fellow workers as Reffos, Balts, Wogs, Krauts, Eyeties, Dagos and any number of other derogatory titles.

None of these names seemed to overly bother the Europeans, though some new arrivals found the Australians' inability to distinguish between different nationalities irritating. Germans and Poles, bitter enemies in their home countries, disliked being collectively referred to as 'Wogs', and Hungarians and Czechs were annoyed at being dismissed as 'Balts'. But for the most part, the Europeans understood that the Australians' attitude was a product of insecurity and ignorance. Australia had no bordering countries, no immediate neighbours whose languages and cultures differed from their own. The European Snowy workers, unlike their counterparts in the cities, were not a lonely, stigmatised minority. They were not easily threatened. Buoyed by the strength of their numbers, they recognised the Australians for what they were: naive.

Cooma, the largest of the Monaro townships, with easy rail access from Sydney and Canberra, had been selected as the Authority's headquarters. Satellite townships of prefabricated houses and facilities were erected to the north and the east of the town. As the migrants continued to pour into the township, Cooma became a microcosm of Europe and proximity forced its local inhabitants to recognise and accept their new neighbours. In the nearby rural townships of Adaminaby, Berridale and Jindabyne acceptance was more gradual, with many of the townspeople fearful of the unfamiliar and 'different'.

But it was the workers themselves who first forged the bond that slowly spread throughout the mountains and valleys and plains. Workers started referring to themselves simply as 'Snowy men' and, although there was occasional friction, the Authority's fears of fierce racial disharmony proved groundless. Commissioner Hudson's policy from the outset had been one of assimilation, and his presence remained a daily driving force for harmony throughout the region.

By the early 1950s mobile houses were already replacing tents in many work camps. The prefabricated structures, built on sled bases and known as 'snow huts', were transported to each new site as the work progressed. In areas where labour was required over a long period for a particular phase of the project, mobile settlements became townships with married couples' quarters and prefabricated cottages, and single men's huts and barracks. There were canteens, mess halls, and entertainment facilities, and an overall sense of permanency prevailed as 'Snowy people' formed bonds that would last a lifetime. Communities flourished, gardens were carefully tended and the simplest of houses became nurtured homes.

It was to one of these townships that young Pietro Toscanini arrived in early 1954.

Twenty-year-old Pietro had been bewildered when he'd arrived at the picturesque railway station of Cooma and walked through the gates to the forecourt overlooking the town below. They'd told him in Sydney that he was going to the Snowy Mountains. But where were the mountains?

Where was the snow? He'd anticipated a replica of his native alpine Italy, but all he could see were distant low-lying hills surrounding a vast plain, in the centre of which sat a shabby town with makeshift settlements sprawling either side. The heat, too, confused him. It was so hot that he was sweating beneath the fine wool suit he'd purchased before he'd left his home country. It was the only suit he possessed, the latest fashion with tapering collar and trouser legs, and he'd worn it to impress his new employers.

He'd been comforted, though, by the crowds of fellow passengers pouring through the gates into the forecourt, speaking all manner of languages other than English. He might have been in Europe, he'd thought, and he'd found it most reassuring. The several days he had spent in Sydney prior to his departure for the Snowy had not been pleasant.

'We speak English here, mate,' he'd been brusquely informed when he'd tried to buy a beer in a pub. But hadn't the man realised he'd been trying to speak English? he'd wondered. He'd said 'please' and 'thank you', two of the terms he knew, like 'hello' and 'goodbye', and he'd since discovered that 'bira' sounded very like 'beer'. And then the man had looked him up and down and muttered a snide remark to the others at the counter. Although Pietro had been unable to understand the actual words, he'd known it was a derogatory comment on his appearance. Why? His new suit was far smarter and more fashionable than the shapeless baggy trousers worn by the men in the bar. Pietro had decided that the man, along with most of the other Sydneysiders he'd met, simply did not like him, and he'd wondered why.

He'd made friends on the train trip. Or rather the men who had spoken to him had made friends with him. Shy by nature, Pietro had not joined in the conversation, although the three were seated nearby and speaking in Italian. He'd unashamedly eavesdropped, though, relish-ing the sound of his mother tongue.

Two of the men, who appeared in their mid-thirties, were brothers. They had been chatting animatedly to each other and the third man had introduced himself to them. He didn't look Italian, but spoke the language fluently. It turned out he was a Czech from Prague, but his wife was Italian. His name was Frydek and he was a geologist, he told the brothers, but he would have to work two years as a labourer under the government's Displaced Persons contract before his qualifications would be accredited. He was going to send home every penny he earned, he said, so that his wife and baby son could join him.

The brothers, Luigi and Elvio Capelli, were carpenters brought out by Legnami Pasotti's firm to join the hundreds of other Northern Italians contracted to build houses and barracks for the Snowy workforce.

The conversation had been in full swing when the elder of the two Capelli brothers, Elvio, had turned to Pietro. 'And where are you from, my friend?' he'd asked.

Pietro had been embarrassed. He hadn't thought his eavesdropping had been so apparent.

'Milano,' he'd stammered self-consciously. He wasn't really from Milano. Not originally. He was from the mountains. But how could he tell them that he could not remember the first half of his life? He hoped they wouldn't ask too many questions.

'Ah, Milano,' Elvio had enthused. 'We, too, are from Milano, what a small world, eh? Come and join us, what is your name?' He hadn't been aware of Pietro's eavesdropping at all, he'd merely recognised the young man as an Italian, and a Northerner at that, but he was aware that the boy was lonely, in need of company, and that he appeared a little shy.

Elvio was a sensitive man and, realising that Pietro didn't wish to be interrogated, he'd quickly reverted to general conversation; then, when they reached Cooma, he announced that they were all good friends and they must keep in touch.

'We are to be based in Cooma,' he said to Pietro. 'What about you?'

'I don't know,' Pietro replied. 'A work camp somewhere. It's called Spring Hill. I'm to be met at the station.'

They'd bade each other farewell on the railway platform, Pietro promising he would visit his newfound friends, and then he'd walked through the gates and stood on the forecourt, patiently waiting to be found by the person who was to meet him.

The crowd had dispersed until finally there'd been six men left, two chatting in Hungarian and the others, of inde-terminate nationality, wandering about impatiently. Finally, an Australian in a grubby open-necked shirt, shorts and sandals, who had been lounging against a nearby Land Rover, walked up to them. He was carrying a clipboard.

'G'day. You the blokes for Spring Hill?'

He'd ticked their names off the list and, together with the five other men, Pietro had been piled into the back of the canvas-covered Land Rover and driven through the centre of Cooma on his way to the work camp.

Cooma had intrigued Pietro. It was not large, but it was not at all the shabby town it had appeared from the railway station. To his right was a neat, green park where families picnicked and children climbed the railings of the small rotunda in the centre. The main thoroughfare was busy with traffic, the pavements bustled with people milling about awning-fronted shops and on either side of the broad, dusty boulevard stood graceful hotels with balconies of ornate iron lace.

Pietro barely had time to drink it all in before he'd found himself clinging to the Land Rover railings as it bounced its way over rough gravel roads towards the settlement approximately fifty miles from Cooma. The trip would take about an hour and a half, the driver had told them.

'Good day for it,' the taciturn Aussie had remarked, 'takes about four hours in winter when the weather's

crook, and sometimes you have to wait until the snow-
ploughs have been through.' Then he'd lapsed into silence.

The men – a German, a Pole, a Norwegian and the two
Hungarians – had chatted jovially during the trip, mostly
in passable English, and Pietro had been able to offer
nothing more than his name and 'how do you do', a
greeting which he had mastered to perfection. The huge,
blond Norwegian had slapped him on the back and said
'You will be right, mate,' in a grotesque imitation of an
Aussie accent and the others had laughed.

'Welcome to Spring Hill.' The Australian who'd greeted
them was a lean, fit man of around forty, with a pleasant
smile, but a manner that clearly indicated his authority.
'I'm your boss,' he'd said with a brisk handshake all
round. 'Name's Rob Harvey. You men speak English?'

The others had all nodded, and as the boss had clasped
his hand Pietro had stared at the ground, shaking his head
in embarrassment.

'No worries, mate.' Good-looking kid, Rob thought, bit
on the skinny side, though; he'd need toughening up.

Rob Harvey, Site Engineer, was responsible for overseeing all the work sites at Spring Hill, liaising with the
Norwegian contractors, the myriad sub-contractors, and
the Authority itself, namely Commissioner William Hudson.
But, although well placed among the hierarchy, Rob chose
to live in the 'wages' camp with the workers, rather than
the 'staff' camp that housed the engineers and clerical
employees. He liked to keep in direct contact with the men
and take a personal interest in each of his workers.

'You Italian?' he'd queried, looking Pietro up and down,
and Pietro had finally raised his eyes and nodded.

'I'll put you on Lucky's team – Lucky speaks every
lingo under the sun. Come on, I'll show you blokes your
accommodation.'

From that day on, Pietro's life had changed. He loved
Spring Hill. He'd expected tents. The interpreter in Sydney

had explained to him that he was going to a 'work camp', and a work camp meant tents. But Spring Hill was a town of eight hundred people. There in the wilderness, among the red gums, the blackbutts and the silver birch, with the mountains forming a backdrop and the river flowing nearby, were streets and rows of neat, prefabricated staff cottages with front verandahs and gardens. And the adjacent camp, although less sophisticated, was equally impeccable, with lines of barracks and single cabins, ablution blocks, a huge mess hall, and a wet canteen where the men gathered over their beers at night.

Pietro had been allotted the end room in a line of barracks, and he kept it in pristine condition. Of a similar size to the one-man cabins, the rooms in the barracks were small, each housing no more than an iron-framed bed and a tallboy and lowboy made of plywood, but Pietro was inordinately proud of his new home. He'd acquired blue curtains for his window, an orange bedspread for his pallet, and a small blue mat with orange trim for the floor so that everything matched. They looked quite new, although they weren't.

'They is old, Pietro, I am soon throw them out, please you take them,' Vesna had insisted in her colourfully broken English.

It was Lucky who had introduced him to Vesna and her husband, Miroslav, who lived in one of the staff cottages. They were Yugoslavs, and Miroslav was an engineer. Pietro had been surprised and a little overawed when Lucky had taken him to their home, but then Lucky had done so much for him. It seemed sometimes that Lucky had adopted him and, although there was only sixteen years difference in their ages, Pietro had quickly seized upon Lucky as the father he couldn't remember.

'Tell me about yourself,' Lucky had said over their beers in the wet canteen on Pietro's third night.

Pietro had worked hard for the past three days. He'd

wanted to. Language barriers appeared to present little problem to the others, the men communicating with gestures or yelling for others to interpret if necessary, but although there were a number of Italians among the forty-man team, Pietro had found it difficult to join in the general camaraderie. His natural reserve had made him reclusive. So he'd decided to prove his worth another way. He would show them that, despite his slight build, he was strong. Strong and not afraid of hard work. And the work had been very hard.

There were many work sites around Spring Hill. The first of the Scheme's major projects, the Guthega dam, power station, three-mile tunnel and interconnecting steel pipeline, was due for completion the following year, and the race was on.

Assigned to Lucky's team, Pietro's job had been in the smaller of the tunnels, loading the skips after firing. The aqueduct system, designed to pick up the maximum run-off from tributaries feeding into the Snowy River, required many miles of tunnels, far smaller than the massive ones through which the river itself would be channelled. The run-off water would eventually be piped through these tunnels into the nearby dam already nearing completion.

The face was drilled with jackhammers, the holes loaded with gelignite, then fired. An hour later, after the ventilating system had cleared away the fumes, the workers re-entered the claustrophobic tunnel, barely two yards high, and with hands and shovels they collected the debris, using spalling hammers to break up the rocks too big to lift. Then they pushed the skips along rail tracks to the spoil dump outside.

'Come on, Pietro, tell me about yourself,' Lucky had again prompted in Italian when the boy had remained silent. 'You're a hard worker, I can see that much,' he'd added encouragingly. 'What's your background?'

Pietro had looked self-consciously around the wet canteen, the air thick with cigarette smoke and the unintelligible conversation of men. A card game was going on in one corner and, in another, men were laying bets on an unknown wager; no-one was paying them any attention.

'I worked for a year on a construction site in Milano,' he'd said, then returned his attention to his beer, hoping the simplicity of such a reply would suffice.

But it hadn't. 'So you're from Milano?' Lucky appeared most interested.

Pietro had been impressed by the man from the moment he'd met him, as most people were. Lucky was far more than a foreman: he was everybody's friend. A German, he also spoke English and Italian fluently and seemed to have a passable knowledge of any number of other languages, which made him a bit of a mystery. But he shrugged off enquiry, simply saying, 'I have an ear and an interest.'

Physically strong, Lucky would have been handsome, had it not been for the puckered scar on his temple that made his left eye droop like a bloodhound's. Lucky had natural authority and an intense charm, qualities which had served him well when he'd arrived with the first batch of Snowy workers in '49.

Looking up from his beer, Pietro had felt himself succumb to the keenness of the enquiry and the eager intelligence in Lucky's gaze, which even the disfigured eye could not disguise. Perhaps he was merely flattered that a man such as Lucky would find him of interest, but Pietro had a sudden desire to admit to the mystery of his life. He had told others his story before. In Milano he'd made no secret of his memory loss, although he had not relished the discussion it occasionally invited. But during his job interviews, both in Italy and Australia, he had been careful to admit to none of his past, fearful that it would affect his employment prospects.

'In a way I am from Milano, yes,' he answered carefully. 'I lived there for many years, but it was never my home. I come from the mountains.'

His considered response had clearly intrigued Lucky, who forgot that he'd finished his beer and had been about to get another. 'Where in the mountains?'

'I do not know. I can remember only the snow, and the mountain peaks so high they block out the sun. And in the spring, the rocks and the grasses and the flowers, and the pine forests in the valley below. And I can remember the goats.'

He didn't want to dwell upon the goats. During the occasions when jagged fragments of memory returned, the goats were the clearest image of all. Pietro liked the goats, but he didn't welcome them when they became too vivid – when he could see their teats and feel the rubbery warmth in his hands as he milked them – for such clarity invariably preceded a seizure. He could never remember what images followed the goats, but when the fit had passed, he was always left with a sense of horror.

Through his shirt, Pietro fingered the sturdy piece of leather strap which rested against his chest, an automatic gesture. He always wore it on a thin length of twine around his neck. When he felt a fit coming on, he would place it between his teeth so that he would not bite through his tongue.

'I cannot remember my home, or my family.' His tone became matter-of-fact. It was never wise to become emotional, and he did not intend to tell Lucky about the fits. 'I can remember nothing but the Convent of the Sacred Heart where they took me when I was eleven years old. I was told that I had been wandering the streets of Milano living on scraps from rubbish bins in the alleys behind restaurants and cafes. I don't know how I got there, and they told me that I could say nothing but my name, Pietro, over and over. It was many months before I spoke any more, they said.'

Pietro was gratified by Lucky's avid attention – he had wanted to impress his new friend – but he didn't wish to sound sorry for himself, so he smiled. 'There were many war orphans at the convent, and they played us music on the gramophone, so I called myself Toscanini.'

'You must forgive me, Pietro. I am too nosy, I always have been, it is a flaw in my nature.' Lucky had seen the flicker in the boy's eyes as he'd embarked upon his story, and he chastised himself. There were many on the Snowy who had pasts they did not wish to revisit. The boy had been traumatised and he should not have pushed him. 'I am sorry.'

'But there is no need to be,' Pietro insisted, surprised by Lucky's obvious remorse. 'I wished to tell you my story.'

'One day I will tell you mine, my young friend.' Lucky grinned as he rose, tapping a finger to his bloodhound eye. 'How I came by this, eh? But for now, I will get you another beer.'

Ever since that night, Lucky had taken Pietro under his wing. He had encouraged him to attend the English classes held in the mess hall two nights a week, and Pietro had applied himself diligently. And when Lucky had invited Pietro to the home of his friends, Miroslav and Vesna, he had encouraged the boy to practise his new language. Pietro had been shy at first, but it had been Vesna who had put him at his ease.

'My English is too bad,' she had said, and when her husband had laughed, she had demanded, 'Why is wrong?'

'My English, too, is bad,' Miroslav had corrected her.

'Yes, most bad,' she had agreed. 'So we is practise together, Pietro.'

It had been easy after that, and Pietro had become good friends with Vesna as they clumsily helped each other master the language.

She told him her background. She was Serbian, she said, and Miroslav was Croatian, and they came from towns just a mile either side of the border. But they hadn't met in the old country; they had met in Australia eighteen months before.

'All my life Miroslav live two mile away,' she laughed, 'and I meet him first week I am in Brisbane.'

Miroslav had been in Brisbane for three years when they'd met and, having served out his two-year Displaced Persons contract, had received his accreditation as an engineer. They had fallen in love the moment they first met, Vesna said, much to the disapproval of their respective families. Miroslav's brother, who had also emigrated, had severed all ties with him.

'The Serbs and the Croats,' she said, 'is much hate. But for Miroslav and me, we leave this behind. We is Australia now. Is new life here.'

Pietro vehemently agreed with her. He, too, was embracing his new life, feeling himself grow stronger with each week that passed. Just as the physical labour honed and strengthened his body, so the company of his fellow workers and the gradual ability to communicate strengthened his belief in himself.

But it was Lucky who had made the deepest impression upon him, for it was Lucky who had taught him to love the landscapes of his new country.

On a Sunday, several weeks after Pietro's arrival, the two had travelled the countryside together in one of the Land Rovers to which Lucky appeared to have constant access. He had earned the right. He was Rob Harvey's most valued foreman, not only because of his communication skills and his popularity with the men, but for the fact that he doubled as a motor mechanic. Although not officially qualified, there was very little Lucky didn't know about cars. They were his obsession, and he would happily spend all his recreational time tinkering with engines that needed attention. Rob Harvey quite rightly considered it only fair that Lucky should have a vehicle at his ready disposal.

They had driven into the mountains and pulled up beside the banks of the mighty Snowy, and Lucky had

painted the pictures in Italian for Pietro. Normally he
insisted upon speaking English to further the boy's education, but he'd wanted to communicate his passion.

'During the snowmelt, Pietro,' he'd said, 'she roars
down the mountain like herds of wild white horses. She is
magnificent.' He'd been silent for a while, before adding
with a touch of regret, 'I sometimes think it is sad that we
are harnessing her.' Then he'd started up the Land Rover
and they'd driven still higher, to where the track ended and
where, far above them, the craggy tips of the Snowies were
clothed in white.

'Your new mountains, Pietro. Perhaps not as high as
your alps in Italy, but just as splendid, do you not agree?'
Pietro had nodded, and Lucky had said, 'They are your
home now.'

As they'd wound their way back down the track, Lucky
had waved through the windows, an all-embracing gesture
at the trees passing by. 'Just look at them,' he'd said admiringly, and Pietro had. They were so varied, he'd thought,
different from the alpine forests he could still vaguely
recall. Some were black and stunted, while the pure white
trunks and graceful limbs of others shimmered in the sun.

'The trees are like women, Pietro,' Lucky had smiled.
'See how the blackbutt bends? She looks plain now, but
when winter comes she will accept her burden of snow
with ease, for she is a contortionist and she knows she is
pretty in white. And the snow gum,' he'd added, with a
mock frown of disapproval, 'the snow gum is shameless.
She is a hedonist, basking in the sun. She is white and
virginal now, but in the early autumn, she will flaunt her
summer tan and turn a deep shade of terracotta.' He'd
laughed out loud, thoroughly enjoying himself.

'And now I will show you Monaro country. It is a good
time of year for you to see it, before the snow covers the
high plains.'

When they were back in the valley, his mood had again

become serious. 'You thought this land was barren when you first arrived, Pietro, but you were wrong. There are whole worlds that live in these hills and plains.'

And he'd driven Pietro through a landscape that made him breathless with its beauty and variety. A landscape of rolling hills and grassy valleys. Of escarpments overlooking vast, treeless plains where the orange heads of the kangaroo fronds mingled with the silver-gold of the native grasses to ripple in the summer breeze like a massive multi-coloured river.

'It is so alive,' Pietro said as they gazed across the plain. He was reminded of the children's picture book Sister Anna Maria had given him for his thirteenth birthday, *Animals of Africa* it had been called. 'It looks like a sea of lions' manes,' he said. The countryside was taking on a new life to Pietro as he viewed it through Lucky's eyes.

Then they were in the granite belt, where huge mottled grey stone sculptures grew out of the soil, infinitesimally larger with the passing of each century as the ground was washed away from beneath them.

They wandered among the clusters of giant boulders strewn about the rocky plains, many the size of houses. 'Perhaps, in a thousand years, they might be the size of skyscrapers,' Lucky had mused. 'But then perhaps they will be dust. Who can tell?'

Here and there, the countryside was dotted with the stamps of man's intervention. The picturesque groves of imported poplars had been planted as memorials to fallen soldiers following World War I, Lucky had explained. Although they had a shorter lifespan than the indigenous trees, the poplars were nonetheless hardy, the mature tree sending up suckers and reinventing itself well before its demise, in order to ensure the survival of its species.

'A fitting choice for a memorial to the dead,' he'd said.

During the drive back to Spring Hill, Lucky had been aware that his passion for the countryside had been passed on to the boy, just as he had intended, and he was glad.

'This land and its history are ancient, Pietro,' he said, 'as ancient as time itself. But as a civilisation, it is only just being born, and we are a part of that birth. The birth of this country is our own rebirth. It will nurture and protect us, and we will repay it with our love, for we are free here. Free of all that haunts us,' he said meaningfully. He had not brought up the subject of Pietro's past since their early conversation and he had no intention of doing so now. 'Free to build a new life in a country without hate.'

The day had indeed had a profound effect upon Pietro. On their return to camp in the late afternoon, he'd felt light-headed and, with Lucky's words still ringing in his mind, strangely reborn. It no longer seemed to matter that his childhood was lost to him.

Pietro Toscanini couldn't remember a time when he had been happier. He belonged here, he thought. Here in the Snowy Mountains and the high plains of the Monaro. He was part of this country now, just as Lucky had said. And he would prove himself worthy of it. He would embrace this land. As Lucky had.

CHAPTER TWO

It was Saturday afternoon and Cooma was buzzing. Cooma was always buzzing these days, particularly on Saturdays. But this was no ordinary Saturday. This was Show Day Saturday.

For well over seventy years, Cooma's annual two-day Agricultural Show had been a major social event for the entire rural community. In earlier times, farmers had walked their stock into town, proudly parading their prize cattle and sheep down the main street. These days the stock was mostly brought in by trucks. In the Agricultural Hall, wool and fresh produce were exhibited alongside the cakes and condiments and needlework of the ladies; in the ring, events from gymkhana and showjumping to wood-chopping and livestock parades took place non-stop, each duly followed by the presentation of coveted ribbons and prizes; and of course there were games and rides for the children.

Since the arrival of the Snowy Mountains Authority and its huge contingent of workers, however, the Cooma Show had grown into a far bigger and grander affair. The SMA itself had become involved. There were displays of heavy machinery and mining equipment and, in a specially erected tent, films of the Scheme were shown. But it was the Snowy workers themselves who had had the most impact on the show, as hundreds upon hundreds paid their three shilling entrance fee at the gate and poured into the Cooma showgrounds.

The ever-increasing crowds quickly attracted the attention of the travelling show circuit, and sideshows became a crowd favourite, as did the regular horse riders who travelled the countryside competing at all the rural shows, of which Cooma's was the biggest. The Snowy workers, inveterate gamblers, were only too keen to place a wager on the rider of their preference in every event imaginable, from races to rodeo to showjumping, and even dressage.

For locals and new arrivals alike, the two show days of the year were a highlight, and this particular Saturday, March 20, 1954, was no exception. The 79th Annual Cooma Show was proving bigger and better than ever.

In the ringside stands, audiences cheered as sturdy horses cleared each newly raised bar. Wide-eyed children with sticky-pink fairy-floss faces wandered among gaudy stalls clutching kewpie dolls and cheap china statues. Mingling with the ever-present smell of fried sausages and onions were the more exotic aromas from the several European food stalls, and above the hubbub and the merry-go-round music of the calliope, the voices of the spruikers could clearly be heard touting the attractions of coconut stalls, shooting galleries and sideshows.

'Line up! Line up! Is there a local boy wants to give it a go? Line up, line up and test yourself against the greatest fighting legends in the country!'

Of all the sideshows, Jim Sharman's boxing tent was the most favoured by the Snowy workers. Crowds gathered by the dozens, all ready to lay bets on who'd make the requisite three rounds.

On a makeshift platform outside the tent stood several

professional boxers, formidable men, strong-bodied in
their satin shorts, tough-faced, defying challengers, and, as
Jim Sharman continued to tout through his loudhailer,
bearing the most ludicrous of names and claims.

'Wild Billy Burrum Burrum, never been beaten!' he
declaimed of an Aboriginal boxer who dutifully squared
up. The crowd gave a cheer – Billy was always popular.
'And two-time All Ireland Champion, the one and only
Patrick Murphy!' Jim yelled, pointing to another who
danced on the spot and jabbed the air with his fists, the
Irish among the gathering applauding loudly even as they
laughed and muttered to each other 'what a load of shite'.

'Name your man! Three rounds, ten bob a round if you
can make it. An extra quid if you can beat my man. Who
wants to prove himself? Do I have any takers?'

'Go on, Luigi.' Urged on by his mates, Luigi was about
to put up his hand, but Elvio stopped him, flashing a
knowing look at Pietro and Lucky, who both grinned.
Luigi was always itching for a fight and it was always
Elvio who held him back.

Pietro had eventually made good his promise to visit the
Capelli brothers, whom he'd met on the train from Sydney
to Cooma. He'd been reluctant at first, but when Lucky
had promised he'd accompany him, he'd finally taken the
plunge. Now, after several trips to Cooma and many a
beer together, the four men had become friends.

At the showground, Luigi had met up with half a dozen
workmates, also Italians employed by Pasotti's and based
in Cooma. Insisting on heading straight for Jim Sharman's
tent, they were disappointed now when Elvio stopped his
younger brother from accepting the challenge. They themselves were not prepared to volunteer, but they would have
liked to have seen one of their own in the ring.

A strong young man in khaki shorts and shirt boldly
stepped forward. He'd come for the specific purpose of
fighting, and he'd brought eight of his friends along to

back him up. 'I take Patrick Murphy,' he called in a thick, guttural accent.

'Brave lad! Good on you, mate!' Slinging a comradely arm around the shoulder of the young man, Jim hauled him out in front of the crowd. 'Here's a local prepared to take on the two-time All Ireland Champion, let's hear it for him!' he shouted through the loudhailer, and a cheer went up. 'What's your name, son, and where are you from?'

'My name is Erik,' the young man said, and he waved to his mates who yelled back enthusiastically. 'I am from Cooma.'

'Course you are, mate, course you are,' Jim said with boisterous approval. 'But where are you from before Cooma?'

'Kassel.'

'And where's that?'

'Germany.'

There were more supportive yells from Erik's friends, all of whom were German, and there were loud boos from another quarter – specifically the Italians, with Luigi leading the troops.

Pietro was surprised – surely they should all be backing the Snowy man? – and he cast a quizzical glance at Lucky. But Lucky just shrugged.

'Well, good on you, Erik. Good for you, mate!' Jim grabbed Erik's hand and held it high in a gesture of triumph as he addressed the crowd. 'This brave young bloke is going up against Patrick Murphy, two-time All Ireland Champion! Chances are we have another Max Schmeling right here in our midst!' he yelled, and the Germans bellowed at the mention of their own world champion. 'Line up! Line up!' Jim enthused, inciting the crowd. 'Showing on the inside! Showing on the inside! The All Ireland Champion meets the new Max Schmeling!' And, with a quick survey of the numbers gathered, he gave a nod to his man at the door of the tent, a further nod to his boxers and, clamping an arm firmly around Erik, he led him inside, still yelling through the loudhailer for the benefit of the crowd. 'Come on, son, let's show you the ropes! Line up! Showing on the inside! The All Ireland Champ meets the new Max Schmeling!'

Two other young locals, lined up earlier, were already awaiting their turn in the tent, but Jim decided he'd put Erik on first; the crowd reaction to him was excellent.

While the eager audience poured in, Erik was taken aside to be gloved by an assistant and Jim muttered his instructions to 'Patrick Murphy'.

'Let him go the three rounds, Col, I want to milk the crowd.'

Colin 'Patrick Murphy' Jenkins nodded his understanding; he'd guessed as much the moment the cheering and jeering had started.

Jim Sharman's boxers, despite their ludicrous claims to fame, were indeed professionals adept at choreographing a fight. They knew how to prolong the action and how to take a dive, and they always obeyed their instructions, the principal one being that no punter was to be badly hurt. Jim couldn't afford to lose his licence.

Pietro, Lucky and the Italians were among the first to enter the tent and took ringside spots beside the makeshift roped-off square in the centre. Erik's friends, keen to spur on their mate, quickly jostled their way to the front on the opposite side.

The tent was packed. Money rapidly changed hands as men laid bets on whether Erik would last three rounds. The other professional boxers, now clad in robes and doubling as bouncers, wandered the periphery of the ring keeping the crowd several feet from the ropes, while Jim stood in the centre bawling instructions.

'Stand back, give them air, don't crowd the ring.' Then finally, as the mob settled, came the dramatic announcement: 'And now let's hear it for . . . Patrick Murphy! Two-time All Ireland Champion!' The Italians and the Irish vociferously applauded Patrick Murphy as he stepped into the ring and danced about, gloved hands delivering forceful air-punches. The others reserved their applause for the local contender.

'And here he is! Will he make the three rounds? Has he got the stamina? Let's hear it for our latest contender . . . Erik! The new Max Schmeling! All the way from Germany!'

Along with the Germans, the majority of men cheered their fellow Snowy worker as he climbed into the ring, but Luigi and his mates voiced their disapproval at the top of their lungs and, as the applause died down and the men went to their corners, the Italians continued to boo loudly.

'Enough! Enough!' Jim eventually roared. 'Give it a rest, give the boy a break, and let's commence . . .' A dramatic pause . . . 'Round One!' He delivered the signal. The bell rang. The men came out of their corners and the fight was on.

Erik was fit and strong. Two years' heavy physical labour on the Snowy had brought him to peak condition and, having won a number of amateur boxing championships in his home country, he was not altogether inexperienced.

None of this went unnoticed by Colin 'Patrick Murphy' Jenkins. The kid was an amateur, sure, he thought, but not your regular mug. In fact, Erik was just the sort of bloke who could land a lucky punch. Col blocked and sparred, buying time, watching the young man like a hawk and, when he sensed the audience needed a bit more action, he landed a right to the face. A glancing blow, not too hard, just enough to urge the kid and the crowd on.

The Italians cheered Patrick Murphy's punch even louder than the Irish, and Erik's friends countered by roaring encouragement to him in German. Then the other men gave voice to their fellow Snowy worker and the cheers of

Patrick Murphy's supporters were all but drowned out. 'Give it to him, Erik!' the men yelled. 'Go on, mate, you can do it!' And, fired up by the crowd, Erik did.

It was just what Col wanted: the kid was suddenly behaving like a mug, giving it all he had. Col could read him easily and he feinted twice before allowing one of the blows to glance him. The kid was going wild, the Germans were cheering, the Italians booing, and if the kid didn't watch it, Col thought, he'd run out of steam well before round three. He held him in a clinch so that the kid could get his breath back, and the bell rang end of round one.

During the next round, Jim Sharman, refereeing in the centre of the ring, kept his eyes and ears open to the mood of the crowd, as he always did. The Germans and Italians were yelling abuse at each other now, but Jim didn't mind. It was what he loved most about the Cooma Show. Everywhere else, from the big Royal Shows of the cities, to the smallest of rural community fairs, everyone rooted for the local boy. Here in Cooma there was the added excitement of faction against faction – it was a good crowd-pleaser. He gave the secret hand signal to Col to cop a couple more punches. The mob could do with an extra thrill – Erik was fired up and they were loving it. Col dutifully copped two more punches and the bell rang end of round two.

Halfway into round three Erik had tired himself out to such an extent that even Col's clinches, designed not only to give the kid air, but to signal to the crowd that he, too, was tiring, weren't really doing the trick. The kid was supposed to make it through, and if something didn't happen soon, Col thought, the crowd would sense a sham.

The two of them danced clumsily in the ring, locked together, and Col looked over Erik's heaving shoulder for Jim's hand signal. A lucky punch, it said. He'd thought as much. It irked him, it always did, but this time more so than ever. He pushed the kid away, got in three sharp jabs, none of which, he knew, would do any harm, before leaving himself open for the uppercut. He pulled his head up and to the left, going with the punch so that it would do little damage. Then he dropped.

The fight was over, and Patrick Murphy lay on his back attempting to struggle to his feet while Jim counted to ten. Then, when he stood, seemingly unsteady on his feet, conceding defeat, the crowd went wild. The Italians jeered at the All Irish Champion, and the Germans and the others cheered Erik as Jim held his arm high, announcing the winner.

With jeers and cheers ringing around the tent, Col leaned against the corner post, pretending a fatigue he didn't feel. Bugger it, he thought. The kid'd earn an extra quid for winning the fight instead of just seeing out the three rounds, and he'd be a hero to his mates. Col wondered what his own mates in Sydney would say if he told them he'd thrown a fight to a bloody Kraut. They wouldn't understand, he didn't himself, it only ever happened in Cooma. But shit, that was part of his job, he'd had half a dozen fights already today, and there'd be more to go, so no point dwelling on it.

As the mob poured out of the tent fifteen minutes later, two of the Germans hoisted Erik onto their shoulders, unintentionally barging into the Italians as they did so, which annoyed Luigi.

'It was set up,' he said to his mates, very loudly and in English, so that the Germans could hear. 'The fight, it was rigged.'

There was a tense moment, as Erik signalled his friends to put him down and the Germans squared up to the Italians.

'You are a bad loser,' one of Erik's mates said.

Luigi was about to come back with a further retort – he was in the mood for trouble – but Elvio interrupted. 'It was a good fight,' he said. And then Lucky stepped forward.

'*Ja. Das war ein gute Kampf, mein Freund,*' he said to

the Germans and he offered his hand to Erik. '*Sehr gut, Erik.*'

'*Danke schön.*' Erik returned the handshake and the moment passed, the Germans agreeing with Lucky that it had been an excellent fight, chatting to him in their mother tongue, patting their hero on the back and eventually dragging Erik off to ply him with beer.

Luigi was left scowling, and his workmates looked even grimmer, casting openly antagonistic glares at Lucky, whom they'd not met before.

Lucky decided, diplomatically, that it was time to part company. 'I am going to see Peggy,' he said in Italian to Pietro and Elvio. 'I promised I would – she is working in the Agricultural Hall.'

Pietro nodded. He would far rather go with Lucky than remain with the brothers' friends, but Peggy was Lucky's girlfriend and he didn't wish to intrude.

'I will see you at Dodds?' Elvio asked, and Lucky responded with a smile of recognition. Of the many pubs in Cooma, Elvio knew that Dodds Family Hotel was Lucky's favourite hangout, just as Lucky himself knew that the brothers usually drank with their mates at the Railway or the Cooma. The offer to meet at Dodds was Elvio's unspoken apology for his workmates' unfriendliness.

'Of course,' Lucky replied. 'I will be there in an hour.'

When he'd gone, Luigi announced that he and the others were off to the Railway, but Elvio declined to join them. He would wander around the showgrounds until it was time to meet Lucky, he replied pointedly. 'What do you say, Pietro? Shall I challenge you to a shooting contest?' Pietro thankfully agreed.

The Capelli brothers parted a little coldly. Luigi knew that Elvio was cross with him for his perceived rudeness to Lucky, but he'd intended no insult to Lucky at all. Lucky was their friend. Lucky was different. It was those other German *bastardos* he couldn't abide.

'What was that about?' Pietro asked, as he and Elvio headed off for the shooting gallery.

'Italians and Germans,' Elvio shrugged. 'They do not mix.'

'Here they do, don't they?' Pietro queried. He had not encountered any such friction at Spring Hill. 'Here we are all Snowy men.' He glanced back at the tent where Jim Sharman was once again touting through the loudhailer, his boxers lined up on the platform, Patrick Murphy having made a remarkable recovery. 'We should have been backing the Snowy man in the fight.'

Elvio smiled. At times Pietro seemed bordering on simple, he thought, which was not surprising given the boy's sheltered upbringing, but his simplicity was refreshing in its innocence.

'You are right, Pietro,' he said, 'but people cannot change overnight. Some find it difficult to leave their hatred behind. I, too, have no liking for Germans,' he admitted, 'but it does not mean I wish to pick fights as Luigi does. That is an unfortunate part of his nature.'

'But you and Luigi both like Lucky,' Pietro persisted, genuinely puzzled. 'And Lucky is a German.'

'Lucky is different.'

'Why?'

'Lucky is a Jew.'

'Oh. Is he?' Pietro had never met a Jew. Not that he was aware of. There had certainly been no Jews at the orphanage throughout his schooling, nor during the four years he'd stayed on at the Convent of the Sacred Heart as a gardener. And during his twelve months at the building site in Milano, there had been no Jews. But then perhaps there had been, he thought; how would he have known? And then it occurred to him that there must be many Jews working on the Snowy and that he'd probably met lots of them, it was just that nobody had ever bothered pointing them out to him.

'Does that mean that Lucky is not a real German then?'
he asked as they arrived at the shooting gallery, and Elvio
laughed as he dug some coins out of his pocket.

'You ask too many questions, Pietro,' he said, giving
the money to the man behind the counter, who passed him
two rifles. 'Questions too complicated for me to answer.'
He handed one of the rifles to Pietro. 'Here,' he said in
English, 'my shout.'

In the Agricultural Hall, Lucky pushed through the crowds
that meandered about the exhibits and flower displays,
weaving his way as best he could towards the kitchen
where he knew Peggy would be working hard with the
team of ladies serving refreshments.

The vast hall had seen better days but was still impressive. Upon its official opening in 1887, the pavilion had
been described as 'the finest in the Colony south of
Sydney' and over the years it had served Cooma well. Now
known as the Agricultural Hall, it was not only a showground pavilion but a regular venue for balls and all other
manner of social events. It was currently even serving as a
temporary school. The influx of Snowy children had
rendered the town's only public school sadly inadequate,
and the new school was still under construction, so, on
weekdays, canvas partitions were erected in the hall to
form makeshift classrooms. Draughty in the cold, stuffy in
the heat, they had earned the title 'Tent City' from teachers
and students alike. But, uncomfortable as the conditions
were, it was evident to all that the ever-versatile pavilion
was once again proving itself invaluable to the people of
Cooma.

Peggy was at the far end of a queue of several women
working at the large kitchen bench. She was carving a leg
of mutton, and the dexterity with which she handled the
huge knife seemed at odds with the neat, sharp-featured
little woman that she was. Standing there in her neat apron

and her tidy floral dress, her tidy brown hair secured in a severe bun at the nape of her neck, her butcher-like expertise with the carving knife was most incongruous.

Peggy Minchin, upon first impression, was not unattractive; rather, she was unapproachable. To most, she appeared a mixture of frosty and fragile, when, in truth, she was neither. She was feisty, outspoken, and above all efficient. Peggy Minchin was efficient at everything she tackled, which today included carving mutton. Shaving away at the leg, she was nearly down to the bone, and a pile of meat lay neatly stacked on the cutting board beside her.

The women were making sandwiches in conveyor-belt fashion, one slicing the loaves of bread, another buttering the slices and adding homemade chutney, the third in the line inserting Peggy's freshly sliced mutton and cutting the thick sandwiches in two. The final member of the group, the young daughter of one of the women, ran to and fro with fresh supplies and, when there was a substantial pile of sandwiches, she collected them on a platter for sale at the counter, where another team of ladies was making and serving tea from a large urn in the corner.

'G'day, Lucky love.' The big woman slicing the bread didn't halt in her actions, but gave him a breezy grin and a jerk of the head. 'She's up the end there.'

'Thank you, Edna. Good afternoon, ladies.' Lucky nodded politely to each of them, receiving tight smiles of recognition from Mavis and Vera. It wasn't that they disapproved of Lucky himself. Lucky was well respected among the locals. He'd been working for the Snowy for years now and was one of the better assimilated foreigners. Extremely so, in fact: his English was perfect. But Mavis and Vera could not condone the relationship that appeared to have developed between Lucky and Peggy Minchin over the past several months.

'He's courting her!' Vera had said disbelievingly when

the two had been spotted around town several weekends
in a row, dancing to the band at the Snowy Mountains Inn,
or gathered around the piano at Dodds, Peggy leading the
singalong.

'*She's* courting *him*, you mean,' Mavis had retorted,
outraged. 'Brazen, I call it. She's a *schoolteacher*! It's
shameful.'

'And he's a *German*, what's more.'

They both agreed that made it far worse.

Mavis and Vera were not the only ones who disapproved. Several parents of local children had complained to
the school. 'Teachers are expected to set a good example,'
they maintained, and the principal had been reluctantly
forced to suggest to Peggy, with all the tact he could muster,
that she be a little more 'discreet' in her private life. Peggy
had asked no questions, she knew just what he was talking
about and her response had been simple. If she couldn't
keep company with whoever she wished, she said, then she
would seek employment elsewhere. The principal, who'd
had no argument with the situation in the first place, hastily
backed down. Cooma was desperately in need of teachers.
They couldn't afford to lose one, and certainly not the best
they had. From that day on, he'd turned a deaf ear to any
further complaints about Peggy Minchin and 'that German'
and most of the outrage had died down. But there were still
some like Mavis and Vera who whispered disapprovingly
among themselves and on occasion made sure it was loud
enough for others to hear.

Today was no such occasion, however, because Edna
was there.

'Go on, Lucky,' Edna called over the babble of noise,
'get her out of here, she hasn't had a break for four hours.'

Edna had seen Peggy's face light up. When Peggy had
stopped attacking the mutton for a brief second and
flashed Lucky a smile, she'd looked downright beautiful,
Edna thought. God but that girl was in love. 'Besides, she's

way ahead up her end. Just look at it, will you. I've never seen anyone carve a leg better.'

Having noticed the pile of sliced mutton, Edna stopped working and looked at her own stack of sliced bread. 'You're slowing up again, Mavis,' she said. Then she scowled at the fine veil of chutney Mavis was carefully wiping over each slice. 'And you're spreading it miles too thin.'

'Just trying not to waste it, that's all,' Mavis replied through pursed lips. This particular jar of chutney was from her own batch, and she always spread it this thin at home.

'The men like it thick – you've got to pile it on. I told you that before.'

Edna could see that Mavis was miffed, but she didn't care, Mavis was always miffed about something, and, returning her attention to the end of the counter, she noticed Peggy's hesitance as Lucky whispered in her ear. The girl felt guilty about leaving her post, Edna realised.

'Oh go on, love,' she urged, 'you two get out of here. We'll have to be packing it in soon anyway.'

Young Tess arrived with the platter to collect the sandwiches. 'That was the last leg, Mum,' she said, 'we're out of mutton.'

'There you are, you see.' Edna shrugged in an I-told-you-so way, and Peggy laughed.

'All right, it's meant to be. I'm off.' She quickly untied her apron, threw it on a packing case in the corner and grabbed Lucky's hand. 'Come on, let's go.'

'Goodbye, ladies.' Lucky rolled his eyes, the bloodhound one looking particularly alarmed as he pretended to be physically dragged away. Tess laughed and Vera was about to do the same until she caught Mavis's eye. She quelled her laughter and joined Mavis in another tightly polite smile.

'Are you bringing him to the ball tonight, Peg?' Edna called just before the couple disappeared through the door.

'You bet I am, Edna,' Peggy called back. 'You bet I am.'

The polite smiles vanished as Mavis and Vera exchanged looks of amazement. Surely she wasn't going to bring her German boyfriend to the P & A ball! But they didn't dare say anything in front of Edna. Edna was a force to be reckoned with, and one who approved of change. It was Edna who had suggested that the Pastoral and Agricultural Association should consider including European food stalls at the show. 'Something different – we need to change with the times,' she'd said. As usual, few had chosen to disagree with Edna, and Mavis and Vera certainly weren't about to start now, so they returned to their sandwiches. But they would talk about the matter in depth later on, Mavis would make sure of that. Peggy Minchin really was going too far.

Lucky and Peggy found a relatively quiet spot behind the pavilion.

'I've missed you,' he said. It had been three weeks and he longed to gather her to him and feel her body against his. He would have done so. Lucky was a passionate man and had no qualms about openly expressing his feelings, but he was aware of her position and the censure of local society, and took care not to compromise her.

'I've missed you too.' It was Peggy who initiated the kiss. She was suddenly in his arms, her face upturned, her mouth inviting him, and before Lucky knew it their lips had met. The kiss was brief. Even as she'd acted instinctively Peggy had been aware that her behaviour was outrageous. But short though the moment was, it held a wealth of passion and, when they hastily parted, both were a little breathless.

'Have a seat,' Lucky said, pulling over one of the many wooden crates strewn about and hoping, for Peggy's sake, that no-one had seen them. There were a number of people around, but they seemed to have paid no heed as they busily gathered up crates themselves in preparation for packing. The show was nearing its end and in an hour or so they would start clearing the hall for that evening's ball.

Peggy sat. She didn't look around – she refused to – but casual glances from the corner of her eyes assured her that none of her many pupils had been present to witness her indiscretion. Thank goodness for that. She'd rather shocked herself.

Lucky overturned a crate and, as he sat, he decided to get straight to the point. 'I cannot go to the ball with you, Peggy,' he said.

'Why not? You said that you would.'

'I said that I *might*.' He hated to disappoint her and he had intended to go. He'd been looking forward to it; he'd brought his best suit into town and it was hanging in the wardrobe at the hostel. But he'd seen the looks on the women's faces as he'd left the kitchen. They'd been horrified. And it had occurred to Lucky that he'd not heard other workers boasting in the past about having gone to the show ball. On Saturday show night they all went to the pub. It might well cause a great deal of trouble for Peggy if she took him along.

'None of the other Snowy men ever go to the ball, do they?' he asked.

'Of course they do,' she replied with an all-encompassing wave of her hand. 'Lots of them, dozens, all nationalities . . .'

He captured her hand mid-air and smiled as he interrupted: 'Lots of them, dozens, and all nationalities from the SMA, you mean, don't you, Peggy?'

'Yes, of course,' she said. 'But that doesn't . . .'

'And along with the SMA hierarchy there will be the show committee. And then there will be the farmers, and the competitors and the exhibitors . . .'

'And anyone else who buys a ticket,' she briskly concluded.

'But there won't be any Snowy workers, will there?'

'Then it's high time there were. Can't you get any of your friends to buy a ticket?'

'They'll be at the pub, as they always are.'

'Well, that's their bad luck,' she said dismissively before starting on another tack, facetious this time, although she sensed she was losing the battle. 'Just think, Lucky, you'll be the envy of Spring Hill – as my guest you get to go to the ball free.'

He squeezed the hand he was still holding, forcing her to be serious. 'I don't think it is wise for you to take me along, Peggy. I don't mean for myself,' he added, aware she was about to interrupt again. 'I mean for you. I saw the looks on the faces of those women in there.'

Peggy realised that she had misunderstood his reluctance. She had presumed he felt self-conscious at the prospect of mingling with the locals and the farmers and the SMA bosses. She should have known better: Lucky had the confidence to rise above the petty class consciousness that still persisted in many areas.

'I'm sorry, I've been bossy, haven't I?'

'Of course,' he grinned. 'You always are.'

'Once a schoolteacher . . .' She gave an apologetic shrug. 'Thanks for worrying about me, I appreciate it.' She did. Few people had ever worried about her; it was a refreshing change. 'But you don't need to, you know. I can look after myself.'

'Oh yes, I'm aware of that.' Lucky nodded vehemently: he'd seen her in action many a time over the past three years since she'd arrived in Cooma. Most people had. It was a known fact that Peggy Minchin could be quite aggressive, particularly when she perceived an injustice. When a busy shopkeeper favoured locals over Europeans, as many very often did, Peggy would loudly announce 'they were here first!', embarrassing everyone, particularly the Europeans who would have preferred to wait patiently until the crowds died down and who, often struggling with an inadequate command of the English language, hated suddenly being the focus of attention.

Once, early in their relationship, well before they'd become lovers, Lucky had offered Peggy a friendly word of advice on the matter, suggesting that she could perhaps be a little more 'sensitive' in her approach. Peggy had been vociferous in her disagreement. 'People need to be taught,' she'd said, 'both the locals and the Europeans. The longer the Europeans fail to exercise their rights, the longer the locals will walk all over them.'

Unable to refute such a statement, Lucky had never broached the subject again. He respected Peggy for her spirit and her sense of justice and the strength of her beliefs. But, as his respect had slowly blossomed into something deeper, he had seen beyond the facade. It was a pity, he thought, that Peggy Minchin was unable to believe, with equal strength, in herself as a woman. And over the past several months, since they'd become lovers, he often wondered if there were others who guessed, as he had, that beneath the ever-efficient exterior and the outspoken confidence, Peggy Minchin was, at heart, the most vulnerable of women.

'Come on!' She jumped up. He was looking thoughtful and she had a feeling he might be weakening. She dragged him to his feet. 'Come with me tonight, I dare you! There'll be a band.' Her eyes, always so piercingly blue and intelligent, sparkled, childlike with hope, and the smile that urged him to say 'yes' was, to Lucky, irresistible, the tiny dimple in the right cheek hinting at the daredevil sense of humour which he knew always lurked beneath the surface. 'Come on, Lucky, give in. You know how you love to dance.'

She had no idea, he thought, how truly beguiling she could be. She didn't know that, like this, animated and vital, she was very, very pretty. He liked to tell her so, although he was aware that she didn't believe him.

'Pretty Peggy Minchin,' he laughed, pushing back the stray wisp that had escaped its confines and picturing her hair splayed out on the pillow; Peggy had lovely hair. 'Pretty pretty Peggy, how could I possibly resist?'

She returned his smile. These days she no longer shrugged off his compliments or laughed self-consciously as she first had. Not that she believed him. She was not pretty, she never had been. But she believed that Lucky thought she was and, inexplicably, in his company she felt pretty.

'I'm glad,' she said, 'I like to be irresistible.' She was as irresistible as she was pretty, she thought, but if she appeared so to Lucky, then that was all that mattered.

Peggy had never had any illusions about her appearance. She looked like a schoolteacher; she had since she was eighteen. Neat, efficient, thin-faced and at times stern, just the way a schoolteacher should look. It had never bothered her. In fact, she'd decided early on that she rather liked her image; it fitted who she was. Teaching was, after all, more than a chosen profession, it was a vocation. At least it was to Peggy. Which was why, following her Sydney graduation, she had volunteered for an outback posting where she'd remained for the following ten years. Outback children, Peggy maintained, were like the land: as starved of opportunity and inspiration as the drought-ridden country was starved of water, and her greatest joy was to watch them blossom like the country did after rain. The only time Peggy ever waxed lyrical was when she spoke of her 'calling', as she termed it.

Upon answering the desperate plea for teachers needed in Cooma, Peggy had been confronted by a new form of pupil far more challenging than those suffering the privations of an isolated existence. In the ill-equipped, over-crowded classrooms were many European youngsters who had witnessed and lived through shocking times, some having arrived directly from displaced persons camps.

They were frightened and insecure, and they trusted no-one. It was the greatest test Peggy had yet faced and, dedicated as she was, she rose to the occasion. Her new students became her children, and gradually even the most damaged responded to her strength, her discipline, her care, and her utter devotion.

It was Peggy's blind devotion to her calling which had, over the years, deprived her of any personal life. She had deliberately lost her virginity to a young physical education instructor when she was in her mid-twenties, feeling it was high time she found out what it was all about, but she had never been in love. Nor had she sought a husband; she had no desire to be dependent upon a man, and at thirty-three she had settled quite comfortably into her role as a spinster. Then along had come Lucky. He'd been just a friend at first, an intelligent, well-educated man with whom she shared stimulating conversations and chess games. He remained just a friend for two whole years while she denied to herself there could possibly be any attraction. And then he kissed her. A little over three months ago now. And that kiss had changed Peggy's life.

'Don't bother coming to pick me up,' she said, efficiency once again the order of the day. 'I'll meet you out the front of the hall at half-past eight, things don't really start happening until around nine, does that suit?'

'It does,' he replied with a mock salute, and he walked her back inside the pavilion, refusing the offer of a cup of tea in the kitchen. 'I'm to meet Pietro at Dodds,' he said. 'I left him in the company of some rather hot-headed Italians, although I knew he'd far rather come and see you.'

'The Italians will do him more good – Pietro needs a bit of toughening up.'

The women were selling the last of the sandwiches and starting to clear things away. In less than two hours the hired professionals would be arriving to decorate the hall for the evening.

'See you at the ball, Edna,' Lucky said loudly, before turning to Mavis and Vera. 'Good afternoon, ladies.' He bowed slightly, gave each of them a winning smile, then flashed a barely perceptible wink at Peggy and left. Mavis and Vera, aware they were being observed, didn't quite know where to look.

Peggy and Edna exchanged a quick glance of amusement before getting on with their work. How could she possibly have assumed Lucky's reluctance to go to the ball stemmed from insecurity? Peggy thought. Lucky of all people!

'I've got nothing against Germans. Live and let live, I say.' Cam Campbell was a man's man. Or rather that was how he perceived himself to be and how he wished to be perceived by others. A good bloke who called a spade a spade and wasn't afraid to speak his own mind. 'So long as a bloke's honest I don't give a bugger where he comes from. Good to meet you, mate. Cheers.' He clinked his beer glass resoundingly against Lucky's and both men drank.

Heavy-handed as Cam Campbell's bonhomie was, he appeared sincere and Lucky was grateful to the man for rescuing him. Peggy had left him stranded with two P & A lady committee members early in the evening, saying she was off to check on Edna and the volunteer caterers and she'd be back in a minute.

'But I thought you weren't working tonight.'

'I'm not. They might just want a quick hand setting up, that's all,' and she'd disappeared in the direction of the kitchen.

Half an hour later, as the members of the local band started tuning their instruments, Lucky had found himself still marooned with the lady committee members. Having shared with him their admiration of the decorations – the streamers, the balloons, the floral arrangements and the festive atmosphere of the hall in general – the ladies had embarked upon an intensely personal discussion about a particularly cantankerous judge in the show's needlework section, and then they'd been joined by two of their male counterparts who'd discussed with equal intensity the improvements required to the main arena fence, and the fact that it must certainly be discussed at the next general meeting. Lucky had by that time been so assiduously ignored that he'd felt invisible, which he'd considered most fortunate. But then several farmers had arrived, one of them keen to discuss the collection and care of birds sent by rail for the poultry section and, as Lucky introduced himself, aware that no-one present would remember his name, he'd suddenly become very visible.

'You're a German, aren't you.' It had been an accusation rather than a question, and although the others had been silently nursing their own vague discomfort in the German's presence, they had been most embarrassed by the poultry farmer's overt hostility.

'Yes, I am German.'

'Thought so.'

That was when Cam had come to the rescue. He'd slapped the poultry farmer on the back. 'Look after your birds, Bill, that's what you're here for.' Everyone knew that Bill was a bit barmy when it came to Germans. His younger brother had died by his side at the Somme, so it was pretty understandable. 'Come on, mate,' he'd said to Lucky, 'let's go outside and grab a beer.' Out in the showground he'd headed for the nearest liquor booth and insisted on shouting the first round. 'Lucky you said, right?' He handed Lucky his beer and they edged clear of the crowd around the booth.

'Yes.'

'I'm Cam. Cam Campbell.' They shook. 'I've got nothing against Germans . . .' and Cam launched into his hail-fellow-well-met routine.

A successful farmer with a large family property not far

from Adaminaby, Thomas 'Cam' Campbell was a big, beefy man in his late forties, ruddy-faced with a smile both confident and likeable. Highly respected as one of the finest horsemen in the area, he was popular among his peers, and Lucky, like most, found himself warming to the man.

'You work for the Authority, I take it?' Cam queried after they'd clinked and taken a swig from their glasses.

'No, I'm a labourer, I work for Selmers,' Lucky said, referring to the Norwegian contractors handling the Guthega dam project. 'I'm based at Spring Hill.'

Cam was surprised. He'd assumed that the German, a cultivated man judging by his faultless English, was one of the experts brought out from Europe by the SMA. But he wasn't deterred by discovering the bloke was a labourer; he liked him all the more for it.

'Well, good on you, Lucky,' he said. 'There're plenty of decent honest blokes working here on the Snowy,' and he raised his glass in a toast of approval, 'which is more than I can say for the bloody SMA bosses!' Then he downed half his beer in several swift gulps before steering the conversation, with all the subtlety of a sledgehammer, to his favourite subject, as he always did when he had a captive audience.

'I tell you, mate, the SMA top brass are a pack of lying mongrels and I wouldn't trust them as far as I could spit.' He skolled the rest of his beer as if to emphasise the point; and besides, it was Show Night and Cam was in a drinking mood.

Lucky followed suit, draining his glass. He didn't really want to drink at this speed, but he knew the rules.

'My shout,' he said, and together they wove their way through the crowd back to the liquor booth, Cam talking all the while at the top of his voice.

'They think they can get us all on the cheap, but they'll have their work cut out with me, I can promise you . . .'

There were SMA employees everywhere, and mostly from the upper echelons of the hierarchy, but Cam couldn't care less who heard him. In fact, he hoped they did. He'd stated his case to the bosses loud and clear enough, and he'd state it again to anyone who'd listen. 'They can't buy me out for thirteen quid an acre and they know it. It's downright bloody robbery what they've done to some around here.'

Although Lucky rarely mixed with the farming community, he was kept well in touch with the events of the day by Rob Harvey, and he knew exactly what Cam was talking about. Despite the fact that it was still some years before the scheduled completion of the dam at Adaminaby and the flooding of the area, the Authority had been buying up the land since 1949 and there was much contention among the locals. 'The farmers do have a genuine gripe,' Rob had said. 'The SMA's taking advantage of them and the cockies'll come out the losers.'

To ensure discipline and avoid accusations of favouritism, Rob Harvey maintained a certain distance from his workers at Spring Hill, but he stretched the rules where Lucky was concerned, the two regularly meeting up for a beer in Cooma. Both well-educated men with a strong love of the land, Rob and Lucky shared a friendship of like minds, and Rob was thankful to have someone to whom he could speak openly. Loyal as he was to his employers and to the Scheme in general, there were areas which didn't entirely meet with his approval, the method of land purchase being just one of them. 'They're striking each deal individually,' he'd told Lucky, 'and taking advantage of the farmers' lack of negotiation skills. It's all a bit dodgy, if you ask me.'

'Thanks, mate.' Cam accepted the beer Lucky handed him and they again edged clear of the liquor booth.

'But I believe there are many receiving double that price now,' Lucky said after the obligatory clink and the 'cheers'.

Rob had told him as much. One or two of the farmers, Rob had said, were determined to hold out until the very last minute, which was causing a few headaches for the SMA. 'Good on them, I say,' Rob had added.

'And I hear the price is still going up,' Lucky said after he'd taken a swig from his glass.

Cam wasn't sure whether he was gratified or disappointed by the German's awareness of the state of play; he'd rather looked forward to explaining things from his point of view. But then, he thought, the German seemed like a very intelligent bloke, and so he decided to move on to his other pet topic, which was a little more sophisticated.

'Yeah, well, they'll need fifty quid an acre before they'll shift me,' he said. 'But I'll tell you something else for nothing, Lucky.' He lowered his voice, more for dramatic effect than anything. 'There's a conspiracy going on with that mob.'

'Oh? Really?' Lucky was most interested.

'Yep.' Cam was pleased that he'd captured the German's attention. Despite his wonky eye, there was something about the bloke that commanded respect, he thought. He was a man's man, Cam decided, that was it. 'Right from the start of the Scheme,' he said, 'when they approached us farmers, they told us that the alpine pastures'd be virtually unaffected.' He snorted derisively. 'Dumb cockies, that's what they think of us, the bastards. And they're right, we are. Or rather we were: we bloody well believed them. How dumb's that?' He took several gulps of beer to calm himself down. 'The high country's important to us, Lucky,' he explained, 'it's our summer grazing land. We take the cattle and sheep up there to feed on the new grass after the thaw, and we leave them up there for a good five months. That way the lower land regenerates and we get top feed for the herds during winter.'

Lucky remained attentively silent, aware that Cam Campbell was bent on letting off steam and didn't require a reply, but he was recalling a particular conversation he'd had with Rob Harvey. It had been several months ago now, shortly before young Pietro had arrived at Spring Hill, and he and Rob had been sitting upstairs at the Australian Hotel. 'Life is going to change for the Snowy River men,' Rob had said, looking down at the broad avenue of Sharp Street and the convoy of trucks carting supplies newly arrived by rail to the work camps out of town. He'd been in a reflective mood, as he often was with Lucky. 'In a few years, there'll be no more stockmen droving sheep and cattle by the thousands up to the high country. There'll be no more herds of wild brumbies rounded up on the plains. It'll be the end of an era.' He'd looked sad as he'd said it. 'The days of the mountain horsemen are numbered, Lucky. The trouble is, no-one's told them that yet.'

'And now they're talking about banning us from the high country,' Cam continued, outraged. 'They reckon the stock's causing soil erosion. Soil erosion! How's that for a joke?' He was getting carried away again. 'Have you seen the damage those bastards are doing up there? They're murdering this land, and they know it. What's more, they know that *we* know it. And *that's* why they're trying to ban alpine grazing,' he finished triumphantly. 'It's got bugger all to do with soil erosion! They don't want us up there because they don't want the truth to get out. It's a conspiracy, mate!'

The man's passion was understandable and Lucky was sympathetic to his predicament, but he didn't at all agree with Cam's theory. It was a simple fact that thousands of stock wandering the mountains would certainly cause erosion problems, and eventually siltation of the dams, which in the long term would affect the power stations. He'd said as much to Rob Harvey. 'It is the price of progress, Rob,' he'd said realistically, even as he'd agreed with Rob that the passing of the mountain man's era was regretful. 'But there may be a far greater price to pay one day. Who can tell what the future has in store for an undertaking as vast as the Snowy Scheme?'

Their conversation that day had remained vivid in Lucky's mind because it had been the one and only time either of them had spoken negatively about the very reason they were all there in the mountains.

'To alter the course of a river is to play a dangerous game with nature,' he'd said, not sure how Rob, staunchly loyal to the Scheme, would respond. 'Engineering projects in other parts of the world have proved it to be so,' he'd added, as if to back himself up in case he'd offended.

But no offence had been taken. Rob had merely wondered, yet again, why a university-educated man like Lucky continued to work as a labourer when he'd long since served out his Displaced Persons contract. Lucky himself always shrugged off any queries, saying it kept him fit. Rob had nodded in his lackadaisical way, 'Yep, it could be a worry.'

As Cam Campbell continued rabbiting on about his conspiracy theory, Rob's words came back to Lucky, and he rather wished it was Rob he was talking to now. Cam's one-sided view was wearingly dogmatic.

Deep down, Rob Harvey had agreed with Lucky's comments on the Scheme's possible long-term repercussions. Having initially studied geology and zoology before deciding on an engineering degree, Rob was more environmentally aware than most. 'You can't take all the water from one place and dump it somewhere else without asking for some sort of problems down the track,' he'd said.

The two had remained quiet for several moments, both feeling somehow disloyal – they were, after all, Snowy men – and it had been Rob who'd broken the guilty silence.

'Course I might be wrong,' he shrugged. 'I probably am.'

'You hope you are,' Lucky smiled.

'Too right, I do.' And they'd drunk to it.

'A bloody conspiracy, that's what it is!' Cam concluded

now, looking about belligerently, prepared to challenge any disagreement, but as the band struck up in the nearby pavilion no-one was paying him the slightest attention. 'They're not only a bunch of crooks out to rob us of our land, they're liars and hypocrites into the bargain. Well, bugger them! Bugger every bloody one of them!' He drained his glass and then nudged Lucky boisterously. 'Hey, you haven't finished your beer, mate. Drink up, my shout.'

Lucky, who was not a heavy drinker, looked at his untouched beer. The thought of downing it and embarking upon a third inside twenty minutes made him feel slightly bilious, but he knew that to knock back the offer of a beer was considered almost as rude as not returning a shout. Sighing inwardly, he took a few sips from his glass. No matter how 'assimilated' he might appear to the locals, and many congratulated him on the fact that he was, he knew he would never become accustomed to the drinking etiquette of the Australian male.

'Lucky!'

Saved, he thought thankfully as Peggy ran up to him and grabbed his hand.

'I'm terribly, terribly sorry, I didn't mean to desert you for so long, but they were short of help setting up and . . .' She broke off as she registered Cam Campbell. 'Oh hello, Cam.' She released Lucky's hand and shook Cam's warmly. 'I didn't see you at the show, but then I was stuck in the kitchen most of the time. I heard you picked up half the blue ribbons in the cattle section as usual,' she laughed.

'Hello, Peggy.' He didn't return her laugh. Cam Campbell's face was a mask. The shutters had gone down as his eyes flickered from Peggy to Lucky and back again. He couldn't disguise his shock and outrage and he didn't attempt to. Peggy Minchin was having it off with the German. But she was a school mistress! The most proper, the most respectable of school mistresses, a woman whom Cam had deeply admired. She'd taught his own daughter for

two years; young Vi still worshipped the ground 'Miss
Minchin' walked on, and 'Miss bloody Minchin' was having
it off with a Kraut. The way she'd looked at him when she'd
grabbed his hand. Brazen. Cam couldn't believe it.

So much for not giving a bugger where a bloke came
from, Lucky thought, and so much for the hypocrisy of the
SMA. The animosity that emanated from Cam Campbell
was palpable; the man was the biggest hypocrite of them all.

Lucky had suffered many a bigot in the past, particularly when he'd first arrived in Australia. Bigotry was
nothing new to him and he felt little more than annoyance at having been so easily taken in by Cam Campbell's
bluster. But he was angry for Peggy. Why should Peggy
be judged by the company she kept? And he was angry
with himself. He should not have come to the ball, he
should not have placed her in this compromising situation. Above all, he was angered by his powerlessness. He
dared not call the man a fraud, much as he longed to –
any form of confrontation would create a scene, and that
would be far more damaging for Peggy. So he smiled
instead.

'There is no need to apologise, Peggy,' he said. 'I have
been excellently entertained by Mr Campbell.' He couldn't
bring himself to call the man by his nickname, and as he
turned to Cam the smile froze on his lips.

You smarmy bastard, Cam thought. Pretending to be a
good, honest, working bloke, sharing a beer, listening to
a man pour out his troubles, and all the time you're
fucking the school mistress, you dirty rotten Kraut. Cam
wanted to belt him one.

'Thank you for looking after Lucky, Cam, I'm most
obliged.' Peggy's smile was bright and her crisp schoolteacher's voice held no added edge. 'How's Vi?'

'You tell me. Since she's moved into town you'd see
her more often than I would now, wouldn't you?' Cam's
animosity was plainly not reserved for Lucky.

'Yes, of course I would,' Peggy agreed, undeterred, 'and I do. But you'll have seen her yourself during the show, and you must be very proud. She won several events, I heard.'

'Two jumps and one dressage. She only entered three this year.'

'Cam's daughter, Vi, is a wonderful horsewoman,' Peggy said to Lucky. 'It runs in the family.' Another bright smile. 'And she's looking so pretty lately, isn't she? I see her around town a lot. Quite the young lady.'

'She should be back home where she belongs.'

'Don't worry about her too much, Cam, she's just turned eighteen, she wants to grow up.' Peggy's tone, while still briskly polite, was caring. It always was when she spoke of her ex-students. Each and every one was special to her, and Violet Campbell was no exception. 'She'll come back when she's ready.'

He did not respond. To think that less than a year ago he'd been telling young Vi to heed every word Peggy Minchin uttered. 'You listen to Miss Minchin, Vi,' he'd said time and again, 'she's a real lady, and she's got brains, what's more.' Well Miss bloody Minchin had now lost the right to offer any form of advice whatsoever where his daughter was concerned.

Cam was staring sullenly at the ground, so Peggy didn't wait for a reply. Turning to Lucky, she said, 'The band's playing and you haven't even asked me to dance.'

'May I have the pleasure?' he asked.

'You may.'

As she took his arm and they walked off to the pavilion, Lucky didn't look at Cam, but he could sense the farmer's eyes burning a hole in his back.

He whirled her onto the dance floor and into a speedy quickstep to the tune of 'Don't Let the Stars Get in Your Eyes'. Lucky was an excellent dancer and, as the band continued to play up-tempo numbers for most of the bracket, Lucky and Peggy didn't even think of taking a break – they danced to every single one. It was only when they'd finished waltzing to 'How Much is That Doggie in the Window', and the band announced it was taking a break, that they were forced to leave the dance floor.

'I have never danced for so long and with such energy – I'm thoroughly exhausted,' Peggy panted as they walked outside to buy a soft drink from one of the booths.

She was radiant. She didn't know it, Lucky thought, but she was wearing her femininity like a badge. Her bosom heaving, her face glistening with perspiration, her eyes gleaming excitedly, she looked as wanton and womanly as she did after they made love. He wished he could capture the image, he would have liked to have shown it to her. Not that she would have believed him, he thought – she would simply have said that she looked 'untidy'.

But, as he watched her, Lucky realised that he'd learned something new about Peggy tonight. His fears that he might compromise her had been unwarranted. She didn't need his protection. She didn't want it. She had brought him to the ball for the very purpose of social confrontation. By openly admitting to their relationship, she had defied others to disapprove, and he had a feeling that she'd enjoyed testing them. Even those who'd been found wanting, like Cam Campbell. Lucky realised, possibly for the first time since he'd met her, what a truly liberated woman Peggy Minchin was.

'"Charmaine".' As the band struck up the first chords of its Mantovani bracket, Peggy put her glass of lemonade on the counter and started swaying to the music. 'Golly it's a pretty tune, isn't it?'

He offered her his arm and wordlessly escorted her back into the pavilion. If only, he thought, she could be liberated from her views on herself.

I wonder why you keep me waiting, Charmaine, my Charmaine . . .

A singer who sounded remarkably like Perry Como had

stepped up to the microphone – it was young Chris, a local boy who was very popular with the crowd.

I wonder when bluebirds are mating, will you come back again . . .

It was a slow waltz and, no longer concerned about appearances, Lucky held Peggy close. If the odd disapproving look from others didn't bother her, then it certainly didn't bother him.

I wonder if I keep on praying, will our dreams be the same . . .

Peggy felt him draw her closer than he usually did when they danced in public, and she was glad that he was throwing caution to the winds and no longer being overprotective. She didn't want Lucky to feel he was in any way responsible for her.

I wonder if you ever think of me too. I'm waiting, my Charmaine, for you.

Or did she? she wondered briefly as their bodies moved about the floor in perfect harmony with each other and the music. But just as briefly she dismissed the notion as fanciful romantic nonsense. She and Lucky were strictly 'an affair' and she knew it.

It was one o'clock in the morning when they left the ball, Peggy swearing she couldn't dance another step, which was a lie – she could have, but she wanted to be alone with him. They talked non-stop during the ten-minute walk down Murray Street to the small weatherboard house she rented just around the corner from the school. They agreed that the evening had been an unmitigated success and that they'd both enjoyed every minute of it.

'And you certainly achieved your purpose,' Lucky said meaningfully.

'Which was?' She stopped and looked at him.

'What is that wonderful English saying? You have . . .' Lucky also halted while he searched for the phrase. 'You have put a cat among the pigeons. Yes, that's it. That's just what you have done.'

'And that was my purpose, was it?'

'Yes, I believe so.'

She laughed. She wasn't really sure if that had been her conscious intention. 'Well, if it was, and if I did, then I'm glad,' she said defiantly. They started walking again. 'But I don't actually think I upset many, Lucky,' she added. 'People are less narrow-minded than they used to be. The Snowy has taught them tolerance.'

Lucky didn't agree. 'What about Cam Campbell?'

He'd chosen the perfect example and Peggy had no immediate answer. She'd always liked Cam, and she didn't want to admit that the force of his reaction had surprised and disappointed her.

'Cam is a product of his times,' she said carefully. 'He's an old-fashioned man, set in his ways, and we shocked him. I suppose I fitted his image of the perfect school-teacher and . . .' She tailed off with a shrug and a laugh. 'Let's face it, Lucky, I fit the schoolteacher image for most people, and so I should, I've worked all my life to do just that, so no wonder the poor man was shocked.'

Lucky didn't reply as they arrived at the house. In his mind, there was no legitimising Cam Campbell's behaviour: there had been too much hatred in it. And the legit-imising of hatred was something Lucky had seen far too often in the past.

Later, however, when they'd made love and he lay on his side, one leg nestled between her thighs, raking his fingers through her hair splayed on the pillow, he decided that the man was not worth taking seriously.

'I wonder what Cam Campbell would say about his perfect schoolteacher now?' he smiled.

'I dread to think.' Peggy laughed, breathless, still recov-ering from the passion which continued to surprise her. 'Let's not tell him.'

The discovery of Peggy's passion had surprised them both. The first time Lucky had kissed her, tenderly and with affection, he'd been making no conscious sexual advance, and he'd been taken aback by the hunger of her response. He'd also been aroused, and when they'd made love, he'd been further surprised, and further aroused, by the depth of her passion.

But Peggy's surprise had far outweighed his. Peggy Minchin's discovery of her sexuality had been a total awakening. Her one previous experiment with a man had been a disappointment and she had never explored her own body, never fantasised about its potential. The fact that it could be brought to rapturous orgasm with relative ease had never crossed her mind – such states of sexual euphoria belonged only in books. Now, three months later, the force of her passion remained a never-ending source of amazement and pleasure.

He kissed her softly, and lay back, cradling her in his arms. Soon he would drift off to sleep, and she would remain, head nestled against his shoulder, until she could hear the change in the rhythm of his breathing; then she would gently ease her body away from his. They would sleep for several hours, Lucky rising before daylight to return to the hostel, trying unsuccessfully not to wake her, and insisting that she remain in bed. 'Sweet dreams, pretty Peggy,' he would whisper before he left.

She could hear the steadiness of his breathing now, and feel the rise and fall of his chest beneath her fingertips. Carefully, she slid to the other side of the bed. Her body was still unaccustomed to sleeping in close proximity with another.

Sated as she was, she always tried to stay awake, just for a little while. She liked to relive her rapture, to relish the fact that never in her life had she felt so alive, but sleep usually claimed her after only a few moments.

Tonight, however, was different. Tonight sleep eluded

her, her brain refusing to wallow in rapturous recall and choosing instead to think of the evening's events.

Was Lucky right? she wondered. Had she been making a statement? Had she deliberately set out to 'put a cat among the pigeons' as he'd said? And, if so, what had been her aim?

As the answer occurred to her, Peggy felt herself cringe with embarrassment. By so openly flaunting her relationship with Lucky, she was forcing not only the township to accept them as a couple, but also Lucky himself. Had it really been her intention, to seek a commitment from him? She hadn't been aware of it at the time, but if that had been her ulterior motive in inviting him to the ball, then it had been very wrong of her. She had thrown herself at him the first time they'd kissed, and not once had there been any talk of commitment. He had never told her he loved her, and she had never burdened him by professing her own love; it would not have been fair.

She lay in the dark chastising herself. She would apologise to him as soon as he awoke, she told herself. He had, after all, been scrupulously honest with her.

Peggy knew that much as Lucky had embraced his new life in the Snowies, he was not ready to embrace a new wife, and he probably never would be.

'I am unable to let go of the past, Peggy,' he had said that very first night after they'd made love. And he'd told her about his wife. She had perished at Auschwitz, along with their daughter. He should have perished too, he'd said, except someone else went in his place.

'My best friend,' he'd told her. Then he'd smiled humourlessly, and his voice had been tinged with self-loathing. 'Lucky by name, lucky by nature, that's me. I am here because my best friend died in my place, and because a Nazi was a lousy shot.' And, as she had lain silently in his arms, he had told her his story.

CHAPTER THREE

'Samuel. Samuel, can you hear me? You're alive, Samuel. You must wake up. Can you hear me, Samuel? You must wake up.'

Samuel Lachmann's eyelids flickered open as he felt himself gently rolled onto his back and his head was propped against someone's shoulder. He blinked several times, unable to see through his left eye, which was clouded by blood. He flinched and jerked his head away from the beam of light.

'Slowly. No quick movements.'

He lay propped against the stranger for several seconds, trying to remember where he was and what had happened. His head and his left arm throbbed with pain. He realised he was in the apartment. He could see the legs of the dining table in the low beam of the torch. Puzzled, he squinted at the person who was whispering to him in the dark.

'It's me,' the voice said, and the torchlight was directed upon a face he knew well, 'it's me, Efraim.'

Efraim Meisell. What was Efraim Meisell doing in the apartment? Samuel was bewildered. The Meisells and the Lachmanns no longer visited each other, even though they lived just across the square. Young Naomi stole over for the occasional English lesson with Ruth, but the Meisells and the Lachmanns hadn't visited each other for a whole year – it was too risky.

'We need to get you out of here. They come back to collect the bodies at first light.'

They! Samuel sat bolt upright. He knew who 'they' were and, with sudden and horrifying clarity, he knew what had happened. He could see it. Ruth on the floor, the rifle aimed directly at her head. He staggered to his feet, clutching the dining table for support.

Efraim scrambled up beside him. 'Slowly, you must move slowly or you'll faint; you've lost a lot of blood . . .'

'Ruth. They shot Ruth!'

'No, they didn't.' Efraim said it with force, but Samuel continued to look at him in wild disbelief. The memory was so clear. Ruth, the rifle, then the explosion. But he could not remember anything after that.

'They didn't shoot her,' Efraim insisted. Samuel had the look of a madman. 'Naomi saw them take her away.'

Swaying unsteadily on his feet, Samuel remembered throwing himself at the SS man with the rifle. That was when he'd heard the explosion.

'Can you walk?' Efraim asked. 'Lean on me,' and without waiting for an answer, he draped Samuel's right arm over his shoulder and clasped him tightly around the waist.

Samuel ignored the pain as they slowly made their way towards the door. 'They took Rachel too?'

'Yes.' Efraim was aware that the question was rhetorical, but he knew Samuel needed to ask it and, more importantly, that he needed to hear the answer out loud. 'They took Rachel. And they took Mannie as well.'

Confusion mingled with Samuel's pain. His head seemed on fire. Mannie? Why would they take Mannie? He wasn't a Jew. He opened his mouth to enquire, but they were at the front door and Efraim hushed him as he switched off the torch. Then, silently, they edged out into the darkness of the hall.

Ten minutes later, ensconced in the cellar of the ground-floor flat opposite, Sharon Meisell bathed the caked blood from Samuel's face and, careful not to start up the bleeding, she applied disinfectant to the open wound where the bullet had splintered his cheekbone and raked an ugly furrow along the side of his head.

'It will leave a nasty scar but it will mend,' she announced. 'You are fortunate you did not lose an eye, Samuel.'

'An eye?' Efraim said. 'He is fortunate to be alive.'

Efraim and Sharon were accepting the inevitability of what had happened and concentrating on the present, but Samuel was not. Despite the pain which threatened to engulf him, he was barely aware of Sharon's ministrations as he listened to young Naomi Meisell.

When the Nazis had first appeared in the street outside, it had been apparent that the object of their raid was the apartment building opposite, and Naomi had ignored her parents' orders to go with them to their hiding place in the cellar. She had watched through the gauze curtains of the front room instead, and she told Samuel in precise detail everything she had witnessed. Eighteen-year-old Naomi prided herself on her precision and eye for detail and it had a purpose. When she escaped Germany, she had no intention of fleeing to safety with her parents; she would join the nearest resistance group she could find.

There had been five of them, she told Samuel, one man in plain clothes whom she judged to be Gestapo, and four uniformed SS. 'One officer and three troopers,' she said. They had marched Ruth and Mannie out of the building, and little Rachel had been in Ruth's arms. The three of them had been unhurt, she hastily assured him. Mannie had been carrying a suitcase and he had had his arm around Ruth.

'Mannie was protecting her, Samuel.'

As Sharon started cutting away his shirt in order to examine the flesh wound in his upper arm where the other bullet had passed through, Samuel continued to fight against the pain, seizing instead upon the shred of hope Naomi had fed him.

'Of course,' he said. 'That's why Mannie went with them. Mannie will save her.' Noticing the look that passed between Efraim and his wife, he realised how unrealistic he must sound to them. But they didn't understand. 'Mannie is a lawyer,' he said, 'a distinguished lawyer from a respected Aryan family.'

As the idea formulated in Samuel's brain, he started to feel light-headed, possibly from his wounds, or from loss of blood, or perhaps . . . just perhaps . . . from the dizzying possibility that there might actually be hope. He felt driven to convince them of his argument.

'When Manfred Brandauer pleads on Ruth's behalf,' he insisted, 'they will listen!'

The only sound in the room was the slop of the water in the bowl as Sharon started to bathe Samuel's arm.

They didn't believe him, he thought, and who could blame them? He knew what they were thinking. Plead for what? There were no grounds to plead on a Jew's behalf.

'Ruth's mother was a Gentile.' He tried to sound as if he was pulling an ace from his sleeve, but he knew that his voice lacked the ring of triumph. 'And she looks Aryan . . .' he could hear himself sounding more desperate by the second '. . . that will help when Mannie makes his plea.'

Sharon stopped bathing the wound and glanced at her husband, who nodded. Efraim, too, knew it had gone far enough. Both of them turned to their daughter.

'Mannie was wearing your coat, Samuel,' Naomi said. 'He was wearing your coat with the Star of David on it.'

Samuel's hopes died in that instant. He'd known they'd been implausible, born of wishful desperation, but they'd been something to cling to. Now, with the enormity of his friend's sacrifice, came the recognition of the inevitability of his wife's death, and all hope deserted him. Like the hundreds of thousands before him and the hundreds of thousands yet to follow, Samuel Lachmann felt himself drowning in despair.

He didn't leave Berlin with the Meisells, although Efraim secured him false papers. His head wound made him conspicuous, he said, and he insisted he would pose too great a threat to their safety as a travelling companion. The family had already risked far too much on his behalf, he told Efraim. In saving his life they had risked their own and he was forever in their debt.

'You were not intended for death, Samuel,' Efraim said, embracing him in farewell. 'It was God's will you should live. You are a lucky man.'

Lucky? Lucky to have lost his wife and daughter? Lucky to live the rest of his life in the knowledge that the man who had been a brother to him had died in his place? Samuel could taste the bitterness like bile on his tongue as he returned Efraim's embrace. He wished Efraim hadn't saved him; he wished that he'd died that night. But he allowed Efraim to believe he still cared about life, it was only fair. He would live secretly in the cellar, he said, and when his wounds had healed he would make good his escape. Then he bade the family farewell.

Samuel did not live in secret. He flaunted his existence, venturing out daily, and his enquiries about the departures from Grunewald Goods Train Station were dangerously blatant. A chain of information existed for Jews seeking loved ones, witnesses surreptitiously passing along the grapevine the names of those they had seen rounded up for transportation. It was advisable to be discreet, however: word could reach the Nazis who were always keen to identify anyone asking questions. Samuel's lack of discretion yielded swift results and, after several days of persistent investigation, he discovered the information he sought.

Early in the morning after their capture, Ruth and Rachel and Mannie had been seen herded into the cattle trucks along with the hundreds of others who had huddled on the railway platform throughout the night, their destination Auschwitz.

Samuel decided to leave Germany.

The night before his departure, he visited the second-floor apartment across the square, his purpose not one of sentiment but practicality. He needed supplies, most importantly whatever cash he could lay his hands on, and he hoped that the meagre savings Ruth had put aside were still in the tea canister where she kept them.

The door was not locked, but then why should it be? Only he and Ruth had keys to the apartment. He turned on the overhead light, heedless that such advertisement of his presence might be imprudent. Everything remained exactly as it had been, with one exception. There was a large, dark stain on the floorboards beside the dining table. But that was all it was, just a stain. Where was the blood? Who had cleaned it up?

Frau Albrecht, Samuel thought, recalling how, several days previously, as he'd been leaving the Meisells' flat, he'd looked up at the second-floor apartment opposite to see a figure watching him from behind the living room curtains. He'd known immediately, by the glint of sunlight on silver hair, that it was Frau Albrecht. He'd been surprised. He'd never thought of the Albrechts as pilferers, but why else would Frau Albrecht be in his apartment? War obviously made thieves of even the most respectable, he'd decided, and he hoped she hadn't discovered the money in the tea canister.

Now, as he looked at the stained floorboards, he pictured Frau Albrecht on her hands and knees, scrubbing away with furious intent. Of course she'd have cleaned up the mess, he thought scornfully, she wouldn't have been able to help herself. Frau Albrecht was fastidious, and pools of congealed blood were not only untidy, they were unhygienic.

Samuel had always felt disdain for the conservative, elderly couple who'd owned the other apartment on the second floor for twenty years. The Albrechts' front door was virtually opposite the Lachmanns', but so assiduously did they avoid Samuel and Ruth that meetings in the hall were rare, and on the odd occasions when they misjudged their timing, they would nod politely to Ruth and pointedly ignore Samuel.

'Of course they ignore us, Samuel – they have to.' Ruth's defence of the couple had been vociferous from the outset. 'I think they're very brave,' she'd added with that edge to her voice that defied disagreement. The Albrechts had been friends of her father's, she'd explained, and when it had become dangerous to be friends with a Jew, they had distanced themselves. As mere neighbours it would be easier for them to plead ignorance should it prove necessary.

'And ignorance is bravery?' Samuel's reply had been scathing, but Ruth's retort had been equally so.

'Yes, Samuel,' she'd said. 'In failing to report us they could be accused of harbouring Jews and sent to their deaths, so yes, their ignorance is most brave.'

Samuel had shrugged his acknowledgement, but she hadn't convinced him. Like his best friend, Mannie, Samuel believed people should stand up and be counted. 'Too many are pleading ignorance,' both men agreed.

Now, as he pictured Frau Albrecht scrubbing the blood from the floorboards, Samuel wondered whether playing ignorant had proved too much for the Albrechts. Had it been the Albrechts who had denounced them? he wondered. But as quickly as the thought occurred he put it aside. He would go mad if he tried to allot blame; he and

Ruth had been living on borrowed time for so long they had brought about their own undoing.

The money was in the canister. Along with the handful of coins was the neatly folded ten-reichsmark note he'd earned that last day working at Hoffmann's Garage. The note had been crumpled and covered in grease when he'd handed it to Ruth, he recalled, and he could hear her good-natured chastisement as she carefully wiped it with a warm dishcloth and folded it into a square. 'Really, Samuel, you are the messiest man I know.' She hadn't been able to clean the grease off completely, he noticed, the money was still slightly stained.

Mannie's knapsack remained on the kitchen bench where he'd left it and Samuel took it into the bedroom. He packed some items of clothing, a torch and his penknife, and then, from the top drawer of the dresser, he lifted out a photograph of Ruth. He would have liked to have had one of Rachel too, but there were no photographs of the child. The past two years had not been a time for taking photographs. What was the point? To have them developed would have been far too risky.

The picture of Ruth that he kept in the top drawer was Samuel's favourite. It was the one Mannie had taken on campus, outside the library. Mannie had been characteristically methodical, searching for the perfect light, the perfect angle, the perfect composition, and Ruth had made fun of him, posing and pulling silly faces, until finally she'd burst into exasperated laughter. 'Oh for God's sake, Mannie, press the button!' Mannie had, and he'd captured the very essence of Ruth, which, as Samuel knew, had been his intention all along.

Samuel slid the photograph into his pocket. The picture was as representative of Mannie as it was of Ruth, for Mannie's love was in it. Mannie had loved Ruth, Samuel had always known it. He'd even told Ruth. 'You do realise that Mannie's in love with you, don't you?' But she laughed, not taking him seriously, and he never mentioned it again. It wasn't fair to Mannie, he thought.

He went back to the kitchen in search of food supplies, although he doubted he'd find any. He opened the bread box. Bare. He'd expected it. Frau Albrecht. But then he supposed it was sensible: the bread would have been mouldy by now. He opened the cupboards and, to his surprise, the packet of powdered eggs was there. So were the tins and, most surprising of all, the coffee. Then he noticed, beside the small brown paper bag, the money. A neatly stacked pile of coins rested on top of two ten reichs-mark notes. He counted the amount. Thirty reichsmarks in all. Not a vast sum, but substantial enough in these strait-ened times.

Samuel had numbed his mind to everything around him from the moment he'd entered the apartment. He could not afford to do otherwise. But the money unnerved him. The sheer unexpectedness of it had caught him off-guard. He slipped the notes and coins into his pocket, and con-centrated on the practical matters to hand, loading the food supplies into the string bag which Ruth kept in the top drawer, wrapping a sharp knife in a tea towel and packing it, together with several other kitchen utensils, into the side pocket of the knapsack. He must not allow himself to be distracted. Now was not the time to question the money, or the donor, or the reasons.

String bag in one hand, knapsack over his shoulder, he crossed through the living room to the front door, flicked off the light switch and stepped into the hall. He pulled the door to, hearing the click of the latch, and started towards the stairs. Then he heard the click of another latch as a door opened quietly behind him. He turned. Frau Albrecht stood in the hall, the silver of her hair shining in the light that streamed from her apartment. She looked so frail, and so very, very old, he thought. She hadn't looked that old the last time he'd seen her, surely. The war had aged them all, but Frau Albrecht more than most.

They stood barely ten paces apart, and although not a word was uttered, Frau Albrecht's eyes spoke to him. A faded milky blue, they appeared huge in the fragile parchment pallor of her face, and all her confusion, despair and helplessness was mirrored in them. How had it ever come to this? her eyes asked, and it seemed they were begging his forgiveness.

Samuel nodded his thanks for the money. We are all lost, he thought as he stared into the old woman's eyes. The whole world is lost.

Frau Albrecht remained standing in the hall, watching him as he walked away.

He left Berlin the following day.

Samuel's aim was to reach Switzerland and his father. Recklessly indifferent to capture, he travelled openly, hitching lifts, jumping trains, producing his false papers whenever necessary, anticipating exposure at every turn and sometimes even wishing for it. But it seemed he was charmed. His head bandaged, the dressing which Sharon had applied now grubby and ill kempt, he was certainly conspicuous. Perhaps people presumed he was a wounded soldier returned from the front. How ironic, he thought. Or perhaps his survival was due to the sheer perversity of life: if one didn't care whether or not the worst happened, then it didn't. Perhaps it was as simple as that.

When eventually he arrived in Zurich his father was elated. Having received no news of his son for eighteen months, Leonard Lachmann had assumed the worst. And over the ensuing two years, as Samuel found employment and settled into a regular pattern of existence, Leonard was relieved that his son appeared to be getting on with the business of living. In truth, Samuel was not. He was simply going through the motions.

Samuel Lachmann was a tortured man, grieving for his wife and child and haunted by the past. Above all, he was a man plagued by guilt: guilt that he had not been taken with his family; guilt that his best friend had forfeited his life for their protection; and, above all, guilt that he was alive when the three people most dear to him had gone to their deaths.

But, when the war finally ground to its conclusion and the Allies claimed victory over Germany, a fresh torture presented itself to Samuel. He was taunted by the faintest rekindling of hope.

Reports from the liberation fronts exposed the hideous truths of the death camps. But they also spoke of survivors. Among the unbelievable horrors of man's inhumanity were survival stories which beggared description. Could Ruth be one of them? Samuel wondered. Could she be alive?

He pictured her. She would be singing to Rachel. In Italian, her favourite language, 'the voice of Puccini and Verdi', she would say. And, as he pictured her, he heard her. She was singing her favourite aria from *La Bohème*, softly, in her true, pretty voice, and Rachel was clapping her hands, out of time with the melody. Was Mannie with them? he wondered. And, as he pictured Mannie, Samuel heard his voice too. He was reading a bedtime story to Rachel. It was 'The Snow Queen', of course. How strange that the child never tired of hearing it, that she reacted with the same degree of fear and delight each time Mannie read it to her.

Samuel tried to haul his mind back to reality, but the images and the voices wouldn't let him. He was becoming obsessed. Everywhere he looked he saw Ruth and Rachel and Mannie. He didn't believe they were still alive, but the slender thread of possibility was driving him insane, and he knew there was one way only to free himself of his wild imaginings. He must learn the truth. He must explore all avenues, discover witnesses if he could. He must know how they died.

The Jewish Agency for Palestine, an organisation newly

formed with the express purpose of reuniting and re-
settling Holocaust victims, informed Samuel of Camp
Foehrenwald, roughly fifteen miles south of Munich. Originally a village built in 1939 to house the forced labour at
I.G. Farben's camouflaged munitions plant in the nearby
woods, Camp Foehrenwald now served a very different
purpose. The village and surrounding area had been taken
over by the United Nations Relief and Rehabilitation
Administration and was one of the largest displaced
persons camps in Germany. It no longer housed workers,
but survivors. And a great number of the survivors had
come from the death camps, including many from
Auschwitz.

Ruth and Rachel Lachmann and Manfred Brandauer
were not listed among the residents at Camp Foehrenwald,
Samuel was informed over the phone, but the Jewish
Agency for Palestine had compiled an extensive Survivor
List at the camp, and already many families were being
reunited through contacts made there.

Samuel returned to Germany. At last he had a purpose,
a direction to follow, and, as the train approached
Munich, he started to feel a flicker of genuine hope. His
imaginings no longer seemed so far-fetched.

In the camp's main office, he carefully scanned every
name on every page of the Survivor List, but Lachmann
and Brandauer were absent. In the central hall, he studied
the massive noticeboard with its hundreds of names of
displaced persons and its plaintive pleas of those seeking
the fate of relatives. There were even several names he
recognised. Louis Halpem was one. Samuel had known the
Halpem family quite well many years ago in Berlin. Louis
had been a friend of his father's. *Does anyone have news
of my daughter Frieda Halpem?* Louis's note read. *She was
sixteen years old when we were separated at Buchenwald.*
There were many such messages on the board, and Samuel
added his own. *Does anyone know what happened to*

Ruth and Rachel Lachmann and Manfred Brandauer?
They were transported to Auschwitz in July, 1943.

He asked among the residents of Camp Foehrenwald,
specifically those who had been in Auschwitz, but no-one
could give him any information. Most were sympathetic,
wishing him good luck in his search while plainly holding
out little hope of success, but several responses were quite
brutal.

'Who can say what happened to them?' one man
shrugged. 'The Nazis didn't keep records of those who
went to the ovens.'

'A woman with a baby?' another scoffed. 'No chance.
They shot the babies as soon as they arrived, and usually
the mothers as well.' Having witnessed his own wife and
child shot in front of him, the man saw no point in soft-
ening the blow for Samuel. 'Young mothers of dead babies
don't make good workers,' he said.

Defeated and depressed, Samuel was about to leave
when the Agency representative, a kind enough woman
but eminently practical, suggested that he should look at
the record of deaths witnessed by survivors. 'It's not a very
long list,' she added, 'there were not many who survived
to become witnesses.'

Samuel couldn't believe he hadn't even thought to
enquire about such a list, and realised that his newfound
hope had made him naively optimistic. He had been
searching among the living, when he should have been searching among the dead.

As the woman had said, the list was not extensive, but
it was thorough in detail, as the Agency wished to avoid
any confusion of the facts. Alongside each name was the
cause of death, the place where it had occurred, the date if
known or an approximation if not, and the identity of the
person who had witnessed the death.

Samuel's eyes remained glued on the papers now quivering in his hand. There was no mention of Ruth Lachmann

or her daughter, nor could he see Martin Brandauer, but the name Lachmann was there. Alongside it was the identity of the survivor, a man named Ira Schoneberger. Ira Schoneberger had witnessed the execution of Samuel Lachmann by firing squad at Auschwitz-Birkenau in the month of October, 1943.

The grief and guilt Samuel had suffered in the knowledge of Mannie's sacrifice returned tenfold as he stared at the record of his own death.

'But why Australia? It's so far away.' Leonard Lachmann was aware of the answer even as he asked the question. For over a year his son had trekked throughout Europe, from one displaced persons camp to another, seeking news of his wife and daughter, and the futility of his search had all but broken his spirit.

'A new life in a new place,' Samuel said. 'It's the only hope I have. Even here in Zurich I'm too close to the past, I must leave Europe.'

Leonard was saddened at the prospect of losing his son to such immense distance, but he agreed that Samuel was right. Europe was still in turmoil, the memories of hate and horror too raw. He hoped that in Australia Samuel might find himself again, that the strength and the confidence and the buoyancy of spirit his son had always possessed might return in a new country where such qualities would be called upon.

'Come in, mate.'

Samuel entered the office, and the interviewer from the Snowy Authority, a jovial man, middle-aged and overweight, indicated the chair.

'Take a seat,' he said as he circled the desk.

'Thank you.' Samuel did, and the two of them sat.

'How long have you been in Australia?' Stan was making pleasant conversation – he liked to put migrant applicants at their ease before he started on the official interview.

'Eighteen months. Only six months here in Sydney, though. I was in Brisbane for a year before I came south.'

'Your English is good.' It was, Stan thought. In fact, the bloke sounded very well educated. But then Stan had bumped into quite a few foreigners who were, surprisingly enough. 'Where are you from originally?'

'Germany. Berlin.'

'Ah. Right.'

It was Stan's theory that all Germans couldn't be bad, and he made a habit of trying hard not to let any bias show when he interviewed one of them. The poor bastards copped enough flak as it was, in his opinion. Besides, apart from the buggered-up eye, this one looked like a nice enough bloke.

'Well, let's go from the top, shall we?' He smiled his broad assurance that he wasn't one of those who made judgements, opened the manila folder on his desk, and picked up his pen. 'What's your name, for starters?'

'Lachmann. Samuel Lachmann.'

'Right you are.' Stan printed the name clearly on the application form. 'Luckman, Samuel,' he said.

Samuel watched from the other side of the desk as the pen formed the words upside down, and he didn't bother correcting the man.

'Luckman, eh?' Stan looked up with another hearty grin to prove he wasn't a bad guy. 'Do they call you Lucky?'

The question took Samuel by surprise and he paused for a moment to consider his answer. 'Yes, that's right,' he said. 'They call me Lucky.' And he smiled as he realised he'd said it without bitterness.

CHAPTER FOUR

Pietro was in love. Or so he professed to Lucky. And for an innocent like Pietro who wore his heart on his sleeve, Lucky knew that it was serious business.

'I admire your choice, my friend,' he said. 'She's very pretty.'

Pietro flicked back his hair with a quick jerk of his head in the manner he'd recently adopted to conceal his self-consciousness, but secretly he was pleased. Lucky's teasing, and his own acceptance of it, was a measure of their friendship. When any of the other men made fun of him, as they sometimes did, without malice, simply because his naiveté made him fair game, Pietro would walk away, flicking his hair back furiously in an attempt at bravado as he nursed his hurt. It was different with Lucky. He trusted Lucky.

'But beware of the father.' Lucky's tone was still teasing and he rolled his bloodhound eye melodramatically in the way that always made Pietro laugh, but his warning was genuine. Why, he inwardly sighed, of all the girls in Cooma, did Pietro have to fall in love with Cam Campbell's daughter? Not that it was really surprising, he supposed. Violet Campbell worked behind the counter of one of the busiest shops in town, she was eighteen, pretty and on constant display. Every young man for miles around was probably in love with Vi Campbell

'Beware? Why beware, Lucky?' Pietro had not met Violet's father, but Violet herself had said that he was 'a fine man', those had been her very words. He was puzzled. 'Why I must beware for Mr Campbell?'

Lucky decided to back-pedal. Pietro was an impressionable young man and it would be wrong to feed him preconceived notions about the man whose daughter he seemed bent on courting.

'No real reason,' he said. 'I'm sure you will be fine.'

But he wasn't going to get away with it that easily. 'Why, Lucky? Why you not like Mr Campbell?'

'Because he does not like me.' Lucky decided to be truthful.

'Why?'

'Because I am a German.'

'Ah yes.' Pietro nodded, the answer was understandable. 'Many Australian do not like the Germans.' Then his face lit up. 'But I am Italian.'

'And he'll like you, I'm sure.' Perhaps he would, Lucky thought. Perhaps Cam Campbell's intolerance was reserved purely for Germans. He doubted it, but he smiled his assurance anyway.

A thought occurred to Pietro. 'Why you not tell him you are a Jew? You tell him you are a Jew, then he like you.'

Pietro's logic sometimes escaped Lucky and he decided not to pursue it, just as he decided to stop worrying. There was little he could do about the current situation. Pietro was an immigrant, and whether it was Cam Campbell's daughter he courted, or the daughter of any other local, he was bound to receive the same reaction. Even the most open-minded Australian men, Lucky had observed, developed instant double standards when it came to their daughters. But then wasn't it the way with all fathers? If the girl was his daughter, he'd probably be the same.

Lucky's mind jarred to a halt as he thought of Rachel. If she had lived, she'd be thirteen. A dangerous age, thirteen. Nearly a young woman. He tried to picture her but, as always, he couldn't. If he'd had a photograph of her as a child, then perhaps he'd be able to imagine the girl she might have become, but as it was he could summon no image to his mind.

Lucky deeply regretted not having a photograph of his daughter. Not for maudlin reasons. He would not have wept over it – the time for weeping had long passed. But he would have liked to have had proof of her existence. Sometimes it seemed as if Rachel had never lived.

The only reminder Samuel Lachmann had of his past life was the single photograph he possessed of his wife: the photograph that his best friend Mannie had taken with such loving care. He no longer kept it in his wallet as he had in the early days – wallets were renowned for disappearing. Many a drunken night in a Cooma pub had seen a man divested of several weeks' wages. At first the photograph had lived tucked into the frame of the shaving mirror which he'd hung on the wall of his one-man cabin. But when his natural desires had got the better of him and he'd started paying an occasional visit to the prostitutes who regularly came down from Sydney, it had felt wrong to return to the image of Ruth, so he'd put the photograph away in the top drawer of his lowboy. These days he rarely looked at it, even though, strangely enough, Ruth was on his mind more than she had been for years.

Lucky's affair with Peggy Minchin was the first real relationship he'd had with a woman since his wife's death over a decade ago, and it aroused in him many sensations that left him unsure. Was he in love with Peggy? Or was he in love with the feelings she evoked in him? He was a sensual man, he had had several casual affairs and many sexual encounters over the past ten years, and he had been content to do so. Now Peggy was reminding him there was far more to share with a woman than lust and the pleasure the female body had to offer. At night, he enjoyed the warmth of her in the bed as he drifted off to sleep, and in the morning, when he awoke early, he liked to watch her sleeping beside him. During the days they spent together, he delighted in her intelligence and conversation and the sheer happiness of her laughter. And when he caught her unaware, before she had time to look away and compose herself, he was moved by the undisguised love he saw in her eyes. But sometimes the strength of her love frightened him. Could he return it? Was he deluding them both and offering Peggy false hope in continuing the affair? He wasn't sure whether his feelings for her were genuine or whether they were the result of the memories she evoked. Memories of a life shared with a woman he'd loved many years ago, in a different world when he'd been a different man. Lucky didn't know what to do. Peggy Minchin's love was a responsibility he was not ready for.

He envied Pietro. Love at first sight was so unquestioning and uncomplicated. 'I love Violetta the moment I see her,' Pietro had confided to him, and Lucky had recalled the day he'd introduced himself to Ruth on campus. 'You're Ruth Stein, languages,' he'd said. 'Samuel Lachmann, engineering.' He'd held out his hand and the moment their eyes had met, he'd known she was the one.

'Hang on a minute. You've given me too much.'

Pietro's introduction to the woman of his dreams had been far more gauche. He'd been halfway to the door when she'd called out to him.

'Is all right,' he said, turning back.

'No it's not.' The cash register resounded with a ting as she pressed the button and the drawer sprang open. 'You gave me a quid, not ten bob,' she said ferreting out the change. He must have got his notes mixed up, she thought, a lot of the foreigners did.

He cursed himself. He hadn't looked at the note he'd given her, and there were at least half a dozen people waiting for her to serve them. It was a busy Saturday and the two other assistants, a young man and a young woman, were attending a horde of customers at the far end of the long wooden counter that stretched the entire length of the shop. He shouldn't have bought anything, he thought as the panic rose, he should have just browsed through the catalogues like he normally did. He didn't need two new pairs of trousers and he didn't even know if they were his size. He'd pretended to check when she'd handed them to him, but he hadn't really. He'd acted on impulse, just wanting to be near her, assuming that he'd be able to make a quick getaway in the general hive of activity.

'Is all right.' He started again for the door.

'Don't be silly, you have to take your change.' Crikey, Snowy workers were rolling in it, she thought. Ten bob was more than a week's wages to her.

Before he knew it she was around the other side of the counter and a dozen eyes were watching them.

'Hold out your hand,' she said, and automatically he did. 'Seven and threepence from one pound . . .' She placed a threepenny coin in the palm of his hand and started counting out the change. 'Seven and six . . . eight shillings . . . nine shillings . . .'

Trying desperately to ignore the collective critical gaze of the other customers, he focussed upon his hand, and her fingers as they methodically placed the coins there. But her fingers were slowing down now and so was her voice. He knew she was challenging him to look at her, so he did. Breathlessly. He'd never been this close to her before. So close that he was mesmerised by the dusting of freckles across her finely shaped nose, he could have counted each individual one.

'Ten shillings . . .' Her eyes didn't leave his and, as she gently pressed the final coin into his palm, she smiled.

Pietro's heart skipped a beat. During all of the time he'd spent browsing in the shop, he'd never seen her smile that way at anyone else, he was sure of it. The sky-blue eyes that looked at him from beneath sandy lashes seemed to signal a promise, and the curl of the prettily shaped mouth a special invitation. He was so spellbound that he forgot to flick back his hair in a gesture of nonchalance.

It was Violet who broke the spell, snapping the ten shilling note she held between her fingers with all the expertise of a bank teller. 'And ten bob makes one quid.' She held it out to him and he took it.

'Thank you,' he said, flicking back his hair as he shoved the change into the pocket of his trench coat.

She smiled the smile he'd seen on many an occasion: bright, personable and efficient; she was popular with the customers, particularly the young men. She even flirted with them sometimes, so long as they weren't rude. Just in fun, always proper, never letting things get out of hand. Then she said something, and Pietro wasn't sure if he'd heard her correctly.

'I knock off for lunch in half an hour.' She said it under her breath, very quickly, and suddenly she was back behind the counter. 'Sorry to keep you waiting,' she was saying to the next customer in line.

'You're Italian, aren't you?' They were her first words half an hour later when she stepped out into Sharp Street where he was waiting by the open shop doorway in uncertain anticipation, still wondering whether he might have misconstrued what she'd said.

'Yes.' They moved away from the doors to make way for the steady stream of customers going in and out. 'My name is Pietro Toscanini,' he said.

'Violet Campbell.' She'd taken to calling herself Violet lately, but it had little effect upon the locals who all knew her as Vi. She held out her hand and he shook it. Violet liked the way European women offered their hands – she thought it was sophisticated – and these days she always initiated a handshake, even though most Aussie blokes thought it too forward. But then Aussie blokes had a lot to learn about manners. 'I've seen you in the shop,' she said. 'Lots of times.'

She had. He'd been coming into the shop once a fort-night for nearly two months now, and she couldn't fail to notice him: he was very handsome. He'd leaf through the catalogues on the stand near the door, or he'd peruse the merchandise on display. Behind the counter, samples of every grocery and hardware item in stock were exhibited on the myriad shelves that stretched the length of the shop from floor to ceiling. Other goods were displayed on the counter itself: jars of lollies, ladies' handcreams, boxes of soap and candles, bottled sauces and tins of cooking oil were all carefully arranged between machines and appara-tuses that sliced and chopped and measured and weighed. The shop appeared to sell every item imaginable.

'Can I help you?' she'd asked him once as he'd examined the jars of chutneys and pickles stacked on the end of the counter near the windows, but he'd given a quick shake of his head and returned to the catalogue stand. Another time, when he'd had his face buried in a catalogue, she'd called, 'Want to order something? Need any help?' But once again he'd given a shake of his head, and a minute or so later he'd left the shop. She'd come to the conclusion that he couldn't speak English and that he was shy. A lot of the foreigners were like that, she'd found.

Then one afternoon she'd caught him out. During a moment's respite in an otherwise busy day, she'd been sitting on a stool by the windows listing the items that were in short supply while Trish and Mick, her fellow assistants, had been looking after the several customers at the other end of the counter. Leaning on her elbows, twirling her copper curls between her fingers and intermit-tently chewing on the end of her pencil, she'd looked up and caught his eye. He wasn't perusing the shelves at all – he was looking at her. And, as he'd guiltily averted his gaze, she'd realised that he had never really been perusing the shelves, that he'd always been looking at her. She was flattered. And from that day on she'd proffered him the brightest of smiles as soon as he'd arrived. 'Hello there,' she'd call, and he'd return a quick nod before diving for the catalogues. She'd never dared push any further, for fear of scaring him off. But when the workers came into town on the weekends, Violet always looked forward to seeing the handsome young foreigner. He was an admirer, one with far more taste than some of the others who made lewd remarks to which she never responded. He made her feel special.

'Where you would like lunch?' Pietro asked, and she looked blankly at him. 'Is your lunchtime. You said.'

'Oh, I'm not hungry; shall we go for a walk?'

It was a fine day in late March, but the heat of summer had gone, and Violet buttoned up the cardigan of her blue twin-set as they walked through the lunchtime crowd that thronged Cooma's main street. She initiated the conversation with questions. Where was he based? she asked. Spring Hill, he said, he'd been working on the Snowy for nearly three months now. And where was he from? Milano, he said, a big city in the north of Italy.

He looked like a film star, she thought, dark-eyed and romantic, and she liked the way he flicked his hair from his face – it was debonair. She'd like to go to Italy, she said, she intended to travel one day. Heavens above, she'd never even been to Sydney, but she wasn't going to tell him that.

Centennial Park, just a block away, was crowded and Violet could see several people she knew, so she decided to head for the creek instead, where they could sit on the grassy bank overlooking the water. Pietro automatically followed her lead as she chatted away. Her family had a property near Adaminaby she said, as they turned down

Bombala Street beside the park, but since she'd been working at Hallidays she lived with her aunt in town.

'I like working at Hallidays. Mr Halliday's a good boss, and it's a very good store, one of the best in town. I get to meet so many interesting people.' The smile she flashed him was a personal compliment. 'I like living in Cooma too,' she said, 'it's so cosmopolitan.' It was a word she'd learned recently – her Auntie Maureen used it a lot – and Violet thought it sounded very sophisticated.

Pietro didn't know what 'cosmopolitan' meant, but he nodded anyway. 'Is nice place, Cooma,' he agreed, enjoying her company and feeling more relaxed by the minute. He was proud to be seen with her. Several young men had called 'G'day, Vi' as they'd passed and he'd been aware of their admiring glances.

Violet's prettiness had come as a surprise to everyone, especially her family. Throughout her childhood she'd been a freckle-faced tomboy who could outride and outrun every one of her male peers. And, as a late developer, with a chest as flat as a board at the age of sixteen, it had appeared she was destined to remain a tomboy. Then, shortly before her seventeenth birthday, she had blossomed, overnight it had seemed to her confused father. Already taller than average, her body had suddenly filled out to match her height until, like a healthy young mare, she was perfectly proportioned. Her face, too, had taken on a womanly glow, the Irish antecedents on her mother's side clear in the colouring of her hair and skin. She was pretty rather than beautiful, but it was the bloom of youth and the sheer animal health of Violet Campbell that made her so attractive.

At the junction of Massie Street, as they neared the creek which meandered through town, a young woman crossing the road called, 'Hello there, Vi.'

'Hello, Grace,' she called back. 'That's Grace Tibbert,' she said, walking down the slope to where the bank was strewn with the early autumn leaf litter from the now bare-limbed trees. 'She was two years ahead of me at school. She's a receptionist at the Department of Main Roads now.' Violet said it with the utmost respect.

'Vi,' Pietro said thoughtfully, as he took off his trench coat and spread it out on the grass for her.

'Yes?' She was so impressed by the offer of his coat that the response to her name was automatic.

'People, they say Vi.' He'd noticed that her fellow assistants and many of the customers at the shop also called her Vi.

'Yes, but I prefer Violet,' she said rather primly as she sat. 'Thank you for the coat. Won't you be a bit cold?' He was in a short-sleeved shirt.

But he appeared not to hear. 'Violet is more pretty,' he agreed and he sat on the ground beside her. 'In Italia we say Violetta.'

She was entranced, it sounded so beautiful. 'Violetta,' she said, but the way she said it, it didn't sound beautiful at all. 'Say it again.'

'Violetta.'

Her intention to impress forgotten, Violet studied his mouth as he spoke the word. She loved the way his tongue seemed to rest on the 't'.

'It's much nicer than Violet,' she said. 'Say it again.'

'Violetta.' He sounded each syllable slowly.

She laughed, delighted. 'Say something else in Italian,' she urged, her eyes once again trained on his mouth.

Her enthusiasm was so beguiling that Pietro no longer felt in the least self-conscious. '*Sei tanta carina*, Violetta,' he said softly. And, watching her eyes focussed on his mouth as he formed the words, he fell hopelessly in love.

'What does it mean?' Violet asked, breathless in her admiration. 'What did you say?' She thought that never, in the whole of her life, had she heard anything so romantic.

'I say you are very pretty, Violetta.'

'Oh.' Her attention switching from his mouth to his eyes, she was taken aback by the intensity she saw there, and she found herself momentarily spellbound, just as Pietro himself had been in the shop. 'Thank you,' she said. Then, with an awkward laugh, she looked away, diverting her attention to the willows that graced the opposite bank, and the spell was broken. But not before it had been well and truly cast. Violet was feeling a little shaken.

'Is true.' Pietro's confidence remained surprisingly intact. He was sorry if he'd embarrassed her but he'd been stating the truth.

'Are your mum and dad still in Italy?' She reverted to the safety of small talk.

'They are dead. The war.'

'Oh.' She didn't know what to say. She'd intended to ask about brothers and sisters as well, but now she didn't dare – they might be dead too.

Realising he'd embarrassed her further, Pietro took up the baton. 'Your family,' he said, 'you have brother? Sister?'

'Two brothers,' she said, smiling her gratitude. 'They're older than me, they help Dad on the property.'

'Tell me of your property.' Pietro hugged his knees to his chest and hunched forward eagerly, like a child awaiting a story, and Violet, once again on home ground, relaxed. Her family were cattle graziers, she said, they had been for generations, then she launched into a full account of her childhood.

He reacted in all the right places and in all the right ways. He was concerned to hear that she'd fractured her collarbone in her first gymkhana when she was ten years old, and impressed when she told him she'd got back on the horse and won the event anyway. 'It was the way Dad taught us,' she said with a touch of pride. And he laughed when she told him how she'd smuggled Beth, the blue heeler, into the house in the dead of night so that she could have her puppies on the sofa.

'I was only six so I didn't get into trouble,' she said. 'Dad actually thought it was funny, but Mum wasn't too happy. A bitch having pups is pretty messy, I can tell you.' She wondered briefly whether it was quite proper talking about birth to someone who wasn't from the country, but she needn't have worried.

'I know this,' he said, his laughter stopping abruptly. 'I help my goat have her baby.'

'Really?' She was surprised. 'You said you came from a big city.'

He was surprised himself. He'd forgotten about his goat's baby, and the image that had flashed through his mind had startled him. *His hand emerging from the animal's womb, having turned the baby that had been pointing in the wrong direction.* How had he known to do that? Who had taught him? *His hand, covered in blood, the blood dropping scarlet onto the snow.* It was an image he'd not seen before and he didn't want to think about it. It was too dangerous. Automatically, his fingers strayed to his chest, and the strip of leather he could feel resting there beneath his shirt.

'Before Milano,' he said, 'was farm. No matter. Go on,' he urged. 'Tell me more.'

She told him about the winter of '49, when her father had been out rounding up stray cattle and hadn't come home for nearly a week. 'He was caught in a blizzard,' she said. 'Mum was really worried, but I knew he was fine. I'd only just turned thirteen, but I knew it. I was right, too. He'd been holed up in a cattleman's hut living on rabbits. My dad's a really good shot,' she added boastfully, 'and a week later he walked in the front door and said "bad weather up there".'

Again, there was pride in her laughter, and Pietro noticed how much her father featured in her conversation. 'You love your father very much,' he said.

'Oh yes, my dad's my hero.' Her dad had been her hero for as long as she could remember, which made the current rift between them all the more upsetting. 'He's a fine man,' she added. She'd heard it said many times ever since she'd been a little girl – 'he's a fine man, your dad, Vi' – and she'd always believed it. That's why she hadn't liked the glimpses she'd seen of him lately; she hadn't found them fine at all.

'And your farm,' Pietro said, noticing that she'd become thoughtful. 'You love your farm very much.'

She nodded, still distracted enough not to correct him. She would ordinarily have said, 'We call it a property. Farmers grow crops – we're graziers, we run cattle.' She liked informing people of the difference.

'Why you come to town?' He could tell that he'd gained her attention with the question. He'd jolted her from her thoughts, and he hoped she didn't mind. He hoped she didn't consider him too inquisitive, but he was very interested in her story. 'You talk much love of your father and your farm,' he urged. 'Why you leave? Why you come to live in Cooma?'

She hesitated. He'd not offended her by asking; she'd have liked to have confided in him. 'I'm not sure,' she said, and it was the truth. What else could she say? 'I don't want a life like my mother's.'? That's what she'd thought at first. But then did she want a life like Auntie Maureen's? That's what her father most feared, she was sure of it, that she'd go the way of his own sister and leave the land. But she didn't want to be a career woman like Auntie Maureen. She didn't know what she wanted, it was too confusing. She only knew that she wanted her father to love her and to treat her the way he had when she was a child, instead of burdening her with his mistrust and suspicion.

'You watch yourself, girl,' he'd said to her, only last week, just before he'd headed home after the Cooma Show. He'd never called her 'girl' before, and he'd been even more aggressive than when she'd announced her intention to get a job and move into town. 'It'd be just for a while, Dad,' she'd said at the time, astounded by his belligerence. Fortunately her mum had intervened. 'Be fair, Cam,' Marge said. 'You gave the boys time off when they finished school.' He'd muttered something about it being 'hardly the same', but he'd had to give in. And then, when she'd been thrilled to see him in town for the Show, he'd been angry all over again. As if she'd done something wrong. 'And I'll tell you another thing,' he'd said, 'you keep away from Miss Minchin.'

Keep away from Miss Minchin? She wasn't sure if she'd heard right. 'Why?'

'You just do like I say. You keep well away from her, girl, you hear me?'

'But you always told me to listen to every word she said.'

'Well, I changed my mind, didn't I? I don't want you hanging around her.'

'But why?'

'Because she's not a good influence.'

'Why?'

'Because I bloody well say so, that's why!' And he'd stormed off without even a goodbye.

'I suppose I just wanted a change,' Violet said now, aware that Pietro was waiting for her to continue. 'I'll go home one day, it's where I belong.' But home to what, she wondered. She'd hated the several months after she'd left school. 'You stay and help your mother, Vi,' her dad had said at dawn as he and the boys had set off to work the property. And, along with the drudgery of cooking and cleaning, her mother had started her on an intensive course in book-keeping. 'A bloke on the land needs a wife who can do the books, Vi,' Marge had said, quoting her own mother-in-law. 'Grandma Campbell taught me and now I'm teaching you. You'll be running a property of your own one day.' Marge was proud of her bookkeeping skills. The terror her mother-in-law had instilled in her long forgotten, Marge was proud to be a Campbell woman.

Violet had been shocked by the sudden change in her circumstances. It had seemed only yesterday she'd been treated like a son, accorded the respect of a son by her father, who'd loudly applauded when she'd outridden her older brothers. 'That's my Vi,' he'd always boasted. But he no longer treated her like that. She was aware that she'd matured quickly, but that was hardly her fault. And while she enjoyed suddenly being attractive to boys and even occasionally flirting with them, she didn't feel she'd done anything to warrant her father's suspicion, and she wished that her mother would stop schooling her to be someone's wife. Things were moving too fast.

'I like working at Hallidays,' she said brightly. She wished she could have spoken more openly to Pietro. It would be nice, she thought, to talk to someone other than Auntie Maureen, someone nearer her own age, but she didn't know what to say. 'It's a very good store, one of the best in town. And Mr Halliday's a very good boss.'

'Yes. You say.' She was changing the subject – he'd offended her. 'I am sorry.'

'Why?'

'I ask too much questions.'

'No,' she said hastily; he looked so contrite. 'No, it's fine, honest.' Then she had a sudden thought. 'Do you know what the time is?'

Pietro looked at his watch. It was the first he'd ever owned and it had cost him a whole fortnight's pay. He usually made a show of consulting it, hoping people would notice what a fine watch it was, but he didn't this time. He'd offended her so deeply that she wanted to leave. He felt terrible, and automatically he flicked back his hair. 'It is twenty minutes before one o'clock.'

'Oh crikey, I have to go.' She jumped up – she was only

supposed to take half an hour for lunch and she was already ten minutes late.

'Yes.' Pietro stood, picking up the coat, looking away as he shook the grass from it, hoping that she wouldn't notice how wretched he felt. He put the coat on. 'I am sorry,' he said again, giving another flick of the hair as he turned to her.

This time she didn't find the action debonair at all. He believed that she was trying to get away from him, and the flick of his hair was an attempt to cover his embarrassment, she thought, taken aback by her own insightfulness.

'I really am late, Pietro.' It was the first time she'd attempted his name. She'd been too inhibited before – it was so Italian-sounding and she knew she'd get it wrong. But it didn't matter now if she got it wrong, she wanted desperately to put him at ease.

Saying his name, however, was not enough. 'Yes.' His response was polite; it was plain he didn't believe her.

Then Violet heard herself say, 'There's a dance at Dalgety Town Hall the Saturday after next, why don't you come along? Do you like to dance?'

'I like to dance very much.' His smile was tentative, but hopeful.

Marvelling at her audacity, Violet continued, 'I'm going with Trish and Mick. Trish and Mick work at the store, you would have seen them there.' He nodded. 'Well, Mick's got a car and he's driving us, I'm sure he wouldn't mind if you came too.' She had no right to make such an offer, she realised. Mick might well not wish for another passenger; after all, he didn't even know Pietro.

'No, is all right, thank you. I go with my friends Lucky and Peggy.' Pietro couldn't wipe the grin from his face. 'Lucky and Peggy, too, like very much to dance.' Confidence restored, he offered her his arm. 'I can walk you to the shop?' he asked.

She hesitated for only a moment. What the heck, why

not? she thought. Let her be late for once – Trish and Mick sometimes took a full hour for lunch when Mr Halliday wasn't there, so why shouldn't she? Besides, she was interested in hearing about Lucky and Peggy. She accepted his arm. The Aussies never offered their arm, and it was such a stylish thing to do.

'I've met Lucky,' she said as, arms linked, they walked up the slope towards the street. 'He's been into the store with Miss Minchin a couple of times, he's very nice.'

'Yes, Peggy, she is his girlfriend. And Lucky, he is my very best friend,' Pietro announced proudly. Anyone would be proud to have Lucky as his best friend.

Violet felt the vaguest sense of shock at the term 'girlfriend'. 'Girlfriend' inferred that Miss Minchin and Lucky were a couple and, although she'd seen them together on several occasions, she had never considered them a couple. She'd simply been pleased that Miss Minchin, whose social life seemed to revolve around ladies' committees, had a friend. She'd ignored the whispers that it was not proper Peggy Minchin be seen with *that man*, assuming the criticism was due to the fact that *that man* was a German. What was wrong with Miss Minchin having a friend who was a German? she'd wondered.

'One bloke is as good – or as bad – as another, Vi,' her father had said when the New Australians had first come to the area. 'It's not up to us to judge a person because they look or speak a bit different from us. Even the Germans,' he'd said. 'The war is over, and we've got to let bygones be bygones.' It was one of the reasons why everyone said her father was a fine man, she'd thought at the time.

She now wondered briefly whether there might be another set of rules when it came to a 'couple'. Could that perhaps be the reason for her father's sudden disapproval of Miss Minchin? Violet was confused, both by the possibility of her father's double standards and by the thought of Miss Minchin being someone's girlfriend.

'G'day Vi.'

'Hello, Hazel.' She returned the greeting of the middle-aged woman passing by, a friend of her Auntie Maureen's. It was all too much to think about right now, Violet decided, she'd think about it later. But she noticed Hazel's look at her arm curled through Pietro's. Well, let Hazel talk, she thought, let them all talk. There was nothing wrong with accepting someone's arm.

'I'll see you at the dance,' she said as they arrived at the shopfront, 'Saturday after next.'

'Yes.'

'Goodbye, Pietro.' She said his name easily, without any inhibition, and as he smiled she noticed that he didn't flick back his hair.

'Goodbye, Violetta.'

She walked into the shop, and for the rest of the afternoon she thought about so many things, but mainly how handsome he was when he smiled.

'You keep your hands off our women, you dirty Wog bastard!'

As the Aussie staggered past, punching wildly, the Pole stepped neatly to one side. He'd agreed to come out into the street rather than cause disruption at the dance, although he had no idea what he'd done wrong.

The night air stung with the spiky chill of autumn, and puffs of steam came out of men's mouths as they gathered in the dim street. The nearby pub afforded no light, although the chinks beneath its doors and the soft glow through its windows signalled there was action in the back bar. The men could see plainly enough, though, by the light which poured through the open front doors of the Dalgety Municipal Hall opposite, where a local band from Cooma thumped out 'The Boogie Woogie Bugle Boy of Company B' with surprising expertise.

The attractive colonial-style pub and the ugly squat

stone building with DMH proudly inscribed above its door were the only two buildings of any note in Dalgety. Apart from a number of cottages and a small shop, there was nothing else. But as a river-crossing town on a major stock route, Dalgety's pub and its old town hall saw a great deal of action. Tonight was no exception.

The Aussie lunged, and missed, again. Among the dozen or so men, several were trying to reason with their drunken mate while the others, although not bent on violence, looked at the Pole with venomous dislike.

'Take it easy, Ken,' one said.

'Jesus, give it a rest, Kenny,' said another. 'He was just dancing, there's nothing wrong with that.'

'Nuthin' wrong! He's trying to pinch our women like all the rest of the bastards.' A number of the men were clearly in agreement. 'Come 'ere, you Wog prick, and fight!' As he once more lurched forward, a friend grabbed his arm.

'C'mon, mate, we'll take you home.'

The well-meaning interference caught Ken off-balance and he sprawled heavily, face down, on the rough gravel road.

'Oh shit!' He scrambled to his knees, a hand to his bloodied nose. 'Oh shit.'

Sergeant Merv Pritchard watched from the shadows of the Buckley's Crossing pub. Well, hopefully that'd put an end to it, he thought. He hadn't wanted to intervene unless it was absolutely necessary. No point in locking up Ken just for causing a disturbance. He was only like this when the grog was in him, and the Pole could obviously handle himself. Good of the bloke to step outside when he'd done nothing wrong, of course, but then that was the generally accepted rule. No fights inside. Even a bar brawl, it was understood, was to adjourn to the street.

Being a cop in the Snowy Mountains required a great degree of diplomacy, Merv had found. You couldn't afford to throw your weight around needlessly, even if you had the muscle to do so. And big Merv Pritchard had more than enough muscle to down any bloke foolish enough to take him on. But the ten-man force stationed at Cooma was also required to police the smaller outlying towns and the mountain camps and, in such a male-dominated society, it would have been asking for trouble to come on too heavy. The whole area was a potential tinderbox of violence, and the coppers found it wiser to turn a blind eye to many an activity which elsewhere would have attracted police attention. Particularly gambling. The men needed to gamble, the coppers realised; it was their major form of entertainment. So the raids staged on the SP betting racket run out of the sports club in Cooma were purely for show, orchestrated well in advance and designed to cause minimal bother for all concerned. And the two-up games at the mountain camps, and the boxing matches and card games in which big money changed hands, were ignored unless violence came into play.

The coppers were also well aware that the men needed women, so a blind eye was turned to prostitution as well, so long as the girls weren't too ostentatious. If prostitutes set themselves up discreetly in town for the several days of their stay and arrived and left the camps under the cover of darkness, they, too, were ignored for the most part. It was the pimps the coppers came down on hardest – they didn't like the pimps, turning up with their caravans, a queue of men stretching for hundreds of yards waiting their turn. The pimps were the scum of the earth.

And as for the brawls . . . Well, you had to turn a blind eye to most of the brawls, Merv thought, watching Ken's mates haul him to his feet. Men needed to get it out of their system. Strange, though, that it was the Aussies who caused the majority of the problems. The Aussies and the Paddies – the Irish, too, liked a bit of a stir. Jesus, you'd expect the Europeans'd be the ones to cause the trouble, wouldn't you? But apart from the Yugoslavs, there was little to worry about. And even when the Serbs and the Croats had a go at each other they didn't match the antagonism of the Aussies. Funny about that, he thought for the umpteenth time.

Merv kept his eye on the Pole as Ken was dragged away. He was pleased to see one or two of the men apologise. 'Sorry, mate,' he heard one of them say. But most of the others gave the Pole a dirty look as if it had all been his fault. When they'd shuffled off, he saw the Pole adjust his jacket and run a hand through his hair, preparing to return to the dance. Merv would have liked to have congratulated the man on his behaviour, but he decided against it. He'd seen the Pole's acceptance of the situation. The Pole was a fit young man with the knowledge that he could defend himself against a drunk, but he had suffered Ken's attempt to bully him as if it were his lot in life. As if it were something he was meant to endure. And Merv knew that this was the sort of man who would fear him if he were to step out of the darkness. He'd seen it often before, the panic in a man's face when confronted by a uniform. A uniform was a reminder of a police state, or perhaps of something far worse, some hideous war experience beyond Merv's comprehension. Unlike the Aussies, always quick to buck at authority and to whom a uniform could be like a red rag to a bull, Merv had found there were many New Australians who envisaged a policeman only as a persecutor. It was this element which required the greatest diplomacy of all, big Merv Pritchard thought as he watched the Pole walk back in to the dance.

Merv lit up a smoke. He could hear the murmur of men behind him in the pub. The odd guffaw of laughter, quickly stifled. It was ludicrous. They knew he was out here in the dark keeping watch on the dance and the general proceedings, and he knew they were in there drinking illegally. It was nine o'clock – they'd been illegally drinking for three hours, but Merv didn't anticipate trouble. They'd be taking it easy by now, aware that there was no rush. It was the six o'clock swill that did it. Ever since the wowsers had forced early closing way back in 1915, men had been schooled to pour beer down their throats as fast as was humanly possible before the bars shut at six pm. It was why Ken, falling-down drunk as he usually was by six, especially on payday, had set out to pick a fight at the dance. It was why men went home and bashed up their wives. That was the aspect of police work that Merv hated the most. Domestic violence was a bastard to deal with, and in his opinion the six o'clock swill had a hell of a lot to do with it. There was talk of a change in the legislation, a call for later licensing laws and, as far as Merv was concerned, the sooner it came the better. In the meantime, the pubs managed to cheat. They had 'cockatoos' on the lookout, there was a secret knock on the door, a back room was reserved for after-hours drinking, and on it went. Yet another area the cops turned a blind eye to.

He glanced across at the town hall. A pretty girl had stepped outside. It was Vi Campbell, he realised. Jeez, who would have thought she'd turn into such a looker? And a bloke was with her. Handsome young bugger – Italian by the looks of it. Christ alive, she'd taken him by the hand! She was leading him down towards the river at the back of the town hall. Merv hoped there wouldn't be any shenanigans – Jesus, what the hell would Cam have to say about that? He ground his cigarette butt out with the heel of his boot. Bit of a turn-up for the books, he thought; he'd never considered Vi that sort of girl. Despite her looks, she was still a baby at heart, an innocent young kid. At least that's what he'd thought. Oh well, it was none of his business.

The night, though chilly, was clear and windless, and the light of the moon shone on the still, black water ahead as Violet and Pietro walked hand in hand down the rough track without talking.

'The Snowy River,' Pietro said when they arrived at the open grassy banks where graceful willows dipped their branches to the water's edge. 'She is so beautiful.' He had adopted Lucky's habit of referring to the river always in the feminine.

'Yes,' Violet agreed, and she slipped her hand out of his under the pretext of huddling her coat more firmly about her, although she wasn't really cold. It had seemed perfectly natural to take his hand as they'd left the hall; after all, he hadn't known where they were going. 'This way,' she'd said, when they'd decided to get away from the unpleasantness that had pervaded the dance. Now, standing alone hand in hand, she hoped he hadn't found her too forward.

'You are cold?' he asked anxiously, and he started taking off his own coat.

'No, Pietro,' she laughed, her self-consciousness forgotten, 'don't you dare give me your coat, I'd feel terrible.'

Why would she feel terrible? he wondered, still poised with his coat half off.

'I'm not cold,' she insisted as she saw him hesitate. 'Honest, I'm not!'

'Very good.' He shrugged his coat back over his shoulders and they stood in silence once more, looking at the river.

'Does that happen very often?' Violet asked after a moment or so.

'What?' he queried. He knew what she was referring to, but he wanted to buy a little time, to come up with the sort of answer Lucky might have. He'd been taken aback himself by the man's aggression. *Think you're something, don't you, mate, in your fancy clobber?* That's what the drunken Aussie had hissed at him, and Pietro had again wondered why his fine wool suit should receive such criticism, just as it had in Sydney. *Well, you can go back to your own country, all of you Wogs, we don't want you here*, the Aussie had muttered before disappearing into the crowd.

Pietro had witnessed such antipathy before on several occasions, but it had never been so overtly directed at him, and he'd been bewildered: he didn't know what he'd done to warrant it. Then, half an hour later, the same drunken man had forced the Pole, who had been dancing with an Australian girl, to leave the dance floor and go out into the street with him.

'You know,' Violet prompted. 'People trying to pick a fight with you. Why did that bloke behave like that?'

'He did not like I am with you.' Pietro was aware that his reply sounded abrupt, and not at all the way Lucky would have put it, but he couldn't come up with the right English words. He couldn't even come up with a proper reason, he realised. Did the man consider him a threat? If so, why? He wished Lucky was with him, but Lucky hadn't attended the dance; he'd already arranged to play chess with his doctor friend in Cooma, he'd said, and then he was dining with Peggy. Pietro had driven down to Dalgety with Elvio and Luigi Capelli in the brand new Chevrolet they'd bought in Sydney and of which they were inordinately proud. It was just as well he'd come with Elvio and Luigi, he now thought, the drunken Aussie was a bully and he would not have dared take on the Italian brigade. He'd hissed his insult privately to Pietro on the dance floor.

'Oh, is that all?' Violet was suddenly dismissive. Of course, that was it, she realised. 'He was just jealous,' she said. 'A lot of the Aussies are.'

'Why he is jealous?'

'Because you New Australians have such good manners.' She smiled, pleased that she'd sorted out the reason for the man's venom, which she'd found disturbing. He was drunk and jealous, it was as simple as that. 'Where did you learn to dance, Pietro? You're a very good dancer.'

Pietro decided to put the incident behind him, for the moment anyway. If it didn't bother her, then he would not allow it to bother him, although he felt the situation was not as simple as Violetta appeared to believe. He would discuss it with Lucky, he thought.

'Sister Anna Maria, she teach me,' he said.

'A nun taught you to dance?' She wondered if he was joking.

'Yes. At the Convent of the Sacred Heart in Milano. Sister Anna Maria, she teach me many things.'

'Oh.' An orphanage, Violet thought, remembering that his parents had been killed in the war. She felt guilty. She shouldn't have asked him questions.

But Pietro wanted to tell her about himself, as much as he was comfortable with anyway. He wouldn't tell her about the farm and the goats though, that would be too dangerous.

'Sister Anna Maria, she was like mother to me,' he said. 'And she was good teacher,' he added earnestly. 'I learn to read and to write at school. And Sister Anna Maria, she teach me to dance. And she teach me . . . how you say . . . *good manners*.' He smiled. 'She was very pretty, Violetta, like you.'

Pietro also remembered how, as a young boy, when he'd emerged from one of his fits, it had always been Sister Anna Maria comforting him, bathing his face and rocking him in her arms. In the early days Mother Superior had been cross with Sister Anna Maria for singling him out as her favourite. But when the doctor had diagnosed his epilepsy, Mother Superior had allowed Sister Anna Maria to pay him special attention, and so she had become the mother he had never known. He would have liked to have told Violetta all that, but he didn't dare mention his fits – it might frighten her away. Or, worse still, talking about them might bring on a seizure, and he hadn't had one since he'd been in Australia. So he told her about the convent instead, and the beautiful gardens he'd tended there, and Milano, a big city, he said, even bigger than Sydney. And he told her how, when he'd been working on the building site, he'd read in the newspapers that they were seeking workers in the Snowy Mountains of Australia.

'So I come to Sydney,' he said, 'on a boat. A big, big boat.' He held his arms out wide to signify just how big, and Violet laughed.

'And then I come to Cooma.' Pietro had not spoken at such length and with such enthusiasm for as long as he could remember; it was pouring out, he seemed unable to stop. 'When I come here I am . . .' he couldn't think of the word '. . . *confusione*,' he said in Italian before rattling on. 'Where is this mountains, I think, where is this snow?' He shrugged expressively, hands in the air, and, even in the dim light of the moon, his expression was so comical that Violet burst out laughing. He laughed along with her.

'I am glad now I come here,' he said, his burst of energy finally spent. He looked out at the river. 'I love this place.'

'I'm glad you came here too,' she said.

He turned to her. She seemed to be hardly breathing, he thought as her eyes met his. Did she want him to kiss her? He would like to, very much, but did he dare? He wasn't sure if he was good at kissing. There had only been that one time, with the prostitute in Milano, when his work-mates had taken him to a brothel, insisting it was time he lost his virginity. He'd liked the prostitute, she'd been nice. And she'd called him her handsome boy. '*Mio carino*,' she'd said and when he'd kissed her, clumsy in his excitement, she'd told him to go slowly. '*Lento*,' she'd said, '*lento*.' And when he'd slowed down, enjoying the feel of her mouth, she'd said, '*buono, buono, mio carino*.' He'd liked kissing her, but when she'd guided him into her, everything had happened so fast. She'd felt indescribable, something he'd dreamed about, sinful as it was, and then suddenly everything had been over. He'd wanted to lie in her arms and feel her soft skin, but she'd jumped up from the bed and started washing herself with a flannel, and water from the basin on the wooden dresser. She hadn't been unkind, just businesslike. '*Non ti preoccupare, carino virgine mio*,' she'd laughed. She'd told him that it would be better next time, and then before he knew it he'd been outside in the street, his workmates thumping him on the back and congratulating him.

Violetta was still looking at him, she had remained motionless. She wanted him to kiss her, he was sure of it. He put a tentative hand on her shoulder. Still she didn't move, and very slowly he brushed his lips against hers.

His mouth felt so soft, Violet thought. She'd wanted desperately for him to kiss her, but even as she'd willed it to happen, she'd hoped it wouldn't be like the time with Craig McCauley. She'd been willing Craig McCauley to kiss her too, just so she could know what it was like. It had been three months ago, behind the pavilion hall during the school fundraising dance, and it had been horrible. He'd stuck his tongue in her mouth – halfway down her throat it had felt – and he'd grabbed at her breasts as he'd shoved her into the wall and ground his pelvis against hers. He'd been panting and sweaty and she'd felt his hardness sticking into her through her thin summer frock. She hadn't been frightened. Only last year she'd gone to school with Craig McCauley, and she was sure she could still belt the living daylights out of him if she wanted to. So why didn't she? she'd wondered as she put up with his mauling. Finally, she'd forced him away from her, and he seemed to come to his senses. 'Sorry, Vi. Sorry,' he'd panted before disappearing into the dark.

She'd thought about Craig's kiss for the past three months. At night, in her bed, she'd rolled her tongue around her mouth imagining it was his and she'd been repulsed, but she'd also been fascinated. Was that what kissing was like? Real kissing that led to sex? The pursed-lips kisses she'd exchanged with boys in childish times, experimental to both parties, had never been like that. She remembered feeling his penis, hard against her, and, while that, too, repulsed her, she couldn't get it out of her mind.

Now, she felt Pietro's lips open slightly, and she opened her own in return, waiting for the tongue, not sure whether she dreaded it or wanted it.

Lento, Pietro thought, remembering the prostitute's instructions, *lento*. And, without breaking the gentle rhythm of the kiss, he put his arms around her.

Violet's eyes were closed, she felt as if she were floating, aware of nothing but the softness of their mouths and the warmth of his arms, and slowly her hands crept up to his chest.

Pietro was aware of everything. He was becoming aroused and he fought against it. He could feel the swell of her breasts beneath her coat, and he was careful to keep his groin away from hers so that she wouldn't feel his erection. Finally he drew away; he must not allow things to go too fast, he must not frighten her.

She remained for a moment, eyes closed, lips parted. 'Violetta,' he murmured, softly stroking her hair.

Was it over? She opened her eyes. She wanted more. She had been prepared for the tongue, it would have been tender, like his lips; she would have welcomed it.

'Is time we go back,' he said.

'Yes,' she agreed.

He wanted to tell her he loved her, but he knew it was too soon to say the words, so he took her hand instead and they walked back to the hall.

CHAPTER FIVE

It was June, 1954, and the first leg of the mighty Snowy River Scheme was nearing completion. The Guthega project comprised a 110-foot-high concrete dam, a three-mile tunnel, 3,200 feet of steel pipeline, aqueducts to maximise the flow of water into the dam, and a reinforced concrete power station, which had been commenced in November 1951 and was officially scheduled to start operation in early 1955.

'If we can make it by February, we'll be right,' Commissioner William Hudson said to Rob Harvey as they stood among the gathering beside the power station. 'February'll see us only a few weeks behind schedule.'

Hudson was a good-looking man, tall, with a strong-boned face, a fine head of greying hair and the easy confidence of one to whom command came naturally.

'It'll be a big day,' Rob remarked, 'when the Snowy comes to life.'

'You're not wrong.' It would be the biggest day of his own life, Hudson thought. The life of the Snowy and William Hudson were by now irrevocably entwined.

Gathered with them on the rocky hillside were other senior representatives from the Snowy Mountains Authority and Selmer Engineering, the Norwegian contractors. All were stamping their feet and hugging their coats tight to their chests.

'Wish they'd hurry it up a bit,' Hudson said, but it wasn't the cold that was making him impatient. He flashed a quick smile of anticipation at Rob, not bothering to disguise the touch of anxiety in his excitement. He shared his feelings freely with Rob Harvey; the two were often in liaison and he liked and trusted the man both professionally and personally.

Rob returned the smile. Today was a big occasion all right, he thought. The second in just a matter of weeks. It had been barely a month ago that the workers had celebrated the Guthega-Munyang tunnel breakthrough. The completed connection between the power station and the dam three miles away had been cause for great jubilation. When the final explosion had broken through the hillside, the Norwegians had passed around their specially imported Akvavit and everyone had joined in the partying until cries of 'Skål!' had echoed all about the countryside.

And now the top end of the hierarchy was gathered for another great occasion. The structural work on the station was almost completed, the turbines and generators had been erected, the two 30,000 watt transformers installed, and the Guthega Power Station was about to undergo its first test: the trial run of its mighty turbines. Momentous times, Rob thought as he trained his eyes on the mouth of the massive pipeline.

The collective gaze of most of those present had been trained on the pipeline for quite some time. *Any moment now*, minds had been ticking. The few who had become impatient and wandered off in search of a nook or a cranny away from the chill wind missed the initial drama of the moment.

Suddenly, like a geyser, the water burst from the bone-dry mouth of the pipeline with unbelievable force. It hit the stores building on the other side of the bridge with such power that, in an instant, the building was blown away by the sheer strength and ferocity of the torrent. Jaws dropped – no-one had seen anything like it before. Rob Harvey hardly dared blink, it had happened so quickly, and he was aware that Commissioner Hudson beside him was staring with equal amazement.

'What happened?' someone queried. The several who had been sheltering from the cold and not paying attention during those few crucial seconds were dumbfounded. One moment the store had been there, and the next it had disappeared. Along with 40,000 pounds worth of tools, as it later turned out.

No-one was hurt and the situation was quickly brought under control, the Selmer engineers admitting that perhaps the trial hadn't gone precisely as planned. Perhaps the demonstration had proved that a little modification here and there was necessary, they agreed, but, all in all, the test was considered a great success.

'Well, at least we know it works,' Hudson muttered to Rob Harvey. 'Let's grab a beer at the pub in Jindabyne.'

'We might be working for the Americans soon,' Lucky said to Pietro as they took their crib at the campfire site which the workers had cleared in the snow not far from the tunnel entrance. There had been a heavy fall the previous night and the countryside was at its most spectacular. There was no breeze, and trees stood motionless in mantles of lace. Sounds were hushed, and the snow lay smooth and unblemished, the ground resting breathlessly still beneath its blanket of dazzling white.

As part of the Guthega project, the aqueduct system, and its series of tunnels upon which Lucky and his team were working, was also nearing completion, and Rob Harvey had discussed with Lucky the fact that their job with the Selmer Company would soon be over. Rob had already been approached by the American contractors who were keen to have him on board as soon as he was available the following year, and Rob was equally keen to keep Lucky and those men of Lucky's choice with him when he made the transition.

Lucky automatically swapped his salami sandwich for Pietro's liverwurst, the two sharing their crib as many did. The packed lunches of fruit, cake and sandwiches were doled out at the Spring Hill settlement each morning before the men left for work, and favourites were readily exchanged.

The team was gathered around the campfire, squatting on the logs and rocks that they'd cleared of snow, pouring tea from the billy can and warming their hands against their tin mugs. They were taking their crib while the ventilating system cleared the tunnel of fumes from the last firing. When Lucky declared the all-clear, they would push the skips along the rail tracks into the tunnel where they would load the spoil.

The men were loudly discussing horses and the line-up at Randwick that coming weekend, and Lucky was trying to cheer Pietro up. He'd been a bit down lately, something to do with Violet, Lucky was sure. The boy was plainly lovesick, but he wasn't going to ask. A lover's tiff perhaps? Pietro would tell him if and when he wished.

'Wouldn't you like to work for the Americans? It's rumoured they will pay big overtime – you would make more money.'

Pietro looked up from his sandwich, a flicker of interest in his eyes. More money would be good, it would impress Violetta, and perhaps she would change her mind. Yes, he would like to work for the Americans, he thought.

The American conglomerate, Kaiser-Walsh-Perini-Raymond, known as 'Kaiser', had been contracted for the next major series of constructions on the Snowy, and although work was not due to commence until December,

senior Kaiser staff had already arrived in Cooma. Those in
the know were aware of the Americans' expertise. The
Yanks intended to import modern machinery, the likes of
which had not been seen on the Snowy before, and their
work methods were radically different. The Yanks would
offer bonuses – their adage was 'time is money' – and
workers could get rich. Lucky was one of those in the
know, via his good friend Rob Harvey.

'The Yanks are contracted for the Eucumbene-Tumut
tunnel and the Happy Jacks and Tumut Ponds dams,' Rob
had said, 'everyone knows that. But Bill Hudson reckons
he's going to hand over the dam at Adaminaby to them if
he can. He's sick to death of the Department of Public
Works and their bullshit – it's been five years now and
they're way behind time.'

Rob had been recounting to Lucky the conversation
he'd had with Commissioner Hudson at the Jindabyne pub
following the fiasco of the Guthega Power Station trial.

'Hudson reckons it'll cause a bureaucratic furore, taking
the contract off the DPW and handing it to the Yanks,'
Rob had told Lucky, 'but he's right. Jeez, you can't have a
public institution responsible for one of the biggest rock-
fill dams in the world; it's got to go to those who know
what they're doing. And Kaiser sure as hell does. All this
is strictly confidential, of course,' he'd added, and Lucky
had nodded – it went without saying.

'I will work for the Americans, yes,' Pietro said, his face
brightening at the prospect. 'If I make much money,
perhaps Violetta allow me to meet her father.'

So that was it, Lucky thought, but he said nothing.

'Why she not wish me to meet him, Lucky?' Pietro
asked. They spoke always in English these days, at Pietro's
own insistence. He'd become more determined than ever
to improve his language skills since he'd met Violet.

'How do you know she doesn't want you to meet him?'

'Ah. Of course. I do not tell you.' Pietro pretended that

he'd forgotten to discuss the issue. He hadn't forgotten at all – he discussed everything with Lucky – but they'd spent less of their leisure time together of late, and even when they did meet up, he'd been too distracted by his problems, unsure how to voice them. Now, having brought up the subject, he couldn't wait to unburden himself.

'Two month now I go out with Violetta, each second week it is that I see her.'

Lucky nodded, he knew that. He'd lived through the first kiss the two had shared by the river, and also their forays to the pictures, and their dinners and dancing at Dodds Family Hotel. Pietro had recounted every detail to him. But the boy had been introspective over the past fortnight, and Lucky had presumed that things had gone a step further, that perhaps Pietro and Violet had become lovers and that their intimacy was no longer something to be shared. He'd made no enquiry, respecting his young friend's privacy, but he'd been concerned when Pietro had appeared unhappy.

'Each time I see her,' Pietro continued, 'I ask to meet her father. I wish to tell him I court his daughter, this is proper.' Pietro desperately wanted Lucky's advice; he had only the lessons of Sister Anna Maria to go by, and they had been ringing in his head for the past two weeks.

One day you will be a man, Pietro, and you will fall in love, Sister Anna Maria had said. Her voice had been very strict, and her hands around his wrists had felt like steel as she'd eased him away. It had been shortly before his fourteenth birthday and he'd just wanted a cuddle, or so he'd thought. But he'd suddenly been aware of the feel of her, of her womanly softness, and, to his shame, she had somehow known it.

And when you do fall in love, Pietro, you will respect your intended according to the laws of the church. You will seek her father's permission to court her legitimately, and you will never . . . never, do you hear me . . . attempt to take advantage of her.

Overwhelmed with guilt as he'd been at the time, Pietro had nonetheless sensed that Sister Anna Maria was more cross with herself than with him, although he hadn't known why. She had never again spoken to him harshly, but she had never again cuddled him either. From that day on, she had ceased to treat him as a child, preparing him instead for his adult life in the world that existed outside the convent.

'Is right I ask permission of her father, yes?'

Pietro was plainly begging for assurance, but Lucky was at a loss for the right answer. His position as the boy's adopted father figure seemed suddenly invidious. What was he expected to say, what advice should he give? He wished Pietro could just have an affair like any normal, lusty young man, but Pietro was different, and Lucky knew it. He was a true innocent, unaware of the prejudice of others, and he was set on courting Cam Campbell's daughter. Hell, no wonder young Violet was so reticent: she obviously feared her father's reaction, and no doubt rightfully so. Elopement, that'd solve the problem, Lucky thought. The two of them should just run away together. But it was hardly a responsible option to suggest. He tried to buy time.

'You love her very much, Pietro?'

'Oh yes, I love her.' Pietro's eyes glowed with adoration. 'And she love me, I am sure of this.' He scowled again, troubled. 'So why she not wish me to meet her father? Why she not wish me to tell him I court her?'

Back to square one, Lucky thought. 'I don't know. Have you asked her?' He glanced at his watch. It had been nearly an hour since the firing, the tunnel would be cleared of fumes and it was time he called the men back to work. Just as well, he thought. He didn't have the right advice, and who was he to offer it anyway? He didn't even know how to handle his own relationship with Peggy.

'Yes, I ask her,' Pietro said. 'She say she speak to her Auntie Maureen. She live with her aunt,' he added, 'and I have been to her house. Twice now I have been to her house.'

'Yes, you told me.' He had, several times. He'd met Violetta's Auntie Maureen, he'd said, and he'd liked her.

'I like Maureen,' Pietro continued, 'she is nice. And Maureen, she say to Violetta that she must be patient. She tell me too, the second time I meet her. I must "bide my time", is what Maureen tell me. She say I must trust her. She say she will help "when the time is right". What that does mean, Lucky? When the time is right?'

'It means that it's sound advice, and that you must trust her.' Lucky tossed the dregs from his tin mug out onto the snow as he stood.

'You think so, yes?' Pietro looked up in deadly earnest; Lucky's every word was of the utmost importance to him.

'Yes, I certainly do. Maureen sounds like a very wise woman.'

'This is good.' Pietro rose to his feet, nodding thoughtfully. He felt happier knowing that Lucky approved of Maureen's advice.

Breathing a thankful sigh of relief and blessing Violet's Auntie Maureen, Lucky disappeared into the tunnel with Karl, his second-in-charge.

Karl Heffner, an Austrian in his mid-thirties, was the most experienced miner on the team, having recently arrived from Europe where, since the war, he'd been working on the alpine railway tunnels in his home country. The two men would 'bar down' the freshly exposed tunnel ceiling, checking for any weakness that could result in a cave-in, and freeing the loose rocks so the men were not at risk from falling debris.

Pietro stood by the skips at the spoil dump with the rest of the team, waiting to be given the go ahead. The others were grabbing a final smoke, but Pietro was still lost in his thoughts. Lucky's words had been exactly the same as Violetta's.

'Auntie Maureen is wise, Pietro,' Violetta had said. 'We must trust her.'

He'd wanted to trust Maureen; she had been very nice to him.

'Hello, Pietro, I'm Maureen, I've heard a lot about you,' she'd said on their first meeting.

She was a strong, capable woman in her mid to late forties. Thickset, with iron-grey hair, she had once been handsome, but she no longer cared about appearances, opting instead for practicality and comfort.

'Auntie Maureen is a career woman,' Violet had told him in private. 'She left home when she was eighteen, the same age as me, and she studied nursing at Sydney Hospital.'

Violet had wanted Pietro to know as much as possible about her Auntie Maureen before the two of them met. It was imperative they become friends, she'd thought, her aunt could prove a valuable ally. Against what, Violet wasn't sure. She only knew that she feared telling her father she was seeing a boy. Any boy, let alone an Italian.

'Auntie Maureen married a city bloke when she was in her twenties,' Violet had said. 'He was in real estate, and I met him once when I was just a kid – I thought he was awfully handsome. But they broke up a few years ago, I don't know why, and she came back to Cooma. She's a senior nurse at the hospital here now.' Violet knew there had been a disagreement between her father and aunt when Maureen had refused to return to the family property, buying a cottage half a mile out of town instead, but she'd decided not to tell Pietro that. Every time she mentioned her father Pietro asked when he could meet him.

'My auntie never had any kids, Pietro, so I s'pose I'm a bit like a daughter to her. And she's like a best friend to me; I tell her things that I could never tell my mother.'

Pietro had recognised Violetta's desperate desire for him to like her aunt, and it had been easy to do so: her aunt was a nice woman. He had been very polite upon their first meeting. They had talked about Cooma and his work at Spring Hill, and even his life at the Convent of the Sacred Heart – Violetta had told her aunt all about him. Pietro had resisted the urge to query Maureen about her advice to Violetta, which he'd found bewildering. She had told Violetta to be patient, and he wondered why. Why would Maureen not want her brother to know that Pietro wished to court his daughter with the most honourable of intentions?

But on their second meeting, over cups of tea in the kitchen at the rear of the little stone cottage, he'd blurted it out.

'Why we must be patient, Maureen?' he had asked. 'Why I cannot meet Violetta's father?'

She hadn't answered for a moment or so. She had glanced at Violetta, and then when she had turned back to him, there had been sympathy in her eyes and her voice had been kind.

'You must bide your time, Pietro,' she had said.

'Why I must bide my time?' He'd felt frustrated, he wanted a clearer answer than that. 'Why I must . . .'

She'd interrupted, still kindly, but firmly. 'You must bide your time and you must trust me.' He'd started to say something, but she'd continued: 'I will help you, I promise. And when the time is right, I will approach my brother for you.'

When would the time be right? Pietro had wondered, but he'd known he must push no further, and he'd left after the next cup of tea, dissatisfied with the outcome of their meeting.

Lucky and Karl reappeared, and the men slung their shovels and spalling hammers into the empty skips and started pushing them along the rail tracks into the tunnel.

Pietro concentrated on the task at hand. Until a man's eyes became accustomed to the half-light afforded by the generators, it was easy to stumble. He put all thoughts of Violetta out of his mind, but he had made his decision. He would bide his time. Lucky had said he must heed Maureen's advice, and he always listened to Lucky.

In the gloom of the narrow tunnel, the air was thick and the work was hard. It was always hard, the men shovelling the debris into the skips, lifting rocks by hand, breaking up those too big to be lifted with their hammers, the relentless sameness of their labour repeating itself day in, day out. Wet-weather coats were quickly discarded, then woollens and sweat shirts until the men were working bare-chested or in singlets. Hours passed, sweat flowed, the workers no longer chatted among themselves; the only sounds were the crash of rock against metal and the grunts of men's labour. Finally, the skips were loaded and ready to be pushed the 400 yards through the tunnel to the spoil dump. Clothes were hauled on again in preparation for the cold outside.

The skips were heavy now, and cumbersome. They were harder to push uphill and easier to lose control of downhill, and there were places where the slope of the tunnel was quite pronounced – it was wise to take care. But despite all Lucky's nagging, at times some of the less disciplined men became inattentive, particularly at the end of the shift. At the end of the shift men were tired and looking forward to a beer, and Lucky knew that was when accidents were most likely to happen.

It was the end of the shift now, or it would be when they had unloaded the spoil, and, from the rear of the line of men and skips, Lucky could see several workers at the skip just ahead chatting, paying no attention to the fact that there was a slight bend ahead and an incline in the tunnel that ran 200 yards down to the entrance. He yelled at them, but it was too late. The skip had developed a momentum of its own. It barged forward, one of the men falling to his knees as he fought unsuccessfully to control it.

'Runaway skip!' Lucky yelled and, further down the line, men repeated the call, bracing themselves against the tunnel walls.

Pietro was next to Karl Heffner when it happened. Another young man, no older than himself, a new arrival and inexperienced, whom Lucky had purposely teamed with Karl, panicked. He didn't move fast enough, standing indecisive for a moment, frightened by the sudden chaos and the claustrophobia of the tunnel. Karl lunged forward and grabbed him, throwing him against the wall. Then there was the clash of metal against metal as the runaway skip collided with the one in front, and Karl screamed, his leg ripped open. He fell, striking his head against the side of the skip, and lay unconscious on the ground beside the tracks.

The collision had momentarily halted the runaway skip, and the men fought to control the two now locked together and threatening to career down the tunnel on a collision course with the next skip ahead. Other workers scrambled to their aid, and Pietro knelt beside Karl; he was alive, groaning, already regaining consciousness.

Then Lucky was there, taking command. 'Get him outside, Pietro,' he said, before issuing directives to the men, telling them to clear the way for Pietro, checking there were no other injuries among the workers.

Pietro hauled Karl across his shoulders in a fireman's lift and headed for the daylight at the end of the tunnel. He bore the weight with ease – Karl was not a big man and Pietro was young and strong – but he moved with care, wary of the narrow rock walls and the risk of further injury to the man he was carrying.

Outside, he headed for the clearing, Karl still groaning, semi-conscious.

Kneeling beside the campfire, Pietro rolled the man from his shoulders and laid him on the ground, looking back at the tunnel as he did so to check if help was on its way.

Lucky and two other members of the team, the Czechs Franta and Bedrich, had emerged and were running towards him.

Pietro had been about to tend to Karl, but as he'd looked back, he'd seen the blood on the snow, a bright trail of red, stark against the white. He stood and looked down at himself. Beneath his open wet-weather coat his clothes were saturated. He was drenched in blood. Horror overwhelmed him. A terrible, unknown horror, but the sensation of it frighteningly familiar. Adrenalin pumped through his body; he wanted to run, but he couldn't. He was unable to move, unable to control the involuntary twitch of his muscles and the quivering of his fingers as he stared at the trail of blood in the snow. He remained frozen, unaware of Lucky and the others as they arrived at his side.

The men paid him no heed as they knelt beside Karl.

'Use your belt,' Lucky ordered one of them, clamping his hand around Karl's upper thigh where the leg had been ripped open and blood pumped from the artery. 'Get the Land Rover,' he said to the other, who then raced off.

Franta wound his belt around Karl's thigh, tightening it to form a tourniquet, and gradually the bleeding eased off.

As Lucky examined the gash to the forehead where Karl had hit his head in falling, he was aware of Pietro standing motionless beside him, not even watching them, doing and saying nothing, just staring out at the snow. What the hell was wrong with the boy? He'd performed well getting Karl out of the tunnel, but why had he done nothing to stem the bleeding? Why had he just stood there while the man was bleeding to death?

The head wound was not deep and Karl was regaining consciousness. His eyes flickered open and he saw Lucky.

He muttered something in German and tried to sit up.

'*Es wird alles wieder gut*, Karl,' Lucky assured him. '*Nichts bewegen.*'

The Land Rover pulled up next to them and the Czechs lifted Karl into the back as gently as possible, Karl gritting his teeth with the pain. Franta remained in the back of the vehicle and Bedrich returned to the wheel. Lucky didn't have to tell them to get Karl to the doctor at Spring Hill as quickly as possible.

'Keep releasing the pressure on the tourniquet,' Lucky instructed Franta, although he was aware that, too, was unnecessary – the Czech knew what he was doing.

As the men drove off, he turned to Pietro. He'd been about to reprimand him, but he realised that something was terribly wrong. The boy's hands were shaking, his whole body was twitching.

'Pietro.' Worried, Lucky grasped him by the shoulders, and in an attempt to break through the boy's trance-like state, he spoke in Italian. 'Pietro, my friend, what is it? Tell me, what is wrong?'

The firm grip of Lucky's hands, and the sound of his voice and of his own mother tongue reached through Pietro's horror and brought him to his senses. He could feel the pulsing in his temple and the awful tic in his left eye, and he prayed there was enough time to get away on his own before the fit overtook him. He wrenched the focus of his eyes from the blood upon the snow, and saw the men and skips emerging from the tunnel. The first of the men were already making their way over to the campfire. He was in control now, but for how long? The fit could come upon him at any moment. He must get away, they must not see him.

'Help me, Lucky, I beg of you. Help me to get away. They must not see me.' He said it in Italian and his eyes implored Lucky desperately.

'Yes, yes, of course, my friend, I will help you.' The boy was as white as a sheet, but at least he seemed normal. 'I will take you to the creek.' He led Pietro several paces away. 'Stay here,' he instructed. Then he turned back to the men who had arrived at the campfire and said in English, 'Franta and Bedrich have taken Karl to the doctor. It's a bad leg wound, but I think he'll be all right.'

The men muttered their relief to each other; they'd seen the trail of blood and had feared the worst for Karl.

'I'm taking Pietro to the creek to get cleaned up. You boys have a smoko break.'

'Well done, Pietro,' the men called, 'yeah, good on you, mate.' And they gathered about the campfire, others joining them, talking nineteen to the dozen about the accident and how it had happened. They took little notice of Lucky and Pietro as the two made their way to the creek several hundred yards from the site.

Lucky kept a firm hold on Pietro's arm, aware that the boy was shaky on his feet, but they didn't make it to the creek. Barely fifty yards away, in a small copse of trees out of sight of the men, the last of Pietro's strength deserted him and he sagged to his knees.

Lucky squatted beside him, regretting his instinctive impulse to do as the boy had so desperately wished. He'd behaved rashly, which was unlike him. Pietro needed medical help.

'We must take you to the doctor, Pietro.'

'No, no. It will pass, I promise.' Away from the others, Pietro's panic had subsided, but his hands were shaking as his fingers fumbled for the piece of twine about his neck. He drew out the strip of leather from beneath his bloodied clothing, trying to close his mind to the stickiness and the sickly smell. He sat back in the snow and pulled his wet-weather coat around him. 'I would like you to leave me, Lucky.' It was becoming an effort to speak, and his voice sounded strange. 'They do not take long. So others tell me.'

'What does not take long?'

'My fits. It is epilepsy.' He saw the concern in Lucky's eyes, and became agitated. 'I can still work,' he insisted. 'I am a good worker, Lucky, you know that. I have not had a fit since I have been on the Snowy. Something has made this happen, something I saw . . .' The blood on the snow. And he could no longer close his mind to the stickiness and the sickly smell of his clothing: he was drowning in blood. But he mustn't think about that: he must convince Lucky that he was strong and capable and able to work . . .

'Be still, Pietro, be still.' Lucky tried to quieten him. The boy's eyes were rolling back into his head.

'Go. Please go.' His voice was strangled now, barely coherent. 'Please, Lucky. It is not a good thing to see.' He placed the piece of leather between his already chattering teeth, he could feel his jaw start to clench.

'No, my friend, I will not go.' Lucky sat beside him. 'I will stay with you.'

Then the convulsions started. Pietro's muscles spasmed, his body suddenly rigid. Then his limbs lashed out, kicking and clawing, and his bared teeth gnawed angrily at the leather, spittle foaming from his mouth. Small, stifled growls of torture came from the innermost core of his being and his eyes rolled back into his skull as if trying to define what madness lay there.

Lucky watched, terrified. And, as he watched, he wondered what it was that Pietro had seen. What had brought to life this hideous torment?

CHAPTER SIX

Pietro Lorenzi had always been a strange boy, and his mother, Lucia, had tried hard to protect him from his father's disappointment.

When his wife had finally borne him a son, Franco Lorenzi had given thanks to the Heavenly Father; after two miscarriages and one stillbirth, he had wondered what crime it was he'd committed to so offend God. Several days after the birth, he'd made a special trip from their little log hut on the mountainside into the village, travelling on the old donkey, and he'd placed the few meagre coins he could ill afford in the church donation box.

But, as the boy Pietro had grown, he had proved a weakling, prone to illness, and when, five years later following two more miscarriages, Lucia had given birth to the child that would prove to be their last, Franco's prayers for a strong, healthy son had gone unheard. She had borne him a daughter and again Franco had wondered why he was so out of favour with God. Then, when Pietro was six years old and had the first of his fits, his father had seen it as a curse from above.

'We are being punished,' he said. 'The child is not normal.'

Lucia did not see her son as a punishment from God. She loved the boy even more for his infirmity, and she tried every way she knew how to protect him.

'He is different, Franco,' she pleaded. 'He has a way with animals. He is good with the goats, the goats love him, you know it.'

Franco couldn't deny that she was right, the boy was a natural goatherd. 'Then let him stay with the goats,' he growled. 'He can live with them and share his madness with them, beasts together.'

But Lucia knew her husband would not throw the boy out into the snow to live with the goats. The goats were the one bond they shared and Franco was teaching his son the ways of a goatherd, even how to assist in the animals' birthing. Franco was frightened, that was all, she told herself. Pietro's fits disturbed him; he always left when the first signs appeared. As soon as the boy's eyes started rolling in his head, Franco stormed out of the hut and prowled the countryside until it was over. Pietro's fits disturbed Lucia too; they were fearful to behold. Once he bit his tongue so badly that it took her an hour to stop the bleeding. After that she learned to wedge a piece of rag between his teeth before the madness took hold. But frightening as the fits were, Lucia always stayed with the boy, comforting him when he had regained his senses.

By the time Pietro was eight he was able to recognise the signs. He knew when a fit was coming upon him, and the desire to avoid his father's disgust outweighed the comfort his mother offered. Whenever possible, he would escape to his secret hiding place. He would wriggle under the two front steps of the hut and then squirm on his belly to the hollow in the ground where he could roll onto his back and look up through the gaps in the wooden floor-boards above. He could hear the thump of his father's boots overhead, and he could see them. Or his father's stockinged feet if the boots were muddied and his mother had made him leave them outside. And he could see the worn soles of his mother's shoes, which she had had for as long as he could remember, and Catie's chubby little bare feet. He could hear the muffled sounds of their voices too, and at first he had worried that he might scream out. He wasn't sure if he screamed when he had his fits, he could remember nothing once they had passed.

But no-one ever heard him. No-one ever knew that he was there in his shallow grave in the darkness. He would wedge the piece of rag in his mouth, and suffer his fits alone, his father none the wiser.

As the fits appeared less frequent, the household became happier, and Pietro grew stronger and more confident. His little sister, Caterina, no longer ran away from him in fear, and, at long last, his father accepted him.

God was not punishing him after all, Franco thought, when nearly a year had passed and there had been no sign of the madness. The boy was nine years old, he was strong now, and healthy. At last Franco had the son he had prayed for, and he lavished attention on the boy.

'In the spring I will take you to the village with me, Pietro,' he said, 'and perhaps we will buy a donkey.'

His wife smiled. The old donkey had long since died, and there was not enough money to buy another, but she liked to see Franco share his dreams with his son.

She looked at the glass jar on the bench in the corner. There was barely a handful of coins in it. Each time Franco returned from the village with their meagre supplies in his haversack, Lucia would put the money left over from the purchases into the jar. But, without the old donkey, Franco could carry only one barrel of cheese down the mountain; the donkey had carried four. It was a vicious circle. They needed another donkey.

'And we will buy a saddle,' Franco boasted. He had never owned a saddle. 'A real saddle, and I will teach you to ride.'

He built a fine, wooden donkey for the boy. He was an excellent builder and he had built their hut with his very own hands when he and Lucia had first come to the mountain. The donkey had stirrups made of goat hide, and for reins Franco used the strong leather belt he'd bought from the village shoemaker.

Pietro loved his wooden donkey, and he taught four-year-old Catie how to ride it, shortening the stirrups for her and holding her firmly in the cloth saddle as he rocked her back and forth.

He still had his fits, secretly under the hut, and when his mother worried about the shadows beneath his eyes, he would lie to her. He would never admit to the knife-like pain in his head that always followed a fit, fearing that she might guess the truth. But he was happy now, and the fits were indeed becoming less frequent. Perhaps one day they would leave him forever.

Pietro was eleven years old when the priest came to the house. It was winter, and he and his father had just delivered Rosa of her baby in the wooden shelter among the trees down by the river. Rosa was Pietro's favourite goat, the one he allowed himself to love, for she was the family pet and they would never eat her. He had known for a long time that the stews his mother brewed in the big iron pot were made from the very goats he tended. His father had told him.

'It is the way things are, Pietro,' his father had said the day he had forced Pietro to watch the slaughter of a goat. 'It is how we live.' The animal had died quickly, a swift slash of the killing knife and its throat had been slit, then his father had hung the carcass up by its hind legs from the branch of a tree. The meat needed to be bled, he'd told Pietro. 'One day you must learn to do this yourself,' he'd said.

Pietro had had one of his fits that afternoon.

He'd come to accept now that the killings were a part of life, but he dreaded the day when he'd have to perform the task himself. And he never told Catie about the goats.

'Pietro delivered Rosa's baby!' Franco announced with pride as they came in from the snow to the warmth of the hut where the fire crackled in the stone fireplace and the hearty smell of stew filled the room.

He slung his coat from his shoulders and was about to hang it on the peg beside the door, but he stopped in his tracks as he saw the man in the cassock. A priest was sitting in Franco's own chair at the head of the wooden table, sipping a mug of hot goat's milk.

The priest set down the mug and rose from the chair. 'Franco,' he said, extending his hand. 'I am Father Brummer.'

Franco had never shaken hands with a priest before. He visited the church every time he went into the village, attending the service and offering his confession, and during confession he always assured the priest that he said his rosary regularly and begged God's forgiveness each night. But he had never approached the priest personally when he had seen him in the street. He had been too much in awe: a priest was a man of God.

Franco handed his coat to his son and stepped forward. 'Father,' he said, accepting the priest's hand with the utmost reverence. 'It is a great honour.'

'The honour is mine, my son,' the priest smiled. 'Your wife has welcomed me into your home and I am most grateful.'

The priest was a fine-looking man and he spoke beautifully; he was a gentleman, Franco could tell. A gentleman and a man of the cloth. Franco felt deeply honoured that such a man should be in his house.

'Father Brummer is going to stay with us, Franco,' Lucia said, beaming with pride. 'He is in hiding from the Russians.'

Franco looked at her as blankly as she had looked at the

priest when he had told her the same thing, so she turned to Father Brummer. 'You tell him, Father, I do not have the words.'

She didn't understand, the priest thought, neither of them did. But then the war would have had little impact on the peasants in this remote mountain area.

'The war is over, Franco,' he said.

'Ah. That is good, yes?'

'Yes, it is very good, there has been too much death. But for some, there is still cause for fear. The Russians now occupy Eastern Germany. Indeed, they occupy much of Europe,' he added.

Franco glanced at his wife, who nodded as if she knew what the priest was talking about, and Father Brummer continued.

'The Communists do not take kindly to a man of the cloth,' he explained, 'and many German priests are being sent to Siberia.'

Franco was surprised: the priest was a German? But he spoke Italian like a gentleman. 'You do not speak like a German, Father,' he said admiringly.

'I shall take that as a compliment,' the priest laughed. 'Now, enough talk of war. This is your son, Pietro, yes? What a handsome young man.' He held out his hand to the boy and they shook.

Franco and Lucia looked at each other incredulously. To think their young son had shaken hands, man to man, with a priest. Why the boy had only just turned eleven.

'Now tell me about this Rosa whose baby you have delivered, Pietro.' The priest glanced at Lucia, smiling as if he were sharing a joke with her; she had told him one of the goats was giving birth.

It was Franco who answered, proud of his son. 'The baby was coming out the wrong way and Pietro turned it around,' he said, patting him on the back. 'He is a good boy.'

Pietro looked at the floor, embarrassed to be the centre of attention, but basking in his father's praise.

They cleared the little bedroom which Pietro and Catie shared, lifting one of the beds out into the main room of the hut. Caterina would sleep there, Franco said, and they would make a bed on the floor for Pietro. The children welcomed the idea. They would be warm by the remnants of the fire.

The priest tried to insist that it should be he who slept on the floor, but Franco and Lucia would not hear of it.

'You will be comfortable in this bed, Father.' Franco patted the wooden head of the small bedstead. 'I made it with my own hands.'

'You are an excellent carpenter, Franco,' the priest said.

That night, as the family sat down to their meal, Franco offered Father Brummer his chair at the head of the wooden table. 'It is only right,' he insisted.

The priest was most complimentary about the stew.

'I grow the potatoes and turnips myself, Father.' Lucia was not normally boastful, but she was proud of her garden. 'Even in the winter. In the spring and the summer we have many other vegetables.'

The priest was also complimentary about the table. 'Made by your own hands?' he queried, and Franco nodded, but he was distracted. He was wondering how he should broach his request.

When they'd finished eating, Lucia gave the children permission to play, so long as they weren't noisy, and Pietro helped Catie climb up onto the wooden donkey. He had outgrown the toy now, but he derived pleasure from Catie's enjoyment of it. He longed for the real donkey he and his father would buy on their next trip to the village. This time his father had promised, and even his mother had agreed that they now had enough money in the glass jar. She would forgo her new shoes for the donkey, she'd said.

When Lucia had cleared away the bowls and was washing them in the basin on the bench in the corner, Franco made his bid. 'Father . . .' He spoke quietly, hesitatingly, not sure if he had the right to ask. 'We are good Catholics, we say our rosary each night and we pray always for forgiveness . . .' Then he halted.

'That is good, Franco, and God will be listening.'

'But we do not go to church often. My wife never, the village is too far and the trip back up the mountain is too hard for her . . .' He halted again, sure that Father Brummer must know what he was trying to say and hoping that he didn't think him presumptuous.

'God understands, Franco.'

But Father Brummer had not understood, Franco thought, and he blurted the words out. 'Would you hear our confessions, Father?'

The priest paused, and Franco was worried. Then he said, 'I would be honoured, my son. For as long as I am here, I will hear your confessions. Yours, and your wife's, and those of your children.'

The priest had changed their lives, and Pietro didn't like it. It was the priest who now sat in his father's chair at the table each night, and each night it was the priest who said grace instead of his father. The priest told them stories as they dined, and Pietro knew that his parents were impressed. Each Sunday for the three weeks since he had been with them, the priest had heard the family's confessions as, one by one, they knelt before him. Even little Catie, although Pietro wondered what sins she would have to confess. He worried that God might punish him for not telling the priest about his fits, as his fits were surely a sin. The thought weighed heavily upon him, and he hated confession. But he maintained his secret, and he always obeyed his father's instructions, kissing the hem of the priest's cassock after confession, as a sign of reverence.

Both his father and his mother deeply revered the priest, and Catie loved him. It was the priest who now played with her, rocking her on the wooden donkey. But Pietro did not like the priest.

'He is jealous, Father, forgive him.' His mother made excuses for his surliness, and his father berated him in private.

'Father Brummer is a man of the cloth, Pietro,' he said angrily, 'and he shook your hand – that is a great honour!'

But Pietro couldn't warm to the priest, and he couldn't disguise his feelings. He couldn't smile when the priest tried to charm him, telling him about the great cities he knew, about Berlin and Rome, and other places that Pietro had never heard of. And, as his father's anger grew, Pietro became more and more unhappy.

'Milano,' the priest said one night after they had shared their evening meal. He and Franco had also shared a bottle of red wine, and the priest was feeling mellow. Catie was asleep in her parents' bed, and Pietro was sitting at the table with the men while Lucia washed up the bowls at the bench. Father Brummer had insisted Pietro have a small glass of wine with them; he was nearly a man now, after all, he had said jovially.

'When the spring thaw comes, we could take the boy to Milano and show him a big city, Franco, what do you say?'

The prospect overwhelmed Franco. He had never been to Milano himself, and to go there with the priest! He was sure Father Brummer was only humouring the boy, but the fact that he would suggest such an idea was a great compliment.

'Perhaps we could, Father. Although Milano is many kilometres away.'

'A hundred kilometres only,' the priest said dismissively. 'That is nothing – men have walked far greater distances. When you buy your donkey, Franco, we could pack our supplies and follow the river to the south. You and me and Pietro, what do you think about that?'

Franco's eyes lit up – the priest's enthusiasm was always infectious. But from her bench in the corner, Lucia smiled indulgently. Franco was so gullible. Father Brummer was simply trying to include Pietro in their conversation, as he so often did. She glanced at the boy, wishing he would respond, but he was staring at the priest with fear and suspicion. It embarrassed her.

'You would like Milano, Pietro,' Father Brummer said, and once again he conjured up images in an attempt to gain the boy's interest.

But as the priest talked, Pietro wasn't listening, he was lost in his own thoughts. Why would the priest suggest travelling together when the spring thaw came? The priest had said that he would be leaving their house when the spring thaw came. Did it mean that he intended to stay with them? Pietro didn't like the thought of that at all. He looked at the priest's handsome face, animated and confident as he painted pictures of the great city of Milano, and he disliked him more than ever. He didn't trust the priest.

Then he heard his father's roar and the sound of his father's chair toppling over as Franco sprang to his feet. He felt the angry blow of his father's hand across his face, and he sat quivering from the shock of it.

'You will not look at Father Brummer in that way!'

His father, too, was shaking. With a rage that Pietro had never seen before.

'You will not look at a man of the cloth with such insolence!'

Towering over him, his father raised his hand as if to strike him again, but the priest intervened. 'No, Franco,' he said as he stood, 'do not hit the boy.'

Pietro could feel the vein in his temple throbbing, and the tic in his left eye starting to twitch. And he could see the priest watching him, studying him closely, as if he also recognised the signs. He knew that he must get out. He must get to his secret hiding place before the fit overtook him. He pushed his chair away and ran to the door, but his father charged after him, dragging him back into the room, shaking him roughly by the shoulders. His mother was screaming, and so was Catie who had appeared at the open doorway, and his father was yelling words at him that Pietro could no longer hear.

'Let him go, Franco,' the priest said. The boy's eyes were rolling back in his head.

Lucia, too, had seen the signs. 'He is having one of his fits,' she cried, running to Pietro in time to catch him as he crashed heavily to the wooden floor. 'Fetch me a piece of rag, Franco, quickly.'

Franco ran to do her bidding. But, as Lucia forced the rag into the boy's mouth, he turned away in disgust and disappointment. His son's madness had returned, and he was sickened by the sight. He picked up his daughter who was crying and carried her into the other room, where he sat with her, cradling her head to his chest. Through the open door, he could see the priest watching as the boy kicked and thrashed about on the floor like a demented animal, and he wished the priest would look away. But he didn't. The priest stood silently witnessing the boy's shame, and Franco's humiliation was unbearable.

When the attack was finally over, and the boy lay limp and exhausted, Lucia wiping the spittle from his face, Franco tucked the little girl into bed and told her to stay there.

'I am sorry, Father,' he said, returning to the room.

'Why are you sorry?'

'That you should see such a thing. My son's madness. The shame of it.'

'There is no shame in his illness, Franco. I have seen seizures like his before. How long has he been suffering them?'

Lucia answered for her husband, as she sat on the floor, her arms about Pietro. 'He used to have them often when he was a little boy, Father,' she said. 'They started when he was six years old. But he has not had a fit for over two years now, isn't this so, Franco?'

Franco nodded, still not able to look at the boy whose eyes were beseeching his forgiveness.

'Is this true, Pietro?' the priest asked, and when the boy remained silent he repeated the question. 'You have had no attacks for over two years, is this true or is it not?'

Pietro slowly rose, his mother also, her arm still protectively about him, but he shrugged it away. He stood alone, unsteady on his feet, trying to ignore the sharp pain in his head. 'Yes,' he said, although he knew that the priest did not believe him, 'I have had no attacks.'

'I think that you are not telling the truth, Pietro,' the priest said gently, and Pietro looked down at the floor, unable to meet the accusation in his parents' eyes. His parents believed the priest, and no matter how much he denied it, no matter how hard he lied, they would continue to believe the priest. He said nothing.

The priest addressed himself to Lucia and Franco. 'I know something of Pietro's illness,' he said. 'Attacks such as his do not disappear for years and then suddenly manifest themselves again. He suffers from a condition which will likely remain with him until adulthood, and possibly for the rest of his life.' He took Pietro's arm. 'Come, my boy, sit down. You are weak.'

Pietro allowed the priest to lead him to the table and seat him in a chair. The priest sat beside him, and his mother joined them, but Pietro could see his father, still glaring silently at him, and he hated the priest for ruining his life.

'You must not hide yourself away, Pietro,' the priest said. 'It is not safe for you to be alone when you have your attacks, you could harm yourself.'

The priest was aware that he was not getting through to the boy, but then he had been unable to make an impression upon the boy since he'd first arrived. No matter, it was the parents' trust he needed to ensure.

'Come, Franco, join us,' he said, and Franco sat at the table, sullen and hard-faced. 'There is no sin in your son's illness, my friend, you must believe me. And there is no shame in it either.'

Franco listened to the priest; it was the first time Father Brummer had ever called him 'my friend'.

'And Lucia,' the priest said, turning to the wife, 'you must not put the rag in the boy's mouth, he could choke on it.'

'But he bit his tongue once, Father, so badly that . . .'

'Yes, yes, I know, but we must find something more suitable.' The priest looked around the room and spied the wooden donkey. He crossed to it, pulling the strong, leather belt of its reins through the hole in the donkey's mouth. 'This would be excellent,' he said. 'Do you have a sharp knife, Franco?'

Franco went obediently to the bench in the corner and fetched his killing knife from the drawer.

'You do not mind?' the priest asked, doubling the end of the belt over, the knife poised beneath it.

'No, Father.'

The priest sliced off a short section from the end of the belt, the sharply honed blade cutting through the thick leather with ease. 'It is a fine knife, Franco,' he said. Then he returned the knife to the drawer and brought the piece of leather to the table where Pietro remained sitting in silence, his mother beside him. He put it on the table. 'When the boy has another fit, Lucia, you must place this between his teeth. And Pietro . . .'

The priest sat beside him, his face so close that Pietro could feel his breath. He didn't look at him.

'If you feel an attack coming upon you when you are

alone, Pietro, this is what you must place in your mouth, do you understand?'

'Answer Father Brummer!' Franco snapped when the boy remained silent.

'Yes, Father,' Pietro said. 'I will place the piece of leather in my mouth.'

'Good. This is excellent.' The priest stood and handed the leather strip to Franco. 'Feed some string through the hole in the end, my friend, so that your son can wear it around his neck at all times. It is best to practise care, is it not?'

From that day onward, Pietro wore the piece of leather on a string around his neck, and over the next six weeks, in his secret hiding place, he used it. He had two more attacks in that time, both with very little warning. They came upon him more swiftly and ferociously than ever before and he barely had time to slither beneath the house and prepare himself. He blamed the priest. But the priest was right about the leather strap, he discovered. It was far more effective than the piece of rag, which he'd often found himself gagging on as he'd regained his senses.

Pietro now spent more time with the goats than he did at home with his family. The priest was always in the house, and he did not wish to keep company with him. He would rise early and milk the goats, tethering them one by one in the shelter among the trees down by the river, the warm, rubbery feel of their teats somehow comforting. Then he would carry the pail of milk back to the hut and put it on the bench where his mother would later prepare the cheese. He would breakfast with his family, his father ignoring him for the most part, and then he would leave before the priest awakened, returning to the goats.

The morning was cold, and Pietro hugged his coat about him as he carried the pail from the shelter. But despite the cold, the snow was dazzling in the sun's early rays and he squinted from the glare; soon the spring thaw would come, he thought. Pietro prayed that the spring thaw would see the departure of the priest, although he knew that even if the priest left, things would never be the same.

He walked up from the river very slowly. He always carried the pail with care, but this time he walked more slowly than ever. He could feel the pulse throbbing in his temple and he wondered how much time he had before the fit would strike. They came on so quickly these days that he couldn't risk taking the milk to the hut. He should have left the pail at the shelter. He set it down in the snow – he would come back for it later. He must get to his secret place.

He clambered up the bank, but, as he came into view of the rear of the hut, he could see his father with the priest. What was the priest doing up at this hour?

He circled around the trees as he made his way to the front steps and, sliding beneath them, he slithered on his belly to his hiding place, where he turned onto his back and waited.

His mother and Catie were preparing breakfast. He could see his mother's old shoes, and Catie's slippers that his father had made of goat hide, crossing to and from the table directly above him.

Several minutes passed. The tic in his left eye started, and he placed the strip of leather between his teeth. Then someone else entered the room. Pietro could see the shadow of another pair of shoes at the door. But they were not the boots of his father, and they did not thump as they crossed to his mother and sister who were laying the table together. They were the priest's shoes, and they trod very softly. So softly that he could not hear them at all as they arrived beside the shoes of his mother.

Pietro's jaw clenched and his eyes rolled back, and he heard and saw nothing more. He failed to hear the crash of the chair and the thud of the bodies as they fell to the floor. And he did not see the priest's shoes cross quietly to his parents' bedroom.

The priest moved quickly and purposefully. He took the peasant's identity papers from the dresser where he knew the man kept them. He took his birth certificate and his marriage certificate too; he'd been prepared, he knew where everything was. He took the haversack from the peg behind the door and bundled some of the man's clothes into it, then returned to the main room. Taking the knife from the table where he'd left it, he stepped over the bodies and crossed to the bench in the corner where he poured water from the jug into the basin. He washed the knife and put it into the haversack's side pocket along with the papers, and the money that he poured out of the glass jar. From the larder, he packed a supply of bread, salted goat's meat and cheese, and then he left. The whole exercise, including the killings, had taken only minutes. But then, he was an expert. There was only the boy to dispose of. He set off for the goat's shelter down by the river.

Pietro could hear his name being called and he opened his eyes, unsure of where he was; it always took him several moments to recover his senses.

'Pietro! Pietro! Pietro!'

The voice kept calling his name. He took the leather strap from his mouth, alarmed. He was under the house, he'd had a fit. The voice was nearby. Did they know he was here? Was that why they were calling him? But it was not his father calling him, he realised, it was the priest's voice. He peered out from his hollow in the ground and saw the priest's shoes. They were silhouetted in the light that shone through the front steps. Pietro lay back, very still. He could not leave his secret hiding place while the priest was standing on the steps.

'Pietro! Pietro! Come here, my boy!' the priest called. 'Your father wishes to see you!'

Why was his father not calling for him himself? Pietro

wondered. Something was wrong. Through his open coat, he could feel his shirt wet against his skin, and he knew it was not the sweat and drool that resulted from his fits. Something was dripping through the floorboards above. In the darkness, Pietro could not see what it was, but there was a sickly smell that he recognised. It was the smell of the goats when his father hung them up to bleed. He was drenched in blood.

Pietro lay in his shallow grave, unable to move, listening to the priest call out his name. He didn't know how long he stayed there, but it was long after the priest had stopped calling and all was silent that he finally crawled from beneath the house. He walked up the two front steps and opened the door.

His mother and sister lay where the priest had left them, on the floor beside the table, their throats efficiently slashed with the killing knife. Just like the goats.

He ran, his mind numb, unwittingly heading for the river, and as he did, he tripped over the body of his father. There was a trail of blood on the snow where the priest had dragged it out of sight among the trees.

Pietro continued to run. He ran and he ran. Away from the horror. Away from the images his brain refused to recognise.

CHAPTER SEVEN

The fit did not last long, although to Lucky, watching, powerless, unable to help, it seemed interminable.

As Pietro came to his senses, he looked around vaguely, wondering why he was sitting in the snow, wet and uncomfortable. Someone had been calling his name. 'Pietro! Pietro!' Over and over. Then he realised he'd had a fit. Often when he emerged from a fit, it was to the sound of someone calling his name.

'Pietro.'

The voice was concerned. Lucky was kneeling beside him. What was Lucky doing here?

'Pietro, are you all right?' he asked in Italian.

'Yes. Yes, I am fine.' He wasn't, his head was splitting and he was exhausted, but he started to struggle to his feet.

'No,' Lucky stopped him, 'rest for a minute. You're still weak.'

'I am sorry.' Pietro looked away, mortified, aware that Lucky must have witnessed his attack.

'Why? What do you have to be sorry about?' When the boy still refused to meet his eyes, Lucky persisted, gently but firmly. 'There is no crime in your epilepsy, Pietro, but we must do something about it.'

Pietro was startled. How did Lucky know about his epilepsy? Had he told him himself? He couldn't remember. He remembered carrying a man out of the tunnel, but he could remember nothing after that.

'We must take you to the doctor, we must seek help . . .'

'No! No-one must know about my fits. You must swear to me, Lucky! You must promise to tell no-one. It must be my secret.'

'Ssh, be still, be still.' The boy was alarmed, and Lucky put a reassuring hand on his shoulder. When Pietro had calmed down, he asked, 'Why must no-one know? Why must it be a secret?'

Someone else had asked him those questions many years ago, Pietro recalled.

Why do you wish no-one to know, Pietro? Sister Anna Maria had asked. She had discovered him in his hiding place in the garden and she had witnessed his fit. She had called for the doctor and Pietro had admitted to the truth. *Why have you kept it a secret?* she'd asked when the doctor had gone.

Pietro had told her that his fits were a sin. *They are shameful*, he said. And when she'd asked him why he believed such a thing, he hadn't been able to tell her.

Pietro no longer believed that his fits were a sin, but he could not eradicate the sense of shame he felt when he knew someone had witnessed them, much as he tried to convince himself it was merely embarrassment. Now, however, there was a reason far greater than embarrassment, or even shame, which dictated the need for secrecy. Here on the Snowy, where he was happier than he had been for as long as he could remember, it was of the utmost importance that no-one know of his illness.

'They would not let me work,' he said. 'If they knew of the fits, they would not let me work on the Snowy.'

Lucky's silent response was confirmation to Pietro, and an edge of desperation once again crept into his voice. 'But I have not had a fit since I have been on the Snowy, I swear it, and I am a good worker, Lucky, you know I am.'

'Yes, yes, Pietro, I know this.' Lucky was in a quandary. The boy was quite right, he would be considered a safety hazard, and Lucky was already wondering where to place him on the team to ensure he was no risk to himself or others.

'Promise me you will say nothing. Please, Lucky, I beg of you.' Lucky's silence was frightening.

'I promise to say nothing on one condition . . .'

'Yes?' He would agree to anything.

'That you will come with me to the doctor . . .'

Pietro's hopes were dashed. He might as well announce his illness directly to his employers. 'But the doctor would report me.'

'We will not go to the doctor at Spring Hill,' Lucky continued. 'I will take you to see Maarten Vanpoucke in Cooma.'

Pietro had not met Doctor Vanpoucke, the Dutchman with whom Lucky played chess. Could Doctor Vanpoucke be trusted not to report his condition to the SMA?

'Maarten has no ties with the Snowy Authority,' Lucky assured him, aware of the reason for Pietro's reluctance. 'He never has – he came to Cooma before the Scheme was even started. There would be no report to Selmers or the SMA.' When the boy still hesitated, he added firmly, 'This is the condition for my silence, Pietro.'

Pietro nodded.

'Good. I will speak to Maarten, and we'll make an appointment for this Saturday. Now come,' Lucky helped him to his feet, 'we must get back to the others.'

Pietro saw that his clothing was drenched in blood, and he remembered the accident. 'Karl,' he said, concerned. 'How is Karl?'

'He has a bad leg wound, but he will live.'

'That is good, I am glad.' Pietro looked down again at the mess of his shirt. 'He is very fortunate. Such a lot of blood.'

The following Saturday afternoon, Lucky and Pietro visited Karl in Cooma Hospital, after which Lucky had arranged for them to see Doctor Vanpoucke in his consultation rooms just a block away. Maarten Vanpoucke had been most obliging. 'Saturday morning's always busy,' he'd told Lucky. 'Best I see the boy after surgery hours when I can give him more time. Why don't you bring him with you when you come to the house?' The two men played chess every third Saturday afternoon. 'I'll examine him before I thrash you,' he'd laughed.

Pietro sat by Karl's bedside, the odd man out while Lucky and Karl conversed in German. Karl had been told that Pietro had carried him from the tunnel, and had thanked him profusely in his barely comprehensible English. Then he'd broken into German, as he and Lucky discussed the damage to his leg. It would be some time before he could report back to work, Karl said.

'A severed tendon, they had to operate. And they tell me that I will walk with a limp.' Karl shrugged philosophically; he was a tough little man. 'Still, men have suffered far more than a limp, eh, Lucky?' he remarked with characteristic irony. There was always a touch of cynicism about Karl, as if he wanted it known that he was one step ahead of whatever life had in store.

'This is true,' Lucky smiled, 'you've a lot to be thankful for – things could have been far worse.'

Pietro was bored; he couldn't understand a word of the men's conversation. He was restless too, nervous about his meeting with Doctor Vanpoucke – he didn't relish discussing his fits with anyone, least of all a stranger. He looked at his watch. Two whole hours before he was to meet Violetta.

Lucky caught his eye and signalled that he wouldn't be long, and Pietro wandered out into the waiting room. Perhaps he'd get a coffee. His face lit up when he saw Maureen. She looked different, he thought, in her neat, white uniform. Not at all like the woman he'd previously met, homely and comfortable in her floppy trousers and big checked shirt. She was talking to a young nurse. Pietro wasn't sure whether he should say hello. But she noticed him and waved, so he stood politely waiting, and, when she'd finished giving her instructions to the girl, she turned and greeted him warmly.

'Pietro.' She crossed to him and her handshake was energetic. Everything about Maureen was energetic. She was a positive woman, strong, practical and good-humoured, with a what-you-see-is-what-you-get attitude. 'You're quite the hero, I believe. I heard all about Karl. You've come to see him, I take it?'

'Yes, but his English, it is more bad than me. Lucky and Karl they speak German, so . . .' He shrugged.

'Well, why don't we grab a cup of tea?' she suggested. He looked lost, and in a strange way Maureen felt responsible for Pietro. 'I drove in today, so I'm early. I'm not actually on duty yet.'

She only drove to the hospital when she was on night shift, she told him as they made their way to the newly constructed canteen. Or when the weather was awful, and today was both. 'Night shift and nasty,' she said, 'so I drove.' Normally she walked. 'My twenty-minute constitutional,' she said, patting her sturdy frame and laughing. 'Heavens above, I can certainly do with it.'

Pietro wasn't sure what a 'constitutional' was but he laughed anyway, pleased to find that Maureen was as easygoing in her nurse's uniform as she was in her floppy trousers.

'We've been undergoing extensions for the past several years,' Maureen told him as he followed her down the corridor. 'Extra wards and nurses' quarters.' She didn't explain that the ever-increasing stream of patients the hospital had to accommodate were mostly accident victims from the Snowy workforce.

'And a canteen,' she announced as they arrived at the sterile, spotlessly new room with its shiny Laminex-topped tables. 'We're rather proud of our canteen.'

They took their cups, her tea and his coffee, to a table in the corner.

'Violet tells me you're going to the pictures tonight.'

'Yes. Marilyn Monroe. Violetta very much like Marilyn Monroe.'

'She certainly does,' Maureen agreed dryly, wondering if Pietro knew this would be the third time Violet had seen *Gentlemen Prefer Blondes*. She recalled how, when her niece had first come to stay, she'd asked her what she wanted to do with her life. The girl had appeared to have no idea; she didn't want to be a grazier's wife, she said, and she didn't want to be a career woman either. 'I'd like to be a film star like Marilyn Monroe,' she'd said, and Maureen had had a sneaking suspicion that she wasn't joking. Maureen worried about Violet.

'I bet you're a bit partial to Marilyn Monroe yourself, Pietro,' she grinned, 'most men are.'

He considered the matter carefully. 'Yes, I like Marilyn Monroe,' he replied in all seriousness, 'but Violetta is more pretty, I think.'

Pietro was a greater source of worry than Violet, Maureen thought, sipping her tea.

'My friend Lucky say you are a wise woman.' Pietro's coffee sat forgotten – it was far more important to tell Maureen that she had Lucky's seal of approval.

'Oh?' The non-sequitur baffled her.

'You say I must "bide my time". Lucky, he agree. He say you are wise.'

'Oh, I see.'

'So I do what you say.' Pietro nodded. 'I wait until "the time is right". You will tell me when this is, yes?'

Dear God, why had she said that? She'd simply been buying time, and now the boy was pinning his hopes on her. She smiled, trying to think of a reply, but Pietro's attention was distracted. He was looking over her shoulder and waving. She turned to see Lucky at the canteen door.

'Lucky,' Pietro said, as he crossed to their table. 'I just speak of you. This is Maureen. *Scusa*,' he added apologetically, 'Mrs Miller.'

'Maureen's fine,' she said. 'Hello, Lucky.' She offered her hand.

'I tell Maureen you say she is wise,' Pietro said as the two shook.

'And she is. Most wise.' Lucky gave Maureen a meaningful nod. 'Sound advice, in my opinion. Very sound.'

'Thank you.' So this was the German Peggy Minchin was seeing. Good-looking bloke, Maureen thought, though she wondered what had happened to his eye. 'Will you join us, Lucky? Cup of tea? Coffee?'

'I would love to,' Lucky replied apologetically, 'but I'm afraid there is no time. Pietro and I have an appointment.'

'Yes. I am sorry.' Pietro sprang dutifully to his feet and, when the men had said their goodbyes, Maureen was left staring vacantly at the untouched coffee and sipping her tea while her mind dwelled, yet again, on the dilemma of Violet and Pietro. Lucky obviously shared her reservations: he, too, believed that Pietro should not be so eager to declare his intentions. But why? she wondered. Was it because Lucky feared her brother's reaction? Perhaps he saw through Cam's facade of bonhomie and 'all men are brothers'. Or was it because he sensed Violet's frivolous nature? Maureen was more concerned about the latter herself.

Maureen Miller had come to the conclusion that she

really didn't understand young women like Violet. She'd tried to, but she had no grounds for identification. Perhaps if she'd had a daughter of her own, she sometimes thought . . . But then she hadn't, had she? As an eighteen-year-old herself, she had never been addicted to the cinema, nor had she devoured magazines about film stars nor lived in a world of romantic make-believe. She'd known exactly what she wanted to do with her life at the age of twelve when a nursing career had beckoned, and for the following six years she'd simply marked time until she could follow her path. Young women like Violet were beyond her comprehension, and she worried about the ramifications of such a rose-coloured view of the world. Was Violet unwittingly toying with Pietro?

'He looks like Gilbert Roland, only even more handsome,' Violet had raved when Pietro had started coming into the shop. 'No, he looks like Rossano Brazzi,' she'd corrected herself, 'only much younger.' Maureen had laughed; she'd found it amusing then. She didn't any more. Not since things had taken a serious turn.

'I'm in love, Auntie Maureen,' Violet said these days. Pietro was no longer a carbon copy of her Hollywood idols; but she now cast herself in the role of female lead. 'When he kisses me, I feel like I'm Joan Crawford. Truly!' she insisted emphatically, as if expecting her aunt to laugh, although Maureen didn't. 'He makes me feel like I'm the most beautiful woman in the world.'

Maureen loved her niece. She valued the fact that Violet spoke freely to her, the way she never would to her mother, and she was careful not to be too dismissive of the girl's romantic notions, frivolous though she found them. What right did she have to be dismissive anyway, she thought, she with her childless, failed marriage? Perhaps Violet really was experiencing true love. Although she doubted it. Violet was a child. But she was a child in a woman's body. She'd blossomed overnight from a tomboy with an obsession for horses to a young woman with an obsession for romance. It was a lethal transformation, and the one most likely to pay the price was not Violet herself, but young Pietro. Would he last the distance in her affections, or would she tire of this particular romantic illusion and choose another hero?

In buying time with her advice, Maureen had sought to protect Pietro, but it was now evident that, with the endorsement of his good friend Lucky, the boy was relying entirely upon her. Dear God, she'd even told him that she'd approach her brother when the time was right.

Well, in the unlikely event that it should come to that, she would do so, Maureen thought, draining the last of her tea. She would stand up to Cam; they'd had their run-ins before. In the meantime, it was unlikely he'd hear of his daughter's liaison. He purchased his supplies at Adaminaby and wouldn't make another trip to Cooma until well into the spring. By that time Violet's infatuation might be a thing of the past. Why risk the wrath of Cam Campbell unnecessarily?

Maureen looked at the clock on the canteen wall; she wasn't officially on duty for another whole hour. It was true she'd driven the Holden in because she was working the night shift and the weather was threatening, but that wasn't why she was early. With Violet at the store, the house was empty and Maureen preferred the hospital. Indeed, her life seemed purposeless elsewhere. It had for some time now, ever since Andy left. A whole three years.

She rinsed the cups in the corner sink and left them to drain. Early or not, there was much to be done – they were shockingly understaffed. She'd catch up on some paper-work before it was time to start on her rounds.

'You are in excellent health, Pietro.'

Doctor Vanpoucke had completed his general exam-ination and now leaned back in his leather armchair, crossed his legs, tapped his fingertips together and, beaming through horn-rimmed spectacles, gave Pietro an encouraging smile.

'So, tell me about yourself.'

He was well spoken, with a slightly stilted accent that was as much Australian as it was Dutch; having arrived in the area before the flow of migrant workers, Maarten Vanpoucke occasionally joked that he was a 'true Aussie'. He had chosen the quiet township of Cooma for what he termed his 'semi-retirement', away from the big hospitals in which he'd practised. Here he could work at his leisure and enjoy the best of both worlds, he said: the Australian summers and the snowy winters which were so reminiscent of Europe. 'So much for leaving behind the hustle and bustle, though,' he'd remarked to Lucky. 'It now seems that half of Europe has come to Cooma.'

Pietro didn't know where to begin. He was in awe of Doctor Vanpoucke and he wished Lucky was with him, but Lucky was sitting alone in the waiting room outside. There were no other patients, and the doctor's receptionist had gone for the day. 'A quick check-up first, and a bit of a chat,' the doctor had said, 'then I would like you to join us, Lucky.'

Maarten Vanpoucke was an impressive-looking man in his early forties. Elegantly grey-haired, with a body tending to the fleshy, he bore the appearance of one who enjoyed the finer things in life, and his house in Vale Street attested to the fact. It was a two-storey building built of local stone, with a large bay window on the ground floor and an upstairs balcony with iron lacework railings. It was most imposing, and even the downstairs rooms from which he conducted his medical practice were elegantly furnished.

Pietro sat carefully on the edge of his chair, frightened his boots might scuff the glossy polish of its carved wooden legs. The doctor gave him another avuncular smile.

'Where I should start?' Pietro asked.

'You must start from wherever you remember,' the doctor said. 'That would be the convent, would it not? Lucky has told me that you have no memory of your early life, is this so?'

'Yes. Is so. Is the Convent of the Sacred Heart in Milano I remember.'

Doctor Vanpoucke was very attentive as Pietro told his story, and gradually the boy relaxed. He told the Dutchman all about the convent, and about Sister Anna Maria and how she had found him having one of his fits, and how she had called in the doctor.

'The doctor ask Sister Anna Maria what happen,' he said. 'He ask her many things. Then he say to her is epilepsy.'

'I see. And you had experienced these fits before?'

'Oh yes, many time. In the shed of the convent garden. Is my secret.' Pietro told the doctor about the signs, the tic in his left eye, the pounding in his temple. 'I know before it happen,' he said, 'and I hide. I put the leather in my mouth . . .' He ferreted beneath his shirt for the twine; he was enjoying talking to the doctor now. 'Is here. See?'

'Ah yes,' the doctor said. Lucky had told him about the strip of leather and how the boy had placed it between his teeth. 'It is most wise of you, Pietro.' He examined the scarred leather. 'This has seen much wear,' he said sympathetically. 'Did Sister Anna Maria give this to you?'

'No.' Pietro shook his head. 'I do not know who give this to me. I have this when I come to the Convent of the Sacred Heart. Sister Anna Maria, she say it is . . .' he searched for the word in English, but gave up, '. . . *pratico*, and she say for me to keep it.'

The doctor laughed. 'It is indeed practical, Pietro, and I suggest you hang on to it, but I hope you will never need to use it again. Shall we ask Lucky to come in?'

Pietro was no longer inhibited by the doctor and his fine

house and his chairs, but he was more in awe of the man than ever. Was it possible the doctor could cure his fits?

'Yes. Please,' he said.

While Lucky answered the doctor's questions, Pietro remained silent. During the recounting of the accident in the tunnel, he nodded verification, but when it came to the fit and what Lucky had seen, Pietro stared at the floor, squirming with embarrassment. When Sister Anna Maria had talked to the doctor at the convent, he had been taken aside; now Pietro was hearing every sordid detail.

'Forgive me, Pietro,' the doctor said, recognising the boy's discomfort, 'but I need to know exactly what happens during your fits for a correct diagnosis. A witness is essential.'

Finally, Maarten Vanpoucke leaned back in his chair, legs once again crossed, fingertips once again tapping and, over his spectacle rims, he addressed himself to Lucky.

'Pietro has told me that he has warnings of his attacks, a tic in his left eye, a throbbing in his temple . . . perhaps a pain in the stomach?' he suggested, turning to the boy. 'Would this be correct, Pietro?'

Pietro was dumbfounded. Yes, sometimes he did have a pain in the stomach. How did the doctor know this? He nodded.

'These are not warnings as such,' Doctor Vanpoucke said to Lucky. 'Pietro is already experiencing a simple partial seizure on the right side of the brain. It is not something he is able to control, but it gives him time to escape, a time when he is still lucid, before the grand mal strikes. Now Lucky, you told me you believe something triggered this particular attack you witnessed.'

'Yes,' Lucky replied. 'Pietro told me himself. He said something made it happen. Do you remember, Pietro?'

Pietro didn't. Both men turned to him, but he had no answers.

'The accident,' Doctor Vanpoucke said, 'carrying the

man from the tunnel was very stressful, it's under-standable. We must try to avoid such triggers whenever possible.' Maarten Vanpoucke always used the royal medical 'we' when it came to advice, people found it comforting. 'But we have something even more "practical" to hand.' He smiled at Pietro as he emphasised the word, then leaned forward and, taking his favourite fountain pen from its niche, he opened his prescription pad. 'Your illness can be controlled with medication, Pietro,' he said as he scribbled. 'I am writing you a script for Dilantin.' He tore off the page and slid it across the highly polished desk. 'You will take this to the chemist, and he will give you some pills. You will take one of these pills every morning and every night.' The eyes behind the horn-rimmed spectacles stared solemnly at Pietro. 'You will do this for the rest of your life. Do you understand me, Pietro?'

Pietro's own eyes were wide with amazement, he scarcely dared believe it possible. Was it really this simple? He looked at Lucky, seeking affirmation, and Lucky nodded.

'You will visit me regularly for the next six months and if all is going well, as I'm sure it will, then you will need to come and see me only when you require a new prescription.' Maarten Vanpoucke stood, signalling the end of the consultation.

'You mean I have no more fits?' Pietro remained glued to his chair, looking from the doctor to Lucky in disbelief.

'If you take your medication, I see no reason why you should have any further seizures. Now, Lucky,' Maarten suggested with a smile, 'shall we adjourn upstairs? It is surely my turn to win.'

At the door, Maarten took Pietro's hand in both of his and shook it. 'Good luck to you, Pietro, although you will not need it. We will monitor your progress and keep a check on your medication and, between the two of us, you and I, we will conquer your illness.'

Pietro stammered his thanks and left. He stepped out into Vale Street where the biting winter wind ripped at his clothes and people walked bent double, chins tucked against chests. But Pietro didn't notice the wind. He was euphoric, in a daze. His life had changed, just like that.

'I would like to keep a close eye on the boy,' Maarten said in the upstairs lounge room as he poured their drinks and Lucky set up the chess board. 'At least for a while – his amnesia is worrying. He's said nothing to you of any memory prior to the convent?'

'He told me once that he came from the mountains.'

'Oh really?' Maarten wondered why the boy had said nothing to him of the mountains. Then he remembered that it had been he himself who had opened their conversation with queries about the convent, so it was hardly surprising. 'A memory prior to the convent,' he said, handing Lucky his glass of beer. 'Most interesting. What did he recall?'

'Nothing really, just the mountains. And the goats, he said he could remember the goats. Nothing more. He couldn't remember his early days in Milan either. Evidently he was found wandering the streets, and that's when he was taken to the orphans' home.'

Scotch in hand, Maarten sat opposite Lucky. '*Proost*,' he said in Dutch.

'*Prosit*,' Lucky responded in German. They smiled, clinked glasses and took a swig of their drinks. 'I never brought up the subject again,' he continued thoughtfully. 'I sensed fear in him, and I felt guilty that I'd asked him about his past. Of course I didn't know about the epilepsy then. If I had . . .' he tailed off apologetically.

'How could you possibly have known,' Maarten assured him. 'But the boy has certainly been traumatised, and it may well be some subconscious memory that triggers his attacks. I am of the opinion, like you, that Pietro should avoid reminders of his past life whenever possible. But of course,' he shrugged, 'there may be others who differ. Modern psychiatric opinion might suggest that the boy confront his demons – there are such therapies practised these days. I could refer him to a Sydney psychiatrist perhaps? If that's what you wish?'

Lucky was startled. Why was Maarten seeking his permission? Why should he have any say in the matter?

'The boy obviously sees you as a father figure,' Maarten explained, noting Lucky's reaction. 'He will do whatever you say . . .'

'No, no.' Lucky shook his head emphatically, he wanted no part of it. 'You're the doctor, and he'll do what *you* say.' Fond as he was of Pietro, Lucky was tired of being a father figure. Besides, he agreed wholeheartedly with Maarten. If Pietro's mind was mercifully blocking out some hideous past, then why open the doors and let it back in? Lucky only wished there were doors to his own past which he could close forever. 'No psychiatrists,' he said.

'As you wish.' Maarten nodded. 'We'll let sleeping dogs lie. All for the best, I think.' He placed the glass of Scotch on his coaster beside the chess board. 'Now I take it I can't tempt you to stay for dinner? Mrs Hodgeman is cooking roast beef.'

Maarten's housekeeper lived with her son, who served as a gardener and handyman, in the self-contained flat downstairs, behind the consulting rooms. Each time the men played chess Maarten extended the invitation for Lucky to join him in whatever meal Mrs Hodgeman was preparing that night, and each time Lucky declined. They both knew why, although neither of them ever mentioned Peggy.

'Thank you, Maarten, it's most kind, but no.'

'Then let us begin.'

Maarten was bemused, as he always was. The school-teacher was beckoning Lucky, though he couldn't for the

life of him understand what a lusty man like Lucky saw in
Peggy Minchin. A worthy woman, of course; Maarten
knew her socially. He treated a number of her pupils, who
adored her, and a number of their parents, who respected
her: Peggy Minchin was a fine teacher and an asset to the
community. But as a woman? As a lover? Maarten was
mystified. He was a lusty man himself, and he found any
association between eroticism and the neat little schoolteacher not only ludicrous, but faintly obscene.

'I believe it's your turn to open play,' he said. Lucky
appeared a little distracted.

'Oh. Yes.' Lucky moved his pawn to bishop four. He
hoped the game wouldn't take too long, his heart wasn't
really in it.

He'd told her that he might be late. He was meeting
Pietro at the hospital and then playing chess with Maarten,
he'd said. 'The game might drag on, you should eat
without me.'

'I'll wait.'

'But we didn't have lunch – you'll be starving.'

'Who needs food?' she laughed. And as he kissed her,
feeling her naked body against him in the warmth of the
bed, he started to make love to her again. She aroused him
so quickly and easily when she was like this, shameless and
abandoned.

'You're more wanton than ever at lunchtime,' he'd
whispered.

'Yes, I know. Isn't it shocking?'

'Your move,' Maarten said.

'Oh. Sorry.' Lucky forced the image of her from his
mind. 'Daydreaming.'

The night was cold, and Pietro put his arm around Violet as
they walked along Sharp Street. The wind had died down
and there was a stillness in the air, the feeling of snow. But
snow in Cooma was not romantic; it invariably led to sludge

the following morning. They crossed the stream and walked up the hill, towards Maureen's cottage, which sat beside the main road to Sydney, half a mile out of town.

Violet was chatting nineteen to the dozen. She'd seen all of Marilyn Monroe's pictures, she said, but she liked *Gentlemen Prefer Blondes* best – she'd seen it three times now.

'I am sorry,' Pietro said. Why had she not told him?

No, no, she protested, she wanted to see it another three times, it was the best picture in the world, and Marilyn Monroe was much better than Joan Crawford, and Bette Davis. Then she went on to list her favourites. 'Doris Day's my second best favourite,' she said, 'and I like Grace Kelly, and Rita Hayworth too, because they're so beautiful.'

They arrived at the cottage, pretty with its white-painted stone walls and its quaint little picket-fenced front verandah and blue-trimmed window frames.

'You are more beautiful than all of the film stars, Violetta,' he said as he kissed her.

Her heart stood still. She was Marilyn and Doris and Grace and Rita, all in one. 'Do you want a cup of tea?' she asked.

'Yes. Thank you.' Pietro was pleased. She had never asked him in for a cup of tea before. Not at night. Whenever he'd seen her home after a dance or the pictures he'd kissed her goodnight at the bottom of the steps which led up to the little fenced verandah, and then he'd walked back to the hostel.

She opened the front door. The house was in darkness, and she switched on the lights in the front lounge room.

'Maureen, she is asleep?' he whispered.

'No, she's at the hospital, she's on night shift.'

'Ah yes.' Maureen had told him herself, of course. In the excitement of the day he'd forgotten.

They walked through to the kitchen where they hung their coats on the pegs by the back door, and Violet filled the kettle. He sat at the table watching her as she set out the teapot and cups. She was so beautiful.

She could feel him. She could actually *feel* him watching her. It was as if he were touching her. But he wasn't.

Violet hadn't planned to ask Pietro in for a cup of tea, the invitation had popped out unexpectedly. But she knew that she wouldn't have asked him if her aunt had been home. Just as she knew that her aunt would not approve of her entertaining Pietro alone late at night.

'He's a nice young man, Violet,' Maureen had said in her direct fashion. 'I like him very much. And I'm glad that he looks like Gilbert Roland or whoever, and that he makes you feel beautiful, but you mustn't get too carried away with romance when it comes to the physical, you know what I mean?'

Violet had hoped that Auntie Maureen wasn't about to give her a lecture on sex like her mother had done before she'd left home. But Maureen hadn't.

'You do know what I'm talking about, don't you, Violet?' she'd asked.

'Yes, of course I do.' Auntie Maureen sometimes treated her as if she were simple, Violet thought, but she didn't really mind. Auntie Maureen was just being Auntie Maureen, it wasn't her fault that she had no sense of romance.

'Good, we'll leave it at that.'

Violet had been thankful. She hadn't liked hearing her mother talk about sex, she'd found it sordid. True love wasn't about 'men having their way and women paying for it'. At least that's what she'd thought at the time. But since she'd been seeing Pietro she'd started to wonder what it would be like if she let him 'have his way'. When he kissed her, he not only made her feel beautiful, he made her feel something far more, although she didn't tell Auntie Maureen that. There were some things she couldn't discuss, even with Auntie Maureen. Some things had to be experienced.

She lit the gas stove and set the kettle on the burner, and as she felt him watching her, she wondered whether tonight would be the night. Was that why she had asked him in for tea?

She had stopped talking. It wasn't like her, he thought.

'Grace Kelly, I think she is very good,' he said. 'And Gary Cooper, I think he is good also. I see *High Noon*, we have this picture in Spring Hill when I first come to the Snowy.' She had turned to him, but still she was silent, and he wondered why. 'My English then it is bad, so I do not understand what they speak, but Grace Kelly and Gary Cooper, they are very good I think.'

'Do you want to see my room?'

'Yes.' It came as a surprise, but he supposed he did; she seemed to want him to.

Taking him by the hand, she led him out onto the back verandah and through the door to the sleep-out at the rear of the house.

'This is my room,' she said.

It was a tiny room, just a single bed with a small chest of drawers and a tallboy. Apart from the pink chenille bedspread and the pictures of film stars sticky-taped to the walls, it reminded Pietro of his barracks room at Spring Hill.

'Is nice,' he said.

She maintained her hold on his hand as she sat on the bed, so he sat beside her. He noticed the fluttering of her pulse at the base of her throat and he felt his own pulse rate quicken as she leaned towards him, her head slightly tilted, her lips parted, her eyes closed. She wanted him to kiss her. Here, in her bedroom. It wasn't right, he knew it, but he couldn't resist.

Pietro was aroused the moment their lips met. He was aroused every time they kissed, but he always maintained his self-control, carefully avoiding contact so that she shouldn't be aware of his erection. Now, he felt a touch of panic as her arms circled his neck, drawing him closer and closer, then taking him with her as she lowered herself back onto the bed. He knew he should break away, but he couldn't. She was rubbing her breasts against him, and her mouth was more urgent than it had ever been, her tongue darting across the ridge of his teeth, beckoning him, teasing him.

Violet couldn't believe that she had actually put her tongue in his mouth, tentatively at first, then demandingly, wanting him to do the same. She wanted him to kiss her the way Craig McCauley had kissed her that time behind the pavilion. And she wanted him to touch her breasts the way Craig McCauley had tried to before she'd hurled him off her. Why did she want this? She'd found Craig McCauley repulsive, and Pietro was gentle and romantic and everything that love should be. So why was she rubbing herself against him and pulling him down on top of her as she lay back on the bed?

She was breathless, they both were, and Pietro was losing control, he couldn't help himself. He cupped a hand around her breast, feeling the hardened nipple through her cotton brassiere, and she moaned. Then, before he knew it, they were lying on the bed, locked together, and he was thrusting his body at her.

The feel of his erection startled Violet and she gasped. Rock hard, it ground itself against her pubic bone. She wasn't repulsed, but she was shocked; his hardness frightened her. She was about to lose her virginity.

Pietro stopped, something was wrong. He looked at her briefly, at her wide, startled eyes, and he heard the voice of Sister Anna Maria.

You will respect your intended according to the laws of the church, Pietro. You will seek her father's permission to court her legitimately, and you will never . . . never, do you hear me . . . attempt to take advantage of her.

He swung his legs over the side of the bed and sat with

his head in his hands. 'I am sorry,' he said. 'I am sorry, Violetta.'

Violet wriggled her way to sit beside him. What had happened? She'd been prepared to do it, although she was thankful now that it hadn't happened. Why had he stopped?

'Pietro . . .' She put her hand on his knee.

'No, no.' He pushed it away. 'I am sorry. I am very, very sorry, please forgive me.'

'Pietro . . .' she pleaded, but, eyes trained on the floor, he refused to look at her. 'Pietro, please . . .'

Slowly, he turned to her.

'I asked you into my room,' she said. 'It was my fault. I am to blame.'

'No.' He shook his head firmly. 'No, is not you to blame. But it must not be this way. Is wrong this way.'

'Yes, I know. And I'm sorry.'

'I love you, Violetta.' Finally, he said the words that he'd been longing to say for the past two months. 'With all my heart, I love you.'

It was the most romantic moment of Violet's life. Far, far more romantic than anything she had seen on the screen. She ignored the urgent whistle of the kettle coming from the kitchen. 'I love you too, Pietro,' she said.

CHAPTER EIGHT

The countryside was riotous with blossom. It was the first week of September, and the dusky mustards and gaudy golds of the various wattles mingled with the whites and pinks of the flowering plums and cherries, heralding the arrival of spring.

The change of season brought a renewed vigour to social activity; roads were more accessible and the workers' trips into town more frequent. It was also easier for those wishing to make the journey out to the work camps, and spring brought with it an influx of pimps, prostitutes and professional gamblers. All of which made Merv Pritchard's job that much harder.

'Hello there, Merv, how'd you be?'

'G'day, Jack.' Big Merv Pritchard stepped out of the police car and nodded to the muscular Irishman who was leaning against the wall of the administration hut, chatting to his offsider and having a smoke. 'I'm fine, thanks. What brings you two to Spring Hill?' His query was facetious and required no answer – as if he didn't know what brought Flash Jack Finnigan and his fellow card sharp to Spring Hill on payday.

'Oh, just catching up with a few mates, you know how

it is.' The Irishman, a roguishly handsome man in his mid-thirties, gave an easy grin and dragged on his cigarette.

'Sure I do.' Merv smiled pleasantly enough, but his eyes issued a warning which Jack acknowledged; the men understood each other implicitly. Then Merv disappeared inside the admin hut for his meeting with Rob Harvey.

Jack Finnigan was the most successful of the local gambling kings, and well liked throughout the work camps where he and his offsider, a taciturn Latvian known as Antz, travelled intermittently. Jack ran his operation like a legitimate business, which it was as far as he was concerned, and he had his own code of ethics. If a married man was foolish enough to lose everything he had, then Jack would give him a sizeable amount back with the warning, 'always leave some to send home to the wife'. If the same man was to repeat his folly, then Jack would bar him from future games, refusing to take his money.

Jack's motives weren't altruistic: he knew only too well that one of the rules by which gambling was tolerated was that the men should have money enough left to send to their families. But he was nonetheless perceived as a good bloke by all, and he reinforced the perception with generous donations and sponsorships. Churches and hospitals had a great deal to thank him for, as did a number of local youth organisations and football clubs. As a result, the police turned their well-practised blind eye to his lucrative business in the townships and work camps, aware that it was a case of 'the devil you know'. Jack's card and dice games flourished, and the ever-popular traditional two-up, played throughout the work camps, was a different sort of game when the Irishman was there. Flash Jack was prepared to meet the wager of every serious punter present and the stakes went higher than ever. He also organised sporting competitions and boxing tournaments, occasionally competing in the latter himself, 'for the fun of it'. And it must have been, for when Jack competed, the money was more than likely on him and he stood to lose a bundle. It was a well-known fact that, not only was Jack Finnigan a master in the ring, he would never throw a fight in order to pick up the winnings. Flash Jack Finnigan was an honest bloke, the men said, and they were right. In his own way, Jack was.

'Saw Flash Jack and his mate outside,' Merv remarked to Rob Harvey after they'd greeted each other and he'd settled himself in the chair on the opposite side of Rob's desk.

'Yeah.' Rob nodded, knowing Merv's remark was not confrontational, but rather a friendly warning to keep an eye out for trouble. 'We were just chatting.' Rob himself wasn't a gambler but, like Merv, he understood the men's need for distraction in their sometimes lonely and always isolated world.

'And there's a caravan parked on the back road about half a mile out too. Nobody in it, but I take it a pimp's arrived.'

It wasn't a question – Merv didn't intend to put him on the spot – so Rob smiled and shrugged his ignorance, although he knew the men had been queuing up outside the caravan throughout the night.

'I'll send him packing as soon as he opens for business,' Merv said.

'Fair enough.' Rob involved himself in neither the gambling nor the prostitution which was readily on offer, but he could sympathise with those who did, particularly those wanting for female companionship.

Having spent all his working life in the company of men, Rob Harvey was self-conscious with women, even those who found him attractive, and many did. When he felt the need for female companionship, he didn't visit the prostitutes in town, but made a discreet trip to Sydney. Not to the brothels, but to the more upmarket bars where women were impressed by men from the Snowy. Everyone knew that Snowy workers spent up big – a ten pound note was called 'the Snowy quid' in Kings Cross – and as a result Rob was able to conduct his transactions decorously. He never discussed money, always giving the woman her promised 'present' in an envelope as she left his hotel room, the mutual pretence that she wasn't really a prostitute being maintained throughout. Like so many others, Rob Harvey was a lonely man.

But Merv hadn't come here today merely to discuss the necessary vices of men. There'd been an outbreak of thieving over the past several months – tools and copper cable had been vanishing at an alarming rate. Pilfering from the company was not uncommon, copper cable regularly went missing – copper fetched a high price – and there were always farmers keen to buy tools at half their market value from the workers who smuggled the stolen goods into town. But the current spate of thieving had been on a larger scale than normal and more professionally organised. Rob and Merv had been doing their homework.

'You were spot on,' Merv said. 'It's Slim Parker all right. We've been keeping a watch on him, and one of the boys saw him unloading the stuff in his garage, bold as brass.'

Wayne 'Slim' Parker was a small-time sub-contractor. A local with an eye to the main chance, he'd put himself into hock, bought a '49 Fargo and for the past two years had arrived every month, rain, hail or shine, to deliver his supplies of tobacco, Arnott's biscuits, Vegemite, tomato sauce and every other manner of work camp necessity. From the outset, it had been easy for him to load the empty truck with a few added goods for the trip back. But lately he and his mates had become greedy.

'We didn't book him,' Merv continued, 'I wanted to wait until we could tie up your end.'

'It's an Aussie mob,' Rob said, and Merv rolled his eyes in mock surprise. 'Yeah,' Rob agreed. Whenever there was a scam, it was invariably the Aussies, and it really pissed him off. Why couldn't they just do an honest day's work for an honest day's pay like the migrants did? He'd sack them when they were caught, and he hoped they'd do time – it'd serve them right – but of course that'd all depend on the magistrate. 'I'll give you their names,' he said. 'They're stashing the stuff in a work hut near the old tunnel site.'

Half an hour later, the policeman left, the plan being to wait until Slim's next delivery, so they'd catch the men in the act.

As he drove off, Merv decided that while he was out here he might as well pay another visit to the pimp's caravan. The bastard wouldn't be open for business in broad daylight so he wouldn't be able to book him, but at least he could piss him off. God, he hated the pimps. Scum of the earth.

The caravan remained deserted, however, pulled over by the side of the road, locked and empty. But the pimp would be back for business tonight. And so will I, Merv thought as he climbed into the police car.

From behind a clump of wattles, Al the Frenchie watched the copper drive away. He'd been strolling back from Spring Hill after a card game with some of the workers just off the morning shift when he'd heard the car coming around the bend behind him. He'd automatically ducked out of sight, probably unnecessarily, but it was a habit of his. Just as well, he'd thought, when he'd seen the police car. How come the coppers were on to him already? Word had never got out this quick before. Good thing he'd holed the two girls up at the pub for the day.

Al cursed the copper. He wouldn't be able to work out of the van tonight, and the van always turned over top money, far more than the pub, particularly on payday. He didn't dare risk it, though – the bastard copper was bound to turn up.

Alain Duval, known as 'Al the Frenchie' on his home
turf in Sydney, had been a small-time but relatively successful Kings Cross pimp for the past five years. No-one
really knew where he came from. He probably wasn't
even French. His English was fluent, but his accent was
an indecipherable mixture of European-Australian, and he
spoke a hybrid gutter language that befitted his trade.

It was the way Al wanted it: he liked to be a mystery.
Besides, he felt that he added a touch of glamour to the
backwater that was Sydney. He longed for the Berlin of
the twenties, before the war, when he'd been nineteen and
beautiful. Canny too. It had been an easy step from prostitution – men, women, he hadn't cared so long as they
paid – to running his own racket. Everyone had wanted
him then, he thought. They'd wanted to fuck him, they'd
wanted to be fucked by him, and most importantly they'd
wanted to be a part of his life, so it had been easy to fuck
them back. Berlin loved beauty in those days. Berlin had
been the most erotic, most decadent city in the world. But
the war had fucked them all, hadn't it? Now he was no
longer beautiful. A lifetime of debauchery had caught up
with him and he knew it showed. He was forty-eight years
old and he ran a team of doped-up hookers in Kings Cross.
Life was shit. But at least he was still canny.

Al the Frenchie was indeed more cunning than most of
his contemporaries. He'd been practising his trade in the
Snowies for a number of years and he was yet to be
caught. His visits were fleeting; he stayed for only several
nights and was gone by the time the word had got around.
He considered himself a valuable commodity on the
Snowy: the workers needed to be serviced, and he was
there to provide the women to do it. Shit, he thought, the
hookers were hopeless on their own; they were slags, with
no sense of business. But the Snowy was also a source
of fascination to Al. All those Europeans working themselves into an early grave, he thought, earning a good quid

it was true, more than they would in their home countries, but to what end? Accidents were rife, they lived for a quick visit into town every third payday weekend, and there was always a queue a hundred yards long outside his caravan. Shit, he thought, who'd want a life like that? Australia, the land of opportunity. Well, it was. For those who knew how to take advantage, and he did. In Al the Frenchie's view, there were those who earned their money the hard way, and there were those who profited from their labour.

As Al watched the copper drive off, it irked him to think that he'd come all the way out to this arse-end of the world just for a one night stand. What the hell, he thought, there were other ways to make money. It was payday, Flash Jack Finnigan was at Spring Hill and there'd be big dough around tonight. He'd stay for the game, he decided. There'd be other strange faces turning up at the camp – Jack had a regular following, and all sorts fronted for play wherever the Irishman went. He wouldn't call attention to himself, he'd watch from the sidelines, he decided, and who knew, perhaps he'd come out the winner in the end. Workers were renowned for being careless with their cash and Al's fingers were nimble. They always had been. Ever since the good old days in Berlin.

'Come in spinner,' the boxer called.

Behind the corrugated iron hut that was the wet canteen, dozens of men were gathered around the ring of steel cable staked to the ground. Two men stood on the flattened surface in the centre and, as the boxer stepped back and the spinner raised the wooden kip in his hand, the crowd fell silent.

With a deft flick of the wrist, the pennies resting on the kip were sent spinning high into the air and, as they landed, the boxer stepped forward. The coins were resting heads and tails up.

'No throw,' he announced, to the spinner's annoyance –

it had been the third 'no throw' in succession. The boxer called in a new spinner, as the rules demanded after three 'no throws', and the kip changed hands. The babble of men's voices resumed, until the next cry. 'Come in spinner.' And, for a brief moment, silence once again reigned.

Flash Jack stood among the crowd, to all intents and purposes just another punter, but his presence was forcing the stakes higher. Men pooled their bets, knowing that Jack would meet their wager, and the common aim was to beat the Irishman. Jack never controlled the two-up games – that was another understood regulation by which gambling was tolerated. Two-up was run by one of the workers, to protect the men from professional gambling sharks who might use weighted coins or manipulate the game in some way to their advantage. Jack abided by all the rules.

'Heads!' the boxer called.

'Lucky by name, Lucky by nature, eh?' Flash Jack Finnigan called across the ring, as he doled his money out to the runner.

Lucky returned a smile, accepting his winnings from the runner. If he'd had a quid for every time someone had said that, he thought . . . But he had to admit, these days he agreed with them, life was good. And tonight he was certainly having a run of luck. Not that it would have bothered him overly if he weren't. He'd lost and won heavily on two-up in the past.

Lucky had never been a gambling man in his younger days, and he still didn't consider himself one. But like the others, he earned big money and, like all those with no family commitments, there was little to spend it on. What else was there to do with one's time, locked out here in the company of men? Besides, he enjoyed the simplicity of two-up. He played it with equal simplicity: he chose to bet heads or tails and then he stuck with it. The game usually favoured one or the other. Tonight it was heads – fourteen out of the last twenty throws had been heads – and he was doing well, a hundred and sixty quid to be exact, close to two months' wages. He'd stick it out for another ten throws, he decided. Then he'd call it quits, since he was on the morning shift.

Jack Finnigan continued to back the spinner, who always tossed for tails; he was sure that the run on heads had to end. And Lucky bet a further twenty quid, again on heads, a number of the men pooling their fivers and tenners to join him. Lucky was on a winning streak, they'd decided, and Jack Finnigan, who was meeting the wagers and backing tails, was the loser. It was a good game for many tonight.

Al the Frenchie stood quietly at the back of the crowd. He didn't bet – he never did, he considered betting a mug's game – but he watched the play closely. The man with the bung eye was clutching close to two hundred quid in his hand, and he was one of those careless with money, Al could tell.

Out of the nine following throws, five landed heads. Lucky was still well and truly a winner, but his simplistic rule of play wouldn't do him any favours if the next toss came up tails. It was his last bet for the night and he wanted to be adventurous, so he put a hundred quid on heads.

It was a lot to place on one throw and Lucky's supporters voiced their approval loudly, pooling their own bets and looking to Jack Finnigan. There were smaller side bets going on, but the big money was all resting on the Irishman. Three hundred quid in all. Would he match it? Of course Jack did.

'Tails,' he said, nodding to them and flashing his easy smile. What the hell, losing at two-up kept him onside with the men. Antz'd be picking up a fortune in the wet canteen where a manila game was currently in progress, and he'd shortly be joining him to set up a pontoon table.

'Come in spinner,' the boxer called.

Silence again, as the pennies spun dizzyingly, seeming to halt in mid-air before starting their downward spiral. Then they landed, one with a gentle thud, the other rolling several feet before coming to rest.

'Heads,' the boxer announced. The men who'd been following Lucky's lead roared.

The Irishman shook his head good-naturedly as he counted out the notes. 'You're breaking the bank, Lucky,' he called, and the men gave another cheer – that'd be the day.

Al the Frenchie watched the runner cross to the man with the bung eye first before doling out the rest of the winnings to the other punters. He watched while bung eye gave Jack a wave and made his farewells. Several tried to persuade him to stay, but bung eye said he was on the early shift, and his mates slapped him on the back before turning their eyes to the next toss of the pennies.

Al edged around behind the crowd. Bung eye was stuffing about three hundred quid into his pockets as he walked off. Not a bad night's takings, Al thought – the girls would have scored around the same with one night's work in the van. If he could pull it off, it'd make his trip to Spring Hill worthwhile. He watched bung eye walk up the slope away from the mess hut and the wet canteen, towards the lines of huts and barracks. He didn't follow him, but walked off towards the bushes at the edge of the settlement where he could observe bung eye's progress without being observed himself. He had no intention of mugging the man; apart from the backhanders he dished out to the girls when they needed it, Al avoided violence like the plague. But it wouldn't do any harm to find out exactly where bung eye was headed.

He kept to the bushes, dodging among them, following the man's progress. He watched as bung eye walked along the road past the lines of barracks towards the row of snow huts. A single cabin, he thought. Promising. Then he watched as bung eye kept walking past each of the huts before disappearing into the one at the very end. Al couldn't believe his luck. Things were looking distinctly possible.

Al the Frenchie's presumption that he'd go unnoticed at the game had proved erroneous from the outset. Certainly there'd been men other than Spring Hill residents present, at least a dozen or more workers from other camps, and Al had been careful to hang back at the rear of the crowd, but word had been passed down the line nonetheless. One of the men who'd visited the caravan the previous night had recognised him and sent out a warning that the pimp was at the game, and Al had become aware of the odd muttered remark, the nudge of an elbow, a pair of eyes darting in his direction. They wouldn't rat on him, he knew it, they wouldn't want the girls to be sent packing, but he'd quickly abandoned any thoughts of pick-pocketing. Pity. It would have been so easy. The men were slack with their money and their wallets, he'd even seen one man's pay packet sticking halfway out the back of his hip pocket. Unscrupulous as some were with company property, there was no thieving in the camps. The workers trusted each other. Al had done a quick rethink and stayed put, a mere observer of the action.

Now, as he watched bung eye close his cabin door, Al decided to come back in the morning. He'd heard him say he was on the early shift, and if the coast looked clear when the workers had gone, it'd be relatively simple; he'd done it before, the men rarely locked their doors.

He returned to his caravan. The copper would have been and gone now, realising the van wasn't open for business. The bastard would be back tomorrow to move him on, but Al would be long gone by then.

Early the following morning, the two-up ring was deserted, but inside the wet canteen, dense with cigarette smoke and the smell of stale beer, the card games continued; the heavy-duty punters were there for the long haul. Jack and Antz had worked throughout the night, and would no doubt work throughout the following night too. As the day wore on, they would take it in turns to grab half an hour's kip in the back of Jack's Mercedes – it was all they needed. Jack and Antz could deal cards for twenty-four hours straight with no more than a catnap in between. They'd trained themselves to do so. The official ruling that gambling was permitted only on pay night was regularly overlooked and the card games could go on for several days, the keenest of the punters paying others to work their shifts. Jack and Antz needed all the staying power they could muster.

'Franta, he tell me you win big last night,' Pietro said when Lucky had completed a head count of his work team. The men were milling around the trucks not far from the mess hut, about to head off to the work site, a good half-hour's drive from the settlement.

'I did.' Lucky climbed into the truck's cabin. 'Want to ride in comfort? First in first served.' Lucky always drove the lead truck, and it was always his catchphrase when he offered the passenger seat. Pietro piled in beside him while others of the team clambered into the open back. 'You coming to Dodds tomorrow? I'll be shouting the bar.'

'I will be there, yes,' Pietro said. 'I take Violetta to Dodds for dinner and dancing.'

'Good. Then we'll meet up for a couple of beers before-hand.'

There was a signalling tap from behind and Lucky checked in his rear vision mirror to see that the men were all safely seated before pulling out into the street, the several other trucks following in convoy.

'So how was your night, Pietro?'

'Is very good. Vesna, she cook me dinner, after we practise our English. Vesna, she is very good cook, I think.'

Lucky smiled to himself. Pietro would have to be the only man on the Snowy who chose English practice in preference to a Flash Jack Finnigan gambling night. But then Pietro never gambled. He never had. He didn't know how to.

Nine hours later, the trucks returned and the men piled out, tired, grubby, but in excellent humour. It was a Friday and Jack Finnigan was in Spring Hill.

'Will you be coming to the game tonight, Lucky?' Franta the Czech asked as they walked up towards the barracks.

'I think I'd be pushing it, two nights in a row,' Lucky smiled, 'but I'll see you for a beer in an hour or so.'

He walked past the barracks and the row of snow huts to his cabin, intending to collect his towel and fresh clothes and head straight for the ablution block. He'd get there early so he wouldn't have to queue for a shower.

He knew he'd been robbed as soon as he opened the door – the thief hadn't been subtle. But whoever it was had been quick and efficient, he realised, in and out of the hut within a matter of seconds, it appeared. The top drawer of the lowboy sat upside down on the floor, its contents tipped out beside it. Nothing else had been touched; the thief had immediately found what he was after. Lucky knelt and sifted through the mess of papers and toiletries that lay scattered about. His wallet was there, but the hundred pounds he'd put in it wasn't, and neither was the envelope in which he'd put the rest of the money, intending to bank it.

In the five years he'd been working on the Snowy, Lucky had never known of a worker's room being burgled. Men's possessions were safe in the work camps; they trusted each other. It was only when they went into town that they needed to be wary.

He was angry, but he was also bemused. The thief was a stranger, he thought, a stranger who'd been at the game, and knew he'd won big. But the strangers who'd been gathered about the ring, pooling their bets along with the locals, had been men from other work camps, and they'd arrived together. He even knew a couple of them, he'd shared a beer with them in Cooma. They wouldn't stoop to such an act.

Lucky had been so intent on the game that he hadn't heard the whispers about the pimp, and the only other strangers he could think of were Jack Finnigan and his offsider. It wouldn't be Jack, he knew that. Whether or not Jack was the soul of propriety he made himself out to be was perhaps a dubious point, but Jack Finnigan would certainly not risk soiling his reputation. The dealer maybe? The Latvian called Antz? Doubtful, but who could say?

As he sat on the floor, replacing his possessions in the drawer, Lucky cursed the man who had robbed him. Not so much for the money – easy come, easy go, he thought – but for the arousal of his suspicions, for the betrayal of trust which existed in this unique society of men in the wilderness.

He picked up the envelopes that were strewn about, and his pad of airmail writing paper. He'd forgotten it was there – he hadn't written a letter for three years, not since his father had died. And he'd stopped corresponding with his old friend Efraim Meisell when he'd first come to the Snowies. He'd severed all ties with the past, even with the man who'd saved his life, he thought guiltily, as he placed the writing pad in the drawer. Then he saw the photograph, sitting on the floor. He'd forgotten that was there too. He picked it up. Ruth, radiant, captured laughing and exasperated by Mannie's patience. He studied the photograph for quite a while before slipping it into his wallet. There were some ties with the past that would never be severed, he thought.

Lucky stood and slid the drawer back into the lowboy.

He'd shower and then join the others. He'd have to borrow some money to see himself through till next payday. The thief had cleaned him out – the bastard.

'You're a bastard, Al, that's what you are. A low, thieving bastard.'

Al cowered against the dresser in the corner, eyes darting towards the French windows that led to the balcony, but dismissing escape as an option. It was dark outside and even if he made it onto the balcony he'd probably break a leg jumping to the street one floor below.

The shock of his hotel door being kicked open and the appearance of the enraged Irishman had terrified Al, and his mind was racing. What the hell was Jack Finnigan doing in town? He was supposed to be in Spring Hill. How had the Irishman known where to find him? How did he even know his name? The men at camp must have told him, but why would Jack leave his game in full swing? Why would a few hundred quid nicked from a punter be of any importance to Flash Jack Finnigan?

Shit, Al thought, if only he'd left town earlier. But Friday was a top night for local trade, and he'd sent the girls off to do the rounds of the barracks at Cooma East. He'd been so sure he was safe. Nobody could prove he'd nicked bung eye's money, and even if they suspected him, the workers from Spring Hill didn't come into town until Saturday. He'd intended to be well away by dawn. Shit, shit, shit, he thought, if only he'd left earlier.

He tried to dredge up an air of nonchalance. The one option open to him was to bluff it out, and he relinquished his hold on the dresser, squaring his shoulders and running a casual hand through his hair.

'That was quite an entrance, Jack. You gave me a fright, I have to admit.' He painted a smile on his face, but his pulse was racing – there was murder in the Irishman's eyes. 'I don't believe we've actually met, although of course I know who you are. Everyone knows Flash Jack Finnigan.' The ingratiating laugh came out more of a strangled giggle. 'It's a pleasure to meet you. The name's Alain.' He offered his hand. 'Alain Duval.' And he stepped forward straight into Jack's fist.

Jesus, what had happened? He was flat on his back, a ringing in his ears, one front tooth missing, several others loosened, and he was looking up at the powerful thighs of Flash Jack Finnigan standing over him.

'Save your smarmy shite, you low thieving bastard, just give me the money.'

Al sat up and scuffled on his backside into the corner by the dresser, blood dripping from his chin.

'What money, Jack? I don't know what you're talking about, I swear it . . .'

But in two strides, Jack was once again towering over him.

'No, don't hit me,' Al begged. 'Please. Please. I've got money. You can have it. You can have all of it. Don't hit me again. Please.'

The Irishman leant down and grabbed him by the shirt collar and, as Al was hauled to his feet, he felt the trickle of urine down his legs.

'No, no, please. It's there. The black bag in the top drawer. You can have it all.'

'I don't want it all, you lowdown scum.' Jack released his hold on Al and took the black zippered bag from the drawer. He opened it and upended the contents onto the top of the dresser, hundreds of pounds spilling out, notes floating to the floor. 'I won't have your girls working their fannies off for nothing, although Christ alone knows what pittance they get to keep for themselves.' He counted out three hundred pounds. 'That's around what you nicked from Lucky's cabin, isn't it?' he said, folding the notes into a wad and shoving them into the inside breast pocket of his jacket.

'I don't know what you're talking about, Jack. But take it, it's yours. Take all of . . .'

The Irishman's fist once again crashed into his face, and Al felt the cartilage of his nose crumple. He started to slide down the wall, but Jack grabbed him again, by the throat this time, and held him up.

'You'd let others take the blame, wouldn't you, you wormy bastard? Well, I've a mind to kill you right here and now. I'd be doing everyone a favour.' He balled his hand into a fist. 'You don't deserve to breathe other people's air.'

As Jack Finnigan hauled his arm back, Al gave a strangled scream.

'No, Jack! No!' He tried to turn his head away but the hand around his throat tightened its grip. He squeezed his eyes tight shut, his face contorting as he gasped for breath, waiting for the killer blow. But it didn't come. He waited, heart pounding, but still it didn't come. He opened his eyes, barely able to see through the blood and tears. The Irishman remained poised, arm drawn back, fist at the ready. Waiting.

Waiting for what? Al's mind screamed. A confession? He could have it. He could have anything. 'I took it, Jack,' he blubbered. 'I took it, and I'm sorry.' He was gagging and sobbing simultaneously. 'I'm sorry, Jack, I'm sorry.' The circle of urine was widening about the floor where he stood.

Jack released his grip on Al the Frenchie's throat. 'I tell you what you'll do . . .' he began, but Al once again started to slide down the wall. 'No, no,' he barked, 'you're not to fall. Not yet.'

It was an order, and Al clutched on to the dresser for dear life, whimpering, doing his best to remain standing, although his legs were like jelly.

'You'll leave, and you'll not come back, you hear me?'

Al nodded, dribbling blood, not daring to speak.

'As of tomorrow,' Jack continued, 'word will be out, around every work camp, around every town, and if you so much as show your face, I'll kill you for the lowlife rat you are. Do you understand me?'

Al nodded again.

'Say it, scum.'

'I promise, Jack.' Al the Frenchie's reply gurgled its way out through blood and mucus. 'I won't come back, I swear I won't.'

'Good. We understand each other. You can fall down now.'

Al didn't see the fist this time, but he felt it hit him in the midriff like a pile-driver, and he collapsed to the floor clutching his broken ribs.

The Irishman stepped back to avoid the pool of urine that was threatening his Italian leather shoes. 'I'll leave you now, Al,' he said, 'right there where you belong. Lying in your own filthy muck.'

It was ten o'clock when Jack's Mercedes pulled off the main road and wound its way into Spring Hill. The trip to Cooma and back had cost him three hours. Three hours when he could have been making a bundle at his pontoon table. The visit to the pimp had been an expensive exercise. But he was proud of his actions. Even as he'd tipped the pimp's money out onto the dresser, he had not been tempted to recompense himself for his loss. He would give no-one rise to accuse Jack Finnigan of thievery. Not even a lowlife scumbag like Al the Frenchie.

In the wet canteen, where the indefatigable Antz remained at his station, the men cheered Jack's arrival. They didn't know why he'd disappeared or where he'd gone. Even those who'd told him about the theft of Lucky's money and the pimp being at the game had not assumed for one minute that Jack would take action. Why should he?

A bunch of the men started crowding around the pontoon table.

'Give me a few minutes, lads, I'll just grab a beer.' Jack wasn't going to grab a beer at all, he never drank when he was dealing, but he'd spied Lucky seated at a crowded table in the corner. He'd hoped the man hadn't retired for the night – it would have cost more valuable game time finding him in his barracks.

Lucky was mildly drunk, which was unusual, he rarely had more than a couple of beers. But the men had been so outraged by the robbery that they'd all insisted upon shouting him a round. Every time he'd tried to leave, someone had insisted it was their turn, and he hadn't been able to resist the camaraderie. He'd been relieved to hear about the pimp. Of course he'd known all along that the thief wasn't one of them, but it had been a relief nonetheless, it had restored his faith in mankind. Well, the mankind that was the Snowy anyway, he thought a touch blearily. He was feeling very mellow in the company of his mates, but he was heartily sick of the taste of beer.

'Can I see you for a minute, Lucky?'

'Hello, Jack. You're back,' he said rather foolishly, looking up at the Irishman. 'Where've you been?'

'Had to make a little trip. Can I have a moment of your time?'

'Sure.' Lucky rose unsteadily to his feet.

'Let's go to the bar.'

'Oh. Right.' The Irishman was going to buy him a beer, Lucky thought. He really couldn't stomach another one.

They edged through the crowd of men, Lucky wondering how he could politely refuse the shout, but when they got to the far end of the bar, Jack didn't offer him a beer at all.

'Got a little present for you,' he said. And with the sleight of hand possessed only by magicians and master card dealers, the Irishman transferred the wad of notes from the inner breast pocket of his jacket to the outer chest pocket of Lucky's shirt. No-one, including Lucky, had seen the transaction. Jack's hands had simply flickered in the air as if he were making a gesture. 'Three hundred quid, that's what the pimp nicked, right?'

'It was a bit less actually.' Lucky was mystified. What had just happened? Something had landed in his pocket, he could feel it through the cotton of his shirt.

'Well, it's three hundred quid now.'

Lucky dipped his hand into his pocket, about to draw out the money, but the Irishman stopped him.

'No, don't,' he said. 'No need to advertise. We're just righting a wrong, that's all.'

But Lucky drew the money out anyway. He stared at it, dumbfounded, a thick wad of notes, how had it got there? God, but he must be drunk, he thought. He shook his head, further mystified as to why the Irishman should feel it necessary to reimburse him for the theft. 'It's very kind of you, Jack, but I can't take it. I can't take your money.'

He handed the wad of notes back, and the Irishman appeared about to accept it. But he didn't. Instead, he took Lucky's hand in both of his, and folded his fingers around the money.

'It's not my money,' he said. 'It's yours.'

Lucky tried to protest further, but Jack wouldn't listen.

'It's yours, Lucky, I promise you. I got it from the pimp. He said he was sorry. So put it away, all right?'

'You got it from the pimp?' Lucky's look of incredulity was bordering on comical, and Jack grinned his flashy grin.

'Indeed I did, and he was most keen to give it to me.' The Irishman's grin faded as quickly as it had appeared. 'He'll not be showing his face around here again, you can tell your friends that. I'll have no thievery at a Jack Finnigan game.' Then he gave Lucky a comradely pat on the shoulder. 'Now the men are impatient and the cards are calling, if you'll excuse me.' And he headed off to the pontoon table, leaving Lucky clutching the wad of money and staring after him in amazement.

Jack Finnigan was pleased with the turn of events. True to form, his actions had not been as altruistic as they'd appeared to others. They never were, for there was an element of self-interest in everything Jack did. And what was wrong with that? He was a businessman, after all. Certainly, when he'd taken off after the pimp he'd been in a towering rage: the scum had damaged his reputation, even threatened his livelihood. If word got out that Jack Finnigan's gambling events attracted thieves to the work camps, he'd be banned. Jack had wanted to kill the lowlife scum bastard.

But, during the drive into town, he'd realised that the episode could prove an invaluable public relations exercise if he went about it properly. And he had. Bugger the money he'd lost during the three-hour visit to Cooma, he now thought, the pimp had done him a favour. Lucky was a man well-respected throughout the camp, one to whom the others listened, and he would tell the men what had taken place in just the right way. He would tell them that Jack Finnigan had taken care of the pimp, that he'd returned the money quietly, without seeking praise, and that he'd banned the scum from ever showing his face again. All of which would get back to the bosses – word travelled like wildfire in the camps.

I'll have no thievery at a Jack Finnigan game. It had sounded good, the Irishman thought, and it would sound good to the authorities too, when they heard it. He must remember to bandy the line around a little in case Lucky forgot to quote him – the man had had a few drinks.

CHAPTER NINE

Cooma's pubs were the hub of the community. Townsfolk, Snowy workers, shearers and farmers alike all flocked to the pubs, and each had its own unique character. The Prince of Wales was big and showy, dominating Sharp Street. The Alpine, further up the road, offered fine accommodation in its 'Humela House', attracting the Snowy administrators and engineers, and on the opposite side of the main street, the ever-popular Australian, known affectionately as 'the Aussie', remained a favourite with everyone.

But it was Dodds Family Hotel, just a block away in Commissioner Street, that held the record in beer sales. Of all the Cooma pubs, Dodds, with a regular weekly delivery of forty kegs, outsold its closest rivals by a good five kegs a week, irrefutable proof of its ranking in the popularity stakes.

Dodds was a family hotel in every sense of the word. It was raucous, certainly, as every Cooma pub was, but the bar was warm and welcoming, the restaurant boasted good food, and there was a singalong around the piano in the lounge after dinner. Dodds was a reflection of the Duncan family who owned and ran it.

Bob Duncan was a tough, hardworking man with a dry sense of humour that endeared him to his patrons. He and his equally hardworking wife, Rita, had four children, and it was Rita Duncan herself who was one of the pub's main attractions. Rita was a devastatingly pretty, effervescent woman who treated everyone as family. She was, furthermore, a virtuoso on the piano and led the evening singalongs with infectious charm. Bob considered 'Reet', whom he loved very dearly, worth her weight in gold.

'Took her a while to get used to being a publican's wife, though,' he'd say, and Rita would laugh. Bob liked to dine out on the watermelon story. It had been in the early days at their pub in Lismore when, during the height of midsummer, Bob had been aghast to discover his young wife handing out platters of watermelon to the customers. When she'd protested that it was such a hot day and watermelon was cooling, he'd said, 'So's beer, love. That's why they're here, to drink beer. I don't think the watermelon's a good idea, Reet.' He'd laughed. 'If you want to give them anything, give them salted peanuts,' and he'd ragged her about it ever since.

Lucky arrived at Dodds in the mid-afternoon. It was two days after his two-up win and he was intent upon shouting the bar as he'd promised, but on entering the pub's entrance hall with its grand granite staircase leading to the upstairs accommodation, he didn't turn right to the bars, but disappeared into the main lounge to the left, in search of Bob Duncan. He found him in the dining room to the rear of the lounge, discussing the menu with the new chef who'd arrived on the train from Sydney that morning.

'Would you look after this for me, Bob?' Lucky handed the publican the envelope in which he'd put the two hundred pounds he intended to bank.

'Sure, I'll shove it in the safe.' Bob regularly looked after workers' money. Sometimes a heavy drinker would hand over his entire pay packet, in which case Bob would dole him out some spending money for the night. Come morning, when the man thought he'd lost the lot or been robbed, Bob would reproduce the cash, still intact in its pay packet. Lucky was not one of the heavy drinkers who needed to practise such caution, but Bob had heard about the two-up win.

'Do you want me to bank it for you?' he asked – he did the banking for his favourite regulars too.

'If you wouldn't mind, yes, thanks, I'd appreciate it. I had a win at two-up,' Lucky grinned, 'a big one.'

'So I heard.' Bob hadn't been about to say anything, but as Lucky had proffered the information . . . 'I heard about Jack Finnigan too. They say the pimp left town in one hell of a mess. Go on through to the bar, I'll just pop this upstairs.'

News travels fast, Lucky thought as he crossed back through the main lounge towards the saloon bar.

He wasn't wrong. Pietro and several others from Spring Hill were already in the bar, and all the talk was of Jack Finnigan, as every new arrival was filled in with the story, the townsmen and the men from Spring Hill each telling their side.

'You should have seen the pimp, he could hardly walk, the hookers were carrying him out of the pub,' one man said.

Al the Frenchie had had to wait all night for the girls to return from work, and his ignominious departure in the early hours of the morning had been witnessed by many.

'His face was pulp,' another added. 'One of the hookers had to drive.'

'That's what you get for crossing Jack Finnigan,' a worker from Spring Hill said. 'Jack won't have thieving at his games. And he gave the money back to Lucky on the quiet, without even expecting so much as a thank you.' The man noticed Lucky's arrival. 'Isn't that so, Lucky?'

'It is.'

'There'll be no thieving at a Jack Finnigan game!' the man announced in a true imitation of the Irishman, and several of the other Spring Hill workers gave a cheer. 'That's what Jack said, isn't it, Lucky?'

'That's right.' Those had been the Irishman's very words, Lucky recalled, but he'd said them in private. Lucky had not quoted the man verbatim when he'd told the others what had happened, and he wondered how the phrase was now being bandied about.

'Now there's a man of honour for you, bejaysus,' a thick Irish brogue said in his ear, and Lucky turned to meet the approving grin of Peter Minogue.

Peter Minogue was arguably the most famous and certainly the most highly paid waiter in Cooma. He was another of Dodds' attractions, and a close friend of Jack Finnigan's. Along with their Irish heritage, the two had much in common. Like Jack, Peter was a strong man – on the palm of one hand he could carry several trays of full beer glasses, one tray balanced on top of the other. And, like Jack, he was a showman. Peter drove flashy cars, and he liked to entertain the men with his darts skills, splitting a match three times, or landing the darts with lightning speed between the boldly splayed fingers of young Robert, the publican's fourteen-year-old son. He regularly forgot to collect his wages from Bob Duncan, making far more money than he could spend in tips from patrons who willingly paid for the service and entertainment he provided.

'Jack's a true Irish gent, that's for sure,' he now said, picking up the three trays that sat on the bar and raising them showily with one hand to shoulder height. 'There'll be no thievin' at a Jack Finnigan game!' he stated loudly for the benefit of the entire assembly. Then he gave a wink to Lucky. ''Tis a fine statement indeed,' and he sailed off to the lounge where the heavy tippers were waiting to applaud his entrance.

'Drinks are on me,' Lucky called to the bar, and as the

men cheered both him and Jack, Lucky thought what a
clever man Jack Finnigan was. It had been Jack himself
who had bandied the phrase about, he realised. Peter
Minogue had obviously guessed as much too – his signal
had been unmistakable. The wheels had been set in
motion, and Flash Jack Finnigan was swiftly becoming the
stuff of legend.

An hour or so later, Lucky left to call on Peggy and,
early that same evening, the two of them returned to
Dodds where they joined Pietro and Violet in the dining
room. The four had dined together on previous occasions,
Violet most impressed to be seen on an equal social footing
with her former schoolteacher.

'I think it's time you called me Peggy, don't you?' Peggy
had smiled on the first occasion when Violet's conversation had been peppered with 'Miss Minchins', and Violet,
far from being intimidated, had made sure that she said
Peggy's name very loudly when there was anyone she knew
within earshot.

She no longer did so. These days there was an aspect to
Peggy Minchin which was of far greater interest to young
Violet Campbell than the elevation of her own social
status. Peggy Minchin and Lucky were lovers. She could
see it in Peggy's face. Previously, she had found the thought
of her former school mistress in a 'relationship' a source of
fascination, but now, as Violet looked at Peggy across the
dining table, she knew that Peggy Minchin was in love, in
every sense of the word.

'You look beautiful, Peggy,' she said. Her schoolteacher
had never looked beautiful before, but these days she did.
And especially right now. Had they just made love? Violet
wondered. Was that why? She envied Peggy.

'Thank you, Violet,' Peggy answered briskly. She didn't
look beautiful at all, she thought, but she was aware of the
girl's scrutiny, and she was a little unnerved. Was it really
that obvious? Less than an hour ago, she'd been in a state

of sexual delirium, her naked body locked with Lucky's, and Violet seemed to sense it. 'That's very kind of you to say so.'

'I mean it. You look really, really beautiful.'

Violet's smile was special, a sharing between two women, and while Peggy felt exposed, she couldn't help but respond to the girl's intimacy. She smiled back, then quickly returned her attention to the men, hoping they hadn't noticed the exchange. They hadn't: Lucky and Pietro were deep in conversation. Little Vi Campbell had certainly changed, Peggy thought, and it was more than the unexpected blossoming of her body. There was something eminently sexual about young Violet.

After dinner, the four of them retired to the main lounge where the real fun was about to begin. The bars had officially closed, in accordance with the law, but serious drinking continued in the lounge under the guise of a supper licence. Unwanted plates of cheese and biscuits and sandwiches were doled out with the alcohol, and a 'cockatoo' was placed on watch outside. If the warning sounded and a copper arrived on the scene, there must be no evidence of excessive drinking. Everything must appear to be in order, and every person must appear to be eating.

When they begin the beguine, it brings back the sound of music so tender . . .

It was Rita Duncan's favourite song and she played it with feeling, even though she'd been at the keyboard for three hours solid with barely a break.

It had been a good night. Most of the patrons were happily inebriated, and there'd been no trouble. Bob Duncan and Peter Minogue had evicted one drunk who'd been intent on picking a fight. The man would happily have taken any potential contender out of the bar and into the street, but it would have presented a problem nonetheless. A fight in the street would attract the attention of the coppers, and that must be avoided at all costs. Fortunately no-one had taken him up on his offer.

Now, dozens were gathered around the piano singing along, and several couples were dancing. It was nearly midnight and the lounge would soon close.

Peggy and Lucky's bodies were one as they moved to the rhythm of the music. They were excellent dancers, and quite evidently in love. Peggy no longer agonised over their relationship, openly admitting to herself that she loved him in a way she had never dreamed possible, and she didn't care who else knew it. It wouldn't last. She had no expectations – he had offered her none. But if Lucky was to be her one great affair, then she would enjoy it as much as she could. And, when it was over, she would get on with her life as efficiently as she always had. It was simple, she told herself. It was simple because it had to be.

As Violet swayed to the music, she watched Peggy and Lucky dance. She wished Pietro would hold her close like that, but he always avoided any contact from the waist down, and she knew why. The night of her attempted seduction remained clear in Violet's mind. There had been no repetition of their passion – if anything, that night had doused his ardour altogether. Pietro kept her virtually at arm's length these days, he no longer even opened his mouth when he kissed her, and Violet was becoming very frustrated. She knew that she loved him – he was her romantic ideal, the man she'd dreamed of – but she wasn't sure whether she wanted to marry. Not just yet. There was one thing she *was* sure of, though. She wanted him to make love to her. She tried to edge her body a little closer as they danced.

Pietro felt her hand move from his shoulder to the back of his neck, and he felt her groin ease closer to his. He twirled her quickly in time to the music – he was a good dancer and she wasn't, so it was easy for him to avoid the connection. There must be no connection, he had told himself. Not until they were married. And for that he must see her father. The time was right, Pietro had decided, and he intended telling Maureen so. He would go and see Maureen tomorrow at her house before he left for Spring Hill, and if Maureen did not agree to present his case as she had promised, then Pietro would do so himself.

Till you whisper to me once more, darling, I love you and we suddenly know what heaven we're in . . .

As she played, Rita Duncan looked at the couples dancing. They were so in love, she thought. And they were dancing to 'Begin the Beguine'. How perfect. Rita was an incurable romantic.

'Cam Campbell, what a pleasant surprise! What brings you to town?'

It was pretty obvious, wasn't it? Cam thought – he'd just stepped out of Learmont's Menswear with a load of shirts tucked under his arm. 'Bit of shopping,' he said. What business was it of hers anyway? But he smiled in his customary amiable fashion. 'How are you, Mavis?' he asked, preparing himself for the inevitable fifteen-minute monologue – God, but the woman could talk. He usually tried to avoid Mavis when he saw her in the street.

'Any fitter and I'd be dangerous,' Mavis said. Her thin face wreathed into a smile and she gave a girlish laugh, her form of innocent flirtation. She liked Cam Campbell, such a man's man and she wished her Brian was a bit more like him. 'I've just come from a P & A meeting,' she continued, 'and your name came up again. We could do with you back on the committee, Cam, you're sorely missed.'

Cam had lasted all of six months on the Pastoral and Agricultural Association's Committee, and it had been a whole year ago, but Mavis said the same thing every time she managed to corner him.

'Too busy, Mavis.' His reply was always the same too.

'Yes, I know, such a pity, but you won't stop me from

trying, you know – we need men like you on the committee.' She changed subjects without drawing a breath; it was
a talent of Mavis's. 'I saw Vi on Saturday. Well, of course
I see her all the time, I'm in Hallidays nearly every day of
the week. She's turned into such a pretty girl, hasn't she?'
The question was rhetorical and she sailed on, 'But when
I saw her on Saturday night, all dressed up, I must say I
was most impressed. She and her young man make a lovely
couple.'

Young man? What young man? Cam thought, but he
said nothing. Mavis was a garrulous fool of a woman, but
she was also a gossip-monger who liked to cause trouble.
He waited for her to go on.

'I've seen them quite often around town, they've been
going out together for some time now, I take it?' This time
the question was not rhetorical, and Mavis looked at him
with feigned innocence, awaiting his answer. She was
dying to find out if Cam knew about his daughter and the
Italian. But Cam's face was unreadable.

'Yes, I believe they have,' he replied. He was damned if
he'd give the interfering cow the satisfaction of knowing
that she'd dropped a bombshell. 'Vi's eighteen now, Mavis.
I trust her, and I don't meddle in her life.'

'Of course, and so you shouldn't.' He knew, and he
approved, Mavis thought. Well, fancy that. But then Cam
Campbell had accepted the foreigners right from the start.
She decided that flattery was the best tactic. 'I must say,
Cam, I admire your open-mindedness. Of course I've
always believed, like you, that we should welcome the
migrants into the area,' she added, although she didn't
believe anything of the sort, 'but to welcome them into
one's family, so to speak . . . well, you're certainly living up
to your principles . . .'

Mavis knew she'd gone too far. Her flattery had back-
fired on her, the man looked angry. She'd offended him.
'I'm not being critical, I know you believe that all men are

equals, and I'm sure you're right. It's just that I can't help feeling . . . and perhaps it's wrong of me, that . . .'

'Yes, Mavis. It's wrong of you.'

He walked off and Mavis was left feeling most put out. She'd been trying to be helpful. If he hadn't known about his daughter, then it was high time someone told him, she'd thought. And if he had known, as it appeared he did, then she'd been prepared to be malleable. If he'd been upset, she'd have commiserated with him; as he wasn't, she'd flattered him. And it hadn't worked. She couldn't win.

Cam dumped his shirts into the back of his Holden ute and strode off towards Hallidays. His daughter going out with a bloody foreigner? Over my dead body, he thought.

'G'day, Cam, haven't seen you for a while.'

Frank Halliday was seated beside the windows. It was Monday and Frank was taking an inventory following the busy weekend.

'G'day, Frank.' Cam propped himself casually in the open doorway; he could see his daughter further down the counter, stacking tins on the shelves. 'How's business?' He had no intention of creating a scene in front of the shopkeeper, or anyone else for that matter.

'Can't complain. You after Vi?'

'Yes, if you could spare her for a sec.'

'Take your time, we're not busy. Hey Vi,' Frank called, 'your dad's here.'

Violet's face lit up in a smile as she turned. 'Dad!' She dumped her armload of tinned tomatoes, circled the counter and ran to him. 'I didn't know you were in town,' she said, throwing her arms around his neck and hugging him.

'I was going to call around the house later and surprise you and your auntie.' Cam returned the embrace, briefly and uncomfortably. She was too old to hug him like that, particularly in public.

Violet, aware of his self-consciousness, broke away. In the instinctive pleasure of seeing her father, she'd forgotten for a moment that things had changed. She wished they hadn't. She wished her father would still hug her the way he used to.

'That'd be beaut,' she said brightly. 'Can you stay for tea? Auntie Maureen'll be home by four, she was on the early shift today.'

'We'll see. Do you want to pop out for a cuppa?'

Violet looked at Frank Halliday.

'Go on with your dad, Vi,' Frank nodded, and she quickly ducked back behind the counter to collect her handbag – Violet never went anywhere without her lipstick and comb.

'Like I said, Cam, take your time,' the shopkeeper added. 'We're never busy on Mondays.'

'Thanks, Frank, most appreciated.' Cam smiled, and he and Violet stepped out into the street. But the moment they were outside, his smile disappeared, and he took his daughter by the arm and started walking her briskly in the direction of the Holden.

'What's the matter, Dad?' she asked, but she'd already guessed. Her father had heard about Pietro.

Cam said nothing until they arrived at the ute. He opened the passenger door. 'Get in,' he said.

'I thought we were going for a cuppa.'

'I want to talk to you, Vi.'

'We can talk over a cup of . . .'

'Privately. Get in.'

Violet did as she was told, and her father slammed the ute door a little harder than was necessary. He was furious, she thought. But she wasn't going to let him frighten her, she decided. She'd done nothing wrong.

Cam drove across the creek and out of town, away from the eyes of passers-by, and stopped the ute by the side of the road and turned to her.

'Right. Now tell me about this bloke you're going out with.'

She looked him square in the eyes. 'His name is Pietro,' she said. 'Pietro Toscanini.'

A Dago, he thought. My daughter's going out with a bloody Dago. But he controlled himself, as any good, responsible father would. 'How long have you been seeing him?'

'Five months.'

A whole five months! Jesus Christ, he'd kill the Wop bastard. 'And why wasn't I told?'

'I haven't seen you since the Show, you haven't been into town . . .'

'There's such a thing as the telephone, Violet, you could have rung your mother and me.'

She turned away and gazed rebelliously out the window. Although she liked others to call her Violet, she hated it when her father did so – it meant she was about to get a lecture. Well at least he was only mad because she hadn't told him she had a boyfriend, she thought, he didn't seem to mind that Pietro was Italian. She'd worried that, for all his talk, he might not be as broadminded as he professed when it came to his own daughter.

Cam was infuriated by her silence. How dare she ignore him and stare out the window. 'Look at me, girl.'

She did. And her look was cold. 'Girl' was far worse than 'Violet'. She hated him calling her 'girl' more than anything.

'What have you got to say for yourself?'

'Nothing. What is there to say?'

Cam was uneasy; she wasn't behaving like his little girl. Vi would normally protest, 'Don't be mad at me, Dad, I haven't done anything wrong.' Her self-composure worried him, she seemed too grown up. Did it mean she was sleeping with the boy? His baby girl and a Dago Wog bastard, he was sickened by the thought.

'How far's it gone?' His tone was gruff, and the question sounded blunt, tasteless, but he didn't know how else to ask it.

'I'm not sleeping with him, if that's what you mean.' Violet could see the relief in her father's eyes and she would have liked to have added, 'but I want to.' Just to shock him. But she didn't.

'Of course you're not, I didn't think for a minute you were,' he said. 'I trust you, Vi.' He started the ute. End of conversation. 'But you're not to see him any more, you hear me?'

'Why?' Perhaps she'd been right after all, Violet thought. 'Because he's Italian?'

'Of course not. You're too young, that's all.' Cam checked the rear vision mirror and did a u-turn.

'We love each other, Dad. He wants to marry me.'

There, she'd said it. And she'd well and truly got his attention now, she thought as the ute slowed to a halt.

Cam turned off the engine. Then he sat and waited, his face giving away nothing.

'Pietro's been wanting to ask your permission for ages, but Auntie Maureen thought it was best to wait until we were sure.'

'Oh yes?' Maureen, he thought. Bloody Maureen. He should have known better than to leave his baby girl in the care of bloody Maureen. She'd messed up her own life and now she was going to mess up his daughter's. Well, bugger that. 'And you're sure now, are you?' he asked, studying her carefully. Something wasn't quite right, he thought, there was too much bravado about her, as if she were trying to shock him, and convince herself at the same time.

Violet's answer was strangely indirect. 'Pietro came to see Auntie Maureen yesterday,' she said. 'I wasn't there, but they talked, and Auntie Maureen promised that she'd go out home and see you.'

'Did she?' Bloody Maureen and the Dago prick appeared

to have it all figured out, he thought. God alone knew why. 'And you *wanted* her to come out home and see me, did you?' Cam kept his voice steady, though he'd have liked to strangle his sister: why hadn't Maureen just told the Dago to piss off? 'You want to marry this bloke, is that it?'

Auntie Maureen had asked her the very same question, Violet thought. She hadn't really been sure of the answer then, and she wasn't sure now, but her reply was the same.

'Yes,' she said.

Cam continued to study his daughter. She looked vulnerable. Lost and uncertain. She wasn't sure of herself at all, he thought, and he breathed a sigh of relief. He'd been worrying about nothing. It was a bloody joke, the whole thing. Romantic bullshit. The girl went to the pictures too much, that was the problem.

'Don't you worry, baby girl.' He put his arm fondly around her, uninhibited this time, and for a moment he held her close. 'Don't you worry about a thing, we'll sort this out.' Then he started up the ute.

He hadn't called her 'baby girl' for a very long time, and he hadn't cuddled her like that either. Comforting as she'd found it, and relieved as she was to have avoided his anger, Violet sensed that things hadn't gone quite according to plan. Her father was treating her like a child, he wasn't taking her seriously.

'I love Pietro, Dad,' she said. She'd said the same thing to Auntie Maureen when Auntie Maureen had told her she had only two options.

'Marry him, or stop seeing him, Violet, it's that simple.' Her aunt had spelled it out bluntly. 'Make up your mind.'

'I love him,' she'd said. And, without insisting on any further discussion, Auntie Maureen had nodded knowingly. Something had passed between them, Violet had thought, and she'd been grateful for her aunt's understanding.

Cam glanced affectionately at his daughter. She was just

a kid, he thought. 'Of course you do, baby girl, but don't you worry, I'll have a chat to your boyfriend and Auntie Maureen, we'll sort things out.'

They'd sort things out all right, he thought. He wanted to kill his bloody sister, and he wanted to kill the fucking Dago too. They'd given him one hell of a scare there for a minute.

He dropped Violet back at the store. 'See you later, love,' he said as she climbed out of the ute. He'd go to the Billiards Club, he decided, and while away the time with some of the blokes until Maureen got home from the hospital. Four o'clock, Violet had said.

She was about to ask him if he was going to come home for tea, but the ute pulled out from the kerb. 'Bye, Dad,' she called instead, and he waved at her through the open window.

Violet stood in the street and watched as the Holden drove off. She expected to see it turn left into Vale Street, on its way to the hospital only a couple of minutes' drive up the hill. But it turned right instead. There was time for her to warn Auntie Maureen. She ferreted about in her purse for some coins and walked to the public phone box just down the street. Mr Halliday didn't mind his staff using the store's telephone so long as they were brief, but Violet didn't want anyone overhearing.

'Dad's in town,' she said when Maureen's voice came on the line, 'and he knows about Pietro.'

There was a moment's pause. 'Ah well,' Maureen said in her practical fashion, 'it'll save me a trip out there. What did you tell him?'

'That Pietro wants to marry me.'

'And what was his reaction?'

'He didn't get mad. But he didn't seem to take me seriously, Auntie Maureen. He said he'd sort things out with you, so I thought I'd ring before he turned up at the hospital.'

'Thanks, Violet, I'm glad you did. Just as well to be prepared. I'll see you at home.'

'But Auntie Maureen . . .'

'I have to go now, dear. Don't you worry. Everything'll be fine. Bye.'

Violet returned to work, confused. Her future was at stake and everyone was telling her not to worry, that everything'd be fine.

Maureen was thoughtful as she replaced the receiver. Cam wouldn't come to the hospital, she knew that much. If he was going to confront her, as she was sure he would, he wouldn't risk causing a scene in front of others, he wouldn't want to be caught out. But it was odd that he'd appeared not to take the situation seriously. Cam Campbell would be livid at the mere thought of his daughter going out with an Italian.

Maureen knew that, for all his pretence of egalitarianism, her brother had a different set of values when it came to his family. In fact, when it came to his family, Cam was a man of strict convention. He saw himself as the patriarch. It was Cam who made the rules in the Campbell family, and woe betide anyone who bucked them. Maureen had bucked all the rules when she'd left the land for a career in the city – it had been against the Campbell tradition. Campbell women worked like men until they were of a marriageable age, then they wed local farmers or graziers and bore them children to take over the property. But Maureen had married a busi-nessman at the age of twenty-three, and she'd paid the price when she'd come home two decades later.

'That's what you get for marrying a city slicker,' her brother had gloated. 'No loyalty.'

'Andy and I loved each other and we still do, Cam. We had a good twenty years together, there are no regrets.' Her reply had been delivered with composure; even as a child, she had never let him rattle her. She was two years his senior and she'd always played the older sister with a superiority that she knew infuriated him.

'Oh come off it, Maureen, how can you defend the bastard? He dumped you for a younger sheila, why don't you admit the truth?'

She'd hated him at that moment, even though she'd known he was angry on her behalf. 'The truth?' she'd replied coldly. 'Andy wants children. He's always wanted children, I could never give them to him, and now she can. That's the truth, Cam.'

It hadn't been the truth at all, but Maureen would never admit to the hurt she felt, not even to Andy, with whom she'd parted on amicable terms, and certainly not to her dictatorial brother.

She and Cam had had a row that night when she'd told him she was not coming back to the property. He hadn't been able to comprehend her preference for long hours at the hospital and a modest house in town. He'd called her disloyal and accused her of having no sense of family, but Maureen had refused to budge in her decision.

They'd eventually called a truce further down the track when she'd offered to have Violet come and live with her. Cam had been grateful, albeit begrudgingly. It wouldn't be for long, he'd said. It was just some passing whim of Vi's, she'd be back home in a few months, he was sure. But, despite his gratitude, he still hadn't been able to resist laying down the law.

'Don't you go giving her any fancy ideas, Maureen,' he'd warned. 'Vi's not like you; she belongs on the land.'

Maureen had refused to be dictated to. 'She'll make up her own mind, Cam,' she'd said, but secretly, she'd agreed with her brother. Young Vi was not like her. The girl had no ambition and Maureen had been certain that she would return home within the year. In true Campbell tradition Violet would marry a local and produce an heir, just as she was destined to do.

It now appeared that both she and Cam had been wrong, Maureen thought as she left the reception desk and returned to the wards. The relationship between Violet and young Pietro could no longer be dismissed as a young girl's romantic illusion. Was that why Cam had not taken his daughter seriously? Well, he'd better start doing so, she thought. Whether or not the girl genuinely wished to marry was beside the point; she was on the verge of sleeping with the Italian. And Maureen would have to tell her brother that. She didn't relish the prospect.

At the end of her shift, she changed from her uniform into her comfortable trousers and shirt; it was spring, the weather was fine and she'd walked to the hospital. She set off briskly, enjoying her twenty-minute constitutional, and as she finally strode up the hill towards the cottage she was pleasantly out of breath.

She recognised the ute parked in the street, and slowed her pace. He was sitting on the front steps, leaning against the small white picket fence of the front verandah.

'G'day, Maureen,' he said, but he didn't smile.

'Hello, Cam.'

He rose as she walked to meet him. 'We've got some talking to do.'

'Yes, I know. Come on in.'

She opened the front door, which wasn't locked, and he followed her inside.

'Do you want a cup of tea?' she asked, leading the way into the kitchen.

'No, I bloody well don't.'

So it was going to be like that, she thought. It was pretty much what she'd expected. Cam's belligerence could be quite intimidating, and his anger even frightening, but Maureen refused to be daunted.

'You won't mind if I have one then?' She busied herself filling the kettle.

Her imperturbability irritated him. 'What the hell's been going on behind my back?'

'Your daughter's been falling in love. All proper and above board, I hasten to add.' She put the kettle on the stove. 'She's eighteen, Cam, it's quite normal.'

'And you knew he was a Dago, right?'

He was showing his true colours right from the start, she thought, and the sneer in his voice annoyed her.

'Yes, I've met him a number of times. He's a very nice young man.'

She knew she shouldn't have sounded so arch – it was a red rag to a bull – but she hadn't been able to help herself. His fist hit the table.

'Jesus Christ, woman,' he yelled, his face flushed with anger, 'what the hell are you playing at?'

Maureen didn't light the gas stove; she decided to forget about the tea. 'Calm down, Cam,' she said, crossing to the table. 'It won't serve anyone's purpose if you lose your temper.'

He had no intention of calming down. 'What do you think you're doing, encouraging my daughter? How dare you interfere.'

'In what way have I interfered?'

But he wasn't listening. 'You gave up any rights in this family years ago when you pissed off to Sydney. I won't have you disrupting Vi's life with your smartarse liberated ideas. I don't give a shit if the Dago's a *nice young man*, do you hear? He's not coming anywhere near my daughter!'

He was prowling around the kitchen now, and she wished he'd sit down so they could discuss the whole thing in a civilised fashion. She wanted to sit herself, it had been a long day, but she didn't. She said nothing, leaning against the table instead, waiting for him to get it out of his system.

'Jesus, Maureen, I don't understand you,' he went on. 'Vi's just a kid, she listens to you, she admires you, she drinks in every bloody word you say. How could you encourage this bullshit?'

His sister's silence was having its effect. Cam was running out of steam.

'Christ, you're an intelligent woman. Can't you see that's all it is? She doesn't want to marry him. It's romantic bullshit. It's all in her head.'

'Yes, that's what I thought to start with.' She hoped he was calm enough to talk sense now, and she sat. 'But it's not in her head any longer, Cam. Sit down. Please.'

He sat. And Maureen wondered how to address the true issue without her brother once again exploding.

'When Violet first started seeing Pietro, I was sure it wouldn't last.' She noticed the flicker in his eyes at the mention of Pietro's name. This wasn't going to be easy, she thought. 'She told me he reminded her of an Italian movie star, and, like you, I thought it was just a romantic fantasy on Violet's part.'

Cam forced himself to stay silent, but his sister wasn't winning any points. She should have pissed the Dago off right from the start, he thought.

'And I agree with you,' Maureen continued slowly, trying to find the right words, 'I'm not altogether sure that she really wants to marry him. Not yet anyway . . .'

Jesus Christ, he thought, whose case was she arguing, his daughter's or the Dago's? The girl hadn't slept with the bastard, and if she didn't want to marry him, then where was the problem? Why was she wasting her breath talking about the bloody Dago?

'Don't get me wrong,' she added, 'I'm convinced that she loves him . . .'

Outside, Violet walked up the steps to the back verandah. Mr Halliday had been very understanding when she'd asked if she could leave early.

'You go along, Vi,' he'd said; she rarely asked for favours. 'You get home early and make your dad's tea.'

That had been the excuse she'd used, even though she wasn't sure if her dad was coming to tea.

As she'd approached the house, she'd seen her father's utility parked out the front, and she'd known the two of them would be inside, talking about her. It hadn't been her deliberate intention to eavesdrop as she'd walked around to the back of the cottage. She often entered via the verandah, freshening up in her room before going inside. But this time she didn't go to her room, and as she opened the back door, she did so quietly.

'. . . in fact I'm sure that she loves him very much,' Maureen said.

Violet heard her aunt's voice quite clearly through the flywire screen, and she hovered by the doorway only several yards from them, out of sight but within easy earshot. She felt guilty to be eavesdropping, but glad that Auntie Maureen was so openly pleading her case.

'. . . and I know that Pietro loves her, and that he genuinely wants to marry her . . .'

If she mentioned the Dago's name once more he'd hit her, Cam thought. Whose bloody side was the woman on?

'. . . but I think the prospect of marriage frightens Violet,' Maureen said.

'Of course it does!' He finally exploded. 'She's a kid, for Christ's sake!'

'No, that's just it, she's not!' Dear God, she'd have to spell it out, Maureen thought; she'd been trying to edge around the subject tactfully. 'She's a woman, Cam. And she's in love! Don't you understand what I'm saying?'

He was halted in his tracks. What was she inferring? Had his daughter lied?

'Vi told me they weren't sleeping together,' he said, his voice menacingly quiet.

'They're not. Not yet. But only because Pietro wants to wait until they're married.'

That was it! He jumped to his feet. 'I don't give a shit

what the bloody Dago wants, you stupid woman!' he yelled. 'He's not getting my daughter!'

'She'll sleep with him anyway, Cam!' Maureen hadn't wanted to raise her voice, but it seemed the only way to get through to him.

It worked. He stared at her, taken aback.

'This isn't just one of Violet's romantic fantasies, it's gone much further than that,' she continued. 'She's in love with the boy and she's going to sleep with him whether you like it or not. You have to give your permission for them to marry.'

'Over my dead body,' he snarled.

She stood, exasperated. 'Your daughter's on the verge of losing her virginity, Cam, and there's nothing you, or anyone else, can do about it.'

'Oh isn't there just? I can kill the fucking Dago, that's what I can do.'

'And what good would that do?' Her frustration was getting the better of her; it was becoming a slanging match. 'What if the next boy she falls in love with doesn't want to marry her? Would you prefer to see her run off with some buck to a cheap motel? Because that's what she'll do. If it's not Pietro, then it'll be some other young stud . . .'

His open hand lashed out and struck her hard across the cheek. She staggered off-balance, then recovered herself, and there was a moment's silence, brother and sister staring at each other, both shocked by his action.

'You tell the Dago to keep away from my daughter,' he said finally. 'And you tell my daughter if she sleeps with him I'll disown her.'

She watched wordlessly as he walked to the door.

'I didn't mean to hit you,' he said without turning back.

Violet heard her father's footsteps walking away, and then the sound of the front door closing. She stood in silent dismay as her world crashed around her. Her father's blatant bigotry had horrified her. He'd been her hero all of her life, but he was a fraud and a hypocrite. She'd been horrified, too, when she'd heard him strike his sister. But it had been her aunt's words that had cut Violet most deeply, and the tears welled as she stood staring unseeingly at the flywire door.

Was that really what Maureen thought of her? But yesterday, when she'd told Maureen that she loved Pietro, they had shared an understanding. Or at least she'd thought that they had. She'd thought they'd shared a special moment, as only women could. Like the moment she'd shared with Peggy Minchin in the restaurant. Just a look, when each knew what the other was thinking. But she'd been wrong. There'd been no shared understanding. Maureen considered her a shallow, empty-headed girl bent on losing her virginity; a girl who would run off with some buck to a cheap motel.

The tears slowly coursed their way down Violet's cheeks. Maureen was wrong, she thought. She wasn't like that at all. She wanted to lose her virginity, yes, but she wasn't using Pietro in order to do so. Maureen thought that she was, and Maureen was clever, but it wasn't like that, Violet told herself. She couldn't and she wouldn't believe it.

'Violet.'

Maureen was appalled when she stepped out onto the verandah to discover Violet standing motionless, crying silent tears.

'Come inside, dear. I'll get us a cup of tea.' The girl had heard, Maureen thought guiltily.

Violet, unprotesting, allowed herself to be ushered into the kitchen where she sat at the table and, while her aunt lit the gas stove, she wiped away her tears with the back of her hand. She didn't want to cry in front of Maureen.

'Violet . . .' Maureen set the teacups out on the table and sat opposite the girl, not sure what to say, but about to start with an apology. Violet, however, got in first.

'I know you think I'm stupid,' she said quietly, studying

her teacup, avoiding Maureen's eyes. 'And you're probably right. I'm not clever like you, I never will be . . .'

Her aunt was about to interject.

'. . . but I know when I'm in love,' Violet continued. 'And I'm in love with Pietro.' She redirected her eyes from her teacup to her aunt, and her look was candid. 'You're right, I want to sleep with him, but it's more than that. I love him.'

The girl had made the same declaration just yesterday. '*I love him,*' Violet had said, and Maureen had found the girl's sexuality alarming, like an electrical pulse sending messages through the air. She'd chastised herself for not having registered the warnings earlier. It was a common case with late developers like Violet – hormones suddenly ran wild. The girl was aching to lose her virginity, she'd thought, and she'd looked no further than that.

But things were not that simple, she now realised, as Violet's eyes met hers with a candour and maturity Maureen had not seen there before.

'I know you think I'm empty-headed and romantic,' Violet said directly and without any form of accusation, 'but you see, Maureen, I believe in romance.'

The use of her Christian name without the 'auntie' title was strangely affecting, and Maureen felt riddled with guilt for having hurt the girl as deeply as she plainly had.

'I believe that romance and love are the same thing,' Violet said. 'They are for me. I don't want to sleep with Pietro just to lose my virginity.' Her lip trembled slightly, her composure was starting to crack. 'And I wouldn't run away with some buck to a cheap motel.'

Maureen was mortified, at a loss for words. But Violet stemmed the tears that threatened. She took a deep breath, regained her dignity, and continued.

'You think my romantic view of the world is shallow, and perhaps it is. But it doesn't mean that my love is shallow. I just look at things a different way from you. I like romance in my life, and you don't.'

It was a simple statement, and it was true, Maureen thought. She couldn't remember a time when she'd experienced even the slightest sense of romance. Passion, yes, in the early days with Andy. She'd slept with him before they were married, she'd been the one to instigate it. And she'd experienced love. She'd loved Andy deeply, she still did, they'd been partners and soul mates. But romance? She'd had no time for romance, her life had been governed by practicality and commonsense for as long as she could remember.

'I will marry Pietro,' Violet said. 'I want to. I was frightened before, but I'm not any more, Dad's helped me make up my mind.' A rebellious edge crept into her voice. 'I'll marry Pietro whether Dad likes it or not.'

Maureen hoped Violet wasn't marrying Pietro simply to spite her father, but she quelled the voice of reason. She was being over-practical again, she warned herself, now was not the time.

'Your dad's not a bad man, you know, Violet,' she said.

'Yes he is.' The girl's tone was more than rebellious now, it was hard. 'Dad's a hypocrite.'

'Only where his family's concerned. He thinks he's being protective.'

'And he hit you.'

'Yes,' Maureen admitted, 'but he did it because I was saying things about you he didn't want to hear. I think he frightened himself more than me.'

'You're very forgiving, Maureen.' Violet wasn't. She could still hear her father's voice: *I can kill the fucking Dago, that's what I can do.* She'd never forgive him for that.

'I'm sorry for what I said, Violet.'

'I know. And it's all right.' Violet smiled her pretty, childlike smile. 'It's all right. Really.' She and Maureen had

an understanding now. A real woman's understanding.
Violet was happy about that much at least.

Lucky's winning streak continued. Two months after his
two-up triumph, he and Maarten Vanpoucke picked the
winner of the Melbourne Cup.

Rising Fast had been Maarten's choice. The Melbourne
Cup was the one time of the year Maarten gambled, and
he took his selection very seriously, studying the field, the
owners, the jockeys and the track conditions. This year,
however, he'd considered there was no need to study up.

'Rising Fast,' he'd said to Lucky. 'He's won this year's
Caulfield Cup and the Cox Plate – he's a champion. And
Purtell's a fine jockey, he won last year's Cup on Wodalla,
we can't go wrong. I'm putting fifty pounds on Rising Fast
to win.'

Lucky had gone along with the idea and they'd placed a
hundred quid on the nose. It had become an annual event
to pool their bets. This year it had paid off.

On the Saturday following the Melbourne Cup, Lucky
collected their winnings and arrived at Maarten's around
four in the afternoon, as they'd arranged. Maarten met
him at the front door flourishing an unopened bottle of
vintage Taittinger.

'What a horse, eh?' the Dutchman said as he ushered
Lucky up the main staircase and into the lounge room. He
started opening the champagne. 'The Caulfield Cup, the
Cox Plate and the Melbourne Cup all in one year – he'll go
down in history.' The cork popped loudly.

'Pity he was the favourite.' Lucky took his bulging
wallet from his pocket. 'But we still did very nicely.' He
grinned, about to count out the money.

'All in good time,' Maarten said, pouring the champagne
into the flutes sitting on the sideboard beside the ice-bucket.
'To Rising Fast.' He handed a glass to Lucky, who dumped
the wallet on the coffee table and joined in the toast.

'To Rising Fast,' he said, and they clinked.

For the next ten minutes or so they chatted enthusiastically about the race. Maarten was in a most effusive mood, and not only because of their win. Lucky had finally agreed to stay and dine after their chess game – it was a first.

'You can't turn me down this time, Lucky,' he'd insisted over the phone. 'It was a history-making race, they'll be talking about this horse fifty years from now. We must celebrate.'

'Of course we must, I'd be delighted to stay for dinner. Thank you.' Lucky had accepted the invitation with good grace, although he'd hoped he wasn't creating a precedent; he'd far rather spend his evenings with Peggy. But he felt guilty always declining Maarten's invitation; for all the Dutchman's charm he appeared to have few friends.

'Tell me, how's young Pietro?' Maarten asked, topping up their glasses and replacing the champagne in its ice-bucket. 'He hasn't been to see me for over six weeks.'

'He's probably been distracted,' Lucky replied. 'He's in love.'

'Ah well,' Maarten laughed, 'that explains it.' But he was serious as he added, 'He must be due for another script by now. He's been meticulous with his medication, I take it?'

'I presume so.' Lucky had no idea.

'I'd like him to visit me once a month as we agreed,' Maarten peered over his spectacle rims in professional doctor mode. 'It's advisable I keep an eye on his condition. Perhaps you could remind him, Lucky?'

'Yes, of course I will.' It was obvious he was still perceived as the boy's father figure, Lucky thought, but he was grateful to Maarten for his concern. He would chastise Pietro for neglecting his monthly check-up.

'Well, let's get started.' Maarten placed the ice-bucket and champagne on the table where the chess board was laid out. 'The sooner I beat you, the sooner we eat.'

Lucky joined him at the table and they sat.

'Mrs Hodgeman is preparing veal knuckles in red wine,' Maarten said. 'A specialty of hers, and a favourite of mine.'

'You're a genius, Mrs Hodgeman,' Lucky said five hours later as he mopped up the last of his gravy. The food had been superb. 'I haven't eaten a meal like that since the old days.'

'Goodo, sir, I'm glad you liked it.' Noreen Hodgeman beamed with pleasure. She was a tough little woman in her mid-forties with an Aussie accent that belonged in a shearing shed. 'It's one of the doctor's favourites,' she said as she started clearing away the plates. 'Shall I leave it half an hour before serving sweets, Doctor? Fruit flan,' she said with a special smile. It was obviously another of Maarten's favourites.

'Yes, thank you, Mrs Hodgeman, and tell Kevin to fetch another bottle from the cellar, if you wouldn't mind.' Maarten drained the last of his specially imported Bordeaux into his empty glass; Lucky's was still half full.

'Right you are then,' and she disappeared with the empty bottle.

Lucky had always liked Mrs Hodgeman. She was a bizarre mixture. She was an outback woman, yet her attitude to her employer was both maternal and servile, and Lucky found it amusing. He sensed she liked him too, but she'd refused to call him Lucky when he'd suggested it. 'Ah no, sir,' she'd said, 'this is the doctor's house, I like to do things right. Heavens above I owe him that. I dunno where I'd be without the Doctor.' A widowed farmer's wife, her husband killed in the war, Noreen Hodgeman had been Maarten's housekeeper for the past five years and, as he'd also employed her son and given them both a roof over their heads, she'd had every reason to be grateful. It was obvious that she now adored Maarten and she played the roles of mother and servant with equal dedication.

'Where did Mrs Hodgeman learn to cook like that?' Lucky asked when she'd gone. He'd been fussed over with cups of tea and cake in the past, but he'd never experienced Mrs Hodgeman's cooking.

'Books,' Maarten said, and he laughed at Lucky's reaction. 'It's true. She knows I like European food so she's made a study of it. I must say it's a relief. When she first came to me I got so sick of mutton stews and lamb chops with boiled vegetables.'

Several minutes later, Kevin arrived with the wine. He was a big, thickset young man in his early twenties, and gauche, like an overgrown boy. He rarely said a word and Lucky hadn't known what to make of him upon their first meetings. Whenever he'd tried to introduce polite conversation, he'd been met with a stony silence.

'Don't bother,' Maarten had said finally, 'he's not all there.'

'Oh.' Lucky hadn't realised. He wished Maarten had told him earlier.

'What's that wonderful Australian expression?' Maarten had said. 'He's not the full quid,' and he'd laughed.

Ever since then Lucky had gone out of his way to be nice to Kevin, and he'd quickly registered that the boy was not sullen at all, but painfully shy.

'Hello, Kevin,' he said now as Kevin arrived with the wine.

Kevin nodded and gave him a quick smile before concentrating on the corkscrew and the wine. Kevin liked Lucky. He put the opened bottle on the table and left in silence.

'Drink up, Lucky, you've ground to a halt,' Maarten said jovially.

'I have, you're quite right. Not for me, thanks.' He waved aside the bottle that Maarten held poised over his glass. The Dutchman had drunk virtually all the previous one; half a bottle of champagne had been quite enough for Lucky.

Maarten didn't seem to mind. He topped up his own glass and toasted the air. 'To Rising Fast,' he said yet again, forgetting that he'd said it at least half a dozen times. 'The horse of the century.'

'Which reminds me, I owe you some money.'

Lucky rose from the table and fetched his wallet. He was wondering how long it would be before he could politely make his exit; Maarten was getting happily drunk and it was nearly ten o'clock. He resigned himself to the fruit flan, however. It would be rude to leave before the dessert, although he felt he couldn't eat another thing. But his mind was on Peggy now, and her promise was beckoning. 'I'll be ready and waiting no matter how late you are,' she'd said suggestively when he'd told her not to wait up.

He took the bundle of notes from his wallet and placed them on the table in front of Maarten.

'There you go,' he said, 'the honour's all yours.' And he sat.

'What were the odds? Five to two, weren't they?' Maarten asked. 'That should make it three hundred and fifty pounds between us, including the one hundred we laid on for the bet.' The Dutchman appeared instantly sober – money was serious business to Maarten Van-poucke. He unfolded the wad of notes.

'I can't remember,' Lucky said. 'He was five to two on the tote, but I think the bookie gave us better odds than that. I didn't count it when I collected it, how much is there?'

A photograph was sitting in the middle of the notes he'd unfolded, and Maarten picked it up and stared intently at it. 'Is this your wife?' he asked slowly.

'Yes,' Lucky said. He'd forgotten the photo was there; it must have got mixed up with the money when he'd shoved it in his wallet, he thought. He must return it to the safety of his cabin which these days he kept locked. Wallets were far too easily stolen. 'Yes that's Ruth,' he said.

The Dutchman studied the photograph. Lucky had told him that his wife had died at Auschwitz. But Lucky was wrong, Maarten thought. He knew this woman. This woman was very much alive. Or she had been the last time Maarten had seen her.

BOOK TWO

Book Two

CHAPTER TEN

Ruth was enjoying the warm desert breeze blowing through the car's cabin as they drove along the Jaffa Road to Jerusalem. The early November weather was pleasant: the scorching heat had long gone, the days were comfortable and the nights were cool. Not that she minded the intensity of the heat; she was well accustomed to it.

Far in the distance, she could see the city. So many new buildings, she thought, although she'd known there would be. The Jewish settlement to the west had been expanding at an extraordinary rate even in 1948 when she'd last seen the city, barely a month before the State of Israel had officially come into being. Now, over six years later, the settlement appeared to have doubled in size.

Six years, she thought – had it really been that long? She lived barely a half-hour drive from Jerusalem and yet for a whole six years she'd chosen not to return. She could have done so whenever she'd wished – Moshe regularly made the trip into the city. In the early days he'd always asked her to come with him, but each time she'd said no. Occasionally she'd accompanied him into Haifa, where she'd done some shopping and visited the synagogue, more to please him than herself, but she no longer maintained the pretence of finding interest in either shopping or synagogues, preferring to remain at the orchard. Now, when Moshe went into town, he no longer asked her if she wanted to accompany him.

She glanced at him. He was deep in thought as he drove, but, sensing her look, he turned to her.

'I told you you'd see some changes,' he said, indicating the distant city.

'Yes,' she agreed. 'It's very beautiful.'

The two once more lapsed into silence, his eyes on the road, hers on the city.

It was extraordinarily beautiful, she thought. The new buildings already resembled the old – built, as they were, of the same local limestone, they appeared as timeless as their predecessors. In the midst of the parched, biblical landscape, the rocky oasis of Jerusalem seemed to grow out of the very stone upon which it sat, stark and pale like bleached bones.

Ruth had first arrived in Palestine in November of 1947, shortly before the United Nations' vote for the Partition of Palestine into a Jewish and Arab state, and before the final departure of the British governing forces. Initially unaware of the depth of conflict seething around her, it had been the ancient beauty of Jerusalem that had made such an impression.

'Yerushalayim has that effect upon everyone who comes here,' her uncle had said in Hebrew. Walter Stein no longer spoke his German mother tongue unless it was necessary, and Ruth was fluent in Hebrew. 'But its timelessness holds a special purpose for we who have returned to the homeland of our people, Ruth. It is here that you will find yourself.'

Walter had felt a deep responsibility, both paternal and spiritual, for his niece. She was his blood, his name. The poor child had reverted to her maiden name in a desperate bid to obliterate the memory that she had once been married with a child. She was a lost creature, and he had welcomed her into his home like a daughter. Having brought up his two children in the strict Orthodox traditions of Judaism, Walter had been convinced that the strength his niece required to rebuild her shattered life was to be found in the faith she had deserted long before.

Her uncle was kind and well-meaning, and Ruth had dutifully attended the synagogue each Shabbat and taken care to observe the rituals, but it had all been meaningless to her, mere gestures of courtesy to her uncle and his family in whose home she was living. The faith she had grown up with had died in Auschwitz. For Ruth, there was no God – there could not possibly be.

But perhaps there was some truth in her uncle's words, she'd thought as she wandered the narrow streets of the old walled city, in awe of its history and its architecture. Perhaps here, in this ancient place, spiritual heart for Jew, Muslim and Christian alike, she might find some kind of peace within herself, something to fill the void of despair in which she'd been lost.

The miracle of liberation and her own survival had meant little to Ruth Lachmann. There had been nothing to live for, and the nightmares had haunted her . . .

The cattle car. Mannie supporting her, Rachel on his shoulders; the stench of vomit and faeces. The old woman on the floor unable to get up, wailing, then silenced, trampled to death.

The doors thrown open. The blinding glare of daylight. Dogs barking, jaws snapping. 'Raus! Raus!' Nazis screaming, cudgels flailing. The air thick with a hideous sickly smell.

The march to the head of the ramp. The SS officer in his smart, black uniform directing the traffic with a flick of his riding crop. 'Links. Rechts.' Mannie cudgelled and dragged from her.

*The queue of old people and women with children.
Clutching Rachel's hand, trying to hide the child behind
her. The SS soldier snatching at a baby in a woman's arms,
the woman fighting back, not letting go. Two shots. The
woman and baby dead on the ground, the child still in its
mother's arms.*

*Then Rachel ripped from her and, above the chaos, the
shrill scream of her child's terror. Lunging forward,
reaching for her daughter. The soldier raising his rifle. Her
own scream mingling with Rachel's . . .*

Ruth always awoke before she heard the shot. But it
didn't save her from the image of Rachel. Her tiny, lifeless
body lying next to the woman whose baby remained
clutched in her arms. Ruth envied the woman.

The image returned relentlessly throughout her waking
hours. Without warning, and with an accompanying click,
like the shutter of a camera, it would flicker on and off in
her brain. And after her liberation, when her daily focus
had no longer been on the fight for survival, the image had
seemed never to leave her. Her mind had been free to dwell
on the image of her murdered child and the purposeless-
ness of her own existence. Even her work as an interpreter
with the American occupying forces had provided no distraction. Rachel was always there, lying beside the woman
with the baby.

It had been easier in the camp, Ruth often thought.
There she had learned to exist on hate. Ira Schoneberger,
who had fought so desperately to encourage her will to
live, had finally discovered the right avenue of persuasion,
although his early attempts had met with little success.

'Survive, Ruth!' he'd told her at first. 'Survive. If you
die, they win. You're young, you can have another child.
Every one of us who survives is a victory. And those who
go on to bear children are the greatest victors of all.'

His advice, well intentioned as it was, had meant
nothing. Ruth hadn't wished to survive and she had no

desire to bear another child. But she had decided that she would live long enough to save Mannie. Through her relationship with Klaus Henkel, she could do it, she was sure. Henkel had the power over life and death. Henkel would save Mannie, and then she would be free to give up her own battle for survival. But Klaus Henkel, the Nazi who had preserved her from certain death, had not saved Manfred Brandauer.

'Mannie is dead,' Ira had told her bluntly. 'They shot him yesterday, and it was Henkel who ordered it.'

She hadn't believed him at first. 'But Klaus promised me Mannie would be safe,' she'd said, desperately. 'I told him that Mannie was not a Jew, I told him that Mannie was Stefan Brandauer's son. Klaus said that he knew Stefan. Stefan was a fine man who had served the German government well, he said. He promised to . . .'

'I saw it, Ruth, I was the doctor in attendance. The wall of death beside Block 10, a firing squad of four, at three o'clock in the afternoon.' Ira had been ruthless in his detail. 'The soldiers told me it was Henkel who ordered the execution.'

She had known it was true, even as she'd tried to persuade herself that Ira was wrong. Ira was never wrong. Ira could always be relied upon for correct information.

Ira Schoneberger, although a Jew and an inmate, had been given the freedom of the camp. A highly qualified doctor, he'd proved useful to Josef Mengele and Klaus Henkel, and he'd ingratiated himself with the Nazis, even to the point of agreeing with Mengele that his hideous experiments were invaluable to the future of medical science.

Ira's survival had depended upon his sycophancy and willingness to betray his own people, but Ruth had proved his weak spot. He had fallen in love with her, and would do anything to save her. The privileged position Henkel had assigned Ruth at the hospital had made it easy for Ira to meet secretly with her. She'd had no idea of his feelings for her, and he had no intention of declaring them – it was too dangerous – but he'd welcomed her as another tool in his survival kit. The anticipation of his meetings with Ruth had helped keep him alive, and he had passed to her the drugs and supplies that she then smuggled out to her fellow inmates. Ira would never have risked smuggling the drugs on his own, but giving her a further purpose to live had been to his advantage. Through Ruth, Ira Schoneberger had unwittingly been a lifeline to many of his people, all of whom detested him and considered him a traitor.

He hadn't wanted to tell Ruth of Mannie's death for fear she would lose her own will to live, but he'd known that she would find out eventually, and he'd needed to feed her a fresh purpose to survive.

'You've tried to believe that Henkel is different, Ruth,' he'd said after comforting her in her grief and shock. 'But surely you must know that he's not. Surely you must have felt the malevolence in the man.'

She had. Even when Henkel had wooed her, massaging her shoulders with caring expertise, singing along gently to 'Barcarole' as the music played on his gramophone, she'd had the feeling he could break her neck with equal expertise if she displeased him.

'Klaus Henkel is different from the others in only one way,' Ira had said. 'He is more evil than all of them. Mengele himself fears Henkel, I can sense it. The man is so diabolical that even the Angel of Death fears him – imagine that!'

Then, as he'd planned, Ira had set out to fuel her hatred with all the reason and persuasion of which he was capable. 'We must live to see Henkel brought to justice, Ruth – it is our duty to do so. The Germans are losing the war. I hear Mengele and Henkel talking freely about it in the Experimentation Block where there's no-one but me to hear them. They're worried.'

His mention of the Experimentation Block had been deliberate and he noted her reaction. She'd had no idea that Klaus Henkel was directly involved in Mengele's experiments.

'And when the Germans have been defeated, we must be alive to tell our stories and see Henkel and the rest of his kind hang,' he'd urged. 'Use him, Ruth. Use Klaus Henkel to survive. But hate him. It's your hate that will feed you and keep you alive.'

Now as the car neared Jerusalem, Ruth could see the ancient fortifications of the Old City and the domes and spires of the mosques and churches that lay beyond, the great golden dome on Temple Mount glinting spectacularly in the afternoon sun. The Dome of the Rock, one of Islam's most sacred sites, dominated the skyline of the old walled city from every possible viewpoint.

She recalled her hope that sacred Jerusalem might bring her some peace. How naive she'd been. Hatred and violence had abounded throughout the whole of Palestine.

The hate Ira Schoneberger had successfully fuelled in her had been rekindled in Jerusalem, and Ruth didn't want to go back. She knew that seeing her cousin David would arouse memories she'd been trying to obliterate for the past six years, memories that rivalled even the horrors of Auschwitz. But most of all she dreaded the thought that Eli Mankowski might be at the funeral. It was quite probable he would attend, she thought. He and David were comrades in arms, after all, and Eli might well wish to pay his respects.

'It will be hard for Sarah.'

Ruth had been so preoccupied with her thoughts that Moshe's voice startled her.

'Yes. Very hard. She'll miss him.'

'Hard for Rebekah and David too.'

'Rebekah yes, but I don't think David will grieve for long.' Her tone was cold, as it so often was lately. 'David will be too busy to bother with grief.'

She returned her attention to the old walled city, aware that she'd sounded rude and dismissive. She shouldn't have – Moshe was only trying to make polite conversation – but she'd been brusque with him ever since he insisted she attend her uncle's funeral.

'You owe it to Sarah, Ruth,' he'd said. 'She and Walter took you into their home; David and Rebekah are your cousins, your blood. It is essential you attend as a mark of respect.'

He'd spoken to her as if she were a recalcitrant child, and she'd been annoyed. Of course she was aware of the debt she owed her aunt and uncle, but she owed no debt to her cousin David, or to his friend Eli Mankowski. Why must she be forced to suffer their company? She'd agreed to go, but was angry that Moshe appeared to have no idea what he was asking of her.

Moshe took his eyes from the road to glance at her as she gazed resolutely ahead, ignoring him. He knew what was occupying her thoughts, and it certainly wasn't the death of her uncle. Nor was it her Aunt Sarah's impending loneliness. She was wondering if Eli would be at the funeral. A stab of the old jealousy returned, but Moshe pushed it aside. She didn't love Eli any more than she loved him, he thought. Ruth was incapable of love. She had told him so all those years ago, and it had been arrogant of him to presume he could change her. But Eli Mankowski had held a power over her, and Moshe had always envied the man for that. Any reaction, even the repulsion she now professed to feel for Mankowski, would be preferable, Moshe thought, to the remoteness he himself was forced to endure.

He wondered sometimes whether he still loved her. She was beautiful certainly, he thought, watching her now, the wind playing havoc with her sun-bleached hair; a tanned arm resting half out of the window; her body lean and healthy. But Ruth had a tortured mind, and little wonder.

Moshe had hoped somehow that he might be her saviour. But he hadn't been able to break through her coldness. He had the feeling she would leave him soon and, when she did, he wondered how much he would care.

Ruth felt his eyes upon her, but she continued to ignore him. His unhappiness was of his own making, she thought. She had warned him. But she couldn't help feeling guilty. She had accepted his protection, she had even welcomed the father image he'd represented – twenty years her senior, Moshe was certainly old enough to be her father. Now that same paternal manner was a source of irritation. She would have to leave him soon, it wasn't fair of her to stay.

Ruth's hatred of Klaus Henkel and her obsession with Eli Mankowski had drained her of any capacity for love. And now there was Moshe. Poor Moshe who had been left with the dry husk of a woman, incapable of tenderness. She felt sorry for him.

She had known love once. Before the world had gone mad there had been Samuel; she'd been tender then. But that woman was dead. The person who had once been Ruth Lachmann had ceased to exist years ago.

CHAPTER ELEVEN

'**R**uth Stein, Eli Mankowski.'

The young man sitting alone at the table in the far corner of the cafe looked up as if he'd only just noticed them, although he'd seen them as soon as they'd stepped through the door.

'Eli, this is my cousin Ruth.' David concluded the introduction with his usual easy charm, but Ruth registered the exchange of looks between the two men. David had obviously told Mankowski all about her, she thought, just as she had been told of the great Eli Mankowski, the Polish freedom fighter who, though not yet thirty, was one of the leaders of Lehi.

'He fought in the Warsaw ghetto uprising, Ruth,' David had said. 'He's a hero and one of our top unit commanders. He's also one of my best friends,' he'd added boastfully.

'It's a pleasure to meet you, Mr Mankowski.'

He made no attempt to rise, she noticed, but his nod was courteous and he offered his hand. They shook and she sat opposite him. 'David has told me a great deal about you,' she said.

Eli was impressed by the directness of her manner. Her eyes told him that she knew he was also aware of her past, and that she expected no sympathy. She spoke Hebrew fluently too, he noted; so many of the European new-comers spoke only Yiddish. He'd expected a broken woman – she had, after all, lost her husband and child to the Nazis – and he'd been prepared to offer his con-dolences and dismiss her as a possible recruit. But he changed his tack. David had been right, he thought, she was promising.

'You have been attending meetings, David tells me.'

Mankowski was studying her keenly, but not in the way men usually did – there was none of the customary defer-ence to beauty in his manner. He was appraising her as a potential fighter and, refreshing change as it was to Ruth, she found it daunting.

'Yes,' she answered. 'I've been receiving instruction for two months now.'

'Tell me about Lohamei Herut Israel.'

'Lohamei Herut Israel was founded by Avraham Stern in 1940 as an offshoot from Irgun Tsvai-Leumi . . .' Ruth recited what she had been taught of the Fighters for the Freedom of Israel group into which she had been accepted on a trial basis. Her meeting with Eli Mankowski was the first step to her acceptance as a full active member of Lehi.

To a casual observer, the three sitting at the table in the corner could have been any of the university students that frequented the cafe. They were young, vital, good-looking, and deep in conversation as university students always were. The girl's natural beauty, of which she appeared unaware, shone like a beacon, and the handsome young man with whom she'd arrived bore the easy air of one who had a way with women. The third member of the group, dark-haired, thickset and heavy-browed, was not hand-some in the conventional sense, but the supreme con-fidence of his demeanour made him an arresting figure.

As Eli Mankowski tested Ruth's knowledge of Lehi, the Jewish Nationalist group considered by many to be terrorist and radical, he lounged back in his chair, adopting the manner of an arrogant student, his guise for the day; it was why he'd chosen the cafe. Eli was always careful with his body language. He was a chameleon. If they'd been meeting in one of the training centres, his manner would have been that of the fanatic he was.

Fifteen minutes later, satisfied with her schooling in Lehi history and doctrine, his line of questioning became more personal. Where did she live? Were those with whom she lived sympathetic to their cause?

Before Ruth could answer, David interrupted. 'She lives with me and my family, Eli, I told you, remember? My father's apartment in Beit Yisrael.'

Ruth noticed the steely glint in Mankowski's eyes, but David was oblivious to it as he gave a light laugh and continued.

'Poor Ruth, she knows Father would be furious. She's had to resort to the same subterfuge I've suffered for two years, but she's managed very well . . .'

'Let Ruth answer for herself, David.' Eli's tone was not unpleasant but patronising, that of a teacher to an over-talkative child.

'Oh.' David, unbothered by the reprimand, gave an apologetic smile. 'Sorry.'

'Do you feel guilty, deceiving your uncle, Ruth?' Eli would have preferred to put him more firmly in his place. He didn't particularly like David, but it was to his advantage to maintain the semblance of friendship. Despite his rather frivolous facade of 'young man about town', David was committed to the cause and extremely useful. Well-educated, from a good family, his father a respected gold-smith and a pillar of society, David Stein's background and considerable charm were impressive to many, and he had proved an excellent recruiting scout.

'Yes, I do feel guilty.' Ruth wasn't sure if it was a trick question. Was it wise to admit to her guilt? But she decided to answer in all honesty. She'd hated the lies over the past two months. Stealing off to the meetings with David each Shabbat when her uncle and aunt thought they were at the synagogue. Lying to fourteen-year-old Rebekah when her young cousin had asked why she wasn't attending Rabbi Yeshen's service with the family. 'David and his university friends attend a different synagogue, darling,' she'd said, 'and I promised I'd go with them.' It had been loathsome, but easy. Her aunt and uncle were trusting, and David, a highly accomplished liar, had been paving the way for the past two years.

'Your uncle is not sympathetic to our cause, I take it?'

Eli cast a glance at David, warning him not to answer for his cousin, and David maintained an obedient silence, although he wondered why Eli should ask such a question – Eli Mankowski knew Walter Stein's stance on the Zionist movement.

But Eli was testing Ruth's loyalty, both to her uncle, and to the doctrines of Lehi. She didn't disappoint on either count.

'My uncle is a good man, and he has strong Zionist beliefs,' she said, 'but he is conventional. He disapproves of the tactics employed by Lehi and Irgun, particularly following the bombing of the King David Hotel last year. He believes we must follow the Haganah's official policy of restraint.'

'And you, Ruth?'

'The Haganah have served the Yishuv well with their support of illegal immigration and the protection of new settlements,' she said, referring to the underground military organisation the Jewish community had formed in the 1920s. 'But they have become too complacent, too co-operative with the British and their non-aggression policies.'

'And when the British leave . . . ?'

Ruth realised she was being tested not only on her knowledge but on the depth of her commitment. 'We will need a force more aggressive than the Haganah offers,' she said. 'We will need Irgun Tsvai-Leumi and Lohamei Herut Israel.'

She said what she knew Eli Mankowski wanted to hear, but as she looked into the intense black eyes, she felt a passionate desire to serve. She yearned to belong somewhere, to be useful. Lehi offered her a purpose for her life.

Eli smiled. She was quoting her instructor perfectly, but there was something far more important in Ruth Stein than her aptitude as a student. She was malleable. Perfect material, he thought. And he would enjoy moulding her, he decided, noticing all of a sudden how extraordinarily attractive she was.

'Your training will begin one month from now,' he said, 'in late January at Kibbutz Tsafona.'

David's jaw dropped in disbelief. He'd been a member of Lehi for two whole years. He'd scouted for recruits, distributed propaganda leaflets, pasted posters on public bulletin boards, all of which could have had him arrested by the British. He'd even attended light-weapon practice at Ra'anana's orchards where a training base was established. Like every Lehi member it had been his dream to participate in military action, but whenever he'd begged to be sent to one of the kibbutzim that served as secret guerrilla training camps, Eli had told him he wasn't ready. Why then was Ruth so instantly acceptable?

'Just a minute, Eli, that's not fair . . .' he said petulantly, but he was cut short.

'Don't worry, you'll be going too.' There would be fewer questions asked in the Stein household if Ruth were to make the transition to the kibbutz with her cousin. Two committed young Israelis working the land together – Walter Stein would approve of that. The man would entrust the care of his niece to his son, although why, Eli couldn't imagine. David was a spoilt child with no thought for anything but his own pleasures. But then, Eli reminded himself, children seeking pleasure made very good soldiers when their bloodlust was up.

'David, my dear friend,' he grinned, attractively boyish, the heavy-browed face transformed, 'I wouldn't send Ruth off to war without you beside her. Cousins fighting side by side, blood protecting blood like Spartan brothers.' He turned his smile upon Ruth. 'Poetic, don't you agree?'

Eli Mankowski was right. Walter Stein was in favour of his son and niece working on the kibbutz, particularly his son. It might toughen David up a bit, Walter thought – the boy was spoilt. Sarah pandered to him too much.

'For twelve months,' he said, 'it will do you good. Then I hope you will apply yourself to your work with a little more discipline.'

The previous year, David had completed the accountancy degree he'd reluctantly started at Mount Scopus Hebrew University, but Walter had found his son's commitment to the family business – in proud anticipation of which he'd named Stein and Son – sadly lacklustre.

As for his niece, Walter considered the kibbutz would do Ruth the world of good. The hard physical labour of farming would distract her from her terrible preoccupation with the past.

Walter's wife, Sarah, did not agree with her husband, particularly where Ruth was concerned.

'But Moshe is going to propose any day now, I'm sure,' she said. 'Ruth will have a far better future with him than with any of the young men she's likely to meet on a kibbutz. Moshe's wealthy, he has his business in Haifa and he's talking of retiring to his orchard soon. It would be the perfect life for her.'

'She doesn't love him.'

'She can learn, Walter. Love takes time.'

Walter shook his head wryly. The remark was so typical of Sarah. She had always been eminently practical and ruthlessly honest. She had said very much the same thing to him twenty-five years ago in Berlin when she'd agreed to become his wife.

'I'm very fond of you, Walter,' she'd said. 'And I respect you; you're a successful man. I shall be a good wife to you, and I shall come to love you in time.'

He'd had to be satisfied with that, despite having been desperately in love with her. There had been other eligible suitors – Sarah was of good family, intelligent and beautiful – and he'd found some comfort in the knowledge that she'd chosen him.

He smiled now as he looked at her, approaching fifty and still beautiful. She'd been true to her word in every way. She'd devoted herself to his comfort, his children and his business. And she loved him with a deep, unquestioning loyalty.

'Why don't you suggest to Moshe that he make his move within the month,' he said, 'and we'll leave the decision in Ruth's hands?'

Walter was of the personal opinion that his business associate and friend, Moshe Toledano, was far too old for Ruth, but Sarah had been dismissive of that argument too. Age was immaterial, she maintained, Moshe was an honourable man and would be a fine provider.

Life's choices were clearly defined for Sarah, Walter thought. He had the feeling they were not quite so simple for his niece.

Ruth was aware of her aunt's well-intentioned meddling. Subtlety had never been Sarah's strong suit and she'd been singing the praises of her husband's friend, Moshe, for months.

'Such a successful man,' she'd said from the outset, 'so sad that his wife died five years ago. The sooner he marries again the better, in my opinion. Every man needs a good woman to help shoulder his burden in life, and he'd certainly make an ideal husband.'

Ruth hadn't been sure whose case her aunt was championing at first, hers or Moshe's, but she hadn't taken the matter seriously – Sarah was a compulsive matchmaker. Besides, she'd thought, Moshe was old enough to be her father; indeed his manner towards her seemed more paternal than anything. She was sure that he, too, would pay no attention to Sarah's heavy-handed hints.

For the first month or so after her arrival in Palestine, Ruth had enjoyed Moshe Toledano's company. A Palestinian by birth, he and his brother ran a family import-export business inherited from their father, based in Haifa. Moshe made weekly trips to their agent in Jerusalem, always dining with the Steins when he did so. He'd offered to show Ruth the city and the surrounding countryside which he knew so well, and she'd found him not only an informative companion, but a welcome distraction from her troubled state of mind.

'I was born here in Palestine, Ruth,' he'd told her. 'So was my father and my father's father. We are part of this land.'

He'd taken her on an excursion to the Dead Sea, and during the drive back to Jerusalem he'd expounded upon the beauty of the harsh landscape which he fervently loved. He'd also talked of his sympathy for the plight of the Arabs.

'I have many Arab friends, I grew up with them. We Mizrahi Jews have lived in peace with our Arab brothers for centuries. We have shared the same love for this land.'

She'd become accustomed to Moshe's rather dry history lessons and his tendency to lecture. The passion with which he'd spoken that day had seemed intriguingly out of character.

'I welcome my brothers, the Ashkenazim, in their return to their spiritual homeland,' he'd said, referring to the European Jews who had continued to flood into Palestine following Britain's Mandate to govern after World War I. The flood of immigration had become a torrent after

Hitler's rise to power. 'And I welcome the creation of the State of Israel. But the creation of an Arab State is not being given equal attention; the Partition of Palestine is an empty promise. The money and the might of America supports Israel, and the Arab State of Palestine is simply words on paper. The Arab will be forced from his land and he will no longer live in peace with the Jew. There are fearful times ahead for us all.'

He'd told her that he intended to escape the conflict. He was contemplating an early retirement to his citrus orchard half an hour from Jerusalem, he'd said.

'I have no wish to take sides; the thought of it saddens me. The orchard is a place of peace, a haven from the hate that already invades this country.'

Ruth had wondered why he was sharing his views and his plans so intimately with her, but she had found the man interesting.

Moshe Toledano and his views had ceased to be of interest, however, when, at her cousin David's suggestion, Ruth had started attending meetings and had become immersed in the study of Lehi.

Conversely, Moshe's visits to the Stein house had increased in regularity – he was there every second day. He had business in town, he said, he was staying at the King David Hotel. That was when Ruth had realised that, with the endorsement of her Aunt Sarah, Moshe had come to look upon her not as a friend at all, but as a potential wife.

Now, less than a month before she was to start her training at the kibbutz, the man's intentions were evident, and his company stifling. They had nothing in common, Ruth thought, and his views, which she'd initially found interesting, now offended her. How could he be a Jew and sympathise with the Arabs? Even in the early stages of her Lehi conditioning, Ruth found the notion traitorous.

'The cholent is good,' Moshe said.

'It is only as good as the guests,' Sarah responded.

Walter and young Rebekah smiled, acknowledging the compliment and the response, but Ruth didn't. She pretended not to hear them and concentrated instead on the stew of meat and beans and sweet potatoes, although she wasn't hungry.

The cholent received the same compliment and the same response every Friday night. It was the normal polite exchange between guest and host. But since when was Moshe a guest? she thought. He'd been devouring cholent at the Stein house every Friday night for months – surely that made him one of the family. Ruth wished she could have avoided the tedium of the evening meal and Moshe Toledano, but David hadn't allowed her the easy escape route when, having announced he was dining out with friends, she'd privately asked if she could join him. 'Sorry, it's men only,' he'd said, and she'd known from the smirk on his face that he'd arranged an assignation with one of his many girlfriends.

'I'll clear the table.' She bounded to her feet the moment the meal was over.

'No, no, dear.' Sarah rose. 'Rebekah and I will do that, you entertain your uncle and Moshe.'

It was the same every time, Ruth thought, sinking back into her chair. She tried to look interested as Walter and Moshe chatted, and she tried not to notice that Sarah and Rebekah were clearing the table at breakneck speed. Thank goodness only two weeks to go, she thought. She couldn't wait to be at Kibbutz Tsafona, serving the cause, away from this empty existence.

Then, suddenly, the dishes had been cleared, her aunt was placing before her a tray with a *kum kum* of Turkish coffee, milk and sugar with, ominously, two cups, and her uncle was rising from his chair.

'If you'll excuse me, Moshe, Ruth my dear, I have some business to attend to in my study.'

But her uncle never went to his study straight after the meal, Ruth thought, and where was Rebekah? She'd disappeared from sight.

As Walter was ushered out of the dining room, Sarah was unable to resist a meaningful glance over her shoulder, and Ruth realised that this was the moment she'd been dreading.

'May I?' Moshe asked, picking up the *kum kum*.

'Thank you.' She watched as he poured the coffee. 'Milk and . . .'

'. . . no sugar,' he said. 'Yes, I know.'

There was a proprietorial air about him that she found irritating.

He carefully poured just the right amount of milk – he knew that she liked her coffee strong. Then he handed her the cup, his craggy face grave.

'I'll get straight to the point, Ruth,' he said, and she steeled herself for what was coming next.

Moshe himself was feeling uncharacteristically nervous. He wouldn't have been two months ago, he thought. Two months ago, he would have been hopeful of his chances. She'd been a lost young woman then, interested in learning about him and his country, and he'd wanted to protect and nurture her. First as a friend, then he'd fallen in love, and with Sarah's encouragement, he'd believed that he might have some hope. But Ruth had changed, he'd noticed. She seemed stronger, and he was thankful for her sake, but her attitude towards him was different these days. She was remote, disinterested, and he didn't know why.

'As you know, I'm anticipating an early retirement to my orchard . . .'

'Yes, you want to escape taking sides.' She hadn't been able to help herself.

'I'm sorry?' he asked, bewildered.

'You're a Jew but you want to escape the commitment of being one.'

'I don't understand you, Ruth.'

'The reclaiming of our historical and spiritual homeland, Eretz Yisrael – you don't believe in fighting for it.' She hadn't intended to sound so belligerent, but his complacency annoyed her.

So that was it, he thought. He was relieved to discover that her change in attitude towards him was not personal. She'd been influenced by some radical set, he told himself, probably David and his university friends who sat around in cafes talking intensely and doing little else. Moshe didn't take them seriously, particularly David, whom he found superficial.

'I leave the fighting to the fanatics,' he smiled, picking up the *kum kum*. 'I am a confirmed pacifist, and always will be.'

'Yes. I know.' She wondered if it was intended as a joke, but Moshe never joked. What an arrogant statement, she thought.

He didn't notice the coldness of her gaze as she watched him pouring his coffee.

'It is a peaceful life I should like to offer you, Ruth,' he continued, adding milk and sugar to his cup, 'a life free of the conflict that surrounds us.' Methodically he stirred the coffee with his teaspoon, feeling self-conscious, aware of the disparity in their ages and hoping he wasn't making a fool of himself. 'I wish to offer you a life with me on my orchard.' He knew that he sounded stilted and formal, but he didn't know how else to voice himself. Finally, he looked up from his cup to meet her eyes. 'I am asking you to be my wife.'

She found his manner pompous, and felt an intense desire to shock him. She would have liked to have yelled, 'I don't want a peaceful life. I don't want a life free of conflict. I intend to fight for our homeland, like every Jew should, and I'll kill if I have to!'

But she was courteous instead. 'You do me a great

honour, Moshe, but I cannot accept.' She was thankful to
see him finally stop stirring his coffee. There was the tinkle
of silver on china as he replaced the teaspoon on the
saucer. 'I do not love you.'

He hadn't thought that she did. But in time perhaps she
would. Many a successful marriage had been based on
affection and respect. He was about to say as much, but
before he could do so, she quite firmly terminated any
further discussion.

'I thank you for your proposal and the honour you do
me, but I cannot become your wife, and I cannot live with
you on your orchard. I am sorry.'

'I see.' He picked up his cup and sipped at his coffee.
Cannot meant *will not*, he thought; she had no wish to
accept the life he offered her. But he was grateful for the
courtesy of her reply, and thankful that she hadn't made
him feel like a self-deluding old fool.

'Well, we'll say no more on the matter,' he replied. 'And
I trust that we will remain always good friends.'

'Of course.' She breathed a silent sigh of relief.

'As your friend, Ruth, I hope you know that you can call
upon me at any time should you be in need of help.'

'I know.' She was glad now that she hadn't given way to
the outburst that had threatened. Misguided as she found
his views, he was a kind man, and a man of dignity.
'Thank you, Moshe,' she said.

Kibbutz Tsafona, twenty minutes' drive east of Haifa,
housed a thriving community of two hundred. The surrounding landscape, arid as it appeared, was surprisingly
fruitful, yielding healthy orchards of citrus fruit, figs, and
groves of olive trees.

Wooden-framed buildings with tin roofs, tiled floors and
white painted interiors formed the accommodation, with
separate barracks for men and women, smaller huts for
married couples, and a nursery where children over the age

of three were brought up communally. There were outlying buildings that housed workshops, garages and store
depots, and in the middle of the commune stood the largest
structure, the chadar ochel. The chadar ochel, where the
workers gathered for their daily meals, was more than a
dining room – it was central to the community's social
existence, often doubling as a recreation space or lecture hall.

Kibbutz Tsafona, although relatively newly established,
was self-supporting. Along with its orchards, it maintained
vegetable gardens and livestock in the form of goats and
sheep, and the work was constant and hard. But no-one
minded. The majority of the community were young,
mainly in their twenties and thirties, and they considered
themselves *chalutzim*, pioneers, like those original settlers
of the Hashomer Hatzair kibbutzim in the 1920s. And,
like those before them, they too were working the Land of
Israel and creating a new society based on social justice
and equality.

But, among the *chalutzim* who farmed the land, another
breed of Israeli resided at Kibbutz Tsafona. A breed
accepted by the young farmers as their future protectors,
but whose activities were conducted at a camouflaged
camp a few miles from the settlement. At the kibbutz itself,
there was no evidence that close to fifty of its members
were Lehi, most of them new recruits, secretly training in
guerrilla warfare. They wore no distinguishing uniforms,
they carried no weapons, and the American jeeps and soft-
top GMC cargo trucks known as 'Jimmies', which transported them to their training camp, were identical to those
used by the settlers themselves. The jeeps and trucks were
largely donated by American Jews eager to assist their
Israeli brothers and sisters in the reclamation of their
ancient homeland; in fact, American Jews did much to
fund the kibbutzim and, indirectly, Lehi.

Under the command of Eli Mankowski and his
lieutenant, Shlomo Rubens, Lehi Unit 6 comprised a

communications expert, an acquisitions officer, an engineer specialising in explosives, and two squads of twenty fighters. Ruth Lachmann and her cousin David Stein were among the latest recruits.

Ruth embraced her new life from the moment she arrived at the kibbutz. She became strong and fit, her body responding to the rigorous daily training sessions, but of far greater importance to her was the response of her mind. The nightmares faded, along with the past and the woman she'd once been, as she devoted herself to the collective ideology of Lehi and the part she now played in the future of Eretz Yisrael.

The day started early for both farmer and fighter, and the new young recruits quickly discovered that, like the settlers, their work was arduous, unrelenting and demanding.

After breakfasting in the chadar ochel on yoghurt, pickled fish, bread and fruit, the fighters were transported by Jimmies to the training camp three miles from the kibbutz. Situated in a valley surrounded by low hills and rocky outcrops, the camp's location was remote, but no chances were taken with its possible discovery. All training devices – the targets, the barbed wire, the climbing apparatus and other equipment – were stored in caves or out of sight among the rocks, and the cache of weapons was housed in a well-concealed bunker. A cave in the side of a hill had been extended by detonation, and behind the camouflaged netting of its entrance was their motley collection of firearms – mostly German, others stolen from the British. Alongside the Luger and Walther pistols, the K98s, and the Erma sub-machine guns, sat the Webley & Scott revolvers, the .303s, and the Mills Bomb standard British hand grenades.

Before the heat of the day set in, the morning started with rigorous exercise. The several seasoned fighters worked out briefly before starting on target practice and assault tactics, but the new recruits spent two hours mind-lessly stepping in and out of car tyres, climbing ropes and crawling under barbed wire. There was weaponry training, further instruction in the use of plastic explosives and the construction of Molotov cocktails and other incendiary devices, and, finally, their own target practice and assault course. As they drove their knives into straw-stuffed hessian dummies, the eager young recruits found it a rewarding conclusion to an arduous morning.

Normalcy descended at lunchtime when the unit returned to the kibbutz. Fighters and farmers dined together on meat and potatoes, the main meal of the day. But when the kibbutz workers retired for their three-hour siesta, the chadar ochel became a military headquarters. It was the one time Lehi activities infiltrated the kibbutz.

Guards were placed at strategic lookout points, and no maps or demonstration equipment was produced during the meetings, which could have appeared to be lectures on farming to a young kibbutz collective. In reality they were lectures in military tactics, planning sessions and, above all, conditioning in Lehi ideology, the most important aspect of the recruits' training.

Eli Mankowski and his lieutenant, Shlomo Rubens, who at thirty-eight was the oldest member of the unit, worked well as a team. The experienced and pragmatic Rubens, having recognised Mankowski's leadership skills, had accepted the younger man's quick rise in the ranks and was content to serve as his lieutenant. Eli, in turn, respected Shlomo's expertise in terrorist tactics and the effectiveness of his motivational techniques. Competition was encour-aged and a reward system set in place. Strict discipline was instilled throughout the unit, authority delegated to those deserving of it and punishment meted out to those found wanting. But it was Eli Mankowski's personal zeal that was the unit's prime motivational tool. Under Mankowski's fanatical leadership, the unit was indoctrinated with a fierce sense of comradeship and a steadfast belief in the task at hand.

'We belong to this land, and this land belongs to us!'

At the conclusion of each two-hour session, Eli would fire up his troops with all the fervour in his possession.

'We are Lehi and our mission is pure. Rid our homeland of those who threaten it. Do not shirk in our duty. All ends justify the means.'

The actual words of his daily address varied, but the content was always the same. In Eli's personal interpretation, and in true Lehi belief, the command of the Torah, 'Obliterate – until destruction' allowed for no moral hesitation on the battlefield. And as he raised his fist in encouragement, the entire unit joined in the final chant.

'Obliterate – until destruction. We are the future!'

Following the meeting, well before the settlers resumed work, the unit would again depart for the camp where they would continue training until dusk. Then, upon their return to the kibbutz, normalcy would once more reign as fighters and farmers shared their light evening meal of cold meat and salads, before gathering around the campfire.

An active social life existed at Kibbutz Tsafona, particularly in the evenings when, gathered about the *finjun*, young musicians strummed guitars and played piano accordions while others sang along. After a heavy day's work for all, the mood was one of fun, and the members of the unit were encouraged by their commander to socialise with the settlers. Eli Mankowski believed that socialising was an important reminder to both parties of Lehi's purpose as the protector of Israelis and their land. Fraternisation of any sexual nature was, however, firmly forbidden, as was any such fraternisation between male and female soldiers.

The young man on the piano accordion was playing 'Tum Balalaika', one of the favoured campfire songs, and Eli tapped his foot in time to the rhythm.

'*Tumbala, tumbala, tum balalaika . . .*'

The members of his unit sang the chorus with gusto.

The partying around the *finjun* bore all the appearance of young kibbutz workers bonding after a hard day's labour, and it pleased Eli. But these two breeds of Israeli, the fighter and the farmer, were worlds apart, he mused. Both shared a passion for their homeland, but one was trained to kill for it.

Soon they would be put to the test, Eli thought, and they would not be found wanting. He looked approvingly at the fit young bodies, proud in the certain knowledge that their minds were equally attuned to the challenge ahead. The new recruits had been in training for six weeks, and for the past fortnight teams had successfully carried out minor sabotage missions. An Arab village had been raided for supplies, a bridge detonated, and two Arab wells poisoned; nothing of any particular military significance, but as training exercises and morale boosters, immensely successful.

He'd had a little trouble with the first mission, he recalled, the poisoning of a well, but even that had proved to his advantage. A new recruit assigned to the team had questioned the directive. The young man had argued that, before the recent outbreaks of Arab–Jewish hostilities, his family had drawn water from the same well. He was sure that some Jews still did.

'The Arab and the Jew cannot drink from the same well,' Eli had told him. He'd said it for the benefit of the assembled unit. The man had already signed his own death warrant.

'But if we poison the well, we may kill Jews,' the man had argued.

'There are martyrs to every cause,' Eli had replied, 'and all ends justify the means.'

The next morning, when the man had disappeared, no queries had been made, even by the youngest and newest recruits. They had passed another test, one which Eli had not yet placed before them. They had accepted, unquestioningly, that there was no place in Lehi for non-collective thinkers. Eli had been grateful to the man.

The piano accordionist upped the tempo as a guitar joined in. It was David Stein, an accomplished guitarist, and the crowd applauded as the two performed their duet.

David Stein had proved a surprise. A confirmed womaniser, Eli had expected that he'd have to get rid of young David. But, despite the number of female settlers who found him attractive, David's prime target had ceased to be the conquest of women; he hadn't even found them a distraction. David Stein couldn't wait to do battle, Eli thought with satisfaction. Sabotage was not enough for him – he longed to kill.

Tum balalaika, play balalaika, tum balalaika, it will be joyful.

The voices of the gathering swelled as the song came to its conclusion and, despite the raucousness, or perhaps because of it, Eli could hear, quite clearly, the one true voice among them all. Ruth Stein. She had a pretty voice, he thought, watching her as she sang.

The fact that he continued to find Ruth Stein desirable had proved another surprise to Eli. There were several good-looking women among the eight female members of the unit, but he barely noticed them. To Eli, a fighter was a fighter, regardless of gender, and now that the recruits had completed their training, the women were barely distinguishable from the men. But he remembered how impressed he'd been upon first meeting Ruth Stein. He'd noticed her looks then, hadn't he? He'd relished the prospect of moulding her. He'd thought at the time that it was her mind that had interested him, but perhaps it had been her body after all. It was difficult to separate the two now, he thought. The power he had over her mind was teasingly erotic when he applied it to her body. But he shrugged off the notion as a fleeting fancy; there could be no double standards in his unit. Sex was not an option.

He continued to study her, however, waiting for her to turn and meet his eyes, as he knew she would.

There was a burst of applause, the song had finished.

Ruth turned and caught the full force of his gaze. She was unable to look away. But then no-one was able to look away when Eli Mankowski's concentration was focussed upon them. They weren't meant to. They would remain transfixed, like a working dog awaiting the signal of its master, seeking approval, dreading disapproval. And Eli always sent a sign to the subject of his attention.

For Ruth, the sign was one of approval. Eli clapped his hands softly several times, as if joining in the general applause, but she knew he was applauding her alone. Then he nodded, just the once. She returned the nod, and he looked away.

The exchange meant everything to Ruth. It was a reward; he was pleased with her. She didn't know why, perhaps he'd enjoyed her singing, although how he'd heard her above the others was a mystery. But most of all, she recognised the intention of his signal. The nod had been one of camaraderie, encouragement for the part she would play in the mission tomorrow night, and she felt honoured to have been so specially singled out. The thought of the mission excited her, and she couldn't wait to prove herself worthy of her commander's approval.

Eli was satisfied that she had received his message. Tomorrow she would be tested to the full, and encouragement had indeed been his intention – Ruth Lachmann was of paramount importance to the operation. Her non-Jewish appearance and her multilingual skills made her an invaluable member of the ten-man team assigned to the theft of British ammunition and explosives.

As David and the accordionist started up again, Eli no longer heard the music. His mind was on the significance of tomorrow's operation. This was to be no training exercise or unit morale booster. Irgun and Lehi had joined forces, and additional ammunition was imperative for the raid to be staged five days from now. A raid which both groups considered would change the face of the Arab–Israeli war.

Eli and Shlomo Rubens had seen fit to communicate their orders, received from the joint Irgun and Lehi head-quarters, to no-one but their fellow officers. The unit had no need for advance information; politics and strategy were for those in command. Blind obedience was the order of the day. The members of Unit 6 would address each directive as it was issued and, for the moment, it was the theft of British ammunition and explosives from the Haifa docks, with the aid of a team of Irgun fighters.

The military supplies had been delivered to the docks the previous morning and had been due for collection and shipment to Britain later that same day. Irgun Intelligence, however, had intercepted a message from the British vessel that it was undergoing emergency engine repairs at sea, and that its arrival would be delayed for three days. With the raid looming, and a severe shortage of ammunition, the situation was most opportune. Eli had assigned a sur-veillance team to keep watch throughout the preceding night, and, just two hours before, during a briefing session at the training camp, the officer in command of the team had made his report.

The shipment of arms and ammunition was stacked on the northern side of the main wharf, he'd stated. There was no barrier on the seaward side where the cargo would be loaded aboard the vessel, but on the other three sides the shipment was surrounded by coiled barbed wire approximately five feet high. There was a wooden-framed gate set in the barbed wire and, inside the compound, a prefabricated military hut. Five British soldiers had remained on guard duty throughout the night, a sergeant and four privates. Their commanding officer, a captain in rank, had left them on duty at around 21:00 hours and had not returned until after midnight.

'Let us hope he's a creature of habit,' Eli had remarked, 'one less to take care of. But no matter if not,' he'd shrugged, 'we will be prepared,' and he'd assigned an assault force of six men. But his orders were explicit: there was to be no killing; they could not afford any reprisals from the British. And, to be on the safe side, those assigned to attack would be dressed as Arabs.

Not that it really mattered, Eli told himself as the next campfire song finished to another round of applause. The British cared nothing about the theft of arms and supplies, by either Arab or Jew, and so long as there were no killings there would be no reprisals. The only reason he had chosen to disguise his assault force was in case one of his hot-blooded young fighters got carried away and slit a British throat in his excitement. And who could blame him?

Eli detested the British, he always had. These days, more so than ever. Since their Mandate was coming to an end, the British had ceased to care what the Arab did to the Jew. A raiding party of Arab villagers had ambushed a Haganah convoy and killed thirty-six Jewish fighters only the week before, and the British had done nothing. Some of the fighters had been executed, their heads and sexual organs mutilated, but the British hadn't cared. The British cared about nothing but their own imperial superiority. And now that they were no longer to govern Palestine, they couldn't wait to get out. Well, good riddance, Eli thought, the sooner they were gone the better. When the last of the British had left the country, the path would be clear for him. Through his proven commitment to Lehi, he would pave his way to a position of power within the new State of Israel. Eli Mankowski was a man of ambition.

The evening was winding down. The music had ceased, some were chatting quietly, others retiring for the night.

As she was about to leave, Ruth glanced at her commander, perhaps in the hope of another special sign of encouragement, but none was forthcoming. As David said goodnight to the others, he, too, glanced at Eli; most members of the unit did. But the commander remained squatting by the dying campfire, deep in thought as the party dispersed about him.

Eli was aware of the glances, but he was not in the mood to communicate. From the corner of his eye he watched Ruth and David as they walked off together to their respective quarters, and he wondered if they were talking of tomorrow's mission. David, he knew, had been aching to be assigned to the assault force. But Eli could not afford to risk David Stein's lust for blood. Not yet. The killing of a British guard would invite investigation, which could well jeopardise the forthcoming raid. Five days from now, David Stein would have ample opportunity to kill, Eli thought. For tomorrow's mission, he must be content in his relegated position as driver.

'Tomorrow is just the beginning, Eli.'

It was several minutes later that Shlomo Rubens broke into his thoughts. Shlomo was the one member of the unit not in awe of him, but then Shlomo was in awe of no-one.

Only the two of them were left beside the glowing embers of the campfire, and Eli looked up at Shlomo where he stood. He was a big man, strong and implacable, and his implacability served him well as a fighter – Eli had seen him in action. Shlomo Rubens was a perfect killing machine, a good man to have by one's side in battle.

'Yes,' Eli agreed. 'Tomorrow is the first step in a new war for us.'

They remained silent for a moment, both contemplating his statement. It was a new war indeed. No longer a war of Haganah defence against Arab brutality, but a war of aggression by the fighters of Irgun and Lehi.

Shlomo turned to go. Tomorrow would be a big day at

the training camp. There would be a further report from the surveillance team, and then the assault would be repeatedly rehearsed before the evening's mission. Shlomo Rubens believed in an adequate quota of sleep.

'Goodnight,' he called abruptly over his shoulder. Eli would probably sit by the fire for the next several hours, he thought, then he'd be up before dawn. The man seemed to survive on no sleep at all.

'Goodnight, Shlomo,' Eli automatically called back. His eyes were trained on the campfire's embers, but he wasn't seeing them. He was envisaging the next day's mission, as he would repeatedly throughout the night and the following day.

A ten-man team. Six to attack from beneath the wharf, one lookout on the top floor of the vacant warehouse, one driver and team mate in the Jimmy parked at the fishermen's wharf a mile away, and a decoy, the final member of the team.

Stealth and speed were of the essence. There would be no radio communication; the lookout would signal the Irgun boat by torchlight. There would be no use of firearms except as cudgels, and no use of knives except by way of threat. The British must be overcome swiftly and silently, and they must be left incapacitated but alive. The success of the plan depended a great deal on the decoy. And the decoy was to be Ruth Stein.

CHAPTER TWELVE

Moonlight shone silver on the black harbour waters as Ruth walked along the darkened dockside. To her right, she could see the vacant warehouse where the lookout would be waiting, signal torch at the ready, and ahead, to the left, the main wharf jutted out into the harbour. In the gloom she could not make out the shipment and enclosure, but halfway along the wharf she could see the glow of a lamp.

After weeks of training in sturdy trousers and men's shirts, she was conscious of the unfamiliar feel of her skirt and blouse – the skirt a little too tight, the blouse exposing her skin to the gentle spring breeze off the water. Her feet seemed slightly unsteady, too, in the strangeness of high-heeled shoes. Or perhaps it was nerves, she thought. But she didn't feel nervous. She felt energised and focussed, and more alive than she'd been in years.

She turned left onto the main wharf and walked towards the glow of the lamp, aware of the tapping of her heels, wondering if the assault force could hear her. They might well be beneath her very feet right now, and she pictured them, climbing among the beams and pylons, making their way under the wharf to take up their positions in preparation for the attack.

She could see the compound clearly now. Coils of barbed wire, silhouetted in the light of the lamp that hung from a pole beside the gate, and, beyond the wire, the huge shadowy shapes of crates and boxes piled high. She didn't alter her pace, but walked on.

'Halt! Who goes there?'

The voice came out of the darkness. She guessed the accent to be that of a Londoner, but she couldn't see the soldier. She couldn't see any of the guards.

'I am sorry . . .' she said in the heavily French-accented English she'd been practising all afternoon. 'I mean no harm . . .'

'Step into the light.'

She walked the twenty yards to the gate and stepped into the pool of light.

'Identify yourself,' the Cockney voice barked.

'Simone Renet,' she said. 'Please . . . I mean no harm.'

Tom Baker lowered the .303 he'd had trained upon the shadowy figure of the intruder and, through the barbed wire, he eyed the woman up and down. She was a looker, he thought, she had to be a pro. He walked the several yards from the guard hut, where he'd been standing, to the gate and the spillage of light.

'You're a bit off the beaten path, aren't you, love?' he said.

Ruth gave the nervous laugh of a frightened woman relieved to see a friendly face.

'*Bonsoir*,' she said. It was the sergeant, she noted. The lookout had reported that the captain, a creature of habit as Eli had hoped, had left at nine o'clock as he'd done the preceding two nights. But where were the other four guards? In the glare of the light, she couldn't see them.

'You French then?' the sergeant asked.

'*Oui*,' she smiled, 'I am French.'

'Long way from home, aren't you? What can I do you for?' He gave her a wink and laughed at his joke, but the innuendo was plain.

Ruth played ignorant. '*Oui*,' she said, 'I am very long way from home. That is why I come here. You can help me? Please?' As she looked appealingly at him, she could hear movement further along the enclosure. Like moths to a flame, the other guards were coming in for a closer look.

'I'll do whatever I can, love, that's for sure,' Tom said, aware of Cliff and Bill sidling up behind him. 'What you after then?'

'A ship, it will leave from here soon, yes?'

'Yeah, that's right.'

'I wish for passage to Europe.' She could see the figures of two of the guards standing behind the sergeant, just out of the spill of light. 'You can help me?' she implored.

'Well, now . . .' Tom cast a lascivious glance at Cliff and Bill. 'That depends on our Captain, doesn't it? He's the chap you'd need to see, but he's not here right now. Would you care to wait?'

She appeared to hesitate. 'How long he will be?'

'Oh, I shouldn't say more than ten minutes or so, what do you reckon?' Tom looked a query at the two soldiers. They were standing either side of him now, plainly visible and openly gawking at the French woman's breasts.

'Oh yeah,' one of them said, 'the Captain'll be back any minute now.'

Bill had got the message loud and clear. The Captain wouldn't be back for a good hour yet, he'd be dining out with his mates who were stationed in the nearby barracks. Plenty of time for them to have some fun. He turned and gave a nod to Stan and Godfrey, who were in the shadows behind him, their eyes glued on the French woman.

'You want to come in then?' Tom asked.

Again, she hesitated, looking from man to man, uncertain, and Tom thought that perhaps she wasn't a prostitute at all. The swell of her breasts beneath the open-necked blouse and the shapely legs beneath the short skirt had distracted him. She was French, he told himself, and French women dressed different from English women. There was a real touch of class about her, he thought.

Behind the three soldiers, Ruth could make out the shapes of two other figures.

'Oh I do not know I can wait,' she said, looking about nervous and uncertain, a vulnerable woman.

''Course you can, love,' Tom said reassuringly, 'come on in and we'll make you a cup of tea.' He nodded to Bill who opened the gate.

'A cup of tea,' she said, 'that would be nice.'

As she was ushered through the gate, Tom made the introductions.

'I'm Tom,' he said, 'and this is Bill and Cliff.' The men nodded and ogled and she nodded in return. 'And this is Godfrey and Stan,' Tom said as the other two soldiers joined them.

'Hello,' she smiled. Five guards, the full complement, excellent, she thought.

'Put the lamp on, Stan,' Tom said, as he took her arm. French women always liked you to take their arm, he thought. Well, they did in the pictures – he'd never actually met a French woman before.

Stan went on ahead as Tom escorted her through the dark, the others following, to the prefabricated hut.

'So where you from, love? Gay Paree?' Tom said it as a joke for the benefit of the men, but she nodded.

'*Oui*. I am from Paris.'

'Oh, really!' He cast a none too subtle look at his mate Bill. *You know what they say about women from Paris*. 'Gay Paree, the city of love, I'm told.' Tom considered himself a bit of a wag.

They'd reached the guard hut, which was suddenly illuminated, Stan having lit the kerosene lamp inside.

He stepped out into the compound and held the door open for her, but she seemed reluctant to enter.

Tom, presuming she was nervous, gave her arm a comforting pat, trying not to stroke the bare skin as he would have liked to have done.

'Don't you worry, love,' he said heartily, to put her at her ease. 'We'll plead your case with the Captain when he gets back, he listens to us, he does.' As if the Captain ever listened to a word they said! The Captain was a pig. 'He's a good man, isn't that right, Bill?'

'My oath he is.' Bill was a Yorkshireman. 'Captain'll see you right, don't you fret about that.'

'Oh I would be so very grateful.' She looked around at the men, careful to engage the eyes of each one. 'I will do anything to get home,' she said. Then she aimed the promise directly at Tom: 'Anything at all.'

Blimey, if that wasn't an offer, Tom thought, then he didn't know what was. She wasn't bloody nervous at all, her look was as bold as brass, and his cock was already rising to the occasion.

'I'm due for me break about now,' he said. 'Come on in and I'll get you that cuppa.'

She stepped into the hut and he followed her, with a wink to the boys.

As the sergeant closed the door behind him, Ruth quickly undid the buttons of her blouse, giving the men who were watching through the window a show of their own as they waited their turn.

'Jesus!' Tom exclaimed. He'd been about to make the pretence of lighting the primus stove, but when he'd turned from the door, there she was, blatantly bare-breasted. Her blouse was open, she wasn't wearing a brassiere, and Tom thought that, in the whole of his life, he'd never seen such a great set of tits. He fell upon them, convinced that all his Christmases had come at once.

'Oh Jesus . . .' His hands were all over the place, he was

fumbling with his trousers and trying to grope her breasts at the same time.

Then, suddenly, she was taking over for him. She had his trousers undone, she had his cock in her hand and she was wriggling her skirt right up to her waist.

Oh, Jesus Christ, he thought, she wasn't wearing any panties. He was going to come any moment, and he wasn't even inside her. He thrust himself furiously between her thighs, feeling her mound and pubic hair. 'Oh God,' he muttered, 'God, God, God.'

Leaning back against the wall of the hut, Ruth hooked a leg around the man's buttocks, and, fingers encircling his clumsily frantic penis, she guided it to its target. But her peripheral vision was trained on the window, and the four men watching, wide-eyed and open-mouthed. Suddenly, there was movement behind them and the brief sounds of a scuffle.

'*Oui, oui,*' she whispered passionately in his ear to muffle the noise, clutching at him as he finally entered her. But Tom hadn't heard a thing, he was on the verge of explosion, and when she glanced back at the window, the men had disappeared. Ruth found it comical – one moment they'd been there, the next they'd dropped out of sight.

The man was nearing his climax, and she moaned, feigning excitement, while, over his heaving shoulders, she watched the door of the hut quietly open.

Head thrown back, mouth gasping, Tom gave a series of guttural groans. He was mid-ejaculation and still thrusting, when he felt the barrel of a pistol rammed deep into his mouth, the muzzle jamming hard against the back of his throat. He gagged. Horror-struck, his eyes sprang open. Ruth had the insane desire to laugh.

Then, as swiftly as it had appeared, the barrel of the pistol was withdrawn and the butt of the Luger struck the side of Tom's head. He slithered down her body to the floor, and a man in Arab dress stood there in his stead. It was Eli Mankowski.

Their eyes met for a brief second. Eli gave one sharp nod of approval, gestured at the kerosene lamp, then wordlessly dragged Tom outside.

Ruth adjusted her clothing, extinguished the lamp and followed him.

In the compound, the four guards lay unconscious, already bound and gagged, and robed figures were crouching, waiting.

Shlomo Rubens bound and gagged the sergeant, and Ruth, upon Eli's silent instruction, stepped briefly into the light by the gate. It was the prearranged signal to the lookout whose binoculars were trained on the compound. He in turn would signal the waiting Irgun boat.

The guards were dragged out of sight behind the crates and the fighters set about carting supplies to the edge of the wharf for loading. It was Ruth's duty to watch for the warning signal from the lookout, should the captain be observed returning.

The team worked in silence, selecting the supplies which Eli indicated in the dim shielded glow of his torch. The larger crates were ignored. Much as they would have welcomed the heavy weaponry, they didn't have the time to load it. It was the boxes of ammunition, plastic explosives and British hand grenades they were after.

Five minutes later, when the fishing boat pulled into the wharf, the six Irgun fighters aboard helped with the carting and loading and, within thirty minutes, they were clear of the docks and on their way to the fishermen's wharf a mile down the coast where the Jimmy would be waiting. The only member of the team remaining at the docks was the lookout.

Satisfied that the captain was nowhere in sight, the lookout set off on foot to join the others, where, by the time he got there, they would have finished unloading the supplies into the truck.

It was shortly after midnight when Captain James Portman wandered down the wharf towards the compound. He'd had several nips of arak with his friends at the cafe which stayed open until all hours to accommodate the soldiers from the nearby barracks, and he was feeling quite mellow. The interminable night yawned before him, but he'd have a bit of a snooze in the guard hut, he thought, then in the morning they'd be off. He couldn't wait to get out of this abominable place.

Odd, he thought. No sentry. Were all five of the bastards asleep?

He pushed the gate open. Silence, eerie, not a soul.

'Sergeant?' he snapped. But there was no response.

He drew out his Webley & Scott revolver as he crossed to the hut. The door was ajar; he kicked it open, weapon at the ready. No-one there. He walked around the perimeters of the compound. The place was deserted. Where the hell were his blasted men? Then he saw them – bound and gagged, all but one wide-eyed and struggling with their bonds. Good God, James thought, what had happened?

He released his sergeant, then stood back while Tom Baker released the next man.

'What the hell happened?' he asked.

'We were ambushed, sir,' Tom said as he frantically untied Bill. Shit, what the hell *had* happened? he wondered. One minute he'd been up the French woman, then there'd been a gun in his mouth and he couldn't remember anything more.

'That's quite apparent,' his commanding officer remarked caustically. 'But by whom?'

Tom was at a loss for words. Fortunately Bill, freed of his gag, broke in.

'Arabs, sir. More than a dozen of them, I'd say.' Bill had caught a brief glimpse of Arab garb before he'd been silenced. 'They jumped us from behind – must have climbed up the side of the wharf.' He busied himself releasing the next man, Godfrey, who was still unconscious.

Bloody Arabs, James thought. 'Inspect the shipment, see what's missing,' he ordered his sergeant.

'Sir, I think Godfrey's dead,' Bill said.

All eyes turned to Godfrey.

Oh God no, James prayed. Now there'd be an investigation, he wouldn't get away in the morning, he'd be stranded in this godforsaken hole.

'Get a light, man, get a light,' he ordered, and his sergeant ran to the hut for a torch.

Five minutes later, when Godfrey regained consciousness with a groan, James felt immense relief.

'Check the shipment,' he ordered his men, while he tended to Godfrey's head wound.

The men eagerly jumped to their captain's command, thankful to escape further questioning for the moment. While they checked the crates, they agreed that there would be no mention of the French woman.

As he inspected the first aid kit, James cursed the fact that the report of the theft in the morning would delay their departure. But at least it wouldn't take long, and then they'd be out. He couldn't have cared if the Arabs had taken the whole damn shipment. Let the Arabs and Jews wipe each other off the face of the earth, he thought, just get me out of this hellhole.

It was only when the Jimmy was well clear of Haifa that silence was no longer mandatory. Arab dress discarded, the truckload of young people could well have been any group of kibbutz workers returning from a night in town.

The young fighters, seated with Shlomo and the supplies in the back of the Jimmy, talked excitedly about the events of the night. The mission had gone according to plan and they were proud of themselves.

They had every right to be, Shlomo thought, they'd

exercised discretion, just as they'd been ordered; no hot-headed youngster had killed indiscriminately. But he knew they'd wanted to. And they'd want to even more next time around. They'd been blooded – well and truly.

As they talked among themselves, Shlomo noted that they avoided any mention of what they'd seen, albeit briefly, through the hut window. There were a few mean-ingful glances but, out of deference to Ruth, seated with Eli and David in the front cabin which was open to the rear of the canvas-topped truck, no reference was made to the seduction of the sergeant. It was as it should be, Shlomo thought. Like them, Ruth was a fighter and she'd been doing her duty as one of the team. Any lewd refer-ence would have been out of place. But these were young men with healthy libidos, no doubt frustrated by their current vow of celibacy, and Shlomo had no doubt there would be quite a deal of lascivious chat among them when they were on their own.

The three in the front cabin said nothing. When the ban of silence had been lifted and the others had started talking, David, driving, had plied Eli with questions. He'd wanted a blow-by-blow account of the mission, but Eli's responses had not been encouraging. He had answered gruffly and monosyllabically and then stared out of the side window, and they'd quickly lapsed into silence. Eli was such a moody bastard, David thought, sulking.

Ruth was grateful for the silence. Seated between the two men, aware of the nearness of Eli Mankowski, and trying to avoid any physical contact, she felt charged with an extraordinary energy. The danger was past, but adren-alin still pumped through her, and with it the strangest of urges. She desperately wanted sex. Beneath the short skirt, her nakedness responded to the truck's motion, and she longed to be penetrated, to rut like an animal. Her wanton seduction of the sergeant had in no way aroused her – she'd been focussed upon her purpose and the sexual act had been meaningless. But now, as the truck bounced over the rough desert road, her whole body was pulsing, and the unavoidable contact her thigh occasionally made with Eli's made her more aroused. She hoped he couldn't sense it.

Eli could. Her excitement was palpable, and it was having a profound effect upon him. Heightened sexual awareness was not uncommon after a mission – he experienced it at times himself – but it was always controllable. At least it had been in the past. Now, as he stared out the window, the image of her exposed, her skirt around her waist, consumed him. In the brief second when the sergeant had slumped to the floor and Eli had seen Ruth in her nakedness, the sight had meant nothing to him. He'd admired her commitment. Her orders as decoy had not specified fornication, and the lack of underwear was proof that she'd been prepared to go as far as necessary to distract the guards. She'd obviously put on a show for the watching soldiers as well, and he respected her for it. Now, feeling her beside him like a bitch on heat, he couldn't get the image out of his mind.

They drove directly to the training camp where they unloaded the ammunition and explosives by torchlight, and Eli ordered Ruth to stand watch in the cave which served as a lookout over the approach to the valley.

A wise and tactful decision, Shlomo decided as he watched her set off up the narrow track, the boots she'd exchanged for her high-heeled shoes incongruous with the short skirt and revealing blouse. The lookout cave was well out of earshot and it would give the men an opportunity to speak openly; they needed to let off steam.

Several minutes later, Eli himself wandered off into the night, and Shlomo thought nothing of it. Eli Mankowski never shared his men's enthusiasm after a mission, invariably choosing to be on his own.

Eli took her where she stood, against the wall of the cave, just the way he knew she wanted to be taken. Her legs wrapped around his waist, her boots pressed into his buttocks, the rocks digging into her back. When it was over, he left without saying a word.

As he circled behind the cave and approached the camp from a different direction, Eli refused to acknowledge any sense of guilt. He had broken one of his own cardinal rules: no sexual fraternisation among the unit. Any two of his fighters found guilty of the same action would have been instantly dismissed. But Eli had always placed himself above the others, and he told himself that one momentary lapse meant nothing.

But the following night, gathered about the *finjun*, Ruth's sexuality once again beckoned, and the knowledge that he could have her whenever he wanted was irresistible. He walked off to the distant grove of olives, knowing that, given time, she would join him.

No-one commented upon his departure. They knew the commander often preferred to be alone, particularly before and after a mission, and rumours that something big was in the planning abounded, since the commander and his lieutenant had left in the jeep that morning and had not returned until the evening meal.

Shlomo Rubens found Eli's distraction eminently understandable. The two of them had spent most of the day in meetings with Irgun and Lehi leaders at the secret joint headquarters recently set up in Jerusalem. The raid was only three days away, and the next day they would brief the unit. Eli had a lot to think about.

Eli's mind was far from the impending raid, however, when Ruth joined him in the olive grove an hour later. Again, they coupled like beasts, feeding off each other's lust. And again, when it was over and she'd left him, he refused to acknowledge any abuse of his leadership, but prided himself instead. Ruth Stein's uncharacteristic behaviour was proof of the power he had over her mind and her body, he told himself – it was a measure of her dedication to both him and the cause.

It didn't occur to Eli to question the power Ruth Stein may have had over him. Eli was not only a fanatic and a megalomaniac, but a master of self-delusion.

Ruth, too, didn't question her actions. The drive in her was compulsive. She was obsessed with Eli and everything he represented. So long as he wanted her, and in whatever capacity that might be, she was his.

'Our orders are to liquidate the enemy,' Eli announced. 'No prisoners will be taken. All men will be destroyed, as will any other force that opposes us.'

The briefing was held at the training camp – as specific missions were never discussed in the chadar ochel – the fighters squatting in the dust before their commander and his officers.

The strategy of aggression, Eli told them, was in direct retaliation to the Arabs' take-no-prisoners policy and the mutilation of Jewish fighters. The goal in capturing the village was also to improve Jewish morale and obtain supplies for Irgun and Lehi bases. But, knowing that his young fighters were eager to do battle, Eli had decided to place his main emphasis upon revenge.

'The raid will symbolise a new era,' he declared forcefully. 'It will be a warning to our enemies and a sign of liberation to our people. No longer do we rise only in defence. The joint forces of Irgun and Lehi will, from this moment on, attack all those who pose a threat to our homeland. Arabs will pay with their lives for the Jewish blood they have spilt!' He raised his fist and each of his fighters did the same as they joined in the chant.

'Obliterate – until destruction. We are the future!'

The target of the joint attack was the village of Deir Yassin, an Arab Muslim stonecutter community of approximately seven hundred and fifty inhabitants. Situated on a rocky hillside west of Jerusalem and a mile or so south of the Tel Aviv highway, the village lay inside the United Nations' proposed Jerusalem international zone, its terraced stone houses descending to a corridor of flat land which led to Jewish Jerusalem's western suburb of Givat Shaul.

The village's strategic position made it the perfect subject for attack but, during the briefing, there was a great deal Eli did not impart to his fighters.

Deir Yassin had come under much discussion between Irgun and Lehi forces and the Haganah, Israel's military organisation. Upon being approached by the two guerrilla groups with a view to a coordinated attack upon the village, Haganah leaders had rejected the idea. They'd agreed that the capture and subsequent takeover of Deir Yassin would suit their plan to convert the pathway from Givat Shaul into an airstrip – but a truce existed, they said, which prevented an assault upon the village. Deir Yassin had been steadfast in honouring a Haganah-sponsored agreement to refrain from hostilities with neighbouring Jewish areas in exchange for protection from Jewish attack. The village was docile, the guerrillas were informed.

Irgun and Lehi refused to budge, insisting they would take Deir Yassin with or without military support, and, finally, Haganah Jerusalem Commander, David Shaltiel, washed his hands of the matter.

I have nothing against your carrying out the operation, he wrote to the guerrilla leaders, aware that the takeover of Deir Yassin was, after all, to the Haganah's advantage. He further refused his own intelligence chief's urging to notify the town that the truce was over, maintaining that he would not endanger a Jewish operation by warning Arabs.

Eli Mankowski saw fit to communicate none of this detail to his unit, and Shlomo Rubens agreed. In keeping with Lehi's policy of blind obedience, it was wiser they be

kept ignorant of the facts, and it would make little difference in any event, Shlomo thought. The fighters were
young and hot-blooded – they would follow Mankowski
wherever he led them and do his bidding, whatever it
entailed.

The attack was planned for early Friday morning on
April 9, just two days away, and, after weeks of covert
operations, the members of Unit 6 couldn't wait to meet
their enemy face to face.

Eli and his principal officers did not return to the kibbutz
that night, but camped out at the training centre where a
meeting had been arranged between the Lehi and Irgun unit
commanders. Battle tactics were finalised, and ammunition
from the stolen British cache was divided among the other
guerrilla groups.

The following day, the fighters, like the farmers, retired
to their barracks for the afternoon; they would be leaving
the kibbutz at midnight to prepare for the dawn raid.

While the rest of the kibbutz observed siesta, Eli and
Ruth again met in the olive grove. She was prepared, as
before, for him to take her in silence and when their desire
was sated to dismiss her without a word. But this time was
different.

Slowly, he undid the buttons of her shirt, and exposed
her breasts. He studied them, running his fingers over the
already erect nipples. On the previous occasions, he'd paid
no attention to her breasts – he hadn't looked at her at all
during the ferocity of their coupling.

She waited, breathless.

'Are you eager for battle, Ruth?' he asked, still intent on
her breasts.

'Yes.' She was eager for whatever he wished.

'You're a true fighter now; you may be told to kill. Does
the prospect excite you?'

The prospect of being told to do anything by him
excited her.

'Yes,' she said.

'Are you ready to kill?'

'Yes.'

'Do you *want* to kill?'

The focus was no longer upon her breasts, although his hands remained there, fingers manipulating her nipples, the manic black eyes commanding, dictating, controlling her.

'Yes.'

'Say it.'

'I want to kill.'

'Say it again, Ruth.' His eyes didn't leave hers as he undid the buttons of her work trousers and slid them down over her hips. 'Say it again for me.'

'I want to kill.'

'And again.'

Her trousers slid around her ankles. He was undoing his own now, his eyes still transfixing hers. She could feel his erection against her.

'I want to kill.' She shook a foot free of a trouser leg, and parted her thighs for him.

'Again,' he said as he lifted her, her legs instantly wrapping around him, trousers hanging from one foot and flapping against his buttocks.

'I want to kill,' she panted through clenched teeth. She said it over and over as he entered her, and Eli, insane with lust and a sense of his own power, drove himself into her with brutal force.

Five minutes later, when she'd gone, he was left to reflect upon what he considered had been an extremely interesting exercise. It was unlikely Ruth would be given the chance to kill; the women of the unit were detailed as backup. With a shortage of weapons, the female fighters were to remain at the rear and gather much needed firearms and ammunition from the casualties. But he would like to see Ruth kill, he thought, and he wondered briefly whether he might place her in the frontline after all. Then he chastised himself: it had been a test, that was all, just a game really.

He mustn't let things get out of hand, Eli thought as he left the olive grove. He'd proved his power over her, it was enough.

Irgun and Lehi leaders anticipated an easy victory in the capture of Deir Yassin. Given the township's non-hostile status, the villagers would be offered the chance to flee, and a truck with a loudspeaker would take the path westward, broadcasting warnings in Arabic and urging flight to the nearby Arab township of Ein Kerem. Any who remained to oppose the invading forces were to be liquidated, but the guerrilla commanders assumed such opposition would be minimal and easily contained.

The Lehi were to approach Deir Yassin from the east. One Irgun section was to advance west from the Jerusalem suburb of Bet Hakerem and approach the strategically positioned Sharafa ridge overlooking the township, and another Irgun section was to approach the village from the south.

At dawn's first light, the concealed units advanced on the town while, on the westward path, the truck's loudspeaker urged the villagers to flee.

To the east, Eli Mankowski and his unit covered good ground, undetected in their advance, but to the south their Irgun counterparts were not faring so well. A village guard had sighted them.

'*Yahud!*'

As the guard yelled a warning that Jews were approaching, an Irgun fighter prematurely gave the starting signal, machine-gun tracer bullets announcing to the other advancing units that the battle for Deir Yassin had commenced.

The guerrillas attacked, and chaos ensued. Above the

sound of gunfire and grenades, the Arabic broadcast could not be heard. The driver of the loudspeaker truck sped up in an attempt to enter the village, but the vehicle careered off the road and into a ditch. There would be no warning broadcast.

From out of the stone houses, panic-stricken villagers poured into the narrow streets, many in their nightclothes. Women who'd been working in the bakery fled up the hill to seek refuge in the *mukhtar*'s house. The multi-storeyed *mukhtar*'s dwelling sat at the summit of the town, and as the panic continued, others ran there, some clutching children.

The Irgun fighters, like the Lehi, were young, some of them not even twenty years old, and they ran wildly through the streets, firing at everything that moved, lobbing hand grenades in the doors of open houses, yelling the guerrilla Hebrew phrase '*achdut lochemet*': 'fighting in unity'.

But there was no unified fighting. Command and control had been lost and with it any form of disciplined attack.

Many young male villagers successfully escaped to gather at the Sharafa ridge where they effectively repulsed the Irgun advance from the west. The township rallied its defence force, snipers taking up positions in the *mukhtar*'s house and the higher buildings in the west of the village.

The Irgun unit was finally forced to withdraw in order to regather its troops for a renewed assault, and, as they retreated, fearing attack from the rear, they shot every Arab they saw. The elderly, the wounded, the women clutching their children, even the children themselves. They slaughtered indiscriminately.

To the east, Eli Mankowski's Lehi fighters had penetrated the village, securing themselves among the sturdy houses and stone fences. When word of their successful advance reached the others, Irgun forces joined them. Leaders conferred. It was seven o'clock in the morning, which meant the Sharafa ridge should have been taken and the township secured. But the Arabs controlled the ridge, four guerrilla fighters were dead, a number were injured – some out of reach and unable to be evacuated – and one commander lay mortally wounded. The attack had been chaotic and undisciplined.

The combined units massed for a concerted assault and Shlomo Rubens ordered announcements to be made from the salvaged loudspeaker urging the villagers to surrender. He also dispatched word to Haganah's Camp Schneller in Jerusalem. The guerrilla forces needed help, he said. If the Haganah could take the ridge, it would enable the fighters to evacuate their wounded under the cover of fire.

Then Eli gave the command. '*Achdut lochemet!*' he cried. The fighters surged into the street, their screams of vengeance soon mingling with the cries of women cowering with their children in houses exploding around them, or fleeing terrified through the gunfire in a desperate attempt to save the children they carried.

Shlomo Rubens was methodical in his attack, choosing not to waste his precious grenades on those villagers who posed no threat. The fighters were allotted only two grenades each, and Shlomo intended his for the *mukhtar*'s house and the higher buildings on the western side of the village where the Arabs were maintaining a successful defence. Nor did he waste his ammunition, but killed only those who opposed him, leaving the slaughter of women and children to the younger fighters whose bloodlust was beyond control.

Shlomo had seen it before in young, inexperienced fighters: this lethal mixture of fear, anger and a blind desire to kill; but he was not critical of the wholesale murder being unleashed around him. Indeed, the original Lehi proposal had suggested the liquidation of the entire village as a warning to the Arab population in general, and Shlomo himself would have obeyed such an order. But the proposal had been tempered to specify 'all men and any other force that opposes us' – the women and children offered no opposition.

He was deeply critical, however, of the appalling waste of ammunition and, as he dived to the ground, he inwardly cursed the young fighter who lobbed a hand grenade into a house too close for comfort. Given the current situation, with the Arab fighters holding their ground, such a cavalier use of explosives, which were short in supply, was intensely annoying.

The house erupted and, from a nearby building where she'd been hiding, a young woman ran out onto the street. She was yelling, demented; it was the home of her sister and her sister's children, she wailed.

The fighter who had thrown the grenade – it was David Stein, Shlomo noted – shot the woman twice. She fell to the ground – one bullet lodged in her lungs, another in her belly – and lay squirming, gurgling, drowning in her own blood.

A further waste of ammunition Shlomo thought, and he ducked behind a wall to view the narrow junction of streets and the surrounding buildings for any legitimate threat. Ahead of him, he could hear Eli screaming, 'Obliterate – until destruction. We are the future!', others readily taking up the call.

Eli was encouraging his men's bloodlust, but not because he himself was out of control, Shlomo knew it. Eli's purpose was plain. He had argued keenly for the instigation of the original proposal and, despite orders to the contrary, he intended to honour it. Eli Mankowski wanted no Arab left alive. Every inhabitant of Deir Yassin was to be annihilated, including the elderly, the women and the children, and he was whipping his fighters into a frenzy to accomplish that end.

Opposite, at a corner of the junction, an Arab sniper had exposed his position on the first-floor rooftop of a cottage, kneeling to take aim at the attackers who passed below. Shlomo trained his sights on the man and fired.

The sniper disappeared from view, and Shlomo backed against the wall of a nearby building, waiting for a moment, just to be sure, eyes scanning other buildings, seeking possible danger.

From the nearby pile of rocks which had once been a house came the unsettling sound of a woman keening. Three Arab fighters lay dead, and in the centre of the small, dusty junction was sprawled the body of the young woman. She was no longer squirming, but it had taken her several minutes to die, and Shlomo noticed, for the first time, that she was heavily pregnant.

He made his way quickly up the main street, dodging around the piles of rubble, to join the battle that raged ahead.

Ruth and two other women had been following in the rear of the attack. They had dragged a wounded Lehi fighter to the safety of a deserted building to await evacuation, and they had collected two rifles and ammunition from Arab casualties.

As Ruth had pulled the rifle from the hands of one man who appeared dead, he had clutched at it, his eyes wild in his death throes. But it meant nothing to her – he was the enemy. She'd thought about shooting him, but hadn't, leaving him in the sea of his blood; he was already a dead man.

She'd heard the screams of women and children, but had taken no notice. It was natural the women and children would flee in terror; she'd concentrated on the fallen fighters, both guerrilla and Arab.

When she came upon the pregnant woman lying dead in the street, blood flowing from her distended belly, she was taken aback. The woman was young, barely eighteen, her face contorted in agony. She must have been caught in the crossfire, Ruth thought. But it looked as though both bullets had been fired directly at her – surely that wasn't possible?

The two fighters with her ignored the young woman – to them she was just one of the enemy – and set about gathering the weapons from the three Arab men who lay dead. Only one had a firearm, but they took the knives from the other two.

Then, between the bursts of gunfire and explosions only several hundred yards away, Ruth heard the voice of the woman in the bombed-out house nearby. An ululating lament, songlike and mournful, it beckoned her. She held the .303 rifle she'd taken from the dying man at the ready and approached the hole that had once been a doorway. She nodded to the other fighters, who sidled up beside her, all three of them with their backs to the stone wall, their weapons poised – it could be a trap.

Ruth listened for any signs of danger, but there was only the crying of the woman. She cocked her rifle and stepped quickly inside, moving away from the light of the entrance.

The woman was kneeling on the floor, rocking her dead infant in her arms, covered in the child's blood. Beside her stood a little girl of no more than six, silent, sad-eyed and bewildered.

At the sight of Ruth, the woman staggered to her feet, still clutching her mutilated baby, and pushed the little girl behind her with a bloodied hand, trying to shield the child, while desperately pleading for her daughter's life.

Ruth lowered the rifle and stepped outside, leaving the woman to her grief. She tried to shake off the sickening feeling that engulfed her. This was war, there were always unexpected casualties, she told herself.

But the young pregnant woman, little more than a girl herself, still lay in the street, a vile condemnation, and Ruth could not extinguish the image of the mother and her mutilated baby. These were not the enemy.

She started running towards the sounds of battle, paying

no heed to the calls of her two fellow fighters who urged her to come back. She needed to see for herself. She needed to know that these hideous acts had been a mistake.

But when she reached the thick of the action, she discovered they were not. Scenes of incomprehensible slaughter unfolded before her eyes. Oblivious to the gunfire that ricocheted about her, she watched in horror as madmen killed indiscriminately. Some fighters who had run out of ammunition used knives to dispatch their innocent victims. She saw her own cousin open fire on a group of helpless women as they fled for the safety of a shop doorway. One of the women fell.

David wished he had a grenade to lob into the shop, but he'd used the two he'd been allotted. He fired another three shots through the door and another woman fell. He would have continued firing on them until they were all dead, but he was angered to discover that he'd run out of ammunition. He slung his rifle over his shoulder, took his knife from its scabbard, and charged towards the shop.

A woman gathered her three-year-old in her arms and ran out of the doorway, but she was not quick enough. She was stabbed in the chest, the knife narrowly missing the little boy, who dropped from her arms as she fell to her knees. Even as she reached for her child, the knife struck again.

David raised the knife a third time to slice the woman's throat and finish her off, although, as she vainly clutched for her child, she was already dying. But someone was grabbing his arm, screaming. He turned, ready to plunge his knife into his aggressor, but it was Ruth. For a split second he wondered why Ruth would stop him in his liquidation of the enemy, then he hurled her aside and headed for another woman who was fleeing the shop.

Ruth picked up the child and ran to the corner of a nearby building, where she sheltered against the wall, shielding the little boy as best she could.

Two of the women escaped; the other three were murdered mid-flight. One was shot and the others were knifed to death. The frenzy was at its peak.

Fifteen minutes later, the guerrillas moved on, cutting their murderous swathe through the streets of the once peaceful town. The broadcast urging the villagers to surrender had gone unheeded. It had been meaningless. Fighters and villagers alike knew there would be no prisoners and, as the fighters neared the western side of the village where the Arabs maintained a brave defence, their frustration at not successfully securing the town drove them to further acts of carnage. Children were lined up against walls and executed in the style of a firing-squad. Women were knifed to death as they tended the wounded. Frenzied fighters even plunged their knives into those who lay already dead. The slaughter and insanity continued unabated.

Ruth remained frozen. She didn't know how long she'd stood there, transfixed by the sheer horror of what she had seen, but the child whimpering in her arms brought her to her senses. Comforting the little boy, burying his head against her shoulder, she crossed cautiously to where the mother lay, still moving, her fingers stirring the dust as if seeking her child. The woman was alive. Perhaps if she dragged her to safety, she might survive.

But as she knelt beside the woman, Ruth realised that she was beyond saving. Her eyes were already glazing over, even as her fingers continued to clutch at the dust.

'Your child is alive,' she whispered, hoping that the woman could hear her. She shielded the infant from the sight of his mother but leaned close to the woman, praying that she would see her son before death clouded her vision. 'Your little boy lives. He will survive.'

The fingers stopped stirring, the last light of life died in the eyes, and Ruth had no idea whether the woman had heard her, or whether she had seen her son.

'Put the boy down, Ruth.'

She looked up. Eli Mankowski stood barely ten yards away, his face impassive.

'Eli . . .' She struggled to her feet, the child still in her arms. '. . . you must stop them . . .' Speaking seemed difficult, she felt strangled, breathless in her urgency. '. . . they've gone insane . . . they're murdering innocent people . . . women and children . . . you must stop them . . .'

'I said put the child down.' His voice was as chillingly expressionless as his face.

She didn't move.

'Why?' she asked, although his dreadful implacability signalled the answer. The slaughter was no mistake, she realised – Eli Mankowski had sanctioned it. In all probability he had ordered it.

'The child is the enemy. He must die like the others. Put the boy down.'

'Since when have children been our enemy?' She could barely get the words out.

'Every Arab is an enemy to the Jew, Ruth, you know that.'

It was the voice of reason. He'd used it incessantly throughout her indoctrination. It had made sense to her then, but now it so repulsed her she was unable to respond. He went on, weaving his own demented form of magic, convinced he still had her in his power.

'The boy will grow to be a man, Ruth, he will kill Jewish fighters, he will threaten our land. They must all die. The women who breed and the boys who become men, every Arab is our enemy.'

'Only to madmen, Eli. Madmen like you and your kind.'

She'd found her voice, and outrage lent her strength. 'What makes you different from the Nazis, tell me?' She spat the words at him. 'You saw the extermination of your own people in Poland, you fought in the ghetto in Warsaw, you lived through it all, and now you and your kind wish to exterminate another race, so what's the difference? Tell me that. What gives you the right? Which particular god made you superior?' She realised that she'd been yelling, and the child was crying. She stroked his head, calming her hysteria as much as the boy's alarm, aware of her own terrible guilt. The young pregnant woman, the mother with her mutilated baby, the woman freshly dead on the street beside her, whose child she clasped in her arms . . . she'd been a part of it all. The cause she'd believed in was responsible for this.

'We are worse than the Nazis,' she said. What right did she have to distance herself? She had been one of Eli and his kind. 'What we are doing is unforgivable, and I beg you to put a stop to the killing. If you can,' she added weakly. She knew it was impossible, she could hear the demented screams in the distance, 'Obliterate – until destruction', she had chanted the same slogan herself. 'I beg you, Eli, do whatever you can to stop the slaughter.'

He had remained unmoved throughout her outburst, it was impossible to gauge his reaction, and she could do nothing but wait and pray that she might have made some impact.

Eli was bemused. Her passionate address had fallen on deaf ears, but he wondered how she had so escaped his control.

'Put the child down, Ruth,' he said.

'And if I refuse?' How could she have expected other- wise, she thought, and she clasped the boy closer.

'I will shoot it right where it is and you'll both die.' He raised the Luger and pointed it at the boy, where he sat nestled against her breast.

'Very well.'

Slowly, she leaned down and lowered the little boy to the ground, his hand clasping tightly to hers; in his young mind the woman who held him was the only tangible thing in his world and he wasn't going to let go.

Her eyes fixed upon Eli and the weapon that was now trained on the child. She shuffled the boy behind her and, as she eased her hand from his, he seemed to understand. He buried his head into the back of her knees, clutching her trousers with both tiny hands, eyes squeezed shut, breathlessly still. He was hiding, the way he did when he played with his cousins.

As Ruth stood erect and faced Eli Mankowski, the image of her daughter Rachel flashed through her mind. The queue on the ramp, *'Links! Rechts!'* Mengele's commands, the flick of his riding crop. She'd shuffled Rachel behind her in much the same way and, like the boy, Rachel had clung to her skirt with both hands. It hadn't worked then, and she didn't expect it to now.

'You are aiding and abetting the enemy, Ruth. As a traitor, I could have you executed.'

Again Eli's voice betrayed no emotion, but she could see the flash of anger in his eyes, and the thought that she'd broken through his composure gave her a peculiar satisfaction.

'It is within my rights to execute you myself,' he said.

'Then do it, Eli.' This time she would meet her death with the child, she thought. It was right. She waited for the shot. She welcomed it.

Eli was no longer bemused, he was dumbfounded by her defiance. He raised the Luger, training the sights directly between the eyes which were brazenly daring him.

The pistol remained poised, Ruth remained motionless, and seconds ticked by like a lifetime as Eli realised that he couldn't kill her. What was wrong with him? One gentle squeeze of the trigger, that was all it took. How had he allowed this to happen? How had she come to hold such sway over him? All the more reason to kill her, he told himself – if she lived, she would be a witness to his weakness. But the finger on the trigger remained as frozen as the woman who stood before him. He was powerless, and he detested her for it.

He lowered the pistol, turned his back on her, and walked away towards the sound of gunfire.

Ruth watched him go, half expecting him to turn and shoot her where she stood. But he didn't.

She gathered up the child and headed back towards the eastern side of the village. She had no plan, apart from getting the boy to safety.

Across the street, standing at the corner of a narrow lane, she saw the two female fighters and realised that they'd witnessed the confrontation between her and Eli. She held the little Arab boy closer. Did they, too, think she was a traitor saving an enemy life? Were they as crazed as the men? They were armed; perhaps they might feel it their duty to kill the child. She didn't look at them as she hurried by, but she felt vulnerable. She wished she still had her rifle, but she'd dropped it when she'd run to the woman's defence.

The two watched in silence as she passed.

Several minutes later, she came to the junction where the pregnant woman had been lying in the street. The woman was still there, but others were gathered around her. They were placing her gently on a hessian cloth. The mother of the mutilated baby was there too, kneeling beside the pregnant woman, who was her sister. The mother was still covered in blood, but she no longer carried her baby. An elderly man standing beside her held in his arms the small bundle of the child's body wrapped in cloth, and he was overseeing the proceedings with an impressive authority. The women, six in all, were gently keening but there was no sense of hysteria as four of them, upon his orders, grasped the corners of the cloth and prepared to carry the pregnant woman from the street.

The man was the first to see Ruth. He barked something at her which she didn't understand and all eyes turned towards her. The keening stopped, the women were silent, malevolent in their grief, condemning her.

The man again barked the words, his tone even more aggressive this time, as he gestured at the boy she held on one hip.

The hatred in the group was palpable and Ruth felt a rush of fear. They could kill her with ease. They could tear her to pieces and they had every right to do so.

Carefully, she lowered the boy to the ground, but he refused to let go of her hand, grabbing it with both of his. She was unable to stand straight without pulling herself free from his grip, which she was reluctant to do.

She looked over at the man. He gestured for her to bring the child to him. Clumsily bent over, with the boy still holding on with both hands, she led the infant to him.

The man passed the small bundle of his grandson's body to his wife who was standing beside him. Then he leaned down to pick up the boy.

As Ruth relinquished her hold, the child started crying and reached out for her, but the man lifted him into his arms and spoke soothingly to him, stroking the boy's head until the cries became whimpers.

The women did not move; eyes flickering from the man to Ruth, then back again, all awaiting his command. He gave an order and gestured to the road which led out of the village to the east. Ruth was free to go.

She avoided the guerrilla command post on the outskirts of the village and, as she left the township, she avoided the main road. For a long time she could still hear the sounds of gunfire behind her as she cut across the low rocky hillsides on her trek to Jerusalem.

CHAPTER THIRTEEN

Maarten Vanpoucke continued to study the woman in the photograph.

'When was this taken?' he asked, peering closely at it through his spectacles.

Lucky was puzzled by the question, and he wished Maarten would give the photograph back; he was not accustomed to sharing his photograph of Ruth.

'At university in Berlin,' he said rather shortly, 'not long after we met,' and he held out his hand for the photograph.

'Forgive me.' The Dutchman smiled apologetically as he passed it to him. 'I didn't wish to be intrusive, it's just that I couldn't help admiring her. She is very beautiful, your wife.'

'Yes,' Lucky agreed, slipping the photograph into his wallet. 'She was. Very beautiful.' He felt embarrassed. He'd been impolite and he hoped he hadn't offended the man.

But Maarten's attention was distracted. Mrs Hodgeman had appeared bearing a large silver tray.

'Ah, the flan,' he said, rubbing his hands together approvingly as the housekeeper placed the tray on the table. 'Look at that, fit for a king. And a work of art, wouldn't you agree?'

Lucky did. The fruit flan was huge and looked like a stained-glass window.

'I shall serve, Mrs Hodgeman,' Maarten said, lifting the dessert plates from the tray, 'thank you.'

'Right you are, sir.' The housekeeper left beaming.

'A small portion for me, Maarten, please.'

But the Dutchman apparently was not listening as he carved a large section from the corner of the flan, lifted it with the cake slice and placed it ceremoniously on one of the plates.

'Now tell me all about young Pietro – he's in love, you say?' He slid the plate across the table to Lucky.

Lucky took a deep breath, preparing to embark upon both the flan and Pietro's love affair. The night was losing its savour. He would have to demolish the flan or he would hurt Mrs Hodgeman's feelings, and he would have to circumvent Pietro's love affair, which had taken a complicated turn.

'We're lucky to have Lucky.' Propped on one elbow, Violet played with the patch of hair on his chest – she loved the way she could twirl the hairs in the very centre into a perfect curl.

'Maureen also,' he said, 'we are lucky to have Maureen.'

It was unusually sweltering for early November, and their bodies glistened with the heat of the night and their own exertions as they lay entwined on the narrow bed in Violet's little room on the back verandah.

He ran his fingers over her skin, tracing the curve of her spine, relishing the feel of her breasts against his ribs as she cuddled beside him. The perfection of Violet's body was a constant source of admiration to Pietro who spent every waking hour these days marvelling at his good fortune. To think that such a woman returned his love! He was the luckiest man on God's earth.

'It is me is lucky,' he said, stroking the damp locks back

from her face, running a finger over the freckles of her nose.

'It is I,' she corrected him in her schoolteacher voice. Violet was a stickler with his English – he'd asked her to be – and she made a game of it.

'It is *I* is lucky,' he said.

'It is I *who am* lucky,' she persisted, sounding very like Peggy Minchin, then she bent and kissed the perfect curl of hair on his chest, wriggling against him as she did so.

It didn't take much to arouse Pietro.

'You also is lucky?' he teased. But he corrected himself immediately: 'You also *are* lucky,' he said in all seriousness.

Violet pretended to be shocked as she noticed his erection. 'Again, sweetie?' She always called him 'sweetie' when she was being playful or flirtatious; it was a term she'd picked up from the American pictures. 'So soon?' But she giggled delightedly as she lay back on the bed. Violet loved making love.

And to think that such a woman was his wife, Pietro marvelled as he covered her body with his.

Pietro and Violet had been married for one month, but this was the first weekend they had spent together since their marriage and brief honeymoon in Sydney. Pietro's trips into town were less frequent now as he worked harder and longer, signing on for extra rosters in his determination to make as much money as he could as quickly as he could. He intended to buy a house for Violetta.

Only Lucky and Maureen knew of their marriage. Lucky and Maureen had been their witnesses when they'd exchanged their vows at the Registry of Births, Deaths and Marriages in Cooma.

It had been Violet who had suggested they marry in secret, and despite his initial misgivings, Pietro had finally agreed. Particularly when even Maureen had told him it was the only path open to them.

'But I must seek permission of Violetta's father,' he'd doggedly insisted.

'We've already approached him and he won't have a bar of it.' Maureen's reply had been brutally honest – it was time to put an end to Pietro's fruitless persistence.

'A bar?' He'd been confused. A bar was where men drank beer.

'He won't let me marry you, Pietro,' Violet had said, her tone as adamant as her aunt's.

'But he has not met me, your father. How can he . . .'

'He'll never let me marry you. Not for as long as he lives.'

Pietro had felt rather stupid as he'd suddenly guessed at the truth. Why hadn't it occurred to him earlier?

'This is because I am Italian, yes?'

Both women had nodded, and Pietro had been devastated. What did this mean? Sister Anna Maria had told him that if he ever wished to marry, he must seek permission from the father of his intended. Did this mean he could not marry Violetta?

'So I will marry you without his permission,' Violet had said.

He'd stared at her, speechless, and Maureen had interceded before he could argue further.

'Violet is of age, Pietro. It is her decision to make, not her father's. And she loves you very much.' Following her confrontation with her brother, Maureen had been impressed by her niece's strength and resolution. Violet had grown up, she knew her own mind.

'Perhaps, when you are married, my brother might come to his senses and learn to accept you as his son-in-law,' she'd said. 'In the meantime, I will help you in whatever way I can.' Then she'd left them alone in the kitchen.

'Will you marry me, Pietro?' Violet had asked.

From that day on, nothing else in the world mattered to Pietro. Violetta wished to be his wife.

Back at the work camp he'd asked the Roman Catholic priest, who visited Spring Hill weekly to conduct the mass and hear confession, if he would marry them. But the priest had said no. Violet was not a Roman Catholic.

'You cannot marry a woman who is not of the Roman Catholic faith, my son.' Father O'Riordan had spelled out the rules in no uncertain terms; he considered Pietro a rather simple young man. 'The Church does not recognise such a union.'

Pietro hadn't liked the priest's peremptory tone.

If Violet were to convert, Father O'Riordan had said, then they could marry. But it would take some time, he warned. Violet would need to be instructed, she would need to learn her catechisms, then she would be baptised, after which she would take her first Holy Communion.

'You must be patient, my son,' he'd said in what he considered to be an understanding manner; he could sense Pietro's annoyance. 'You young people like to rush into things, but marriage is not something to be taken lightly.'

Both the comment and the priest's patronising attitude had further annoyed Pietro. He did not take his marriage lightly at all.

'I will ask someone else to marry us,' he'd said abruptly.

Father O'Riordan's response had been severely reprimanding.

'I must warn you, Pietro, if you marry outside the jurisdiction of the Roman Catholic faith, the Church will not recognise your union.'

'Then that is how it must be.'

Father O'Riordan had assumed Pietro's rebellion was the result of youthful impatience, but he'd been wrong.

Educated by the nuns at the Convent of the Sacred Heart, Pietro had never questioned the teachings of the Church. Now he did. God did not belong to the Roman Catholics, he thought. God was everywhere. God belonged to everyone, and everyone belonged to God.

God would bless his marriage, with or without the sanction of the Roman Catholic Church.

Violet, worried that he might regret his decision, said she would convert to Catholicism. She didn't mind. 'Really,' she insisted.

But Pietro had made up his mind. 'God is not a Roman Catholic,' he'd said, and he would not be swayed.

Their honeymoon in Sydney had been the most thrilling event of Violet's life. They'd caught the train in the morning, just an hour after the service at the Registry office and they'd held hands all the way. Violet was breathless with anticipation, admitting that she'd never been to Sydney before.

Pietro had booked a suite at the Australia Hotel and when they had arrived in the early evening they had been exhausted.

But after showering before dinner, they'd quickly discovered they were no longer tired. Nor were they hungry.

'You are beautiful,' Pietro said. He'd stepped out from the bathroom with a towel modestly tucked around his waist to discover Violet, who had showered before him, standing in nothing but her panties, surveying the selection of dresses she'd hung in the wardrobe. She hadn't heard him – she was in a state of dilemma.

'I don't know what frock to wear,' she said, worried. 'I've never been to a posh restaurant before. Do you think it'll be really dressy?'

He'd dropped the towel and taken her in his arms, and the frock dilemma had been forgotten.

'I love you, Pietro,' she said afterwards as they lay side by side on the crumpled bed. It had hurt a little to start with, but she'd known it would, and he'd been gentle. She'd heard that the first time was never any good, and she'd expected to be disappointed. But she hadn't been. Sex agreed with Violet. It was everything she could have hoped for – and more.

'I love you also, Violetta. I love you with the whole of my life.'

She wasn't sure whether he meant with the whole of his heart or for the whole of his life, but it didn't matter, it was the way he said it. She had never heard anything so romantic, not even in *Casablanca*.

They ordered room service – mountains of toasted sandwiches which they ate naked in bed, and chocolate milkshakes which they slurped noisily through their straws when they got to the bottom of the glass. Then they ordered two more. Violet thought it was all wonderfully worldly and decadent.

And they talked. They talked endlessly. About when they'd first met, how he'd come to Hallidays store just to look at her, and how he'd been so shy that she'd had to make the first move.

'I bet you thought I was forward,' she said. 'Go on, I bet you did. I was one of those easy girls, that's what you thought.'

'No, no,' he insisted, 'I think that I cannot believe it. Already I am in love with this beautiful girl, and she wishes to walk with me? I am amaze.'

'Amazed.' She corrected him automatically, forgetting the schoolteacher voice.

'Yes. I am amazed.'

'That was the day I fell in love with you,' Violet solemnly declared; she had decided that it was. 'It was the way you said my name that did it.'

'Violetta.'

'I swooned.' She put a melodramatic hand on her heart, and to emphasise the point dropped back on the bed, arms wide, in a mock faint, and he laughed. But then, whimsy quickly discarded, she sat bolt upright and said in deadly earnest, 'It's true, Pietro, I nearly did swoon, honest. It was the most romantic thing I'd ever heard. Until now,' she added.

They talked of their first kiss, by the Snowy River at Dalgety, and the conversation took a more serious turn.

'You're very experienced, Pietro. How many women have you had?' It was a direct question, but she felt as his wife she now had the right to ask.

'I am no experience,' he laughed, and she didn't correct him. 'I am ·near a virgin. I am with one prostitute in Milano, my friends they take me to her. I am no good,' he smiled, 'she is nice, she try to teach me, *lento*, *lento*, this mean slowly, but it is over,' he snapped his fingers, 'just like that.'

Then Violet found herself telling him about Craig McCauley, how she'd been repulsed by his mauling her behind the pavilion, but how she'd wanted to know what it would be like. How, when Pietro had kissed her by the river, she'd wanted him to go further. No topic was sacred to Violet now; she wanted him to know everything about her, and she wanted to know everything about him. She told him about her father, and the confrontation she'd overheard between him and Maureen.

'He called you a Dago, Pietro,' she said.

'It is no matter.' He cuddled her to him; she seemed upset. 'I am called Dago many times. It is just a word, I pay no heed.'

'And he said he'd kill you if I kept seeing you.'

It was difficult, Pietro thought, to pay no heed to a man who threatened murder, but he pretended to shrug it off and continued to comfort her.

'It is words, Violetta, nothing more. Your father, he does not mean them.'

'Yes, that's what Auntie Maureen said. She said he's just being protective.'

Pietro was relieved to hear it. 'Of course that is so. He is a man and you are his daughter.'

'I hate him.'

'It is wrong to hate your father.'

'Well, I do,' she said rebelliously. Then, feeling much better at having unburdened herself, she decided it was

Pietro's turn. Apart from the convent, she knew nothing about his childhood, and Violet didn't like mysteries. Besides, she thought, there should be no secrets between a husband and wife.

'How old were you when your parents were killed in the war?' she asked tentatively, hoping she wasn't being insensitive.

'I do not know exactly,' he shrugged. 'I think perhaps I am eleven.'

'Then you must remember them.' She was pleased that he didn't seem to mind her asking, and she wanted to picture him as a little boy with his mother and father. 'What were they like?' she asked ingenuously. 'I bet your dad was handsome like you – Italian men are so good-looking. And your mum probably looked like Gina Lollobrigida.'

'I do not know what they look like. I cannot remember them.'

Then Pietro told her his story; he, too, believed there should be no secrets between a husband and wife. But there was so little to tell, he said, he only wished he could share more of his past with her.

Violet huddled on the bed, spellbound and incredulous. It was incomprehensible to her that Pietro had no memory of his early childhood.

'That's terrible,' she said. 'So you don't even know if you have brothers and sisters?'

'No. I know nothing. I wish that I did.'

'You said there was a farm,' she reminded him. 'You told me that once. "Before Milano there was a farm", that's what you said.'

'Yes, I remember the farm. Only a little. I cannot remember the house where I live, but I remember the mountains. So big.' He looked up at the ceiling and gave one of his extravagant and all-encompassing gestures. 'So big, more big than the Snowies. And I remember the pine forests in the valley and the flowers in spring. And in winter, all covered in snow. And I remember the river, and, near the river, my goats.'

Pietro felt no fear in recalling the goats – he was too eager to share whatever remnants of his childhood he could remember with Violet, who was listening, enthralled.

'I love my goats,' he said. 'And I am good with them,' he added proudly. He had been too – he could remember how they'd come to his call. 'My goats they love me also. They stand very still when I milk them.' His hands curled into gentle fists: he could see and feel the rubbery teats in his fingers.

It was the dangerously vivid image which had often, in the past, preceded a seizure, but Pietro felt no threat. He'd been meticulous in taking his medication each morning and evening and he'd had no warning signs for months now. He no longer wore the strip of leather hanging from its string around his neck, although he always kept it in his pocket. Whether as a safeguard, or because it had simply become a part of his life, he wasn't sure.

Now, as he allowed himself to dwell on the images of the goats, smelling their rich animal odour, hearing their milk squirt against the side of the pail, he felt nothing but comfort in the memory.

'I have a special goat, she is my favourite.' He could see her, dun-coloured, gentle. Rosa was not mean-spirited as the others sometimes were. 'Her name is Rosa. I deliver her baby.' He saw his bloodied hand sliding out of the animal, the kid slithering along with it. But the image did not upset him. He heard Rosa bleating with the pain, he saw her raising her head off the ground, a further cry of relief, then the look of gratitude in her eyes as she lay back, exhausted. Rosa knew that he had helped her.

'Violetta,' he said excitedly. 'I remember Rosa.'

'Yes, you just said. She was your favourite, you delivered her baby.'

'No, no, you do not understand. Never before do I remember Rosa. Is just now, here with you, that I remember her.' Pietro was elated. 'Is you, Violetta. Is you have done this.'

She didn't know exactly what it was she had done, but she was happy that he seemed so excited by it.

'Do you not see? I wish to share my past with you, and it is because of this that I remember Rosa.'

The significance suddenly dawned on Violet.

'I will help you, Pietro,' she said, and she hugged him with all the passion of her newborn purpose. 'I will help you remember.'

Genuine as Violet's fervour was, she couldn't help imagining the scene as it would look on the screen. She would devote her life to helping her husband regain his past; it was the noblest cause imaginable. For a moment she was Bette Davis.

Pietro was unsure of the main source of his elation, whether it was the fragment of returned memory or the non-threatening image of the goats. But he related the two. He was free from his fits, he thought. He was free to remember without risking the onslaught of a seizure.

That was the one thing he had not shared with Violet. He had not told her about his epilepsy. He had felt wrong in not admitting to his illness before their marriage, but he had worried that Violet might not wish to marry him if she knew of it. Now a huge weight was lifted from his shoulders. He was not ill any more. His epilepsy was a thing of the past.

The next morning they'd walked down to Circular Quay and caught a ferry to Manly. Violet had categorically declared that there was nowhere in the world as beautiful as Sydney Harbour.

'I know I haven't actually been to other places,' she'd said defensively, although he'd made no query, 'but I've seen them at the pictures. I've seen Rome and Paris and

London at the pictures, and I've seen New York too. And Sydney Harbour's much prettier.'

At Violet's insistence they'd visited Taronga Park Zoo and, on their return to the Quay, they'd explored The Rocks where, at a souvenir shop, Pietro had bought her a miniature statuette of the Harbour Bridge and a tiny stuffed koala like the ones she'd seen at the zoo. Violet had gawked in awe at the Harbour Bridge. 'It's even bigger than it is in the postcards,' she'd said incongruously, but he'd known what she meant. The bridge had had much the same effect upon him when he'd first laid eyes on it. How long ago that seemed, he'd thought. And yet it wasn't really. It was barely eleven months since he'd arrived in Sydney, and three weeks later he'd been on the train to Cooma. And now here he was, earning more money than he thought he'd see in a lifetime and married to the most beautiful girl in the world. Australia was most certainly the land of opportunity.

Upon his return to Spring Hill, many noted a change in young Pietro Toscanini. The boy had become a man. He was no longer withdrawn and there was an assurance in his manner. Several of his mates who knew that he'd spent the weekend in Sydney, made ribald comments about what he'd got up to in the big smoke. Pietro said nothing, but grinned good-humouredly.

'Marriage suits you, Pietro,' Lucky commented out of earshot of the others. 'You're a new man.'

'Violetta, she has changed my life.'

Pietro said nothing to Lucky of the other factor that had changed his life, for he knew that if he told Lucky he was no longer ill, Lucky would insist he visit Maarten Vanpoucke, and Pietro had decided that there would be no more doctors. There would be no more pills either, he'd decided, and he stopped taking his medication – there was no need for it. He was healthy now, as normal as the next man, and he wanted no reminders of the illness and the shame that he'd put behind him.

Having refused Maarten's offer of port with his coffee, Lucky was relieved that the evening was finally drawing to its conclusion. He'd conquered the fruit flan, although he now felt bloated, and he'd steered the conversation away from Pietro's love life to an interesting discussion about the American contractors. Maarten had agreed that Kaiser would have an immense impact upon the region.

But now, draining his glass, the Dutchman again reverted to the topic of Pietro.

'I am glad that young Pietro is happy in his personal life,' he said, 'it will help keep anxiety at bay and avoid triggers which could lead to a seizure. But I worry that he is perhaps being slack with his medication. I will check my records, but I'm sure he's due for another script.' He was about to reach for the port decanter.

'I'll have a word with him, I promise.' Lucky rose from the table, it was time to make his escape. Maarten was labouring the point, determined to get drunk and eke out the evening. 'Now, if you'll forgive me, I really must go.'

'Yes, yes, of course.' The Dutchman looked at the clock on the mantelpiece as he stood. 'My goodness, I didn't realise how late it was.'

As they stepped out onto the first-floor landing, they found Mrs Hodgeman's son, Kevin, loitering uncertainly by the door. The housekeeper had retired, as she usually did when the doctor stayed up late, and it was invariably Kevin who cleared and washed the dishes.

The Dutchman nodded briskly. 'You may clear the table.'

'Goodnight, Kevin,' Lucky said, and the gauche young man gave his bashful smile, a mixture of self-consciousness and pleasure.

The two men walked down the main staircase to the hall and shook hands at the front door.

'Thank you, Maarten, for a most delightful evening.'

'My pleasure indeed, we must do it again soon.'

'And do thank Mrs Hodgeman for me. The food was magnificent.'

'She'll be delighted to hear it.'

As soon as the Dutchman had closed the door, Lucky took off at a sprint for Peggy's house only several blocks away, where she lay dozing and dreaming and waiting for him.

Maarten Vanpoucke returned upstairs to the dining room.

Kevin was methodically placing the dessert plates and glasses onto the silver tray, wary of the delicate bone china and crystal, each movement painstakingly slow. He picked up the decanter.

'Leave the port,' Maarten said as he sat.

Kevin did, setting it down very carefully.

'And the glass.'

Kevin's eyes flickered between the two port glasses on the tray. Fortunately he could pick the one that was the doctor's, as Lucky had not drunk any port. He replaced the glass on the table and left.

Maarten poured himself another port. He took off his spectacles and placed them on the table, rubbing eyes which felt weary, then he leaned back in his chair. There was such a lot to think about.

His mind returned to the woman in the photograph. Was Ruth still alive? It was quite probable. If so, he wondered where she was.

CHAPTER FOURTEEN

As they drove through the suburban streets of Jerusalem, Ruth glanced at Moshe. He hadn't spoken for the past several minutes and she presumed he was sulking.

'I'm sorry,' she said stiffly, 'I didn't mean to be so brusque.'

Yes she had, he thought – even her apology sounded stilted. But he forgave her.

'It's all right,' he replied. 'I can understand your nervousness.'

She felt another irrational surge of annoyance, but tried not to let it show. Everything Moshe did and said grated. He didn't understand at all; if he did, he wouldn't have insisted she go to the funeral. And dismissing her trepidation as 'nervousness' was infuriating, damn him – she was becoming more terrified by the moment. How would she react, coming face to face with her cousin? The last time she'd seen David he'd been knifing a woman to death. And what if Eli were there? Moshe didn't understand. He never had. She knew that now.

Ruth had contacted Moshe Toledano a week after her return to Jerusalem, convinced that he was the only person

in whom she could confide. They'd met at the King David
Hotel and, distraught, she had poured out her story. From
her indoctrination at Kibbutz Tsafona to her affair with
Eli Mankowski and the massacre at Deir Yassin, she had
spared no detail, however sordid or gruesome, and he'd
listened, not once interjecting.

News of Deir Yassin had been published in the press and
Moshe had followed the reports closely, also gleaning inside
information from his powerful business associates. In a
post-battle press statement Irgun and Lehi had claimed a
great victory, but in truth it had been the Palmach troops,
the elite fighting arm of the Haganah, who had quelled the
Arab resistance, accomplishing in one hour what the guerrilla fighters had failed to do throughout the entire morning
of their initial attack. But the guerrillas' slaughter of innocents had continued for a further two days and, of the Arab
dead, two-thirds had been women and children. The Jewish
Agency in Tel Aviv had condemned the attack, but there
were rumours that there would be no criminal prosecution
or inquest by the British, whose final departure from Palestine was due in only a matter of weeks. The reason, Moshe
had heard, was that, as the attack and subsequent massacre
had been instigated by the Revisionist underground militia
rather than by the official Zionist leaders, nothing more
than a police investigation was required.

The massacre of Deir Yassin had confirmed Moshe's
worst fears. There would be no turning back now, he'd
thought. Already, in direct retaliation, Arabs had
ambushed a Jewish medical convoy and murdered over
seventy people. The wheels of destruction had been set in
motion and who knew where or when it would end.

But he'd made no comment as Ruth had told her story,
and when she'd finished and stood before him, emotion-
ally drained by the weight of her confession, he'd remained
silent.

Ruth had expected his condemnation. She had been

involved with the murder of innocent *falachim*, Arab
peasants who'd simply been going about their lives, and
guiltily she'd awaited his verdict, hoping for some kind
of absolution. Moshe, with his sympathy for both sides,
was the only person, she thought, who could possibly
understand.

But Moshe had offered neither judgement nor absolution.

'It is this senseless violence I had wished to save you
from, Ruth,' he'd said finally. 'And I still do.' Then he'd
repeated his offer. As his wife, he could provide her with a
peaceful life, he'd said, away from the horrors of the war
that would devour Palestine.

Ruth had found his detachment extraordinary. Had her
revelations of the hideous brutality she'd witnessed meant
nothing more to him than a renewed opportunity? It
seemed somehow obscene that, after hearing her story, he
could discuss something as mundane as marriage. And yet
the prospect of escape to a life of nothingness suddenly
appeared irresistible to Ruth.

'How can I become your wife, Moshe, if I do not love
you?'

An empty question, he'd thought – he could see that she
already knew there was only one answer.

'You need me.' To Moshe Toledano, love and need were
perfectly equated: he wanted her, she needed him, and a
love of some form would develop over time.

'No,' she'd said, 'I will not become your wife, and I will
not bear your children. But, if you wish, I will live with
you on your orchard.' Then she'd shocked him with her
own unequivocal offer. 'I will perform all the duties of a
wife. I will cook for you, I will work by your side and I will
share your bed.' She would owe him that duty, she'd
thought. And why not? She'd been a whore to Klaus
Henkel and Eli Mankowski: her body was already a commodity, and it was a cheap price to pay for a peaceful

existence. 'If it is companionship you wish, Moshe, in all its forms, I am willing to provide it.'

And Moshe's arrogance had allowed him to accept. A woman like Ruth Lachmann, he'd thought, would not be content to live in sin for long. She would marry him eventually.

They were not far from her uncle's house in Beit Yisrael, and Moshe, having accepted her apology, tried to put her at her ease.

'A lot has changed in six years, Ruth,' he said.

'Yes, I can see that,' she replied, deliberately mis-understanding him, looking out at the new buildings.

'I mean people,' he said. 'People like David.' He made no mention of Eli Mankowski – in the six years they'd lived together they'd never once spoken the man's name – although he knew it was Eli she was thinking of. 'People do change,' he said. In any event, he wasn't referring to Eli. He doubted whether Mankowski would ever change – from what he'd heard the man was an insane fanatic. But he'd noted her scathing tone when she'd mentioned her cousin and he felt obliged to assure her there was nothing to fear. 'David was young,' he said, 'and easily influenced at the time.'

At the time, she realised, meant Deir Yassin. It was a subject which never came under discussion, and although she knew he meant well, she wished he would stop.

'He's changed, Ruth, you'll see. David has grown out of his radical phase.'

Grown out of killing, do you mean?

'He's been working with his father for three years now, Walter was so glad when he came back to the fold.' Moshe had often seen David Stein during his trips into town, and although he still didn't particularly like the man, he'd maintained the semblance of a friendship for the sake of his old friend, Walter. Out of deference to Ruth, however, he'd never mentioned the fact – David was another subject never discussed.

'David will be taking over the family business now that Walter has gone.'

Good for David.

He wished she'd say something. 'You've changed too, Ruth,' he said encouragingly. 'You're a different person, you've adapted to a different life.'

Adapted? Oh no. Oh no, I haven't.

'I know, Moshe,' she agreed, anything to stop him talking. 'I know I have, and it's thanks to you.'

He smiled, glad to be appreciated, and took a left turn into the street which led to her uncle's house.

Adapted, she thought. No, she'd never adapted. If only she could. That was her trouble, she'd never learned to adapt. Ira had tried to teach her, but it had been a skill she had never mastered.

In her loneliness over the past years, as she'd tried to reconcile herself to a life with a man she didn't love, Ira Schoneberger had become Ruth's constant companion. She heard his voice and pictured him in her mind as she'd desperately tried to heed his advice. She even had conversations out loud with him when she was on her own. Perhaps she was going mad, she'd thought, but she'd found comfort in Ira's words.

'I intend to become a chameleon,' he had told her, 'when I am free.' Ira had always said 'when' and not 'if'. 'I shall change my colour to suit my environment, I shall become whatever people wish me to be. If I am in a country intolerant towards Jews, I shall change my name and live accordingly. And if I go to America, which I believe is very sympathetic to the Jewish plight, then I shall tell my story to anyone who wishes to hear it. Who knows what lies ahead for us all? To survive successfully, Ruth, one must adapt.'

She had tried. She'd tried her hardest on a daily basis,

year after year. But, unlike Ira, Ruth had been unable to
adapt, and the nothingness of her life with Moshe
Toledano had become a prison.

'Ruth!'

As they pulled up outside the apartment, Rebekah ran
out to greet them. She'd been watching for their arrival
through the front downstairs window.

Ruth climbed from the car and embraced her young
cousin, grateful for Rebekah's uninhibited display of affection. The two had maintained contact over the years by
letter, but she'd been unsure of the reception she might
receive in person. There was no awkwardness, however;
Rebekah's welcome was warm and genuine, and there was
a hint of tears as she clung to Ruth.

'Just look at you.' It was Ruth who finally broke the
moment, holding the girl at arm's length and looking her
up and down admiringly. 'Every inch the young sophisti-
cate.' Rebekah had certainly inherited the dramatic good
looks of her mother, Ruth thought: always a pretty child,
she was now a striking young woman. 'So tell me,' she
asked briskly, aware that the girl was trying to control the
threat of tears, 'how did your exams go?'

'I'm fairly confident.' Rebekah smiled, thankful for the
small talk.

'You're being modest. Moshe tells me you're bound to
top the course again this year.' Twenty-one-year-old
Rebekah had just completed the second year of her
medical degree at Mount Scopus Hebrew University.

Her emotions now in check, Rebekah was able to speak
her mind. 'I'm glad you're here, Ruth,' she said, 'it would
so please him to know that you'd come.'

The grief for her father's death was etched in her face,
and Ruth was moved.

'I'm glad I'm here too,' she said sincerely, casting a look
in Moshe's direction, both apologetic and thankful.

Arm in arm, the women walked up the path to the front

door, chatting as freely as they always had, and Moshe followed behind them, pleased by their reunion and his own vindication.

The moment Ruth stepped into the hall and was confronted by her aunt, however, the awkwardness she'd been expecting was instantly readable. It was clear that, even on the occasion of her husband's funeral, Sarah Stein wished to communicate her disapproval.

Sarah surveyed the group coldly. She was cross with her daughter – Rebekah's effusiveness was unfitting behaviour for one in mourning. Furthermore, it was offensive she should so warmly welcome her cousin, a woman who had besmirched the family name by living in sin with a good man who wished to marry her.

She ignored her daughter and greeted Moshe only briefly. Then, offering no words of welcome to her niece, she waited for Ruth to make the first move.

'*Shalom*, Aunt Sarah.' Ruth crossed to her aunt and kissed her on both cheeks. 'It is a sad day,' she said.

'Yes,' Sarah replied stiffly, accepting the show of respect with the dignity it warranted. 'A sad day indeed.'

'I loved him. Very much.'

'Yes. I know you did.' Recognising her niece's sincerity, Sarah relented just a little. She couldn't understand the girl, and she never would, but Walter had. They'd argued about it, she remembered.

'She's disgracing the family name,' she'd said.

'How is she disgracing it?' he'd asked. 'She's not flaunting her relationship – she's gone into hiding.'

'That's not the point . . .'

'It's exactly the point,' he'd insisted. 'She's been tortured for years by the death of her husband and child, perhaps Moshe and his orchard can provide some sort of peace.'

'Then she should marry him.'

'There are some who can't marry without love, Sarah.' He'd said it with no deliberate intention to wound, but she'd recognised it as a personal remark, even a criticism, and it had hurt just a little.

Over the years, Ruth's incomprehensible decision not to marry had continued to meet with Sarah's disapproval, but she had never brought up the subject again.

Now, thinking of her husband and confronted by her niece, Sarah felt herself mellow. As Walter would have wished, she had no doubt.

'He loved you very much too, Ruth,' she said. She offered no embrace, no display of affection – she was too wearied by grief – but she could tell by the look on Ruth's face that the words were enough, and for the moment she was glad.

'Now come into the kitchen,' she said, leading the way. 'David is making us a pot of tea before we leave.'

Ruth braced herself.

He was setting out the cups and saucers on the large kitchen table as they entered, and Ruth's initial impression was that he seemed bigger.

'*Shalom*, Moshe,' he said looking up from the tea things. Then to her, '*Shalom*, Ruth, it's been a long time.'

'*Shalom*, David.'

He *was* bigger, she realised. Not yet fat, but fleshy, the finely chiselled cheekbones of his youth were gone, and the athletic frame was now that of a man approaching middle age. But David was not even thirty, she thought, relieved somehow that he looked like a stranger.

'I'm sorry about your father,' she said dutifully.

'Yes, it came as a shock to us all. He was only sixty-three.'

David's reply was equally dutiful, for the sake of his mother, but he was glad to see Ruth, and abruptly he changed the subject – he was sick of being maudlin.

'You're looking good,' he said, and as he smiled Ruth was jolted into the past. His smile was as confident, as winning and as boyish as it had always been, and it was flirtatiously intimate, like a lover hinting at a shared secret. It unnerved her.

'You're looking well yourself, David,' she said, aware that she sounded unnaturally prim.

'Yes,' he replied, patting his waistline, 'a little too well. The good life has agreed with me.'

Sarah was finding the conversation too frivolous for her liking. 'Rebekah, will you pour the tea,' she asked, more an order than a request.

'No, no,' David halted his sister as she crossed to the teapot which sat on the bench by the sink, 'it's still drawing, Mother, give it a few more minutes. I'll just pop outside for a cigar, be back when it's ready. Ruth, will you join me? There's so much to catch up on, isn't there?' And before his mother could reply or Ruth could demur, he'd taken her by the arm and led her out onto the patio, Sarah glaring her annoyance.

'I didn't know you smoked,' Ruth said when he'd closed the door.

'I don't really, it's more to impress than anything.' His grin was cheeky as he took a Corona from the solid silver case which he kept in his breast pocket and lit it with his solid silver lighter. Then he struck a pompous pose and puffed ostentatiously, the quintessential businessman, but a boy showing off, and again an intimacy he was sharing with her. She didn't react.

'I just wanted a chance to talk with you alone,' he said, dropping the pose.

Why? she wondered, but she made no enquiry.

'It's good to see you, Ruth. Are you happy?'

'No.' She didn't want to look at him. He no longer appeared a stranger. The eyes in the fleshy handsomeness of his face were all too familiar and they brought back ugly memories. She gazed out at the street instead.

He waited for her to continue, but she didn't. 'Oh, I'm sorry to hear that.' He was surprised; he'd presumed that she was happy. Moshe hadn't led him to believe otherwise, but then Moshe was a man of few words. At least he was with him. David had the impression that Moshe didn't very much like him – not that it mattered: he didn't much like Moshe. He'd suspected at one stage that the man was jealous of his relationship with Ruth; Moshe had been so overprotective of her.

'I'm her cousin, for God's sake,' he'd said when Moshe had repeatedly prevented him making contact with her. 'I'm no threat!'

'Yes, you are,' Moshe had finally told him. 'She doesn't wish to see you or to hear from you – she wants no reminder of her time with Lehi.'

He'd been taken aback. No-one outside the group, including his parents, knew of his or Ruth's association with Lehi. 'How much did she tell you?' he'd asked.

'Everything.'

David looked at her now, gazing out at the street, assiduously avoiding his eyes. 'So why are you not happy, Ruth?' he asked.

'What is it you want of me, David?' She still refused to look at him. 'Why did you wish to speak to me alone?'

It was futile, he realised, to continue with the niceties.

'Has he made contact with you?' he asked.

She pretended ignorance. 'Who?' she replied, fixing her eyes on the unattractive apartment block opposite.

'Eli, of course.'

'I haven't seen him since that day.'

'Well, I didn't expect you'd seen him.' There was a touch of irritation in his tone. 'No-one has. But has he been in touch? Do you know where he is?'

'No.' At last she looked at him, trying not to let her relief show. 'So he's not here? He won't be at the funeral?'

'Good God no, he dumped me along with everyone else.' The irritation was replaced by bitterness. 'I haven't seen or heard from him in six years. The rumour is he left

Palestine in '48. I thought at least he might have contacted you, of all people.'

Why me 'of all people'? she wondered, surely David didn't know of her sexual relationship with Eli Mankowski? No-one knew. Eli himself would certainly never have spoken of it.

'There is no reason why Eli should contact me,' she said. He was looking at her shrewdly, trying to read her reaction, hoping she'd give something away. He didn't know the truth, she realised, he was just guessing. She met his eyes directly. 'I meant less than nothing to Eli. There would be no reason for him to remain in contact. Unlike you, David, I was not a good fighter.'

The condemnation in her voice failed to register, but, satisfied with her answer, he stopped studying her and puffed on his cigar, flicking the ash over the railing.

'They still talk about him, you know. Some say he fled Palestine fearing there'd be reprisals over the attack . . .'

He used the term 'attack', she noted, not 'massacre'.

'. . . although that seems a little out of character, don't you think? But whatever the reason, he's deserted us. Perhaps he was never as committed as he pretended to be, perhaps it was all just a game to him.' David snorted contemptuously. 'He's probably hired himself out as a mercenary to whichever cause has offered the highest bid, "Eli Mankowski, the great freedom fighter!"' He painted a sign in the air, relishing his derision of the hero who had abandoned him. 'I don't think he cares who he's fighting or what he's fighting for. Eli just needs to be part of a war . . .'

'I'm going inside,' Ruth said, 'the tea will be ready now.'

It had been a fine funeral, Sarah thought. The service had been conducted with all the dignity befitting a man of Walter Stein's standing and she'd been most gratified by the numbers in attendance. She thanked Rabbi Yeshen as they stood on the steps of the *chevra kadisha*, and then he left her to accept the condolences of those queuing to pay their respects before the family and friends departed for the cemetery.

As the mourners respectfully filed past Sarah and her children, Ruth stood to one side with Moshe. She knew very few of those in attendance and, unaccustomed to social gatherings, was glad to be excluded. Then she saw a couple who seemed familiar. She hadn't noticed them in the crowded funeral parlour, just as they had not noticed her.

'We wish you long life,' they both said to Sarah.

Their backs were to Ruth and she couldn't see their faces, but she knew them just the same, and she recognised the woman's voice.

'We arrived only last week,' the woman was saying, and she was speaking Yiddish, not Hebrew. 'We've been in Switzerland these past years. And yesterday, when we heard the news of Walter's passing, we felt we must come and pay our respects. He was such a fine man.'

'Thank you.' Sarah accepted the tribute graciously. It was good of the Meisells to go to such trouble so soon after their arrival, she thought, and particularly as she'd not seen them in fifteen years. Not since she and Walter had left Berlin shortly before the outbreak of war. 'It's so kind of you to come.'

So the Meisells had survived, Ruth thought, and she felt a surge of pleasure at the sight of her friends from Viktoria-Luise-Platz. Memories of the hardships they'd endured together returned: the furtive meetings she'd had with Sharon, the dangerous excursions they'd made to forage for food, always hiding the Star of David on their coats. She remembered the secret English lessons she'd conducted with their daughter and she looked around the crowd, but Naomi wasn't there. She hoped that Naomi, too, had survived.

She waited until the Meisells had finished paying their respects and, as they walked down the steps towards the street, she excused herself from Moshe and followed them.

'Sharon, Efraim,' she said, 'it's so wonderful to see you.'

She'd never witnessed such amazement. Jaws agape, they stared at her, then at each other, then back to her. It was almost comical, she thought.

'Ruth? Ruth Lachmann?' They had recognised her immediately, but Efraim's statement came out more a question – he was incredulous.

'Yes, that's me.' The sound of the name she'd denied herself all these years was not painful, not from Efraim. From Efraim, it gave her pleasure.

'Ruth!' Sharon hugged her fiercely, then stepped back to survey her again, as if she still couldn't believe her eyes. 'We thought you were dead.'

'Well, that's to be expected,' Ruth said. 'The Lachmanns and the Meisells, we were the last ones left, weren't we?' And as she said it, she remembered the clatter of the Nazis' boots on the stairs, the fist on the door, Samuel holding her close in the darkened kitchen. 'I thought that, in all likelihood, you were dead too, that's why it's so wonderful to see you . . .'

'No, no,' Sharon interrupted, 'I mean that we *knew* you were dead, there was no question about it. We knew you'd been taken away, Mannie too; Naomi saw it all through the front window . . .'

'Naomi's not with you?' This time it was Ruth who interrupted, and Sharon immediately read the concern in her query.

'Naomi is safe,' she reassured her. 'She came to Israel over a year ago, she's working on a kibbutz. She says she likes farming.'

Ruth wondered whether it was Kibbutz Tsafona, and whether indeed young Naomi Meisell was a farmer or a fighter. Somehow she suspected the latter. Naomi had always been a rebellious girl; she recalled how she'd admired her passion.

'Escape is not enough,' Naomi had said, 'we need to fight back.'

As Sharon continued, Ruth's mind remained on Naomi and she wasn't paying full attention.

'. . . And we knew you'd been taken to Auschwitz, the spies at the railway station told Samuel, and then all those years later, after the war . . .'

Samuel? The name broke into her thoughts. *Which Samuel? Samuel who?* She was bewildered as she looked back to Sharon.

'. . . when he was trying to find news of you and he discovered the witnessed report of Mannie's death, he naturally believed, as we all did . . .'

'Who was trying to find me?'

'Samuel.'

Ruth looked at her blankly. *Samuel who?* her mind once again asked.

'She doesn't know, Sharon.' Efraim, who had been silent as the women talked, realised that of course Ruth didn't know. How could she? She was as ignorant of her husband's existence as he was of hers. 'Ruth doesn't know that he's alive.'

'Who's alive?' she asked. Not her Samuel – they were wrong, she'd seen him. She could still see him, lying on the wooden floorboards, the pool of his blood creeping around the leg of the dining room table.

'Samuel is alive, Ruth,' Efraim said. 'The last letter I had from him was in 1949. I still have it. He's living in Australia. In the Snowy Mountains.'

'We're going now, Ruth.' There was a note of censure in Sarah's voice as she appeared by Ruth's side; she very much disapproved of the social chit-chat taking place. She left the rebuke hanging in the air and glided past, followed by her son and daughter, Moshe lingering, waiting to accompany Ruth.

'The Snowy Mountains?' It was not real, Ruth thought, she was in a dream. Samuel was alive? 'I didn't know they had mountains in Australia,' she said vaguely, 'or snow.'

Moshe wasn't sure if he'd heard her correctly, it was such an odd thing to say.

'Time to go, Ruth.' He took her arm, she seemed distracted. 'Please excuse us,' he added politely to the couple.

'Of course,' Sharon replied. 'Are you all right, Ruth?'

'The Snowy Mountains, you say?'

'We really must go,' Moshe said firmly. She appeared reluctant to leave, and he could see Sarah waiting beside the shining black limousine, glaring in their direction. He applied a little pressure to Ruth's arm.

'Yes,' Efraim said. 'A work camp called Spring Hill near a town called Cooma.'

A work camp, Ruth thought, neglecting to say goodbye to the Meisells as she allowed herself to be led away. A work camp, how strange.

'Ruth, what's wrong?' Moshe muttered. She was behaving most oddly.

But she didn't hear him. A work camp called Spring Hill near a town called Cooma, she thought. But the war was over. What was Samuel doing in a work camp?

Chapter Fifteen

'It all sounds a bit dodgy to me,' Maureen said, 'and I'm sure it will to him. I think it might be time to tell him the truth, dear.'

Violet shook her head adamantly.

'You're going to have to some day, Violet. It can't stay a secret forever.'

'Not just yet,' Violet waved a hand airily, not wanting to think about it, 'in the New Year.'

It was Cam they were discussing, and the problem of Christmas. Violet's mother and father expected her to spend the festive season at the property, the Campbell Christmas was always a family affair. But Violet had other plans: she and Pietro were going to Sydney.

'I shall spend Christmas with my husband,' she'd grandly announced. Violet loved saying the word 'husband', and as Maureen was the only person to whom she could say it, she used the term whenever possible.

'He's taking me to Sydney, Auntie Maureen.' She'd dropped the grand manner in her childlike excitement. 'And he's promised we'll stay at the Australia Hotel, and we'll catch a Manly ferry and go to the zoo and do all the things we did last time. It'll be like our honeymoon all over again! And I'll be able to wear my wedding ring.' It irked Violet that she had to keep her wedding ring hidden away in the drawer of her bedside table. 'And everyone will know I'm married to the handsomest man in the world.'

'And what will you tell your mum and dad?' Maureen had expected her question to bring Violet crashing back to earth, but it hadn't.

'I'll tell them that Trish from the store won a magazine competition and the prize was a trip for two to Sydney.'

'What if they check with Trish?'

'They can't. She's got three whole weeks off – her grandma's dying in Adelaide.' There had been a triumphant ring to Violet's voice. 'She left yesterday and she won't be back until the New Year.'

'A magazine competition?' Maureen had been highly dubious, and that was when she'd said it all sounded a bit dodgy.

Violet, however, remained unfazed. 'They have them, you know, competitions like that, in magazines, I've seen them.'

'Well, you'd better get your facts right, is all I can say.'

Apparently Violet did. She went home for her brother's birthday the following Sunday, told her parents of her plans, and upon her return, announced to her aunt that it was all sorted out.

'And he fell for it, your dad?' Maureen asked in amazement.

'Not at first. He wanted to know all about the competition, who was running it, what magazine and all that.'

'So what did you do?' She couldn't help it, she was fascinated.

'I showed him that.' Violet dumped a copy of *The Women's Weekly* on the kitchen table. 'Short Story Competition' it said on the cover. 'Win a trip for two to Sydney'. 'That's what gave me the idea in the first place,' she admitted.

'Good heavens above.'

'Dad got really snaky,' Violet continued. 'He said I was letting down the family and I was too young to go to Sydney, and then Mum jumped in. She said the family could live without me for Christmas and I was nearly nineteen years old and it was the chance of a lifetime. All downhill after that.' She laughed, obviously suffering no pangs of conscience.

'What a clever little liar you've become,' Maureen remarked, a mixture of admiration and censure.

'I know,' Violet said with great pride. 'I should have been an actress.'

Pietro hadn't been able to get a suite at the Australia Hotel. He'd tried to book the same one as last time, he told her, but there were no suites left. Christmas was a very busy time, they'd said when he'd telephoned, and he was lucky to get the last room available. It was a pleasant room, they'd told him, on the third floor, and it looked out over Martin Place.

'I am sorry, Violetta,' he said as she peered from the window enthralled.

'I don't mind, it's cosier. Crikey, Pietro, just look at all the people!'

As he'd promised, they caught a Manly ferry and visited the zoo and The Rocks, where this time he bought her a pretty silk scarf. They did everything they'd done on their previous visit – Violet was obviously a creature of habit when it came to Sydney – and her energy was boundless.

Upon their return to the hotel, Pietro felt unnaturally tired and his head was aching, but he said nothing to Violet, not wanting to spoil things for her.

'We shall have room service?' he suggested hopefully; he didn't relish the thought of dining in the restaurant.

'Of course.' To Violet it was a foregone conclusion: 'Toasted sandwiches, lots and lots of them, and chocolate milkshakes.'

They showered together and she wriggled sensually as he soaped her body, giggling at the effect she knew she was having on him. They towelled each other dry, and by the time they reached the bed Pietro's lethargy was forgotten.

After they'd made love, she dozed off in his arms, and Pietro, whose head was once again throbbing, felt himself drift thankfully into a deep slumber.

Violet, her energy finally depleted, slept more soundly than she'd expected, and it was pitch dark when she awoke. She sat up startled, wondering what it was that had awoken her so abruptly and, for a moment, wondering where she was. Then she heard it again and realised it was his call that had awakened her.

'Pietro . . .' And a second or so later, 'Pietro . . .'

She was in the hotel room and, in the bed beside her, Pietro was calling out his own name. But it didn't sound like him.

'Pietro . . .' He called out again. 'Pietro . . .'

It was as if someone was calling *to* him, she thought. Someone else. From far away. The sound was rhythmic, repetitive, the way a person might call for a lost dog.

She leaned over to look at him – he'd rolled away from her in sleep. Was he having a nightmare?

Violet didn't know what to do. He'd never talked in his sleep before. But then this was only the third weekend they'd spent together in the few months of their marriage; perhaps he often talked in his sleep. Should she wake him or not?

'Pietro . . .' The call again, not loud, but unsettling. 'Pietro . . .'

Well, she certainly wouldn't be able to sleep with that going on all night, she thought. Besides, it was time to order the toasted sandwiches.

She jumped out of bed and turned on the light.

'Pietro, wake up,' she said, shaking him by the shoulder,

not too roughly, but firmly enough. Then she jumped back, startled, as he sat bolt upright, staring ahead, apparently not seeing her.

'I'm sorry, sweetie,' she said soothingly. He was alarmed and she regretted having woken him so brutally. 'You were having a nightmare.'

It was Violetta, he realised. He'd wondered what had happened and where he was. He looked blinkingly around the room, the light seemed dazzling.

'Was I?'

'Yes. You were talking in your sleep, yelling out your name.'

'My name?'

'Well, not yelling really. Calling. You were calling out "Pietro", over and over.'

He could hear it now, the voice that used to come to him sometimes after a seizure. 'Pietro! Pietro!' But it hadn't been him. Someone else had been calling his name. Then he saw the shiny shoes standing on the wooden steps. Nothing else. Just the shoes and the steps, and he heard a man's voice calling his name. But it wasn't a nightmare, he thought. It was a memory.

His headache was still with him, and he put his fingers to his temples trying to ease it away.

'Violetta,' he said excitedly, 'there is something I remember.'

True to her promise, Violet had tried to help him recall the past. She'd talked of her childhood, encouraging him to think of his, hoping it might trigger some memory. Once when she'd talked about her first pony and her love of riding, he'd thought that he could remember a wooden horse. 'No, no, a wooden donkey,' he'd corrected himself.

Violet had considered it a breakthrough. 'Like a rocking horse,' she'd said. 'And a rocking horse would be inside a house, Pietro. Try to think of the house.'

But it hadn't worked. If anything her encouragement

had had an adverse effect. The memory of the wooden donkey had disappeared, and only the goats remained.

Violet was now once again on a mission.

'What do you remember, Pietro? Tell me everything, quickly, before it goes away.'

He told her about the shoes and the wooden steps. A man's shoes, he said, standing on the steps, and a man's voice calling his name.

'Wooden steps,' she said. 'That's a house – try to remember the house.' If he could remember the house, Violet thought, then he might remember his parents, or his brothers and sisters, and everything else that went on inside a house. A house was a home – it meant family.

'Wooden steps leading where?' she asked. 'A front door? A back door?'

He kept rubbing his temples, trying to ease away the pain; if the ache in his head went, then perhaps he would remember. But all he could see was the light through the steps and the man's shoes as they stood there.

'I am beneath the house,' he said. 'I cannot see the door.'

'It's a cubby,' Violet said excitedly. As a child he'd had a cubby under the house, just like she had, she thought. 'Come out of the cubby and walk up the steps,' she urged, but he didn't seem to hear her.

'I see floorboards above me,' he said, 'and light.' He concentrated hard on the gaps in the floorboards and, through them, he thought that he could see feet. He was about to tell Violetta, but he stopped, horrified as his body started to tremble and he felt the familiar flicker of his left eye.

'Go on,' Violet urged.

His heart was pounding, he was overcome with dread. That Violetta should see him! Did he have time to get away? Perhaps he could lock himself in the bathroom. He tried to remain calm; the more agitated he became, the quicker the seizure would be upon him. He climbed out of the bed; he was shaking now, and beads of sweat had formed on his brow. He ferreted through the pockets of his jacket slung over a chair and found the piece of leather strap.

'Pietro, what is it? What's wrong?' She was alarmed.

He fell, his body already beyond his control – there was no time to get away.

She screamed and knelt beside him, then grabbed at her clothes on the chair, prepared to run for help. But he stopped her.

'No, Violetta,' he said, through teeth already chattering. 'Stay with me.' Resigned to the awful fact that she would witness his fit, he was determined that no-one else must see him. 'Do not be frightened, it will not last long.' And, as his jaw started to clench, he placed the leather strap between his teeth.

Pietro was right; the seizure did not last long, but to Violet it went on forever. Naked and helpless, she hugged her knees to her chest, drawing herself into a ball, rocking backwards and forwards and sobbing hysterically as she watched the violent convulsions of her husband's body, convinced that Pietro was dying.

When it was over and she realised that he wasn't dead, she tried to pull herself together. She must do something. She fetched a wet flannel from the bathroom and, cradling him to her, she wiped away the sweat and spittle from his face.

'I'm here, Pietro,' she whispered, tears coursing down her cheeks, 'I'm here.'

Someone soft and gentle was holding him, whispering words of comfort, and for a moment Pietro thought it was Sister Anna Maria. But the words were in English and Sister Anna Maria did not speak English. Then, as the world slowly came back into focus, he realised it was Violetta, and she was crying.

'Sssh.' He tried to sit up, to wipe away her tears, but his

energy was sapped and he lay back exhausted. 'A moment,' he said, 'a moment and I will be all right, you will see.'

'Oh Pietro.' She was openly sobbing again, overcome with relief. 'I thought you were dying.'

'Sssh . . . sssh . . .' He held her hand.

They remained where they were for several minutes, naked, vulnerable, each fighting to regain control. When her sobbing had stopped and when Pietro felt he was strong enough, she helped him to his feet and they sat on the bed, hugging the coverlet about them.

He told her about his illness, the fits he'd had as a child at the convent and the diagnosis of his epilepsy.

'Is that why you can't remember?' she asked.

'Perhaps it is the epilepsy. I do not know.'

She was riddled with guilt: she had prompted the attack by trying to help him recall his past. But when she said as much, he vehemently protested.

'No, no, Violetta, is good I remember. I wish to remember.' He did, since he'd met Violetta, he desperately wished to know about his childhood and who he had once been. 'Is good that you help me.'

She looked unconvinced – his epilepsy frightened her – but Pietro was insistent. His fits were rare now, he told her, he'd had only one attack since he'd been in Australia, and after the doctor had given him pills, he'd had not even a warning sign.

'And so I stop taking these pills,' he said. 'I no longer need . . .'

'Then that's why you had the attack,' she said, a mixture of accusation and relief.

'I do not know,' he answered.

'Well, of course it is, Pietro. It was bloody stupid to stop taking the pills.'

She sounded cross. More cross than he had ever heard her sound, and Pietro felt wretched. He was profoundly sorry that he had not spoken of his illness – he should have told her from the very beginning, he admitted.

'But you see, Violetta,' he protested, anxious for her to believe him, 'I think that I am better. I have no fit for a long time. It is not like before. I think to myself that it is past. And it will be. I promise. You will see.'

She looked at him shrewdly. 'You thought I wouldn't marry you if I knew, didn't you?'

'Yes,' he said, shamefaced.

'Well, I would have. I love you, Pietro. For better or for worse and till death do us part, for ever and ever, I love you.' It wasn't a scene from a film and she didn't think of Bette Davis; Violet was in deadly earnest, and the dialogue was all her own. 'But you should've told me, just the same,' she added.

'I am sorry, Violetta.'

She kissed him. 'As soon as we get back to Cooma,' she said, 'we're taking you to the doctor.' Then she added, concerned, 'You don't look too good. How do you feel?'

'I feel hungry,' he replied. He didn't – he felt as if he'd been run over by a truck and his head was still aching – but it didn't matter. She loved him, and he was happy. 'I feel like toasted sandwiches,' he said.

'Ah, Pietro, a long overdue visit.' Maarten Vanpoucke smiled a welcome as he went to show the boy into the consulting room; it was his last consultation of the day and he'd told his receptionist to go home after she'd let him know Mr Toscanini had arrived for his appointment. Then he noticed Violet as she rose from her chair. 'And you must be Pietro's young lady; Lucky's told me all about you.'

Pietro and Violet shared a quick look – there were some things Lucky hadn't told his friend the doctor, as they'd known Lucky wouldn't.

'Is all right if Violetta come in with me?' Pietro asked.

'Of course, if that is what you wish . . .'

'Yes, please.'

'Violet, isn't it?' Maarten asked. He'd seen her in Halli-days shop from time to time, a pretty little thing. 'How do you do, I'm Doctor Vanpoucke.'

'How do you do, Doctor.' Violet was disappointed that he didn't offer his hand. She knew he was European, although he didn't really sound it, and European men shook hands with women. She would have initiated the handshake herself, but he was a doctor and she wasn't sure if it was quite right. 'I've seen you at the store,' she said as he ushered them into his consulting room. She was disappointed, too, that he hadn't mentioned the fact himself – she'd served him many times. 'I work at Hallidays.'

'That's right, of course you do,' he smiled.

Gratified, Violet returned the smile. He was quite good-looking, she thought, for an old bloke anyway; he had to be over forty.

'And you know my aunt too; she works at the hospital.'

'Oh yes?' He gestured at the chairs and they sat.

'Maureen Campbell,' Violet said proudly, 'she's my auntie.'

'A fine woman,' Maarten said.

A bossy woman, he recalled. He didn't know Maureen Campbell well, just as he didn't know any of the locals well – it was the way he preferred it. But he remembered how, not so very long ago when there had been a severe shortage of doctors in Cooma, she had politely suggested he might give more time to the hospital than he did. Equally politely, he'd put her in her place, informing her that, as he had chosen an early semi-retirement, he preferred to work his own hours. He'd been aware of her criticism but he hadn't cared. There would always be a shortage of doctors in Cooma and he would always live according to the way he wished, regardless of the opinions of women like Maureen Campbell who devoted their every waking hour to the hospital because they had little else in their lives.

'A fine woman and a fine nurse.' He sat behind his desk and opened Pietro's medical file.

Violet flashed Pietro an I-told-you-so look – she'd known that Doctor Vanpoucke would be impressed. 'Auntie Maureen practically runs the hospital, Pietro,' she'd said, 'and it helps to have friends in high places.' She'd heard the phrase somewhere and she'd relished the ring of it.

When Violet had announced she was coming with him to the doctor, Pietro had at first been reluctant. There were no longer any secrets between them, but he wasn't sure how he would feel about discussing his illness in front of her.

'But we're married now, sweetie,' she'd gently reminded him, 'and your problems are mine.' Pietro had changed his tune in an instant. He'd never had anyone to share his problems with before. Now he had Violetta.

'So, Pietro,' Maarten said, 'you're long overdue for a new prescription. I presume you've been lax with your medication.'

Pietro nodded guiltily, and Violet answered for him.

'That's why we're here, doctor,' she said. 'He had a fit the other day and I bet it's because he hadn't been taking his pills.'

'It is possible, but not necessarily the case,' Maarten replied shortly; he'd have preferred it if the girl had allowed Pietro to answer. 'How long is it since you stopped taking the Dilantin?' he asked.

'Three months.'

'And have you recently suffered any headaches or lethargy?'

The doctor was writing it down and Pietro wanted to get the facts right. He understood 'headaches', but he wasn't quite sure about the next word and he hesitated.

'Have you felt tired lately?' Maarten's pen remained poised.

'Yes, a little, and I have some headache.'

'There, you see,' Violet said triumphantly as the doctor returned to his notes. 'It's because you weren't taking your pills, I told you, that's why you had the fit.'

'I doubt it.' Maarten's response was icy. 'Not taking the pills may have contributed to the fatigue, but I doubt it was the cause of the attack.' The girl was as vacuous as she was pretty, he thought. 'Tell me about the seizure, Pietro.'

'I am sleeping . . .' Pietro paused, giving the doctor time to make his notes.

'So the attack occurred while you were asleep?'

'No, no, I am awake, I know that it will happen. Always I am awake, and always I know that it will happen.'

'You had the same warning signs then? As you've had in the past?'

'Yes, I know it is coming. I have a dream and . . .' Pietro stopped himself just in time. He couldn't say 'and Violetta woke me' as he'd been about to. The doctor would know they were sleeping together and that was not right – the doctor did not know they were married and he would judge Violetta. '. . . and when I wake, I remember this dream.' He paused again, trying to be meticulous in his recollection, he must tell the doctor every single thing he remembered.

'And it was your dream that brought on the seizure?' Maarten prompted.

'No, no.' The doctor had misunderstood, Pietro realised. 'I am happy with the dream, because it is of the past. It is real. I feel good that there is something I remember.'

So the boy's past was coming back to him, Maarten thought. How very interesting, particularly under the circumstances.

'And what is it you remember, Pietro?'

'I remember shoes. Man's shoes. They are standing on steps, and the light is shining through the steps where I can see them. And I can hear a man's voice calling my name.'

The doctor nodded encouragement, and Pietro was pleased.

'I am beneath the house,' he said, 'I can see the floorboards above me.'

The boy had been hiding under the house.

'I think that perhaps I am in a . . .' Pietro couldn't remember Violet's word for it, and he looked to her for assistance.

'A cubby.' Violet dived in, thrilled to be of assistance. 'Pietro had a cubby under the house as a child, and I told him he should walk up the steps to the door. I said if he could see inside the house, he might remember, but that's when he had the fit.'

See inside the house. Is that what the boy did?

'So you were with him at the time of the seizure?' the doctor asked, and Violet froze, realising that she'd given herself away.

The girl had suddenly become important, and Maarten seized upon the moment. 'Tell me about the attack,' he said. 'Come along, Violet, there's a good girl.' Good God, she was going coy – what the hell did it matter if she was sleeping with the boy? 'Tell me everything that happened. It will be very helpful, believe me.'

Violet realised that Pietro was about to jump to her defence and she stopped him with a shake of her head. Embarrassed and caught out as she was, she had no intention of telling the doctor that she and Pietro were married. Until their announcement to her parents, their marriage would remain a secret.

'What do you want to know?' She looked squarely at Doctor Vanpoucke.

'You said the fit occurred when you were encouraging him to recall the past, to enter the house, is that right?'

'Oh.' Violet felt dreadful. So the doctor thought it was she who had brought about the attack. 'I didn't mean to do anything wrong,' she said. 'Pietro and I often talk about the past . . .'

'Yes, yes,' Pietro agreed, not liking to see Violetta upset. 'I wish to remember . . .'

'But that was before I knew about the epilepsy . . .' Violet was becoming agitated. 'I didn't mean to . . .'

'Calm down, my dear,' Maarten said soothingly, 'you meant well and it was very caring of you to try to help Pietro remember.'

It might even have been medically helpful, Maarten thought. It was possible Pietro's fits were not epileptic at all, but pseudo seizures brought about by his repression of the past. Freud himself would argue that the boy's trauma should be revealed to him. It was certainly a fascinating case.

'You have nothing to feel guilty about, I assure you.'

The doctor's bedside manner was well-practised and Violet felt herself relax.

'So tell me,' Maarten said, his full focus now upon the girl, 'what was Pietro's reaction to the discussion of his past? I am most interested.'

'It all started with the goats.' Violet, vindicated, enjoyed the doctor's attention. 'Pietro remembered his favourite goat Rosa and how he'd delivered her baby. Didn't you, Pietro?'

Pietro nodded. 'Yes, I remember Rosa, and how I help her with her baby.'

The boy had recalled more than the shoes and the steps.

'What else did you remember, Pietro?' the doctor asked, but it was Violet who answered.

'For a little while he remembered a wooden donkey, and I told him that something like that would be inside a house. But when I told him to try to see inside the house, he couldn't remember the donkey any more. Isn't that right, Pietro?'

Maarten interrupted before she could continue; the girl was annoying him again.

'So you recalled your goat Rosa and her baby, and, at one stage, a wooden donkey. Was there anything else?'

The boy shook his head. 'No, that is all I remember.'

'And at the time these memories returned, you had no warning signs and no fit?'

'No.' Pietro smiled gratefully at Violet. 'Violetta, she help me to remember. Is good, yes?'

'Perhaps.' The girl was not altogether as silly as she appeared, Maarten thought, the boy's past was returning. But she was treading on dangerous ground.

'Let's get back to the recent seizure, shall we?' he asked, returning his attention to the girl. 'Pietro was lucid before the attack? He warned you that it was going to happen?'

Violet nodded. 'He told me not to be frightened, and he put a piece of leather between his teeth . . .'

Maarten waited for her to continue.

'He said it wouldn't take long, but it went on forever and I didn't know what to do. It was awful . . .'

'Yes, yes,' he tried to curb his impatience, 'it is not a pleasant thing to witness –'

'I thought he was dying, honest I did.'

'Of course, most understandable. Now, Violet,' he said, 'without upsetting yourself, I'd like you to tell me everything you witnessed, before, during, and after the seizure.'

He proceeded to ask her specific questions, and Violet answered in detail. Responding to his queries, she described the particular movements Pietro had made during his attack, and she confirmed that when it was over he had been lucid.

'He told me about the epilepsy,' she said, 'he'd never talked about it before, and then when he said that he'd stopped taking the pills,' she looked accusingly at Pietro, 'well, that's when I knew . . .'

'Yes, yes.' Maarten wasn't at all interested in her opinion. 'And during the actual seizure, did you try to converse with him?'

'No.' Violet was amazed. 'You mean that I could have? I could have talked to him, and he could have answered?'

'It is perhaps possible.'

Maarten had become more intrigued by the minute, and increasingly of the opinion that Pietro's fits were not epileptic. The boy had said they never occurred during sleep, that he always had warning beforehand, and the girl had said that he was lucid immediately afterwards. Even Violet's descriptions of the movements he made during the attack were in keeping with a pseudo-epileptic seizure. It was impossible to be sure, of course, Maarten thought, but the trauma of the boy's background strongly indicated it. How interesting it would be, he pondered, to induce a seizure here and now; Freud would certainly recommend it.

Maarten was an avid believer in Freud's methods and, had it been any other case, he would have considered such action. But under the circumstances, he'd be flirting with danger. A pity – the results might have been quite thrilling.

'Now, Pietro, I think we'll continue with your medication,' he said, taking his prescription pad from the top drawer of his desk.

Violet's eyes widened in surprise. Surely there was no question about it: Pietro had had his fit because he hadn't taken his pills.

'And if at any time you decide, of your own volition, to cease your medication,' Maarten stopped scribbling and looked up, 'then you will do so gradually. If you stop taking your medication abruptly, you will get headaches and feel tired. Do you understand me?'

The doctor's horn-rimmed spectacles had slid down his nose and, as he peered over the rims, his eyes were stern and admonishing.

'Yes, I understand,' Pietro said apologetically, averting his eyes from the doctor's and wishing the doctor would look away.

'Good lad.' Maarten smiled approvingly at the boy. If

his diagnosis was correct, there was no need for anti-
epileptic medication, but as he couldn't be sure, it was
wisest to prescribe it. That's what made the boy's case so
intriguing, he thought, tearing the script from the pad.
Pietro actually *wanted* to recall his past, regardless of what
he might discover. Most unusual. Those suffering pseudo
seizures were usually looking for attention or an avenue of
escape, and the boy was seeking neither. He was a perfect
subject for psychoanalysis.

As the doctor rose and circled his desk, Pietro and Violet
quickly sprang to their feet.

Maarten gave the prescription to Pietro and shook his
hand briefly. 'Good to see you, Pietro.' It was best for all
concerned, he thought, that the boy be kept in ignorance
and continue to believe that his fits were epileptic in origin.
'You too, Violet. Give my regards to your aunt,' and he
ushered the young couple quickly out of the surgery door,
Violet a little offended that the doctor hadn't shaken her
hand too, particularly as she'd been so helpful.

Maarten returned to his desk and watched the couple
through the bay windows as they walked down Vale
Street, hand in hand.

So the boy had been under the house.

He pictured the squat hut, several narrow wooden steps
leading up to the door. He'd never thought to look under
the house; there hadn't been space enough there for the
boy to hide. And all the while he'd called the child's name,
the boy had been watching his shoes on the steps.

He felt no threat that Pietro had re-entered his life – on
the contrary, he found it a fascinating situation. The
moment Lucky had told him about the young man named
Pietro who'd had a seizure and had placed a strip of
leather between his teeth, he'd wondered at the coincidence. He'd seen the boy alone in his consulting rooms
just in case, although he knew that, even if it were the
same boy, Pietro would not recognise him. He'd made sure

that no-one recognised him these days – and he himself
had not recognised the child in the young man. But he had
recognised the leather strap.

'*If you feel an attack coming upon you when you are
alone, Pietro, this is what you must place in your mouth,
do you understand?*'

He remembered the very words he'd said as he'd given
it to the child. The leather had not been worn then, it had
been shiny and new, cut from the reins of the wooden
donkey that stood in the corner of the room. He'd used the
killing knife which the peasant father had fetched from the
drawer of the bench where the mother prepared the food.

How extraordinary, he'd thought as he'd looked at the
scarred leather.

It was interesting now to consider that perhaps his diagnosis of the child may not have been fully correct.

'*He suffers from a condition which will likely remain
with him until adulthood, and possibly for the rest of his
life.*'

That was what he'd told the peasant couple and he'd
believed it at the time – the boy had appeared a classic
case. But Pietro's childhood epilepsy may well be a thing of
the past, he thought. The aberrant firing of the brainwaves
may have ceased and the boy's seizures could now be
psychologically-triggered. Particularly if he'd been traumatised by the sight of his murdered family, which it seemed
he had. He must have entered the house.

A most intriguing case – so little was known about
pseudo epilepsy, he would have loved to investigate
further. If only he were not so personally involved.

He cleared away his papers and rose from his desk. It
was remarkable how the past continued to catch up with
him in this remote outpost, he thought as he locked his
consulting rooms and walked upstairs.

In the lounge room, he poured himself a large Scotch and
topped it up with a finger of water. The irony of his situation

amused him. Over recent years he'd become surrounded
by his past – who would have believed it possible? He'd
escaped from the world which would condemn him, and
had exiled himself to one of the farthest regions on the
globe, the Snowy Mountains of Australia, but the world
had followed him.

How could he have known when he'd arrived in the
backwater of Cooma in 1948, that barely a year later
Europe would be on his doorstep? Now, at the end of
1954, the Snowies and the Monaro were populated by
more Europeans than Australians. And among the hordes
of migrants were refugees from displaced persons' camps
and Holocaust survivors, some quite possibly bearing the
brand of Auschwitz on their wrist.

He'd felt threatened to start with and he had kept to
himself, rarely working at the hospital, being selective
with his patients, mingling very little, and had wondered
whether perhaps he should leave the area. But the prospect
of once again being on the run like a common criminal
had angered him. Why should he run? He'd made a home
for himself here and he liked it in Cooma. Besides, the
surgery he'd undergone in Buenos Aires had made him
unrecognisable as the man he'd once been. And in Cooma
he blended with the potpourri of nationalities far more
than he would elsewhere in Australia where foreigners
were regarded with suspicion at worst and fascination at
least.

His reasoning had proved correct. The very European
element that he'd initially feared had become his protection, and he defied them now, every single one of them.
When he saw a face in the street which he thought vaguely
familiar, as he occasionally did, he no longer felt threatened. Those who were not looking, he thought, tended not
to see. And why would they look anyway? What would
they wish to see? They didn't want reminders of their
nightmares – they wanted a new life. It was ironic, he

thought, that of all the places he could have chosen to hide, here was where he was safest.

The door opened and a tantalising aroma wafted in from the kitchen.

'Dinner in one hour, Doctor?' the housekeeper asked.

'Thank you, Mrs Hodgeman.' He sniffed the air appreciatively. 'A stew. Lamb shanks, I take it?' They were his absolute favourite – the one Australian specialty of hers he'd insisted she keep on the menu.

'Yes, sir. And a sherry trifle for sweets.'

'Excellent.'

As she closed the door behind her, he returned to his thoughts. The boy was a wild card, to be sure, but he was the least threat of all. Even if Pietro were to regain his memory, he would not recognise him. The boy was a freak coincidence, nothing more. Pietro had no links with the death camps. The boy and his family had merely been in the avenue of his escape. Most opportunely, as it had turned out.

He drained the glass and crossed to the dresser. How extraordinary that Lucky had proved such a catalyst, he thought, pouring himself another Scotch. His friendship with the man had always been risky and perhaps he should have exercised more caution – Lucky was a Jew, with friends who were possibly Jewish. But he'd taken care never to socialise publicly with the man, to always keep their relationship within the confines of his home, forgiving Lucky the accident of his birth in exchange for the stimulation of his mind and his expertise at chess. And now Lucky, the one person to whom he had opened his home, had brought the boy back into his life. And he'd brought *her* too. Or at least the memory of her. Most extraordinary.

Lucky had told him several years ago that his wife had died at Auschwitz, and he'd wondered briefly whether he might have known the woman; the thought had been dangerously amusing. He'd made the appropriate sympathetic comments and the subject had not been mentioned again. He'd never thought for one moment that the woman might be Ruth.

He downed half the Scotch in two swift gulps – he'd been drinking more heavily of late. He had thought that he'd eradicated Ruth from his mind, but clearly he hadn't. Just one glimpse of her and his obsession had returned. Since the night he'd seen the photograph, he hadn't stopped thinking about her. And as she had flooded his mind daily, she had brought with her the past.

Chapter Sixteen

Klaus Henkel was born to serve in the Waffen SS, the elite fighting arm of the Schutzstaffel. The Waffen SS comprised the most fanatical adherents to the Führer's divine purpose – the preservation and protection of the German race – and its members were instructed to flout the rules of war: their motto, 'Give death and take death', was a licence to commit atrocities. Young Klaus Henkel couldn't have been better qualified, both to serve the cause and to employ the methods of the Waffen SS: he fervently believed in Aryan superiority and he enjoyed the licence to kill.

While serving, he found himself happily reunited with his good friend Beppo, and just as they had competed during their early university days, so they competed in the field of battle. In accordance with the motto of the Waffen SS, Klaus and Beppo gave death ruthlessly and risked it with a careless courage. Both were wounded in the course of their respective duties and were unable to return to combat. Klaus was bayoneted in the back and his lung punctured, an injury which he was assured would leave him with no permanent damage, but his recovery would take some time. Deskbound during his recuperation, he was frustrated in his desire to return to the front.

Both Klaus and Beppo were decorated for their conduct in battle. While stationed on the Ukrainian front, Beppo was awarded the Iron Cross Second Class, then, following his second campaign, the Iron Cross First Class. Klaus received the Iron Cross Second Class following his service deep behind Soviet lines, and both men received the Black Badge for the Wounded and the Medal for the Care of the German People.

It pleased Klaus that his life so paralleled that of his good friend Beppo, a man two years his senior, and the common zeal with which they had embraced the party during their student days in Munich remained their bond throughout their service.

Born and raised in the North Rhine near the Dutch border, the only child of middle-class parents – his father German and his mother Italian – Klaus Werner Henkel had been a highly intelligent child. From an early age, he'd spoken fluent German, Italian and Dutch, his precocity encouraged by his socialite mother who'd enjoyed showing off her 'child prodigy', as she'd called him. His father, Gustav, a doctor, had been a remote figure in his early life, leaving the rearing of his son to the wife upon whom he doted, and Klaus had rarely mingled with children his own age. His cosseted upbringing, however, had caused problems when he'd first attended school. Accustomed as he was to the company of adults, he had considered himself superior to his peers, and as a result he'd suffered at the hands of bullies. It had been then that Gustav had taken over his son's education. A hard man and a strict disciplinarian, he had instilled in the boy the desire for perfection in all areas, from the playing fields to the classroom.

'Be the strongest and the best at whatever you do, Klaus,' he'd said. 'When you are the strongest and the best, no-one can bully you.'

In his drive to earn the approval of his previously distant father, Klaus had been a diligent student, outshining his classmates both athletically and academically.

Gustav's advice had proved correct: Klaus had no longer been bothered by bullies, but his success had not earned him the popularity he expected. The others were in awe of him – they feared him, and Klaus had discovered that he liked it that way. He enjoyed instilling fear, it gave him a sense of power. He was different from the others.

In 1930, shortly before his eighteenth birthday, he had passed his Abitur with outstanding honours and had been awarded a scholarship to study medicine, majoring in psychology, at the University of Munich. It was there that he'd met his good friend and fellow student, Josef 'Beppo' Mengele who, at that time, was studying philosophy prior to turning his sights towards medical science. And it was there, in Munich, the capital of Bavaria and the heart of the growing National Socialist Movement, that the two had become inspired by the political revolutionary, Adolf Hitler. Intoxicated by Hitler's frenzied speeches and his visions of a new German Empire populated by a German super-race, the two young students, Henkel and Mengele, had joined the nationalistic organisation known as Stahlhelm, or Steel Helmets, and had cemented their common devotion to the cause of the future Führer of Nazi Germany.

Following his active service with the Waffen SS, Klaus lost touch with Beppo as he impatiently bided his time until he was deemed fit enough to return to battle. Then he received a proposal that changed his mind altogether. Notification arrived from the Race and Resettlement Office in Berlin that, at the request of his friend and mentor Captain Josef Mengele, a position was on offer. Klaus informed them he was delighted to accept.

It was early 1942 and a new policy, Endlösung, had been introduced. 'The Final Solution' had been formalised in Berlin by the upper echelons of the Nazi hierarchy: the plan to construct vast concentration camps across Europe. These camps, Klaus was informed, would hold untold opportunities for dedicated Nazis committed to the cause.

Within a year of his posting to Berlin, Klaus was asked by his friend Beppo to join him as his assistant on a new assignment and, in May of 1943, Doctors Josef Mengele and Klaus Henkel, in their respective ranks of Captain and Lieutenant, departed for the Nazi concentration camp at Oswiecim, recently renamed Auschwitz, in Poland.

The death factory that was Auschwitz-Birkenau offered unlimited medical opportunities to Mengele, whose mission was to perform research on human genetics. His goal was to unlock the secrets of genetic engineering, and to devise methods of eradicating inferior gene strands from the human population as a means of creating a Germanic super-race.

Klaus, as Beppo's assistant, found the work inspiring, but his own interest lay in the opportunity for psychological study which had never before been available to medical science. Here at Auschwitz, human beings replaced guinea pigs and rats and monkeys, and the frustrating, futile experiments previously performed upon animals now resulted in conclusive evidence. For the first time, Klaus was able to examine the human threshold of pain, marvelling at how it varied so vastly from subject to subject. He could observe the effects of torture and learn to pinpoint the fine line where the majority would succumb to madness. Interestingly, the findings were not finite – there was always the subject whose mind seemed capable of retaining its sanity until death finally claimed it. And, above all, he could observe on a daily basis the varying survival instincts of those existing in conditions of such deprivation it was difficult to comprehend both their ability and their will to live. The human mind was a source of inestimable wonder to Klaus Henkel.

Of equal satisfaction to him was the efficiency of the entire exercise. To be cleansing Germany of its racial impurities while also advancing medical science on all levels was in his opinion an extremely tidy and effective arrangement.

Surrounded by double rows of electrified fences, the vast complex of Auschwitz-Birkenau was the size of a small city. In the concentration and labour camp of Auschwitz were endless rows of wooden barracks, each of which housed up to a thousand inmates, hundreds of thousands in all, and in the adjoining extermination camp of Birkenau were the gas chambers and the huge furnaces whose chimneys relentlessly belched smoke. The railway line divided the camps, and trains arrived daily through the towering entrance arch into the confines of Auschwitz-Birkenau. The selection procedure was simple: the new arrivals were herded from the cattle trucks and up the wooden ramp to where Josef Mengele, who had personally undertaken the task of selection, would indicate Birkenau to the right or Auschwitz to the left. Between seventy to ninety percent of new arrivals were directed to the right, where they would be ordered to strip in preparation for their de-lousing shower – the shower in actuality a gas chamber. It was an uncomplicated and economical process, and one which Mengele enjoyed.

Klaus embraced his new life at Auschwitz, although it was some time before he could acclimatise himself to the rancid stench that suffused the place. He never did quite manage to get it out of his nostrils. It got into his clothes too, and into the very pores of his skin. But it was a small price to pay, when all was said and done. He was serving his Führer and ensuring the future of a superior Germany – he could learn to live with an unpleasant smell. Besides, his officer's quarters were excellent, and there was the companionship of his good friend Beppo.

He was thankful for the stimulation of Beppo's company and their mutual interests, for he had little in common

with the other Nazi soldiers. Most seemed to be louts with
no breeding or, worse still, men with no stomach for the
job at hand. Klaus had serious doubts about the commitment of some who made a habit of getting drunk or taking
drugs when rostered on train-arrival duties. The selection
process and its accompanying culling of babies and infants
obviously upset them. Klaus himself did not altogether
approve of Mengele's summary execution of children so
immediately upon arrival; it was messy, he thought. If
mothers were lulled into a sense of security, it would be
far more orderly in the long run. However, orders were
orders, and he had his eye on those soldiers who didn't
have the stomach for their duty – some would certainly
have to go.

Of course there was the other extreme: the thugs who
liked to show off, bashing unnecessarily, shooting indiscriminately. It was not an efficient way to go about things
– it caused panic. When applying oneself to a task, Klaus
thought, there was no need to show off.

It was an area of criticism which, strangely enough, he
applied also to Beppo. In Klaus's opinion, Beppo had a
tendency to strut his self-importance during the selection
process. Standing at the head of the ramp in his shiny
boots and his immaculate black uniform, buckles and
badges gleaming, Beppo was clearly intent upon creating
an image. White-gloved and brandishing his riding crop
like a conductor's baton, he would whistle while he
directed the traffic. And he would always wear his medals.
Klaus, who was invariably present during the selection
process, never wore his, and he found it rather ostentatious of Beppo to do so.

But then Beppo had always been vain, he reminded himself. Even in their university days Beppo had been obsessed
with clothes and appearances. They'd joked about it.

'Clothes do not make the man, Beppo,' he would say.

'Nor does the body, Klaus.' Beppo's response was

always lightning fast and his laugh triumphant. 'You are far more vain than I.'

It had been true, Klaus had to admit. He hadn't seen it as vanity at the time, but perhaps Beppo had been right. He was proud of his body and he kept it honed to perfection. His body was his temple. Well, if that was vanity, he thought, then so be it – his body served him well.

They'd both been attractive to women. Beppo, the slim, dapper young man, tawny-skinned and with the dark eyes of a Latin film star, and Klaus, the Aryan with his sandy hair, blue eyes and athlete's body.

Beppo's charm had usually won out with the women, and Klaus had always given in with good grace; he had no desire to compete with his friend over something so trivial. Women meant nothing more to him than sex, and he'd been willing to relinquish any claim and move on to the next – there was always another waiting.

There had been one time, however, which he remembered clearly. The time when he had felt a particularly strong lust for a girl and had decided that she was not Beppo's, but his. He had told Beppo so.

'She is mine tonight,' he'd said. 'You can have her tomorrow.'

And Beppo had acquiesced without a word. From that day on, both had recognised a slight shift in the balance of power. Beppo, as Klaus's senior in years and rank, had always been the leader, but when it came to direct confrontation it was Klaus who was the stronger.

Klaus supposed now that he should forgive Beppo the medals which he wore during the selection process. It was simple vanity. Besides, he no longer had the right to judge a man for his vanity: he himself had been disguising the prematurely grey streaks in his hair with henna for the past two years, although he would never have admitted it to Beppo.

He couldn't help feeling critical, however, of other traits in his friend which were manifesting themselves at

Auschwitz. Beppo's mood swings and sudden fits of temper were non-productive and unprofessional, in Klaus's opinion. In fact they bordered on indulgent. Beppo's power over life and death had gone to his head, he'd become self-indulgent. Particularly in his sexual degradation of the women, which was a pity, Klaus thought, for in degrading the women, Beppo degraded himself.

Mengele had insisted from the outset that the women spared for their good looks and possible use as prostitutes be stripped nude and paraded before him. One or two other doctors would be present to perform physical examinations for any signs of sexual disease, but Mengele would delight in degrading the women far more than was necessary. One by one he would ask them intimate details about their sexual lives, and Klaus found his friend's lewd enjoyment of their humiliation unsettling. Most of the women were Jewish and, in private, Beppo always referred to them as 'dirty whores', yet it was clear that he found them in some way desirable. Such behaviour provided a surprising insight into Beppo's character, Klaus thought. How could a man like Josef Mengele find the humiliation of such women sexually titillating? The women were Jews.

Klaus did not voice his disapproval, nor did he allow it to affect his friendship with Beppo. He couldn't afford to. Beppo was too important to him, both as his friend and his senior officer. Nothing must upset the delicate balance which existed between them.

Then the woman arrived.

Klaus noticed her the moment she was herded from the cattle truck along with the rest. She stood out among the horde, fair-haired and patrician and, even in her fear, very beautiful. The dogs were snarling, the soldiers were yelling, and many of the new arrivals were screaming in terror. But the woman was silent. She took the child from the man standing beside her and made her way up the ramp with the others, the man supporting her, although she held herself proudly. She was a woman of breeding, Klaus thought – she didn't look Jewish; she looked Aryan. So did her husband. But then, Jews came in all guises, he told himself as he dragged his eyes from her to survey the rest of the scene from where he stood near Mengele at the top of the ramp. That was the problem: Jews were too smart for their own good.

But his eyes kept returning to the woman as she and her husband reached the point where the crowd was split into two queues, Mengele quietly whistling and directing with his riding crop to the right or the left. The woman's husband tried to stay with her, but he was cudgelled and dragged to the queue on the left, and Klaus kept watching her as she drew nearer in the line that comprised the old and infirm and women with babies and infants. It was a pity that such beauty had to go to the gas chamber. He saw her place her infant on the ground and edge the child behind her, the little girl clinging to her skirt. Little good it would do either of them, he thought. Closer and closer she came, and he couldn't drag his eyes away from her.

There were some who were becoming hysterical, realising the significance of the queues. It was always at that point that things became chaotic, Klaus thought. If only people could conform and respond in an orderly fashion, it would be so much more efficient. Hysteria would not alter the outcome of their lives, or their deaths, all of which were predestined. And hysteria always affected the thugs on duty. He glanced either side of him at the Nazi soldiers who stood, rifles poised. Yes, they were longing to kill.

As the hysteria reached fever pitch, one of the soldiers grabbed at the baby in the arms of a young mother standing directly in front of the woman. The mother refused to relinquish the baby, Mengele gave the order, and the soldier shot them both.

Then the same soldier pulled the child from behind the skirt of the woman who was desperately trying to shield it. He threw the infant down on the ramp and shot it, then turned to shoot the woman who, in lunging forward, had fallen beside her child.

'Nein!'

It was not Josef Mengele's voice that barked the order, but Klaus Henkel's, and the soldier, rifle still poised, glanced at his commanding officer.

Mengele nodded abruptly and resumed his direction of the traffic, but he was not pleased. He had been about to halt the execution himself – he, too, had noticed the woman's beauty – but Klaus had usurped his authority, and he didn't like it.

Klaus stepped forward and, taking the woman by the shoulders, gently lifted her to her feet. She did not resist, but stood shaking, her breath coming in small strangled gasps as she stared at her child. She was in a state of shock. She didn't resist as he led her away, her head craning back for a last glimpse of the infant.

At the gates of the Auschwitz compound, he handed her into the care of one of the *kapos*, those inmates who had been allotted duties, very often of a most un-savoury kind, in exchange for their lives. The *kapo* would take the woman, along with the other females who were to be spared, into the building known as The Sauna. There, before being showered, the hair would be shaved from their heads, their armpits and their groins. Klaus would have liked to have saved the woman from such indignity, but he had pushed his authority far enough, he decided.

When he returned to the ramp, Mengele refused to look at him, and Klaus noted that he'd stopped whistling. Beppo was displeased, he thought, but he didn't care. For whatever reason – perhaps simply as a tribute to her beauty, he wasn't sure – Klaus had wanted the woman spared. He wondered if Beppo would take him to task for his insubordination.

But nothing was said over the ensuing days, although Klaus registered a slight coldness in his friend's attitude towards him. No matter, he thought, Beppo would recover from the slight. He would not allow it to affect their relationship.

Three days later, however, there was a further confrontation, and again it was over the woman.

A dozen or so of the best-looking females were to be paraded naked before Mengele for the customary examination and interview, and Klaus, who had for the past several weeks absented himself from the proceedings, this time attended, sure that the woman would be present.

She was, standing among the group of frightened women whose nakedness was rendered more stark and vulnerable by their shaved heads and groins. But unlike the others who clung together, eyes downcast in shame and humiliation, avoiding the gaze of the doctors, trying to edge behind each other and cover their nakedness with their hands, the woman stood unashamed. She stared vacantly into space as if she were not there in that bleak room with its bare floorboards and its ominous examination table upon which sat a metal bowl with medical tools of the trade and neatly folded grey army blankets. Klaus wondered whether perhaps she'd lost her mind or whether she might still be in shock.

He'd ordered one of the female *kapos* to keep a special watch on the woman in case of any suicide attempt, and the *kapo* had been faithful in her duty, never letting the woman out of her sight, knowing that her own life was at stake if she did. The woman, whose name was Ruth, the *kapo* had told him, didn't talk to the others, and she didn't eat. The others took the food from her but she didn't appear to care. She obeyed orders, the *kapo* said, but she seemed in a daze.

Klaus looked at Mengele. Mengele couldn't take his eyes from the woman, which was hardly surprising – her body was flawless. Even the bare dome of her skull did little to detract from the perfection of her beauty. Klaus did not want to hear the questions Beppo would ask her; it was not right to treat a woman of such breeding in so degrading a manner, he thought.

Mengele signalled the woman to approach him. She appeared not to comprehend the order, then one of the other women, thankful that she herself would not be the first to undergo the ordeal, prodded her and she stepped forward. Still unashamed and seemingly unaware of her nakedness.

Mengele looked her up and down approvingly. He was about to ask her how she did it with her husband. How many times a week, what position did she prefer, was her husband a good lover, was he faithful, had she herself had other lovers? But he didn't even manage to voice the first question before Klaus interceded.

'This is an extremely interesting case psychologically, Josef.' Klaus never used Beppo's nickname in public, nor in the presence of the other camp doctors, two of whom were present. 'As you can see by her demeanour, she appears to be in shock. I should like to interview her personally . . .' He crossed to the examination table. 'Alone,' he added as he picked up one of the folded grey army blankets and shook it out, '. . . with your permission, of course.'

He placed the blanket around the woman's shoulders, and she looked at it momentarily as if it were something quite foreign, then, comforted by the feel of it, she pulled it closely and protectively about her body. It was a healthy sign, Klaus thought.

'With my permission, Klaus?' Mengele's voice was laden with menace and there was a dangerous glint in his eyes. Klaus hoped he wasn't about to throw one of his tantrums; it would be so undignified, particularly in the presence of the other two doctors.

'Naturally.' He met Mengele's gaze and held it steadily, his eyes signalling Beppo that it would be unwise to make a scene. 'With your permission, of course,' he said.

The room was deathly still, the doctors waiting for Mengele's anger to vent itself, the women sensing the tension.

Mengele's gloved fingers hovered over the flap of his holster. He wanted to take out his pistol and shoot the woman between the eyes just to teach Klaus a lesson. He would certainly have done so if any other of his subordinates had so flouted his authority.

'I would be most grateful, Josef.' Klaus's tone was both friendly and respectful, the perfect balance between medical comrade and loyal fellow officer, but his eyes told Beppo to leave the pistol where it was.

The moment passed, and Mengele turned away.

'Permission granted,' he said curtly, to the surprise of the doctors, and he nodded towards the next of the inmates who, arms cradled about her body in an attempt to hide her nudity, shuffled forward.

'Thank you.' Klaus nodded respectfully and ushered the woman towards the door, ignoring Mengele's contemptuous glance.

They stepped outside where the midsummer sun beat mercilessly down on the barren grounds of the camp.

'Ruth, isn't it?' he asked, softly.

She reacted to the caring voice and the sound of her name, and as she looked at him the cloud of uncertainty cleared from her eyes a little.

'Your name, it is Ruth, is it not?' Gently, he repeated the question.

'Yes, my name is Ruth,' she said.

'So you decided to keep the Jew whore to yourself, Klaus.'

It was the following morning and Beppo had called him into his office the moment he'd arrived at the

Experimentation Block. Klaus had avoided the officers' mess the preceding night, dining alone in his quarters, giving Beppo time to cool down. But the moment they were alone in the well-ordered room with its polished wooden desk, its filing cabinets and its shelves lined with jars of specimens, Mengele's anger had been apparent.

Klaus made no reply. Beppo was obviously still upset. It was wisest to let him get it out of his system, he thought.

'Did you enjoy her last night? What was she like? A tigress? I'll bet she was wild in bed – that sort of Jew whore would be.'

Klaus wished that Beppo would get to the point and reprimand him for his insubordination, but the man was whipping himself into a rage. It was typical of Beppo's behaviour these days.

'I interviewed her, Josef,' he replied evenly, 'just as I said I would.'

It was true. He'd taken the woman to his quarters and clothed and fed her, although she'd eaten little. Then he'd talked to her quietly, and she'd responded well – in fact, far more lucidly than he'd expected. The man who had arrived with her, she'd said, was not her husband and he must be saved.

'He is not my husband and he is not a Jew,' she'd insisted. 'He is a Roman Catholic and he is Aryan – he does not belong here. You must save him! Please, I beg you!'

How quickly she'd recovered her senses, he'd thought. She'd recognised him as her saviour, and already she was capable of the lie that might save her husband. He admired her cunning – it made her even more fascinating.

'You *interviewed* her.' Mengele's tone dripped sarcasm. 'And in which particular *position* did you interview her?'

Klaus was becoming annoyed; again he wished that Beppo would get to the point.

'What exactly is it I've done that so angers you, Beppo?'

The enquiry was made in all apparent innocence, but the use of the nickname was deliberately provocative, and Mengele exploded, just as Klaus had intended he should.

'How dare you take it upon yourself to undermine my authority in such a way, and in the presence of my colleagues. How dare you so flaunt the chain of command!'

At last, Klaus thought, they were dealing with protocol.

'Forgive me, Josef. It was wrong of me, and I apologise most sincerely. It will not happen again.'

Mengele stopped in his tracks; he'd been about to rant further.

'I am yours to command, you know that,' Klaus said. 'I will obey your every order always, as is my duty.'

He had Mengele's full attention, he could tell, and he was glad that they'd sorted out his abuse of Beppo's command, but now they needed to deal with the specific issue which was of interest to him.

'In the meantime, however, Josef, I have a favour to ask of you,' he continued. 'I would like your permission to study this woman . . .'

'To *study* her!'

Mengele gave a short derisive laugh, but Klaus took no notice.

'I find her an interesting case. I believe she is a perfect subject for psychoanalysis . . .'

'Don't expect me to believe such shit, Klaus. You don't want to analyse her, you want to fuck her. You want to keep her to yourself and fuck her every night without sharing her around. Be honest, for God's sake.'

Mengele's face was twisted with scorn. For a handsome man he looked extremely ugly, Klaus thought.

'Very well, I'll be honest,' he said. 'You are quite right. I wish to keep the woman to myself.'

Beppo was not right at all, he thought, he did not want to fuck the woman. But more importantly, he did not want the others to fuck her. He would not allow the woman to be abused by the thugs.

'I have never asked a favour of you, Beppo, but I would like you to grant me this request.' His tone was mild, but his eyes sent the strongest of signals. *The woman belongs to me*, his eyes said, *no-one else is to touch her*. 'I would like it very much.'

Mengele met the force of his gaze.

'And what will you do, Klaus, if I refuse?'

'What could I possibly do? You are my commanding officer.' Klaus smiled, and the smile was that of a friend to a friend. 'I would abide by your decision, of course, Beppo. I would always abide by your decision.'

They stood for a moment, then Mengele broke eye contact, turning away to sit at his desk. 'Oh for God's sake,' he said as he took a file from the tray in front of him, 'keep your Jew whore, Klaus, what do I care?'

The woman called Ruth became an obsession to Klaus Henkel. He told himself at first that she was simply an interesting case study; her beauty was pleasing, of course, but she was a Jew and of no sexual interest to him. He allotted her regular and easy work in the infirmary, and when he realised that she was stealing drugs and extra food rations for her fellow inmates, he ignored it, for her own safety. Some women serving as prostitutes had suffered at the hands of their fellow inmates, and it was highly likely that the other prisoners found her preferential treatment suspect. As a valuable provider, they would not dare vent their wrath upon her, even if they believed her to be a German whore.

But she was not a whore. He had not touched her.

She was summoned to his quarters several nights a week, where he would give her the use of his bathroom. She would scrub herself clean and she would dress in the bathrobe he provided for her, the grey-striped dress of the Auschwitz inmate discarded for the several hours she was there. Then she would drape the silk scarf over her shaved head, and he would forget that she was a Jew.

She'd been puzzled when he'd first handed her the white silk scarf.

'I am not cold,' she had said.

She'd understood, however, when he'd gestured at her bare skull. It appeared that he found her unsightly, and she'd obediently draped the scarf over her head like a prayer shawl.

She would sit in the big comfortable armchair, her legs curled under her, while he sat on a hardback chair at the table, and he would play music to her on his gramophone. His favourite recording of all was the Comedian Harmonists' rendition of 'Barcarole' from *The Tales of Hoffmann*, and he would sing along to the lyrics, softly and melodically. He would offer her good food, and she would eat sparingly. Despite her deprivation, food appeared to be of no major interest. Until the night he told her she could take it with her.

'Have it later,' he said.

'I will,' she replied, and she shovelled it into the paper bags he provided.

They didn't speak as the music played. He was content to watch her while she stared into space. She made no pretence of listening, and he doubted whether she was hearing the melodies at all. When he'd turned off the gramophone they would talk a little, or rather he would, about music and literature and the arts in general – always things of beauty, as if they were chatting in a Berlin salon. Occasionally he would talk about himself and his devotion as a doctor to the preservation of life, carefully distancing himself in her eyes from Mengele and the rumoured medical procedures that were conducted at the Experimentation Block. She would answer politely enough but monosyllabically for the most part, and always, when she was once again in her grey-striped dress and about to leave, she would plead for her husband.

'Is there any further news about Manfred, Klaus? When will he be freed?'

It hadn't taken her long to call him by his name. The enticement, he'd discovered, had been the promise of her husband's freedom.

'He is not my husband and he is not a Jew,' she'd pleaded over and over, 'he is a friend who has sacrificed himself for me. He does not belong here, Herr Doktor. Please, you must save him!'

'Klaus,' he'd said. 'You are to call me Klaus, Ruth,' and his suggestion had carried the promise that it might expedite matters. She'd called him Klaus from that day on.

He'd come to believe, however, that she might not be lying.

'His name is Manfred Brandauer,' she'd said, 'and he is the son of Stefan Brandauer, the prominent politician. You must surely have heard of him.'

Of course he'd heard of Stefan Brandauer. He'd met the man in Berlin on several occasions during his university days, a well-known Jew-lover who'd been rightfully sent packing in 1936.

'Ah yes,' he'd replied, 'Stefan Brandauer, I knew him. A fine man who served the German government well.'

So this was Stefan Brandauer's son. She was wrong, he decided, the man most certainly belonged here. Another Jew-lover like his father, he deserved no clemency. Let him suffer along with his friends. Klaus gave no further thought to the matter.

But the more she pleaded, the more suspicious he became. Manfred Brandauer was her lover, he decided. Why else was she so desperate to save him? And the stronger his suspicions grew, the more his jealousy consumed him. He'd have Brandauer shot, he decided. But then, if he did so, his negotiating power would diminish;

she believed that he intended to save her lover. He was in a dilemma.

Klaus had come to recognise his obsession; he could no longer dismiss it: he wanted Ruth more than he'd ever wanted a woman. But he wanted her to come to him of her own volition; he did not wish to force himself upon her. It would be demeaning to them both, he had decided.

So he wooed her. While the music played and she stared vacantly at the wall, he massaged her shoulders and he sang to her, always 'Barcarole'.

'Schöne Nacht, du Liebesnacht, o stille mein Verlangen . . .'
He had a good ear and a pleasant tenor voice.
'Süsser als der Tag und lacht die schöne Liebesnacht.'

It was impossible to tell what she was thinking. She reacted to the singing the same way she reacted to the music, as if she didn't really hear it, and she suffered the massage, neither flinching from his touch, nor relishing it. Then, as always, before she left, she pleaded for Brandauer's release, and, as always, he placated her with the promise that he was doing what he could and that these things took time.

Klaus's desire was driving him mad, and one night he decided that he could wait no longer. But he broached his ultimatum with care.

'Mengele has not shown a great interest in Brandauer's case, I must admit,' he said, 'although, as you know, I've spoken to him on a number of occasions. To Eichmann also.' He had not spoken to Eichmann, and he could just hear Beppo's hoot of derisive laughter if he ever brought up the subject. 'So your Jew whore wants you to save her lover, Klaus,' Beppo would say. 'Why don't you just put a bullet through his head and be done with it?'

The prospect had been more than tempting for the past two months.

'What do we do then?' Ruth asked. 'There must be another course of action, Klaus. Where do we go? Who do we see?'

We. He felt a flicker of amusement at her use of the word, and he admired her audacity. *We* are not going anywhere, he thought, *we* are not seeing anyone. You are here in Auschwitz, my beauty, and you are alive at my whim.

'Without direct permission from a senior camp commander, Ruth,' he said carefully, 'to free someone from Auschwitz is no easy task. There is the bureaucratic process which needs to be addressed, the proof of mistaken identity . . .'

'But I gave you his address: Viktoria-Luise-Platz in Berlin. His papers will be there. I gave you a list of his Aryan friends who will vouch for him. There is solid proof of his identity . . .'

'I know, I know,' he said reassuringly, although irritated; the only time she showed any passion or vitality was when she spoke of Brandauer. 'I will contact Berlin Headquarters tomorrow and set the wheels in motion.'

'Thank you, Klaus,' she whispered, and there was the shadow of a smile in her gratitude. She believed him. 'Thank you, thank you.'

She was seated in the comfortable armchair, as always, in her robe with her legs curled under her, and, as he crossed to sit on the arm beside her, she looked directly into his eyes. He trailed his fingers through the soft spikes of her hair – she no longer wore the silk scarf, it was not necessary, he had decided – and he thought how incredibly young she looked. Young and gamine, like a girl on the brink of womanhood.

'We are in this together, Ruth, we are a team,' he said, caressing her cheek and her throat. Tenderly, like a lover.

'Yes.'

He could see it in her eyes. She had been expecting this moment.

'Perhaps, as a team, you and I . . .' He lowered his face to her, and she parted her lips in anticipation of his kiss.

'Yes,' she said. 'I will do anything you wish.'

It wasn't the way he'd wished it at all, he thought, but at least the stalemate had been breached. He was thankful that he hadn't had Manfred Brandauer shot – the man had proved useful.

But, several weeks later, he was once again cursing Brandauer. His promise of the man's freedom, and her subsequent gratitude, had not unleashed any passion in her. She responded to his lovemaking in the same mindless way she responded to his massage, and Klaus found it deeply insulting. In his bed, her mind was elsewhere, no doubt with Brandauer, he thought. Well, she'd sealed her lover's death sentence. His patience had been tried for far too long, he should have had the man shot months ago. And perhaps, he thought hopefully, following the demise of her lover, whose life he had so diligently fought to preserve, perhaps in her grief she might seek his consolation.

Having made his decision, he ordered the execution for three o'clock the following afternoon, a firing squad of four. He himself would not be present to give the command, which was a pity – he would have enjoyed it.

He summoned her to his quarters the day after the execution, prepared to break the news to her gently and to offer his heartfelt sympathy over the death of the man who had been wrongfully imprisoned and whose freedom they had both so keenly sought.

But she made the announcement herself. 'Manfred Brandauer is dead.' She said it the moment she stepped in the door. 'He was executed by firing squad yesterday.'

He was annoyed that she'd already heard of Brandauer's death; he'd underestimated the grapevine system that existed in Auschwitz. And he was further annoyed by her lack of etiquette. She had not showered and changed into the bathrobe, and he had no wish to communicate with her while she was dressed in her prisoner garb. But he quelled his irritation.

'I know. I heard this afternoon, I had no idea Mengele had ordered it. I'm sorry, but there was nothing I could do, it was too late.'

She was staring at him strangely. Her grief was evident – he could tell that she'd been weeping – but there was something else in her eyes which he'd not seen before. Was it accusation? Impossible. She couldn't know that he had ordered the execution.

He turned away, refusing to speak to her any longer while she wore the grey stripes that pronounced her status. The sight of the uniform disgusted him.

'Go and clean yourself and change into the bathrobe,' he said.

She did not immediately respond to his order as she normally did, and although his eyes remained averted, he knew she was staring at him with that same look of accusation. Then she walked off abruptly to the bathroom.

She couldn't possibly know, he thought. Who would have told her? Certainly not the soldiers who had formed the firing squad – they would not confide in a Jewish inmate. And nor would Schoneberger, the attendant doctor. Schoneberger would never threaten the comfortable relationship he shared with the Nazis. He was too much of a survivor; a loyal sycophant to his masters, he was despised by his own kind.

She didn't know. Her accusation was a manifestation of her grief, he decided. She held all Nazis, himself included, responsible for her lover's death.

Five minutes later, she returned in the bathrobe. Her short-cropped hair, wet and tousled, framed her face beautifully, he thought. She was once again 'his Ruth' and he was prepared to play out the charade.

'It is a tragic occurrence, Ruth,' he said. 'I cannot understand why Mengele would issue such an order, but he's a strange man. Perhaps we pushed him too far with our demands, who can tell?' He shrugged, enjoying the use of *we*. Let her bear a little of the guilt, he thought. She had, after all, in her own way, brought about Brandauer's death. 'Mengele does not like to be dictated to. Perhaps . . .' He gave another heartfelt shrug. 'Perhaps if we had not been so aggressive in our attempt to save him, Manfred might still be alive.'

'Don't call him by his first name. Please.'

He was nonplussed.

'You have never called him by his first name before. Please don't do so now.'

The look in her eyes was far more than accusation, he realised, it was hatred.

'What is it, Ruth?' How dare she look at him like that. Didn't she realise he could send her to the gas chamber? 'Is there something you wish to say to me?' She remained silent and he prompted her further. 'A question you wish to ask, perhaps?'

'No, there is nothing I wish to ask.'

She was not going to confront him, which was wise, he thought, he'd have sent her to her death if she'd dared. But the hatred was still there, and the rebelliousness in her excited him.

'Very well.' He smiled. 'Shall we forgo the music tonight? I think, under the circumstances, comfort of a more physical nature would be apt, do you not agree?'

He felt her tense as he put his arm around her, but she allowed him to lead her towards the bedroom. He was aroused. Their relationship had undergone a change for the better after all. If he was never to succeed in gaining her love, at least he was no longer merely a means to Brandauer's freedom. Her hatred, he thought, was vastly preferable to her indifference.

Manfred Brandauer's name was never again mentioned, and over the ensuing months the charade continued. He still wooed her – it had become a ritual which he enjoyed. He still sang along to 'Barcarole' and massaged her shoulders, but these days she no longer stared vacantly at the wall. He was aware all the while of her hatred and he continued to find it a source of arousal. In the past she'd cared nothing for her own life; she had existed purely to save her lover – but now she wanted to live and he was her means of survival. He owned her, body and soul. And after all, he told himself, hatred was a powerful emotion, very akin to love. One day she would come to realise that.

Nineteen forty-four was not a good year for Germany. The tide of war had turned and when the Allied Forces landed on the Normandy beaches on June 6, defeat appeared inevitable. Months dragged on and, as Christmas approached, all hope was lost. How could it have happened? Klaus wondered. How could the right and might of Germany possibly have failed? But somehow the days of the Third Reich were over.

'I am leaving Auschwitz tomorrow,' he said.

It was Christmas Eve, and she was sitting in the bathrobe which was now hers, in the armchair which he'd come to think of as her domain, and she was looking extraordinarily beautiful. It would be their last night together.

'Yes, I gathered that.' She'd noticed the priest's cassock draped over the chair and had seen the identity papers lying openly on the desk; he hadn't bothered to hide them. So Klaus Henkel was going into hiding in the guise of a priest, she thought, how ironic.

His departure appeared to be of little concern to her, he realised, but surely he deserved her thanks – he'd preserved her life for a whole eighteen months. Perhaps she would show a little more gratitude when he told her of the plans he'd made for her own safety.

'There is a transport of workers departing for Bergen-Belsen tomorrow,' he said. 'You will be one of them; I have had you listed.'

'Why are you sending me to Bergen-Belsen? Auschwitz will be liberated any moment now.'

He didn't know which irritated him most, her arrogance or her prescience. How did she know that the enemy was on their doorstep? Inmates were not privy to news from the outside world. But he refused to demean himself by asking how she'd come by such information.

'And exactly who do you think will "liberate" Auschwitz, Ruth?' he sneered. 'Your friendly allies, the Americans?' He rose from his hardback chair by the table and crossed to the gramophone. 'No, no, it will be the Russians who will enter Auschwitz.'

The familiar melody flooded the room, 'Barcarole', the harmony group singing softly, unobtrusively, but he didn't sing along with them this time. He walked silently to stand behind the armchair and ran his fingers through her hair.

'And you know what the Russians will do to a beautiful woman like you?' He was no longer annoyed. The feel of her hair soothed him. It was shoulder length now, and like flaxen gold – how he loved her hair. 'They will defile you, Ruth. I will not let that happen.' He encircled her skull with his hands. 'I would kill you myself before I would allow the filthy Bolshevik pigs to defile you.'

His fingers strayed to her neck and her throat, and she remained quite still as he slipped the bathrobe from her shoulders.

'But you will live, Ruth,' he said, massaging her gently, tracing the bones of her spine and her shoulder blades. 'You will go to Bergen-Belsen, which will be liberated by the Americans. And for the rest of your days, you will remember that you owe me your life.'

He waited for her to say something; he deserved some expression of gratitude, surely. But none was forthcoming.

'Get up.'

She rose.

He circled the chair to stand in front of her. He looked

at her breasts, then untied the belt of the robe. It slid to the floor and she stood naked before him.

'Surely I deserve some thanks, Ruth.'

'Yes. I'm sorry. Thank you.'

'Thank you who, and thank you for what?' he asked, irritated by her lack of respect.

'Thank you, Klaus, for saving my life.'

There was no animation in her: she spoke the words like an automaton, and he felt a sudden flash of rage. Then he saw that there appeared no hatred in her either; her face was a mask. He curbed his anger and reached out a hand to caress her.

'Ah well,' he said, his fingers tracing the curve of her breast, 'actions speak louder than words, do they not?' He pulled her gently to him, her body compliant. 'There are other ways you can show your gratitude.' He kissed her, and her lips obediently parted.

'Love me,' he whispered.

Just as obediently, she embraced him.

'Love me, Ruth, love me.'

Her hands were caressing his back. She wanted him, he could sense it in her touch, she had never caressed him like this before.

'Love me, love me,' he repeated over and over, his excitement mounting as he felt her respond.

He fumbled with his trousers, freeing himself, kneading her breasts, his tongue seeking hers, his desire stronger than it had ever been. She was his, she was offering herself to him, he could feel it. Her thighs were parting as he thrust himself at her. He could feel her breath, she was panting; soon she would moan, he wanted to hear her voice.

'Love me, Ruth, love me.'

There was no time to undress or to take her into the bedroom, his need was too urgent, he would have her here on the floor, and he would hear her, lost in pleasure. He broke away from the embrace, ripping at his trousers, then he made the mistake of looking at her.

Her eyes held nothing but pure contempt.

At the sight of her undisguised loathing, his rage exploded and he struck her across the cheek with all the force he could muster, sending her reeling across the room and smashing into the table.

'Whore!'

He threw himself upon her.

'Filthy whore!' He covered her body with his, pinioning her wrists to the floorboards. 'You think you're different from the others?' he screamed, in insane rage. 'You think because I grant you favours you can look at me in that way? You belong in the ovens along with the rest of your tribe . . .' He spat in her face. 'You filthy Jew whore!'

She made no attempt to struggle free, but her chest was heaving, she was gasping for air. He could see she was terrified and the insanity of his rage lessened a little. Good, at last she knew her place – a Jew was meant to feel terror.

'Would you like to know what the Russians would do to you, Ruth?' He slapped her face. 'Would you like that? I'll show you, shall I?' He slapped her again and she whimpered with fear. He felt a stab of pleasure. He rolled her over on her belly.

'Kneel,' he said, taking off his trousers. 'Kneel and spread your legs.'

'No,' she begged, 'please, Klaus . . .'

But he hauled her to her knees. It was too late to beg for favours. He pushed her head to the floor, ripped her buttocks apart and forced himself into her. She screamed with the pain.

'Do you like being taken by the Russians, Ruth?' he panted. 'They're animals, the Russians, pigs, every one of them. And this,' he grunted as he sodomised her, 'this is what they do to Jew whores.'

When it was over and he was dressing himself, he

watched her crawl on her hands and knees to cower in a corner of the room. She was bleeding, he noticed: a thin trickle of blood ran down her thigh. He crossed to the gramophone which was making scratching noises; the record was probably ruined now.

It had not been the way he'd wished, but she'd brought it upon herself, she had pushed him beyond his limits. He rarely lost his temper, he preferred to remain in control at all times. It was most regrettable that she had so angered him.

'Wash and dress yourself,' he said.

He must put her out of his mind, he thought. He would be leaving the camp the next day. All had been arranged and he must concentrate on his escape plan. Mengele had already left Auschwitz, and the Russians could arrive at any moment – he was running out of time.

Several minutes later, she returned from the bathroom wearing her faded striped uniform.

'Come here,' he said.

She approached him fearfully, and she flinched when he put a hand to her face.

'No, no,' he assured her, 'I am not going to hurt you any more.' Tenderly, he touched the cut on her temple where she had struck the table. 'You will be safe in Bergen-Belsen,' he said. Then he ran his fingers through her hair for the last time. 'It was not meant to happen like this. You should have loved me, Ruth.'

CHAPTER SEVENTEEN

In 1944 a secret meeting of top German industrialists and bankers was held at the Maison Rouge Hotel in Strasbourg. It had become clear that the Third Reich would not survive the war, and their new aim was to ensure the safety of their Nazi leaders, along with Germany's wealth. The future resurrection of the party depended on safeguarding the nation's assets, much of which had been acquired through plunder, and aiding Nazi officials in their escape to havens outside the country, where they would be safe from prosecution for war crimes.

The meeting led to the genesis of a highly efficient organisation which, following the war, would be called the Organisation Der Ehemaligen SS-Angehörigen, or 'the Organisation of Former SS Members', but which would become widely known as 'Odessa'.

The organisation's basic plans were quickly set in place. By the end of the year, funds were arranged, safe houses set up, false identities available, and escape routes devised.

Klaus Henkel had opted to escape rather than remain hidden in Germany and, as a highly valued doctor and committed Nazi, he'd been among those to receive preferential treatment. He had obtained funds, the false identity of Catholic priest Father Paul Brummer and explicit instructions on the two principal escape routes.

He was to make his way to a major Italian seaport, he'd been informed, and he could get there by either Switzerland or Austria. Once in Italy he would be relatively safe, but he would have to remain there under an assumed identity until his passage to South America had been arranged.

Klaus had chosen his escape via Austria, deciding that, if he was to be captured en route, he would prefer it to be by the Allied Forces advancing from the south, rather than by the Russians. The Austrian route, he'd been told, was through the small Bavarian town of Memmingen. From there he was to make for Innsbruck, then over the Brenner Pass into Italy and south to the port of Genoa where a sea passage would be arranged for him.

It had all been ludicrously easy, Klaus thought. The priest's cassock, which he'd at first detested, had proved the perfect disguise. People didn't look at a priest, he'd discovered, all they saw were the robes, not the man.

'Good morning, Father,' they'd said as he stepped onto the train.

'Good afternoon, Father,' they'd said as he alighted at his destination several hours later.

He'd smiled beatifically and waved small blessings at them; he'd found it rather humorous. A war was in progress, he'd thought, and yet it appeared he could travel the whole of Europe unquestioned, simply because he was a man of the cloth. How extraordinary.

But he'd had a rude awakening in the alpine town of Innsbruck.

He arrived in the afternoon. It was late December, the height of the skiing season, and the township was crowded.

Again, Klaus was amazed. Holiday-makers, in the midst of a war? And not just locals either – he could hear other dialects and accents. He didn't approve at all. He considered it improper.

He booked into a modest hotel, their last room. He was lucky, the girl told him.

'It's the height of the season, Father.'

'Is it indeed?' he said archly, and the girl gave him a strange look, so he waved her a blessing and said, 'Thank you, my child.'

The following morning was bitterly cold. An icy wind swept down from the mountains and, to the disappointment of the skiers, the chairlifts were closed due to the unseasonal gale which was expected.

Klaus lounged over a newspaper and mid-morning coffee and cake in one of the cosy cafes before he was to catch the midday train. Soon he would be in Italy. How easy it had been, he thought. But as he was crossing the square on his way to the railway station, he heard his name called.

'Klaus! Klaus Henkel!'

The voice was coming from behind him, and he curbed his instinct to run. Then a hand patted him on the shoulder, and he turned.

'Klaus, I was sure it was you, I saw you in the cafe, but I couldn't believe it. I didn't know you'd embraced the priesthood . . .'

The man was in his early thirties and Klaus recognised him. Koenig, he thought, although he couldn't remember the first name. Koenig had been at university with him in Munich in the early thirties. An insignificant young man, he vaguely recalled, one who'd tried too hard, and unsuccessfully, to be liked.

Klaus decided that his best option was to bluff it out. He looked at Koenig blankly.

'. . . I mean, you of all people,' Koenig continued with a

comradely chuckle. He was still trying too hard, Klaus noted. 'You cared for nothing but athletics and politics, if I recall.'

'I am sorry,' Klaus said in Italian, his expression one of bewilderment. 'Do you perhaps mistake me for someone else? I do not understand you.'

Koenig was dumbfounded by the response. It was also apparent that he did not speak Italian.

'Forgive me.' Klaus smiled apologetically, then added in stumbling and heavily accented German, '*Ich kann nicht Deutsch sprechen*. I am afraid I can be of no assistance to you,' he said, again in Italian.

'Oh.' Koenig backed away in his confusion. 'I'm sorry, Father, but you look so like someone I once knew.' Embarrassed though he was, he continued to study Klaus quizzically, as if he couldn't quite believe what he saw. 'Please excuse me.'

Klaus smiled again, benignly this time. 'God bless you, my son,' he said in Italian and, with his by now well-practised priestly wave, he walked off, leaving Koenig staring after him in amazement.

But he did not go to the railway station – he did not dare. He'd been too complacent, he realised, he could no longer afford to travel the easy way, leaving an identifiable trail behind him.

It had become difficult after that. Cutting across country by foot, avoiding the larger towns as he headed south, stealing food where he could and sheltering in farmhouse barns. He was strong and in peak physical condition, but the weather was not kind, and once, in Chiusa, desperate for warmth and sustenance, he'd stayed overnight in the small village inn. He had been prepared to kill the innkeeper should there be any show of suspicion, but there had been none. The innkeeper had been honoured to have a priest staying under his roof.

Nonetheless, Klaus knew that when he reached the

major cities of Milan and, more importantly, Genoa, where he might have to bide some time awaiting his passage to South America, he would need a new identity. The encounter with Koenig had shaken him and he doubted whether once the man had overcome his surprise, he had believed the case of mistaken identity. It was only a matter of time before Klaus Henkel would officially be a wanted man, and when he was, Koenig, who had no loyalty to the party, would most certainly report his sighting.

Then he had come upon the remote and secluded peasants' hut, several miles from the village of Tirano. The timing had been perfect: he'd been exhausted and in need of a safe house where he could rest and see out the worst of the winter. He'd noted, too, that the peasant goatherd was approximately his own age and height and, once he got to know the family, that his papers were in order and easily accessible. It was a heaven-sent opportunity.

They were simple people, devout and trusting, and when they'd served their purpose he dispatched them with ease – all but the boy, whose absence had been an irritating glitch. Not that the boy constituted a threat, he'd thought as he'd set off on his long trek to Milan. The boy was ill, an epileptic, he would no doubt perish up there in the snow without the support of his parents. But Klaus would have preferred to have finished it all off tidily; he didn't like loose ends.

He'd reached the sprawling outer suburbs of Milan on the first of May, and had been shocked when he'd heard the news. Adolf Hitler had committed suicide in his Berlin bunker just the previous day. Klaus had mourned the death of his Führer as he'd skirted the city and headed south to Genoa. Then, barely a week later, when Germany had unconditionally surrendered, he'd mourned the death of the Third Reich.

Upon reaching the city of Genoa, he'd found it easy to disappear. There, in the tough, seething seaport, life was cheap and people cared little for the business of others. He had sought out the contact he'd been given and then he'd booked into a small *pensione* not far from the docks, and become just a part of the mass of humanity as he'd awaited his passage to South America.

More than one third of Argentina's population lived in or around the sprawling metropolis of Buenos Aires on the south-eastern coast of the continent. The vibrant and cosmopolitan city stood apart from other Latin American cities because of the diversity of its architecture, which reflected its European heritage. In the *barrios* of El Centro and La Recoleta, parks and boulevards lined with palatial mansions evoked Rome. In Palermo and Belgrano, the plazas were reminiscent of those in Paris, and in the *barrios* of San Telmo and La Boca, the cobblestone streets and rows of bars, cafes and *cantinas* had a distinctly Italian feel.

The Buenos Aires locals, predominantly of Spanish and Italian extraction, referred to themselves as Portenos, their predecessors having originally settled in the port area following their arrival from Europe by boat. But the Portenos had long since created new *barrios*, each with its own character and history, and it was here that the true identity of the city existed. The essence of Buenos Aires did not lie in the beauty or diversity of its architecture, but in the fierce Latin spirit of its people. The Portenos were intensely passionate, and the very air of the city was charged with their restless energy.

For Klaus Henkel, Buenos Aires had proved far more than a temporary safe haven. He had discovered a whole new life in this vibrant city, in this country which so differed from his German homeland. The months became a year, and he wallowed in the sensuality of Buenos Aires. He loved the heat of its climate, the slow fire of its music, the spiciness of its food and its hot-blooded women. He embraced a newfound hedonism, frequenting nightclubs in San Telmo and entertaining prostitutes at his lavish apartment in La Recoleta. Having quickly assimilated the language, he felt that he'd become one of the locals in this city so given to pleasure, where he could be free from the Teutonic discipline that had governed his existence from the earliest days of his childhood.

During the day, he maintained the respectable facade of Doctor Umberto Pellegrini, the identity supplied for him by the now well-established and highly efficient organisation known as Odessa – and the cover provided for him had proved to be impeccable. Doctor Pellegrini was a dedicated practitioner who worked at the Rosario Medical Clinic, a charitable institution offering medical assistance to the disadvantaged.

The clinic, in the port area of La Boca, was to all intents and purposes funded by the Catholic Church, and indeed, had the Bishop of Buenos Aires been questioned, he would have affirmed the authenticity of such a claim in accordance with his instructions from Rome. In reality, the clinic was not funded by the Catholic Church, but by Odessa, and although the treatment on offer was bona fide, the centre itself served a purpose far broader than medical assistance for the neighbourhood poor.

An escape route for German war criminals known as 'The Monastery Route' had been operating successfully for the past twelve months. Odessa smuggled the fugitives across the unpatrolled Swiss borders into Italy, after which they were moved by Roman Catholic priests from one monastery to the next until they reached Rome. There, Bishop Alois Hudal, the Rector of the College of Santa Maria dell' Anima, had created a virtual transit station for escaping Nazis. New identities and Red Cross passports were supplied, and from Santa Maria dell' Anima the fugitives were dispersed around the globe, particularly to South America where German agents, industry and commerce were well established.

The German General Staff, driven by imperialism, had set up operations in South America many years before Hitler took power in Germany. New industrial plants had been established throughout the Americas, especially in Argentina, which had become the chief focus of German intrigue in South America. By the end of the war, German agents had gained control of mines, banks, railroads, aviation lines, and chemical and steel works. By 1946, under the leadership of its new pro-Nazi president, General Juan Perón, Argentina's munitions industry was virtually controlled by the German industrial conglomerate I.G. Farben. The German war strategists had planned well ahead, and with the vast accumulation of Nazi wealth safely deposited in Swiss bank accounts, they could steadily build their underground network in preparation for the future rise of the Fourth Reich.

As an Odessa centre, the Rosario Medical Clinic served an important purpose in the overall scheme, and its dedicated director, Doctor Fritz von Halbach, had welcomed Klaus Henkel's arrival in Buenos Aires. Henkel, one of the first of the SS to escape, was a committed Nazi and a qualified doctor and would prove a valuable member of the team. Furthermore, the man's ease with the Italian language was most convenient, as it enabled the director to choose a non-German alias for Klaus. Fritz von Halbach believed the image of the clinic should be that of an international body of dedicated people working for the common good of the poor.

Klaus had not previously met von Halbach in person, but he'd known of him by reputation for years. Everyone in Berlin society did. Doctor Fritz von Halbach was an eminent plastic surgeon who, prior to the war, had catered to film stars and the moneyed elite. His picture had regularly appeared in the press: urbane, handsome, wealthy and feted, he was of unimpeachable character and had never been associated with the SS. But among the hierarchy Fritz von Halbach had been well known as an avid Nazi supporter. It had been a lesser known fact that, mingling as he did with the rich and famous, he'd been a valued agent of the German General Staff. And he'd proved his loyalty by abandoning his highly successful practice in Berlin to set up a clinic in Buenos Aires which would serve as part of the underground network a full year before Germany's final defeat. Fritz was a man with the future in mind, and a man who believed that the power of the Fourth Reich would emanate from Argentina.

'It was well planned,' Fritz said thoughtfully. 'He must have bribed a guard to smuggle the cyanide capsule into the prison.'

'Clever,' Klaus agreed, and he nodded, feigning interest. The news of Hermann Goering's suicide that very morning had meant little to him. 'The others will no doubt be envying his escape.'

They were seated in the comfortable armchairs of Fritz's office having a Cognac, as they occasionally did at the end of a work day when Fritz felt in need of a chat. The spacious office, with a lounge area and a bar in the corner, was at the rear of the clinic, well away from the public surgery, dispensary and consulting rooms. It was private and soundproof and housed a separate bedroom and bathroom, occasionally serving as Fritz's quarters, although he maintained a modest apartment nearby. Clandestine meetings were sometimes conducted in the office, but the majority of Odessa business took place upstairs above the clinic where the first floor, complete with offices and a private surgery and operating theatre for Nazi use only, was a hive of activity. Few were invited into the personal domain of Fritz von Halbach. But Fritz made an exception for Klaus. Klaus Henkel was the only man at the clinic whom he considered his intellectual equal.

'Yes, I'm sure they would have preferred a more digni-fied end.' Fritz scowled as he poured himself a second hefty Cognac. 'Von Ribbentrop, Streicher, Keitel, Sauckel and the others, they're to be hanged like common crimi-nals. And in a gymnasium, I believe. Where the Americans were playing basketball only days ago! Two gallows to be used alternately. The indignity of it – it's disgraceful!'

Klaus gave another sombre nod, as if he cared. For the past week, the world headlines had been screaming that the twelve found guilty were to be hanged. He hadn't heard Fritz's inside information about the gymnasium or the twin gallows, but what did it matter? If a man was hanged he was hanged. Who cared where or how it took place? Fritz was obsessed with the Nuremberg trial, and Klaus was bored. It was October 1946, and the trial of the major war criminals, or rather those who had been captured and indicted, had been dragging on for nearly a year now. This was only the beginning, he thought – there would be other trials to follow, and they could go on for many years to come. There'd be dozens more found guilty – it was a foregone conclusion – and they'd all be executed, which was a pity because they'd only been doing their duty. But what was the point in talking about it?

'And they're soon to start on the trials of the Nazi physicians,' Fritz continued, outraged; he'd barely drawn breath. 'Twenty-three doctors have been charged.'

Klaus's ears pricked up at the mention of the doctors' trial. 'Any further news of Josef?' he asked. Beppo was the only one he was interested in.

'Mengele is still in Bavaria, I believe, on a farm near Rosenheim,' Fritz said. 'According to the underground reports, he's relatively safe, but the sooner we can get him to Buenos Aires the better, for his own safety and for the cause. We need men like Mengele: respected leaders; Nazis who will inspire others.'

Klaus drained his glass; Fritz had lost him again. He

preferred it when they discussed football – both were avid followers – or even their respective patients and medicine in general; Klaus enjoyed his work at the clinic and valued the expertise of Fritz's opinion. But tonight the man's mood was obviously one of ideological fervour, as it quite often was, so Klaus picked up the bottle that sat on the coffee table between them and poured himself another Cognac. He'd get a bit drunk and let Fritz rant for a while, he thought, then he'd go to Oswaldo's and find himself a whore for the night.

True to form, Fritz did rant. The talk of Nuremberg and the mention of Mengele had wound him up.

'It is the duty of men like us, Klaus,' he declared, 'men like you and me and Mengele, to fulfil the Führer's prophecy and pave the way for the Nazi Fifth Column in the Western Hemisphere. Universal chaos will consume the world, just as Hitler prophesied, and it will emanate from right here in Argentina where they hate the United States.'

He rose to pace the room, one hand behind his back, the other gesticulating with his brandy balloon. Klaus noted that, for all his elegance, Fritz's behaviour on occasions was reminiscent of the Führer himself.

'When Goebbels pronounced that Argentina had the power to form a union of the South American nations,' he continued unabated, 'Juan Perón, as War Minister, openly agreed, and now that he's President, we must ensure that a South American alliance remains his personal ambition. To the Allied nations, and the world at large, Germany appears crushed, and those who believe they have vanquished us forever are relishing the publicity of the Nuremberg trial . . .'

Fritz skolled his Cognac in one hit, fired anew by his anger over the latest reports from Berlin.

'. . . but the indignity and the wrongful retribution afforded our leaders will be of no consequence in the end. If we have Perón in our pocket and work together for the

common cause, the consolidation of Allied victory itself
will be meaningless. When class is set against class and
nation against nation, chaos will reign as the Führer said it
would, and Germany will rise again in all its military
force.'

Fritz was more passionate than ever tonight, Klaus
thought. Goering's suicide and the fate of the others had
obviously affected him deeply.

Klaus did not share Fritz von Halbach's fervour. The
Reich was as dead as its condemned leaders, in his
opinion, and Fritz's plans for the future meant nothing to
him. He listened attentively nonetheless, interjecting now
and then and nodding at all the right times. But, as he continued to study von Halbach, he wondered how a man of
such gifted intellect, a man so good-looking, so elegant
and sophisticated, could be such a pedantic bore.

In his mid-forties, Fritz von Halbach was a walking
advertisement for his life's work as a plastic surgeon. Fair-
haired, blue-eyed and Aryan to the core, he was the handsomest of men and appeared in his mid-thirties. His body
was fit, his skin unblemished, and Klaus had thought, upon
their first meeting, that perhaps one of his peers had performed some expert surgical rejuvenation. He'd surreptitiously searched for any telling signs, but there were none.

Klaus envied Fritz his youthful appearance. The man
was over a decade his senior, and yet it was Klaus who
looked the older of the two. His rapidly greying hair was
successfully disguised with henna, but it was not so easy to
disguise the evidence of a year's dissipation. His skin was
sallow these days, a result of the fine Cuban cigars he'd
come to enjoy, and his body, in which he'd taken such
pride, was thickening from a surfeit of alcohol and rich
food, indulgences he'd previously denied himself. At first
he'd tried to resist the impact of his lifestyle, cutting down
on his excesses and physically working his body, but of
late he'd abandoned all forms of self-discipline. Buenos

Aires had seduced him. The hedonist had won over the disciplinarian.

'Get on with your life, enjoy it while you can,' the voice of the hedonist whispered to him daily. 'You're thirty-three years old, you've devoted the prime years of your youth to the Reich, you deserve the right to indulge yourself.'

He no longer attempted to resist the voice of the hedonist. It spoke the truth after all: he had served his Führer, body and soul; he had earned the right to a life of his own.

He leaned back in his chair and lit up a cigar, and he joined in the conversation for the next hour. He talked of the Reich's history and offered views which he knew concurred with Fritz's, even though he despised the man when he spoke of his devotion to Nazi Germany. How had Fritz von Halbach served the Reich? Had he faced death? Had he killed for his Führer? No, Klaus thought with contempt, he'd been little more than a fundraiser, a conduit to the wealthy. But he was a powerful man, and it was wise to maintain their close relationship, so Klaus played the game accordingly.

From the outset, he had found it easy to manipulate Fritz von Halbach. He'd observed the man's two principal weaknesses. Von Halbach was vain and he was obsessed, and Klaus had indulged him on both counts, always engaging his intellect, careful not to appear obsequious. Von Halbach was an arrogant man who'd led a privileged and protected life, but he was no fool. It had been relatively simple, and at times Klaus had felt like a puppeteer. He'd rather enjoyed it.

Not tonight, he thought an hour later as he lit a second cigar. Tonight his role of puppeteer was proving tedious.

It was ten o'clock when he left.

'Goodnight, Fritz,' he said at the door. 'It's been a most pleasant evening.'

'Goodnight, Umberto.'

Fritz was adamant that all aliases be religiously maintained. Even during the official meetings held upstairs, a man was always referred to by his new identity. If the habit was observed in private, it avoided public lapses.

When Klaus had gone, Fritz emptied the two cigar butts from the ashtray into a paper bag which he crumpled and placed in the rubbish bin, then he carefully washed out the ashtray. He didn't smoke himself, although most of his contemporaries did. Personally, he found it a filthy habit and the smell annoyed him, but he was prepared to suffer the discomfort in exchange for Klaus's company. It was a relief to find an intellect equal to his own; he'd been starved for conversation the past several years. And he and Klaus made such a good team, serving the cause as they did with a common fervour. Fritz was delighted that Klaus Henkel had arrived in Buenos Aires.

Klaus cut through the cramped back lanes of the working-class *barrio* of La Boca, passing brightly painted, multi-coloured houses with corrugated iron roofs, and poky *cantinas* in which families dined noisily. He always walked to the clubs and bars, leaving his recognisable red Peugeot parked at the clinic; it seemed wiser that way, and besides, he'd probably get drunk.

He turned the corner into the main street where the football stadium towered high and splendid over *la Piccola Italia* as La Boca was known. The stadium was the pride and joy of the *barrio*, and indeed of Buenos Aires. With a seating capacity of 50,000, it had been opened only seven years before and affectionately named *La Bombonera* because it looked like a giant chocolate box. He would go to the match with Fritz this Saturday, he thought, and then he would enjoy the man's company. It was the one time they shared a common passion.

Fifteen minutes later, he was in the neighbouring *barrio* of San Telmo where the cobblestone streets teemed with revellers. Tables spilled out onto the pavements and he had to sidle past the diners. Rows of early nineteenth-century colonial buildings which had once housed affluent Spaniards were now tenements, the wealthy having long before deserted their opulent mansions. But, even in their shabbiness, the ornate stone buildings, with their arched entrances and decorative columned windows, remained impressive. In the tiny upstairs apartments, families lived cheek by jowl, but at street level, lined up competitively and touting for business, were the affluent cafes, bars, clubs and *cantinas*.

Klaus headed directly for Oswaldo's. He'd frequented many tango halls and clubs during his early days in Buenos Aires when the eroticism of the music and the dance had first claimed him, but Oswaldo's Tango Club, where the musicians were superb and where a number of the dancers were discreetly available, had become his firm favourite.

The entrance to Oswaldo's was nondescript – two large wooden doors set in the rear of an alcove beneath the stone arch of a building. But inside was a different matter.

Klaus nodded to the doorman.

'*Buenas noches, señor*,' the man replied as he opened the doors and stepped to one side.

The music assailed Klaus's senses as soon as he entered. On a rostrum at the far end of the wooden parquetry dance floor a seven-piece combo was playing 'The Blue Tango' with all the fiery passion and seductive melancholy peculiar to the tango.

'*Buenas noches, señor*.'

A pretty girl in a flared peasant skirt and off-the-shoulder blouse smiled flirtatiously as she guided him to a table.

'*Buenas noches*, Marie-Luisa.'

He knew her. He'd invited her home with him a number of times, but she'd always charmingly refused, so he'd given up trying. She was obviously not a 'working girl'.

But he tipped her well, encouraging her flirtatiousness, which he enjoyed.

The drinks waiter arrived and Klaus ordered a beer, feeling dehydrated from the Cognacs he'd had with Fritz and the walk from La Boca. He also ordered a whisky chaser and the mandatory bottle of cheap sparkling wine which masqueraded as champagne and which the management sold at an exorbitant price. Then he sat back and watched the couples on the dance floor.

In the garish light of day, Oswaldo's might have looked shabby, but at night its allure was magical. The dance floor was surrounded by candlelit tables, and the slowly turning mirrorball overhead cast ever-changing patterns on the terracotta-hued walls. In each corner stood clusters of huge potted palms, indirectly lit to give a jungle-like appearance, and next to the band's rostrum was a spangled curtain leading backstage. When an exhibition dance was announced a spotlight would hit the curtain and the girls would make a spectacular entrance.

Those on the dance floor were a mixed bunch. Professional dancers partnered men who sought out tango halls for the eroticism they offered, but there were couples who had come simply to dance. Some were young, some middle-aged, and here and there, disguised by the half-light and their own vivacity, were some who could only be described as elderly. With the exception of several of the men partnering the professional dancers, all were accomplished. It was not surprising – the modern tango had been born in Buenos Aires. A combination of the Spanish tango and the milonga – a risqué Argentine dance – it had been considered flagrantly sexual and had been socially unacceptable for years. Now it seemed everyone in Buenos Aires could dance the tango.

Which didn't alter the power of its seduction, Klaus thought as he watched one of the professional dancers expertly guide an apparent newcomer around the floor. It was Elizabeta, a working girl who'd accompanied him home on many an occasion, and she gave him a wave over the man's shoulder. She was an exotic-looking creature, but then they all were, with their heavy eye makeup and their lithe dancers' bodies. And they bore themselves with a sexual arrogance, confident in their ridiculously high-heeled shoes, their strong shapely legs exposed in skirts split to the thigh.

Klaus returned the wave, and Elizabeta smiled before twirling her back to him. Her partner, inept in a sea of expertise, was startled by the speed of the movement but enjoying the feel of her groin against his.

She was doing more than guiding the man in the tango, Klaus thought, she was making love to him on the dance floor, and he was reminded of his own first experience in a tango hall. How could a dance be so erotic and yet legal, he'd wondered, and he'd been convinced that the girl was deliberately arousing him, seeking an offer. But when he'd tried to negotiate a transaction, she'd very icily put him in his place.

'I am a dancer, *señor*,' she'd said with contempt, and she'd walked away.

He'd learned to tango after that, quickly and well. It had come easily to him – he was a natural athlete, balanced and light on his feet. And he'd learned to distinguish which of the girls might be available for other activities. He would not make the same mistake twice, he'd decided – he would not have a dance hall woman look at him with contempt. He'd also learned the correct approach. He treated the dancers as if that's what they were, dancers and not prostitutes – it was the way they liked it. And word got around that he was a generous man, one who treated women well. He rarely made a wrong judgement these days, and even if he did, he caused no offence.

'I cannot go home with you, *señor*, I am married,' a dancer might say, 'but Annita, she likes you very much.'

To Klaus, they were all whores.

Ten minutes later, Elizabeta joined him. Close up, she was even more exotic than she'd appeared on the dance floor, her dark hair pulled back tight, highlighting her impressive cheekbones. The kohl-rimmed eyes, the blood-red silk rose behind one ear and the velvet choker about her throat created a highly theatrical effect, as was the intention. But candlelight was kind. Klaus, who had seen her in harsher lighting, knew that she was showing her age. At thirty, Elizabeta was the oldest of the dancers employed at Oswaldo's and her days were numbered.

He poured her a glass of 'champagne' from the bottle that sat in its ice-bucket on the table. The management did not mind if the dancers sat with the customers, so long as the customers were generous with the 'champagne'. Klaus looked around for the man with whom Elizabeta had been dancing, surprised that she had not joined him at his table, but she answered the question before he could ask it.

'He does not like champagne,' she said with a disdainful shrug. It meant that the man did not know the rules. The girls received a bonus for every bottle of 'champagne' a customer bought them.

Elizabeta chatted and flirted with him as she drank the wine. When she had finished the glass, he poured her another, upon which she excused herself briefly.

'I will be back in just one minute,' she promised, 'you will dance with me, yes?'

'Of course.'

She kissed him on the cheek and departed, glass in hand.

He watched, amused as she pretended to chat with one of the other girls beside a clump of palms, knowing that they were both surreptitiously tipping their wine into a pot plant. They all did it – it was amazing the plants continued to survive.

Upon her return, they danced to an excellent tango arrangement of 'Perfidia', after which he poured her another glass of 'champagne', which she took with her as she excused herself to visit the powder room, where Klaus knew she would pour her drink down the lavatory. It was all part of the game. Occasionally an irate customer would realise what was going on and make an accusation, to which the girl would respond with a fiery denial at the top of her voice and one of the bouncers would appear from nowhere to defend her. It was a humiliating experience for the customer, who either left in high dudgeon never to return, or learned that in the future he must abide by the rules.

Klaus ordered a second bottle of 'champagne' and danced with a number of the other girls but, two bottles later, towards the end of the evening, he returned his attention to Elizabeta. There were no new girls on tonight, which was a pity, he would have liked to have tried a new girl, and a younger one at that, but of those available Elizabeta was the most exciting in bed, so she would have to do.

They took a taxi to La Recoleta, and it was three o'clock in the morning when they pulled up outside his apartment block. A converted nineteenth-century mansion in French-style architecture, it was a handsome building with balconies overlooking the elegant Avenida Alvear.

He led her through the side entrance and up the stairs to his apartment on the second floor, and as soon as he'd turned on the lights and closed the door behind them, he started to undress.

Elizabeta was disappointed. It was going to be another of 'those' nights, another of the nights when he treated her like a whore. She didn't like him when he was like this. She was not a whore, she was a dancer, and the first several times he'd brought her to his apartment he'd treated her with respect. He'd played records on his gramophone and they'd danced, and he'd talked about the music. The Comedian Harmonists were his favourite recording artists he'd told her as they'd danced to a German rendition of 'Amapola' which she'd found rather strange. 'Amapola' was a Spanish song and she hadn't liked hearing it sung in German, but she'd nonetheless taken it as a good omen. 'Amapola' had always been her own special favourite and she'd fantasised about the possible implications of such a coincidence. He was handsome and rich and a gentleman, and it was not the first time Elizabeta had entertained such fantasies.

There had been no mention of money, and as he'd said goodbye at the door, he'd slipped 'a little present', as he called it, into her evening bag. She'd been equally gracious in her acceptance. 'Thank you,' she'd said, 'you are very kind,' and she hadn't even looked in her evening bag until she'd left the apartment. But out in the street, when she'd counted the notes, she'd found each time that he'd been most generous.

He was still generous in the amount that he gave her, but it was no longer a 'present', it was a payment, and he no longer saw her to the door. These days he thrust the notes into her hand and Elizabeta had stopped deluding herself. He was just another man interested only in her body, but she wished he would treat her with a little more dignity.

She started undressing. Perhaps he wanted to make love right here in the lounge room; they'd done so before. They'd danced naked to 'Amapola' that very first time, and she'd fantasised that the two of them belonged together, that she lived in this luxurious home, surrounded by antique furniture and works of art, and that this man was hers. And as they'd danced she'd straddled him, taking pride in the pleasure she offered, her unspoken assurance being that he would receive such pleasure nightly if she were his.

'In the bedroom,' he said. Naked to the waist, he flung his shirt over a chair. 'And don't turn the light on,' he added as he crossed to the gramophone which sat on the heavy oak dresser in the corner.

She obeyed, leaving the door open so that some light spilled through from the lounge room, and as she undressed and slipped naked between the sheets, she heard the music. The Comedian Harmonists again, but this time it was 'Barcarole'. She wasn't sure what to expect. He'd played 'Barcarole' once before as they'd made love and he'd behaved differently. 'Love me, love me,' he'd said over and over, and she had. She'd made love to him fiercely, the way she knew he liked it. But he hadn't liked it that night. 'No,' he'd said as she'd clawed his back and bucked like a wild mare. 'Not that way! It wouldn't be that way!'

Elizabeta now lay in the gloom of the room, hearing 'Barcarole' and wondering what it was that he wanted of her.

He stood naked in the doorway, silhouetted for a moment, then as he closed the door the room was plunged into darkness, 'Barcarole' still clearly audible; he'd turned up the volume just to be sure.

He was fully aroused as he joined her in the bed, there was no need for foreplay, and she opened her thighs to him.

'Love me, love me,' he whispered as he entered her.

She moaned. She would play it differently this time, she decided, and without moving her body, she undulated the muscles of her vagina, clenching and unclenching, caressing him, teasing him, locking him inside her, then releasing him only to suck him in deeper, and deeper.

'Love me, love me,' he said over and over as the image of Ruth consumed him. This was right, he thought, this was the way it would have been if she had loved him.

For a year, Klaus had lost himself in the hot-blooded sexuality of the women he'd brought home from bars and clubs, but lately his fantasies of Ruth had returned. He'd tried to imagine it was Ruth he was making love to, but it had been impossible – Ruth would not respond in such a way. He'd played 'Barcarole' on a number of occasions when he'd taken women to his bed, but their fierce Latin passion and their dark, dramatic looks, the very elements which had so attracted him, had been distracting when he'd thought of Ruth. Tonight it seemed Elizabeta was about to fulfil his fantasies.

'Love me, love me,' he whispered. He was lost in her.

Elizabeta's own fantasies returned with a vengeance. He was hers, she could feel it, he was completely in her power, this was what he wanted. She wound her arms gently around him, stroking his back, feeling him quiver inside her. She moaned again as she drew him in deeper.

'*Te amo*,' she whispered.

The spell was broken in an instant, and she knew it as he growled and thrust himself frantically into her the way he usually did.

The bitch, Klaus thought, why did she have to speak? She'd spoiled the final moment.

He was near ejaculation and Elizabeta obediently met his urgency, aware that her power had evaporated, wondering what she had done wrong.

He rolled away when it was over, silent, his back towards her.

'Don't turn the light on,' he said finally. He didn't want to see her. Minutes ago she'd been golden-haired and blue-eyed and he wanted to relive the moment.

She'd made no attempt to leave, but she realised it was an order so she climbed out of the bed and opened the door to the lounge room, affording enough light to find her clothes.

'There's money in my wallet on the table,' he said, staring at the wall, his back still to her, 'take what you want.'

She longed to scream at him, but she didn't. '*Buenas noches*,' she said with dignity as she pinned the silk rose into her hair.

In the lounge room, she took from his wallet only the

amount he would have given her; she could not afford to lose such a benefactor. But she did not like him. If he were not so generous with his presents, she would refuse to go home with him – he did not deserve her. It was no way to treat a professional dancer of the tango.

CHAPTER EIGHTEEN

New Year's Eve was always a hectic time for Bob and Rita Duncan and Dodds Family Hotel, and the send-off for 1954 was promising to be no exception. It was barely nine o'clock and the dining room was packed, although most had finished eating. The lounge was crowded, as were the bars and the backroom which, officially, were 'closed'. There was still a month to go before late-licensing became legal, but the Cooma cops tended to turn a blind eye on New Year's Eve. Indeed, big Merv Pritchard was firmly of the opinion that it was preferable men celebrate the New Year in pubs rather than at separate drunken parties all over town. 'Easier to control things if they get out of hand,' he'd say.

So Cooma's constabulary was conspicuous in its absence as men spilled out into the street, beers in hand. Merv and his mates would avoid the necessity of booking those who bent the law this evening, but they'd be there within minutes at the first hint of trouble.

As yet there was none, and the pubs of Cooma were doing a roaring trade. None more so than Dodds, and it would get even busier as the final hours of 1954 ticked by. They would arrive in droves, and they would cram themselves into every nook and cranny and sing with gusto, while Rita Duncan would sacrifice finesse for volume as she pounded away at the piano.

For the moment, however, the air was one of expectation. Rita was not at the piano, the singing had not yet begun, and, despite the general din, conversation was possible.

In the dining room, Peggy Minchin was chatting to Maureen. Lucky, Pietro and Violet were seated with them, but they were paying little attention. Lucky had pulled his chair to one side and was in deep conversation with Rob Harvey and an American who were sitting at the next table, and Pietro and Violet were in a huddle with eyes for no-one but each other.

The two women had not previously been well acquainted, but they were enjoying each other's company. Peggy liked Maureen's forthright manner, and Maureen found Peggy an intelligent young woman with an enquiring mind, which was hardly surprising in a schoolteacher, she supposed. She was glad now that she'd allowed Violet to bully her into joining them.

'It's New Year's Eve, Auntie Maureen,' Violet had said, 'and I'm not leaving you at home on your own. You're coming to Dodds with me and Pietro.'

Maureen hadn't wanted to intrude upon the young couple. 'Particularly under the circumstances,' she'd said. 'And besides,' she'd added, 'I never observe New Year's Eve. I'll be in bed by ten.'

'You won't be intruding,' Violet had insisted. 'We're not going to sit there all lovey-dovey. Crikey, it's *New Year's Eve*. It's a *party*. We're having dinner with Lucky and Peggy, and everyone'll be there. You're coming with us, I won't take no for an answer.'

'Listen to you, Miss Bossy Boots,' Maureen had said, but she'd given in, and she was pleased that she had.

While the two women chatted, Pietro sat with his arm protectively about Violet.

'Eh,' he called to a man who barged past, jostling Violet's chair on his way to the bar, 'be careful.' But the man didn't hear, or if he did he paid no attention.

'Oh Pietro, stop it,' Violet said with a smile. 'I'm not made of glass, I won't break.' He'd been like this all day, ever since she'd told him about the baby.

Violet had been sure she was pregnant for the past several weeks and she'd longed to tell Pietro during their holiday in Sydney. But the doctor she'd seen at the hospital just before she left, a close friend of Maureen's, had said it would be another week before tests could prove conclusive, so she'd said nothing. She was thrilled now that she'd kept her secret. The fact that the positive results of her test had come through on the very morning of New Year's Eve was, to Violet, extraordinarily significant, and she'd relished the drama of the moment as she'd announced to her husband their impending parenthood.

'Tomorrow is more than the beginning of a new year, Pietro,' she'd said, 'it is the start of a whole new life for us.' The words had been an echo of any number of her favourite films, but they'd been apt and they'd come from the heart.

Pietro's response had been no less dramatic. He'd dropped to his knees and clasped her to him, his head resting as if in worship against her stomach. Violet had found it splendidly European. But since then, his behaviour had been quite foolish, she thought. On their way to Dodds he'd taken her arm every time they'd stepped off a kerb to cross the street – it was embarrassing.

'You have to stop fussing, sweetie,' she said, as he glared at the receding back of the man who'd barged past.

'I am sorry, Violetta,' he replied. 'But I am worry, you know?'

'Worried,' she automatically corrected. 'Yes I know you are, but you mustn't be, it's silly. If you get worried because someone bumps my chair, we might as well go home right now. In a couple of hours this place'll be packed, there won't be room to move, and what'll you do then?'

'Yes. Of course,' he agreed, but he looked about, his concern deepening.

Pietro's initial reaction when Violet had told him they were going to have a baby had been one of pure joy. But now that the news had sunk in, he was lost in awe. He, Pietro Toscanini, who had neither family nor any childhood memory of one, was going to be a father. He was going to have a family of his own. The prospect was overwhelming, and he longed to tell the world.

'I am to be a father!' he would have liked to yell to all those within earshot, but Violet had sworn him to silence. No-one but Auntie Maureen must know, she said.

'Not even Lucky?' he'd asked hopefully.

'Not even Lucky,' she'd said, shaking her head. 'Not until I've told Dad we're married.' Then she'd hastily added before he could interrupt, 'And I'll go and see him soon, in the New Year, just like I said I would.' Pietro had been nagging her about her father as often as Auntie Maureen had. 'After that,' she'd said as she'd kissed him, 'after that you can tell the world, I promise.'

And so Pietro sat in the crowded pub, surrounded by his friends and workmates, bursting with his news and maintaining his silence. It was difficult, particularly with Lucky sitting right beside him.

'We're off to the bar.' Lucky, Rob Harvey and the American stood, Lucky giving Peggy's hand a gentle squeeze as he excused himself from the table. 'I won't be long,' he said.

It was an Aussie custom which, upon their arrival in the country, Europeans had found most strange. Australian men deserted their women at dances and pubs to gather in isolation and guzzle beer, quite often for the entire evening. And when they, the Europeans, paid attention to the women, inviting them to dance or join them for a drink, it created a great deal of friction. The Aussies didn't like it at all. So why did they leave their women alone? the newly arrived migrants quite justifiably wondered.

Before long, the migrants themselves would become infected with 'Snowy' camaraderie, and they, too, would gather for 'a beer with the mates', but they never fully embraced the Australian custom. The Europeans were happy to join their fellow workers at the bar for a drink or two, but, unlike the Aussies, they always returned to their women.

'Are you coming, Pietro?' Lucky asked.

Pietro would normally have jumped at Lucky's offer – he loved being 'one of the boys' – but tonight he stayed put. 'No, thank you, Lucky, I stay here with Violet.'

'For goodness sake, Pietro,' she said with good-humoured exasperation. 'Go and have a beer at the bar – all the other blokes are.'

'No, no, I stay here,' he insisted. He did not intend to leave Violet's side for one second, but as he watched Lucky weave his way through the mob he wished he could tell him why. Lucky was his very best friend.

Despite the chaos that appeared to reign in the main bar, business was being conducted as efficiently as always. The bar staff moved like lightning, Bob Duncan and Robert Junior changed another beer keg as swiftly as they had the last, and Peter Minogue negotiated the crowds with his usual expertise. Two full trays of drinks, one on top of the other, sailed magically over people's heads as the Irishman squirmed through a sea of bodies on his invisible way to the lounge.

In the backroom, at a table jammed in the corner, a poker game was progressing in deadly earnest. Word had spread like wildfire that Flash Jack Finnigan was at Dodds tonight and a number of heavy gamblers had turned up.

Jack had actually called in to Dodds several hours pre-

viously just to have a New Year drink with his good friend
and fellow countryman, Peter Minogue, before the evening
became too hectic. But he hadn't been able to resist the
opportunity that presented itself, and besides, he didn't
want to disappoint the men.

The stakes were high, and the ever-silent, ever-watchful
Antz stood to one side guarding the table. It was apparent
that, to those hunched over their cards, the advent of 1955
meant little, and they would no doubt remain oblivious to
the bedlam that surrounded them even upon the very
stroke of midnight. Poker was always serious business, but
never more so than in the presence of Flash Jack Finnigan.

The babble of the bar rendered conversation impossible
and, despite the overhead fan, the air was thick with
cigarette smoke. Lucky, Rob Harvey and the American,
a likeable, lanky mining engineer called Rusty, took their
drinks outside. 'I'm meeting up with a few buddies out
front,' Rusty said, so Rob and Lucky decided to join them.

Now employed as a site engineer with the American construction conglomerate, Kaiser, Rob Harvey had included
in his team many of those who'd worked with him on the
Guthega project, among them both Lucky and Pietro. Rob
was well respected by the Americans and Lucky had found
many a new 'buddy' among the Yanks, which was not
unusual – Lucky found buddies everywhere.

It was a hot summer's night, but not oppressively so, and
on the pavement outside, Snowy workers were gathered in
groups, smoking and chatting as they downed their beers.
Some were earnestly 'talking shop', some telling bawdy
jokes and some mingling from group to group.

Rob and Lucky chatted to Rusty and his three American
buddies for ten minutes or so, but as soon as the Yanks
had finished their beers they were off on a pub crawl.

'It's our first New Year's in Cooma,' Rusty said, 'and
we're gonna have a beer at every bar in town. You guys
wanna come?' he asked.

Rob and Lucky bowed out, and when the Americans had left they moved away from the crowd a little, enjoying the respite and the ease of each other's company. They talked shop, as they usually did these days. There was a lot to talk about since the Yanks had come to town.

As had been anticipated, Kaiser and its equipment and work methods had had an extraordinary effect upon the Snowy. In just one month of construction, the massive Eucumbene-Tumut tunnel, twenty-two feet in diameter, was progressing at an unprecedented speed. The Americans had not only imported the most sophisticated machinery, they'd set up a whole new work system designed to offer incentive and encourage competition, in keeping with their 'time is money' adage. Tunnelling went on round the clock six days a week. There was the day shift, from eight to four, the 'swing' shift, from four to midnight, and the 'graveyard' or 'cranky' shift from midnight to eight. The teams were paid a 'footage bonus': the further they advanced past an agreed minimum footage, the more money they received on payday. A large blackboard was set up outside the tunnel entrance and, in endless competition, each shift would mark up its footage, eager to be the best.

Already the Snowy's huge network of tunnels was winding its way through the mountains like a vast underground railway system, but the progress to date had been slow and laborious. Kaiser was bringing about a massive change in the rate of construction. World records for the speed of tunnel excavation would soon be broken and new records for hard-rock drilling created, but with it would come danger, and it worried Rob Harvey. He'd spoken of his misgivings to Commissioner Hudson.

'Safety is being sacrificed for speed,' he'd said. 'It's an invitation to disaster.'

Hudson's opinion had differed. 'We have to move with the times, Rob, and the Yanks are leading the way.

They have the equipment, the knowledge and the organisation – we must learn from them.'

'But at what cost? It's become a race and safety procedures are being ignored.'

'Basic precautions need to be observed, I agree,' Hudson
countered, 'but we've been held back by parochialism far
too long. The days of the government bludge are over and
men need to become canny on their own account.' Hudson
approved of the American attitude, which encouraged the
survival and success of only the fittest.

Now, barely a week after his discussion with the Commissioner, it appeared that Rob's fears had been well
founded.

'I visited the hospital this afternoon,' he said, as he and
Lucky sipped their beers. 'The doctor said that he won't
lose the arm.'

'It shouldn't have happened.' Lucky shook his head. 'He
was a new miner, inexperienced, but it still shouldn't have
happened.'

They were discussing the accident that had occurred
during the morning shift that day, when a man had been
injured in a rock-blasting operation. Lucky was in agreement with Rob Harvey. He blamed the accident on the
American system.

'They consider many basic safety procedures "time
wasting",' he said. 'I've actually heard some of the bosses
use the term.'

'Gedday, Rob, gedday, Lucky – do you want for another
round?'

It was Karl Heffner. Since his own accident six months
before, shortly after his arrival on the Snowy, the Austrian
had worked hard to master his command of English. With
his thick accent, he'd provided many a laugh as he constantly mangled the Aussie colloquialisms he insisted on
adopting. But he continued unperturbed. Ever the prag-
matist, Karl was determined to become a local.

'Not for me thanks, Karl,' Lucky declined the offer; he would rejoin Peggy when he'd finished his beer.

'I'm all right thanks, mate,' Rob said.

Karl looked about, surprised that Pietro was not with them. 'My young cobber is not here?' he asked. Pietro had become his 'young cobber' ever since he'd carried Karl from the tunnel, or rather since Karl had added the term to his ever-increasing list of Aussie expressions.

'He's inside with his girlfriend,' Lucky said.

'Ah. Good.'

Karl joined in the discussion of the previous day's accident, and his opinions, interestingly enough, concurred with those of the Commissioner.

'Is progress, mate,' he said to Rob. 'The Yanks bring progress, and with progress is accidents.' He gave a philosophical shrug. 'Is life, yes?'

Rob nodded. Karl was probably right, but Rob was nonetheless determined that his own teams would continue to observe every safety rule possible, he hoped without jeopardising Kaiser's demands for speed. There had to be a happy medium.

'Now I shout for my young cobber a round,' Karl said five minutes later, and he went off in search of Pietro.

Rob and Lucky were caught up in conversation with a number of other workers as they mingled on the pavement and it was only when the sound of singing reached them that Lucky realised, guiltily, he'd been away from Peggy for over an hour. How very rude of him, he thought, and he left Rob Harvey in the street with the others and went back inside, hoping that she wasn't hurt at having been so deserted.

But as he entered the main lounge he saw her beside the piano with Maureen and Pietro and Violet, obviously enjoying herself immensely. The three of them had left the dining room to get the best seats as soon as Rita Duncan had started to play.

Lucky watched her for a moment from across the room, in her little black dress, her hair pulled back in its impeccable bun. Her arm was linked in Maureen's, and she was singing along with the others at the top of her voice. He thought how he loved the contradictions in Peggy Minchin: the passion and humour that lay beneath the schoolteacher facade, and the bravery too – the fact that, despite the image she so carefully maintained, she didn't really give a damn about appearances. He realised how much he'd missed her. Since he'd been working for the Americans, his trips into town had become less frequent. He pushed his way through the crowd.

It's a brown slouch hat with the side turned up . . .

Rita was playing a bracket of all the old Aussie favourites.

And it means the world to me . . .

As he reached Peggy's side, he leaned down and whispered loudly into her ear. 'Sorry, didn't mean to desert you.'

It's a symbol of our nation . . .

She didn't draw breath, but her smile was radiant as she linked her arm through his and continued to sing.

The land of liberty.

He loved her, he thought, returning her smile and joining in the song. He loved Peggy Minchin unreservedly and it was time to do something about it.

Rita played tirelessly for over an hour.

There's a track winding back to an old fashioned shack . . .

They thronged about the piano, all singing as if their lungs would burst.

I'm going back again to Yarrawonga . . .

Half a dozen different nationalities lent their voices to every song.

Our Don Bradman, now I ask you is he any good . . .

Those who didn't know the lyrics sang along anyway. And then came the favourite.

Give me a man who's a man among men
Who'll stow his white collar and put down his pen
Who'll blow down a mountain and build you a dam
Bigger and better than old Uncle Sam.

Roll, roll, roll on your way
Snowy River, roll on your way
Roll on your way until Judgment Day
Snowy River Roll.

Every person present knew the words to 'Snowy River Roll' – it was the song of the Snowy Mountains Scheme.

At half-past eleven, Rita deserted her post for a moment to pop upstairs and tend to the baby. Two-year-old Paula was refusing to go to sleep and driving the nanny mad.

Those who had gained the best positions by the piano didn't move, but stood eagerly awaiting the midnight singalong.

Ten minutes later, Rita was back, though she'd had little success with the baby, who'd kept playing. It appeared young Paula was intent upon seeing in the New Year, Rita thought as she once again seated herself at the piano.

Shine on, shine on harvest moon . . .

There followed a bracket of standard favourites, and as midnight drew near those from the bar tried to cram themselves into the lounge. It was nearly time for the countdown and 'Auld Lang Syne'.

Pietro, worried, wedged Violet between his arms and gripped the back of the piano, protecting her from the jostling crowd with his body, but she laughed and told him again to stop fussing.

Then the countdown began.

'Three! Two! One!' they all chanted, then 'Happy New Year!' they screamed, hugging and kissing, and hurling the streamers that Bob Duncan and his staff had handed out. Rita started pounding the piano keys with all the power she had left in her.

Should auld acquaintance be forgot, and never brought to mind . . .

They sang for all they were worth, and at the end of the song there was more hugging and kissing.

'Marry me, Peggy,' Lucky yelled above the din, their arms about each other, their bodies jammed together by the rest of the crowd.

She stared at him, not sure she'd heard correctly.

'I said marry me!' he yelled again.

She laughed. 'You don't have to feel obliged to make an honest woman of me, Lucky,' she yelled back. He wasn't serious – it was the exhilaration of New Year's Eve, nothing more.

Her reaction was so in character, he thought as he hugged her. The brittle facade of capable, tough little Peggy Minchin hid such a wealth of insecurity. He would ask her again later.

He did. Two hours later, to be precise.

You made me love you. I didn't want to do it. I didn't want to do it . . .

The excitement had died down. Most of the revellers had gone and several couples were dancing languorously to Rita Duncan's final number which, volume no longer an issue, she played to perfection, a few stray voices singing along.

Lucky glided Peggy across the dance floor to where Pietro and Violet were swaying gently in each other's arms.

'Sorry to interrupt,' he said. 'Oh, keep dancing,' he added as the young couple stopped.

You made me love you, and all the time you knew it. I guess you always knew it . . .

'I need witnesses,' Lucky said as the four of them swayed to the music. 'It appears she won't take me seriously.' He kept dancing, but held Peggy at arm's length as he studied her, the beads of perspiration on her brow, strands of her hair now untidy and attractively free.

'Marry me, Peggy,' he said with a raise of his eyebrows and a mischievous challenge in his voice.

You made me happy sometimes, you made me glad . . .

The music continued, but the four had stopped dancing, and Pietro and Violet stood breathlessly awaiting Peggy's response.

She was silent for a moment, and Violet wondered why on earth Peggy was being indecisive. It was obvious that Peggy Minchin was madly in love with Lucky, and his proposal couldn't have been more romantic.

But Peggy was in a state of disbelief, not indecision. It was often difficult to tell when Lucky was joking. Perhaps it was his bloodhound eye. Sometimes his expression seemed comical, sometimes even dangerous, and right now, he appeared to be daring her to say no. Was he serious? If it was a joke, she thought, then it was in very poor taste.

'I'm asking again,' he prompted. 'Marry me.'

'That's not asking.' She tried to sound flippant. 'That's telling.'

'I love you, Peggy' he said, and it was no longer a challenge, it was a declaration. 'Will you marry me?'

Perhaps it was the moment she'd secretly longed for, she wasn't sure, but it was certainly the moment she'd never believed possible.

'Yes, Lucky,' she said, aware that her voice sounded strange, but she didn't care, 'of course I'll marry you.'

As the two of them kissed, Violet felt on the verge of swooning.

After the hugs and congratulations, Pietro shook Lucky's hand solemnly.

'It is a great honour that you share this with Violetta and me, Lucky,' he said.

'Yes,' Violet agreed, and then the words just popped out, the timing was perfect and they seemed only right: 'We have some news we'd like to share with you, too.' She looked at Pietro, whose face was a picture of amazement and delight. 'You tell them, Pietro,' she said. She knew how important it was to him.

'Violetta is to have a baby,' he said. 'I am to be a father.' Imparting the news to his best friend, Lucky, was the proudest moment in Pietro's life.

The following day, Lucky regretted having accepted Maarten Vanpoucke's offer.

'A quick get-together to toast the New Year,' the Dutchman had said on the phone. Lucky had felt sorry for him; Maarten never socialised at the pub and he seemed to have so few friends – it was little hardship to pop around the corner from Peggy's for a quick drink on New Year's Day. But when he arrived in the late afternoon the chess board had been all set up, and it was obvious that Maarten had presumed they would follow their usual ritual. Lucky hadn't had the heart to say no.

Now the game was in progress, and Lucky's mind was consumed by Peggy. They'd stayed up all night, making love, eating cheese on toast and laughing about whether it was supper or breakfast. And they'd talked.

'Are you sure?' she'd asked, not tentatively, but honestly. 'You don't need to marry me, you know.'

'Pretty Peggy Minchin,' he'd said and he'd kissed her, tasting the pepper and cheese on her lips, 'I have never been more sure of anything in my life.' He'd wondered why it had taken him so long to realise just how much he loved her.

The game was fortunately not in Lucky's favour, and his fatigue and lack of concentration saw an early defeat.

'You're not on your normal form tonight, Lucky,' Maarten remarked, the jovial host as always. He poured himself another champagne; Lucky's glass was still full.

'No, it was a fairly big night, I'm afraid.'

'Of course, New Year's Eve.' Maarten shook his head as if he remembered 'those days'. He was barely six years older than Lucky, but the role of responsible middle-aged man seemed fitting for one in his position. 'I suppose I can't tempt you to stay for dinner? Mrs Hodgeman is preparing a veritable feast.'

'Thank you, Maarten, but no,' Lucky said firmly. 'Peggy is expecting me.'

The schoolteacher, Maarten thought, how interesting, Lucky didn't normally mention the schoolteacher by name, although it was common knowledge they were lovers.

'Miss Minchin, of course,' he said. 'A most worthy woman.'

'Yes,' Lucky agreed, 'most worthy indeed.' He didn't like the patronising edge in Maarten's voice. 'We're to be married. I proposed to her last night and I'm proud to say that she accepted.'

'My dear friend,' Maarten said, rising from the table and offering his hand. 'What wonderful news. My sincerest congratulations.'

'Thank you.' Lucky stood and they shook.

'Well, it's understandable you don't wish to stay for dinner,' the Dutchman said. 'In fact, under the circumstances, I'm most honoured by your visit.'

'It was my pleasure, Maarten,' Lucky said, 'thank you for the invitation,' and again he felt sorry for the doctor.

He felt even worse when Maarten opened the door to the landing and Kevin Hodgeman was standing there, a bottle of red wine in each hand, awaiting instructions in his usual gauche manner.

'Lucky will not be joining us,' the Dutchman announced, and Lucky left thinking that Maarten Vanpoucke must be the loneliest man on earth.

Maarten selected a wine and told Kevin to decant it.

When the young man had left, he sat at the dining table and removed his spectacles. They made his eyes ache when he wore them for long periods. The lenses were slightly tinted and they had a mild prescription which he didn't need, but he felt it wise not to risk plain glass in case someone picked them up by mistake. The spectacles were a nuisance and probably unnecessary, but they'd become a part of his identity, and it was best to maintain the image.

How remarkable, he thought as he drained the last of his champagne, that Lucky should be content with the little schoolteacher. The man had once had Ruth. How could he settle for something so inferior?

He rose and prowled the room restlessly. Thinking of Ruth disturbed him, and especially thinking of her with another man. Had she loved Lucky? She must have – she'd married him. He pictured the two of them together; Ruth offering herself to Lucky the way she never had to him. It was an image that had recurred with monotonous regularity lately, ever since he'd seen the photograph.

He needed a woman, he thought – he would have to find a prostitute. The sex would help, but it was never satisfactory – he always despised the whores for not being Ruth.

He poured himself a glass of wine from the decanter; he'd get drunk again tonight. Why not? And why the hell shouldn't Lucky settle for the schoolteacher? Good luck to him. He'd never find another woman like Ruth. But Ruth had given herself to him, at least the bastard had that. It was a fantasy that had haunted Maarten for years.

CHAPTER NINETEEN

'**G**abriella,' Renaldo called loudly as she walked through the door with a group of her fellow students, 'Gabriella, over here.' She saw him and waved.

'Here she comes, Umberto, now you can meet my sister!' Renaldo raised his voice excitedly above the babble that surrounded them.

It was a Saturday and the two men were seated in the crowded Cafe Tortoni. They sprang to their feet as the young woman joined them.

'Gabriella, this is Doctor Umberto Pellegrini.' Renaldo made the introduction with great pomp and ceremony. He was proud of his sister and proud to have a friend of Umberto's standing.

'Doctor Pellegrini,' Gabriella offered her hand, 'I feel as if I know you. Renaldo never stops talking about you.'

'Umberto, please,' Klaus said, returning the handshake. 'He never stops talking about you either. It's a pleasure to meet you at long last.' He hoped that his voice sounded natural; the words seemed to catch in his throat.

'You see?' Renaldo flung his hands in the air as if he were about to catch something. 'What did I tell you. How beautiful is my sister? She is Eva Perón, yes?'

Gabriella gave a skyward glance at her brother's theatrics.

'No,' Klaus replied, having regained his composure. 'She is not Eva Perón, she is Gabriella Nacimento.'

Gabriella smiled. 'Thank you, Doctor Pellegrini. Umberto,' she corrected herself as he held up an admonishing finger. 'I'm glad to hear it.' Gabriella was heartily sick of being likened to Eva Perón; her brother meant it as a compliment but it was wearing at times. She gave Renaldo a nudge. 'It's nice to be perceived as myself for a change,' she said meaningfully, but Renaldo simply grinned back.

'You are yourself, my dear, believe me.' Klaus said it in an avuncular way; she was twenty-one years old and he must tread carefully. But she was not herself. She was not Gabriella Nacimento; nor was she Eva Perón. She was Ruth.

Her fair hair, attractively pinned high on her head with wooden combs, accentuated the elegance of her slender neck, but he wanted to release the hair. He wanted to see it tumble about her shoulders, the way Ruth's had done when it had finally grown and he'd been free to admire her beauty without the stigma of Jew so startlingly stamped upon her.

Her eyes were not blue like Ruth's but they were equally arresting: hazel, and startlingly light in her clear olive skin. Her features, too, were patrician, like Ruth's, and her bearing regal, as Ruth's had been.

'Will you join us for coffee?' he asked.

She hesitated, looking towards the rear of the cafe where the noisy group of university students with whom she'd arrived were squeezing around the one available table.

'Of course she will.' Renaldo pulled another chair from the adjoining table. 'Do you mind?' he asked the couple sitting there, but he didn't wait for a reply. 'Sit down,

Gaby.' Hands on her shoulders, he plonked her into the chair and sat himself. 'There's no room for you up that end anyway.'

'How can I refuse?' she said with a wry grin to Klaus, who signalled the waiter.

'So tell me about yourself, Gabriella,' he said as he sat. 'You're studying medicine, I believe.'

'Yes, I'm in my second year.'

'A noble profession,' Klaus said with mock seriousness, and they all laughed.

'She was one of the top students in her first year,' Renaldo boasted, forgetting that he'd already told Umberto that. He'd told Umberto everything about his sister, he always talked about Gaby; she was the only member of their family ever to attend university. 'Beauty and brains, Umberto, she's got the lot!' He'd said that a number of times too.

Gabriella looked fondly exasperated, but she was spared having to reply by the arrival of the waiter. When they'd ordered, Klaus continued to steer the conversation in her direction, not really taking in her answers to his questions, but needing the excuse to watch her. A number of times Renaldo took over, and Klaus was forced to drag his eyes away from her. How extraordinary, he thought as he looked from one to the other, that this young woman, so like Ruth, was the sister of Renaldo Nacimento.

Klaus had met Renaldo several months previously, in the early new year of '47, when Renaldo's delivery service had been contracted by the clinic to replace a service that had proved unreliable. He was a flamboyant young man in his late twenties, with the rough and ready charm born of a true Porteno: passionate and vibrant, like the city itself. Klaus had found him fascinating.

'What on earth do you have in common with the man?' Fritz had sneered. Fritz von Halbach found Klaus's new friendship bizarre. 'He's a peasant, he's uneducated. He drives a truck. What in God's name do you find to talk about?'

Everything, Klaus had wanted to say, everything that you with your bourgeois mentality and your Nazi obsession fail to find of interest. He hadn't allowed his irritation to show, but for once he'd decided not to let Fritz off the hook altogether, and his reply had been tinged with condescension.

'Renaldo is self-educated, yes, but he's highly intelligent. He's a natural philosopher, in a way, and very passionate about life, as many of the locals are. I find the combination stimulating.'

'Natural philosopher?' Fritz barked a derisive laugh. 'Just listen to yourself – you're sounding like them. They're common peasants who sit around in bars discussing life and politics, and it's more than indulgent, it's downright dangerous. They need leadership, not free thinkers.'

Klaus refused to be drawn into such a conversation. It would only lead to another of Fritz's Nazi diatribes.

'There is a lot to be learned about local customs and history from men like Renaldo,' he said. 'I am of the opinion that it is advisable to mingle with the locals, to know their ways and to speak their language well.'

Fritz did not relish the inferred criticism. He never mingled, deliberately distancing himself, and he communicated only in passable Spanish.

'Mingle with the locals by all means, Umberto,' he said, his voice icy, 'but beware of becoming one. You cannot have it both ways. That is not your purpose here.'

They parted coldly, and in the months that followed, Fritz continued to make the odd snide remark about Klaus's friendship with 'the peasant', but the subject was not brought up again in conversation. Klaus dismissed the man's hostile attitude as a simple case of jealousy: Fritz had considered their friendship exclusive and he was annoyed to discover that it was not. Besides, Fritz's 'purpose' had long since ceased to be his. The Reich was dead, and while Klaus pretended to play his role, he had no interest in the cause. He gave the matter no further consideration.

But Fritz von Halbach had been quite right. Klaus did want it both ways. He enjoyed his position at the clinic and the respect it afforded him, and much as he would have denied it to Fritz, he felt naturally superior to Renaldo and his Argentine friends. But their acceptance was of vital importance to him. He desperately wanted to become a part of the city that had seduced him, and Renaldo and his friends treated him like one of their own. In their company he was a Porteno – they made him feel he belonged. Klaus Henkel had been quick to embrace the friendship of Renaldo Nacimento.

And now Renaldo had presented him with the greatest gift of all, he thought spellbound as he watched Gabriella. But she'd finished her coffee, he noticed. He needed to do something, anything, to keep her in his company.

'My car is parked nearby . . .' he began, about to suggest that the three of them go for a drive, but he was rudely interrupted.

'Gaby!'

It was the third time the young man had yelled from the far end of the cafe. The others were also waving for her to come and join them, and Klaus was having trouble containing his anger. It was extraordinarily rude; students were such an arrogant bunch, he thought, conveniently forgetting his own raucous university days.

'I take it he is your young man?' he'd enquired the first time the lout had yelled her name.

'No,' she'd said, 'just a friend,' and she'd waved back, pointing to her cup and intimating she'd join them when she'd finished her coffee. And now she had.

'I'd better go,' she said. 'They'll think I'm rude not joining them.'

Will they indeed, he thought. They were an ill-bred bunch who needed to be taught some manners.

'What a pity,' he said, 'I was about to suggest the three of us go for a drive. Are you sure I can't tempt you?'

'Not today, thanks, Umberto.'

'Another day then. I shall look forward to it.' He must tread carefully, he warned himself: she was young – he must not frighten her off. He would need to win her admiration before he made a move. It wouldn't be difficult – her own brother deeply admired him and was always quick to sing his praises. Renaldo would be his unwitting ally.

'It's been a pleasure to meet you, Gabriella,' he said, and he rose from his chair as she prepared to leave. 'If there is any help I can offer at any time with regard to your studies, please feel free to call upon me.'

Renaldo, who had remained seated, raised his empty coffee cup in a toast to his sister, his eyes widening comically. What a generous offer, he signalled, she would do well to take advantage of it. Renaldo himself was openly boastful of his friendship with the eminent doctor, and he considered their relationship an excellent trade. He showed his good friend Umberto the real Buenos Aires, Umberto picked up the bills for him and his friends, and he, Renaldo Nacimento, a simple truck driver with a local delivery service, basked in the reflected glory of their friendship.

'Thank you, Umberto.' Gabriella shook his hand warmly. 'That's very generous of you.' She wouldn't take him up on the offer – she sensed that he was attracted to her and he wasn't her type. He was rather old-fashioned, she thought, and he had to be in his mid-thirties at least, but she was flattered by his attention. She could see why Renaldo was so impressed: Umberto Pellegrini was a man of style. But she wondered what he saw in her brother; much as she loved Renaldo, the two men had little in common.

'Thanks for the coffee,' she called over her shoulder as she left. '*Adios*, Renaldo.'

For the next month or so, Klaus became a weekend habitué of Cafe Tortoni. It had not previously been one of his regular haunts, as it attracted students and bohemians whom he found rather pretentious, but it was where Gabriella met her friends.

He struck up an acquaintance with the waiters who greeted him as he arrived, and he adopted a table in the corner where he would sit with his newspaper and coffee. When Gabriella appeared, he would give her a wave and return to his newspaper, never intruding upon her but waiting for her to come to his table, which she always did. She would stand and chat to him briefly before returning to her friends. Then he would watch her surreptitiously from behind his newspaper, thinking that Ruth would have looked like that in her university days, a golden-haired beauty, free and uninhibited.

After several weeks his perseverance paid off.

'Do you mind if I join you?' Gabriella asked.

'I would be most honoured, Gabriella.'

He rose and pulled out a chair for her, waiting until she was seated before he, too, sat, and his manner was so courtly that she wondered whether he might be joking.

'That is if you can bear a little peace and quiet,' he added with a smile.

There was a timely burst of rowdy laughter from the students' table and she returned his smile. Yes, she thought, he had been joking, and she liked him for it.

They sat talking for nearly an hour, mainly about films and books. He was an excellent conversationalist and she found his company stimulating. Which rather surprised her; she'd only joined him because she felt it her duty. She hadn't wished to appear rude in ignoring the company of her brother's friend week after week.

'Are you coming, Gaby? We're off.'

It was the same uncouth young man, Klaus noted; he'd paused by their table.

'Oh.' She looked up, surprised. 'Already?' She'd lost track of the time. 'Oh, I'm terribly sorry,' she added, 'Umberto, this is José. José, this is Doctor Pellegrini.'

'How do you do, José.' Klaus derived a smug satisfaction from the respect she'd accorded him, and from the flash of José's impatient irritation.

José gave him only the briefest of nods before turning again to Gabriella. 'Are you coming or not?'

He was very proprietorial, Klaus thought. Surely they must be lovers.

'No,' Gabriella said sharply, annoyed by his rudeness. 'I'm not.'

'Suit yourself.' The young man shrugged and joined the others who were milling by the door.

'I'm sorry,' she said, embarrassed.

'Don't be. I was a university student myself once. Students are meant to be brash, it's a mandatory part of the image.' He managed to sound amusing and patronising at the same time and she laughed. 'Can I give you a lift home? You live in La Palermo, don't you?'

She looked a query at him.

'You share an apartment in La Palermo just off Avenida Santa Fe with two other students, am I right?'

She nodded. 'Renaldo, of course – my brother has such a big mouth.'

'He certainly has. He's told me everything about you, many times over.'

'I'm sorry, how terribly boring for you.'

'Not at all. Renaldo's proud of you. He's a good man and a good brother and a very dear friend.' Klaus stood. 'Shall we go?'

'Are you sure?' She was hesitant.

'Of course. I live in La Recoleta, it's not far out of my way.'

'Great. I'd love a lift, thanks.'

It was simple after that. The lifts became a regular occurrence, and she started to spend more time with him at Tortoni's than she did with her friends, to José's obvious chagrin – which pleased Klaus.

Everything was going according to plan, he thought. She preferred his company to that of her contemporaries, she obviously found him attractive, so it was time to move on to the next stage.

'Why don't we skip the coffee today and have an early lunch? There's an excellent place in La Boca where I often dine. It's not fancy, but the food is superb.'

She agreed without hesitation.

He'd deliberately chosen El Pelicano, a small *cantina* by the docks a block or so from the clinic where, during the week, he regularly had lunch. It was not yet midday, the place would be quiet. They knew him well at El Pelicano – the proprietor always made a fuss of him when he arrived. It was his intention to impress her without appearing ostentatious.

'Claudia!' Marcello bellowed for his wife. He was a big man with a big voice and the several other early diners winced, but Marcello didn't care. 'Come, come, Claudia, Doctor Pellegrini is here!' And his fat wife waddled in from the kitchen beaming proudly.

'It is a Saturday, you don't come here on a Saturday, never have you been here on a Saturday,' they both gabbled simultaneously in the hybrid Italian-Spanish they'd adopted thirty years ago upon their arrival.

'I have brought a special guest,' Klaus said and he introduced Gabriella. 'Marcello and Claudia Coluzzi,' he said. 'Good friends and great chefs.'

Marcello roared with delight and escorted them to the Doctor's favourite corner table by the window, where the red-checked curtains were drawn back to display the ever-busy passing parade of dockside workers. Claudia followed, confiding in Gabriella.

'Such a fine man,' she said. 'The work he does for the *barrio* . . .' She flapped her plump hands in the air as if words couldn't express her admiration. 'He is a dedicated doctor, we are all so grateful . . .'

'What is on the menu today that you would especially recommend, Claudia?' Klaus interrupted the woman's flow kindly, but with an apologetic look at Gabriella.

'Ah yes.' Claudia rattled off several Italian and Spanish dishes, describing every ingredient and method of preparation, while Marcello fetched a bottle of the Doctor's favourite wine.

Gabriella was intrigued. Umberto was well off, Renaldo had told her so. He could have taken her to any number of exclusive restaurants if he'd wished to impress her, but he had chosen El Pelicano, a favourite among the dockside workers, run by a working-class family just like her own.

When they'd ordered their food and the couple had left them, she urged him to tell her about his work at the clinic. She hoped he didn't think she was presumptuous, she said, but she was eager to learn.

He talked at length about the clinic and its purpose in serving the poor. It was easy to sound committed: his work there was enjoyable, as well as being a distraction from the single-minded obsession of Fritz von Halbach.

Gabriella was enthralled. She asked him questions about his background, and he invented a whole scenario, deriving pleasure from the fabrication. His Neapolitan parents had not been wealthy, he told her, and even as an impoverished student at university in Rome, he'd viewed medicine as a 'calling'. It was an opportunity to serve humanity, he said. He'd practised in major European hospitals, but he'd never been more fulfilled in his work than he was here in Buenos Aires at the Rosario Medical Clinic. He had her in the palm of his hand, he could sense it, and he said everything he knew she wanted to hear.

The food arrived, a huge dish of steaming paella which

Claudia ceremoniously placed at the centre of the table, and they gave her a round of applause. She served them individually, setting out side bowls for the mussel and clam shells, and then she fetched a crusty loaf of bread on a wooden cutting board.

When she'd gone, Gabriella cut the bread and they ate, but the arrival of the food had not distracted her from her interest in his career. She asked more questions, encouraging him to talk more.

Klaus obliged, and as he did, he recalled his one-sided conversations with Ruth. He remembered how he had told Ruth about his devotion to the preservation of human life. He hadn't meant it at the time; he'd been distancing himself from Mengele, and she hadn't been paying attention anyway. But it was different now. This was how it should have been. She should have been hanging on his every word, just as Gabriella was. The thought inspired him, and he spoke with passion.

Gabriella was captivated. Umberto's dedication paralleled her own youthful ambition. She had always longed to be a doctor, even when it had seemed an unattainable goal for someone of her background. But she had worked hard, winning a scholarship, and her family had joined the struggle, contributing whatever money they could towards her education. She admired Umberto – he symbolised all that was noble in her chosen profession.

'Good God, listen to me, I haven't stopped talking,' he said finally. 'I'm so sorry, Gabriella, I hope I haven't bored you.' He knew that he hadn't.

'No, no,' she insisted, 'you're an inspiration, Umberto. And I'm the one who should apologise, I shouldn't have asked all those questions. You've barely touched your food.'

He poured her another glass of wine and tucked into the paella.

She was thoughtful for a moment. 'One day,' she said, 'if and when I graduate –'

'When,' he corrected her, 'not if.'

'Yes,' she agreed firmly, 'when. When I graduate I'd like to do the work that you do. I'd like to practise at a place like the Rosario clinic.'

'Well, as it happens, I'm dining next week with the director,' Klaus said. The opportunity which suddenly presented itself was irresistible. 'Doctor von Halbach is a very close friend of mine. Perhaps you'd like to join us?'

'I'd love to,' she said eagerly.

'Excellent. Thursday night, I'll pick you up at eight. Are you ready for coffee?'

How simple it had been, he thought. He hadn't intended to ask her out for an evening, not yet: he'd felt he might be rushing her. But the lunch today had changed everything. She was more than attracted to him – she was a young, impressionable woman suffering a severe case of hero-worship. It would be so easy to seduce her. He'd moved on to that stage far sooner than he'd expected to.

Klaus went to Oswaldo's that night. And he took Elizabeta home with him. He'd slept with no-one but Elizabeta since the day he'd met Gabriella. He had trained Elizabeta, or rather she had trained herself. She no longer spoke as they coupled, but she caressed him the way Ruth would have done had she loved him. And she gave herself to him the way Ruth would have given herself, tenderly, deeply, engulfing him. And each time, she departed in silence, leaving him in the dark, alone with his fantasy.

But tonight, the fantasy became blurred. One moment Elizabeta was Ruth, welcoming him into her, the next she was Gabriella, consuming him with her desire. And afterwards, when Elizabeta had gone and he lay in the darkened bedroom, the images of his fantasy became intertwined. He could no longer distinguish between them. Ruth and Gabriella had become one.

Klaus's impatience grew intolerable during the days that followed. He couldn't wait for Thursday. On Thursday they would both be his, and there would be no need for darkness.

'Where are we going?' she asked as she climbed into the car. She'd been waiting for him in the street outside her apartment block, an ugly modern high-rise building, one of a number which jarred among the plazas and parks of Palermo.

It was a sultry night in mid June and she was wearing the lightest evening dress with shoestring straps; she looked very beautiful, he thought. He was delighted to see that her hair was no longer pinned up. Held back from her face with combs, it tumbled down to her shoulders, flaxen gold, just like Ruth's. Soon he would feel it run through his fingers, just as Ruth's had, soft and silken.

'We're dining at my place,' he said, 'Fritz will be joining us in about half an hour.' There was probably no need to continue the charade of a meeting with von Halbach, he thought; she had worn her flimsy dress in order to please him, she would be happy to find that they were alone. But he decided it was best to play it safe.

'Oh.' She was surprised: she'd presumed they'd be going to an upmarket restaurant.

'I hope you don't mind.'

'Of course not.' She didn't, but she felt a bit silly in her best evening dress.

'What a glorious apartment.'

'Yes, it is, isn't it,' he agreed as she wandered about looking at the works of art. 'I don't own it, of course,' he lied, feeling it wise not to appear too extravagant. 'The rental is a shocking indulgence, but it's my weakness, I'm afraid. I like beautiful things.' He looked at her meaningfully, but she was too busy examining her surroundings to notice, so he crossed to the bar and poured two glasses of Dom Perignon from the bottle in the ice-bucket. 'The owner is an art collector. Feel free to have a wander around.'

She peered into the dining room, with its crystal chandelier and huge oak table with seating for twelve, and she walked out onto the stone balcony to look down at Avenida Alvear. It surprised her that Umberto Pellegrini lived in the lap of luxury. Although she knew he was well off, it seemed at odds with his choice of work at the Rosario Medical Clinic. But then, she recalled, at their first meeting he'd struck her as a man of style.

When she stepped back inside, he was waiting for her, a glass in each hand, and he'd placed a tray of tapas on the large coffee table in the centre of the lounge room.

'To you, Gabriella,' he said, handing her a glass, 'to you and your career.'

'Thank you, Umberto.' They clinked and drank.

'Take a seat, help yourself,' he said, gesturing simultaneously at the sofa and the tapas.

She chose to sit in one of the large leather lounge chairs, which rather disappointed him, and he sat on the sofa opposite her.

'What's he like?' she asked, ignoring the tapas. 'Doctor von Halbach,' she added when he looked a little vague.

'Fritz? He's nice enough. A bit short on humour, but then many Germans are, don't you find?' He smiled, inwardly enjoying the joke; his anticipation was making him feel quite light-headed.

He was behaving rather oddly, she thought. 'I've heard of him – they say he was very famous in Europe.'

'Yes, he was a plastic surgeon, hugely successful. The rich and famous flocked to him.' Klaus laughed. 'I think half of Hollywood's been under his knife.'

She couldn't see the humour herself. 'How wonderful that someone like Doctor von Halbach would give up everything to practise at a clinic like the Rosario. I'm looking forward to meeting him very much.'

She was truly naive, he decided. 'Shall we have some music?'

He crossed to the gramophone, and as she put her glass of champagne on the coffee table, she noticed that there were only two side plates set for the tapas.

Carefully, he placed the needle onto the record. There was a little scratching at first . . .

'Do you like the Comedian Harmonists?' he asked.

'*Schöne Nacht, du Liebesnacht, o stille mein Verlangen . . .*'

Then the voices sang in perfect harmony, soft and non-intrusive; he'd kept the volume down.

'"Barcarole", it's my favourite.'

The sound of the German singers seemed to add insult to injury, and she stood. 'He's not coming, is he?'

He turned to her. Good, he thought, she'd realised. It was time to end the charade. And she obviously had no qualms; he'd worried that she might be a little nervous to start with, but she appeared perfectly at ease.

'No, he's not. It's a pity, but he was unable to make it – Fritz is such a busy man – so it's just the two of us.' He smiled as he crossed to her. 'You'll have to make do with me, I'm afraid.'

'I see.'

Her eyes met his directly, just the way Ruth's had, and he admired her dignity, he loved her for it.

'He was never coming, was he?' she asked.

Gabriella was not naive as a rule. Brought up among the tough working class of Buenos Aires, she was street-wise and had been aware of men's desire for her since she was fifteen years old. She'd sensed that Umberto had found her attractive when they'd first met, but since then he'd treated her like the eager young student she was and she'd thought no more about it. Now it seemed he believed they shared a mutual attraction, that his feelings were reciprocated. She was annoyed with herself. How could she have allowed this to happen? How could she have been so foolish?

'No,' he admitted. 'I didn't invite Fritz. I didn't feel he was necessary.'

She should have been angry, but she wasn't. She was sorry for him and she felt guilty. It had not been her intention to lead him on.

'I'm sorry, Umberto . . .' she began.

'Sssh,' he said, and she remained very still as he took the combs from her hair. 'I'm not. I'm not sorry at all.'

He ran his fingers through the flaxen gold; it felt exactly like Ruth's, as he'd known it would. 'You're very beautiful,' he whispered.

She pitied him as he stood there, so focussed on her hair, running his fingers through it reverently as though in worship. It was embarrassing. The man was more than misguided, he was deluded. He truly believed that she desired him.

'I'm sorry, Umberto,' she said, 'really I am.' She wanted to save him from his humiliation, and she stepped back, leaving his hand foolishly poised in the air. 'But I think you've misunderstood our relationship.'

'Oh no I haven't, my dear.' All he could see was the slender body, the shape of her breasts through the flimsy fabric of her dress, the fall of golden hair on bare olive skin. 'I've wanted you from the moment I first saw you.' He wasn't sure if he meant Gabriella or Ruth – again they'd become one to him. 'And you've known it, haven't you?' He reached out and pulled her to him. 'You've known it all the time and you've felt the same way.'

He tried to kiss her, but she pushed him from her. She wasn't frightened. But pity had given way to contempt.

'Take me home,' she demanded coldly. 'Take me home right now.'

Her voice cut jarringly through his fantasy. He didn't like her tone at all – how dare she speak to him that way?

Ruth would never have done so. And how dare she look at him with an expression of contempt. What right did she have? She was no woman of breeding like Ruth; she was a cheap little Argentine whore who'd led him on.

'You're not going home, Gabriella,' he said, closing in on her again, 'until you give me what I want, what you've been promising me for weeks.'

As he grabbed her to him, Gabriella could feel his mouth slobbering at her throat, his hands mauling her body, pulling at her dress, one of the straps breaking. She was repulsed, but she refused to be frightened. She fought back like an alley cat, grabbing his hair by the fistful, squirming in his grasp, trying to knee him in the groin.

'Get away from me!' she screamed, clawing at his face. She'd gouge his eyes out before she'd allow him to rape her. Her nails raked his skin, drawing blood. 'Get away from me, you bastard! Get away! You disgust me!'

It was enough to push him over the edge. The whore was disgusted by him? He exploded, insane with rage. He'd kill her.

He let her go, stepping to one side, nimbly avoiding the knee that lashed up at him, and, hauling back his arm, he smashed her in the face with his closed fist as hard as he could.

Her head snapped back and she spun away from him. For a split second, she seemed to hang motionless, her hair splayed like a fan about her. Then she dropped like a sack of wheat and lay motionless on the floor.

He regained his senses as quickly as he'd lost them. He didn't care if he'd killed her – she'd asked for it – but it would present complications if he had.

He knelt beside her, massaging the aching knuckles of his right hand. She moaned, semi-conscious, and raised her head slightly, gagging for breath, spitting out' blood and shattered splinters of teeth, her jaw plainly broken. Good, the bitch would live – not that she deserved to.

He fetched a towel from the bathroom and draped it around him to avoid the blood, then slung her over his shoulder.

There was no-one around as he carried her out of the side entrance, just as no-one had seen them arrive.

He drove her to a deserted backstreet in Palermo, not far from her apartment block, and left her moaning on the pavement. She could make her way home from there, or someone could find her – it was no concern of his.

He reviewed the situation on the drive home. It was an unfortunate incident, but he doubted there would be any repercussions he couldn't handle. She certainly wouldn't go to the police – she wouldn't dare. Who would believe her if she did? Her status as a medical student meant nothing; she was a working-class girl from the backstreets of Buenos Aires, just a guttersnipe like the rest of them, and he was a highly respected man with impeccable credentials. She would be laughed at if she made any accusations. The only problem would be her brother. Renaldo would most certainly seek revenge. No matter, Klaus thought, his army-issue Luger remained in perfect working order in the drawer by his bed at all times. He would carry it with him when he ventured out at night from now on. If the man attacked him it would be a pure case of self-defence.

Back at the apartment, the gramophone was scratching. He took the record off the turntable – it was ruined. Just like the last time, he thought, he would have to buy another; ironic how things had come full circle. But it had been stupid of him to liken the Argentine whore to Ruth. There was no comparison, there never had been and there never would be. He must not make that mistake again.

He bathed his bruised knuckles and his face. The scratch marks where she had clawed him were quite evident; he would have to invent an excuse tomorrow – Fritz was bound to make a comment.

They came for him shortly after midday: Renaldo Naci-mento and six others.

'Pellegrini, where is he?' Renaldo demanded of the young receptionist behind the counter of the clinic.

The girl was unnerved by the mood of the men. They were plainly out to cause trouble, but she stood her ground. She knew Renaldo, he always greeted her when he made his deliveries and more often than not he flirted with her. She found him very attractive and she'd been hoping for some time he might ask her out. He was being very rude, she thought, no-one referred to the Doctor in such a manner.

'Doctor Pellegrini is not available,' she said primly, 'he is in conference with Doctor von Halbach.'

Renaldo made no reply, but strode into the clinic, the others following. The girl called after them to no effect. She picked up the telephone receiver and dialled frantically.

The men barged along the main corridor, past bays where patients waited outside consulting rooms. Curious glances were cast in their direction, muttered whispers exchanged, but no-one attempted to interfere or call for help. It was best not to get involved.

Renaldo knew his way around. He cut through the large storage room that opened onto the rear courtyard of the building where he parked his truck when he made his deliv-eries. It was also where he delivered the personal supplies to the back door of Fritz von Halbach's office apartment.

'It appears there's some trouble at reception,' Fritz said icily as he put down the receiver. He rose from his chair behind the desk and crossed through the lounge area to the office door. 'Perhaps you'd care to tell me what's going on, Umberto,' he said as he locked it.

Fritz von Halbach was very angry. He would probably have to call in the police to evict the men. Attention would be drawn to the clinic and all because of Klaus Henkel and

some sordid business involving a girl. He'd scoffed at the
man's ridiculous explanation for the scratches on his face.
'She has long nails, your neighbour's cat,' he'd replied
scornfully; he'd heard the rumours. Umberto Pellegrini
had been observed leaving clubs with prostitutes, he'd long
been told, and he had strongly disapproved. But he'd said
nothing. Who was he to tell a man how to live his life? So
long as Klaus was discreet and brought no disrepute to the
clinic, it was no business of his. But now it appeared the
behaviour of Doctor Umberto Pellegrini had brought more
than disrepute – it had brought trouble and the possible
intervention of the police.

'What have you done to so incur the wrath of your
peasant friend and his accomplices?' he asked.

'Renaldo?' Klaus rose, startled. He didn't have the
Luger. He hadn't expected Renaldo to come after him in
broad daylight.

'He's here. With six other thugs, and they're after your
blood.'

Right on cue, there was a pounding of boots on the
back door of the apartment and the sound of splintering
wood.

Klaus made a dash for the main entrance, fumbling with
the lock, as Fritz started dialling the police.

The men charged into the apartment, four of them
grabbing Klaus who was halfway out the door. They
dragged him back into the room, his arms pinioned behind
him, and slammed the door shut. He made no attempt to
struggle – he knew he was outnumbered.

'Put the phone down,' Renaldo said.

Fritz hesitated, but he had no choice. It was outrageous,
he thought as he replaced the handpiece. How dare they
barge into his office like gangsters in an American film?

'What do you want?' he demanded peremptorily.

'Him.' Renaldo pointed to Klaus.

'And what exactly do you intend to do to Doctor

Pellegrini?' Fritz asked, his manner still that of a pompous headmaster.

'We intend to kill him.'

The four holding Klaus started to propel him towards the back door, but Klaus baulked, turning back to Renaldo and the two men standing either side of him. He knew the two men, he'd got drunk in many a bar with them and had many a passionate philosophical discussion in true Porteno style.

'Without allowing the condemned man to speak?' He addressed Julio and Manuel, as if appealing to their sense of fair play, but buying time for Fritz to make a move for the weapon which he kept in his desk. 'Surely I must be given a chance to state my defence.'

'There will be no talk,' Renaldo cut in. 'You will say nothing.'

'Come, come, Renaldo, be reasonable . . .' Klaus glanced meaningfully at Fritz, but the man made no move for the gun.

In two strides, Renaldo was beside him, the flick knife appearing like magic.

'One more word and I slice your throat here and now,' he said, the blade pressed against Klaus's carotid artery.

Again Klaus glanced at Fritz, but Fritz was silent. Why was the man just standing there? Why the hell didn't he do something?

Fritz von Halbach remained watching in silence as they dragged Klaus from the room. He could have stopped them – a loaded Walther semi-automatic handgun sat in the top drawer of the desk right beside him – but he'd made no move for it from the moment the men had arrived. A shooting in his office was the last thing he wanted.

When he heard the kitchen door slam shut, he sat and dialled a phone number. Not the police this time. Whatever rough justice the men sought and for whatever reason, it was obviously not their intention to involve the police. Fritz was thankful. Police intervention was not in the best interests of Odessa and the Rosario Medical Clinic.

They marched Klaus down to the wharf several blocks away. They'd tied his wrists behind him and Renaldo's knife dug into his ribs. The people they passed stood to one side, some turning their backs. To Klaus, who was searching for an avenue of escape, the streets seemed ominously quiet. He noticed that El Pelicano was closed, even though it was lunchtime; from behind the drawn red-checked curtains of the *cantina* he could see Marcello and Claudia Coluzzi watching them as they walked by. It was obvious the whole *barrio* knew he was condemned and that it agreed with the judgement.

At the harbour dockside, among the huge crates and containers awaiting collection by sea, a group of workers was waiting, at least a dozen or more. Judge, jury and executioner, Klaus thought.

The men released him, and he looked about for a direction in which to run, struggling with the rope that bound his wrists. If he could free his hands at least he could take some of the bastards with him, he thought.

The workers formed a circle around him.

'Here are your Porteno friends, Umberto.'

Pocketing his flick knife, Renaldo stepped into the circle, the men making way for him, then closing ranks again. 'Those you so wish to claim as your brothers.' He pushed Klaus in the chest and he staggered back, colliding with José. 'Say hello to your brother.'

José spun Klaus about and smashed him hard in the solar plexus. He doubled over. Then José pushed him back into the centre where he struggled to regain his breath, snarling, enraged, about to charge headfirst at them like a wounded bull, prepared to fight to the last.

But Renaldo had no intention of allowing Umberto Pellegrini to die with dignity.

'You wish to learn our ways, Umberto? I have another lesson for you. Porteno justice.' Renaldo's fist smashed into his face and Klaus felt his nose crumple and his vision fade. He sank to his knees, only to be hauled to his feet by Renaldo and pushed across the circle to the next man.

On and on it went. From Renaldo to another of the men and back again, the blows brutal and unrelenting until Klaus could no longer be hauled to his feet. Then the boots came in.

'Enough!' Renaldo called a halt to the proceedings. He wanted Umberto alive for the final moment. The men stood back and he knelt, the flick knife once again in his hand.

'Can you hear me, Umberto?' He leaned over the bloodied face which was barely recognisable and hissed the words. 'This is what Porteno brothers do to those who harm one of their own. And this,' he said, pressing the tip of the blade against Klaus's stomach, 'this is for my sister.'

Klaus screamed in agony as the blade dug deep.

Renaldo twisted the knife once, then withdrew it, and nodded to the men.

They picked up the body, still writhing, and carried it to the edge of the wharf.

'Die in pain, Umberto!' Renaldo yelled. Then he gave the order, and they threw the bloodied carcass of Klaus Henkel into the harbour waters twenty feet below.

'You are a liability to us, Klaus.'

It was the first time in well over two years that Klaus had heard his real name uttered out loud. He couldn't see who it was – his face was swathed in bandages after yet another surgical procedure. He'd undergone many in the past two months and the pain was constant. He knew the voice, however. It was Fritz von Halbach. Fritz had been tending him regularly as he'd been struggling for survival in the upstairs surgery above the clinic. He could hear others in the room too, the shuffling of feet and the murmur of voices. Several he recognised and he knew that this was a gathering of the Nazi leaders. He wondered what it meant. Through the pain he tried to concentrate on what von Halbach was saying.

'We considered it wise to save you – the discovery of your body would have invited enquiry. But you are no longer one of us. Tomorrow you will be taken to a safe house where you will remain for several months while you heal, and then you will leave Argentina. You will be provided with a new identity and funds, after which we will wash our hands of you. You will never contact Odessa again. If you do, we will kill you.'

Fritz paused as if to let the words sink in, and Klaus expected one of the others to make some comment. But there was none. The decision had been unanimous, there was nothing to discuss. Then Fritz continued.

'You must not attempt to speak – the muscles of your face must remain immobile. Raise your hand to indicate you understand the full implications of what I've said.'

Klaus raised his hand.

'Good,' Fritz said briskly, and Klaus heard the door open and the tramp of feet as the men left the room. Then silence, and he thought he was alone. But he wasn't. Fritz had remained.

'By the way,' he said, 'I have taken the liberty of re-arranging your face. It is to our advantage for you to remain undetected. I hope you will appreciate my handi-work.'

Klaus could hear the sneer of superiority in his voice.

'Goodbye, Klaus. We will not meet again.'

CHAPTER TWENTY

Cam Campbell stepped out of Stewarts store, slipping the small parcel he'd just purchased into his coat pocket. He walked down Denison Street to his ute parked outside the pub. He greeted all those he passed and they greeted him in return. Cam knew everyone in Adaminaby, and everyone knew Cam.

It was sad to think the old town's days were numbered. Sad, Cam inwardly cursed – it was more like bloody criminal! Adaminaby was one of the oldest towns in the region – there were some families who'd been living in the township itself and in the district it served for more than five generations. He was from one of them. And the bloody SMA was going to drown the place! The dam wall was nearing completion and just over a year from now they'd start flooding the town. Then there'd be no such place as old Adaminaby; it'd be lying dead at the bottom of a bloody great lake! Oh sure, they'd drawn up plans for a brand new Adaminaby, but it would never be the same – the old days'd be gone, and all in the name of progress.

Cam Campbell's ongoing fight with the Snowy Mountains Authority over the payout for his land continued. He wouldn't sell up until the very last minute, he'd decided, and he'd come out on top. He already had. He wasn't going to lose his homestead, as it was on high ground well above the area allocated for flooding, and he'd already purchased other grazing lands. But the loss of Adaminaby angered him.

For now, though, on this hot, dry Saturday morning, the wide, sunbaked main street lined with its tin-roofed shops and verandahs remained as it always had: a symbol of rural Australia.

Cam climbed into his ute and headed for Cooma. He hadn't planned on heading there – it had been an on-the-spot decision after he'd picked up his supplies. He'd been about to drive back to the homestead when he suddenly thought of Violet. He hadn't seen his daughter since her Christmas holiday in Sydney. She'd rung to say that she'd had a wonderful time, and had promised her mother that she'd come home for a whole weekend in the New Year – she'd ask Mr Halliday for a Saturday off, she'd said. But it was now late January and still she hadn't come, and Cam had an uneasy feeling that perhaps she might be avoiding him; they'd had a number of altercations over the past several months. It wasn't right for a man to be estranged from his daughter, he'd thought, so he'd popped in to Stewarts store to buy her a present. He was pleased with his choice: a small candle in a frosty pink glass bowl; Violet liked pretty things.

'G'day, Frank.'

Frank Halliday was by the catalogue stand near the door tending to a customer's queries about deliveries, and as Cam greeted him, he looked around the store for Violet, but she was nowhere in sight. The two other regular young shop assistants were behind the counter, busily serving, and there was a girl he hadn't seen before stacking the shelves.

'G'day, Cam,' Frank replied, 'you haven't been around for a while.'

'You know how it is, big towns are a bit much for blokes like me.' Cam gave his easy, matey grin. 'How you going, Frank, keeping well?'

'Oh you know, as well as can be expected.'

Cam was waiting for Frank Halliday to give Vi a yell – 'hey, Vi, your dad's here' – like he normally did, but the man was making no move.

'Vi out the back, is she?' he asked.

'Vi doesn't work Saturdays any more – she hasn't for the past three weeks.' Surely Cam knew that, Frank thought.

'I'm sorry, Mr Halliday,' Violet had said, 'I know how busy Saturdays are, and I hate letting you down, but it's personal family business. I hope you understand.'

The way she'd put it, he hadn't dared enquire further, but he'd presumed that she wanted to go home for the weekends and he'd hoped that her mother wasn't ill.

'Oh.' Cam was obviously surprised by the news, although he tried not to let it show. 'Rightio. Thanks, Frank, I'll see you later then.'

'Yeah, see you later, Cam.'

It wasn't like young Violet to lie, Frank thought, returning his attention to his customer. But he wasn't about to say anything to Cam Campbell; Frank always made it a practice to mind his own business.

What the hell was going on? Cam wondered as he drove to Maureen's. If Violet was no longer working on Saturdays, then why hadn't she come out home as she'd promised?

Violet and Pietro were in the kitchen preparing scrambled eggs and bacon. 'Brunch', Violet called it; she found the term and its connotation sophisticated. 'It's not breakfast and it's not lunch,' she explained to Pietro, 'and it's sort of decadent.' She had to explain 'decadent' then, which had been a bit more difficult, but Pietro had been quick to grasp the general idea, and brunch had taken on a whole new meaning. Brunch was the midday meal he and Violetta had after they'd spent a languid morning in bed, making love and discussing their future. Pietro very much liked brunch.

Saturdays were special. Violet no longer worked at the store, and Pietro didn't apply for shift work on Saturdays. He'd decided that being with Violetta every single weekend, instead of just one out of three, was more important than the extra money Saturday provided. Besides, he'd nearly saved enough for their house: by the time the baby came they would be in their very own home. In the meantime, he arrived at Maureen's each Friday night and left on Sunday evening to start work on the early shift the following day. Saturday had become the most important day of the week.

Aware of the fact, and thoughtful of the young couple's privacy, Maureen had rostered herself on to a regular Saturday shift at the hospital. But her warnings to Violet had become more dire than ever.

'For God's sake, Violet, you have to go home and see your parents. You've got to tell them before you start to show. If you turn up looking pregnant your father'll probably have a bloody heart attack.'

Violet's stance had been sulky and rebellious. 'I'm not giving up a weekend with Pietro,' she'd said. She now had a valid reason for hedging; she longed to avoid the confrontation with her father and oscillated continuously between self-justification and guilt. Her life was happy and she wanted it to stay that way. Why invite unpleasantness? Besides, she was still mad at her father for the things she'd overheard him say about Pietro, and she told herself she didn't care if she never saw him again. But she did feel shockingly guilty about her mother.

'Then get some time off from the store and go during the week,' Maureen had argued. 'I'll come with you, I promise. Please, Violet, you owe it to your mother.'

Violet had finally agreed, but she still hadn't named a day. It was frustratingly typical, Maureen thought. The girl was burying her head in the sand in the hope that it would all just go away.

Violet took the pan to the table and started quickly spooning the eggs onto plates.

'How's the bacon going?' she asked.

'Is good. Is ready.' Pietro turned the sizzling rashers with a spatula, then exclaimed as the fat splattered his bare chest.

'I told you it was dumb to cook bacon without your shirt on,' Violet said, but she loved him wandering about the kitchen shirtless – it was so wonderfully decadent.

'Is no matter.'

Pietro spooned the bacon onto the plates and they sat.

'We could go to the pictures tonight,' she said eagerly. 'There's a beauty on. What do you reckon it is? I'll give you three guesses.'

Her eyes were sparkling with childlike anticipation and she wriggled about in her excitement, the pink silk chemise displaying the voluptuousness of her body to perfection. Pietro laughed – the mixture of child and woman captivated him.

'I cannot guess, you must tell me.'

She struck a dramatic pose. 'From Here to Eternity,' she declaimed.

Pietro wasn't sure if it was the title of the film or part of Violet's performance, so he waited for her to go on.

'It's one of the greatest love stories ever to hit the screen,' she said, quoting the advertising jargon. 'Everyone's talking about it. And it stars Deborah Kerr and Burt Lancaster,' she added importantly.

'Ah,' he nodded, still none the wiser.

'They're two of the biggest stars in Hollywood, Pietro, everyone knows that.'

'Then we must see this film,' he agreed. He didn't care

about Deborah Kerr and Burt Lancaster. He didn't care about anything, so long as he and Violetta were together.

'I can't wait.' She wriggled again and started tucking in to her eggs. 'Oh,' she said, 'we forgot the toast.'

'No, no,' he stopped her from getting up, 'you stay, I will do it.'

But as Pietro rose and crossed to the bread bin, he was startled by a burly figure which suddenly appeared in the doorway.

Cam stood speechless at the sight that confronted him. He'd parked his car out the front and entered via the rear verandah, and the back door which he knew was always left open. There they were – his daughter and the Italian: her in her nightwear and the Dago half naked.

Violet looked up, wondering what had caught Pietro's attention, and saw her father standing only several feet from her husband.

For a split second, all three remained frozen. Then Cam lunged at the Italian.

Pietro ducked to one side and, caught off-balance, Cam staggered into the kitchen.

'No, Dad!' Violet stood and yelled as her father fought to regain both his balance and his dignity.

Cam perused his daughter with distaste. She looked like a whore, he thought.

'Leave him alone!' Violet didn't yell this time, but her voice had the ring of authority. 'You can't touch him!'

Can't touch him? he thought. How dare the little slut put on airs and graces and order him about? 'Can't touch him?' he roared. 'I'll bloody well kill him.'

'We're married.'

Cam had been about to hurl himself again at the Dago, but he was halted by the shock of her announcement.

'You're what?'

'We're married,' she calmly repeated.

'You're married?'

His face was so comical in its disbelief that Violet wanted to laugh.

'We've been married for over three months,' she said, 'and there's nothing you can do about it.'

'Isn't there just,' he snarled. 'I can have the bloody marriage annulled, that's what I can do.'

'No, you can't. I'm nineteen years old, I'm not a child any more.'

'Don't you talk back to me, girlie.' The superior tone of her voice infuriated him, he refused to take any more of her cheek. 'You're coming home with me right now.' He grabbed her wrist and dragged her, protesting, out of the kitchen and through the lounge.

Pietro, who had made no attempt to speak for fear any interruption from him would only anger Violetta's father more, was galvanised into action at the sight of his wife being so manhandled. He raced after them, catching Cam as he opened the front door, grasping him by the shoulder.

'You will let her go,' he said.

'Piss off, you filthy little Dago.'

Cam shoved the Italian roughly aside and hauled Violet out onto the front verandah and through the open gate of its little picket fence. As he dragged her after him down the several steps, she stumbled, but he retained his hold on her wrist – he didn't care if she fell, he'd drag her along the bloody ground and out into the street if need be.

Pietro, who had followed, dived forward and grabbed Violet around the waist, stumbling with her, breaking both her fall and her father's grip as they tumbled to the patchy grass of Maureen's front yard.

'You are hurt?' His first concern was for his wife and their child, and, terrified, he helped her to her feet.

'I'm fine, Pietro, honest.' She would have been anyway, she was as strong as a horse and the fall wouldn't have hurt her, but she was thankful to be out of her father's clutches.

She was about to run back inside and yell for Pietro to

follow. They could lock the doors and leave her father to his fury. She'd call the police if necessary.

But, assured of his wife's safety, something happened to Pietro. Something deep inside him seemed to snap and he lost all control. He'd never known anger – in the whole of his life he'd never raised his hand at another human being – but he screamed with rage as he charged at Cam Campbell.

The collision brought both men to the ground, Pietro landing heavily on top of the older man who was winded. There was the crunch of glass as the little pink bowl in Cam's pocket was crushed to pieces within its tissue paper.

Cam struggled to his feet, fighting to regain his breath, ready to teach the Dago a lesson, but before he could fully recover, he found himself being dragged out of the front yard.

Pietro didn't know how to fight. He hadn't been taught and he'd never had the desire to learn, he'd never felt the urge to fight. But he did now. He dragged the man who would have harmed Violetta away from her, away from the house where she lived and into the street. He'd lost all sight of the fact that the man was her father.

Out on the pavement, Cam had recovered his breath and was prepared to do battle. He was good with his fists and far stronger and heavier than the puny Dago – he'd flatten the kid. But the ferocity of the young Italian was bewildering. The boy didn't fight ethically and he didn't fight dirty, he just screamed and clawed like a wild animal. The kid was a lunatic, Cam decided as he tried to land a punch, which missed. Then suddenly he was on his back and Pietro was straddling him, his hands about his throat, screaming like a madman.

'You harm Violetta and I kill you! You harm her baby and I kill you!'

Cam didn't hear the words, he just heard the demented screaming, and with all his strength he bucked the kid off him, scrambling to his feet, his fists clenched. He'd belt the Christ out of the crazy bastard.

But Violet was by Pietro's side, pulling at his arm, trying to drag him back towards the house.

'Stop it, Pietro, stop it!' she was yelling. Violet was terrified her father would kill him.

It was Violetta, Pietro realised, and she was very upset. She must not be upset – it was not good for her, and it was not good for the baby. The insane rage that had overtaken him abruptly disappeared, and he was left bewildered and concerned.

'I am sorry, Violetta,' he said. He put his arm around her and faced the powerfully built man who confronted him. He'd assaulted Violetta's father. How could he have done such a thing? But Violetta's father should not have treated her in such a way.

'I do not wish to behave like this,' he said, 'is not right. But you do not treat Violetta in such a way. That, too, is not right. I wish to be good son to your family. I wish also to be good husband and good father.'

Cam looked from the Italian to his daughter, and Violet nodded.

'I'm going to have a baby, Dad,' she said.

'We go inside now.' Pietro took her by the arm and led her away. He needed to get inside. He needed to sit down, he was feeling very strange.

Cam stood dumbfounded on the dusty pavement and watched them as they walked arm in arm across the little front yard and up the steps to the cottage.

Violet breathed a sigh of relief as she closed the door. Pietro had behaved heroically, and she would no doubt relish the drama a little further down the track, but for now she was glad it was over.

'Well, at least it's all out in the open,' she said.

Rescued from a private confrontation with her father, Violet had recovered remarkably quickly, but she noticed that Pietro seemed shaken, which she supposed was not surprising.

'Don't you worry, sweetie,' she assured him, 'Dad won't do anything. We just shocked him, that's all.' And she added with a smile, trying to make light of the situation, 'You should have seen the look on his face.'

But Pietro didn't smile, he didn't even hear what she said as he sat on the arm of the sofa. His legs were weak, and his head was starting to throb.

'Oh.' She registered that he'd suddenly gone pale, and wondered if he was about to faint. 'Stay there,' she said, worried, 'put your head between your knees, I'll get a glass of water.'

'No, Violetta.'

She stopped halfway to the kitchen.

'The leather strap,' he said, 'in my coat pocket.' He breathed slowly and deeply, calming himself as he felt his left eye start to flicker.

She raced out to the verandah and her bedroom and when she returned with the piece of leather he was sitting on the floor, his back against the sofa. She knelt and handed him the strap. He was going to have a fit, and the thought of it terrified her; she'd thought his fits were a thing of the past. He'd assured her each time she'd asked, which was often, that he'd been taking his pills religiously, every morning and every evening.

'Is there anything I can do, Pietro?' she asked desperately. 'Tell me how I can help you.'

'You cannot help me, Violetta. Please, you must not be frightened, it will not last long.'

He'd said that to her the last time, and it had seemed to go on forever, she'd thought he was going to die. She felt useless and panic stricken. Should she call for a doctor?

'But there is something you can do for me,' he said.

'Anything. Tell me. Anything.'

'I wish for you to talk to me.'

'Yes,' she nodded fiercely, 'I'll talk to you.' Perhaps if she could distract him, it might avert the fit, she thought. 'What do you want me to talk about?'

Pietro smiled, though his head was now throbbing. 'No, no,' he said, 'when it is happening, I wish for you to talk to me, like the doctor say.'

Of course, she remembered. *During the actual seizure, did you try to converse with him?* That was what Doctor Vanpoucke had asked her, and she'd been amazed when he'd told her there was a possibility she might have been able to make contact with Pietro.

'I wish for you to ask me questions,' Pietro said. 'It is most important.'

Now more than ever, Pietro was determined to discover the key to his past. He was to become a father, and a father needed a history to share with his children. Perhaps this was the way, he thought, and he welcomed the symptoms that he'd dreaded for as long as he could remember.

'I wish for you to ask me about the house, Violetta. Why I cannot see inside the house? I wish to know this.'

His deep breathing was no longer calming him, he was becoming agitated and he could feel his jaw start to clench.

'You will do this for me?' he asked as he placed the strip of leather between his teeth.

'I'll talk to you, Pietro, I promise. I'll ask you questions.'

Violet watched, breathless with fear, as his eyes started to roll in their sockets. Then seconds later, she watched aghast as his body contorted and he thrashed around on the floor, growling noises coming from deep in his throat. She wanted to scream, but she steadied herself and called out to him instead.

'I am here, Pietro. It's me, Violetta, can you hear me?'

The awful convulsions continued, but she didn't give up. Squatting beside him, she called over and over.

'It's me, Violetta. Can you hear me, Pietro?'

Again and again she called to him, and gradually the

thrashing eased and the noises faded until finally all was quiet except for his laboured breathing. He lay rigid on the floor, his muscles twitching involuntarily, his eyeballs rolling back in his head.

'It's me,' she said, 'Violetta. Answer if you can hear me.'

He spoke, and the voice sounded barely human. Through the clenched jaw, the leather strap and the foam of saliva, it was tortured and strange, and the word that he said was barely intelligible. But she recognised it as her name.

'Violetta.'

'Yes. Yes, it's me, Pietro. It's Violetta. I want you to see the house, Pietro. Can you see the house?' She felt fearful, frantic, but she forced herself to say the words clearly and methodically, urging him on.

'The house, Pietro. The house and the steps, and the door. Can you see the house?'

In the dim recesses of his brain, Pietro clung to her voice. And then he clung to the words as they started to make sense. He must see the house, Violetta wanted him to see the house. He willed it into his mind. And there it was. The house and the steps and the door. He had not seen the door before. Only the steps. He tried to tell Violetta.

She wasn't sure of the words, but she knew she'd made contact. He could see the house, she was sure of it.

'Go up the steps, Pietro. Open the door. Go inside the house.'

He tried to do as she asked, but he couldn't. He was unable to go up the steps. He was unable to approach the door. He willed it to open before him but it remained shut, and the harder he focussed upon it, the more the door remained steadfastly closed.

Then suddenly he found himself beneath the house, looking up through the floorboards as he had been before. Violetta had called it a cubby. And to his side he could see the man's shoes standing on the steps, and he could hear the man's voice calling him. 'Pietro! Pietro!' But he didn't want to hear the man's voice, it was getting in the way of Violetta's, and he tried to block it out, to hear only Violetta and to do as she said.

'Open the door, Pietro. Go inside the house.' Violet kept repeating. 'Go inside, Pietro, go inside.'

There was no response, and she was frightened. He was shaking his head, his face tortured with the effort; perhaps she was doing more harm than good.

He focussed on the floorboards overhead. He could see the light shining through them and he tried to will his way into the room above. And then, as he concentrated on the floorboards, he realised that he was seeing them not from below at all. He was looking down at them now. He was in the room: he was in the house.

'I am inside.'

The words were clearer this time, and Violet leaned in close.

'What do you see, Pietro? Tell me what you see,' she urged.

But he could see only the floorboards. He tried to look around the room, but his vision remained focussed on the floor, and he could hear the man again.

'Pietro,' the man said.

The man was not calling him this time. The voice was nearby, it was coming from directly above him. Then something else entered his vision. On the floorboards before him he saw the man's shoes, and they were peering out from beneath the hem of a cassock. He was kneeling before a priest, he realised, and slowly he willed himself to look up, seeing the tassel of the cassock, the priest's hands holding a Bible, then finally the priest's face.

'What do you see, Pietro? What do you see?' Violet asked.

'The priest.'

She wasn't sure if she'd heard correctly, it sounded like 'priest'.

'Tell me what it is that you see,' she urged again.

He could see nothing but the priest's eyes now, looking down into his, burning into his brain. The eyes of the priest frightened him.

'I see the priest!'

The words were coherent. Distorted as they were, she heard them distinctly.

'I see the priest!' He said it again. Then the words became garbled, disappearing into animal sounds and he was once again convulsing. But the convulsions were brief this time. In a matter of seconds the seizure was over and Pietro lay semi-conscious beside her.

She fetched a warm flannel from the bathroom and cradled him in her lap, bathing his face just as she had the last time. But she didn't cry as she had then; she was stronger now.

As he came to his senses, he knew immediately who was comforting him, and he did not even think of Sister Anna Maria.

'Violetta,' he said.

When he regained his strength they sat together on the sofa and discussed what had happened. At first Pietro's recollection was hazy – he was still weak and his head ached.

'I see the house, Violetta,' he said, 'but I cannot go inside.'

'You did go inside, Pietro, you told me you did.'

'Ah yes,' he remembered now the floorboards. 'I see the floor.'

'And a priest,' she reminded him. 'You said that you saw a priest.'

The priest. It all came back. The man's shoes, his voice, the hem of the cassock, and then the priest's eyes, how frightening he'd found them.

'Yes,' he said, 'the priest.' Despite his headache, Pietro was excited; jagged pieces of memory were coming together. 'It is the priest's shoes I see on the steps, I know it, Violetta. And it is the priest who calls my name. I see him in the house, I am kneeling before him, I see his cassock.'

Violet was equally excited. 'It's a breakthrough, isn't it?' she said.

'Yes, yes,' he agreed. He hadn't heard the term before, but he liked it. 'It is what you say, a breakthrough. This priest, I know him, I have seen him. And I do not know why, but I fear him.'

As Pietro spoke, he saw the eyes again, staring down at him as if they could see into his very soul.

'There is evil in the priest's eyes,' he said.

But he had seen these eyes somewhere else, he thought. He had seen them not long ago. Where? He struggled to remember.

. . . you will get headaches and feel tired. Do you understand me?

The doctor, warning him of the dangers if he ceased his medication, the stern eyes peering over the spectacle rims. He'd found the doctor's eyes alarming.

'The doctor, Violetta.'

'What doctor?' Violet was confused.

'The doctor when we see him.'

'Who? You mean Doctor Vanpoucke?'

'Yes. The doctor, he has the eyes of the priest.'

She was nonplussed. What a strange thing to say, she thought. 'But the doctor doesn't have evil eyes.'

'No,' he said. She was right, he told himself, it was foolishness of his own imagining. 'No, no, the doctor he does not have evil eyes.'

Pietro dismissed the image of the doctor from his mind, but the eyes of the priest stayed with him. He must not forget the priest, he told himself: the priest held the key. The priest could unlock his past.

'Pietro?' Violet queried anxiously. He'd gone very quiet all of a sudden.

He had worried her, he realised. It was not good for Violetta to worry. He stood and pulled her to her feet.

'I am hungry,' he said, although he wasn't. He kissed her. 'I would like very much to have brunch now.'

'It's half-past one,' she said as they walked back into the kitchen. 'It's way past brunch.'

The eggs were cold and the bacon congealed, but when Violet said that she'd cook some more, Pietro had a better idea.

'We will go into town,' he said, 'to a restaurant, and we will celebrate.'

'Celebrate what?' He was still weak from the seizure, and there were shadows under his eyes, but he seemed extraordinarily happy.

'Our breakthrough, Violetta.' Pietro liked the new word. 'I remember, is good, yes?'

'Very good.'

'Soon I remember who is Pietro Toscanini, and one day I tell our child. One day I say to this child who I am. This breakthrough is good, Violetta. So we will celebrate.'

'Yes, we will.' Infected by his excitement, Violet decided she would celebrate her own breakthrough. 'We'll go somewhere very public, and I'll wear my wedding ring and tell everyone I see that I'm married. And I'll introduce you as my husband and all the girls'll be madly jealous that I'm married to a man who looks like a film star.'

'But your father . . . ?'

'Dad knows now. He's just got to like it or lump it. That's his problem, I don't care.'

She kissed him, then raced off to the bedroom to change and get her wedding ring from the top drawer of the bedside table.

Lucky and Peggy stepped out of Prouds Jewellers shop into the Saturday bustle of Sydney's Pitt Street, but Peggy didn't notice the passers-by.

'Look, Lucky,' she said as she held out the splayed fingers of her left hand. 'It's even more beautiful in the sunlight.'

'You should have let me buy you something flashier. People will think I'm a miser.'

'No, they won't,' she smiled. 'This is perfect. It's the most beautiful ring I've ever seen.'

It was a very pretty engagement ring – the diamond flawless, the setting delicate – but he'd wanted to buy her something more expensive.

'I can afford it,' he'd insisted. 'Go on, Peggy, get something you can really show off,' he urged.

She laughed at his boyishness, but she'd chosen the ring she'd genuinely wanted, and had not been dictated by thrift as he'd imagined.

'I will not wear something gaudy in order for you to show off, my darling,' she'd said, and he'd had to give in. Peggy Minchin was not one to be dictated to.

'Well, I'll have to find some other way to show off then,' he said as they walked hand in hand down Pitt Street. 'Let's go shopping and I'll buy you a whole new wardrobe.'

'Why don't we go down to the Quay and look at the harbour first?' she said. She didn't want a whole new wardrobe, she just wanted to walk through the streets of Sydney with her fiancé.

Pietro and Violet didn't go to the pictures that night. Pietro was tired, and even Violet felt that the drama of the day outweighed whatever *From Here to Eternity* might have had to offer.

They ate dinner with Maureen instead, gathered around the kitchen table, and Violet chatted endlessly, her lamb chops sitting untouched on her plate.

'I wore it all over town, Auntie Maureen,' she said, waving her wedding ring under Maureen's nose, 'and I showed everyone I saw. The whole of Cooma knows I'm married now.'

'Well, that's one way to go about things, I suppose,' Maureen said dryly. She knew about Cam's visit to the house and the confrontation with Pietro. Her brother had stormed into the hospital.

She'd recognised his anger instantly and had refused to see him in private. She'd taken him to the canteen instead, knowing that Cam would never make a spectacle of himself with others around.

'I hold you responsible for this, Maureen,' he'd hissed while they'd sat in a corner away from the several nurses present. 'How could you stand by and let her marry the boy?'

'Better she have some family support rather than run off and marry him on her own.' Maureen had kept calm, as she always did, and as always it had infuriated him further.

'Why didn't you tell me, for God's sake!'

'It was up to Violet to tell you. I urged her to, but she refused.' He'd been on the verge of explosion and about to interrupt, but she hadn't allowed him to. 'I suggest you welcome the boy into the fold, Cam. You have no alternative. Either that or lose your daughter. And your grandchild,' she'd added. 'Don't forget she's two and a half months pregnant.'

'The Dago's a bloody lunatic! He attacked me!'

'No doubt he had some provocation,' she'd coolly replied. 'He's a very gentle young man under normal circumstances.' Then she'd risen from the table; it was time to get back to work. 'I think you should go home now, Cam. Go home and cool off.' And she'd left him, fuming and helpless, the nurses at the other tables casting curious glances in his direction.

Maureen hadn't told Violet the details of what had transpired at the hospital.

'Yes, I know,' she'd simply said when her niece had

started to recount the events of the morning, 'your dad popped in to see me.' And then she'd sat quietly eating her chops while Violet, still exuberant from the excitement of the afternoon, chatted on about the whole of Cooma now knowing she was married to a man with movie-star looks.

When her niece had finally run out of steam, Maureen returned to the topic of the morning's confrontation, and as she listened to Violet's version, she looked now and then to Pietro for verification.

He stayed silent for the most part, nodding occasionally, but Violet was unable to resist a little dramatic embellishment and eventually he interjected.

'Dad was going to kill Pietro!' It was a direct accusation and Violet made it with force.

'Is not so, Violetta,' he corrected her. 'I attack Violetta's father,' he said to Maureen. 'Violetta's father, he defend himself. He is not going to kill me.'

'Well, I thought he was,' Violet insisted, 'he looked mad enough. And then Pietro had a fit, Auntie Maureen. And I reckon that'd be Dad's fault, getting him all steamed up like he did.'

Maureen knew about Pietro's epilepsy – they had talked openly of it, the three of them. And they talked openly now as Pietro and Violet told her everything that had happened.

'Is breakthrough, Maureen,' Pietro said. 'The priest, he frightens me. But is good I remember, yes?'

'Perhaps,' she replied cautiously.

Maureen was concerned. She could tell that Pietro was pleased with his progress, and she didn't wish to alarm him, but it seemed to her that he and Violet were treading a dangerous path. Any delving into the boy's traumatised past should be handled strictly professionally. Pietro was epileptic and he suffered long-term amnesia; their amateur meddling could have disastrous results.

'But I really do think you should talk this over with your

doctor, Pietro,' she said. 'It is essential you seek professional advice.'

'Yes,' Pietro obediently promised. Maureen was looking at him very seriously, and he respected her opinion. 'Yes, I will do this.'

He would go to the doctor as Maureen advised, but not just yet, he decided. He must focus more on the priest first. If he could discover why it was he so feared the priest, then he was convinced he could discover his past.

Pietro and Violet retired early that night, and they did not make love as they usually did. Violet would very much have liked to, but she was sensitive to Pietro's physical state – he was exhausted. She cuddled up behind him instead, her body contoured to his, loving the curve of his back against her breasts, and the feel of their legs tucked together as one.

Pietro lay staring at the wall, still with the dull headache that had remained with him since his seizure. The priest was still heavily on his mind as he drifted into an uneasy sleep.

The dreams were not long in coming. At first the images were those he'd seen during his fit. The familiar house, and the steps, and the door. Then the floorboards and the shoes and the hem of the cassock. And finally the priest's eyes. Then the images became jumbled, first one, then the other, always ending in the priest's eyes.

The eyes devoured him with their malevolence as the dream became a nightmare. The priest was going to kill him – he had to get out of the house. Then he was running through a world of white, hearing his own frantic breathing and the crunch of his feet in the snow. But the world was no longer white, it had become blood-red. Everywhere he looked the snow had turned red – he was running through blood.

Then, as he felt he could run no longer, he was under the house, looking up at the floorboards. He was safe here.

Here he was away from the blood. But he was not safe. The blood had followed him. It was pouring through the floorboards, drenching him, choking him, he was drowning in blood. And as he lay drowning he heard the priest's voice calling. 'Pietro! Pietro!'

'Pietro.' It was Violet's voice and he awoke with a start. She was kneeling by the bed shaking him, her voice trembling with fear, and in the dim light of the moon through the window he could see that, in her hand, she held the piece of leather strap.

'Is all right, Violetta,' he assured her. 'Is a dream, that is all.' And he took the strap from her.

Violet could have wept with relief. He'd been making the most awful sounds, as if he were choking in his sleep; she'd been sure he was having a fit.

She got back into bed and as they sat cuddled up together he told her about his dream. Violet was horrified, but again Pietro saw it as a breakthrough.

'Is no dream, Violetta,' he said, 'is a memory. The priest, he has done something very bad. I feel his evil. If I find who is this priest, and if I find what is it this priest has done, I find who I am. This I know.'

Neither slept well that night. Pietro tossed fitfully, the images returning. And, beside him, Violet lay half awake, fearful that at any moment his nightmares would become a seizure. She was frightened. Unlike Pietro, she was no longer sure that today had been a breakthrough. She hated the priest.

BOOK THREE

CHAPTER TWENTY-ONE

As the train pulled away from the platform, Rob Harvey sat back and stared out the carriage window. His Saturday night excursion to Sydney had served its customary purpose: he'd picked up a girl in one of the classier bars and they'd gone to his hotel and had sex – it had been over four months since he'd slept with a woman. She'd been a nice girl: they'd had a laugh and they'd talked and, afterwards, she hadn't counted out the money when he'd given her the envelope. He'd enjoyed her company even more than the sex. But when she wrote down her telephone number and told him to contact her any time he was in Sydney, he'd decided he wouldn't. His intimacy with the girl had only served to remind him how lonely he was.

He wasn't thinking of the girl as he stared intently out of the window; nor was he paying any attention to the shunting yards as the train slid past, or the rows of shabby houses and the back yards of Sydney's poorer inner suburbs. He was trying to keep his eyes averted from the woman sitting opposite, and he was finding it difficult. There were just the two of them in the dogbox carriage, and he wished he'd bought a newspaper, or that there were others with whom he could strike up a conversation. It was going to be a long eight hours to Cooma, he thought.

He knew that the woman was travelling to Cooma – he'd heard her ask a porter on the platform. He'd already been seated in the carriage when he noticed her through the window – it was difficult not to. Perfectly proportioned, she carried herself proudly and her short-cropped fair hair framed a face that was strikingly handsome. She was possibly the most beautiful woman he'd ever seen.

'This *is* the train to Cooma, isn't it?' she'd asked.

'That's right,' the porter had said, 'leaves in three minutes,' and he'd opened the carriage door for her.

'Allow me.' Rob had taken her case and lifted it up onto the overhead rack.

'Thank you.' Her response had been polite, but she hadn't smiled. Then she'd sat, her hands folded in her lap, and stared out of the window, even though the train was still stationary. She hadn't initiated conversation and Rob had felt awkward, although he'd understood. Such a woman would invite the attention of men; she obviously considered it necessary to present an aloof exterior. But it was disconcerting nonetheless.

Now, as the train picked up speed, they both maintained their gaze through their respective windows, but Rob sensed that the woman, like him, was not really seeing the outside world. She was in a world of her own, he realised as he watched her in his peripheral vision. In fact, she was so lost in her thoughts that he was able to risk the odd glance before guiltily returning his eyes to the suburbs whizzing by.

Ruth wasn't being intentionally rude to the pleasant man who had helped her with her suitcase, but having now embarked on the final leg of her journey, she needed time to think. She concentrated her attention on the smudgy stain on the carriage window, thankful that the man respected her privacy and was not attempting conversation.

What would she do when she got to Cooma? She hadn't really made any plans beyond reaching the Snowy Mountains of Australia. She would try to find Samuel, yes, but he'd believed her dead for over eleven years. His life could have taken many a path – he may even have remarried, she told herself. Just as she was no longer the girl he'd once known, Samuel, too, would have changed.

Ruth had thought of her husband a great deal over the past three months since she'd discovered he was alive. She remembered the love that they'd shared, but she did not pin her hopes on that love's survival. She had become too practical, too hardened: life held no romantic miracles, and she expected none. But finding Samuel had given her fresh purpose – or perhaps simply something to do, she thought; 'purpose' had become an empty word. Her search for Samuel had, however, brought her to a new country. Perhaps it was this country that held the answer. Who could tell?

Her attention was distracted beyond the carriage window's smudgy stain. They were out of the city now, they had been for some time, but she hadn't noticed. And the vista was breathtaking, rugged rocky ridges towering over huge valleys of native forest that stretched as far as the eye could see. Ruth thought she'd never seen a landscape so vast and majestic.

'How beautiful,' she said, leaning forward in her seat to gaze out at the grandeur.

'Yes, isn't it.' Rob was relieved that she'd spoken at last.

'The trees almost look blue from here,' she marvelled.

'It's the eucalypts,' he said. 'The oil from their leaves lends a haze to the air, and from a distance the forests look blue.'

'Eucalypts?'

'Aussie gum trees, indigenous to this country. There're hundreds of varieties.'

'And the oil from their leaves lends a haze to the air,' she said, thinking how pretty it sounded.

'Yeah, so I believe, and in the right atmospheric conditions and from a distance it makes the trees look blue.' He felt himself relax. She wasn't really aloof at all, he told himself, and she couldn't help being beautiful. 'You're going to Cooma, aren't you? I heard you ask the porter.'

'Yes, I am.'

'It's a beaut town, you'll like it.' He wondered why she was going to Cooma, but he didn't ask. Her reply had been pleasant enough, but he'd sensed that the walls had gone up again. 'Of course there've been a lot of changes with the Snowy.' Eager to continue the conversation, he was about to explain the Scheme to her, but she nodded.

'The Snowy Mountains Hydro-Electric Scheme, yes, I know.' Ruth had made enquiries in Sydney about the Snowy Mountains. Thousands of migrants had been employed there, she'd been told. And Samuel would be one of them.

Rob felt like a bit of a dill. Of course she'd know about the Scheme, he thought, she probably had a job lined up through the SMA in Sydney; he was sure she was a migrant. Her English was perfect, but her accent was slightly stilted. He liked her voice.

'You're going to work for the Snowy, are you?'

'No, I hadn't planned to.' She'd planned nothing beyond her search for Samuel, but it occurred to her that it was a good idea. She would get herself settled first so that she wasn't a burden to him. 'But I think perhaps I shall look for a job,' she said, 'that is, if I can find one.'

'Oh you won't have any trouble,' he said. 'There are tons of jobs going around Cooma and the work camps. I'm Rob, by the way,' it was time for introductions, he thought, 'Rob Harvey.'

'Ruth Stein.' She offered her hand and they shook. She hadn't intended to get into conversation; she usually avoided situations like this. The icy reception she offered men who approached her always cut them off at the pass.

But there was an engagingly genuine quality to Rob Harvey, and she was interested in learning about her destination.

'So tell me about the Snowy Mountains Hydro-Electric Scheme,' she said. 'What exactly is it?'

'It's the biggest engineering and construction feat this country's ever undertaken.' Rob was relieved to no longer feel like a dill. 'A river's being diverted from its path to the sea and channelled through tunnels beneath a mountain range,' he said impressively.

'Good heavens.' She was certainly as impressed as he'd intended her to be, but she was also a little mystified. 'For what purpose?'

'Irrigation of the dry interior,' he said, 'and the harnessing of hydro-electric power.' Rob warmed to his theme as he described the principles of the dams and power stations. Her questions were perceptive and her interest rewarding. As they talked, he forgot to be in awe of her beauty. She was an intelligent woman whose conversation he was enjoying.

'And I've heard that the Scheme employs principally migrant labour,' she said.

'In the main, yes,' he replied. 'There was a shortage of local labour after the war so the government brought out thousands of migrants.' He gave a laconic grin. 'The Europeans outnumber the Aussies on the Snowy now, and it's the best thing that could have happened all round, I can tell you.'

'Why is that?'

'The Europeans have found a new life here, and we've found that ours isn't the only way to live. We can be a pretty parochial bunch, us Aussies.'

She found him a most interesting man. He looked and sounded like the quintessential Australian, or rather the way she'd pictured a quintessential Australian might look and sound. He was lean and fit with the weathered face of one who'd lived in the sun, and he spoke with a lazy drawl. Yet there was a worldliness about him. The contradiction was not unattractive, but there was a self-consciousness to it, as if he wished to disguise his obvious intellect beneath a casual masculinity. She wondered if other Australian men were like that; she hadn't really met any – in the few days she'd been in Sydney she'd kept to herself, wandering about the city, taking in the beauty of its harbour.

They were beyond the leafy Southern Highlands now and she looked out at the dry and rolling hills. The country itself seemed a series of contradictions.

'What an ever-changing landscape,' she said, not realising that she'd voiced her thoughts out loud.

'You wait till you get to the Snowies and the Monaro.' He was glad she was again inviting conversation; she'd gone silent for a while and he'd felt that he might have been talking too much. 'You'll see more landscapes there than you can shake a stick at.'

She smiled at the quaintness of the expression.

It was the first time she'd smiled, and he was once more struck by her beauty. He wondered about her background. Where was she from? Why didn't she smile more often? But he asked no questions; it was obvious that she didn't want to talk about herself. So he talked about the countryside instead, finding a lyricism he hadn't known he possessed. He wasn't sure why; he wasn't trying consciously to impress her. Perhaps he simply wanted to welcome her; she was a newcomer to Australia, and she seemed to him very lonely.

Ruth liked the way he talked. He wanted to share his passion for his country, and she thought how good it was to hear someone speak about their country with a passion that was not possessive. They had spoken about Israel with passion, she remembered, but it was always accompanied by the rancour of ownership. 'This land is ours and we will not share it,' they'd said. They'd killed those who had wished to share it.

Samuel had made a good choice, she thought as she listened to the Australian; he had been wise to come to this country. Rob Harvey had said the Europeans had found a new life here, and she hoped that had proved so for Samuel. She wondered if perhaps Rob Harvey knew him. It was quite possible – Rob worked for the Snowy, he was a site engineer, he'd said. But she would make no enquiries until she was settled. She would not intrude upon Samuel's new life until the time was right.

'Well, that was a quick trip,' he said as the train pulled into Cooma. It was late afternoon and there were now others in the carriage, from various stops along the way, but he'd barely noticed them. He hefted her suitcase down from the overhead rack.

'Thank you, Rob,' she said as they stepped out onto the platform. 'I've enjoyed talking to you very much.'

Still no smile, but he could see that she was genuine. In fact, he wondered how he could have found her aloof – there was not a shred of artifice about her; she appeared quite unaware of her beauty.

'Where are you staying?' he asked, signalling a taxi.

'I don't know, I haven't booked in anywhere. I thought I'd just . . .'

'I'll take you to Dodds Hotel. It isn't the classiest accommodation in town, but it's a family-run pub and they're nice people. They'll look after you there.'

The taxi pulled up and he piled her suitcase into the boot, along with his rucksack.

'Really, it's not necessary . . .'

'Course it is, I'm not leaving you here on your own. Besides, the train was early, I'm not being picked up for another half an hour yet.'

The train hadn't been early at all, and as he opened the taxi door for her he looked around for the Land Rover – it'd arrive any second. Lucky wouldn't be driving it as he usually did – he had taken a couple of days off to go to

Sydney with Peggy and wouldn't be back until Tuesday –
but Karl Heffner was due to collect him. Karl had spent
the weekend in Cooma and was going to drive them back
to the work camp.

The taxi pulled away from the kerb just as Rob saw the
Land Rover turn into the station courtyard. Sorry, mate,
he thought, you'll just have to wait.

He booked her into Dodds, personally introducing her
to Rita and Bob, and as Bob Duncan carried her suitcase
upstairs, he scribbled a couple of addresses on the notepad
Rita had given him.

'There you go,' he said, tearing off the page and handing
it to her. 'That's Kaiser's offices here in town and the other
one's the Snowy Authority headquarters. Give them both
a burl and mention my name – one of them's bound to
come up with a job.'

'Thank you, Rob, you've been very kind.'

'No worries,' he said. 'Well, I'll leave you to settle in.' As
she started up the main staircase, he slung his rucksack
over his shoulder. 'Oh, by the way,' he added as if it were
a casual afterthought, 'I'm coming into town next
weekend, meeting up with a mate for dinner here at
Dodds.' It was a lie, but he wasn't sure if she'd agree to go
out with him alone. 'Perhaps you'd like to join us?'

She hesitated, and he realised that the invitation hadn't
sounded right at all.

'There'll be another lady present,' he hastily added, 'my
mate Lucky's just got himself engaged.'

She remained hesitant, and he thought that perhaps a
cosy dinner with another couple had sounded a bit too
intimate.

'There's always a good crowd at Dodds on a Saturday,'
he said hopefully, 'I could introduce you around, you'd get
to meet some of the locals.'

He was a nice man who was trying too hard, she
thought. She could tell he was interested and she didn't

wish to encourage him, but he'd been so welcoming, she also didn't want to appear rude.

'I'd be delighted, thank you.'

'About seven o'clock then, I'll meet you here in the lobby.'

She nodded and smiled.

The smile was only one of common courtesy, he realised, but at least it was a smile.

It was four o'clock on Wednesday afternoon, and Lucky and his team were just coming off the day shift when Rob Harvey arrived. In their grimy overalls and hardhats the men were gathered around the huge tunnel entrance lighting smokes and chatting while Lucky marked their footage up on the blackboard. He wrote it with a flourish, and they all gave a cheer – they were well ahead of the graveyard shift who'd knocked off at eight that morning.

Rob greeted the others who called 'G'day boss', and then he drew Lucky to one side.

'Are you and Peggy having dinner at Dodds this Saturday?' he asked; he knew that the two of them often did.

'Yes, with Pietro and Violet – there's a band booked to play and we're staying on for the dance.' Lucky presumed Rob was tying up the transport into town; it was customary for them to liaise about transport.

'Oh. Right.' Rob hadn't anticipated the band, or the young couple whom he barely knew, and he was aware that the request sounded strange. 'Would you mind if I joined you?'

Lucky was surprised. Rob Harvey was a man's man. He didn't go to dances, he shared a beer with the blokes in the bar.

'Why not,' he said. 'The more the merrier.'

Rob decided that he'd have to come clean. Lucky was looking at him curiously, wondering why he'd choose to be such an odd man out.

'Well, actually, I'll have someone with me.'

'Ah.' Lucky grinned as the penny dropped. Rob Harvey had found himself a woman.

'Yeah,' Rob admitted a little self-consciously, 'I met her on the train from Sydney, and I thought I could do with a bit of back-up, you know?'

'Sure,' Lucky said, 'we're meeting in the lounge around half-past six,' and he left it at that. He could have ribbed Rob Harvey, but he didn't. He had the feeling that, for all his acute intelligence and his confidence in the work-place Rob Harvey was shy and insecure when it came to women.

It was on the dot of seven that Ruth walked down the main staircase to where he was waiting in the lobby; he'd been there a full five minutes.

'Hello, Rob,' she said.

She was even more beautiful than he remembered, and he was aware of the glances from several men who'd just walked through the front doors. He felt shockingly self-conscious; she was actually too beautiful, he thought, and it made him uncomfortable.

'G'day, Ruth.' They shook hands. 'How's your week been?' He couldn't think of anything better to say.

'I found a job right here in Cooma,' she said, 'with the Snowy Mountains Authority. I'm to teach English to migrants, and it's all thanks to you.'

She'd put him at his ease in an instant and he thought, as he had when they'd got off the train, how surprisingly free of pretension she was.

'That's good,' he said, 'I'm glad.'

'Yes, so am I. I'm glad I came to Cooma. I like it here.'

As they walked through to the main lounge, Ruth told him about her new job. She had to undergo the standard government medical clearance, she said, but that shouldn't take more than a week, and then she could report for duty.

'I'll be working with psychologists too,' she said, 'as an

interpreter. Interviewing migrants with problems, helping them settle in. I'm really looking forward to it.'

He wondered again at her background. She obviously had excellent qualifications. Where did she come from? Where had she studied? But now was not the time to ask. Ahead, at a table in the centre of the lounge, sat Lucky and Peggy with the young Italian and his wife. Rob took a deep breath. He wasn't looking forward to this – he was not one for social chit-chat. He would far rather have talked to her on her own.

'That's my mate, Lucky,' he said, indicating the table, and he took her arm as they wove their way through the lounge.

But Ruth had seen him the moment they'd stepped through the doors. Samuel. His arm around a woman, and plainly in love. There was nothing she could do. She was on a trajectory through a crowded room in a place called Cooma, and she was about to collide with her past.

'G'day, Lucky,' Rob said. 'This is Ruth. Ruth, this is Lucky and his fiancée, Peggy, and this is Pietro, and . . .' Rob faltered embarrassingly – he'd forgotten the name of the young Italian's wife.

'Violet.' It was Peggy who dived in to save the day, wondering why Lucky hadn't.

'How do you do,' Violet said, her hand outstretched.

'Hello, Violet.' Ruth shook hands with all of them. 'Hello, Lucky,' she'd left him till last.

'Ruth,' he said.

'Yes, that's right. Ruth Stein.'

The disfiguring scar on his face shocked her, but she'd been prepared for whatever she might find. She'd been prepared for this meeting for some time now.

Lucky had undergone no such preparation, and he stared at her dumbly, unaware that he was holding on to her hand far too long.

Ruth tried to signal him an apology. She had not

intended it to happen like this, her eyes said. Then she
turned away, withdrawing her hand.

'We need some more chairs.' Rob Harvey thought it was
a bit much, Lucky ogling Ruth like that, and in front of his
fiancée.

'Yes, of course.' Lucky sprang to his feet.

The exchange had gone unnoticed by Pietro and Violet,
who themselves had been openly admiring Ruth.

'She should be in the pictures,' Violet had whispered.

But the moment had not been lost on Peggy. Lucky
and this woman had shared something, she'd sensed it.
Did they know each other? If so, why were they saying
nothing? What did it mean?

Lucky offered his chair to Ruth and he and Rob Harvey
fetched two more from a nearby table. Lucky's mind was
reeling. She was alive, she was here. It was incomprehensible As he sat, he tried not to stare at her.

Rob ordered another round of drinks and they discussed
the luxury of late-night licensing. The long awaited change
had come into being only several days before.

'We were out at the work camp,' Rob said, 'but I'd bet
a penny to a pound there was some partying going on in
town that night.'

'There sure was,' Violet nodded. 'You could hear them
all over Cooma.'

'Here's to the end of the six o'clock swill,' Rob said
as Peter Minogue arrived with the drinks. He raised his
beer glass and the others joined in the toast, explaining to
Ruth the meaning of the term, which she found most
colourful, which led to a discussion of other Australian
colloquialisms.

'Running around like a headless chook.'

'Mad as a cut snake.'

'Flat out like a lizard drinking.'

They all had their offerings, even Pietro, who admitted to
finding it rather confusing, and Ruth finally shook her head.

'I obviously have a great deal to learn,' she said, and the others laughed.

'How long have you been here?' Lucky asked, finally forcing himself to look at her directly.

'I've been in Cooma for a week, but I arrived in Australia ten days ago,' she replied.

'You will like it in Cooma,' Pietro said. 'Cooma is very nice place. You will stay here?'

'Yes, I think so.'

'Course she will,' Rob insisted heartily, wondering why she sounded uncertain. 'Ruth's just got a job with the SMA – she's going to work as an interpreter and an English teacher.'

'Oh.' Violet was most impressed. 'Peggy's a teacher too,' she said.

Peggy smiled. She was trying to join in the conversation, but she was having trouble – her feminine instincts were working overtime. She sensed something between Lucky and Ruth, something unspoken, but electric and palpable. Yet no-one else seemed aware of it. Was it just her own insecurity? Did she find the woman's beauty a threat? Perhaps she was jealous. But she'd never been so superficial in the past. She'd never envied women their beauty; she'd admired them for it.

She continued to reason with herself as they adjourned to the dining room, but her feelings persisted. And Violet didn't help.

'I think we should have champagne,' Violet said when the men asked the ladies what they'd like to drink. 'We have to toast Lucky and Peggy's engagement.' Violet didn't particularly like the taste of champagne – she preferred orange juice – but champagne was essential to romance. 'They only got the ring last weekend. Show Ruth, Peggy.'

Peggy extended her left hand. Was she imagining it, or could she sense discomfort in Lucky beside her? He was no longer being physically demonstrative either, he hadn't put his arm around her once since Ruth had arrived. Peggy felt mortified and she wished Violet hadn't brought up the subject of the ring.

'It's pretty, isn't it?' Violet said. Pietro was going to buy her her own engagement ring soon, now that she could openly wear one, and tomorrow she was taking him home for Sunday lunch with the family. Her mum wanted to meet him, and her dad had calmed down – well, at least that's what her mum had said over the phone – so things were working out fine. And when they bought the ring she'd choose something really flashy. Pietro had said she could have whatever she wanted. Not that she was critical of Peggy's choice – it was very tasteful.

'How exquisite,' Ruth said as she examined the ring. 'It's quite lovely. Congratulations, Peggy.' And she turned to Lucky: 'Congratulations to you both.'

'Thank you,' Lucky replied, and Peggy wondered why she felt a shiver of foreboding.

After dinner, they returned to the lounge where the band was striking up. The best tables had been taken and they had to make do with a small one in the corner where they were rather cramped for space.

'Who cares?' Violet said with gay abandon. 'We're here to dance.' She was in a very flamboyant mood: she was unaccustomed to alcohol and the two glasses of champagne had gone to her head. 'Come on, Pietro,' she said as she whisked him away.

'Peggy?' Lucky knew it would seem odd if he didn't ask her to dance.

She stood, feeling wretched. She could tell that Lucky, who was normally so eager to whirl her onto the dance floor, didn't really want to dance at all.

Ruth and Rob Harvey were left at the table, and he turned to her apologetically.

'I'm sorry,' he said, 'I'm not much of a dancer.'

'That's all right, I'm quite happy to watch.'

They watched together; it was a waltz, and Lucky and Peggy were executing each step like true professionals.

'They're very good, aren't they?' he commented.

'Yes, they are.' Samuel had always been an excellent dancer.

The waltz ended, and the next number of the bracket was a samba. Peggy loved the samba, they both did – she and Lucky loved all the Latin American dances.

'Shall we go back to the table?' she said. She didn't love the samba tonight.

'Sure.'

Normally he would have insisted on dancing the whole bracket, she thought as they returned to the table.

The four of them sat in silence watching the dancers. To Peggy it was a most uncomfortable silence; she was sure that Lucky and Ruth were avoiding each other's eyes. She couldn't bear it any longer, and, painting on a smile, she stood.

'Rob, I insist that you dance with me,' she said brightly, taking him by the hand.

He was forced to rise to his feet. 'I'm not much of a dancer, Peggy, I have to warn you,' he said, embarrassed.

'Then I'll teach you. Come along.' And she dragged him onto the dance floor. She would give Lucky and Ruth time alone to sort out whatever it was that rested so uneasily between them.

A minute or so later, as she glanced over Rob's shoulder and saw the two of them leaning close to each other, deep in conversation, Peggy felt the sickest feeling in the pit of her stomach.

'I'm sorry, Samuel, I didn't mean it to happen like this.'

They spoke softly, and they had to lean in close to hear each other above the noise of the band.

'I thought you were dead, Ruth. I searched everywhere.' As he looked at her, Lucky was engulfed by the past.

'I know. I know you did. But I'm here. I'm alive.' She would have liked to have touched his face – her beautiful Samuel, so scarred. 'I'm alive, just as you are.'

'And Rachel?' He held his breath as he asked the question.

'She didn't survive.'

'Ah.'

He nodded as if he'd expected as much. But Ruth had seen the flicker of hope in his eyes and she wanted to hold his hand, to offer him some comfort. She made no move.

'We mustn't talk any longer,' she said, aware that they were looking conspicuous and that Peggy was watching anxiously from the dance floor. Ruth was guiltily conscious of the fact that Samuel's fiancée had sensed something between them.

'Can I meet you tomorrow?' he asked. 'Some time in the morning?'

'Of course.'

'Centennial Park, do you know it?'

She did, the little park on the corner, right in the centre of town. 'Yes,' she said.

'At ten o'clock.'

By the time the others returned to the table, they were once again sitting in silence watching the dance floor.

Peggy tried to make conversation as she and Lucky walked the several blocks from Dodds back to her cottage. She didn't ask him about Ruth, she had decided not to. She would wait until he told her. Told her what? she wondered.

But he said nothing. And later, as they lay side by side in bed, he remained deep in his own thoughts. By now they would normally be making love. Why weren't they? she asked herself. What had happened? She rolled over on her side, with her back to him.

'Goodnight,' she whispered.

'Goodnight, Peggy,' he replied, and he remained gazing up at the ceiling. He knew she was puzzled, and possibly hurt, that he had made no physical overtures. But he couldn't make love to her – he no longer had the right. And what was he to say to her by way of explanation? I am married? My wife has come back from the dead?

Lucky's mind was in turmoil. His lives had collided – he was two men now. What was expected of him? What must he do?

In the morning he was still preoccupied and there was an awkwardness between them. Peggy cooked breakfast as a matter of course, but they didn't eat much. Peggy thought how they would normally have eaten Sunday breakfast in bed, rolling about and making love among the crumbs.

'I have to go out for a while,' he said.

She started clearing the table. He never went out on a Sunday morning. She knew he was going to meet her.

'Will you be coming back?' she asked. 'For lunch, I mean? Will I get lunch?' She walked over to the sink so that he wouldn't see the tears that had sprung to her eyes. She hated the way she sounded so pathetic. She should have yelled 'tell me what's going on', but she couldn't. She could only wait until he told her it was over.

Lucky registered the strain in her voice and crossed to her, seeing the tears that she tried to blink furiously away.

'Yes, I'll be coming back.' He held her close. She was hurt, confused by his remoteness. He owed her an explanation, but he was confused himself. He didn't know what to say, or how to say it. So he told her the truth about his feelings instead. 'I love you, Peggy Minchin,' he said. 'You are the world to me.'

The words which had meant so much only the previous day now had a hollow ring to Peggy, and when he'd gone she busied herself with unnecessary household chores, filling in the morning until his return, all the while fearing the worst.

Maarten Vanpoucke popped into the newsagents and bought himself a paper to read over his coffee and pastry, as he did every Sunday morning. Then, browsing the headlines, he ambled down Sharp Street towards the little cafe which he regularly frequented just opposite the park.

Ruth walked briskly along Bombala Street. It was a few minutes to ten and she didn't want to keep Samuel waiting, but the park was only a block away now. She could see it up ahead, just the other side of Sharp Street.

She increased her pace but, as she reached the junction of the two streets, she was so intent upon crossing the main road that she collided with a man who hadn't seen her coming, his attention focussed on his newspaper. The man looked up, rescuing his spectacles which had threatened to fall off, and for an instant their eyes met.

'I'm so sorry,' she said. Then she continued on her way.

Maarten didn't move. He stood and watched as Ruth crossed the road. Then he tucked his newspaper under his arm and followed.

'I'm sorry, I'm not late, am I?'

Lucky was sitting on a bench and he stood as she approached. 'Not at all,' he said, 'ten o'clock on the dot. Do you want to walk or shall we sit?'

Ruth looked around. It was a fine day and the park was a popular place on a Sunday: young couples sat on the grass, children played, families gathered. She and Samuel weren't within earshot of others, and no-one was paying them the slightest attention.

'Let's sit,' she said. She took a deep breath. They sat. 'Who's going to start?'

'You,' Lucky said. 'Yours is a more important story than mine.'

She knew he meant Rachel, and calmly, succinctly, as she'd promised herself she would, Ruth recounted the facts exactly as they'd happened.

They shot the babies as soon as they arrived, and usually the mothers as well.

As he heard his daughter's fate, Lucky clearly recalled the brutal words of the Auschwitz inmate he'd met at Camp Foehrenwald.

She told him about Mannie too.

'I tried to save him, Samuel. I had "connections" in the camp, a "benefactor" – that's how I survived.'

She said it with self-loathing, and Lucky was taken aback; it was the first time she'd shown any emotion as she'd talked.

'But it was my "benefactor", the very man whose help I sought, who ordered Mannie's execution.' She stared down at her hands, her fingers laced together, kneading her knuckles, her resolve to remain detached starting to crumble. 'I realised later that I was responsible for Mannie's death.'

'*You* were responsible?' The obvious burden of her guilt was more than Lucky could bear. 'Ruth, he went in my place! It should have been me who faced that firing squad. I am responsible for Mannie's death, not you.'

She looked at him. Poor Samuel, she thought. He had carried his remorse all these years, just as she had. He was trying to spare her now, but he couldn't. He could no more save her from her guilt than she could save him from his.

'My poor love,' she said. Then she smiled and raised a hand to his cheek, gently tracing the cruel course of the scar with her finger. 'My poor, beautiful Samuel.'

A smile, Maarten thought. He had never seen her smile.

From his position beside the rotunda, as he leant against the railings with his open newspaper in front of him, Maarten Vanpoucke studied Ruth's every nuance. The fondness in her eyes, then the smile, and the tender gesture of the hand. Husband and wife reunited, he thought, how touching. He'd ached for her to show him such tenderness. He still did.

'And after the war?' Lucky asked, when he'd told his story briefly and without embellishment; having heard hers, his was of little importance.

'After the war I lived in Israel for a number of years.' She had no wish to talk about Israel and her purposeless existence on the orchard, or what had driven her to an empty life with a man she didn't love. She never spoke of Deir Yassin and the massacre. She never would.

'It was in Jerusalem that I saw Efraim,' she said, changing the subject, 'and when he told me you were in the Snowy Mountains of Australia, I'm not sure which I found more unbelievable: the fact that you were alive, or that there was snow in Australia.'

She asked him questions and he answered in detail. She wanted to know about his arrival in Australia, and about the Snowy and his life at the work camp. He told her that he loved the work, and he loved the country, and he talked about every aspect of his new life, with one exception. Peggy.

Finally, Ruth ran out of questions and Lucky ran out of steam, and they sat in silence, both conscious of the one question that still hung unasked in the air.

'So what do we do?' It was Lucky who voiced it.

'We?' To Ruth, the question had been answered long before she'd encouraged him to talk about his life on the Snowy. '*We* do nothing, there is no "we", Samuel.' An edge of practicality, even hardness crept into her voice as she continued. 'You have a new life and a woman you love. What we had is over. It was a love shared between two different people, surely you can see that? We've changed, you and I.'

They had, he thought. He hadn't been Samuel Lachmann for years, and Ruth, too, had changed, he could see it. Even her beauty had changed. She was more arresting than ever, the bloom of youth replaced by the sexual allure of a woman in her thirties, but her beauty had a remote quality now, a wariness. It was not difficult to guess why, he thought, recalling the self-loathing with which she'd talked of her 'benefactor' in Auschwitz. Her beauty had been the source of her survival, and she'd been left with terrible scars. Gone was the gloriously vibrant, supremely confident young Ruth, and in her place, through no fault of her own, was a woman who didn't particularly like herself – or the world.

'Yes, we've changed,' he said, 'but we can start anew.' Even as he spoke the words, Lucky sensed their emptiness. 'We must, Ruth. You're my wife.'

'No, my dearest, I'm not, and I have no desire to be.' It was the truth, she realised. She'd intended to release him from any obligation the moment she'd seen him so obviously in love in the lounge room at Dodds. But relinquishing any claim was no longer a selfless act on her part. Being with Samuel had brought back the past with a pain too raw. And it would be like this always, she thought: they shared wounds too deep to heal.

'We could never be together again, Samuel,' she said. 'Rachel and Mannie would be with us every minute of every day. I couldn't bear that.'

Lucky had no answer; Rachel and Mannie were with them right now, he thought.

He leaned forward, his elbows on his knees, and looked out over the park, his attention caught by a little boy of around three galloping an imaginary pony on the grass.

They'd both lapsed into silence. Ruth, too, had focussed upon the child who, aware that he was being looked at, galloped towards them. He fell flat on his face several paces away, then sat up, unhurt, but unsure whether or not he should cry.

Ruth rose and picked him up, slinging him on one hip, while the mother, who'd been watching, made her way towards them. The child laughed, accident forgotten.

Lucky noted the ease with which she handled the child. Was she thinking of Rachel? he wondered. If the little boy had been a girl, he might well have been Rachel, they were about the same age.

No, he reminded himself, the little boy could not have been Rachel. If Rachel had lived, she would be fourteen this year.

Ruth was right, he thought, as the women exchanged pleasantries and Ruth handed over the child. Their lives would be haunted by the past. But although he agreed with her, he felt ill-prepared and indecisive. The speed of events left him stunned.

She returned to the bench and sat by his side.

'What shall we do?' he asked, after a moment or so. The decision had to be hers. He took her hand. 'What is it that you want, Ruth?'

'I want what you have.' She looked down at their fingers entwined together. 'I want a new life.' Then she met his eyes with candour. 'I believe I could find it here in Australia, but it doesn't have to be Cooma, if you would rather I left.'

'Of course it has to be Cooma. You have a new job, and you have friends here.'

'Friends?'

'Me.'

She laughed – a flash of the old Ruth which surprised them both – and he delighted in the sound.

'I think that, given the fact you're about to commit bigamy, it might be best if I kept my distance,' she said.

She laughed, Maarten marvelled as he watched from behind his newspaper. She'd actually laughed. He would have given anything to have heard the sound of her laughter.

Lucky's smile faded. He wasn't sure if he'd heard correctly.

'You must say and do nothing, Samuel,' she said. 'You must live your life as you have planned it – there is no necessity for others to know of our past. I am legally Ruth Stein – my passport and my papers are all in my maiden name. I left you behind a long time ago, my darling.'

She was so incredibly strong, he thought, but then she always had been.

'I love you,' he said. 'I will always love you, Ruth.'

'Of course. As I will you. And that's what you must tell Peggy.'

He was dumbfounded.

'Peggy knows, Samuel. She knows there's something between us.'

'But how? How could she know?'

'A woman's intuition,' Ruth smiled at his naiveté. 'We always know.'

'So what do I tell her?' Lucky was stumped. He'd never understand women – but then, what man did?

'Tell her that we're old friends from the past who once loved each other. Tell her as much of the truth as she needs to know: that we met at university, that we were each other's first love. Don't try to hide it – she'll know if you do.'

'Right.' Lucky's nod was dubious.

'You'll manage, Samuel,' she assured him. 'Just be yourself, she'll love you for that. I did.' She rose from the bench. 'I must remember to call you Lucky,' she said. 'It's growing on me; I think it suits you.'

Maarten folded his newspaper. They were leaving the park, heading straight towards him. He stepped behind the rotunda.

'I'll walk you back to Dodds,' Lucky said.

'There's no need.'

'I'd like to.'

As they passed the rotunda he took her arm, but then stopped as a familiar figure appeared before him.

'Lucky.'

It was Maarten Vanpoucke.

'Hello, Maarten.'

'How nice to see you. What a perfect day, isn't it?'

Maarten's manner was effusive: he seemed in the mood for a chat, and Lucky had no option but to introduce Ruth.

'Ruth, this is Maarten Vanpoucke,' he said.

'How do you do,' she responded.

'Maarten, this is Ruth Stein, an old friend of mine from university days in Berlin.'

'Delighted.' He had not introduced her as his wife, Maarten noted, and she wore no wedding ring. So they did not intend to acknowledge their relationship. How extraordinary, he thought, and how opportune. If Lucky was still planning to marry his little schoolteacher, then Ruth would be available.

As the two shook hands, Lucky remembered the night Maarten had seen the photograph. *She's very beautiful, your wife,* the Dutchman had said. It was ironic, he thought, that of all people it should be Maarten Vanpoucke they'd bumped into – no-one else in the whole of Cooma had seen the photograph, not even Peggy; he'd returned it to the drawer of his lowboy. Lucky studied the man keenly for any sign that he might find Ruth vaguely familiar.

'You're the young lady who nearly bowled me over,' Maarten said.

'Oh, was it you? I'm so sorry.'

'No, no, my dear,' he laughed amiably, 'it was my fault entirely; I wasn't watching where I was going.'

Lucky breathed a sigh of relief: there was not a flicker of recognition. But then it was not surprising: Ruth was no longer the carefree young student in the photograph.

'Ruth's just arrived in town,' he said.

'Really? Welcome to Cooma.'

'Thank you. I've only been here a week, but I love the place already.'

'And she has a job as an interpreter and teacher with the SMA,' Lucky boasted.

'In just one week?' Maarten smiled his congratulations. 'Well done.'

'Oh I haven't started – I have to get my medical clearance yet.'

'Indeed? Well, if you wish to cut corners and avoid any delays, I'd be only too happy to oblige.'

'Maarten's a doctor, Ruth,' Lucky explained as she looked a query at him, 'he has a private practice in Vale Street. It's not far from Dodds – I can show you where it is.'

Maarten produced a card from the inner pocket of his jacket and presented it to her. 'Ring my receptionist and make an appointment for next week,' he said. 'Tomorrow, if you like, I think there are one or two holes in the day. I'll give you top priority, I promise.'

'Thank you, Doctor Vanpoucke, that's very kind.'

'Any friend of Lucky's . . .' he smiled, 'and do call me Maarten.' He turned to Lucky. 'And you, my friend, you've been neglecting me sadly of late. Could I inveigle you into a game of chess next Saturday, and dinner perhaps?'

Lucky hesitated awkwardly, put on the spot, as was Maarten's intention.

'I think he'll be dining with his fiancée, Peggy,' Ruth said, 'they usually do on a Saturday, I believe, isn't that right, Lucky?'

'Yes.' She'd said it with such ease, he was lost in admiration. 'We go to Dodds as a rule, it's become a bit of a custom.'

'Yes, of course, how silly of me to forget,' Maarten replied, and he turned to Ruth. 'Lucky's engagement is the very reason for his neglect of me – lamentable but

understandable. Well, it's been lovely to meet you, Ruth.'
He shook her hand again, relishing the touch of her. 'I'll
see you during the week.'

How neatly things were falling into place, he thought as
he left them and strolled up Sharp Street.

CHAPTER TWENTY-TWO

It had taken Marge Campbell a little while to adjust to Pietro. She'd welcomed him as warmly as possible – she had nothing against foreigners, but it had been difficult to come to terms with the fact that her Vi had married one.

On Pietro's first visit the three of them had sat in the front room drinking tea.

'The front room,' Violet had remarked as she'd carried in the tea tray, 'gosh, Pietro, you're getting the royal treatment.'

'Don't be silly, Vi,' her mother had said, 'we always entertain guests in the front room – you know that. Now, Pietro, how do you take your tea?' She'd spoken loudly and enunciated clearly. 'Do you like milk?' And she'd held up the milk jug, just to ensure that he understood.

'He speaks English, Mum, and he's not deaf.'

But after ten minutes or so, Marge had relaxed and she'd found herself warming to the young man. His manners were impeccable and he was certainly handsome; Vi's child was bound to be a looker, she thought.

'Is beautiful, your farm,' Pietro said.

Lucky had given him the use of the Land Rover for the day, and Pietro had been hugely impressed as he and Violet drove through the valleys and over the hills of her father's lands. As he'd driven over the cattle grid and up the broad path to the rambling homestead, with its huge verandahs and groves of poplars, he'd been lost in awe.

'Never do I see a farm so beautiful,' he said to Violetta's mother.

'Property, Pietro,' Violet reminded him.

'Property, yes.' He smiled at Marge. He liked Violetta's mother; she was nice and she looked very like Violetta except much older. And a bit tired, he thought. 'Always I forget is property. In my country, is farm. Violetta she correct me.'

Now that she was getting used to it, Marge found it rather pretty the way he called her daughter Violetta.

'We have farms here too,' she said, 'don't you listen to Vi – she just likes to show off.'

Violet grinned. Her mum had taken to him, she could tell. They were getting on like a house on fire.

'So tell me about your farm, Pietro. Vi said you grew up on a farm.'

Violet flashed a warning at her mother. She'd said no such thing. She'd told her mum that Pietro had lived on a farm as a child, but that his parents had been killed in the war and he'd been brought up in an orphanage.

Marge blushed, realising that she'd put her foot in it.

But Pietro didn't seem to mind.

'My farm is high in the mountains,' he said. 'Much more high than here. And I have goats. I have a pet goat. Her name is Rosa.' Pietro intended to tell Violetta's mother everything he could remember about his farm. He would tell her about the mountains in springtime and how he'd helped Rosa have her baby. But Violetta's mother interrupted him.

'How nice.' Marge decided it was time to check on the roast; Violet's signals were painfully obvious. 'I'll just see how lunch is going. Cam and the boys'll be back any minute; they've been out for a morning ride.' She disappeared to the kitchen.

'Why you not wish I should talk to your mother, Violetta?' Pietro asked, a little hurt. The signals had not gone unnoticed by him either.

'I *want* you to talk to her, sweetie,' Violet assured him, 'I just don't want her asking questions, that's all.'

'Ah,' Pietro said, 'she does not know.' Violetta had not told her mother that he had only fractured memories of the farm, and no recollection of his parents. Perhaps she was ashamed, he thought.

Violet could see he was hurt and she cuddled up to him on the sofa.

'I just want to give them some time, Pietro. I mean, I'm married, I'm going to have a baby – they've got a lot to get used to, without . . . you know?'

'Yes, is correct.' Violetta was right, he thought. He must not seem strange to her family, he must try to fit in.

Marge dumped the oven dish onto the newspaper which she'd laid out on the Laminex-topped kitchen table and turned the legs of lamb with a carving fork. She always cooked two, but the way her boys ate, there was rarely any meat left. She wished she could have added an extra leg with Pietro here, but there wasn't enough room in the oven of the old Kooka. It was time Cam bought her one of those new-fangled stoves that had more space, she thought. Crikey, there wasn't enough room to cook a decent sized roast as it was – she had to keep rotating the other two pans with the vegetables.

She heard Cam and the boys talking on the back verandah as they took off their boots. It was a rule of hers: no work boots in the house, and the men always obeyed – the house was her domain. Then there was the closing slap of the back flywire door and all three of them barged into the kitchen.

'Smells good, Mum.' It was twenty-one-year-old Johnno, the younger of her sons. 'Jeez, I'm starving, I could eat the leg off a skinny priest.'

'Mind your language,' she said meaningfully.

Johnno raised an eyebrow that said 'what language?', but twenty-four-year-old Dave got her drift.

'He's here, is he?'

'In the front room,' she said.

'Strewth, you're laying it on a bit thick, aren't you?'

'Course she's not,' Cam reprimanded his son. 'This is Vi's husband and we'll welcome him into the family the proper way. You just mind your Ps and Qs, Dave.'

Dave and Johnno exchanged a look. Any other member of the family would have been welcomed into the kitchen; the front room was for bunging it on.

'Go and wash up and we'll have a cup of tea before lunch,' Marge said.

'A cup of tea?' Another incredulous reaction from the boys, and this time Cam agreed – the rules didn't need to be stretched that far.

'Give it a break, Marge,' he said. 'We'll have a beer.' And they trooped off to the laundry to scrub up for Sunday lunch.

When Cam had told his wife about their daughter, Marge was aghast.

'You mean she's been married for three whole months?'

'Three and a half. Fifteenth of October – I checked with the Registry Office.'

'And now she's pregnant . . .'

'So she says.'

Shocked as she was, Marge's mind had worked swiftly. 'Oh dear God, that's why she married him.'

'Not according to Maureen: she says Vi's only two and a half months gone.' Cam hadn't dared admit to the earlier warnings he'd had from Maureen about Violet's imminent love affair. But Christ alive, he thought he'd nipped it in the bud. How the hell was he to know it'd get so out of hand?

Then, when he'd told his wife about his run-in with the young Italian, much to his surprise, Marge had turned on him.

'God in heaven, Cam, what have you done?'

'*Me*? What have *I* done? The kid *attacked* me!'

'With no provocation on your part, of course.' Marge knew her husband only too well.

Cam was exasperated beyond measure. Maureen had said the same thing. What was wrong with the stupid cows? Why did everything have to be his fault?

'Jesus Christ, woman, why blame me?'

'Don't blaspheme,' she said automatically. Despite the fact that in becoming a Campbell woman Marge had lost touch with the church, her Irish Catholic upbringing regularly came to the fore.

'It's not my fault Vi married a bloody Dago.'

'For goodness sake, keep your voice down – what would the boys say if they heard you talk like that!' The boys couldn't have heard – they were out rounding up strays – but the mere thought of it sent a shiver down her spine. Cam had rammed home to the boys his 'all men are equal' ideals for years, and now he was about to be exposed as a hypocrite.

'Christ, Marge, it's different when your own daughter marries one.'

It was then that Marge read him the riot act.

'Now you listen to me, Cam. Your daughter's married to an Italian whether you like it or not, and she's going to have a baby. You welcome that boy into this family, and you start showing off around every pub in town about how your little girl's been married for three months and how proud you are. And you make sure everyone knows the very date she married, because when she starts to show

I won't have people saying that my daughter had to marry because she got into trouble. Do you hear me?'

He certainly heard her. He'd never heard her so loud and clear in the whole of their marriage. Cam had always ruled the roost and Marge had always run the house, just as the Campbells had done for generations. But not this time. This time it was her call and there was little he could do about it, because she was right.

'How do I explain why she kept it a secret?' he asked sulkily.

'She didn't. We knew all the time. Vi was being romantic – everyone knows what Vi's like. So she eloped and then she came back and told us. And she wanted to keep it a secret for a while because she likes a bit of drama – that's what you say, Cam. Tell it all around town, go on a pub crawl. Tell them in Jindabyne and Dalgety and Berridale too, and you be sure you tell your mates in Cooma. You can make a joke of it, if you like – you're good at that.'

He was, Marge thought, and he'd get it right. Cam was good at bullshit. It was a term she never used, but it was spot on. She'd check the story with Maureen, she thought. Something sounded very fishy. Why would Violet get married without telling her own mother? The girl had obviously feared her father's reaction; maybe she'd seen through Cam's 'all men are equal' ravings – that was bullshit too.

Cam had wandered off, thoroughly chastened, and Marge had rung Violet and told her to bring her husband home for the Sunday roast.

'I am most sorry, Mr Campbell,' Pietro said, rising from the sofa as Cam and the boys appeared.

'Over and done with, son,' Cam muttered, 'let bygones be bygones,' and he shook the Italian's hand. Dave and Johnno looked on, mystified – they knew nothing apart from the surprising fact that their little sister had married an Italian without telling anyone. 'These are my boys,' Cam loudly announced. 'Dave and Johnno, this is Pietro.'

These were not boys, Pietro thought, these were giants.

Sandy-haired and freckle-faced, Dave and Johnno had their father's powerful build, but they towered over Cam.

'G'day, Pietro,' they both said, and one by one they shook his hand vigorously.

'Gedday, Dave, gedday, Johnno.' Pietro returned their handshakes with equal force.

'You want a beer, Pietro?' Cam asked, as Marge appeared with a couple of bottles and glasses.

'Yes, I like beer very much, thank you, Mr Campbell.'

Cam caught his wife's glance. 'I think under the circumstances, we should make it Cam, son,' he said and he busied himself with the beers, avoiding whatever look Vi might have been giving him.

But the awkwardness soon dissipated – Dave and Johnno, blissfully unaware of the sequence of events, made sure of that.

'Oh come off it, Mum,' Dave said, when Marge told Violet to set the dining room table, 'Pietro's one of the family, isn't he? What's wrong with the kitchen?' The dining room, like the front room, was for bunging it on, and besides, it was Sunday – the Sunday roast wouldn't be the same in the dining room.

It seemed to be the general consensus of opinion and, although Marge had been trying to do things 'the European way' in deference to Pietro, she was quite relieved. It meant she didn't have to be running from room to room with the food.

Lunch was a raucous affair, the boys downing their beers and spearing meat from the huge platter onto their plates with their forks. Pietro had never seen men eat so much meat.

'Want some more spuds, Pietro?' Johnno slid the bowl of roast potatoes across the table.

'Thank you, yes.'

Marge was about to pass him the serving spoon, but Pietro speared a potato with his fork the way he'd seen the others do; he was determined to fit in. Ah well, she thought, it was probably a good sign.

Dave was keen to know how Violet and Pietro had met.

'At Hallidays,' Violet said. 'It was love at first sight.' There was no conscious attempt at exaggeration on her part; it was the way she remembered their meeting. 'I thought he looked like a film star. And he does, doesn't he,' she said proudly.

With all eyes upon him, Pietro was plainly embarrassed, so the boys didn't take the mickey out of him like they normally would have.

'Why'd you keep it a secret, Vi?' Johnno asked.

'You know me.' She shrugged, and her smile was teasing. 'I like a bit of drama.'

That's what Mum had said, Johnno thought. Jeez but Vi lived in a world of her own.

Dave was thinking exactly the same thing. He'd given up trying to figure out his sister, but he'd been keen to meet the Italian; he was very protective of Vi and very much the big brother. Pietro seemed like a nice bloke, though, and Vi was obviously happy, so good on 'em both, he thought. Hell, like Dad's always said, one bloke's as good as another. Bit weird, though, he thought, having an Eyetie in the family.

'You work for Kaiser, don't you?' he asked.

'This is true.'

'What's it like, Pietro, working for the Yanks?' Johnno stopped midway through piling a third serve of meat onto his plate. 'They say they're real slave drivers.'

'No, they are good. And they pay good too.'

The rest of the main meal was given over to a discussion about Kaiser and its radical work methods. The boys were fascinated; even Cam, who had remained relatively silent, found himself interested in what the Italian had to say, and Pietro felt relaxed as he answered their questions. Violet was as pleased as punch.

Then, as Marge dished out the apple crumble and ice cream, the conversation turned to the Cooma Show. It was well over a month away yet, but the Show was the most important event on the yearly calendar and always came up for heavy discussion.

'Will you be riding this year, Vi?' Johnno asked.

'Nup,' Violet replied with ease, 'don't have time to get back into training, we're too busy at the store.' The boys didn't know about her pregnancy. Her mum had said she was not to tell a soul.

'Not even Dave and Johnno,' Marge had warned her, 'not until everyone's got used to you being married, Vi – it's better that way.' Violet had known exactly what her mother meant.

'Bloody shame,' Dave said to Pietro, 'Vi's one of the best horsewomen in the district.'

It led to proud boasts of family sporting prowess; the boys, like their father, were excellent riders and regularly collected show trophies. And then, of course, there were Cam's annual blue ribbons for prize livestock and Marge's awards for chutneys and relishes. The Cooma Show was quite a Campbell affair.

Pietro basked in it all. What a fine family, he thought. Over second helpings of apple crumble, when the talk turned to childhood reminiscences, he persuaded himself it didn't matter that he had none of his own to offer. One day his child would be a part of this family, and would grow up with his or her own memories.

But an hour and a half later, as he and Violet drove back to Cooma, Violet chattering nineteen to the dozen about how successful the lunch had been, Pietro decided that it *did* matter. The fact that he had no reminiscences of his own to share with Violet's family was indeed of little consequence, but it was now more important than ever that his child should know who he was. His child should know that he had once had a family. It was imperative to Pietro that he discover his past.

'So tell me about your background, Ruth.'

Why? she thought. Why did she need to tell the doctor her background? She had no desire to talk of the past.

'Your medical background, of course,' Maarten said reassuringly, pen poised over the patient's record card on the desk before him; he'd registered how quickly her guard had gone up.

'Oh.' Ruth felt rather foolish. 'Yes, of course.'

'Any major illnesses I should know of?' he prompted.

'No.'

'Any family history of heart disease?'

'No.'

'Are your parents still alive?'

'No, my mother died of pneumonia when I was a child.'

'And your father?' He concentrated on his notes, but he sensed her hesitation.

'Accidental death,' she said. Kristallnacht, she remembered it so clearly. 'He was killed in 1938.' The receptionist had given the doctor the form she'd filled out: it showed the country of her birth as Germany, and it was plain that the name Stein was Jewish. Let him make of it what he will, she thought.

He stopped his scribbling and looked at her, his expression one of heartfelt sympathy and understanding.

'There were many accidental deaths in those times,' he said.

'Yes,' she answered shortly.

She was very much on the defensive, Maarten thought. Her manner was altogether different from that of the relaxed young woman he'd chatted to in the park just two days ago.

He asked her several more questions, steering clear of anything she might possibly consider personal, then put down the pen and stood.

'Right, that's enough grilling,' he said in his comfortingly jovial bedside manner. 'Let's see what shape you're in.'

As he sat beside her and wrapped the blood pressure gauge around her arm, Ruth felt relieved that they were getting on with the physical examination. She didn't know why she'd been so tense, but it was always the same when people asked her questions about her past: the walls automatically went up. Heavens above, she thought, the man was only doing his job.

'Ah, 120 over 80, excellent,' he said, and he smiled as if she'd come top of her class. Then, with his pencil torch, he examined her ears, eyes and throat. 'Say ah,' he instructed, making Ruth feel like a child.

It was Maarten who was tense now. He was touching her, actually touching her, it was Ruth's skin he was feeling, and he wondered how she could be so unaware of the electricity which he could sense pulsating between them.

He instructed her to stand and he held the stethoscope to her chest, but he was not listening to the rhythm of her heart. He was watching the rise and fall of her breasts, remembering them naked and how they'd felt, how she'd remained so still and accepting as he'd worshipped her body.

'Turn around.' She did. 'Breathe in,' he said, holding the stethoscope to her back, 'breathe out.' But he wasn't listening to her lungs. He was gazing at her hair and recalling how he'd run his hands through it and how it had felt like silk between his fingers. She wore it short now; he preferred it longer, but he liked the way it displayed her neck. He longed to bend his mouth to that neck, to feel his lips brush her flesh, and his eyes strayed to her shoulders, bare in the sleeveless summer dress, the shoulders he'd massaged with such love all those years ago. He remembered how she'd enjoyed the evening ritual of his massage; she hadn't told him so, of course, but he'd felt her body's response. As he'd caressed her flesh to the rhythm of 'Barcarole', he'd known that for her, too, the music and his touch had become one – it had been something intimate and precious that they'd shared.

He could hear the familiar refrain now and he was on the verge of humming the melody as his fingers hovered longingly over her skin.

He pulled his hand away as sharply as if he'd been burned, shocked back to the present and how close he had come to revealing himself.

'You're in excellent health, Ruth,' he pronounced, startling himself with the sound of his own voice. 'Just the blood test and we're done.'

He took the blood sample, concentrating upon the task at hand, divorcing himself from the past and from the fact that this was Ruth. His Ruth. And then he saw her to the door.

'The results should be back next week,' he said, 'and I'll instruct the clinic to send your X-rays directly to me – your appointment is arranged for tomorrow morning, you said?'

'Yes, that's right.'

'Excellent.' He accompanied her into the reception area. 'Edith will arrange an appointment for you.' He nodded to the grey-haired woman seated at her desk behind the counter, and then returned his gaze to Ruth. 'We'll have the report all finalised on your next visit.'

'Thank you very much, Doctor,' Ruth said.

He didn't remind her to call him Maarten – he didn't trust himself. 'My pleasure. I look forward to seeing you next week.' And he returned to his consulting room, where he stood by the bay windows watching her walk down the street, shaken by the effect she'd had upon him.

* * *

'Miss Stein is here, doctor.'

'Thank you, Edith.' He didn't look up from his notes. 'Give me five minutes and then show her in.'

The moment Edith closed the door, he stopped the pretence of his paperwork and gazed at the mantelpiece clock, counting the minutes, just as he'd counted the days until he'd next see her. The week had passed slowly, but he was prepared this time: he would not allow himself to be caught out again. He must resist the temptation to reveal his identity – she was not ready for that yet; he had to ease himself gently back into her life.

'Ruth.' He rose as Edith ushered her in. 'How nice to see you, do take a seat,' he said, accepting the folder which his receptionist handed him.

As Ruth sat, Maarten opened the folder, settling himself once again behind his desk.

'The results are all here: your X-rays show no abnormalities,' he said, and then he ran through the analysis of her blood test. 'Everything quite within the acceptable limits,' he concluded. 'You have a clean bill of health, I'm happy to say, and I've completed a full report for your employers. It's in there with your X-rays,' he said, passing her a large envelope.

'Thank you, doctor, that's excellent news.'

'Maarten, please.' He smiled and sat back in his chair, friendly, relaxed. It was time to establish a personal relationship. 'So I take it you'll be starting work any minute now?'

'Yes, I'm looking forward to it.'

'As a teacher and an interpreter, Lucky said.'

'That's right, teaching English to migrants and assisting social workers and psychologists.'

'How very interesting.'

She was rising to go, so he quickly stood – he had no alternative.

'I wish you every success, Ruth.'

'Thank you.'

He accompanied her to the door. 'Remind our friend Lucky when next you see him that he owes me a game of chess,' he said in a last bid for some personal contact.

'Yes, of course,' she replied. It was not likely she would be seeing Samuel in the near future, but the doctor didn't need to know that.

'Such a fine man, and such a very dear friend.'

'Yes, he is.'

As he opened the door, Ruth offered her hand. 'Thank you for all your help, Doctor Vanpoucke.'

He didn't insist again that she call him Maarten. It was plain that under the circumstances she wished to address him professionally, and besides, there were two other patients waiting in reception.

'Not at all, my dear,' he said as they shook hands, 'any time I can be of service, you know where to find me.'

As she left, he signalled Edith to give him five minutes before showing in the next patient and, closing the door behind him, he crossed to the bay windows and once again watched her as she walked down the street. Things were not proceeding according to plan at all, he thought.

Maarten was frustrated by the outcome of what he'd initially considered a breakthrough opportunity. Offering his services as a doctor was not working in his favour; she perceived him purely on a professional basis. It was understandable, most patients did, and he supposed it had been foolish of him to expect otherwise. But in order to reassert his power over her, he had to develop a personal relationship – and quickly, he thought. Cooma was a man's town. A woman like Ruth would attract a great deal of attention – they'd be queuing up for her favours.

Rob Harvey arrived at Dodds in a jeep.

'Good heavens,' she said, 'a jeep.' She seemed taken aback.

Oh hell, Rob cursed himself, he'd got it wrong. He'd thought she might find the jeep novel and exciting, but he should have picked her up in the Land Rover.

'Sorry,' he said, 'they can be a bit blowy. Do you want to grab a scarf?'

'Certainly not,' she said, ignoring the offer of his helpful hand and leaping into the passenger seat with a professional agility. 'I like jeeps.'

He wondered when and where she'd travelled in jeeps, but it wasn't his place to ask.

'Where to?' he asked, climbing into the driver's seat. 'Any preferences?'

'Wherever you want to take me,' she said. 'I'm in your hands.'

The jeep had reminded her of Israel and the kibbutz – but she convinced herself that it didn't matter. She realised that she actually did like jeeps: she liked the bounce of them and the wind in her hair. And she was relieved to find that jeeps no longer held any threat in her memory.

Rob took her around the Snowy first, the Guthega dam, and the works in progress, and explained the plans for future development. She was awe-struck by the breadth of the Scheme. But as they drove through Adaminaby and he told her about the planned flooding over the next several years, she said, 'How sad.'

'Yep, you're right,' he agreed.

To Ruth, Rob Harvey was an interesting mix: at times a man of few words, simple and direct; at others, one who was articulate, learned and intelligent. And beneath it all, she sensed a man who was shy with women. Rob Harvey was an individual of intriguing contrasts, like the country of his birth, she thought as he drove her through the valleys and plains of the Monaro and up into the stark high country of the Snowy Mountains.

'Mount Kosciusko,' he said as the jeep bumped over the rough roads and the mountain loomed up ahead: 'the tallest mountain in Australia.'

They drove as far as they could to the upper slopes, and he stopped the car at Ruth's request. They got out to walk to one of the patches of snow that nestled here and there in shady nooks. How long had it been since she'd seen snow? she wondered as she bent and scooped up a handful, scrunching it into a ball. She aimed at the trunk of a blackbutt a good twenty yards away and hit her mark with perfect accuracy.

'Good shot,' he remarked.

'I loved snow fights when I was a child.'

'Oh yes?'

He didn't enquire any further, and she realised how extraordinarily respectful he'd been of her privacy. She hadn't offered one shred of information about herself, and he hadn't asked. Had she really communicated such a desire for secrecy? She supposed she must have, and then thought there really wasn't any need.

'I grew up in Berlin,' she said. 'We had regular family holidays in the Alps when I was a child.' She scooped up another handful of snow. 'But after the war I spent many years in Israel.' She made another snowball and hit the tree trunk again with deadly accuracy. 'No snow in Israel,' she smiled. 'I hadn't realised how much I missed it.'

'You'll get plenty of snow here in the winter months,' he assured her. 'In fact, you won't even be able to travel these roads half the time – not until the snowplough's cleared them.'

'And we're in Australia,' she said, 'isn't that amazing? One doesn't think of Australia as a country with snow. Well, we ignorant ones don't, anyway,' she laughed.

He felt privileged that she'd shared her past with him, brief as the exchange had been; what a different woman she was to the one he'd met only three weeks ago. That woman had rarely ever smiled, and this one was actually laughing.

'Come on,' he said, 'we're not even halfway through the guided tour.'

He drove her across the treeless plains and through the boulder country, explaining the flora and fauna as they went.

'It really should be Lucky showing you around,' he said. 'He's the one with the real gift of the gab, he can paint pictures like no-one I know – I reckon there's a touch of the poet in him.' Then he paused, feeling like a dill. 'But of course you'd know that.'

'Yes,' she said, 'I do.' So Lucky had told Rob Harvey that they knew each other, she thought. It was a sensible move. They had to stick to their story; they'd already told Maarten Vanpoucke, and discreet as the doctor might be, word was bound to get around. It was wise to tell as much of the truth as was possible.

'It must have seemed strange that we didn't mention our friendship that night at Dodds,' she said.

'Not really. Lucky said you were both a bit caught out and that you didn't want Peggy to feel awkward, you know . . .?' He shrugged, starting to feel awkward himself, and hoping he wasn't putting his foot in it.

'Yes, a reunion of old friends seemed a little tasteless at an engagement celebration. Lucky and I were very close during our university days.' She smiled. 'But of course that was a million years ago.'

Her reply was candid and comfortable, and once again she'd put him at his ease; she tended to have that effect on him, he thought.

'He's a beaut bloke, Lucky,' he said.

'Yes, he is,' she agreed.

They returned to Cooma in the mid afternoon – it was Sunday and Rob was picking up several of the men to take them back to the camp.

'So when do you start work, Ruth?' he asked as they drove into town.

'Tomorrow,' she said. 'My medical clearance was finalised last week and I report for duty first thing in the morning.'

'Best of luck,' he said as he turned off Sharp Street into Vale. They were only a block from Dodds now, and he wanted to ask her out to dinner next weekend, but he wasn't sure how to put it. A sightseeing drive was one thing, but dinner was a different matter altogether.

She seemed unaware of his dilemma as they turned into Commissioner Street and he did a u-turn to pull up outside the pub.

'I'll be moving out of Dodds in a week or so,' she said. 'The Authority's lining up accommodation for me.'

'Right, that'll be nice.' Perhaps lunch might be a better idea, he thought distractedly as he walked her to the main doors.

'Thanks so much, Rob. I've had a wonderful time.'

She shook his hand warmly, but the gesture seemed such a closure to the day that he faltered over his invitation.

'Any time. Perhaps we might do another drive next weekend?' It was all he could come up with.

'I'd like that,' she smiled. She had sensed he was working up the courage to offer a more intimate invitation, and she didn't wish to encourage him. She liked him a great deal but she wasn't ready for a relationship.

Well, it hadn't been a 'no', Rob thought, cursing his own inadequacy as she disappeared into Dodds. At least she wanted to see him again.

Maarten Vanpoucke was deep in thought as he walked down Vale Street. He'd stepped out of Hallidays store into Sharp Street just in time to see the jeep rounding the corner, Ruth smiling and talking animatedly to the man driving. It had shocked him. Was she already being courted?

As he crossed Commissioner Street, he saw the jeep pull away from the kerb outside Dodds. He knew she was staying at Dodds; the hotel was listed in her medical file as her current address. Perhaps her escort had merely taken her for a drive in the country. He certainly hoped so; there couldn't be any competition. He had to devise a plan: he needed to socialise with her. Once they developed a friend-ship, it wouldn't take long for him to exert the power which he knew he still had over her. He'd felt it in her presence: even though she herself had been unaware of it, the bond between them was as strong as ever.

It would be Lucky who would provide the link, he decided. How ironic that it should be her own husband who would open the doors for him. And how convenient that he himself was the only one to know of their marriage. At least he assumed that to be the case, and it would certainly work to his advantage. He would make his move next weekend, he thought. Lucky was always in town on a Saturday.

CHAPTER TWENTY-THREE

I t was noon on Monday, midway through the day shift, and Lucky had sent half the crew off for crib after the second firing for the day. They had thirty minutes before they relieved the other members of the team – work never stopped in the Eucumbene-Tumut tunnel. Gone were the days of the lazy mid-morning smoko breaks over billy tea, and although many teams working out in the open still sat around a campfire and boiled a billy, they made sure it was only when the bosses weren't about. If you worked for Kaiser you were allowed just the one half-hour crib break in an eight-hour shift, and sometimes even that was cut short.

There was little talk among the twenty men in hardhats and overalls sitting on the long wooden bench in the gloom of the massive tunnel, their backs to the rock wall, scoffing their hasty meal. They rarely complained about the short crib break; they were there to work, and time meant money. They enjoyed the competitive element and they certainly had no complaints about the pay. Indeed, to the migrants, who comprised the majority of the work-force, the opportunities on offer were beyond all expectations. They had left everything behind to arrive with nothing in a new country, and yet working for the Americans could see them owning a house in six months. Their work ethic was strong and, efficient teamwork being imperative, their camaraderie was intense – they were Snowy men and proud of it.

Lucky himself rarely took a crib break. As shift boss he preferred to eat his meal on the job, and he wolfed a sandwich down while the first of the locos drove in with its train of six cars, and the operator of the huge motorised mucker began the laborious process of shovelling up the rock spoil and loading it into the muck train.

After the firing, a scant five minutes was allowed for the smoke and dust to clear before the lengthy mucking-out process began. When the spoil had finally been cleared, it would be Lucky himself, together with another of the strongest men on the team, who would bar down the face to free it of any loose rock. Then the whole cycle would begin all over again.

The 'jumbo', a huge, three-tiered, steel-framed gantry on which twelve heavy pneumatic drilling machines were mounted, would be propelled on rails up to the tunnel face. The drilling would take place simultaneously, then the drill holes would be loaded with explosives. When the jumbo had been led back on its tracks and the men had retreated a safe distance behind the firing switch, the detonation would take place. The entire process of drilling, firing and mucking out took approximately four hours, so two cycles per shift was the common aim.

Crib break over, Lucky called the men back to work. It was time to relieve the others. They stood downing the last of their cold drinks and lukewarm coffee, Karl Heffner complaining that it wasn't the same as billy tea. In his earnest desire to become a true blue Aussie, Karl had not only developed a love of billy tea, he'd perfected the art of whingeing.

'I hear soon the buggers they give us a thermos for tea,'

he said. 'They issue all workers with a bloody thermos, so no-one will boil a bloody billy.' Along with his Australian idiosyncrasies, Karl had worked hard on his swear words.

'Thermoses, eh?' one of the Aussies scoffed. 'I reckon there'll be a helluva lot of 'em busted if they try to bring 'em in.'

They trooped back to work, all except Pietro, who remained seated at the far end of the bench, his chin lolling forward on his chest, his lunchbox unopened on his lap.

'Pietro?' Lucky said, but there was no reaction from the boy. 'Pietro?' Still no reaction. He was fast asleep, Lucky realised with concern. He grabbed him by the shoulders and shook him. 'Pietro, wake up.'

Pietro awoke with a start, nearly falling off the bench. He'd been in a deep and dreamless sleep, the first dreamless sleep he'd had in weeks. For a moment he didn't know where he was. He looked about, confused and disoriented, then saw Lucky gazing down at him.

'Lucky,' he said, 'I fall asleep, I am sorry,' and he jumped to his feet, stumbling a little, still feeling groggy.

'Sit down, Pietro.'

Pietro looked at the men marching off down the tunnel. 'But crib is over. I go to work.'

'I said sit down.'

Pietro did as he was told and Lucky sat beside him, examining him closely, noting the pallor of his skin and the shadows under his eyes.

'You're not well – what is it? What's wrong?'

'Is nothing. I do not sleep so good, is all. I have more dreams. The dreams like I tell you, you know? Of the priest?'

He'd told Lucky his dreams were a breakthrough – a memory. And although he feared the priest, it was a good thing that he remembered. But he hadn't told Lucky that the dreams were now getting out of hand.

Over the past several weeks, the more Pietro had tried to discover the priest's link to his past, the more his every sleeping hour had become haunted by the man with the piercing eyes. Yet he was no closer to discovering the truth. The previous Saturday, however, two days before, in the little back verandah room with Violet, after he'd lain drowning in the blood, the priest's eyes devouring him, and after Violet had woken him fearful that he'd choke in his sleep, Pietro had been sure of one thing.

'The other night in my dream, Lucky,' he now said, eager to share his discovery with his friend, 'I find out why is it that I fear the priest. The priest, he is going to kill me. I do not know why – this I must discover. Why is it the priest wish to kill me?'

Lucky berated himself for not having paid more attention to Pietro's condition. Whether the priest was simply a recurring nightmare, or whether he was indeed a fragment of the boy's tortured memory, was beyond determination, but one thing was certain. Pietro was distracted and in a state of exhaustion.

'Have you been to see your doctor?' he asked abruptly.

Pietro recognised Lucky's anxiety and realised that his talk about the priest must have sounded all wrong. Lucky was his boss, and they were at work. This was not the time or the place to talk of such things.

'I am sorry, Lucky,' he said. 'Is wrong I talk like this.'

But Lucky was not interested in apologies. 'You haven't, have you? You haven't been to see your doctor.'

Pietro shook his head, and he knew what was coming.

'Have you had any more fits since you've been on your medication?'

'Yes.'

Pietro felt terribly guilty that he hadn't told Lucky about his fits. It had been wrong of him to keep silent, he thought, Lucky had put his own job on the line by not reporting his epilepsy to the Authority a full nine months ago.

'I have a fit in Sydney at Christmas when I am with

Violetta,' he said, staring at the ground as he made his admission, 'and I have another three weeks ago.'

Oh God, Lucky thought, and cursed his own stupidity. He'd been eager to believe the illness could be controlled with regular medication, as Maarten Vanpoucke had intimated; but he'd behaved irresponsibly and had endangered the team.

'You cannot work in your condition, Pietro – you know that, don't you? You're a danger to yourself and to the others.'

'Yes, this I know.'

Lucky had such a huge affection for the boy and he looked so miserable that he longed to tell him everything would be all right, but he couldn't give Pietro any false assurances. The boy had problems beyond all comprehension, and to have a man on the team who was mentally unstable was a risk to the others. But what would happen to him, Lucky thought, if he lost his job – with a young wife and a baby on the way?

'I'm going to organise a vehicle to take you into town,' he said. 'You will go directly to your doctor and you'll take time off work and stay home for as long as the doctor says is necessary. Do you understand?'

'Yes, Lucky, I understand.'

Lucky walked off, wondering what on earth he was going to do. He couldn't allow Pietro to remain on the team – he would have to find him some other form of employment, but where? Doing what? Pietro had no skills other than those of a labourer, but as a labourer he was a liability to his workmates.

Pietro sat there feeling wretched. Lucky was cross with him because he had not told the truth, but he'd been worried that he might lose his job. He should not have come to work today, he thought, he should have listened to Violetta and Maureen.

'I don't want to hear any more about the priest,' Violet

had said when she'd woken him from his dream. 'I hate him.' She'd been terrified by his choking and the sound of his voice calling his own name. 'I don't care if you remember – Pietro, it doesn't matter any more. Maybe it's best to forget. Forget the priest!'

Brunch had not been the same that day. And in the late afternoon, when Maureen had returned from the hospital and remarked upon how tired Pietro looked, Violet had told her why.

'It's the priest, Auntie Maureen, he's had dreams about the priest again, and running through the snow, and the blood and . . .'

Maureen had recognised Violet's distress as genuine; this was no manufactured drama, she knew, and she'd been concerned herself. The boy looked utterly exhausted.

'You haven't been to see the doctor, have you?' she'd asked sternly, and when he'd shaken his head she'd been quite adamant. 'You must, Pietro. You must stay here tonight. Don't report for work tomorrow – we can telephone and say you're not well. Stay in town and see your doctor instead.'

Then Violet had joined in. 'Auntie Maureen's right, Pietro. Stay here and go to the doctor, I'll come with you. We'll go together,' she'd pleaded, 'please, sweetie.'

The two of them had been most insistent. But he hadn't listened.

He should have, he thought. Now he'd been caught out and Lucky, his best friend in the world, would be forced to fire him.

'I am sorry, Lucky,' he said again twenty minutes later as they stood beside the jeep, the engine running, 'I have done wrong.'

'No, you haven't.' Lucky embraced the boy as he'd wanted to do in the tunnel; the poor kid looked so woebegone. 'We'll find a way around it, Pietro, don't you worry. Now you do whatever the doctor advises,' he said as Pietro climbed into the passenger seat. 'And you rest up in town for a few days, all right?'

'Yes.' Pietro was relieved that Lucky didn't seem angry with him after all.

'Young Pietro Toscanini is here, doctor. He doesn't have an appointment, but Mrs Chapman is a little late, so I wondered if . . .'

'Yes, yes, show him in and bring me his file.' Maarten put on his spectacles. Old Mrs Chapman could wait, he thought. She was an irritating hypochondriac at the best of times, and the Italian was such an interesting case.

'Pietro, come in, come in.' He stood behind his desk and gestured at the chair opposite. 'Sit down, my boy.'

Pietro sat.

'Thank you, Edith.' Maarten accepted the file she handed him, and as she closed the door behind her he sat and smiled benignly at Pietro. 'I haven't seen you for some time – have you been keeping well?' He certainly didn't look well, Maarten thought.

Pietro shook his head. 'I do not sleep good,' he said. 'For three weeks I do not sleep good. Since my fit, I have dreams.'

'Ah, so you suffered another seizure? Let me see . . .' Maarten opened the file and glanced through the medical report. 'You had a seizure in December . . .'

'Yes, it is Christmas. I am in Sydney with Violetta.'

'Of course, you both came to see me. And you've suffered another seizure since then, is that right?'

'Yes.'

'Have you been taking your medication?'

'Yes, I take my pills every day.'

'Do you have any idea what might have triggered this seizure?'

Pietro nodded, he remembered only too well. 'I get in a fight, and this fight it upset me.' If the doctor asked for details, he'd say it was in a pub, he thought – he certainly wouldn't tell him he'd attacked Violetta's father.

The doctor didn't ask for details, however; he gave an understanding nod that seemed to say 'boys will be boys', but there was a touch of admonishment in his tone. 'With a condition like yours, Pietro, it is wise to avoid aggression whenever possible. Any form of violence is a possible trigger, do you understand?'

'Yes, I understand.'

'So following the fight, you felt the warning symptoms . . .' Maarten checked his notes again. 'The tic in your left eye, headache, general fatigue?'

'Yes, the fight it upset me and I go inside. Then I feel the fit coming.'

'So you were alone when the attack happened?'

'No, Violetta, she is with me. And I tell her to ask me questions, like you say she can do. I wish for her to ask me about the house. Why I cannot see inside this house. Is most important I remember,' Pietro said earnestly, 'because Violetta, she has a baby and I will be a father.'

'Really?' Maarten looked up from the notes he'd been making and smiled. 'My heartiest congratulations.' The boy seemed happy about the fact, so he supposed congratulations were in order.

'Thank you. Oh, Violetta and me, we have been married many months now,' Pietro added hastily – he didn't want the doctor to get the wrong idea. 'We marry in October; we are married when we come to see you.'

'Well, well, how surprising, again my congratulations.' Maarten wished the boy would get back to the point, he was curious to know if the girl had made contact during the seizure.

'Yes, and I wish for my baby to know who I am. This is why I must remember.'

'Of course, most understandable. So did Violet manage to get through to you?'

'Yes.'

'And did you respond?'

'Yes, I answer her.'

How interesting, thought the doctor as he made a further note on the medical report.

'I do not know that I answer her until after, when she tell me.'

'Naturally,' he nodded, 'it would be most unlikely that you would. But when she told you of your responses, did you recall anything?'

'Yes, I see things.'

'Ah.' Even more interesting, Maarten thought. 'Did you see inside the house?'

'No. I try, but I cannot see inside the house. The door, it will not open. I am under the house, I see the floor, it is above me, and I see the man's shoes on the steps . . .'

'These are images you've told me about before, Pietro, they're here in your report.'

'Yes, yes, I see this before,' Pietro was reliving the sequence of events in his mind, trying to get everything in the right order for the doctor, 'but then I see the floor it is not above me, the floor it is beneath me. I am inside the house,' he said. 'I am kneeling. But I cannot see the house, I can see only the floor. And then I see the man's shoes. And I see a priest's robe. And then I see a Bible that he holds in his hands.'

A cassock and a Bible, Maarten thought, remembering how he'd always held the peasants' Bible as one by one he'd heard their confessions, and how afterwards they'd kissed the hem of his cassock. Amazing, he thought – the boy was regaining his memory.

'And then I look up, and I see him.'

'Who do you see, Pietro?'

'I see the priest.'

'Really? You saw a priest?' Maarten noted it in his report.

'Yes, and the priest he is evil. The priest, he has done something very bad, this I know. But I cannot find out what is this bad thing the priest has done. And now I dream of the priest. Three weeks I do not sleep good – every night I have such dreams.'

'Tell me about your dreams, Pietro.' The boy was becoming agitated, he noted.

'I am under the house,' Pietro said. 'I am drowning in blood. The blood it is choking me. I run away from the blood. I run and I run through the snow, but the snow it is red – everywhere is blood.' The revisitation of his nightmare was painful and he pressed his fingers to his temples as though to ease the pressure.

Elbows on his desk, chin resting on his hands, Maarten studied the boy closely. Knowing Pietro's personal background as he did made this the most fascinating case he'd ever encountered. Interesting that three weeks of nightmares had not triggered an attack, he thought. The boy was prepared to meet his trauma head on, which was extraordinary. And his obvious determination to regain his memory was paying off: he was certainly on the right path. The nightmares were very close to the truth, after all: the boy had been under the house at the time, there had been a lot of blood and he would certainly have run through the snow, possibly even happening upon his father's body. How very, very interesting, Maarten thought.

'And all the time in my dreams, the priest he is calling to me,' Pietro said; he was clearly now in a state of distress. 'He calls and he calls to me. "Pietro! Pietro!" The priest he wishes to kill me. I try to run away from the priest, but I cannot.'

He buried his face in his hands, the images returning with fearful clarity.

'And I see the priest's eyes. Always there is the priest's eyes,' he said. 'They are evil, and they look into me. Every night I see them.'

He fought hard to blank the image of the priest's eyes from his mind. The doctor had said nothing for such a long time now, and Pietro felt ashamed that he'd so lost control of himself. He took a deep breath – he must make sense for the doctor.

'I fear the priest,' he said, sitting up straight, taking his hands from his face, determined to get his facts right. He was about to say, 'This is why I do not sleep good,' but he stopped. The doctor was staring at him over the rims of his spectacles. The doctor's eyes were burning into his face – they were evil. The eyes of the doctor were the eyes of the priest.

Pietro started to shake, his whole body quivering. He couldn't tear his eyes from the doctor's.

'What is it, Pietro? What's wrong? What are you feeling?' Was the boy about to have a seizure? Maarten wondered. Had talking about his nightmares triggered an attack?

Pietro stood abruptly, the chair nearly toppling over. He backed away, shaking his head in fearful disbelief, his eyes still locked with the doctor's.

'You have the eyes of the priest!' he said.

Good God, Maarten thought, how very unexpected. The boy remembered him. It was the last thing he'd expected.

'Come, come, Pietro,' he smiled as he stood, 'this is just your imagination, you're becoming hysterical.'

The boy continued to edge away from him as he circled the desk.

'You must calm down.' Maarten placed his hands firmly and reassuringly on Pietro's shoulders. 'There, now, that's better,' he said as the boy stood motionless, although he could feel him quivering. 'We don't want to trigger an attack now, do we?'

Pietro shook his head. The doctor's manner was comforting and the eyes that smiled at him from behind the spectacles were benign and concerned. It was his mind playing tricks on him, he thought, as it had before when he'd imagined the doctor had the eyes of the priest – he remembered telling Violetta. 'But the doctor doesn't have evil eyes,' Violetta had said, and he'd agreed with her. So why did he still feel such fear? Why did he fear the doctor the way he feared the priest?

'You're upset, my boy, I want you to lie down.'

Pietro allowed himself to be led to the examination bed and he lay down as the doctor instructed.

'Close your eyes, breathe deeply and try to relax,' Maarten said. 'I'm going to give you something to calm you down.'

Pietro did as he was told, closing his eyes and trying to control his breathing. His fear threatened to overwhelm him and he could feel the tic of his left eye. But he must not fear the doctor, he told himself – it was foolish to fear the man who was helping him.

'The transferral of identity is not uncommon among patients suffering anxiety, Pietro,' Maarten said as he crossed to the dispensary. 'The relationship between physician and patient is intimate, and occasionally patients tend to confuse their doctors with some demon figure they find threatening.' He took the syringe and the vial from the cupboard.

Pietro didn't hear the doctor's words – he heard the priest.

You must not hide yourself away, Pietro. It is not safe for you to be alone when you have your attacks. You could harm yourself.

Pietro could see the priest. He held a piece of leather in his hands.

If you feel an attack coming upon you when you are alone, this is what you must place in your mouth. Do you understand?

It was the priest who had given him the leather strap.

Maarten took off his spectacles; they were irritating him and there was no need for them now. He glanced in the mirror of the dispensary cupboard as he filled the syringe. Strange that it was the priest's eyes the boy had fixated upon, and that after all these years he'd recognised those same eyes. Remarkably perceptive too, Maarten thought. He remembered how, when he'd first seen the new face Fritz von Halbach had given him, the only thing he'd recognised in himself had been his eyes. And even then they'd been a different shape, he'd been dismayed to discover – his whole face was a different shape. He'd lost the aquiline bones of his youth, he was not as handsome as he had been, and he remembered wondering if it had been Fritz's idea of a joke.

He put down the vial and tested the full syringe, giving it a tap, a brief squirt of potassium chloride coming out of the needle. It was a pity the boy had to go, but it was necessary. Pietro knew him, and although he could point no finger at the death camps, he was a definite threat. When he regained his memory, as it appeared he inevitably would, his story would arouse far too much attention. Maarten could not afford to be an object of attention. He could leave Cooma, of course, and the boy would be regarded as a simple hysteric, but Maarten had no intention of going anywhere. Not now that Ruth was here.

He continued to talk soothingly to the boy. 'You must not be afraid of me, Pietro,' he said, 'I am your doctor, your welfare is of great concern to me. Rest assured that your fear is purely imaginary.'

The priest had also spoken to him in the same caring way, Pietro thought, and the priest, too, had pretended to have his best interests at heart. But the priest had wished to kill him. In his mind, the priest's voice and the doctor's voice started to blend.

'I'm going to give you something to calm you down,' Maarten said as he sat beside the boy.

The sudden realisation terrified Pietro. The doctor's voice was the voice of the priest!

Then he heard the priest say, 'It will hurt just a little bit to start with, but after that you won't feel a thing,' and he looked up in horror to find himself staring into the eyes of the priest.

'Goodbye, Pietro,' Maarten said.

The eyes of the priest were the last thing Pietro saw as the needle plunged into his vein.

CHAPTER TWENTY-FOUR

The death of Pietro Toscanini shook the whole community. Even those who'd barely known him were shocked by the news. He'd been so young and handsome, they all said, just twenty-two years old – and word quickly spread that his young wife was pregnant. It was a tragedy, a terrible, terrible tragedy, they agreed. It seemed the boy had been epileptic, but how could you tell? He never looked sickly, he'd been fit and strong; but he'd died of a heart attack while having a fit. It was shocking.

On the day of the funeral, the men of Lucky's team, all forty of them, swapped their shifts so they could attend the burial service. As word spread around the district, they came from other work camps and sites, those who'd met the young Italian at the pubs and dances in town. They came from the township too, and from neighbouring towns. Some of them hadn't even known the boy personally, but they were mates of the Campbell family and they came for young Vi.

Nearly two hundred people were gathered at the cemetery, standing a respectful distance from the graveside, leaving room for those who'd been closest to the boy as the service commenced.

Violet was supported by her mother, who had an arm firmly around her waist; the girl's eyes remained fixed upon the coffin which sat over the open grave, resting on two planks of wood, with straps laid out on the ground either side. Not once did her eyes leave the coffin; she seemed numb and uncomprehending. Beside her stood her aunt Maureen and her two brothers, Dave keeping a close eye on his sister after Maureen had murmured to him that she thought Violet might faint.

Cam Campbell, hands clasped in front of him, granite face unreadable, was barely hearing the priest as he embarked upon his litany. Cam was surveying the crowd – he had little time for religion.

He'd expected quite a few migrants would turn up, workmates of Pietro's, but they'd come out in force, he noted. The boy had obviously been popular. He was pleased, too, to see that so many of his own mates had come along to lend their support to young Vi. But he had not anticipated such overall numbers, nor so many dignitaries and local identities. He was impressed. The Commissioner himself, William Hudson, was there, and Rob Harvey and others of the Authority's upper echelons whom he'd met from time to time. He'd had occasional run-ins with them, certainly, but they were powerful men and he respected them. The Yanks were there too, representatives of Kaiser, and among the crowd were many people well known throughout the entire district: Bob and Rita Duncan, and Peter Minogue; Merv Pritchard and his copper mates; Frank Halliday with his two young assistants – even the famous Flash Jack Finnigan had turned up with his offsider, Antz.

Cam realised he was more than impressed as the priest droned on. He was moved. The migrants, the bosses and the locals had all come to pay their respects to the young Italian who had found a new life among them and who had met such a tragically premature death. It was a sign of the changing times, Cam told himself with a touch of guilt, and it was a sign that he should move with them. He glanced at Vi, and the telltale bulge of her belly. What a bloody shame the kid would be born without a dad, he thought. Pietro would have made a fine father.

Opposite the family stood Lucky and Peggy. They were holding hands and Lucky could feel her fingers squeezing his tighter and tighter. He glanced at her, but she did not return his look; head erect, straight-backed, she remained every inch the schoolteacher as she clutched at the lifeline of his hand. Peggy was being stoic, determined not to cry. But her heart ached for Violet, the little girl whom she'd taught who was now staring vacantly at the coffin, barely a woman, widowed and carrying a baby.

Luigi and Elvio Capelli, the brothers Pietro had met when he'd first come to Cooma, had also claimed a grave-side position near Lucky and Peggy. Pietro was Italian, one of their own, and they would help lower his coffin into the grave. Karl Heffner stood beside them; it had been his 'young cobber' Pietro who had carried him from the tunnel and it was his right, too, to help lower the coffin.

Father O'Riordan was glad he'd agreed to conduct the service – it was the finest turnout he'd had for a funeral. Not that he'd considered refusing, of course – the boy had still been one of the flock, after all, even though his marriage was not recognised by the Catholic Church, as he'd advised the boy at the time. He had strongly disapproved of Pietro's flagrant disregard for the doctrines of his faith. But what a grand tribute it was, he now thought as he reached the crucial point in the service; amazing that the boy should have so many mourners paying their respects.

Without drawing breath, he gave the agreed nod to Lucky.

Lucky had been awaiting the signal from Father O'Riordan, and he squeezed Peggy's hand before gently extricating himself from her grip. It was time to lower the coffin. As he crossed and knelt by one of the straps, the Capelli brothers and Karl took their cue from him and crossed also, to kneel at their prearranged positions. Then, as the priest continued his solemn intonation, they took up the straps and stood.

Violet, whose eyes had remained riveted on the coffin, blind and deaf to all about her, was suddenly shocked out of her stupor. The coffin was moving.

Two men stepped forward and slid away the planks, then Lucky, Karl and the brothers started to lower the coffin into the grave.

Violet's mind was no longer a blank – it screamed at the outrage. Her Pietro was in that awful wooden box, and it was being lowered into a gaping hole in the ground. 'You can't do that to him,' her mind screamed. 'You can't do it!' But it wasn't her mind screaming at all, it was her voice – and she hurled herself forward to grab at the coffin, to stop it disappearing into the ground.

Dave caught her in time, grasping her around the waist and they both stumbled forward, Violet falling to her knees and Dave not letting go, terrified that she was about to throw herself into the grave.

As he helped her to her feet, her mother was quickly by her side. Violet had stopped screaming and she didn't try to struggle. She was sobbing now.

'Stop it, please!' she begged, tears of anguish pouring down her cheeks as she looked around at the crowd, desperately pleading with them.

'Don't do this to him,' she begged. 'Please! Please, don't let this happen! Please!'

Then, as she searched among the faces of the mourners, she saw the doctor standing directly behind Father O'Riordan.

Violet stretched out her arm, her finger pointing accusingly at Maarten Vanpoucke. 'You killed him!' she screamed. 'You killed him! You killed my Pietro!'

Dave and Marge tried gently to lead her away, but her full hysteria was unleashed and she yelled dementedly, the finger still jabbing ferociously at the air, pointing directly at the doctor.

'You killed him, it was you. You have the eyes of the priest – Pietro told me! It was you. You killed him!'

Her whole body was sagging from exhaustion, about to fall, and Dave and Marge half carried her away from the graveside. She wouldn't give up: her voice, although weaker, was still raised in accusation. 'You have the eyes of the priest, he told me. You killed him.'

Then Dave picked her up in his arms and carried her over to the car, Marge beside him and Maureen following.

'Don't worry, Cam,' Maureen whispered to her brother before she joined them, 'she'll be all right, I'll take her to the hospital, we'll look after her there.'

Cam nodded, then glanced a directive at his younger son before redirecting his eyes to the proceedings. It was important that he and Johnno stay; the Campbell family needed to be represented.

But they could all hear Violet as she sobbed into her brother's shoulder, 'He killed him, he killed him – he has the eyes of the priest.'

There was an uncomfortable silence after the car drove off, all concerned for the tragic young widow.

Then Father O'Riordan continued with the service. But he was rattled. 'The eyes of the priest?' he was thinking. The poor girl was distraught in her grief; it was obvious, and she had his deepest sympathy, but it was most confusing. Why was she blaming him? What had he done wrong?

'Ashes to ashes,' he intoned as he poured the trowel of earth into the grave, then he paused, uncertain to whom he should hand the trowel; it was to have been Violet, or if the widow had not been able, then her mother.

Cam stepped forward and took the trowel, filling it from the mound of fresh earth beside the grave.

'Dust to dust . . .' Father O'Riordan continued.

When he'd tipped the earth into the grave, Cam handed the trowel to Lucky; Violet had told him that the German was Pietro's best friend.

'. . . certain hope of resurrection to eternal life . . .'

As the service drew to its conclusion, the trowel was passed from one to another. To Peggy, the Capelli brothers, Karl Heffner, and finally to Johnno, each adding their own piece of Monaro earth to Pietro's grave.

After the funeral, Cam stayed long enough to shake hands and accept condolences, then he and Johnno left for the hospital to check on Vi.

The others mingled. The men would shortly go to Dodds and get drunk as they always did after a funeral. There had been a number of funerals for Snowy men, and God alone knew how many more there would be before the completion of the Scheme. They all worked with the knowledge that accidental deaths were a part of their job, but there hadn't been a funeral like that before. The unexpected death of one so young and the sight of his distraught young widow had affected them all, and they stayed, talking in muted voices about the sheer bloody tragedy of it.

Among several of the townsfolk – those who enjoyed a good gossip – there was a touch of sympathy for Maarten Vanpoucke.

'Well, of course Vi would blame him,' Mavis said, trying to sound sympathetic, but inferring a criticism. 'I mean, her husband died in the doctor's surgery, didn't he, and it was so unexpected she'd feel she had to blame *someone*. But it's a bit much to accuse him publicly like that. I'm sure the poor man did all he could to save the boy.'

'For goodness sake, Mavis, listen to yourself,' Vera snapped. 'Poor Vi was hysterical; she was distraught with grief.'

It wasn't like Vera to snap, and Mavis realised that she might have overstepped the mark.

'Oh, the doctor certainly did everything he could,' old Mrs Chapman said.

She had their attention instantly. In fact, Mavis and Vera had made a bee-line for old Mrs Chapman – word had gone around that she'd been at the doctor's surgery when it had happened.

'Well, he would, wouldn't he?' Mavis said with a snide glance at Vera, as if she'd been vindicated.

'Oh yes, and so did poor Edith Beasley. Such a nice woman – she was most upset.' Old Mrs Chapman was regularly at the doctor's: she spent a great deal of time in the waiting room and she'd had many a long and pleasant chat with Edith. 'She's a very good nurse too, even though she's retired. Between them they did everything they could to resuscitate the boy. Such a terrible business,' she tut-tutted and shook her head sadly.

Old Mrs Chapman was having an excellent afternoon. At eighty-four she was desperately lonely and a regular mourner at funerals of people she'd never known. Usually she came and went unnoticed; this was the first time she'd ever been the centre of attention.

'Goodness me, I can't tell you what it was like,' she said, 'sitting in that waiting room, knowing that something terrible had happened.'

Mavis and Vera continued to give her their undivided attention.

Lucky and Peggy were talking with Maarten Vanpoucke. Lucky would take Peggy home soon and then join the men at Dodds where they would pay tribute to Pietro the way Snowy workers did – by reminiscing and getting drunk. But like the others, Lucky had felt it was respectful to stay and mingle before he left.

The three of them were discussing Violet's heartbreaking outburst. Now that the service was over, Peggy had lost her poise and was openly dabbing at her eyes with a handkerchief.

'Yes, yes, the poor girl,' Maarten agreed, 'insane with grief.'

'Strange what she was saying about the eyes of the priest,' Lucky said.

'Strange?' Maarten queried. It had surprised him when the girl had said that. How could Pietro have told her he had the eyes of the priest? The boy hadn't recognised him until that day in his rooms. But if Pietro had mentioned him by name to the girl, then perhaps he had done so to Lucky, the man who was his father figure. 'Strange, in what way?' he asked.

'Pietro told me he had dreams about a priest,' Lucky said. 'He was terrified of the man. Strange that Violet should see you as –'

'As the demon priest?' Maarten relaxed; the boy had said nothing. 'No, no, my friend, not strange at all.' He shook his head, his smile sympathetic, professional and just a touch patronising. 'Pietro told me about his nightmares and his obsessive fear of the mythical priest – it's all in my medical report.' It was, Maarten had made sure of it – the demon priest was further evidence of the boy's mental instability. 'Unfortunately, it was the recounting of his nightmares that precipitated the seizure,' he said sadly, 'and then, of course, the heart attack. It's understandable that Violet, in her distraught state, might see me as the evil figure in her husband's nightmares.'

'Yes, I suppose so,' Lucky agreed. 'Poor little Violet, I hope she'll be all right.'

'Indeed, I worry for her mental state,' Maarten said. 'And she's to have a baby, Pietro told me. I do hope the tragic loss of her husband won't affect her pregnancy. It could well do so, I fear.'

Lucky decided it was time to take Peggy home. Maarten's dire prophecy wasn't helping and a fresh onslaught of tears threatened.

Maarten adhered to his plan that Saturday. Arriving at Dodds at six o'clock in the evening, he stood in the front bar by the windows, where he had a perfect view of all who came and went from the hotel. Lucky and Peggy arrived on the dot of half-past six.

He waited a minute or so, finished his Scotch, then walked through to the lounge. He hoped he wouldn't bump into Ruth. Though he longed to see her, it was not part of his plan to meet her just then.

Lucky was also hoping he wouldn't bump into Ruth as he and Peggy sat and he ordered a couple of drinks from Peter Minogue.

'Did you love her?' Peggy had asked when he'd admitted to the affair he and Ruth had had during their university days.

'Very much,' he'd answered.

'And she loved you.' It had not been a question.

'Yes.'

'You still love each other, don't you.' Again it had been a statement.

'Yes, and we probably always will,' he'd said. He'd been determined to follow Ruth's advice and tell as much of the truth as was possible. 'But we loved each other in different lives when we were different people – we both know that. Ruth said it herself. We have new lives now. And you're mine, Peggy. You're my life.'

He hadn't been sure whether she was laughing or crying as she'd kissed him – it had seemed a mixture of both.

'Well, Ruth has great taste,' she'd said, 'and I'm willing to share you.'

Peggy's reaction to the honesty of his admission had gone very much along the lines Ruth had predicted. It was amazing, Lucky had thought, how women always seemed one step ahead when it came to emotional issues. He would probably have tried to bluff it out, to pretend there had never been anything between them, but Ruth's advice had proved correct.

Nevertheless, when it had come to their customary Saturday dinner at Dodds, Lucky had been in a state of indecision. Should he change the ritual of their weekends? Peggy would want to know why, and what would her reaction be if he suggested not going to Dodds because Ruth was staying there? He wished he could have asked Ruth – she would've known what to do.

What the hell, he thought now as Peter Minogue disappeared to the bar, perhaps Ruth herself had averted the possibility of a confrontation. She knew they regularly dined at Dodds on a Saturday – perhaps she'd taken herself out for the evening. But it was most uncomfortable, he thought, playing these cat and mouse games.

'Lucky, what a pleasant surprise.'

Maarten Vanpoucke had appeared beside their table.

'Maarten, hello.' The two men shook hands.

'And Miss Minchin.' Maarten offered his hand to her too. 'I was having a drink with some friends in the front bar when I saw you arrive, and I realised that I hadn't offered you my congratulations on your engagement. But then,' he added sadly, 'it was hardly appropriate to do so the last time we met, was it?' He smiled at Peggy, 'I must say, my dear, in my personal opinion, you couldn't have made a better choice.'

'Thank you, Doctor Vanpoucke.' Peggy returned the smile politely, but found his charm grating. 'The last time we met' referred to two days ago when they'd buried young Pietro, and Violet had been carted off to the hospital, hysterical. The doctor was rather a cold fish, she decided. 'I tend to agree with you, but then I'm a little biased.'

Lucky sensed her reaction. Peggy was never very good at disguising her feelings – it was one of the things he loved most about her. But he felt sorry for Maarten, as he so often did, and he doubted whether the man had been having a drink with some friends in the front bar at all – Maarten didn't have any friends. In fact, Lucky was surprised to see him in the pub at all. Loneliness must have got the better of him to bring him to Dodds, Lucky thought. He'd probably been sitting in a corner on his own.

'Would you like to join us?' he asked. 'We're having a quick drink before we go in to dinner.'

'Well, if I'm not intruding . . . ?'

'Of course you're not.' It was Peggy who was quick to reassure him. She realised that Lucky had picked up on her brittle tone. She really must watch herself, she thought. She could be so impolite, and Lucky was always sensitive to the feelings of others. 'Please, do join us.'

'I'd be delighted,' Maarten said, 'just one quick beer.' How could Lucky have chosen this one over Ruth? he wondered. And it had been a choice, he was quite sure of it. Observing them in the park, he'd seen the love that Ruth and Lucky shared, and yet Lucky had opted for the little schoolteacher. Unbelievable.

He sensed, however, that the little schoolteacher wasn't quite the mouse he'd presumed her to be. There was an edge to her and, he recognised, an astute intelligence. He wondered briefly what she'd be like in bed.

When Peter Minogue arrived with the drinks, Lucky ordered a beer for Maarten, and it was Peggy who steered the conversation. It was deliberate on her part. She wanted to avoid any discussion of Pietro's death; the doctor would speak of it coldly and clinically as he had at the funeral, and she didn't want to hear his views. Violet was home with her family now, but Peggy was plagued by the memory of her in the hospital the day after the funeral. The girl had been under sedation; blank, emotionless, not wishing to talk. Peggy had found it heartbreaking.

'Well, I really mustn't keep you from your dinner,'

Maarten said barely twenty minutes later as he drained the last of his beer. He didn't want to overstay his welcome and it was time to get to the point. 'Oh, and speaking of dinner,' he said as he stood, 'I have an excellent idea. Next Saturday, instead of dining here, why don't you join me for some home cooking? Mrs Hodgeman would love to demonstrate her expertise, and she gets so little opportunity.' He smiled at Lucky, pulling on his heartstrings – he knew the man thought he was lonely.

Lucky suspected Peggy wasn't all that keen to take Maarten up on his offer – for some reason she hadn't seemed to warm to the man – and he found himself in a dilemma, not wanting to hurt Maarten's feelings.

'That's very kind of you . . .' he started to say, wondering what to say without giving offence.

'Excellent.' Maarten dived in before Lucky could come up with a valid reason to decline. 'And I wonder,' he added as if the idea had just occurred to him, 'whether you might like to ask your old friend Ruth to join us. As a newcomer to town, it might be nice to show her some local hospitality.'

His smile was affable, but he was studying Lucky's reaction – he knew he'd put the man on the spot. Had Lucky made any mention to his fiancée of his 'old friend Ruth'? If not, he'd have some explaining to do, Maarten thought, but either way the man couldn't refuse his offer – it would look far too suspicious if he did. His fiancée might assume there had been something more than friendship between him and his 'old friend' Ruth.

It was Peggy who answered. 'What an excellent idea,' she said, 'don't you think so, Lucky? It would be a lovely welcoming gesture; I'm sure Ruth would appreciate it.' Then to Maarten: 'It's very kind of you, Doctor Vanpoucke.'

'Call me Maarten, please,' he smiled, 'and may I call you Peggy?'

'Of course.'

'Splendid. Well, Peggy, I shall look forward to seeing you all next Saturday. Shall we say around seven?'

He shook hands with them both and made his farewells. How astounding, he thought, that the little schoolteacher herself had been the one to decide.

'She might not be able to come,' Lucky said sulkily when Maarten had gone. 'She might have something else planned – she might not even *want* to come.' He was wondering why Peggy had taken over the way she had.

'She'll want to come. And if she has something else planned, she'll cancel it.'

He scowled. She sounded supremely and annoyingly confident.

'Oh Lucky, stop sulking,' she said briskly in the schoolteacher way she did when he was behaving childishly. 'It's best that Ruth and I get to know each other, at least on a social basis, and this is the perfect opportunity. We live in Cooma, for goodness sake; we can't keep trying to avoid each other. It's ridiculous.'

'How very wise of her. I agree entirely,' Ruth said the next day when he returned to Dodds to tell her about Maarten's invitation and Peggy's response.

'But you said you thought it was best if you kept your distance.' He was confused – she was contradicting herself. 'That's what you said, I remember, those were your exact words.'

She laughed. His expression of boyish bewilderment was one she easily recognised. Though he had such a way with women, Samuel really did not comprehend the workings of the female mind.

'That was before we knew Peggy would be so understanding,' she said; he'd told her of Peggy's reaction to his admission. 'It's different now. I was wrong and Peggy is right.'

'I give up.' He was exasperated – women were a bloody

mystery. They'd both patronised him as if he were a child.

'Samuel,' she said patiently, realising that he was becoming irritated, 'when you dined here at Dodds last night, were you worried that I might appear?'

'No, I wasn't *worried*,' he said, floundering, on the defensive, 'but I was a bit concerned. I thought it might be . . . you know . . . awkward.'

'So did I.'

He stopped floundering and his irritation subsided.

'That's why I went out for the evening,' she said. 'I didn't particularly want to – I normally eat in the dining room downstairs – but I was worried that you and Peggy might be there.'

'I thought of changing our routine,' he admitted, 'but I knew she'd ask why, and . . .' He shrugged. 'It all got a bit too difficult.'

'Exactly, and it'll stay that way if we don't stop being so overprotective. Peggy doesn't want it like that, and neither should we. We're old friends now, and old friends don't avoid each other.'

Lucky's smile was rueful. 'I'm having a bit of trouble thinking of you as an old friend, Ruth.'

'I know,' she agreed, 'me too. But we must try. The past won't disappear – but who knows, perhaps there'll come a day when it won't be so vivid.' She smiled too, although for some strange reason she felt on the verge of tears. 'In the meantime, my darling,' she said lightly, 'we don't have to live in each other's pockets, but we do have to live in the same town.'

He would have liked to have embraced her, just for old times' sake. 'Peggy and I'll collect you shortly before seven,' he said.

'Why don't you make it earlier?' she suggested. 'We could walk. Maarten Vanpoucke's is only fifteen minutes from here, and these early autumn evenings are so beautiful.' He hadn't quite got her drift, she realised, but then it had been another subtle female ploy. 'It'll give Peggy and me time to talk,' she said, 'before everything becomes dinner table chat.'

'Talk?' he asked. 'What would you want to talk about?'

'Oh, fashion, jewellery, hairstyles, that sort of thing – or maybe we'll talk about you. For heaven's sake,' she said as he looked alarmed, 'who knows what we'll talk about, Samuel? It doesn't matter.'

Lucky left feeling distinctly uncomfortable – he was not looking forward to Saturday.

Peggy thought Ruth's idea was excellent.

'Let's not take the car at all,' she suggested as they dressed for Maarten's dinner party. 'Let's walk to Dodds.'

'We're backtracking on ourselves a bit,' he said. Peggy's house was equidistant from Dodds and Maarten's.

'Doesn't matter,' she insisted. 'I'd really prefer to walk, would you mind?'

He didn't mind at all, and they both enjoyed the ten-minute stroll to Dodds, walking hand in hand. It was a beautiful evening; March was always a pleasant time of year in Cooma.

As they approached the hotel, Peggy felt a vague trepidation; she'd known that she would. From the outset, she had been nowhere near as confident as she'd led Lucky to believe. She knew she was right to forge some sort of connection with Ruth, however superficial – they couldn't avoid each other constantly in a town like Cooma – but she was daunted by the prospect of the confrontation.

Ruth was waiting at the front of Dodds when they arrived, even though they were several minutes early. 'How nice to see you, Peggy.' She didn't offer her hand, but her cheek instead; a half-embrace, woman to woman, the greeting of old friends.

'Hello, Ruth.' Peggy felt herself relax.

'Lucky,' the name still felt strange, Ruth thought as she

kissed his cheek. 'Now wasn't I right about walking? What a glorious evening.'

They set off at a slow pace, the women more intent upon talking to each other than their route. Lucky dawdled along beside them, his hand still in Peggy's.

Peggy asked Ruth about her new job, which they'd discussed with Rob Harvey over dinner that night at Dodds. Had she started work yet? Was it interesting?

Lucky realised, guiltily, that he hadn't asked Ruth about her job.

She loved it, Ruth said. She'd been working for the SMA for a week now, and in three days' time she would move to the accommodation they'd arranged for her in Cooma North.

As she responded to Peggy's enquiries, Ruth found herself deeply admiring the woman for her open reference to the night they'd met. Peggy had been hurt and humiliated throughout the entire evening – Ruth had sensed it, now she felt she should apologise.

'I'm sorry about that night at Dodds,' she said.

The words came out jarringly in the midst of what had been everyday conversation, and the three of them halted, Lucky feeling ill-at-ease. Ruth was going too far, he thought.

'We should have said something, both of us.' Undaunted, Ruth continued, 'But it was such a surprise, seeing . . . Lucky after all these years.' She stopped herself saying 'Samuel' just in time.

Peggy noticed the stumble. It was silly, she decided in her eminently practical way, that Ruth should feel such a need to be on her guard.

'He wasn't "Lucky" then, though, was he?'

'No,' Ruth admitted. 'He was Samuel.'

Peggy nodded. 'Samuel Lachmann.' Her pronunciation of the German surname was faultless.

'That's right.' Ruth was surprised, although she supposed she shouldn't be. Samuel would naturally have told his fiancée about his past. She turned to him. 'So how did "Lucky" come into being?' she asked. 'You didn't tell me.'

Lucky stopped feeling self-conscious. Why should he? he wondered. The women obviously weren't.

'An Authority official misspelled my name on the application form,' he said. 'He put "Luckman" and I couldn't be bothered correcting him.'

'And Aussies being Aussies, he was "Lucky" from then on,' Peggy chimed in.

'I like it,' Ruth said.

Peggy was glad they were talking so candidly. 'He can be Samuel to you and Lucky to me,' she said. 'I don't mind.'

'Oh, I'm getting used to Lucky,' Ruth smiled. 'It suits him.'

They both looked at Lucky, and he turned to peer comically over his shoulder as if there were someone behind him. They laughed and he took Peggy's hand once more.

'Shall we keep walking?' he suggested. 'I'd like to reach Maarten's before dinner gets cold.'

They continued on their way, the women still talking, and Lucky thought how alike Ruth and Peggy were at heart. They were strong, unpretentious and scrupulously honest. No wonder he loved them.

It was Ruth who brought up the subject of Pietro. She knew all about the circumstances of his death – her fellow workers had talked of little else for the past week. She'd found it hard to believe that the handsome young Italian she'd met at Dodds barely a month ago was dead, remembering how he and his pretty young wife had spent the whole evening dancing. They'd also told her at work that the girl was pregnant, which had made the news of her husband's death even more shockingly sad.

'I was so sorry to hear about Pietro,' she said to Lucky. 'Rob Harvey told me you were good friends.'

'We were,' Lucky nodded, 'we were very close.'

'How is poor Violet coping?' She directed the question to Peggy.

'She's not,' Peggy replied. 'She's a mess. At first everyone worried she might lose the baby, but she'll keep it, they say, she's physically strong. It's her mental state that's the problem. Oh God, you should have seen her at the funeral – it was awful. She was deranged.'

For the past week Peggy had avoided all discussion of Pietro and Violet. She'd talked to Lucky but no-one else – her guard had gone up the moment the topic was mentioned. She found it a relief now to speak openly to Ruth, knowing she was removed from the grapevine of gossip that was Cooma.

'She accused Maarten Vanpoucke of killing him. She kept yelling "you killed him, you killed him, you have the eyes of the priest" – she was demented in her grief. It was horrible to see.' The scene at the graveside remained etched in Peggy's mind.

Lucky was relieved she was unburdening herself. He knew how deeply she'd been affected and had been concerned by the way she'd closed herself off, even in the company of those who truly cared.

'Pietro had recurring nightmares about a priest who wanted to kill him,' he explained to Ruth. 'And because he died in Maarten's surgery, Violet developed this fixation. In her mind, the doctor became the priest.'

'She still believes it,' Peggy said. She'd visited Violet at the family property a few days earlier and had initially been relieved to discover the girl was no longer under sedation. But it had disturbed her to find that Violet was still in a state of distraction. 'She keeps saying the doctor killed her husband and he has the eyes of the priest. She says it over and over.'

'How terrible,' Ruth said. 'The poor girl.'

They were still discussing Violet when they arrived at Maarten's house, and as they walked through the open gate and approached the front door, Ruth looked at the ground-floor bay windows of the doctor's surgery. That was where the young man had died, she thought, in the very same room where she'd had her examination; it was awful to contemplate.

Lucky rang the bell and it was Maarten himself who opened the front door and greeted them. He'd intended to have Mrs Hodgeman show them in, but he'd become impatient – they were fifteen minutes late.

'Lucky,' he said, shaking his hand effusively, 'welcome.'

'Sorry we're a bit late. We walked.'

'No matter, no matter. Peggy,' he said and made a show of kissing her hand.

Peggy felt self-conscious at the theatrical gesture but she chastised herself. The man was European and in his own home – what right did she have to be critical of a social etiquette to which she was unaccustomed?

'Hello, Maarten.' She turned to smile at Ruth. 'We're to blame for being late; we were too busy talking.'

'Naturally.' How comfortable the women seemed with each other, he thought. 'And, Ruth, my dear.' He kissed her hand also, careful not to allow his lips to linger too long. 'Welcome.'

'Hello, Maarten, thank you for inviting me.'

'My pleasure.' He delighted in her use of his Christian name; he'd thought that he might have to remind her. 'Come in, come in.'

He escorted them through the hall and up the grand staircase.

'What a beautiful house,' Peggy said as they emerged onto a polished wooden landing and Maarten ushered them into the lounge room. It was certainly impressive, she thought, taking in the lavish furnishings, the Persian carpets, the paintings and the objets d'art, although a little too opulent for her taste.

'Thank you, I like to surround myself with beautiful

things.' He didn't look at Ruth as he said it, but he could see her out of the corner of his eye. She, too, was gazing around the room, and he noticed how perfectly she belonged here. A creature of such beauty should be surrounded by beautiful things.

'A comfortable lifestyle is important to me,' he said to Peggy, but the words were directed at Ruth. It was his intention to impress on her the comfort, the life and the style his wealth could offer her. That was why it had been necessary to bring her here. It was a pity Lucky and Peggy had to be involved, but there'd been no other way.

He crossed to the bottle of Dom Perignon which sat in an ice-bucket on the sideboard. 'Do make yourselves at home. Is everyone happy with champagne? Lucky, would you prefer a beer?'

'Champagne's fine by me,' Lucky said. He would have preferred a beer, but he didn't want to halt the man's flow – Maarten was in his element, playing the host with great flair.

'May I?' Ruth asked, gesturing to the open French windows leading to the balcony.

'Of course,' Maarten said, opening the champagne.

He watched her as she stepped outside. This is your home, Ruth, he thought, as he eased the cork from the bottle.

Ruth stood on the balcony, breathing in the air with its first hint of autumn chill. She looked out over Vale Street. Several blocks away to the right she could see the crosses of the Brigidine Convent silhouetted against the clear night sky, but her mind was on the boy and his pretty wife, the way they had danced and been so in love. The talk tonight had disturbed her, and she couldn't rid herself of the couple's image as she thought how young Pietro had died in the room just below. She rejoined the others.

They sat sipping their champagne, and Mrs Hodgeman arrived with a tray of hors d'oeuvres. Maarten heralded her entrance with great aplomb. 'Mrs Hodgeman is our chef extraordinaire,' he said, and Noreen Hodgeman, overwhelmed by the honour, gave a clumsy approximation of a curtsy.

He introduced her to his guests. 'Miss Minchin,' he said, 'Miss Stein, and of course you know Lucky.'

'Nice to meet you, Miss,' she said to each of the women, and to Lucky, 'Good to see you, sir.'

'Hello, Mrs Hodgeman.' Lucky gave her a special grin, aware that no amount of urging would make her call him 'Lucky' – at least not under the doctor's roof. Under the doctor's roof he would always be 'sir'.

Peggy found it bizarre. She realised that Lucky and Ruth, being European, might not find it so, but she certainly did. Mrs Hodgeman was an outback Australian. Her worn and weathered look and her accent said she was a woman of the land – Peggy knew such women well – but her manner, her servility was very strange. In fact, Peggy was finding the whole household strange, a fragment of Europe, complete with its class distinction, transplanted right here in Cooma.

Then Mrs Hodgeman disappeared and Kevin arrived with the wines, which Peggy found even more bizarre. Maarten didn't introduce the young man – he simply announced that they were having beef tonight.

'Which will it be, the Bordeaux or the Burgundy?' he asked as he took the two bottles from Kevin and rose from his armchair to present them to Lucky, who was sitting on the sofa with Peggy.

'Hello, Kevin,' Lucky said. As always, he didn't like the dismissive way Maarten treated the young man, but his friendly recognition did the boy no favours. Kevin ducked his head, more shy than ever with other people present.

'I've absolutely no idea, Maarten,' Lucky said, not bothering to examine the labels on the bottles. 'I'm sure we're all happy to bow to your judgement.'

'Very well, we'll have a palate test then.' Maarten was pleased; he loved a discussion of good wines. 'Decant them both,' he said to Kevin.

Having been careful not to make eye contact with anyone, Kevin virtually backed out of the room.

Lucky didn't dare glance at Peggy. He knew she found Maarten's peremptory attitude offensive and this treatment of Kevin disgraceful, but it was just Maarten's way, he thought. The Dutchman was trying too hard to impress perhaps, but he was lonely, he enjoyed entertaining, and he was behaving in the manner to which he'd no doubt been accustomed in his homeland. Lucky preferred the Australian way himself, and he would freely admit the fact to Peggy when they got home and she ranted about snobbery, but for now he hoped she would exercise a little self-control. When Peggy saw what she perceived as an injustice she could be very outspoken.

'And how is poor Violet, Peggy?' Maarten asked as he picked up a napkin and side plate from the large coffee table and helped himself to the hors d'oeuvres. He'd gathered that Peggy was very close to the girl, and it seemed the right thing to ask, under the circumstances. 'I believe her physical state is stable and she won't lose the baby, is that right?' It was what he'd heard.

'Yes, that's right,' Peggy replied.

'How fortunate,' he said. 'I was very concerned, given her outbreak at the funeral, that there may have been repercussions.'

'There were none.' Peggy's tone was curt.

'I'm so glad,' he replied, faking sincerity. How dare the schoolteacher speak to him like that?

'It must have been very hard for you, Maarten.' Ruth tried to cover the uncomfortable gap in the conversation. She was surprised Peggy had sounded so abrupt. Surely the doctor deserved some sympathy. 'Such a terrible thing to have happened – he was so very young.'

'Indeed, most shocking.' How like Ruth to show tact and diplomacy, he thought; she was a woman of style, unlike the crass little schoolteacher. 'It's always sad to lose a patient, but as you say, Ruth, one so young . . .' Maarten shook his head sadly. 'Edith and I did everything humanly possible, but he was gone, poor boy. Edith herself was most upset. I gave her several days off work to recuperate, she was so affected.'

'Do you think we could change the subject?' It was Peggy, being brittle again.

'Of course, my dear. I'm sorry, I didn't want to upset you.' The little schoolteacher was showing herself in a most unfavourable light, he thought. She was not only plain, she was waspish. He sensed that she didn't much like him. Well, the feeling was mutual, he thought.

'Peggy's quite right,' he said, 'it's not a night to be maudlin. And when all's said and done,' he smiled at Ruth, 'we cannot undo the past, can we?' He looked at her for just a fraction too long, and, not sure what to say, Ruth nodded politely.

Maarten turned to Lucky. 'It's your choice, my friend,' he said. 'What shall we talk about?'

'The Cooma Show,' Lucky said. 'Why not? Everyone else is – only a fortnight to go now.'

It was an innocuous and wise choice, and the awkwardness of the moment passed. Ruth had heard of little else but the Cooma Show for the past week, she said. Well, apart from Pietro, she thought. She was interested to learn all about the forthcoming event, which was obviously of such local significance.

'Peggy's the expert – she's on the committee, has been for years.' Lucky sensed that Peggy was regretting her abruptness. The others didn't realise, he thought, that her brittle manner was simply her way of coping.

Peggy gratefully seized on the chance to vindicate herself. She spoke briefly about the Show's importance to the district and the impact the advent of the Snowy Scheme had had upon it, but she mainly amused them with stories of local rivalry.

They were still talking about the Show when Mrs Hodgeman announced that dinner was ready.

'Shall we adjourn?' Maarten said, and he led the way through to the dining room.

Where was she? Peggy wondered as they entered the room. It certainly wasn't Cooma. A dining table that could have seated twelve was set for four with Dresden china, silver cutlery, damask napkins and crystal wine goblets. A huge floral arrangement was placed at the far end of the table as if to disguise the absence of other guests, and a candelabra with four lit candles sat in the centre, alongside two huge silver domed platters, a crystal bowl of steamed green vegetables, a silver gravy boat and a condiment set. Mrs Hodgeman stood by, waiting for them to be seated, and Kevin hovered beside her, a decanter of wine held reverently in his terrified hands.

Maarten indicated where they were to sit and, as Lucky pulled out Peggy's chair and sat beside her, the brief look she gave him spoke multitudes. He had told her that Maarten was a lonely man, and she understood what he meant now. Maarten Vanpoucke longed for more than company, she thought. He longed for another world.

'Forgive me,' Maarten said, seating himself beside Ruth, 'but with just the four of us I thought we'd keep the meal simple, Australian style, and forgo an entrée. But I promise Mrs Hodgeman will make up for it with dessert.'

Kevin poured a taste of wine for Maarten, and Mrs Hodgeman unveiled the platters – eye fillet already carved, glistening pink, and roast vegetables laid out decoratively in rows. As she started to serve, Maarten swirled the wine in the glass, held it up to the light, sniffed it and gave a satisfied nod.

While Kevin filled the guests' glasses with the utmost care, the conversation from the lounge room continued.

'The best thing about the Cooma Show,' Lucky announced, 'is the ball. I'm sorry, Peggy,' he said in mock apology, 'but you can keep your prize heifers and wood-choppers and showjumpers. For me, it's the ball.' He grinned at her. Remember, his eyes asked, remember when you invited me to the ball and flaunted our relationship the way you did?

'Yes,' she said, her eyes answering that she remembered vividly. How could she forget? 'The ball is always exciting, particularly if you're fond of dancing.' They'd danced till they were ready to drop that night.

The intimacy of their exchange was quite obvious to the others, but of far greater interest to Maarten was Ruth's reaction to it. She was happy for Lucky, he realised as he glanced at her. She was actually happy that her husband had found a new love. The two had severed their ties completely: she was free. Maarten felt exhilarated.

'You must come along with us, Ruth.' Peggy hauled herself back to the conversation, a little flustered, aware that she and Lucky had been eminently readable. 'We could invite Rob Harvey and make up a four.'

Behind his spectacles, Maarten's eyes flashed angrily. How dare the little schoolteacher interfere, and who was this Rob Harvey? Of what importance to Ruth was he? He distracted himself by examining his glass of wine, giving it a swirl, another inhalation.

'Rob Harvey and I are just friends,' Ruth gently corrected Peggy. She wanted no misunderstanding – she wasn't ready to be paired off with anyone yet.

'Oh, I'm sorry, I thought . . .' Peggy realised that in her flustered state she'd been rather tactless, so she decided to make a joke of it. 'Just as well,' she said, 'he's a terrible dancer.'

'So I gathered.' The women shared a smile. It was another reference to the night they'd met and they liked each other for it.

Maarten's anger turned instantly to elation. Ruth had been sending him a message – she wanted him to know she was unattached. She was already attracted to Maarten Vanpoucke; the chemistry they'd always shared was making itself felt.

'I'm very fond of dancing myself,' he said, smiling at the schoolteacher; he forgave her now. 'In fact, I'm quite an expert in the tango.' He turned to Ruth. 'But they probably don't tango in Cooma,' he said, intimating a worldliness they had in common. She must have noted that the two of them were a cut above the others: the school-teacher was crass, and for all his style Lucky had developed a common Australian streak.

'I don't tango, I'm afraid,' Ruth said. 'I never learned how.' Maarten seemed to be inferring they shared a love of the tango, she thought. It was rather odd.

'Ah well,' he smiled forgivingly, 'perhaps I can teach you. I've learned from the best – no-one tangos as they do in Buenos Aires.'

'Oh, you've been to Buenos Aires?' she asked with interest.

'Yes, I worked there briefly after the war for a Dutch medical centre,' he replied. He wondered why he'd brought up Buenos Aires; he'd never spoken of the place since he'd been in Australia. Probably just to impress her, he thought. But it had paid off, he'd caught her attention.

'I've always wanted to go there,' Ruth said. 'Is it as colourful as they say?'

'More so. More colourful than one can imagine.' He would take her to Buenos Aires, he decided. He would take her anywhere in the world she wanted to go.

'Do start, everyone,' he said. He would have preferred to have continued his personal conversation with Ruth, but Mrs Hodgeman had served them all and left the room.

'A toast.' He raised his glass. 'To old friends reunited, and to new friendships forged.'

It was a strange toast, enigmatic, but to Lucky and Ruth

very pertinent and their eyes met briefly as they raised their glasses.

'To friendship,' they all said.

The meal and particularly the wine dominated the conversation, Maarten insisting they try the Burgundy after the Bordeaux, and there was a German Spätlese to go with the dessert – individual crème caramels. Mrs Hodgeman had done herself proud.

They were all quite mellow as they retired to the lounge for coffee, port and petits fours. Maarten turned on the gramophone and Chopin's Nocturnes playing quietly in the background.

'Not for me thanks, Kevin,' Lucky said as the young man offered him a port.

'A Cognac perhaps?' Maarten asked; the women, too, had declined the port.

'Coffee's fine, thanks, Maarten.'

'Ah well,' he gestured at the Cognac bottle, 'it's just me then,' and Kevin fetched a brandy balloon from the cabinet.

When they were all settled with their coffees, Maarten leaned back contentedly in his armchair. 'The king of all instruments,' he said, referring to the piano now playing Chopin's Nocturne in G minor. They all agreed and it led to a discussion of music.

Peggy's tastes were eclectic. She rather liked modern music, she said. She was very fond of jazz, and blues, and even some country. But she couldn't quite come to terms with the latest rock and roll craze.

'There must be something in it, I suppose, to drive the youth mad the way it does, but I'm afraid its attraction escapes me. I'm probably too old,' she smiled. 'It just sounds like noise.'

Maarten had feigned attention, but the schoolteacher's views held no interest for him. 'And what sort of music do you like, Ruth?' he asked.

'I'm very fond of Italian lyric opera,' she said, 'particularly Verdi and Puccini.'

As she said it, Lucky could hear her favourite aria from *La Bohème*, Ruth's true, sweet voice singing Rachel to sleep.

Ruth looked at him and knew exactly what he was thinking. Samuel was remembering. For a second or so they shared thoughts of Rachel, before Ruth quickly returned her attention to her half-finished coffee.

The moment had gone unobserved by Peggy, but not by Maarten. He had seen all too clearly the raw, tender exchange. No, no, he thought, we will not have that. We will have no rekindling of old flames. Their love was dead, a thing of the past: he had the claim on Ruth now. And he had power over her too. She simply needed to recognise it.

The evening was wearing a little thin, Maarten decided. He wanted Lucky and the schoolteacher to go. He needed to be alone with Ruth.

Skolling the last of his Cognac, he stood, brandy balloon in hand, and crossed to where the drinks sat on the sideboard.

'Are you sure I can't interest anyone in a nightcap?' he asked, holding up a bottle and looking a query at them in the sideboard mirror.

As he'd anticipated, the offer prompted their departure.

'No thanks, Maarten.' Lucky rose from his chair. 'I think we'd better be on our way.'

The women also stood.

'So soon?' He turned to face them. 'What a pity.'

'Thank you for an excellent evening.' Lucky shook Maarten's hand.

'Yes,' Peggy agreed, 'and do thank Mrs Hodgeman for us. And Kevin too,' she couldn't resist adding.

'Of course, thank you so much for coming.' Before Ruth could offer her thanks, he turned to Lucky. 'You walked, you said?'

'Yes, that's right.'

'But Dodds is in the opposite direction.' How convenient, he thought. 'You must allow me to escort Ruth back to her hotel.'

'No, no, we're more than happy to do that, aren't we, Peggy?'

Peggy nodded.

'I'm quite capable of walking on my own.' Ruth smiled.

'We wouldn't hear of it, my dear,' Maarten insisted. 'Please do allow me – a stroll in the night air would do me the world of good.'

'Thank you,' Ruth gave in with good grace, there was no other option, 'it's very kind.'

'Not at all, I'll just see Lucky and Peggy to the front door.'

'We can see ourselves out,' Lucky said.

'I insist.'

Lucky and Peggy said their goodnights to Ruth, and Maarten ushered them out onto the landing, turning back at the door.

'I won't be long, my dear,' he said, 'pour yourself another coffee.'

She sat, resigned; she didn't want another coffee.

Peggy left with the distinct impression that Maarten was interested in Ruth. Poor Ruth, she thought. The man was so detestably arrogant.

Through the open door to the landing, Ruth could hear the three of them talking as they walked down the stairs. Then the talking stopped and she heard the front door close.

She wanted to go home; she was weary, but she suspected the man would pursue further conversation.

It appeared she was right.

'Now, where were we?' Maarten asked as he closed the door behind him. 'Ah yes, that's right, Italian lyric opera . . .'

She stood. 'I really think it's time I left, Maarten, I'm rather tired . . .'

'Of course, my dear, of course, just one quick coffee and then we'll be on our way, I promise.'

He poured her a fresh cup from the jug on the coffee table, and Ruth sat again, feeling irritated. The man was becoming wearing.

'Personally I find Italian tenors a little brassy, and sopranos on occasion too shrill,' he said, pouring himself another Cognac, 'but I do believe there is no instrument finer than the human voice, particularly when joined in perfect harmony.'

He studied her in the sideboard mirror as she sipped at her coffee. How glorious she looked, he thought, sitting here in this room which so perfectly suited her. It was where she belonged.

'I'm a great admirer of choral arrangements,' he continued. '"Va Pensiero", the chorus of exiles from *Nabucco* – quite splendid.' He took a swig of his Cognac. 'Verdi, Ruth . . .'

She looked up at the mention of her name, and he smiled at her in the mirror.

'. . . as you said, one of your favourite composers.'

She returned his smile politely. 'Yes, it's a beautiful piece of music.' She would allow five minutes, she decided, then she would leave with or without him.

He placed the brandy balloon on the sideboard and crossed to the gramophone, replacing the Chopin record with another.

Good God, she thought, did he expect her to sit here and listen to music with him all night? She'd said she wanted to go home. The man's arrogance was extraordinary.

'I'm particularly fond of close harmony groups,' he said, 'so long as they're good, of course.'

He took off his spectacles and placed them in his pocket. If the boy had recognised him, he thought, then surely she should. All she needed was a little prompting.

The needle found its groove on the record; there was a slight scratchiness to start with.

He moved behind her chair, watching her in the mirror as the music began.

Ruth leaned forward to place her cup on the coffee table, deciding she would leave right then.

Schöne Nacht, du Liebesnacht . . .

She froze. The Comedian Harmonists.

O stille mein Verlangen . . .

'Barcarole'. Of all pieces, why had he chosen that?

Süsser als der Tag und lacht . . .

She looked up at the mirror and saw he was standing directly behind her.

Die schöne Liebesnacht.

He was smiling, and the eyes that met hers were the eyes of Klaus Henkel.

The cup clattered to the polished wooden floor, coffee spilling onto the nearby Persian carpet.

'*Es war eine lange Zeit*, Ruth,' he said.

CHAPTER TWENTY-FIVE

'It has been a very long time indeed.' He reverted to English. He hadn't spoken German for years, it was too dangerous; he'd even trained himself to think in English. No matter: his desire was plain in any language. 'I've thought of you often.'

He crossed to the gramophone and turned the music down. It played softly in the background, but to Ruth it still sounded strident, taunting her with the past.

'I've longed for this moment,' he said softly as he sat in the armchair opposite hers.

Everything about him was suddenly frighteningly familiar. Indeed, as he'd spoken in his mother tongue, she'd wondered how she hadn't recognised his voice earlier. She was amazed, too, at her sense of calm. The horrified shock of her recognition had brought with it panic and the urge to flee, but she just felt numb. She remained motionless, the cup on the floor beside her, the coffee still seeping into the Persian carpet. There was no escape from Klaus Henkel.

'I've missed you, Ruth,' he said.

She tried to ignore his look of tenderness. 'How did you do it?' she asked. 'How did you so change yourself?'

'I had expert help from a friend,' he said dryly. 'His work served its purpose, but it robbed me of my youth. Whereas you, my dear,' he looked her up and down admiringly, 'you are more beautiful than you have ever been.'

'Why are you doing this, Klaus?'

He thrilled to the sound of her voice saying his name.

'Doing what?' he asked in all innocence.

'Why are you exposing your identity? Why are you risking yourself like this?'

'Risking myself? With you?' He seemed genuinely surprised. 'But you would never betray me, Ruth.'

'And why not?'

He rose from his chair, bemused by the question. She loved him, that was why not. Perhaps she didn't yet realise the force of her love, but she must surely understand that she was caught up in the web of his life, that she belonged to him.

'I saved you, Ruth. I preserved your life. I'm the very reason you're alive.' He crossed to the sideboard and picked up his brandy balloon. 'I saved you on the ramp at Auschwitz. I saved you from the ovens and the hard labour that would have killed you. And I saved you from the Russians who would have defiled you like the pigs they are.' He took a swig of his Cognac.

He was mad, she thought. Had he forgotten their last night together? Had he truly forgotten how vilely he himself had defiled her?

'And the times we shared, remember? They were so precious.' He put the glass down and again circled behind her chair. 'Can't you see them now, those quiet nights – just you and me, and the music?' He started to hum along to 'Barcarole', still playing in the background.

Yes, Ruth thought, she remembered. Just as she remembered the smell of burning flesh, and the thousands of emaciated, dying people, and her daughter dead on the ramp, and Mannie's murder . . .

'Stop,' she said. She could see him in the mirror, his hands poised over her shoulders.

'Of course.' He stopped humming and dropped his arms to his side. It was too soon, he realised. She was not ready yet. But he would wait – he had all the time in the world. He turned off the gramophone and returned to his chair.

What did he want from her? Ruth thought. In his insanity, he appeared to believe she belonged to him. Did he honestly expect her to remain silent, to become his personal property again?

He studied her over the rim of his brandy balloon.

'It's all come as rather a shock, hasn't it, my dear?' he said understandingly. 'But have no fear, I will not rush you, I'm willing to wait.'

She was looking at him in a guarded, mistrustful way, rather like a cornered animal, he thought. She must understand that there was no avenue of escape.

'I will wait for as long as it takes, Ruth. I'm a patient man. But in the meantime I advise you to do nothing rash.'

The cold, steel-blue eyes were unwavering. It was more than a warning, she realised – it was a threat.

'Should you feel the desire to share our secret with anyone,' he continued, 'you would be placing that person in mortal danger.'

She did not avert her eyes, but stared back at him in silence. Good, he thought, she was getting the message. He polished off the last of his Cognac and sat back comfortably in his armchair instead.

'I lead a quiet life in Cooma,' he said pleasantly, 'I like it here. But I have found it wise not to call attention to myself; there are people from the past who live in these mountains. I have already eliminated one threat, and I would do so again without compunction. I will not allow myself to be placed at risk.'

The boy, Ruth thought, sickened by the sudden realisation. *He has the eyes of the priest.* That's what Violet had said. And with a jolt she realised that Klaus Henkel had escaped Auschwitz in the guise of a priest. She remembered seeing the cassock, the identification papers . . .

'You killed Pietro,' she said in a whisper.

'The young Italian?' He gave a light laugh. 'Oh my dear, what a fantastical notion. Why should I? I didn't know the boy.'

Yes, of course, she thought, why should he kill Pietro? What danger could the Italian have been to him? But what had he meant when he'd said that he'd eliminated one threat? Was it simply to frighten her? If so, he'd succeeded.

'No, no, the boy was epileptic and had a weak heart,' he said dismissively. He was pleased that he'd made his point, that she'd understood his warning was no idle threat. He rose and crossed to the sideboard to pour another Cognac.

'I once held your life in my hands, Ruth,' he said, looking at her in the mirror as he poured his drink. 'It's interesting to consider that you now hold mine in yours.' He turned, smiling. 'Well, that's perhaps a little melodramatic of me, but you could certainly make my life uncomfortable. If you were to report me, the Australian Government would do nothing – you have no proof – but I would be forced to leave Cooma, and I don't wish to do that.'

He returned to his chair and leant forward with his elbows on his knees, his full focus upon her as he cradled his glass in his hands.

'You don't want me to leave either, do you, Ruth? Of all the places in the world fate could have chosen to bring us together, it was here in Cooma. Don't you see, my dear? It was meant to be.'

He could see the acceptance in her eyes; she knew it was so, and it pleased him.

'Take me home, Klaus.'

'Klaus,' he said, with nostalgic longing. How he loved the sound of his name from her lips. But sadly, he would have to forgo the luxury of hearing it – it was too dangerous.

'That name is foreign to me these days, Ruth,' he said.'It is a title I no longer respond to. I am Maarten Vanpoucke, you must remember it always.'

'Yes. Take me home, Maarten, I'm tired.'

'Of course you are, my dear, it's been an evening of surprises, and surprises are always tiring, are they not? Come,' he said, and she couldn't avoid his hand as he helped her to her feet. 'We won't walk, you're too weary. I'll drive you home.'

He was the Dutchman during the short drive to Dodds. They talked about mundane things; he asked her about her work and she amazed herself by responding normally.

'You cannot surely intend to remain here,' he said as he escorted her from the car to the hotel's front doors. 'It's most unsuitable. Please allow me to arrange proper accommodation for you.'

'The Authority already has,' she said. 'I'm moving to a small house in Cooma North on Tuesday.'

'Then allow me to assist you. I shall drive you to your new home. What time would be convenient, mid-morning?'

'Yes.'

'Excellent. I shall collect you at . . . shall we say ten o'clock?'

She nodded.

'Have no fear, my dear,' his smile was one of supreme confidence, 'I'm prepared to be patient. You must get to know me all over again. As I told you, I'm willing to wait.' He kissed her hand, and his lips lingered a little longer this time.

'Goodnight, Ruth,' he said.

'Goodnight, Maarten.'

It was well after midnight when she let herself into her poky upstairs room. She made no attempt to sleep; she didn't even bother to undress and get into bed. She sat on the hard wooden chair and thought about Klaus Henkel.

For a while she dwelled on the past. It was impossible not to. He'd brought it back as raw and fresh as if it were yesterday. But after hours or perhaps minutes of tortured memory – she couldn't tell – she forced the horrors aside. There was no point in reliving them. She'd done that many times, for many years and it had nearly destroyed her. She was harder now, and tougher – she must not allow him to lead her down that path. She must think about today, and tomorrow, and her new life here in Cooma. She would not let him cheat her of that life. She had run as far as she could run. She would run no further. And she would certainly not run from him.

She stood and opened the window, peering out at the black sky. It was a moonless night, the air was still, and the street below deserted, with not a soul in sight, but she wouldn't have noticed if there had been. She was thinking how cowardly she'd been to refuse to testify as a witness at the Nuremberg trials. She'd been working for the Americans at the time. It was a protected life – the Americans looked after their staff well – and she'd been in a haze, wishing to avoid at all costs the harrowing experience of reliving terrible memories by testifying. But she'd followed the trials avidly. She'd been surprised to discover that Ira Schoneberger had given evidence.

We must tell our story, Ruth. She could hear his voice still. She hadn't really believed him at the time; she'd known it had been another ploy to inspire in her the will to live, but it had worked. It had saved her. And Ira, the greatest survivor of them all, a man despised by his own kind, a man who'd turned everything to his advantage in order to live, had proved to be a man of his word. She'd admired him for it. She admired him still. More than anyone she'd ever known. It had been Ira who had saved her, not Klaus Henkel. And she could hear Ira's voice as if he were with her now: *You owe it to them, Ruth, you owe it to them all.*

But what can I do, Ira? she thought. The Nuremberg trials are over, I have no proof – the Australian Government could do nothing, Klaus himself said so. If I attempt to expose him, he will simply disappear to another place, another town, another identity – he will be untraceable.

She closed the window, the room suddenly cold.

The boy – had Klaus killed the boy? She had no proof of that either, but she needed to know. She sat on the wooden chair again, adding up every fragment of information she'd gleaned. She didn't know why but the boy preyed on her mind. Had Klaus killed Pietro?

She retraced his steps, one by one. Klaus Henkel had left Auschwitz in the guise of a priest, but he hadn't remained in hiding within Germany as many had, and as she had supposed was his intention. He'd fled to Argentina, a common destination for Nazi war criminals. *No-one tangos as they do in Buenos Aires.* But how had he made his escape from Germany? Via Switzerland or Italy?

The Brenner Pass, from Austria into Italy, was one of the favoured routes of Odessa. The boy was Italian. Where did he come from? Why did he dream of a priest who wanted to kill him?

She ran her hands through her hair, clutching it, pulling roughly at her scalp, trying to feed information to her brain, but there was none to be had; she'd reached a dead end. There was only one other who could help her piece the jigsaw together – at least she hoped he could.

Outside, the first rays of dawn were streaking the sky. Ruth gathered her robe and toiletry bag and stole quietly down the hall to the bathroom where she ran a hot bath and lay in it, her mind now a blank as she filled in the hours.

Lucky and Peggy had just made love. It was eight o'clock in the morning and she would shortly get up and cook them breakfast. They would probably eat it in bed and make love again. Sunday was Peggy's favourite day.

There was a knock on the door. She looked at the clock on the bedside table. Who would be calling on her at this hour on a Sunday?

Beside her, Lucky stirred, still half dozing. The knock persisted and he sat up.

'What's the time?' he asked.

'I'll go.' Peggy put on her dressing gown and walked to the front door.

'Ruth,' she said, surprised.

'I'm sorry, I know it's early – do you mind if I come in?' It had been easy to get Peggy's address, she'd asked at the hotel – everyone knew where the schoolteacher lived in Murray Road.

'Of course. Please, come in.' Peggy tried not to look flustered as she ushered Ruth inside, but her call to Lucky was one of warning. 'Lucky, Ruth's here.' She hoped he wouldn't appear too obviously dishevelled.

But he did. He hadn't heard her warning call, and he walked into the small lounge room having pulled on a pair of shorts, bare-chested and bare-footed, hair awry and obviously straight out of bed. Peggy was aware that she was no better herself, in her slippers and dressing gown, her long hair loose about her shoulders.

The two of them felt decidedly self-conscious.

'Would you like a cup of tea?' Peggy asked, pulling back her hair.

Both their appearance and their embarrassment appeared to have gone unnoticed by Ruth, as did the offer of tea.

'Forgive me for dropping in unexpectedly like this, but I wanted to talk to you.' She meant Samuel, but she addressed them both.

'Of course,' Peggy said; Ruth looked tired, she thought. 'Come into the kitchen and I'll put the kettle on.' She signalled Lucky to get dressed, and as he disappeared into the bedroom, she led Ruth through to the kitchen.

'I'm sorry we left you alone with Maarten last night,' she said, filling the kettle, 'but he didn't give us much option. Did he keep you there for a chat? I had the feeling that he wanted to. Or did he walk you home straight away?'

'He drove me.'

'Oh good.' She lit the gas stove and plonked the kettle on the burner. 'Would you like some breakfast?'

'No, thank you.'

Peggy turned to face her. 'Are you all right, Ruth? You look tired.'

'I didn't sleep well,' she admitted. 'For some reason, I couldn't stop thinking about Pietro. I mean, having met him that time at Dodds, and after our discussion about Violet last night . . . it all kept preying on my mind . . .'

'Yes, I can imagine that it would.' The subject was never far from Peggy's mind.

'Where did he come from, Peggy? Why did he have nightmares about a priest who wanted to kill him?'

'Lucky's the one who can tell you,' she said, as he appeared, doing up the buttons of his shirt. 'Lucky knew him better than anyone.'

'Tell you what, about whom?'

'Ruth wants to know about Pietro.'

'Why?'

She'd known he would ask, but she couldn't tell him the truth – she'd be risking his life, and Peggy's too. *Should you feel the desire to share our secret with anyone, you would be placing that person in mortal danger.* But she had to know about the boy.

'It doesn't matter why, my darling.' Peggy didn't find Ruth's interest strange at all. It was understandable that Ruth would be moved by the tragedy of the young couple she'd met. She was, however, a little concerned by the urgency of Ruth's interest, which had prompted a visit at eight in the morning. The boy's death had obviously triggered some real distress in her, she thought. Peggy nodded encouragingly at Lucky; there was no reason why they shouldn't talk about Pietro.

Lucky didn't mind; if it didn't bother Peggy, then it didn't bother him.

'Where did he come from?' Ruth asked, thankful that she'd first broached the subject with Peggy, and that Peggy had so easily paved the way.

'Northern Italy, the Alps.'

'Where in the Alps?' She wanted to fire the questions at him. Near the border? Near the Brenner Pass?

'He didn't tell me, he didn't know. Pietro was traumatised as a child and he had no memory of his early life.'

Traumatised as a child? She waited for him to continue.

As Peggy poured the tea, Lucky told Ruth everything he knew about Pietro: the presumed death of his parents in the war and the loss of his memory; his homeless existence in the streets of Milan; and his upbringing in the Catholic orphanage.

'When was he discovered in Milan?' she asked, sipping her tea, trying to give the impression that she was calming down – they must surely have wondered at her mental stability after barging in the way she had. But all the while she was sifting through every piece of information Lucky gave her.

'In 1945, when he was eleven years old. It was just after the war.'

The same time as Klaus was making his escape from Germany.

'He couldn't remember his family,' Lucky continued. 'He couldn't remember anything from his childhood except a hut in the mountains and goats.'

Lucky recalled the way the boy had spoken to him. 'Rosa,' he'd said, 'she is my favourite, I help her to have her baby.' It had taken Pietro some time to tell him about the goats, he remembered.

'I presume his father must have been a goatherd,' he said rather abruptly. He didn't want to talk about Pietro any more, and he wondered why Peggy was encouraging the conversation. But then women were women, he thought, they needed to sift through everything and share it among themselves; perhaps it was a part of the grieving process.

'And the nightmares?' Ruth prompted him gently, longing to cross-examine him, but sensing his reluctance.

'What about them?'

'You and Peggy said he had nightmares.' She looked at Peggy, who nodded.

'Yes, that's right. Snow covered in blood, a priest who wanted to kill him . . .'

'Of course, the priest,' she said, exchanging another glance with Peggy. 'What did he recall of the priest?'

Lucky found it strange. Why was Ruth interested in such detail? Morbid curiosity wasn't like her at all.

'Nothing much, a man in a cassock . . . the sound of the priest's voice calling his name . . . the man's eyes. Pietro believed the priest was evil.'

Ruth's mind was working frantically, adding it all up. Could the nightmares be a flashback to the boy's trauma-tised past? Had Pietro encountered Klaus Henkel as a priest all those years ago? And if he had, why would Klaus have wished to kill the child?

'I wonder why the priest wanted to kill him,' she said.

She was unaware that she'd spoken out loud.

'I don't know,' Lucky answered, 'nor did Pietro. But he was sure of one thing. He believed that the dreams were more than nightmares. He believed his memory was returning.'

To Ruth, the words hung in the air. *His memory was returning.* That was why, she thought. That was why Klaus had killed him!

I have already eliminated one threat, and I would do so

again without compunction. I will not allow myself to be placed at risk.

It had been no idle threat. Pietro had recognised Klaus Henkel. Pietro had seen the eyes of the priest.

She took a deep breath to steady herself.

'Ruth, what is it? What's the matter?' Peggy asked anxiously. 'You've gone as white as a sheet.'

Ruth stared at them both. She had an insane desire to blurt it out. The priest killed Pietro! The priest and the doctor are one man. His name is Klaus Henkel!

She stood abruptly. She needed to get away, she had to think.

'I'm sorry, I have to go.'

Peggy and Lucky stood also, Peggy protesting that she must stay.

'Come and lie down, Ruth, you don't look well.'

'No, no thank you. I'm all right.'

She was already halfway to the front door, the two of them following.

'At least let me drive you home,' Lucky said.

'No, I want to walk.' She opened the door, but as she stepped out onto the verandah, he took her arm.

'Please, Ruth, let me drive you, you're in no state . . .'

'No!' She ripped her arm from his clasp. 'Leave me alone!'

They were both taken aback by her vehemence.

'I'm sorry,' she said, mustering her self-control, trying to adopt a semblance of calm to put them at their ease. 'I'm very sorry, I don't mean to be rude, but please, Samuel,' she appealed to him directly, 'please, I want to walk. I need to be on my own.'

Peggy and Lucky stood together on the front verandah, worried and bewildered as they watched her hurry away.

The jigsaw pieces whirled through Ruth's mind, and as she carefully sorted them, trying to put them together, she slowed her pace. She crossed Vale Street, oblivious to the passers-by on their way to the church just up the road.

Pietro had witnessed something as a child. The nightmares, the snow covered in blood, the priest calling his name – whatever he'd seen had been so violent and horrific it had traumatised him so brutally he hadn't even been able to remember his family. Why? And why would his parents have been killed in the war? They lived in a remote hut high in the Alps, far away from the bombs. His father had probably been a goatherd, Samuel had said. There were peasants in those regions who hadn't even known there was a war going on.

She came to a standstill at the corner of the street. Could Pietro have witnessed the murder of his parents?

She knew Klaus Henkel was eminently capable of such a deed. It was exactly what he would have done if he'd sought refuge with the peasants – he would have made sure he covered his tracks.

She resumed walking, mindlessly turning left into Bombala Street, certain of one thing: whether or not she'd guessed his motive correctly, Klaus Henkel had murdered Pietro.

As she came to the intersection of Commissioner Street, she didn't turn left towards Dodds, but crossed over and kept walking.

What was she to do? Pietro's murder could never be proved, but Klaus must be exposed. There were many whose lives had been lost or ruined by his hand, and he had to pay for that. He had to pay for all of them. But how could she do it? She had no proof of his identity, and if she reported him, who would believe her?

She halted briefly at the corner of Sharp Street. In the park opposite, children played, and, although it was Sunday and the stores were closed, the street was quite busy.

Turning left, she started to walk up the main road of town, slowly now, looking at the faces of the people she passed, faces stamped with the diversity of their origins. She listened to their voices, to the miscellany of languages and accents. A bunch of Snowy workers, in Cooma for the weekend and bleary-eyed after a Saturday night on the drink, were in search of a late breakfast at one of the cafes. Several smartly dressed European couples, the men no doubt experts employed by the Authority, passed her, walking briskly up towards Vale Street on their way to ten o'clock mass. People of all descriptions, locals and migrants alike, were popping into the nearby bakery for a fresh loaf, or into the newsagency for the Sunday paper.

So many nationalities, Ruth thought, and all living in a harmony they'd not known in Europe. They'd been at war with each other there, or they had been persecuted and driven from their homelands. Here they had found far more than sanctuary: they'd found tolerance. This was a new world where they could build new lives and create a new heritage for future generations, a heritage that meant their children's children would be born into a society free from hatred and intolerance.

She remembered the atrocities she'd lived through: Auschwitz and Deir Yassin. She'd seen Germans slaughter Jews and she'd seen Jews slaughter Arabs. She'd witnessed the very depths of man's inhumanity to man, and knew such evil did not belong in this new world. But there was a cancer living among them; a reminder of all they'd left behind; one who remained a menacing presence and who would kill without conscience if he perceived a threat to his safety. Klaus Henkel had no place here.

She reached Vale Street and turned left. She was circling back on herself now, but her choice of direction was no longer aimless. Maarten Vanpoucke's house was in Vale Street.

Ruth made her decision. She would confront him, and she would denounce him. If he had murdered Pietro because the boy had recognised the eyes of the priest, then he would surely have to kill her too; she was a far greater complication in his life than the unwanted attention the boy would have drawn to him. And if he were to kill her, he wouldn't be able to explain away her death with the ease that he had Pietro's.

She was very calm as she walked down Vale Street. This was her destiny, she told herself. Fate's purpose in bringing her to Cooma had not been to reunite her with Samuel, but with Klaus Henkel. Klaus himself had said so.

Of all the places in the world fate could have chosen to bring us together, it was here in Cooma. Don't you see, my dear? It was meant to be.

Klaus Henkel's obsession with her would be his downfall.

She wondered if she were prepared to die; she'd hoped to build a new life for herself here. But then, remembering the part she'd played in the shame of Deir Yassin, perhaps she'd never been worthy of a new life. She quelled her fear. Her Lehi training was about to serve a purpose, she told herself. Like every true Lehi fighter she must be prepared to sacrifice herself for the cause – only this time the cause would not be the slaughter of innocents.

She crossed over Murray Street. The Catholic Church was to the right, just past Peggy's cottage; she'd completed the circle. She continued down Vale Street towards Maarten's house only a block or so away.

As she saw it up ahead, she was pleased to note that there were passers-by, some on their way to church, some heading into town. She wanted witnesses when she called him out of his house.

Then she saw the front door open and Maarten appear. Even better, she thought, and she slipped through the side gate to the narrow path that led to the tradesmen's entrance. From the side of the house, she watched him.

Maarten turned and locked the door behind him. He was a man of habit and punctuality. It was a quarter to ten on a Sunday and he would buy his newspaper, and then he would go to the little cafe on the corner opposite the park where he would take his coffee and pastry. He liked to be seated by ten.

He walked through the open front gate and into the street, pocketing his keys.

'Klaus Henkel!'

He stopped as he heard the voice call out.

'Klaus Henkel!'

The voice called again – loud, accusing; it was coming from close by. He didn't look around to see where she was. He made a pretence of checking his watch instead, while he searched for where she might be. He recognised the voice.

'Klaus Henkel! Nazi! Murderer!'

People passing by slowed down and looked around, startled; the words were chilling and many recognised the name. Along with Adolf Eichmann and Josef Mengele, Klaus Henkel was one of the the most sought after Nazi war criminals; it was common knowledge, even to the Australians.

Maarten checked his pockets as if he'd forgotten something, then casually turned to retrace his steps.

Ruth strode out onto the pavement only several paces from him. 'That man is Klaus Henkel!' She pointed an accusing finger. 'That man is a Nazi and a murderer.'

Frank Halliday, who lived just around the corner and was walking down to the main road to buy the newspaper, gawped in amazement. That man was Doctor Vanpoucke, he thought. That man had been coming to his store for years – the woman must be mad.

From the upstairs balcony, Mrs Hodgeman looked down at the scene in the street below. It was Ruth Stein who'd come to dinner just last night. The poor woman must be mad, she thought.

Maarten's expression was also one of amazement.

'Ruth,' he said, 'what on earth is the matter with you?' He gazed around at those who had by now stopped to watch; there must have been a dozen or more. Several were locals who regularly saw him about town. They knew who he was and were obviously embarrassed, but too curious to walk on. Maarten smiled his recognition to them, particularly to Frank Halliday, a pillar of the community who had known him for years.

Then he turned again to Ruth, concerned. 'My dear, you're not well.'

'This man is Klaus Henkel.' She walked right up to him, her announcement bold and clear. 'This man is a Nazi war criminal.'

'Ruth, I am your doctor, and your friend,' he said reassuringly. 'I am Maarten Vanpoucke.' He put his arm around her, expecting her to pull away, surprised when she didn't. 'Now come inside and let me look after you.'

She allowed him to lead her away, glad that he was behaving true to form, as she'd presumed he would. Klaus always believed he had total control. He could have disappeared into his house and she would have been left to harangue the passers-by, embarrassing them, or perhaps making them apprehensive and fearful, but certainly appearing like a madwoman. This suited her purpose far better.

At the open gate, Maarten turned back to the gathering, most of whom were shuffling about awkwardly, pretending they hadn't stopped to watch. He addressed Frank Halliday, although his words were intended for all those present.

'Ruth is a patient of mine,' he said. 'She suffered cruelly at the hands of the Nazis. It is sad to see her so deeply disturbed.'

Frank nodded, feeling conspicuous and profoundly embarrassed. He felt he should walk on – he never got involved; he made it a habit to mind his own business.

Ruth delivered her final accusation directly at Maarten. 'You are Klaus Henkel,' she stated clearly for the benefit of those watching. 'You are a murderer.'

'Yes, yes, my dear.' His tone was one of infinite compassion and understanding. 'Now come along.'

He unlocked the door and took her inside, and those gathered in the street dispersed, muttering among themselves, agreeing that the poor woman was mad. But most were unsettled by the impact she'd had upon them.

It was not unheard of for some new arrivals in the region to display peculiar or confused behaviour now and again, and people were generally sympathetic. Most were also aware of the reported sightings of Nazi criminals throughout the world, and wondered how much of it was hysterical paranoia, part of the sad aftermath of the war. But here in Australia such demented accusations were an unexpected and disquieting reminder of the past.

Ruth was aware that they probably considered her deranged, but they had all witnessed him take her inside the house, she thought. And they would remember that.

The front door closed behind her and they stood in the hall. She said nothing as Maarten grabbed her roughly by the wrist, and she didn't struggle as he opened the door to the left and propelled her into the reception area of his surgery.

Looking down at the front hallway from her carefully concealed position on the upstairs landing, Mrs Hodgeman found the doctor's brutal attitude towards his patient a little surprising.

Maarten released Ruth, locking the door behind them, and roughly pushed her into his consulting room.

It was gloomy, with the drapes drawn over the bay windows, and he flicked on the switch of the overhead light. He locked the surgery door also and, taking off his spectacles, he tossed them onto the desk in a gesture of frustration and anger. It was only then he spoke.

'Why have you done this? Why have you betrayed me?'

She was pleased that he'd dropped the pretence. The Dutchman had gone; he was Klaus Henkel now.

'It's over, Klaus,' she said.

'You think you can do it just like that, a few random words from a madwoman in the street?' He grabbed her again by the wrist and hauled her to the bay windows, thrusting aside the drapes, careless of who could see. 'Look. They've gone.'

She looked out at the street. The dozen or so had left and there was just the odd passer-by, paying no heed, but it didn't matter, she thought. The harm had been done.

'They don't care,' he snarled, pulling the drapes closed. 'They want to mind their own business, as people do. Your little outburst meant nothing! Nothing at all, just the ramblings of a woman demented by the war. That's what I told them, and that's what they believe.'

'I'm sure you're right . . .' Ruth felt supremely in command. He was sounding desperate and already he was cornered. She goaded him with the fact: 'But word will get around, as it does in Cooma. You'll be the centre of attention, and you don't want that. You'll have to leave town. The sooner the better, I would think.'

He'd known he would have to. He'd known it the moment he'd heard her call out his name. He wanted to kill her for it.

'Yes, Klaus,' she could see the murder in his eyes and she acknowledged it, 'you'd better kill me, because if you don't, I'll follow you. I'll follow you and denounce you wherever you go.'

It had been a deliberate plan, he realised. She'd made sure they'd all seen him take her inside; it was why she hadn't resisted, why she'd played along with the game of demented patient. How very clever. And now she thought that, because there'd been witnesses, she was safe. But she wasn't. He'd trusted her; she'd betrayed him and she would die for it.

'So you wish to martyr yourself, do you, Ruth?' he said disbelievingly. 'How very noble.'

'Perhaps I do,' she answered. 'If that's the only way. Someone has to stop you, and it appears there's only me.'

So she *did* wish to martyr herself, he thought. How very surprising. He was willing to oblige, but her death would not serve the noble cause she appeared to believe it would – he had no intention of being caught. Neither would he kill her because she posed a threat. He would kill her for the pure satisfaction of it.

'And what makes you so bent on dying, Ruth? You're young, you're beautiful – it seems a strange choice.'

'It's meant to be, isn't it? Fate, you said so yourself. But fate brought us together in order for me to destroy you, Klaus. There is no place for you here. You're a Nazi and a murderer. There is no place for you anywhere – there never was. You and your kind should never have existed.' She felt so strong as she said it. 'You have innocent blood on your hands, Klaus. You have untold deaths to answer for.'

'I do indeed.' He laughed; he was starting to enjoy himself. 'Oh yes, yes, indeed I do.'

Outside in the surgery waiting room, Mrs Hodgeman's ear was pressed to the door. She'd let herself in – she had a key to every door in the house. She was appalled by what she was hearing. She left to fetch her son Kevin, and to get the gun that she knew the doctor kept in the locked drawer of his study desk; the drawer to which she also had access – she knew where he hid the key.

'And you believe your death will destroy me, do you?'

Klaus was now finding the game most pleasurable. She was brave and noble, a zealot with a mission. How he would enjoy seeing her bravado crumble. How he would enjoy watching her beg for her life.

'Yes, I believe so.'

It was as if she were teasing him, flirting with him; he found it titillating.

'And how should I kill you, Ruth?'

'Perhaps the same way you did Pietro,' she said, wandering around the room. 'This is where you killed him, isn't it? Where exactly did he die? On this bed?' She ran her fingers along the crisp white cotton cover. 'How did you do it?'

She expected a denial; he would surely not admit to Pietro's murder. But he made no denial.

'I know that you killed him, Klaus.' She was emboldened by his silence. 'How did you do it?'

He smiled. Oh yes, he was enjoying this game. 'Shall I show you?'

He raised an eyebrow when she didn't answer. 'I'm quite happy to show you, Ruth,' he said, taking off his jacket and placing it neatly over the back of a chair. He took his time methodically rolling his shirt sleeves up over his elbows, then he crossed to the bench with its sink and dispensary cupboard.

'In fact, I would very much like to show you,' he said, washing his hands and drying them on the towel that hung there, 'if that is what you truly want.'

She watched, mesmerised, as he lifted a vial and a syringe from the cupboard. Her bravado had deserted her, just as he'd known it would.

He looked at her in the cupboard mirror. 'Potassium chloride,' he said, opening the vial. 'Very simple. A heart attack; it was soon over.' He filled the syringe, noting with pleasure that her eyes were focussed upon what he was doing, and that she was terrified. 'It will be a heart attack for you too, Ruth. I would like to assure you that you will feel no pain,' he said, testing the syringe with a flick of his finger, 'but I can't be sure. What you *will* feel, however, is regret. Regret for the uselessness of your death.'

'You'll incriminate yourself, Klaus.' She tried to keep the tremor from her voice. 'You won't be able to get away with it a second time.'

He laughed as he turned to face her. 'A *second* time? Oh my dear, you underestimate me. I've eliminated many. Like Pietro, you have become just one more. But you must understand, Ruth, that your death will be of no consequence. It will serve no purpose. I will disappear as I have in the past, I will become another person. They will never find me.'

In the waiting room, Noreen Hodgeman fiddled frantically with the unfamiliar weapon. She knew a bit about firearms – she'd used a .22 and a .303 on many an occasion – but this appeared a most complicated piece of machinery.

Kevin crept quietly back into the room. 'I phoned them,' he whispered. 'Merv Pritchard's on his way.'

'How do I work this bloody thing?' she hissed.

'You cock it like this.' He showed her how to clasp the toggle bolt between finger and thumb and pull it back. He'd seen Nazis do it in the pictures. Kevin loved going to the pictures, he especially loved American war films, and he'd always had a very good memory for details.

Klaus walked towards Ruth with slow deliberation, relishing her terror and his role as executioner.

'I do not kill you because you are a threat, my dear. I kill you because you have been disloyal to me. You betrayed the pact we had, you and I.'

She backed away as far as she could, then felt the edge of the bed behind her; she could go no further.

'I kill you, Ruth, because it gives me pleasure to do so.'

He reached out for her. She dived desperately to one side. He grabbed her by the wrist with his left hand, the syringe in his right.

Behind them, the door was thrown open. Klaus turned.

In the open doorway stood his housekeeper and her son.

He curled his fingers around the syringe, secreting it in the palm of his hand. 'What is the meaning of this, Mrs Hodgeman?' he said, outraged. 'Can't you see I'm with a patient? Get out at once.'

But Noreen Hodgeman extended her arms, the pistol held unwaveringly in both hands. Looking down the sights of the barrel, she aimed directly at his head.

'Let her go,' she said.

Klaus released his hold on Ruth's wrist, and Noreen Hodgeman took several paces into the room.

'I heard what you said and so did Kevin. You killed that boy. You're a murderer.'

He wasn't listening to her. The weapon that was trained on him was his own SS army-issue Luger. Did she know how to use it? he wondered. Was it cocked?

She could see him studying the gun; she knew exactly what he was thinking.

'Oh it's cocked, all right,' she said, 'you can bet on that. Kevin showed me how.'

Klaus glanced at the simpleton son who'd also stepped into the room.

'He's not as stupid as you think,' she added.

'How very clever of you, Kevin,' he said. The boy was big and probably quite strong, but he could finish him off easily with the needle. If he could only tempt the woman a little closer so that he could grab the Luger from her. 'And you too, Mrs Hodgeman.' He took a step towards her.

'Stay right there,' she ordered. Noreen wasn't having a bar of it. She stayed very still, the pistol unwavering, her eyes trained steadily on the pistol's sights.

'Very well.' He backed away and perched casually on the side of the desk, watching her for the slightest movement. She would falter soon; such a stance and such concentration were tiring.

'You're a bloody Nazi too,' Noreen said. Her Leonard had died at Tobruk fighting the bloody Nazis, she thought, and all this time she'd been working for one! Poor Len'd roll in his grave if he knew. 'I heard that part as well. Kevin and me, we're witnesses.'

'Good for you.' He was pleased she was talking. The more she talked, the more her concentration would falter.

Ruth didn't dare say a word. She could sense he was ready to pounce, and she knew he still held the syringe in his hand, but she couldn't risk distracting Noreen Hodgeman's focus.

A car screeched to a halt outside.

'That'll be Merv Pritchard,' Noreen said. 'Go and let him in, Kevin.'

Kevin did as he was told.

They'd called the police, Klaus thought as he watched the boy walk out into the waiting room. Of course they'd called the police. Why had it not occurred to him that they would?

There was no way out of the surgery, except through the door that led to the hall. As he heard the front door open, Klaus knew there was no escape.

Noreen Hodgeman's concentration finally faltered. She was surprised as she peered down the pistol's sights to see him, shirt sleeves still rolled up above his elbows, casually cross his arms as he perched on the side of the desk. He was accepting his fate very calmly, she thought. He was a cool one, she'd give him that much.

They'd hanged them at Nuremberg, Klaus thought. No military execution, no firing squad. They'd hanged them like common criminals. And that was just what they would do to him. Goering had had the right idea, he thought as he pumped the muscles of his left arm and felt with the fingers of his right hand for the vein. Goering had escaped such an ignominious death.

He threaded the tip of the needle into the vein and positioned his thumb over the plunger of the syringe, but he made the mistake of glancing at Ruth. Just one last look, that was all he wanted, and he was pleased at first. She knew what he was doing, and she was saying nothing. She was saving him, just as he had saved her at Auschwitz.

He pressed the plunger, injecting the potassium chloride into his vein.

'You're a coward, Klaus,' she whispered.

At the very last moment, she had robbed him of his dignity.

EPILOGUE

Nineteen fifty-six was going to be an important year for Australians. They eagerly awaited the much heralded arrival of television, and they anticipated with fervent and patriotic pride a plethora of gold medals at the Melbourne Olympics.

But in Cooma, life went on much as usual. It would be some time before they'd see television, and few would travel to Melbourne for the Olympics. They'd follow it like they did any major event, gathered around the wireless, listening to the ABC.

Progress on the Snowy continued. The fourteen-mile Eucumbene-Tumut tunnel ploughed its way relentlessly through the mountain, and new world records were set in tunnel excavation.

The water started slowly encroaching on Adaminaby. A dam wall over four hundred feet high would one day encompass a water capacity eight times as great as Sydney Harbour, and the doomed town would lie beneath a mighty lake.

There were changes in the workplace. Kaiser brought in thermoses to avoid billy tea breaks – and as fast as the Aussies busted them, the bosses replaced them.

For some there were events of more personal significance.

Cam Campbell and his sons won a record haul of ribbons and trophies in the Cooma Show of 1956.

Lucky married Peggy Minchin. Rob Harvey was best man and Ruth was Peggy's sole bridesmaid; Peggy hadn't wanted a fancy wedding. 'I'd ask you to be matron of honour,' she said to Ruth, 'but the matron of honour has to be married, I'm told.' Ruth kept the joke to herself; she didn't share it with Lucky.

But the most important event on the calendar for Violet was July 26, her son's first birthday.

Her mother Marge decided to make a party of that week's Sunday roast in order to celebrate the occasion. Just family and a few close friends – best to have it on a Sunday, she said, so the men didn't have to go to work.

This time they ate in the dining room, with the doors to the lounge room wide open in order to catch the heat from the open log fire. It was midwinter and it had been snowing heavily all morning.

With ten of them crammed around the eight-seater dining table, Marge wondered whether she should have got Dave to lift the kitchen table in as well. But no-one seemed to mind, so she stopped worrying.

She stopped worrying about the boys' table manners too. Dave and Johnno were paying no deference to the fact they were in the dining room, spearing their spuds and meat with their forks although she'd pointedly handed them the serving spoons.

Marge let herself to relax. Everyone was having a very good time, and she was basking in the compliments coming her way. It was an excellent roast, if she said so herself, but then it was so easy now she had the new stove.

She felt very much the proud matriarch as she looked around the table; her sons on either side of her; Cam at the other end. Violet was seated to his left, Maureen to his right and the baby was sleeping in his bassinet nearby. Cam would turn to rock the bassinet every now and then, no doubt hoping the baby would wake up and give him a smile.

'Don't, Dad, you'll wake him up,' Violet said.

'Sorry.'

God, but he was a sook of a grandfather, Marge thought.

Lucky and Peggy were seated on one side of the table, and opposite them was Ruth. Marge was pleased that she'd brought her friend Rob Harvey along – such a nice man. She hoped they'd get married; he was obviously dotty about her.

Marge liked Ruth immensely. Well, why wouldn't she? she wondered as she glanced at her daughter, happy and healthy. Marge Campbell was more indebted to Ruth Stein than words could possibly express. In bringing Pietro's killer to justice, Ruth Stein had saved Violet's sanity. Funny, she thought, how she used to have a bit of a set against Germans – only because of the war, of course – and now there were two of them sitting at her table. Well, she wasn't sure if Lucky really counted as a German. He'd hardly been one of the enemy – Lucky was a Jew. Fancy her grandson's godfather being a German and a Jew. Who would have thought it? But then her grandson was half-Italian, wasn't he? Who would have thought that too? My goodness, but the Campbell family was becoming sophisticated.

Marge stopped indulging herself, and tucked into her lamb, but she couldn't help feeling proud.

After the roast, Maureen helped clear away the plates while the boys poured themselves another beer – Peggy and Ruth declining the offer – and Cam opened the champagne for the official toast, which would accompany the special birthday cake Marge had made for dessert.

Thank Christ Lucky and Rob Harvey had both brought along more champagne, Cam thought. He'd forgotten

Marge had expressly told him to buy some, although he'd laid on plenty of beer.

'Will you put out the sweets plates, Vi?' Marge called as she followed Maureen into the kitchen.

Violet stood. 'Don't you wake him, Dad,' she warned; she'd seen her father's eyes flicker again to the bassinet.

She left, only to return empty-handed barely a minute later. Cam thought she was checking up on him. He was rocking the bassinet and the baby was awake, and he expected another reproach from his daughter.

'I didn't do anything,' he protested. 'He just woke up.'

But Violet didn't notice. 'It's stopped snowing,' she announced. 'Come and look. Bring the champagne and glasses, Dad, we'll do the toast outside.' She picked up the baby and was gone. 'Mum, Auntie Maureen,' the men heard her calling to the kitchen, 'it's stopped snowing – come outside and look.'

They all joined Violet on the verandah where she stood with her baby in her arms, gazing at the virgin white landscape and the poplars draped in frozen lace. All was still and hushed, there was not a breath of breeze. The sun had come out and the snow that blanketed the valleys and the hills sparkled, fresh and unblemished, in the wintry light.

'Isn't it the most romantic thing you ever saw?' Violet said.

Cam filled their glasses and proposed the toast to his grandson.

'To Pietro Toscanini,' he said.

'To Pietro Toscanini,' they responded as they clinked glasses.

The baby leaned back in his mother's embrace, arms outstretched as if applauding. He was only hungry and ready for his feed, but the gesture seemed appropriate.

'To the new generation,' Ruth said.

'To the new generation.' They drank to that too.

It was just the beginning, Ruth thought.

Rob Harvey slipped his hand into hers. He wondered what she was thinking.

She smiled at him. She would tell him later.

ACKNOWLEDGEMENTS

My thanks, as always and forever, to my husband, Bruce Venables, for his support, encouragement, and downright inspiration.

Thanks, too, to the pals and workmates: my agent, James Laurie; my publisher, Jane Palfreyman; my editor, Kim Swivel; Peta Levett and all at Random House Australia; Colin Julin; and my ever-supportive friends, Susan Mackie, Sue Greaves and Robyn Gurney.

For assistance in the research of this book, my sincerest thanks to Pauline Saxon, Robert Duncan, Denise Chapman of Epilepsy Australia, Warren Brown and Don Palfreyman.

I am indebted to all those who were so friendly and helpful during my first research trip to the Monaro and Snowy Mountains region, and would like particularly to thank local historian Frank Rodwell, and Viv Straw, the General Manager of the Snowy River Shire Council. Thanks also to Barry Aitchison and the pals to whom he introduced me: Keven Burke, Charlie Roberson, Fred Fletcher, Ellis Aitchison and Phil Zylstra of NPWS. And thanks to Leigh Stewart of Stewart's Gallery in Adaminaby and to Annette McGufficke of NPWS.

Among my many research sources, I would like to recognise the following:

Berlin, Frederic V. Grünfeld, Time-Life International, 1977.

Homes on the Range, Frank Rodwell, 1999.

Cooma, a Decade of Change, Alison Howell, Cooma Monaro Historical Society, 1996.

The Snowy, Siobhan McHugh, William Heinemann Australia, 1989.

Snowy Saga, Oswald Ziegler Publications for Snowy River Shire Council, 1960.

Pseudo-epileptic Seizures, Neil Buchanan and Jeffrey Snars, MacLennan & Petty Pty Ltd, 1995.

The photographs of George Miso, Hollywood Studio, Cooma.

'The 1948 Massacre at Deir Yassin Revisited', Matthew Hogan, *Historian*, Winter 2001.

Justice Not Vengeance, Simon Wiesenthal, Grove Atlantic, 1990.

The Plot Against the Peace, Michael Sayers and Albert E. Kahn, Dial Press, 1945.

JUDY NUNN

Floodtide

Four men . . . Four Families . . . Four memorable decades in the mighty 'Iron Ore State' of Western Australia.

The prosperous 1950s when childhood is idyllic in the small city of Perth . . . The turbulent 60s when youth is caught up in the Vietnam War . . . The avaricious 70s when Western Australia's mineral boom sees the rise of a new young breed of aggressive entrepreneurs . . . The corrupt 80s, when greedy politicians and powerful businessmen bring the state to its knees . . .

Each of the four who travel this journey has a story to tell. An environmentalist fights to save the primitive and beautiful Pilbara coast from the ravaging of mining conglomerates; a Vietnam War veteran rises above crippling injuries to discover a talent which gains him an international reputation; and an ambitious geologist joins forces with a hard-core businessman to lead the way in the growth of Perth from a sleepy town to a glittering citadel of skyscrapers.

But all four know one thing – the tides of change are irreversible. And as the 90s issues in a new age when innocence is lost, actions must be answered for.

***Floodtide* is a character-driven, merciless rush of blood from the pen of Judy Nunn, one of Australia's master storytellers.**

PROLOGUE

'There is a tide in the affairs of men which, taken at the flood, leads on to fortune'

Julius Caesar, William Shakespeare

1965

'Beats me why you wanna go swimmin' with sharks.' The bottles of Swan Lager clinked as Tubby Lard took the cardboard box the kid handed him. 'Only a dickhead'd go swimmin' with sharks.'

'Yeah,' his brother Fats agreed from where he stood up the bow, ready to cast off. 'You wouldn't get me down there for quids.'

'Well, of course you wouldn't, you stupid bastard,' Tubby said, gunning the engine and yelling above the diesel's throb. 'You can't bloody swim!'

Mike McAllister grinned as he stepped nimbly aboard the *Maria Nina*. It was good to see the Lard brothers again.

Tubby eyed the kid's backpack. 'Haven't you got any scuba gear?' he asked.

'At twenty feet I won't need it.'

Mike settled himself on the massive wooden, lead-lined icebox that doubled as a seat and trained his eyes on the distant low-lying rocky islands as the vessel pulled away from the jetty. It was a hot, steamy morning, barely a breath of breeze, the ocean like glass. A perfect day for it, he thought, excited by the prospect of what lay ahead.

Contrary to her name, the *Maria Nina* was no sea sprite. She was an old tub, thirty-eight feet long, stinking of bait and desperately in need of a coat of paint. But that was only her exterior. The brothers cared little for appearances; she was solid and reliable and her engine was meticulously maintained. The *Maria Nina* was a grand old dame of the sea.

Tubby and Fats Lard were cray fishermen who worked the Abrolhos Islands off Geraldton on the coast of Western Australia. During their respective early school years both brothers had been called Lardhead, but not for long, because both were good with their fists. Fred, the elder, had readily accepted Tubby as a substitute. Skinny as a rake, he was amused by the contradiction. Bob, also on the lean side and five years his brother's junior, was an avid jazz fan. He considered his nickname a tribute to Fats Waller.

'Hey Einstein,' Tubby called from the wheelhouse, 'get off your bum and put the grog on ice.'

'Oh.' Mike jumped to his feet. 'Sorry.' He loaded the beer into the ice chest. Beside him, Fats started baiting up the dozen or more hooks on each of the set-lines.

'Want a hand?' Mike asked when the beer was stowed. Fats nodded. Fats Lard was a man of few words; it was Tubby who did most of the talking.

Mike and the brothers had met at the pub in Geraldton just three days previously. It had been early evening, a squally wind blowing in from the sea and alleviating to some degree the oppressive heat of a typical dry and dusty December day.

*

'You're off the *Pelsaert*, aren't you,' Tubby said. He and Fats were lounging at the bar of the Victoria Hotel when the kid fronted up to buy a round for his mates.

'Yeah, that's right. Three schooners, thanks,' Mike said to the barman.

Tubby eyed the kid up and down. Handsome young bastard – black-haired, startlingly blue-eyed – he should be in the pictures, Tubby thought. Fit too, but just a kid. 'Bit young for a boffin, aren't you?' He glanced at the table where the kid's mates were seating themselves. They were early twenties he guessed. What were they doing aboard the *Pelsaert*?

'We're students, up from Perth,' Mike said. 'UWA.'

'Ah, right.'

The student part made sense, Tubby thought, but hardly the vessel. He'd seen the MV *Pelsaert* tooling about the Wallabi Islands and upon enquiring had been told it was the State Fisheries' new research vessel on some sort of scientific expedition.

'They give you young blokes a brand new boat just because you go to uni?' He exchanged a look with Fats who was equally incredulous.

'Hardly.' Mike laughed. He didn't find Tubby's direct manner offensive, he sensed the man was genuinely interested. 'We're here to do the hard yakka,' he joked, 'the stuff the boffins aren't fit enough for.'

'There you go, mate.' The barman placed the beers in front of him.

Tubby waited until the kid had paid for the drinks, then homed in again. 'What hard yakka?' Tubby had an enquiring mind and his questions were invariably relentless.

'We catch tammars.'

It was true. For the past five nights, from eight o'clock until two in the morning, the three students had raced relentlessly around East and West Wallabi Islands, lights strapped to their foreheads, wielding giant butterfly-like nets, the object of the exercise being the capture of the small nocturnal marsupials which would undergo study the following day. Keen athletes, the boys had been selected for their physical fitness.

'Whaddya wanna do that for?' It was the first time Fats had spoken. He was no less interested than his brother, but he always relied on Tubby to lead the way.

Mike, torn between delivering the beers and not wishing to appear rude to the locals, cast a look in the direction of his mates. Muzza was lounging back with a smoke, but Ian, upon catching his eye, gave an irritated wave and a scowl that said 'Hurry it up'.

'The boys are getting impatient,' he said, gathering up the beers. Then he added, 'Why don't you join us?'

'Rightio.' Tubby didn't need any further invitation. He rose from his stool, grabbed his glass, and Fats followed. The brothers liked meeting new people.

They gathered at the table, Mike plonking down the beers, Ian pointedly making a grab for his. As Tubby and Fats garnered extra chairs, the boys shuffled around to make room for them. When they'd settled, Mike made the introductions.

'Murray Hatfield, Ian Pemberton and I'm Mike Mc-Allister,' he said.

'Tubby and Fats Lard.' Tubby leaned across the table, offering Mike a gnarled hand. Ian snorted into his beer.

They shook all round, then Tubby raised his glass. 'Welcome to Gero, boys.'

The others joined in the salutation, taking a swig along with him. Ian Pemberton sipped reluctantly. He was a classically handsome young man, despite slightly protruding ears, but his aquiline features so often conveyed disdain that the effect was invariably ruined. Ian was a snob.

'How long ya been here?' Tubby led the conversation, seemingly oblivious to Ian's contempt.

'A week,' Mike told him.

'How long ya stayin'?'

'Another week.' It was Muzza who replied. Like Mike, he was aware that Ian considered the brothers an intrusion – Pembo could be a real pain at times, he thought. Muzza was keen to follow Mike's lead. He always did. Just turned twenty, Muzza was two years younger than the others and Mike was a bit of hero. He gave one of his lop-sided, baby-faced grins. 'We leave next Saturday.'

'Good-lookin' boat, the *Pelsaert*,' Tubby said, Fats nodding agreement. 'I've seen her holed up in Turtle Bay on East Wallabi – you boys livin' on board, are ya?'

'That's right.' Mike flashed a warning glance at Ian, who was scowling at his beer, before changing the subject and asking the brothers about themselves.

They were cray fishermen, Tubby told him, 'Born and bred right here in Gero.' Although Tubby did the talking, Fats joined in with nods to the table at large. Fats did a lot of nodding.

'The Lards have been cray men for three generations,' Tubby said proudly, 'comin' up for four soon.' Tubby was thirty-nine and his son barely ten years old, but the boy's future was carved in stone. 'We scored the boat off Dad when he bought his new humdinger five years back, didn't we, Fats?' A nod. 'The old man's sixty-three, still in the business, still goin' strong.'

Tubby drained his glass and stood. 'I'll get another round, hey.' It wasn't a question and he was already gathering up the empty glasses.

Ian put his hand over his glass, which still had an inch of beer in it.

Muzza jumped to his feet before Pembo could refuse Tubby's offer. 'I'll give you a hand,' he said.

As the two of them left for the bar, conversation at the table ground to a halt. Ian drained his glass in sulky silence. Fats turned expectantly to Mike. His eyes, set deep in the crinkles of a face weathered well beyond its thirty-four years, appeared eager for another question or some sort of comment, but Mike was at a loss as to what to say. Tubby's potted history of the Lard family had been so succinct that no further question or comment came readily to mind.

But Fats wasn't seeking question or comment, he was seeking an answer. He'd been prepared to wait patiently for Tubby to bring up the subject, as Tubby no doubt would, although, in Fats' opinion, Tubby sometimes took a long time to get to the point. But as Tubby wasn't here now, and there was a hole in the conversation, Fats decided to ask for himself.

'Whaddya wanna catch tammars for?'

Mike was relieved that Fats had started the ball rolling; he was unaccustomed to feeling socially awkward. 'For study,' he said. 'It's a research trip.'

Fats nodded, he'd gathered that.

'We're earning extra money during the summer vacation,' Mike went on, 'assisting in the research for a PhD student on a Fulbright Scholarship –'

'What about the tammars?' Fats asked. He didn't really want to know about the scholarship part.

'Well, they're remarkable animals,' Mike explained. 'They thrive here on East and West Wallabi and we want to find out how. You see, there's virtually no fresh-water source on the islands, particularly on West Wallabi. There's no fresh water at all there, except for rain, of course . . .'

Fats kept nodding as the kid talked, taking it all in slowly, sifting the information. He hadn't known that tammars were so interesting.

Ian Pemberton looked at the cray fisherman, nodding like a metronome, and his irritation grew to boiling point. How dare the yobbos crash their party. How dare Mike ask them to the table. And look at him now! Good old

Mike McAllister, everybody's favourite, giving his all to a retard who didn't understand a word he was saying. Ian wanted to deck him. What about the nurses they'd met last night? There was a party on at their flat, starting about now. What the hell were the three of them doing sitting here entertaining a couple of local cretins?

'From an environmental point of view it makes them a very valuable source of study,' Mike said.

'So what is it you do with the tammars?' Fats was fascinated.

'*Protemnodon eugenii* to be precise,' Ian cut in, the disdain in his voice matching the sneer on his face.

Fats turned to look blankly at him, just as Tubby and Muzza arrived with the beers. Ian waited until the glasses had been placed on the table before once again addressing Fats, in exactly the same tone.

'We study the water metabolism of genus *Protemnoden*, species *eugenii*, otherwise known as the tammar.'

There was a deathly silence. Tubby stared at the kid with the bat ears and the pointy face and the built-in bad smell under his nose. He'd sensed his antagonism the moment they'd come to the table, but what had Fats done to rile him? Fats might not be the sharpest tool in the shed, but he was a good bloke, he wouldn't hurt a fly. Well, not unless the fly hurt him, and even then he had to be pushed. Tubby was about to challenge the snotty-nosed little prick, but someone else got in first.

'Stop being a smartarse, Pembo,' Mike said good-naturedly. 'Sit down, Tubby, there was no offence intended. Was there, Ian?' The question was pointed.

'Course not.' Checked by Mike's warning tone and the threat of danger, Ian attempted a smile, which wasn't successful.

Tubby sat. Very slowly, his eyes darting about the group, like a cat ready to pounce.

Fats, too, looked around the table, aware of the sudden

tension. He'd gathered that some sort of insult had been intended, and while he wondered what he'd done to warrant it, he wasn't particularly offended. But he could tell that Tubby was ready to do battle, and he was prepared to join in. Tubby only ever picked a fight when there was good cause for it.

'I'm here on a dual study period myself,' Mike said to the brothers, as if nothing had happened. 'Doing some advance research for my PhD next year, and the topic's right up your alley.'

'Oh yeah?' Tubby said, distrustful. One word in the wrong direction and these little uni pricks wouldn't know what'd hit them. But he couldn't help himself, he was impressed by Mike. It was obvious the other two took their lead from him. Muzza wasn't a bad kid, but he seemed younger than the others and, Tubby suspected, a bit of a 'yes' boy. As for the bat-eared snotty-nosed bastard . . .

'And how exactly would your *advance research* be right up our alley?' he asked, his tone a dangerously supercilious imitation of Ian's.

Mike turned to Fats. 'What do you reckon I'm studying, Fats?'

'Eh?' Fats was caught out; people usually addressed their questions to Tubby.

'The topic I'm studying – what do you reckon it is? What's right up your alley?'

'Crayfish?' Fats asked hopefully.

'Spot on.' Mike once again addressed the older brother. 'As well as the study of tammars, the *Pelsaert* and her crew are doing a pre-season cray census. The object of the exercise will lead to a better estimate of the catchable cray population later in the season, and maybe even the following year as well. Does that interest you?'

'My oath it does,' Tubby said. Any insult was forgotten, the kid had won him.

Twenty minutes later, as they were polishing off the next round of beers – Muzza's shout – Mike was still talking, Tubby was still asking questions, and Fats was still hanging on every word. The brothers knew only too well that the whole of the Abrolhos was a hatchery and nursery area this time of year. All down the west coast the cray season ran from mid-November until the end of June, with the exception of the Abrolhos where it didn't start until mid-March. They'd been wondering what the *Pelsaert* was doing laying pots, and now Mike was explaining the mark-and-recapture techniques employed in the research.

'Tail-punching,' he said. 'It leaves an identifiable mark when they're recaught.'

'Well, bein' a Fisheries vessel, we didn't exactly think you were doin' something illegal,' Tubby said. Fats nodded, although they'd both had their doubts. 'Whatever experiments they're up to, I bet they're keepin' a good few crays on the side,' Tubby had said as he'd watched them blatantly setting their pots, and Fats had agreed.

Mike didn't go into detail about the recent break-through. The discovery of *puerulus* in numbers – the elusive settling phase before the juvenile hard-shelled crayfish emerged – had caused much excitement in academic circles. But it wasn't necessary to explain the finer points; both brothers understood the impact of the research. An advance and accurate prediction in the numbers of mature crayfish would revolutionise their industry.

'Time to go.' Ian replaced his empty glass on the table with a little more force than was necessary. Aware that he'd overstepped the mark earlier, it was the only way he could signal his boredom and irritation. He stood. 'The girls are waiting.' He forced another smile, his second of the evening, and again it didn't work. 'Nice to meet you, Tubby, Fats.'

Muzza looked to Mike for his cue. He was a bit bored himself. The cray fishermen had lost their appeal now that the girls were beckoning.

'Sorry, Muz.' Mike smiled apologetically. 'I got a bit carried away. You go and have a good time.'

Muzza shook hands with the brothers as he rose from his chair, but Ian kept his distance, his eyes on Mike.

'You're not coming?' he asked.

'I never said I was.'

'Jeez, mate,' Tubby said to Mike, nudging Fats as a signal they should make a move. 'If you've got women lined up don't let us stand in your way.'

'You're not.' Mike's tone was definite, but his reply was directed to Ian. 'I told you from the start I didn't want to be in it.'

Fats rose from the table, a decision seemed to have been made. 'Goodo then,' he said. 'My round.'

'No, it isn't.' Mike continued to look at Ian. He was wondering how on earth he'd remained friends with Pembo for the past several years. But he knew the answer. He was sorry for the bloke. 'It's Ian's round. Isn't it, Ian?'

Tubby watched, intrigued by the second or so of power play between the two young men, but it was no competition.

'Sure,' Ian said, 'my shout', and he went off to the bar where he ordered three beers. He and Muzza certainly weren't hanging around with the Lard brothers when there were women to be had. Mike had turned into such a square, he thought. God, Mike McAllister had been the biggest womaniser of them all – the bloke could score in a convent, women always gravitated to him. But he'd changed since he'd met Johanna. What a bastard, Ian thought as he paid for the beers. Without Mike he probably wouldn't score tonight. Mike had always been his lucky draw card, and now he was left with young Muzza who was a loser.

He returned to place the three beers on the table. 'You ready, Muzza?' he asked, and Muzza once again stood.

Mike leaned back in his chair, raising his glass to them both. 'Thanks, Pembo,' he said pleasantly. 'You guys have a great night.'

Ian made his farewells tightly but politely.

'See you, Muzza,' Mike called as they left. 'Don't do anything I wouldn't do.'

'Leaves me plenty of licence,' Muzza called back over his shoulder.

'You sure you don't want to go with your mates?' Tubby's question was incredulous. Why didn't Mike want to chase after women? Crikey, they'd be queuing up for a young stud like him.

'Yep, quite sure. I'm not interested.'

As he said it, Mike realised that he genuinely wasn't. He certainly would have been six months ago – six months ago he would have been leading the troops – but since he'd met Jo, he'd lost the urge to bed other women. Not because he felt the need to remain faithful – he'd made no commitment and neither had she – but for some reason the thrill of the chase no longer seemed important. Funny about that, he thought.

'I've got a girlfriend in Perth,' he said to avoid any further questioning.

'Ah,' Tubby replied, sharing a nod with Fats. The kid was in love – that explained it. He took a long draught of his beer and settled back in his chair. 'So, where were we up to, Einstein?' He could listen to the kid all night.

'The *Batavia*.' Mike decided it was his turn to ask the questions.

'Eh?' The non sequitur took both brothers by surprise.

'Do you know about the wreck of the *Batavia*?'

'Do I what!' Tubby's grin was triumphant. 'She was a Dutch East India trading vessel that founded on the Abrolhos in 1629.' He looked like a schoolboy who'd topped his class; he was glad of the opportunity to show off his knowledge to the kid. 'There was a bunch of mutineers on board and they were going to pirate her, but she hit the reef instead. And after the shipwreck they murdered just about all the survivors.'

'Women and children as well,' Fats interjected, the gleam of morbid fascination in his eyes. 'Them islands is covered in bones.'

It was more historical fact than Mike had anticipated from the brothers. 'Do you know where the wreck is?' he asked.

'Too right.' It was Fats again, suddenly and uncharacteristically articulate. 'Tubby and me was on hand when it was discovered a couple of years back. We know the exact spot, don't we, Tub?'

'Yep, we helped the expedition team when they were diving on it. They needed our local knowledge of the area,' Tubby said with a touch of pride.

'I've heard it's in shallow water, is that right?'

'Around twenty feet or so.'

'Could you take me to it?'

The look Tubby exchanged with Fats was dubious. 'Well, we *could*,' he said tentatively.

Mike presumed the brothers were concerned about money. 'I'll pay . . .' he added hastily.

'Nah, nah, it's not that.' Tubby waved a hand airily. 'It's just that you need the right day. If the weather's crook, you can't make an approach, it's bloody impossible.'

'So if the weather's right, will you take me out there?'

Fats was nodding vigorously. Fats had taken to Mike. But then so had his brother.

'Yeah, if the weather's right,' Tubby agreed.

Mike tried to negotiate a price, but the brothers would have none of it. 'Well, at least let me pay for the fuel,' he insisted.

Tubby shrugged. 'If you like, but we'll be takin' the boat out anyway. We gotta make a living.'

Prior to the commencement of the cray season, the brothers fished with set-lines for dhufish and baldchin grouper, both prize table fish for the West Australian market.

'Okay, it's a deal. And I'll bring along a case of beer.'

'You're on, Einstein.'

Three days later, the squally winds had died down and the weather was perfect.

Tubby followed the deep channel that led from the safe anchorage behind the reefs out into the open ocean. He and Fats would lay their set-lines before taking Mike to the wreck site. The *Maria Nina* churned smoothly through the gentle swell, the sea and the sky so peacefully clear they seemed to merge as one. Mike sat on the icebox helping Fats bait up the lines. An hour or so later, when they'd set them, floats bobbing on the ocean's surface, Tubby turned the vessel about.

'You can only approach the wreck from the open sea,' he said as Mike joined him in the wheelhouse. 'Treacherous bastard of a place – no way you can come into it from the land. That's Beacon Island,' he pointed at the low, rocky island up ahead. '*Batavia*'s Graveyard, it's known as. The wreck's just a mile south of it.'

Mike gazed at the island, barren and desolate like the rest of the Abrolhos. *Batavia*'s Graveyard, he thought, and couldn't help feeling a thrill of anticipation. This was the highlight of his trip. It was strange, he hadn't expected it to be – there'd been far too much else to preoccupy him. He'd been intrigued by the lunatic notion of nightly tammar chasing, and excited by the prospect of next year's PhD study when he'd be working as a field assistant with Dr Bruce Phillips of the CSIRO, the man who'd made the breakthrough *puerulus* discovery. Not once had the *Batavia* entered his mind, and why should it? He'd known little about its actual history when he'd left Perth – only that the site of an old Dutch wreck had created headlines when it had been discovered on the Abrolhos in 1963. But he'd been enthralled by the tales he'd heard aboard the *Pelsaert* on the night of his arrival, the crew members infecting him with their own fascination with the *Batavia*'s brutal past. The very vessel that was accommodating them, he'd been told by the crew, was named after the commander of the *Batavia* himself, Francisco Pelsaert. And then they'd embarked upon the grisly story of mutiny, murder and mayhem.

Ever since that night, young Mike McAllister had viewed the islands of the Abrolhos through different eyes. Ecologically, their make-up was simple – in studying the ecology of the crayfish, he had also studied their habitat – the islands were formed of coral shale and sand built up by the conflicting currents on the shallow plateaus. Plants sprouted from seeds in bird droppings to form sparse vegetation, binding the sand with roots and resulting in a series of low-lying islands that somehow defied the elements. It was that very defiance which he found remarkable. For hundreds of years, these desolate and insignificant-looking outcrops, little more than a combination of reef and sandbank, had withstood the full force of nature. They, and the treacherous submerged reefs surrounding them, had become indestructible demons feared by seamen over the centuries. Infamous graveyards to many a ship and its sailors. In fact, as the crew of the *Pelsaert* had told him, the very name Abrolhos meant in old Dutch, 'keep your eyes open'.

No longer did the islands appear insignificant to Mike. He was seeing them with a sense of history, perhaps through the eyes of a seaman. The islands of the Abrolhos were to be respected. They were a timeless and impressively powerful force in the landscape: pristine, primitive and untameable.

'We're coming in nor'-east on the original course of the *Batavia*. That's the reef up ahead, a bit to port.'

As Tubby's voice broke into his thoughts, Mike looked to where the man was pointing. The only giveaway sign of the reef was a ripple of white frills playing teasingly across the ocean's surface.

'We picked a good day for it,' Tubby said, cutting back the speed until they were idling. 'You can get ripped to pieces out here – in crook weather the place is like a bloody cauldron. Let her go,' he called to Fats who was standing by ready to drop anchor. They were barely a hundred yards from the reef.

When the *Maria Nina* was securely at anchor, Tubby cut the engine. 'We'll hang back fine in this breeze,' he said. 'Grab us a beer, will ya, Einstein?'

Mike lifted out an icy cold bottle. Fats was already handing around three grimy plastic beakers. 'Not for me thanks, Fats,' he said, stripping down to his Speedos.

The brothers swigged on their beers whilst they baited up – two hooks on each handline. They had no intention of sitting idly by whilst the kid explored the wreck.

'She should be about dead ahead of us,' Tubby said as Mike donned his flippers. 'Take your time, we'll be jake, there's good fishin' here.' He couldn't resist adding, 'And where there's good fishin', there's sharks.'

'You wouldn't get me down there,' Fats said, slinging his line over the side and watching it spiral from its reel down into the depths. The fact that their baits might well be an added attraction to sharks was of little concern to either Tubby or Fats. If the kid was mad enough to go swimming in shark-infested waters then that was his problem.

'No worries.' Mike grinned at the brothers' dire warnings. They didn't alarm him, he'd dived many a time with sharks.

He slid over the side and trod water whilst he rinsed his facemask and snorkel. When he was ready to take off, he gave the brothers the thumbs up.

'Good luck, Einstein,' Tubby called, chucking his own line into the water and holding his beaker out to Fats for a refill. He watched the kid's easy style as he swam towards the reef, sliding through the water as if he was born to it. Just like Murray Rose, he thought. The kid was pretty to watch.

As Mike swam, a slow energy-conserving freestyle, his powerful flippers barely moving, he relished the sensation of the water and his sense of oneness with it. He always did. It wasn't something he analysed, but neither was it something he took for granted. He was always aware that in the water he felt as if he were in his element, as if he and the sea shared something special.

Through the surface swirl he could see the reef below, and he made a shallow dive, just about seven or eight feet, to get a clearer view.

Then that exhilarating moment when sound ceased to exist and everything stopped, even time itself. It was what he loved most about free diving. There was no echo of laboured breathing through scuba equipment, there was just him and the world under the sea. A world where colour and action abounded and drama unfolded all in breathtaking silence.

Beneath the dappled silver canopy of sun and sea, the visibility was perfect and the colours vivid. The blues and greens of the corals, the fiery reds of the sponges, the delicately wavering mauves of the anemones, all were as riotously colourful as a spring garden in full blossom. He pressurised and swam a little deeper, following the reef's terrain, through castle-like turrets where gaudily painted fish disappeared like magic, past ledges from which crayfish watched, their protruding feelers the only giveaway of their presence, down canyons where silver schools of skipjack and kingfish maintained their restless patrol.

He'd be around twenty feet now, he guessed, but no sign of the wreck. Time to go up. He stopped swimming and allowed himself to slowly drift upwards, just a gentle flick of the flippers now and then, depressurising as he went, watching the dappled silver above grow closer and closer.

When he broke surface, he heaved in a lungful of air and looked back at the *Maria Nina*. She was a good two hundred yards or so away. He must have drifted with the current. He circled back with slow, easy strokes, regaining his breath, studying the reef beneath him, conserving his energy. Perhaps, even from the surface, he'd be able to see the wreck. Given the calm conditions and the fact that she was lying at only twenty feet, surely it was possible. But try as he might, he could see no sign. Perhaps the brothers had got it wrong, he thought. He dived again, allowing himself more distance this time, he'd go with the flow of the current.

He was down about fifteen feet, once again lost in a world of silence and colour, and his attention was so focused on a vivid blue cluster of staghorn coral that he failed to notice the sinister grey shape that had appeared out of nowhere. It was the disturbed reaction of a school of silver bream that caught his attention, and he turned to see the shark gliding towards him effortlessly with no apparent movement of its body, like a robot on automatic pilot, majestic and omnipotent.

He anchored himself against the reef and watched, prepared to lunge forward in attack should the creature show any interest in him – attack was always the best form of defence. The shark was around ten feet in length. Barrel-shaped, yellow-eyed, with long gill slits and a high tail fin, it was a whaler, a dangerous species. But it paid him no attention as it passed by barely four feet away; he could have reached out and touched it.

He watched as the shark cruised a little deeper, gliding through a shallow valley in the rocks below. Perhaps it was unaware of his presence, or perhaps it was merely uninterested. He continued to admire its shadowy form as it cleared the valley and disappeared into the misty beyond.

Then the glint of something caught his eye, drawing his attention to a shape resting amongst the valley's coral growth. It was a long, cylindrical shape at odds with its surrounds, far too regular to be fashioned by nature. And, as the sun's light played teasingly through the ocean's surface above, it glinted again.

His lungs told him he needed to resurface. He had no time to examine the shape, but he knew what it was. A cannon. He'd found the site. The wreck itself must be nearby.

When he broke surface, heaving in air, he looked towards the *Maria Nina*. In his excitement he wanted to shout to the brothers, 'It's here! I've found it!', but they were paying him no attention. Tubby was heaving a dhufish over the side and Fats, having also struck lucky, was hauling in his line.

He trod water for a minute or so, keeping himself stationary against the current, careful not to drift over the spot while he prepared himself. And when he was fully recovered, he dived again.

The moment he was beneath the surface, he spotted the telltale glint and saw the cannon nestled in its rocky valley below. But as he swam downwards, he realised that the valley wasn't a valley at all. It was the encrusted wreck of the *Batavia*.

There she was, a flattened-out skeleton moulded into her grave. The rocks had hollowed out a tomb over the years, protecting her in part from the destructive forces of tide and surf, and the stern and ribs of the vessel were in an extraordinary state of preservation. He was lost in awe, it was beyond his wildest expectations. He wasn't sure what his expectations had been, but certainly not this.

Briefly, he examined the cannon. It was covered in sea

growth, and he assumed it to be bronze but couldn't be certain. It was the refraction of sunlight through relatively shallow water that had lent it the deceptively metallic glint. The giant anchor nestled nearby also seemed to glint from behind its thick encrustation of barnacles. It appeared to signal a life that belonged to its past glory.

But it was the skeletal remains of the *Batavia* that he found truly overwhelming. For centuries, the Abrolhos had kept her hidden, storing her here, preserving her like a trophy, as if in her amazingly recognisable condition she was proof of their own indestructibility.

He swam over what had been the belly of the ship, aware that he must resurface, that he must maintain enough breath in order to breathe out continuously on the way up and release the air pressure in his lungs. But he wanted to remain a part of it all for just one moment longer, to savour the image. It would never be the same on a second dive.

He locked himself between two of the mighty beams that formed the skeleton of the hull and stayed motionless, feeling himself a part of the vessel. Part of a vessel that was four hundred and thirty-six years old! The thought was staggering. And even more so as he recalled the tales the crew aboard the *Pelsaert* had told him. Names flashed through his brain. Pelsaert, the commander; Jacobsz, the skipper; Cornelisz, the wealthy merchant, the leader of the mutineers who'd tortured and murdered at random. And hundreds of nameless others, soldiers, sailors, passengers – over three hundred had been on board when she'd foundered. He pictured them as he looked about the wrecked hulk that was the *Batavia*. He felt their panic and heard their screams.

He must go up, he told himself, this was foolish. His lungs were now bursting, and he was asking for problems shooting to the surface from twenty feet without depressurising. But what the hell, it wouldn't kill him, he'd wait just a moment longer.

He could see them now, their faces tormented, their screams ringing in his ears. Which voice, which face, he wondered, belonged to Jeronimus Cornelisz? Which one amongst them was the torturer, murderer, killer of children?

He stared at the faces that now came at him from every gloomy corner of the wreck. Men, women, children, terrified and tortured every one of them. He searched amongst them for the face of evil.

It was strange, his lungs were no longer at bursting point. In fact, he felt peculiarly at ease, as if he could stay for as long as he wished. As if he could breathe underwater.

It was then that the last vestige of common sense told him he was hallucinating. He was on the verge of drowning. He kicked away from the wreck and made for the surface, the voices behind him screaming for him to come back, screaming for him to save them. But the silvery glint of the sun was now screaming at him to save himself.

Closer and closer he came to the light. The sun was his life, but it was teasing him. It was so close and yet he was unable to reach it, his lungs once again bursting, panic setting in, a fist of iron clamping around his heart telling him he wasn't going to make it.

Tubby was keeping a watch out for the kid. He hadn't seen him for a while and he was wondering whether he should start to worry. Then he saw him break surface and breathed a sigh of relief. Silly of him to worry, the kid could swim like a fish. But his relief was short-lived. Something was wrong. The kid was clutching at his chest, gasping, his face contorted.

'Einstein!' Tubby yelled. And, sharks or no sharks, he hurled himself into the sea.

Tiger Men

The eagerly awaited new novel by Judy Nunn

'This town is full of tiger men,' Dan said. 'Just look around you. The merchants, the builders, the bankers, the company men, they're all out for what they can get. This is a tiger town, Mick, a place at the bottom of the world where God turns a blind eye to pillage and plunder.'

Van Diemen's Land was an island of stark contrasts: a harsh penal colony, an English idyll for its landed gentry, and an island so rich in natural resources it was a profiteer's paradise. Its capital, Hobart Town, had its contrasts too: the wealthy elite in their sandstone mansions, the exploited poor in the notorious slum known as Wapping, and the criminals and villains who haunted the dockside taverns and brothels of Sullivan's Cove. Hobart Town was no place for the meek.

Tiger Men is the story of Silas Stanford, a wealthy Englishman; Mick O'Callaghan, an Irishman on the run; and Jefferson Powell, an idealistic American political prisoner. It is also the story of the strong, proud women who loved them, and of the children they bore who rose to power in the cutthroat world of international trade.

Tiger Men is the sweeping saga of three families who lived through Tasmania's golden era, who witnessed the birth of Federation and who, in 1915, watched with pride as their sons marched off to fight for King and Country in the Great War.

Available from November 2011

Other titles by Judy Nunn

Araluen

On a blistering hot day in 1850, brothers George and Richard Ross take their first steps on Australian soil after three long months at sea. All they have is each other.

A decade on, and they are the owners of a successful vineyard, Araluen, nestled in a beautiful valley near Adelaide. Now a successful businessman, George has laid down the roots of a Ross dynasty, born of the New World. But building a family empire – whatever the cost – can have a shattering effect on the generations to come . . .

Beneath the Southern Cross

In 1783, Thomas Kendall, a naïve nineteen-year-old sentenced to transportation for burglary, finds himself in Sydney Town and a new life in the wild and lawless land. *Beneath the Southern Cross* is as much a story of a city as it is a family chronicle. With her uncanny ability to bring history to life in technicolour, Judy Nunn traces the fortunes of Kendall's descendants through good times and bad to the present day . . .

Kal

Kalgoorlie. It grew out of the red dust of the desert over the world's richest vein of gold . . . From the heady early days of the gold rush, to the horrors of the First World War in Gallipoli and France, to the shame and confrontation of the post-war riots, *Kal* tells the story of Australia itself and the people who forged a nation out of a harsh and unforgiving land.

Other titles by Judy Nunn

Territory

Territory is the story of the Top End and the people who dare to dwell there. Of Spitfire pilot Terence Galloway and his English bride, Henrietta, home from the war, only to be faced with the desperate defence of Darwin against the Imperial Japanese Air Force. From the blazing inferno that was Darwin on 19 February 1942 to the devastation of Cyclone Tracy, from the red desert to the tropical shore, *Territory* is a mile-a-minute read.

Pacific

Australian actress Samantha Lindsay is thrilled when she scores her first Hollywood movie role, playing a character loosely based on World War II heroine Mamma Tack. But on location in Vanuatu, uncanny parallels between history and fiction emerge and Sam begins a quest for the truth. Just who was the real Mamma Tack?

Maralinga

Maralinga, 1956. A British airbase in the middle of nowhere, a top-secret atomic testing ground . . . *Maralinga* is the story of Lieutenant Daniel Gardiner, who accepts a posting to the wilds of South Australia on a promise of rapid promotion, and of adventurous young English journalist Elizabeth Hoffmann, who travels halfway around the world in search of the truth.